SPACE COLONY ONE

BOOKS 7 - 9

J.J. GREEN

INFINITEBOOK

READER GROUP

THE BOOKS OF SPACE COLONY ONE

RESTITUTION

ONE

Human civilization was laid waste. Where vast, busy metropolises had once thrived, only ruins remained. Decaying skyscrapers jutted up from streets choked with debris, like rotten teeth in diseased gums. Immense areas of urban landscape were burned to ashes or drowned in floods from burst dams and levees. Those relentless survivors, rats and cockroaches, had taken over, preyed upon by dogs turned feral.

Along the highways, vegetation thrust through cracks in asphalt or spread over it, infiltrating roots breaking up the hard surface. Abandoned vehicles rusted almost to oblivion formed desolate, motionless convoys. Once-mighty bridges had collapsed and shattered the roads below.

Explosions from processes run out of control had torn factories apart. Billions of hectares of agricultural land were lost to weeds and scrub. In harbors, sunken ships cluttered the water.

During the daytime, the world was silent save for bird song and noises of insects. At night, the sky was black and the stars glittered sharply.

Amongst it all, humanity clung to survival.

Groups of five or six up to several hundred roamed the lands, scavenging for food from the before-times, when people had bought groceries in shops or ordered it on the fabled 'net'. Sometimes, they hunted beasts, killing them inexpertly with blunt blades, hacking them to death slowly and painfully. Sometimes, they hunted each other.

No one wrote. No one painted. No one invented.

The few who could read studied ancient books, poring over the brittle, yellow paper, trying to make sense of unfamiliar words. On rare happy occasions, such as when a cache of aged cans of unspoiled food had been found, some would sing barely remembered songs—songs of love and longing and loss. But hunger always returned and the singers were silent.

How long life had been like this no one knew, only that it had not always been so. In the past, humankind had dominated the world. Yet the knowledge of how humans had risen to greatness was lost. Some said it was through magic, and a plague had wiped out the wizards and witches. Others said the wealthiest elites had gathered all the Earth's riches and departed hundreds of years ago. Less commonly, it was rumored the crumbling buildings had never housed people but had been the homes of another, superior species, now extinct.

So when the Scythians came, some believed they were returning to reclaim their world.

They announced their arrival by raining fire on the lands. Pulses from their starships blasted into the quiet cities. They attacked forests, starting wildfires that raged for months. They blew apart defunct factories and plants. A dying civilization was beaten into the dust.

When the invaders' ships landed, no one and nothing stood against them. The crescent-shaped shuttles, hulls etched in the signature swirling, irregular Scythian patterning, set down, their hatches opened, and the aliens emerged, heads ensconced in breathing apparatus.

Aubriot jerked awake.

He sucked in a breath and stared at the ceiling, dim in the darkness, trying to remember where he was. Something—some*one*—lay beside him. He reached out and touched bare skin, turned and saw the back of a woman's head on a pillow.

Cherry.

He wasn't on Earth. He was on Concordia. He'd spent nearly two centuries in cryo, flying through space. He'd been revived and lived through... so much. Yet his dream had been as vivid as if he'd never left home.

Cherry stirred. She moved onto her back and then onto her other side, curling onto his chest and draping her arm over him. He patted her shoulder awkwardly. If she weren't half-asleep she wouldn't be so affectionate. Neither of them was comfortable in a romantic relationship, but they were trying. The biggest problem was Cherry's attitude. She didn't seem to appreciate him as much as he deserved. He could have just about any woman in the colony and she knew it. Yet she never looked at him the way she used to look at Ethan when she thought no one was watching. That old sap had been dead years. Surely she should be over him by now?

"What's the time?" she asked.

"Don't know, Bandit." He lifted his head to peer out the window. The horizon shone pale gray. "It'll be dawn soon."

She groaned. "I better get up."

"What's the hurry? Go back to sleep."

"I have to get the harvester out. Going to be working all day today. It's supposed to rain tomorrow. Gotta get the wheat in."

"Ah, okay. I'll give you a hand."

She sat up and looked him in the eyes, her lips curved into a small smile. Her black, bed-head hair hung shaggy around her face. "Thanks, but there's no need. The harvester does most of the work. But I appreciate the offer." She bent and kissed him before climbing out of bed and padding toward the bathroom.

"Are you sure you can manage it one-handed?" he asked.

"I've done it before, remember?" She opened the bathroom door.

"What's the crop like?"

As she turned to answer, her expression was grim. "Not great, but a little better than last year, I think. We won't know for sure until it's in."

The bathroom door closed, and the sound of running water quickly followed.

Ever since the Scythians had destroyed most life on Concordia with their biocide, everything the colony tried to grow struggled to thrive. Kes had said it was because the soil was depleted of micro-organisms. A few bacteria and fungi had a natural immunity to the devastating virus and would multiply to fill the gap left by their dead counterparts, but the process would take years.

Plant life was similarly wrestling to recover. In many places, a single species proliferated out of control in the absence of competitors and predators. Between Annwn and the coast, a massive swathe of the rubbery Concordian groundcover plant shrouded the plain. Billions of sea jellies shaped like starfish filled the oceans. Life had survived, but the planet's ecosystems had been whacked out of balance. When things would return to their former state, the scientists couldn't say.

Aubriot's ear comm chirruped. He picked it up from the nightstand and inserted it.

"Hello?"

"You're coming in to help today, right?"

It was Wilder. The fact that it was before dawn clearly didn't faze her when issuing her reminder. Day and night didn't seem to have any meaning for the young woman, except as an inconvenience when they got in the way of her work.

"Uh, yeah. I forgot."

The breath of a sigh came down the line. "Great. See you soon." She was gone.

He swung his legs over the side of the bed. The shower noises had stopped.

A second later, the bathroom door opened and Cherry reappeared, wrapped in a towel. "You're getting up too? There's no need. I told you—"

"Got other things to do, and I wouldn't get back to sleep anyway." He held out a hand. "Come here."

She sat beside him on the bed. "Is everything okay?"

He put an arm around her shoulders. "I had a dream, a nightmare, really."

Her eyebrows rose in concern. "What was it about?"

"It's not important. I just wanted..." *to hold you for a minute.* He pulled her close. "What do you think Earth's like now?"

"How would I know? I was never there."

He snorted a laugh. "I was forgetting."

"You need to have this conversation with Kes."

"Yeah, you're right."

It would be awkward, though. They'd never been friendly, and Kes didn't seem to have got over the death of his wife. He was a shell of a man, mentally AWOL. The only time anyone ever saw him happy was when he was with his kids.

Cherry said, "Maybe a more important question is what it will be like when we get there. It'll take us years. Things change, and if the Scythians—"

"Things won't have changed that much. I think the way things are on Earth, they'll be the same for a long time. And we could be there sooner than you think."

"What makes you say that? Is there some news I haven't heard?"

"Well, nothing official..."

"Tell me. Go on, spill the beans." She tickled his ribs.

He swatted her hand away playfully. "It's not much, but..." he paused for effect "...Wilder thinks she can do it."

"You're kidding!" Cherry faced him. "Seriously?"

"Would I joke about something like that?"

"Yeah, you would."

He held up three fingers. "Scouts' honor."

"What the hell does that mean? Don't start using Earth English again. You know how I hate it."

"It means I'm telling you the truth."

"We'll be able to jump through space like the Fila?!"

"It's still early days, but probably."

"So she was right? Thank the stars we listened to her."

"Yep."

After the Guardian, Faina, had revealed the Scythians had obtained Earth's coordinates, it had become clear something had to be done to protect the home planet from the vengeful aliens. But with the Scythians' fast ships and head start, the Concordians didn't have a hope of arriving until after the damage had been done, not even with the aid of their friends in the Galactic Assembly.

That was until Wilder had come up with the idea of building a starship with jump capability, similar to their friends the Fila's but able to sustain human life. If they could use the faster method of space travel, they could arrive at Earth before the Scythians.

It was a huge challenge, even for Wilder, who had cracked the secret of anti-gravity, but, after two years' constant labor, she'd come up with the answer.

"How long will it take to build a ship?" Cherry asked.

"At least a year, and it has to be constructed in space, so you might not see much of me for a while."

"I'll cope." She stiffened, as if realizing the coldness of her words. "I mean, I'll miss you, but—"

"It's okay. I know what you mean."

She looked at him fixedly. "We're good, right?"

"Yeah, we're good."

"Okay, I'd better get that crop in."

Two

Cherry slipped open the lock on the shed and pulled out the two heavy wooden doors. Her breath puffed like smoke in the chill air. It was late in the season to be harvesting cereal crops, but the weather had been unusually wet. Damp grain rotted in storage, and the colony couldn't afford to lose any more food.

An empty ache settled in her stomach as she saw the looming form of the harvester, shadowy in the pre-dawn light. The sight of it always reminded her of Ethan. She recalled the first time they'd had a proper conversation, that day out by the lake, when she'd used the pretext of wanting to borrow a plow to talk to him. He'd saved her life that day, or rather, they'd thought her life had needed to be saved. The Fila had tried to grab her in order to take a closer look at this strange new species that had appeared on Concordia.

Later, he'd sat with her in the cab of a harvester when she'd brought in the colony's first crop. Perhaps it had been this very machine.

She blinked and drew her sleeve across her eyes. This was no time for tears.

After mounting the steps on the side of the machine, she opened the cab door and climbed in. It had taken her a while to figure out how to handle the machine with one hand, but a couple of adjustments had made it possible. She'd been glad. She didn't want to give up her role as a farmer. She continued to lead the military, but she was sick of fighting and death. Farming connected her with life and the land, her home.

She started up the engine. The welcome vibration coursed through her bones, and she drove the hulking machine out into the field just as the sun sent its first rays over the horizon.

An hour later, when a quarter of the wheat field was stubble, the engine suddenly quit. Inertia threw her forward, thrusting her midriff against the steering wheel.

She cursed and checked the dashboard screen. Nothing seemed wrong. The engine wasn't overheating, the battery held plenty of power. She pressed the ignition a few times, but the machine didn't respond. Turning off the music she'd been listening to on her comm, she hopped out of the cab. There were mechanics she could call out but fixing the problem herself would save time. Garwin had taught her how to deal with the most common problems with farm machinery.

The first thing to check was the cutters. If they hit something thicker than a twig the engine would automatically cut out. It was a failsafe to prevent nasty accidents and animal bodies contaminating the harvest. Considering most wildlife had been wiped out, it was extremely unlikely anything was stuck between the blades, but it wouldn't hurt to check.

The cutters were clean and empty. Nothing was caught in the feeder house chains or belt either.

She walked around to the front of the machine to open the engine casing. The sun was now high enough to take a good look inside. What had Garwin said? She peered at the mechanical innards. Was the problem simply a connection come loose? She reached in and jiggled each one in turn.

The engine sparked to life and the harvester jumped forward. Realizing her mistake, she tried to snatch her arm out of the way but a protruding bolt, old and sharpened with rust, dug into her skin. Within a second the bolt cut a deep channel down her forearm to her wrist.

"*Shit*! *Damn!*"

The harvester had died again as it sensed no one in the driver's seat, but the damage was done.

She swore some more as she inspected her wound. Blood coursed from it and dripped on her boots. Feeling like a fool, she comm'd her fellow farmers to take over for her, but all were busy taking advantage of the dry weather. It couldn't be helped. She set off for the medical clinic.

The autocar dropped her at its doors just as the clinic was opening. She wordlessly held up her arm to the medic.

After a grimace, he led her through the empty waiting area to an examination room, sat her down, and inspected the wound. "Wait here while I get the irrigation equipment. Gotta clean that out before we close it."

When the door opened again, however, it wasn't the medic who appeared, but Kes.

"Hey," said Cherry. "What are you doing here?"

"I could ask you the same question," he replied, seeming equally surprised.

"What's wr— Oh, I see," he added as his gaze alighted on her bloody arm and clothes. "That looks nasty. I hope it isn't serious."

"I was just giving myself a reminder not to be so damned stupid."

"I'm sorry?"

"Doesn't matter. Have you decided to switch professions and go into medicine?"

"No." He pulled up a chair. He was holding a small tray containing cotton bud sticks and clear tubes with stoppers. "I'm taking DNA samples from everyone who comes into the clinic. Would you mind opening your mouth?"

"Uh, sure."

He wiped a swab on her inner cheek and put it in a tube which he then sealed.

"Why are you sampling our DNA?"

The door opened. The medic was back.

Kes asked, "Do you have five minutes for a chat when you're done?"

She did, and he said he would wait for her outside. After her wound had been cleaned and closed with sticky healing gel, she found Kes in the street.

Annwn was waking up. The traffic had grown busier during her short time in the clinic. It was odd how quickly things had returned to normal after the destruction wreaked by the Scythians' biocide. Though many Concordians had been killed in the attack on Oceanside, most had survived the deadly virus. People had picked up their lives and carried on almost as if nothing had happened. But a current of dread underlay the daily routine. Shocked out of complacency, this latest generation of colonists seemed to finally understand the fragility of their existence.

"What's the big secret?" she asked jokingly. "Or did you only want some fresh air?"

He didn't smile. That didn't mean anything necessarily. Kes rarely smiled these days. She inwardly winced. It was irrational, but she couldn't help feeling somehow responsible for his wife's death.

"This probably warrants a longer talk," he said. "The short version is, we're in deep trouble."

"Don't tell me the Scythians are coming back." She was kidding, but if they were and Kes had somehow received the news before her, Concordia was sunk. Most of its defense capability had been expended in the most recent attack. They had begun to rebuild but it would take years to reach the original capacity.

"Internal trouble," Kes replied. "Where to begin? I suppose it started with the case of a young child who cut themselves. It wasn't a very bad cut but it required medical attention. The problem was—the cut wouldn't stop bleeding. The medics sealed it up, but the child continued to bleed internally."

She wrinkled her nose.

"A doctor brought the case to my attention. Not unreasonably, she thought a Concordian organism might be the problem. If something had infiltrated the wound…" He paused and shook his head. "The child has hemophilia."

"Right. And that is…?"

"An inherited genetic condition that stops blood from clotting. When I figured it out, I became curious. You see, Cariad screened out genetic disease carriers in the *Nova Fortuna* Project applicants. It should be impossible for hemophilia to appear in the colony except as a mutation. The child's case *is* due to a mutation, no question, but it prompted me to complete a survey of genetic diversity. I collected samples from schoolchildren first, then workers, and now patients at medical clinics, trying to vacuum up the few who slipped through the net. Cherry, the preliminary results aren't good. The colony's gene pool is too homogeneous. As time goes on more conditions will manifest. We could forestall the effect by enforcing restrictions on marriages, but it would only delay the inevitable."

She had kind of followed what he said, but not quite. "More people are going to get sick?"

"Yes, and, even more importantly, infertile. It's a common effect of inbreeding."

"I thought that was why Cariad created those extra babies—to prevent inbreeding?" Her memory of the influx of infants, saved by the Fila when the *Nova* was destroyed, was vivid. Everyone at Sidhe had endured months of sleepless nights, regardless of whether they had personally volunteered to take on a baby.

"She tried, but it clearly hasn't worked. The Project was already skirting the edge of minimum numbers required for a healthy population according to genetic science at the time. This was always a possibility."

"Isn't there anything we can do?" Cherry had been feeling mildly optimistic since Aubriot's announcement about the jump engine. Kes's revelation had thrown a dampener on everything.

Before he could answer, she exclaimed, "Ow!" and slapped her neck. On her palm was a squashed, black insect about a centimeter long. Fresh blood stained her skin. Her own blood, she suspected. "Something bit me."

He inspected the mess on her hand. "We've been seeing a lot of those lately, though we haven't named them yet. They appear to be harmless—aside from the biting. We're developing a repellent."

Lifting one side of her upper lip, she wiped the dead insect on her pants. "So the colony's doomed?"

He tutted. "This is why I wanted to speak to you in private. You can't go around saying things like that, you understand?"

"I'm not a moron, Kes."

"I didn't say you were, only..."

"What?"

He sighed. "I don't know what we can do. When I think about the future, about the world I've brought Miki and Nina into, I..." He lapsed to silence.

She touched his arm. "No one knew this would happen."

"Maybe not, but we knew the Scythians would be back one day. I've been irresponsible. I imagined life here had turned out to be like it was on Earth—safe and secure. That couldn't have been further from the truth."

"Look, it sounds like all the colony needs is an injection of fresh blood, right? New genes to supplement our current ones."

"You say that as if it were the easiest thing in the world to achieve."

"Not easy, maybe, but possible. If we manage to get to Earth, we might be able to persuade some people to come back with us."

"*If* we get to Earth. How likely is that in reality?"

"According to what I heard this morning, it's likelier than you think. By the way, I've been meaning to ask you something. Aubriot sometimes calls me Bandit. Do you know why? What does it mean?"

The ghost of a smile flitted across Kes's lips. "Why are you asking me? Surely you should ask him?"

"He won't tell me. I thought it might be an Earth-English thing. Is it?"

"It's better you ask Aubriot," was all Kes would reply.

It started to rain.

"*Shit,*" she muttered.

THREE

The problem with having your pick of alien tech, Wilder had discovered, was that a lot of the time you had no immediate use for it. She'd come to regret her decision to ask for one piece of top tech from each member of the Galactic Assembly in return for a working a-grav generator and specs. A new world for Concordians would have been a better price tag to put on her invention. Planets hospitable to life were scarce, and planets that would sustain humans were probably even rarer, but if the friendly aliens had pooled their knowledge and resources, they might have found something suitable.

As it was, she had loads of tech she barely understood and mostly couldn't use, and the colony was stuck on a planet devastated by a viral biocide. Not only that, the prospect of the Scythians' return hadn't gone away. She'd thought she was being clever, like the person who, when the genie gives them three wishes, uses their first wish to ask for infinite wishes. But she hadn't been clever, she'd been dumb. The allure of new, fascinating, secret technology had seduced her, causing her to neglect the immediate needs of her fellow humans.

Yet it wasn't all bad. Before leaving Concordia, the Fila had explained how their starship jump engines worked, though it had taken months to figure out their translation, and now she knew how to stop the jumps from being dangerous for humans.

Or, rather, she *thought* she knew. She wouldn't be certain until they'd run a successful test. The test subject would have to be a human volunteer. No animals larger than a microbe now lived on Concordia except for people and Piddle and Puddle—and she was certainly never going to risk *their* lives. But perhaps a few creatures with natural immunity to the killer virus had survived out in the wild somewhere. Perhaps they could catch one and—

The lab door opened and Dragan entered, panting. He lived five klicks from the research center and ran to work every morning. Dragan was one of the original team working on the a-grav drive, like Niall Cully. Dragan's pseudonym to maintain his anonymity had been The Artist, a much more grown-up and sensible alias than her own, Deadly After Midnight. She cringed when she thought about it. Still, Dragan was in his thirties and she'd been just a kid.

"Hi," he said after catching his breath. "Did you arrive early or have you been working all night?"

She yawned and stretched. She had to think for a minute before answering, "I got here a couple of hours ago. I woke up while it was still dark and couldn't get back to sleep, so I came in."

"Was it a blast of insight that woke you up?"

"Huh! No. Just anxiety, I guess."

The work to develop the jump drive had been painstaking. There had been no brilliant breakthroughs allowing them to leap forward, just slow, steady progress, detail by hard-won detail.

"Don't worry," said Dragan. "We'll get there." He stepped into the bathroom to shower and change.

The next person to arrive was Niall. He'd undergone a growth spurt in the two years since she had first met him face to face, and he didn't show any signs of slowing down. His personality changed, too. She rarely glimpsed the eager young kid she'd met just before she'd gone with Quinn to the *Opportunity*. Niall had become quiet and serious. She guessed seeing his mother killed by the biocide had something to do with it. That, and the time afterward he'd spent helping a group of vulnerable people survive while the deadly virus spread over the land.

He gave her his usual gruff greeting and immediately settled down at his interface to begin work.

She checked the time. She was expecting a new arrival today, now they were finally getting down to the nuts and bolts of constructing the starship that would take some colonists to Earth.

As if summoned by her thoughts, Aubriot walked in.

She stood up. "Welcome to the team."

"No problem. I'm looking forward to getting my teeth into this."

Niall's head jerked up. He stared at Wilder questioningly.

"He's going to help with the installation of the Parvus's weapon," she explained.

"I didn't know we were installing a weapon," said Niall. "Who made that decision?"

"Me, of course."

"Just like that? Unilaterally? I thought we were working together on this project."

"We are. I..." she hesitated "...I didn't think anyone would object."

"Sounds like you didn't *think* at all."

She blinked. Why was he being so rude?

"Let's see what Dragan has to say," said Niall. "Has he arrived yet?"

"Hey," said Aubriot. "Wilder's the one in charge around here, isn't she? What she says goes."

Niall replied without looking at him, "Thanks for your *input.*"

An awkward pause stretched out. Niall continued to glare at Wilder, his lips set. She stared back helplessly, wondering what she'd done wrong. She wasn't very good at dealing with people. Machines and processes were far easier to understand.

"This is stupid," said Aubriot. "Tell me where to sit, and I'll get st—"

Dragan appeared, his hair still damp from his shower. He halted, taking in the scene, looking from Aubriot to Niall and Wilder. He said hi to Aubriot and then turned to Wilder. "I didn't know we were going to have a visi—"

"He isn't a visitor," Niall interrupted. "He's going to be working with us. Installing an apparently *much-needed* weapon."

"Oh? This is the first I've heard of it."

"I thought so. It's the first I've heard of it too."

Wilder looked at Aubriot pleadingly, hoping he would be sensitive to the tension his arrival had caused, wishing he would leave so the three of them could discuss the problem she'd created. Niall was right. She should have consulted with him and Dragan, but she genuinely hadn't imagined they would mind. Should she gently ask Aubriot to give them time to talk it over?

"Look," said Aubriot, "you're going to need defensive weaponry on that starship. It's a no-brainer. Who knows what you'll find each time you complete a jump? What if you stumble into Scythian territory or encounter a different hostile species? If we can't defend ourselves, we're lambs to the slaughter. So let's forget about your stupid office politics and get started. Is this seat empty?" He gestured at Dragan's desk.

"Uh, no," said Wilder. "You can sit there."

He walked to the place she'd indicated, sat down, and turned on the interface. "I'm pretty familiar with the plans already, but I'll check them over and get up to speed."

"Wilder," said Niall between his teeth, "can I speak to you?"

Aubriot was either oblivious to the anger in Niall's tone or very good at ignoring it.

Feeling forlorn, Wilder followed her friend into the passageway.

"I'm sorry!" she exclaimed as soon as the door closed. "I really didn't—"

"So you already said. That doesn't change the fact that now we're stuck working with him."

"I don't understand what your problem is. Isn't he right? We do need some kind of space weapons, and the one the Parvus gave us in exchange for the a-grav device is perfect." Strictly speaking, it was the only weapon they had, and part of her reason for wanting it was her desire to make use of the alien tech she'd bargained for.

"*How* is it perfect?" Niall asked. "It might be incredibly powerful, but you have to be near a sun to use it."

"No, we don't," she replied excitedly, delighted at the opening to explain her reasoning and defuse his ire. "That's the beauty of what I had in mind. You see, as well as the Parvus's weapon, we can use the energy storage cell with a gigantic capacity I got us. We can gather energy for the weapon from the sun before we set off. If we end up in a battle, we'll be ready."

Niall's expression softened a fraction. He was, after all, a scientist at heart like her. As she'd predicted, the awesomeness of the tech and the utility of its deployment was appealing to him.

She continued, "I really am sorry I didn't ask you and Dragan before inviting Aubriot onto the team. But he does know about this stuff, more than anyone else."

"Maybe, but he's also a complete prick. You know that, right?"

"I do know what he's like, yes." Her memories of traveling to and from the Galactic Assembly's space station were vivid. Aubriot had been almost unbearable to live with, and the long duration and boredom of the space flight hadn't helped. She hadn't been aware his notoriety had spread so far. "Can't you just try to get along with him for the next few months?"

Niall didn't answer. He narrowed his eyes at her and returned to the workroom.

Four

Cherry dug her hand into the wheat she'd harvested, scooped up a portion, and allowed it to run through her fingers. The grains weren't the plumpest she'd ever seen, but they were dry. It was the rest of the crop she was worried about. Stepping out of the grain store, she surveyed her field. The downpour that had started while she was speaking with Kes had soaked the remaining three-quarters of it. Other farmers were in a similar position. There were things they could do to mitigate the problem, but basically the harvest would be a disappointment again this year, and unless the weather turned dry again soon, it could be a disaster.

The destruction caused by the Scythians' biocide seemed to have even affected the climate. She'd never known the season to be so wet and humid. If they didn't get a break of a few days' sunshine, the cereals and other crops could become infested with mold. Mold spores were one of the few things to survive the deadly virus, naturally. They were not technically alive, Kes had explained, so the biocide hadn't affected them.

Something buzzed near her ear, and before she could react a sharp pain lanced from her neck. She slapped the spot. Another of those biting insects had attempted to feed on her. She trotted to her autocar and climbed in. The insects followed. They hung around outside.

Oh, well. The fields were too wet to work today anyway.

She answered a comm. "Hello?"

"Cherry," said Kes, "can you come to the Annwn Town Hall right away? The Leader wants to hold an emergency meeting."

"Sure. I'm not exactly busy. What's it about?"
"Just come."

Barker, the Leader elected shortly after the biocide attack was a short, tubby man in late middle age. He was about as boring an individual as Cherry had ever met. He was always so calm. He didn't seem to experience strong emotions or hold any firm opinions. But perhaps that was what the colonists needed right now—someone who would listen and react rather than force his will on everyone.

Barker's usually mild expression was full of worry. That, in turn, worried her. Whatever the problem was, it had to be bad if it was provoking a reaction in the unflappable man. Had Kes told him about the inbreeding in the population? Was that what this was about?

Wilder was also attending the meeting, along with the two engineers she worked with and Aubriot.

"Thank you for coming at such short notice," said Barker. "I'd appreciate it if you were to keep to yourselves whatever is said in this room today. No minutes will be taken, and if I am challenged about what we're about to discuss, I will deny all knowledge of it. So should you. When you hear the subject matter, you will understand why. Kes, please go ahead and explain what you told me this morning."

Kes's face was grim. "As Cherry already knows, I've been conducting a survey of the human gene pool, and the results aren't good. I'll tell you more about that later. But first, I want to tell you about another survey I've been undertaking. I dispatched drones to collect soil samples from all over Lyonesse and Suddene to find out as much as I can about the pitiful remnants of life on this planet. It's taken many months, but the results are in. I'm sure we're all aware how bad the situation is. Well, it's worse than I thought, much worse. The lack of biodiversity extends to all parts of the ecosystem I've surveyed. In many areas the land is simply dead, entirely devoid of any life. In others, one microorganism has filled the niche and is reproducing exponentially. We've already seen the effects. Crops are struggling to grow. Single species dominate hundreds of square kilometers."

He rubbed his temples and then stared at each of them in turn. "I've never heard of or read about a situation exactly like this, but in similar examples in Earth history, where a non-native species was introduced to an ecosystem without its natural predators, the results were damned disasters. Plagues of mice, rabbits, toads..." He shook his head. "From what I can tell, the situation on Concordia is going to get a hell of a lot worse before it can get better. It will be thousands—possibly tens of thousands of years—before life reaches equilibrium and harmony once more."

"So what?" Aubriot challenged. "As long as we can grow enough food to survive, it doesn't really matter. Who cares if we never see another sluglimpet? I certainly don't."

"Of course it matters," said Niall. "Millions of species have become extinct. The planet is like a biological experiment gone wrong. It's a disaster."

"Still," Aubriot countered, "as long as we're okay, we shouldn't sweat it. Species go extinct all the time. That's how evolution works."

"What happened here wasn't evolution!" Niall's face had turned pale. "It was a crime against nature."

Barker asked, "Can we put the philosophical discussion to one side for a moment? Kes hasn't finished."

"Thanks," said Kes. "I do have more to say. The fact is the state of the planet's ecosystem *does* matter to us. Cherry will vouch for the fact that the harvests since the biocide attack have been the worst in Concordian history. Right?"

She nodded, guessing what was coming next.

"Put simply," he went on, "the best we can expect is for yields to continue to diminish. That's if we're lucky. What's more likely is we'll see entire crops regularly wiped out by swarms of insects or pathogens."

"Bullshit," said Aubriot. "I know you've had a hard time, Kes, but don't drag us all down into your private hell. You're scaremongering. We can spray insecticides and pesticides or find other ways to protect the crops."

"Yes, we can, but it's a stopgap measure. Over the long term, that's only going to make things worse."

"I don't believe it."

"Well," said Kes, his jaw tightening, "go and get your PhD in biosciences, then come and talk to me about it."

"The crops won't grow well in dead soil?" asked Niall.

Kes replied, "They won't thrive, but more importantly, this problem with single micro-organism species proliferating will spell disaster for them, and we'll see more and more cases as life re-establishes on Concordia."

"The colony will starve," said the other engineer.

"Exactly," said Kes heavily.

This new information put his earlier pronouncement about inbreeding in a distant second place. Cherry said, "There has to be something we can do. Otherwise, why are we having this meeting?" She addressed Barker. "You called us here for a reason, right?"

"I did. I especially wanted Wilder and her team to attend because Kes has proposed a solution."

For a man who apparently had the answer to their woes, Kes didn't look very happy about it. "The only answer I can think of is to seed the planet with as many other species as possible. It will result in environmental chaos for I don't know how long, but that's a better scenario than the one we currently face."

"Species from where?" asked Wilder.

"Earth," Aubriot answered. "He means Earth species. It's the only place humans co-inhabit with other species."

Kes nodded.

"So what's the problem?" Wilder asked. "We'll be going there in a year."

"We need to go there sooner," said Barker, "if the colony is going to stand a chance of survival. As I understand it, even if we began to seed Concordia tomorrow it would be touch and go."

Kes sighed and nodded again. "We desperately need other life forms, other food sources. The situation is more dire than I imagined, and the only possible solution is the last thing that was ever supposed to happen. The Mandate stated we were to preserve existing life on the colony planet wherever possible. We can't do that now. We have to turn Concordia into another Earth."

"The Mandate?" asked Niall.

A bittersweet sadness hit Cherry. How ironic it was that something Ethan, Garwin, and she had fought the Woken about so viciously in the early days of colonization was now entirely forgotten. How many Gens had lost their lives fighting for their freedom from Woken and Guardian tyranny? Their names were ancient history.

"It's just an old book," Aubriot explained. "It isn't important. And it wasn't *us* who killed Concordia, it was the Scythians, so let's forget the guilty tears. I say we go to Earth and bring back everything we can."

"We don't have a choice, unfortunately," said Kes. "Wilder, as well as the jump ship, we'll also need a vast storage container, somewhere to put everything we want to bring back. Soil, seeds, plants, insects, perhaps even larger life forms."

The young woman's brows furrowed. "We have enough to do already, just constructing the ship. And now you say we need the ship earlier, and on top of that, you also want us to build something that can support a huge range of life forms, all with different needs?"

"All the colony's resources will be at your disposal," said Barker. "Manpower, materials, you name it. This project is our absolute number one priority."

"What about the Scythians?" asked Niall. "I thought we were going to Earth to help protect the planet against them."

"We can do that too," Aubriot replied. "I don't see a problem."

"I'm glad you don't," Wilder commented, "because I see plenty." She asked Barker, "How much time do we have?"

"Can you do it in three months?"

"No," said Niall. "That's ridiculous."

"*Three months*?!" Wilder exclaimed. Then she said resignedly, "We'll do what we can."

FIVE

"How's it going?" Wilder glided over to Niall, who was supervising the installation of the jump engine.

Even through the tinted visor of his EVA suit, she saw the look he gave her. If she hadn't seen it, she would have *felt* it. Niall had been giving her grief ever since the emergency meeting where she'd agreed to the three-month timescale for the construction of the starship.

"It's impossible!" he'd hissed at her as they'd left the town hall.

"He's right," Dragan had agreed as they descended the steps, though he'd sounded more disheartened than angry. "We've already been working all hours to get this thing done. How can we work any faster?"

"We'll draft more people onto the team," she'd replied. "We've done the hard work. We have the engine specs and the basic blueprint. Now it's only a matter of building everything, and the Leader promised us all the engineers, construction workers, and support staff we need. We also have Aubriot, don't forget."

Niall barked out a short laugh. "If you think *he's* going to make things easier for us, you really are deluded."

"He headed several massive corporations on Earth," Wilder retorted. "He must have been involved in hundreds of projects in his lifetime before he even got started on the *Nova Fortuna*."

"That was a long time ago," said Dragan.

They'd reached the autocar that would take them back to the lab. As they climbed inside, Wilder replied, "Not to him it isn't. He spent the journey to Concordia in cryosleep, and over a hundred years passed while he was traveling to and from the Galactic Assembly. By his reckoning, he only left Earth ten years or so ago."

"As recently as that?" asked Dragan. "I didn't realize."

"That makes it worse," Niall said. "He hasn't had time to adjust to being a normal person. He still thinks he's the boss of everyone. You can see it in the way he talks, acts, in everything he does."

Wilder sighed. "You hate him. I get it. But can you please try to get along with him? Just until we finish building the starship. For the colony's sake, okay?"

Niall hadn't replied, only stared out at the passing landscape.

His attitude toward Aubriot hadn't improved in the ten weeks that had passed since, but he hadn't entered into downright confrontations with the man. She guessed that was something to be grateful for.

"We should have it done before the end of the shift," he replied.

The jump drive took up more than a third of the starship, a far bigger proportion than the equivalent engines on Fila ships. The additional size was due to the alterations they had been forced to make so the ship's passengers weren't squashed like putty during a jump. Quinn had been correct in his guess that the human body wouldn't withstand traveling in a regular Fila ship. She'd thanked the stars they hadn't attempted it. Fila bodies were adapted to an aquatic existence and could withstand massive changes in pressure. By comparison, human bodies were extremely fragile. The drive she'd designed with Niall and Dragan's help created a slower, gentler jump, exerting less force on the organic entities it transported light years in one bound.

She gazed at the huge device, hanging within its casing, and the engineers in their suits hooking it up to its connections. "By the end of the shift? That's fantastic. You've done a great job, Niall. I appreciate it."

"Thanks, but I'm not doing it for you. All this taking everything too fast is for the colony's sake, remember?"

Ugh. Why do you have to be such an asshole? For all his complaints about Aubriot, he was turning out to be an awful lot like him.

"And as a member of the colony," she said, "I appreciate it."

"What's happening with the a-grav?"

"They're behind schedule, but they're making progress."

A-grav wasn't a priority. It wouldn't be needed until the ship departed, and during the construction phase it was actually an impediment. It was far easier to work when tools, equipment, and parts weighed practically nothing.

"Have you decided about joining the mission?" she asked.

"Not yet." He returned his attention to the workers installing the drive.

She didn't understand his reluctance. She'd assumed he would want to go to Earth, if only for the sake of traveling aboard the ship he'd spent years working to design. It couldn't be fear putting him off. Assuming everything went to plan, they would arrive way before the Scythians and would have plenty of time to gather the material they needed to seed Concordia before setting off again. The second trip would focus on protecting Earth from invaders, and he didn't have to take part in that if he didn't want to. "Well, don't leave it too long. I want to complete the manifest by the end of the week. There are plenty of others ready to take your place if you don't want it."

Interest in the prospect of returning to the origin planet had been high among the colonists. She had begun to avoid going out in public because people would come up to her in the street and make their argument as to why they should be included. Most of them didn't have a good reason. It was pure curiosity that drove them. She'd grown tired of pointing this out and had taken to telling them to send her a written comm stating their formal request.

"I'll think about it," said Niall.

She clearly wasn't going to get any more conversation out of him today, so she pushed off from the scaffolding. Directing her movements with bursts of pressurized gas from nozzles in her suit, she headed for the airlock leading to the pressurized section of the ship. This included the bridge, engine room, and living and leisure quarters. The shell of all these areas had been built but the interiors remained scenes of frenzied activity. As she stepped into the passageway, she nearly tripped over someone fixing metal sheeting over the deck struts.

The hand holds on the bulkhead had been the first items to be attached. After opening her visor, she pulled herself along them toward the bridge. She wanted to check in with Dragan. He was working on the conventional engine, needed to maneuver the ship short distances.

Before she reached the area, however, she was abruptly drawn toward the deck, landing on her side. Her EVA suit offered some protection, but the exposed struts still dug painfully into her hips and ribs.

Alarms blared, echoing along the unfinished passageway.

Dammit! Ship gravity had accidentally activated. That would come as a surprise to everyone. She hoped no one had suffered a serious injury.

"Wilder?" It was Niall. "Are you okay?"

Before she could answer, he exclaimed, "Shit!"

"What's wrong?"

The alarms continued to blare. If he replied, she didn't hear it.

She was suddenly weightless again and drifting. Reaching out, she grabbed a hand hold and pulled herself over to the bulkhead. "What's wrong?" she asked again, louder.

"The a-grav extended to the jump drive. It's...Oh no. Oh my god!"

The comm cut out.

After several attempts, she couldn't raise him. She sped down the passageway, returning to the drive section, comming Niall at the same time. He didn't answer. Giving up, she tried Aubriot. "Did the gravity field hit you? Do you know what's happening?"

He was on the ship's hull, involved in the installation of the Parvus's weapons.

His tone was grim as he answered, "The gravity field hit the jump dr—"

"I know! What's happened?"

"What do you think?" he asked harshly.

The answer was obvious, but she couldn't bring herself to admit it. She needed to be told. "I-I don't know."

"Some people got crushed between the drive and the casing. Rescue teams are trying to reach them now."

Six

Thirteen people had died and six suffered permanent injuries from the disaster that occurred during the construction of the *Sirocco*. The event had thrown a pall over everything, and what had been an exciting rush toward the building of humanity's first jump-drive starship had turned into a somber, mournful effort to get the thing done. Now it was built, the Leader was attempting to inject some enthusiasm into his voice as he made the announcement, but his heart clearly wasn't in it.

Kes, who was watching Barker's speech at home, turned off his interface. He had observed the building of the ship from afar, through watching daily vidnews reports and via sporadic contact with Wilder. They remained good friends, but she was incredibly busy and he wasn't into socializing these days. He preferred to spend what free time he had with Miki and Nina. They were his only source of happiness now.

He'd tried to move on from Isobel's death, but he'd found he couldn't, not in any meaningful way. He had taken Cariad leaving him for Ethan on the chin. He'd pulled himself up, dusted himself off, and sought—and found—a new love, a new life in this colony light years from Earth. At the time, he hadn't thought he'd had any choice. How could he justify leaving his family and breaking all their hearts if he didn't make the best of whatever fate threw at him?

But so much had happened, so many unexpected, calamitous events. There had been so much death and suffering. Izzy dying in childbirth had been the nail in the coffin. He wasn't the same man anymore. He would do his job and continue to support the colonization in whatever ways he could, but he had to conserve his little remaining interest in life and focus it on his children.

What an amazing pair of little girls they were. Both reminded him strongly of his deceased wife in looks and personality. Smart, kind, gentle, and caring. He couldn't have asked for better offspring. All he wanted was to be the best father he could, especially considering how he'd neglected Miki in her early years. He didn't like to think about that time—the sense of shame was too great.

"What were you watching, Daddy?" Miki threw her arms around his shoulders.

"The Leader's announcement. The *Sirocco* is finished. She'll leave for Earth soon."

"Ms Marrak told us about that." She climbed onto his lap.

At five years old, she was getting a little big for it, but he didn't object. Ms Marrak was her teacher. "What did she tell you?"

"She said the ship's name is the name of a wind that blows from the south. They called the ship *Sirocco* because a ship that came to Concordia from Earth was called the *Mistral*, and the Mistral is a wind that blows from the north. So one wind blew a starship here..." she lifted her hands to represent the ship and puffed out her cheeks to blow "...and another wind will carry our ship back." She blew to her right. Her hands dropped to her lap and she gazed at him earnestly. "Is that right?"

"That's right. Well done for remembering. That's quite complicated."

Miki had a need to be certain about everything, often checking and re-checking any new facts she learned. Perhaps it was something to do with losing her mother so young. She remembered Isobel, but Kes wasn't sure how many real memories she had and how much she'd filled in from pictures, vids, and stories he'd told her.

She laid her head on his chest. "Is it true you come from Earth?"

He'd never told her where he was from. It wasn't a secret, he simply hadn't thought it was worth mentioning. "Yes, it's true. Who told you that?"

Her little body stiffened. "Some girls at school today."

He had a horrible feeling the conversation hadn't been friendly. "Were they teasing you?"

She nodded. "They said you're an alien because you weren't born here."

He gently lifted her upright. Her eyes were wet and her lips had turned down. "Do I look like an alien to you?"

"Your hair is a funny color."

Bad question. He was the only redhead in the colony. Blond hair and blue eyes still made infrequent appearances, but he'd never seen his brand of 'ginger' as Aubriot liked to put it.

"The girls said I'm half-alien because my hair's like yours."

In fact, her hair wasn't anything like his. It did have a reddish tinge, but that was it. He guessed that, to Concordians, it looked unusual.

"Sweetheart." He pulled her close. "Do I seem like an alien to you?"

She shook her head.

"Back on Earth, people had all different colors and types of hair, and there were many different skin shades too, from very pale to very dark. It's only because so few people came to Concordia that most colonists are black-haired and olive-skinned. Those colors predominated, and that was the way Earth's population was trending too. But a person's hair and skin color isn't important. It's what's in *here* that counts." He touched her chest. "What those girls said to you wasn't very nice. I'll speak to Ms Marrak tomorrow."

The Concordian curriculum probably didn't include any modules on the evils of racism, but it surely had something about discrimination and bullying. It was unfortunate, but wherever they went in the galaxy humans were apparently human.

"It must be nearly bedtime," he said. "Go and brush your teeth and get changed, then I'll read your story."

She hopped off his lap and skipped from the room. Nina was already asleep after a long, hard session in daycare.

His interface pinged. A vidcall request had arrived from Wilder. If it had been from anyone else, he would have ignored it.

The young girl's face was framed by a halo of hair. Her hair was always messy. She rarely combed it, let alone had it cut, but in this case it meant she was in the *Sirocco* and the a-grav wasn't on.

"Hey," he said. "Congratulations."

"Thanks. We finally finished, and only two weeks late."

"The deadline was impossible to meet."

"I know, but it sure made us hurry." Despite her upbeat words, her expression was pensive.

He knew what was on her mind. "Wilder, that accident, it wasn't—"

"I know what you're going to say. It's okay. I don't blame myself."

He wasn't sure she was telling the truth.

"Anyway," she continued with false brightness, "the reason I called is I wanted to know when you'll be joining us. We set out in three days, but you can come up anytime. It's probably better you get here early."

"But I... I'm not going to Earth."

"Of course you are! You have to. You're our chief biologist. How will we know what to bring back?"

"I've prepared a list, and you have plenty of people familiar with the typical range of living organisms. I know because I had to sign off on half of my staff going on the trip. It won't be hard to gather everything you need."

"No, no, no. You have to come too." She looked distraught. "You're the person who discovered the problems with the ecosystem, and you've lived on Earth. You know all the landscapes and seas. You know where to find all the organisms."

"I've given instructions on all that. And Aubriot is also from Earth. He can help you too. I take it he's going?"

"As if anyone could stop him. The way he acts, you'd think this is the *Nova Fortuna* Project and he's boss again. Sometimes, it's like he's the only reason we're going to Earth. Kes, you *have* to come! How am I going to survive weeks aboard the *Sirocco* in his company without you? When we went to the Galactic Assembly, if it hadn't been for you and Cherry, I would have ended up strangling him."

He chuckled. "I'm sure you'll be fine. He isn't as bad as he was, and you'll have plenty more people around to keep him in check. How many are you taking?"

"Thirty-two."

"Is Cherry going?"

"Yes. I think part of her still believes this whole situation is her fault."

"She did make the decision to fight back against the Scythians, but if she hadn't we'd probably be living a worse reality now."

"And she would probably feel responsible for that too," said Wilder. "It's hard to forgive yourself sometimes." She chewed her lip.

"You can say that again. Look, I'm sorry, but I really can't go. My place is here with my children. I can't possibly leave them alone for... How long will you be gone?"

"Only six weeks. That's my estimate, anyway. Two weeks there, two weeks working around the clock to collect what we need, and two weeks back. I thought you would bring Miki and Nina with you. I didn't expect you to leave them behind. They're only little so it won't matter if they miss time at school."

"The trip will be that short?"

"That's the beauty of a jump engine. We'll also arrive years before the Scythians. We'll be able to gather the samples we need to seed Concordia, bring them back, and return to Earth in plenty of time to set up planetary defenses." She gave a short laugh. "I'd love to see the look on their faces when they arrive and our missile silos open."

When he hesitated, she went on, "Promise me you'll at least think about it."

"It isn't only the time involved. I don't want to risk Miki and Nina's safety. The jump drive is new tech. What if something goes wrong?"

Her face fell, and he winced. He hadn't meant to remind her again about the gravity-field deaths.

"We've tested the prototype four times with human volunteers, and we'll be testing the *Sirocco*'s drive twice over the next couple of days. We don't have time for more tests, unfortunately, but I really doubt anything will go wrong. Please, will you at least think about it? You know you're the best person for the job. Wouldn't you like to see Earth again?"

Her last statement hit home. The idea of re-visiting the planet of his birth stirred something in him. But at the same time, the sound of Nina's wailing floated in. She'd woken up.

He had to be realistic. It was simply far too risky to take his children to Earth. Isobel would never have entertained the idea for a minute. And he couldn't leave them behind either. He couldn't bear to be parted from them.

SEVEN

It was starting to rain again. Kes unfolded his umbrella and raised it. How long had people been using umbrellas? The simple technology had to be thousands of years old, and now Concordians, light years from Earth, were still using them on an alien planet.

A few other parents were waiting to pick up their children outside the school gates. The line of moms and dads in autocars stretched down the road. Those men and women wouldn't be getting wet today, but he didn't mind a few raindrops. He liked the short walk home with Miki, listening to her chatter about her day.

The school bell rang and the postures of the waiting parents shifted. The children would be out soon.

Beyond the single-story building, vegetation covered the ground to the horizon, the Concordian equivalent to grass. Low-growing, it was wind-pollinated, like many plants on the planet. Flowering flora hadn't evolved yet, and probably wouldn't for tens or hundreds of thousands of years without human intervention.

The green blanket was a welcome sight in some ways. Up until a few months ago the ground had been entirely bare and wind had been gradually stripping it back to rock, blowing the unsecured soil into the ocean. But the domination of a single species was still concerning.

His conscience twinged as he recalled the mail he sent to Wilder last night, telling her he wasn't going to Earth and his decision was final. Everything she'd said was true. He wasn't one to blow his own trumpet, but he *was* the best person to collect the seeding material. He was also inured to space travel after his experience traveling to the Galactic Assembly. And he had a strong hankering to set eyes on the place of his birth again.

Yet his first duty was to his children. Others could do a perfectly adequate job of selecting the range of organisms required and ensuring their survival on the return trip. He wasn't indispensable.

The first children began to appear through the gates. Kes focused on looking for Miki, the red tint to her hair making her easy to identify.

The rain had stopped. He lowered his umbrella and closed it.

There she was!

She'd spotted him too. She ran to him through the bustling mob, her backpack bouncing.

"Daddy!"

He picked her up to hug her. "How was your day, sweetheart?"

He would gladly have carried her all the way home. In the past he had carried her everywhere. Isobel had warned him against spoiling her, but that had been before she'd lost her mother. He doubted Izzy would scold him now. But even he had to concede she was getting a little too big.

As he put her down, she asked, "What's that cloud, Daddy?"

She'd been looking over his shoulder, out across the sea of green that formed the open countryside. He couldn't see what she meant at first. The sky was full of clouds. Then he spotted it. An indistinct, dark haze occupied a space between the ground and the sky. It wasn't a cloud. Its edges were undefined and it was moving too quickly to be any kind of precipitation.

"I'm not sure," he replied, though he had a sense of foreboding. "Let's go home."

He put her down.

Children continued to stream from the gates. He took Miki's hand and they went along the street. Their home was only five minutes' walk away, but he found himself speeding up. He glanced over his shoulder. Houses obscured his view of the hazy cloud.

"You're holding my hand too tight," Miki complained.

"Sorry." He halted. "Would you like a piggyback?"

"Yes, please!"

He took her backpack and swung it over his shoulder before squatting down. With Miki's arms around his neck and her legs tucked under his elbows, he set off, jogging.

Miki giggled as she bounced on his back. "This is fun."

Next she said, "Ow!"

Then he heard the buzzing.

They were all around them. A second ago the air had been clear. Now, it was full of small, flying black bodies. The insect species that had been growing in numbers, one of which had bitten Cherry outside the medical center, was swarming.

He felt a sharp sting on his face.

He ran.

"Ow! Ow!" yelled Miki. "Daddy, they're biting me!"

They were biting him too. Every area of exposed skin was being attacked.

Even running, they were still a minute or two from home. He squatted down again and told Miki to jump off his back. She sobbed and covered her face. The insects settled on her hands, sinking their proboscises into her skin.

He ripped off his jacket and wrapped it around her, batting the insects away. He scooped her up and ran again, thanking the stars she was wearing pants. His jacket wasn't large enough to cover her legs. He hoped the insects couldn't bite through cloth.

At last he was home. He sprinted up the path leading to his house and slammed his hand on the security panel. As the door began to open, he squeezed through the widening gap and then told it to close again. Then he gave the instruction to close all windows, not remembering if he'd left any open. Miki was still crying, but he was forced to put her down and leave her in the hallway while he raced around the house, checking all the windows were in fact closed and the house computer wasn't glitching. In many countries on Earth windows had been fitted with screens but there had never been any need on Concordia. Here, insect life didn't prey on human beings. Until now.

Satisfied nothing would be able to get in, he returned to Miki. She'd stopped crying, but red bumps were appearing on her face and hands. He hoped her reaction wouldn't be too severe.

She giggled. "Daddy, you look funny."

He felt his face. Bumps were rising on him too.

"How about you play in your room while I make you a snack?"

She trotted away, apparently already over the drama. He would have to find some soothing ointment for the bites, but he had more urgent matters to attend to first. He comm'd Nina's daycare center to warn them. Luckily, the swarm hadn't reached them yet. "You must bring all the children inside and close all the windows and doors."

"Yes, yes," replied the receptionist. "I understand. We'll get on it right away."

Next, he comm'd the Leader. The secretary tried to put him off, but he insisted on speaking to Barker immediately. She put the comm through. Kes explained the situation, and then continued, "I'm guessing it's all the rain we've had, or a plant that hosts the insect for part of its life cycle has spread widely. I don't know. But whatever fed on these insects isn't around anymore, and neither are the organisms they fed on, so they're turning to us."

"I seem to remember receiving a report about this just the other week," said Barker.

"You did. My department is in the early stages of developing a repellent."

"Only the early stages?"

"Yes." Kes paused as he chose his next words carefully. "Leader, I don't think you understand how serious this is. Some people could have a deadly allergic reaction to the bites. You need to put out an immediate alert and tell everyone to stay inside until further notice."

"But what will the further notice be? How the hell are we going to deal with these things?"

"I'm not sure yet, but—"

"Never mind. I get the message. I'll put out a general comm. Thanks for the update. Reception has just reported we're being swamped with calls. I appreciate you getting in touch." He cut the comm.

Kes's gaze remained on the blank screen, not seeing it, his mind elsewhere.

Miki skipped in from her bedroom. "Where's my snack, Daddy? I'm hungry."

The bumps on her hands and face had grown bigger and taken on a deeper crimson hue. He needed to get the ointment, but he had a question for her first.

"Come here, darling." Lifting her onto his lap, he wrapped his arms around her. "Would you like to go on a starship?"

She gasped and turned to face him, her mouth an O of surprise. "A real starship? In space?"

"Absolutely. What do you think?"

The colony was in even more of a crisis than he'd estimated. The next months and years were going to be miserable as the colonists eked out their existence on a planet in chaos. His department might develop a repellent to deter the biting insects, but another ecological emergency would loom, and then another, and the population would lurch from one to the next, clinging to survival.

Could he really trust the task of collecting the needed organisms from Earth to his colleagues? None of them had ever been there. Shouldn't he be doing all he could to safeguard his children's lives, even if it meant taking some risks?

He wouldn't—couldn't—leave them in another's care. Yet to ensure their future on Concordia, he had to take up Wilder's invitation.

Miki jiggled excitedly. "I would love to go on a starship! Can Nina come too?"

Eight

The *Sirocco* hung like a jewel in space—a jewel with an ugly appendage. The appendage was the storage facility for the biological material and organisms to be brought back from Earth. It had inevitably been given the unofficial name, the Ark.

Aubriot's view of the two ships through the shuttle window was his first sight of them whole and complete. After years of preparation, years of dreaming of returning to Earth, his dreams were finally becoming reality. But what would he find there? His nightmare still loomed large in his mind.

Dragan was responsible for the main ship's design. The man clearly had an artistic flair, but the haste involved in the building of the Ark meant function had taken priority over form. The additional vessel lacked any beauty whatsoever.

The *Sirocco* was streamlined, though she would never travel through an atmosphere. Four sections widened out from a narrow tip, curved, and then flared at the tail to house the conventional engine. The jump drive was inside, its position not discernible on the silvery hull. According to Wilder, it needed no exhaust outlet. Dragan had managed to incorporate the Parvus's weapon into the design without affecting the overall shape. One of the hull sections— slightly dimmer than the rest—was the energy-capturing device, and the emitter formed the narrow tip.

The *Sirocco*'s shape was simple but elegant, and there was something about her proportionality that was easy on the eye.

Then there was the Ark.

An enclosed passageway protruded from the *Sirocco*'s side. The storage facility sat at the end, a square, plain box roughly as large as the parent ship. Even its hull wasn't pretty. It was dull, barely reflective. Though he wasn't close enough to see, Aubriot was confident even the rivets holding the thing together hadn't been covered. Strength against the vacuum of space had been the priority. That, and the range of refrigeration and freezing units. There had been no time for anything else.

The *Sirocco* grew rapidly larger until his view was swamped by the glistening hull. A round portal opened, revealing bright lights in the interior. The next second, the shuttle swept through it and he was looking at the bay. The shuttle landed and her engine's vibration cut out.

He and Kes were the last mission members to arrive. Kes's kids had been chattering annoyingly when the shuttle had taken off, but then they'd both fallen asleep, thankfully. While Aubriot walked down the aisle, Kes put the younger kid over one shoulder and was trying to wake up the older one.

Aubriot considered giving the man a hand but decided against it. It wouldn't be wise to set a precedent of helping with his kids. Kes might turn to him when it was inconvenient and kids were pains in the backside at the best of times, especially little ones. Bringing them along was insanity but it was the only way the scientist would agree to come. Aubriot had to admit, when it came to biological stuff, Kes knew what he was talking about.

Of course, if they were his own kids, his feelings would be different. But he couldn't have any, so that was that.

As he descended the steps, an odd feeling hit him. Excitement? Nostalgia? When he'd entered cryo on the *Nova Fortuna*, he'd never imagined he would be returning to Earth one day. Yet here he was. He'd known about and been involved in the preparations for more than two years—hell, it had all been his idea—but it hadn't felt real until now.

The pilot was also disembarking. His name was Zapata, and he would be the *Sirocco*'s main pilot. He was Cherry's choice, so Aubriot assumed he was the best Concordia had to offer.

Aubriot headed for his cabin. Leaving the bay, one of Kes's kids began wailing. Aubriot hurried away, hoping the scientist wasn't his neighbor.

He had half an hour before the first general meeting, when everyone would be introduced. Should he skip it? He already knew all the important people and had no desire to meet any of the others. But if he didn't turn up Cherry would give him grief later.

She wasn't in their cabin, so he wandered along to the meeting early and took a seat at the back to watch as the other participants arrived. The chairs were arranged in a horseshoe around an open area where a holo could display for presentations. A couple of the women caught his gaze as they walked in, holding it a fraction too long. He returned their looks, smiling to himself. All his adult life he'd attracted female attention. He'd never really tired of it, apart from a short time when he'd been depressed.

"Pleased we're finally setting off?" asked Cherry, taking the next seat.

He'd been lounging with his arms out. As she sat down he straightened up and pulled his arms down. "Uh, yeah. Where were you? I thought you said we'd meet in our cabin."

"I was giving Wilder a pep talk. She's nervous as anything."

"What about? Does she think the ship isn't ready?"

"No, this meeting, idiot. She's nervous about addressing everyone. It's the first time she's done anything like this."

"Why? What's there to be scared of?"

"Talking to a lot of people can be nerve-wracking."

"Can it? Does she want me to do it? I don't mind." He began to get up.

"Sit down!" She tugged on his elbow. "Stars, you're not slow to take the lead, are you?"

He put an arm around her, grinning. "I can't help it. I've been genetically programmed to dominate."

"Seriously?"

He shrugged. "Don't know, but it wouldn't surprise me."

While they were talking, Wilder had walked to the front of the briefing room. She looked a mess as usual. She seemed to have adopted the never-brushed-hair-and-unmatching-clothes look as a style. No one else was paying any attention to her, and her eyes searched the faces, as if hoping everyone would magically shut up and listen.

He coughed loudly, so loudly everyone looked at him. When he had their attention, he folded his arms over his chest and stared at Wilder. Like pinballs bouncing from one deflector to another, their gazes traveled from him to her.

She gave him a grateful glance before saying, "Thanks for coming, all of you. We know why we're here, so hopefully this won't take too long. I thought, as there aren't very many of us and we'll be living at close quarters over the next six weeks, it would be worth taking the time to introduce ourselves before I go over the mission."

Aubriot quietly groaned. Cherry elbowed him.

Wilder continued, "We'll go around the room. If you wouldn't mind stating your name, your role on the ship, and anything else you'd like to say, like maybe your thoughts or feelings about the trip."

"Jesus," Aubriot whispered, "she'll be having us singing Kumbaya next. Was this your idea?"

"Just the introduction part," Cherry whispered back. "She added the bit about feelings herself. It isn't so bad, is it?"

"Who cares about *feelings*?" he sneered. "We're here to do a job."

"Cut her some slack, can't you? She's trying her best. She's still a teenager."

"Yeah, exactly. I don't know why the Leader thought it was a good idea to put *her* in charge when there are others with decades of leadership experience. She might be a brilliant engineer, but she isn't a people person."

"And *you* are?"

The first two attendees had spoken. A third person rose to her feet. After giving her name and role—she was a botanist—she started on a spiel about how excited she was to see the birthplace of humankind, talking in a way that promised to go on for some time.

"Fuck this," Aubriot muttered. Not only was he absolutely uninterested in hearing about other people's motivations and desires, he had zero intention of sharing his own. He got to his feet.

"Hey, where are you going?" Cherry quietly admonished.

"Out of here."

He edged along the row, bumping knees and eliciting annoyed murmurs and glances, before he reached the freedom of the passageway.

The first jump was planned to take place in two and a half hours. Then there would be a period of recovery when the medics would check everyone for effects, and the jump drive would build power for the next jump. It would take five jumps to reach Earth. The passengers and crew would sit in capsules designed to protect against the crushing and distending forces of the process. The *Sirocco* was reinforced to withstand the unusual pressure, but the human body was not.

It was too early to go to the jump room, so Aubriot wandered around the ship. He was already familiar with the layout but this was his first sight of her since her construction was complete. He stuck his head in the little refectory with its empty white tables and benches, bolted down in case of a-grav failure. He gave the gym a cursory inspection. It was poky and only had five basic pieces of equipment, but it would do. The next place he reached was the bridge. Only two people occupied it: Zapata and the captain, Vessey.

Vessey was about the only person he would have been interested in listening to at Wilder's stupid meeting. He had no idea why she'd been picked as captain over the obvious choice: him. She was Vice-Leader, but apart from that he didn't know what else qualified her for the role.

"Aubriot," she said as he walked in. "Is the meeting over already?"

"Doubt it. It's going to take them at least another hour to get through everyone's life story."

He sauntered to the screen displaying the view outside the ship. Concordia spun lazily on its axis. He hadn't seen the planet from afar since he'd been aboard the *Mistral*, battling the Scythians. It was hard to believe that in a couple of weeks he would be looking at a similar view of Earth.

"Uh, can I help you with something?" asked Vessey.

She and Zapata were watching as if wondering why he was here. Why shouldn't he be here? If it weren't for him, they wouldn't even exist. There would have been no deep space colonization project, no generational starship, and no Gens.

"Nah," he replied. "Just taking a look around."

He left and went to his cabin, where he idly watched entertainment to pass the time.

NINE

The long, oblong capsules reminded Cherry of the vessel she and Ethan had traveled in to visit the Filas' ocean-bed metropolis. Perhaps that was where Wilder had got the idea for the design. She'd had many long discussions with Quinn about jump tech before he'd left Concordia with the rest of his kind. The aquatic aliens couldn't risk coming into contact with any remaining biocide, and the chances of encountering it were higher for them than land-based life forms.

It made sense, but Cherry had wondered if they were also leaving because associating with humans had brought them so much trouble and loss of life. That made a lot of sense too. Until the arrival of the *Nova Fortuna*, the Fila had lived on Concordia in safety and peace for many years, not attracting attention from the Scythians.

Others were getting into their capsules. Aubriot was already in his and looking impatient.

He could be such an asshole sometimes. Poor Wilder's face had fallen when he'd walked out of her meeting. Not that it was worth telling him about it. He wouldn't care. He would say he'd helped Wilder by getting everyone to be quiet. He had, but...

"Are you getting in or not?" he snapped.

She glared at him and stepped into the open capsule. "You know we might not ever see each other again? Do you really want that to be the last thing you said to me?"

"Wind your neck in. It's been tested. It's safe."

He wasn't usually this mean and nasty. This was Aubriot at his worst. She knew what was bothering him. He just couldn't stand it when he wasn't in charge. He'd hated the fact that she'd led Concordia's military and he'd been second-in-command. If it hadn't been for their close relationship, he would have given her a far harder time of it.

Soon, all the capsules in the jump room were full. Everyone, including the pilot and captain as well as the doctor and medics, would be ensconced for the duration of the jump.

Cherry had completed two trial runs in a capsule and each time had been awful. The experience was much worse than it had been when she'd gone to the Joining Ceremony with the Fila.

It was one minute until the jump. Her capsule's lid descended and sealed with a hiss. A heartbeat later, a circle of nozzles below the seal squirted gel into the chamber. At the same time, a mask extended to cover her nose and mouth. Within seconds, the gel rose over her legs and torso and crept rapidly up her chest. When it hit her shoulders, she couldn't help but gasp, even though she knew she was already breathing the special oxygen-nitrogen mix that would protect her lungs from the jump effects.

The gel surged up her neck. Her pulse was loud in her ears, drowning out the countdown.

How much time was left?

What had it said? Fifteen or fifty? She couldn't remember.

Her chest labored, forcing the oxygen mix in and out of her lungs.

Wet stickiness crawled up her cheeks.

She closed her eyes.

The gel covered her lids.

She couldn't breathe!

She *could* breathe. She *could*.

Forcing her hands to remain still, not to tear the mask from her face, not to beat against the capsule while she screamed, begging to be let out, she willed herself to inhale and exhale steadily.

The jump would take ten seconds. She only had to endure ten seconds, then the gel would be sucked away, the mask would be lifted, and the capsule would open. Just ten seconds. She could do this for ten seconds.

Had it started?

Ten.

Nine.

She couldn't feel anything different. What did it feel like to go through a jump? What had the test volunteers reported? She couldn't recall.

Four.

Three.

Two.

One.

That was it. It had to be over now. She waited for the gel to be removed. Why wasn't the gel leaving the capsule? She couldn't stand it. She groped for the emergency release.

Then reality twisted.

There was no other way to describe it. Her sense of her position in space warped. A split second later a heavy shock shook her, almost bouncing her from her seat. At the same time, an explosive *bang*! reverberated.

Shit!

She opened her eyes. All she could see was the fuzzy lines of the crosspiece in the transparent lid.

Waa, waa, waa!

The alarm had started up. The lighting pulsed.

What had happened?

The jump must have failed. Had the jump drive exploded?

There was no point in waiting for the gel to be sucked away. The mission had to be over. The important thing was to get out of the capsule and off the ship now their safety was compromised.

She reached for release and pressed it.

Nothing.

She pressed again, harder.

Still nothing.

Panic rushed up her throat. Fear crushed her chest.

The threads of self-control she'd clung to for the last minute dissolved.

She screamed.

Pummeling her fists on the capsule lid, she heard her cries as if they were from another person. She kicked and writhed. She had to get out. What if the ship was on fire? What if her air supply was cut?

Why wasn't anyone helping her get out?

Was everyone dead?

A cracking, splintering sound came from her right. Instantly, the gel slopped away. A hand reached in and wiped her face clean, then pulled off her mask.

Aubriot was peering in through a shattered hole. "You okay?"

She took a breath and gasped, "Yes."

He was gone.

The capsule lid was broken. She grasped the edges of the hole and pushed. The flexible material bent outward but didn't break. She had to ease herself through it to climb out.

The jump room was in chaos. While the alarm continued to sound and the lights flashed, people were wandering aimlessly or standing still as if confused, coated in gel. Others were smashing fire extinguishers into capsule lids to free trapped occupants. Wilder stood in the corner, her face pale and her eyes wide.

Cherry couldn't help with the rescue effort. She would never lift an extinguisher one-handed. She stepped through the remains of destroyed capsules and gloopy gel to Wilder.

The girl was trembling.

"It'll be okay," Cherry said.

Only one capsule remained unopened and Aubriot was attacking it. He broke through, dropped the extinguisher, and reached inside. The person moved and turned over.

"Is the ship on fire?" Cherry asked. Wilder would be in comm contact with the *Sirocco*'s computer. "Has she depressurized? Are we in danger?"

Wilder shook her head.

Even if the air supply to the capsules had been severed, so little time had passed it was unlikely anyone had died.

"Don't worry," Cherry continued. "We can figure out what went wrong. You can rebuild the drive and try again. We'll still reach Earth years before the Scythians."

Wilder shook her head again, more vehemently. She seemed to want to say something but couldn't.

"I know it must seem like the end of the world, but it isn't. No one's going to blame you or the other designers for what's happened. Everyone knows you were under tremendous time pressure. The Leader shouldn't have pushed for such a tight deadline."

Wilder croaked, "You don't understand. It's over. It's all over."

"What's over? The mission?"

Aubriot arrived, covered in sweat and gel. He wiped his forehead with his wrist. "Christ, what a disaster! What a mess. We were lucky only a few of the capsules were affected. We could have all died."

"Is everyone all right?" Cherry asked.

"Think so. The docs and medics are doing the rounds. I reckon it was the bump that jammed the releases. It was a helluva kick. Was that the jump drive conking out?" He addressed the question to Wilder.

She nodded, drawing her lips to a thin line.

"Don't take it too hard," said Aubriot, patting her shoulder. "Everyone makes mistakes."

He seemed a little pleased. Cherry predicted that tonight she would be hearing all about how nothing would have gone wrong if *he'd* been in charge.

The alarm cut out and the lights returned to normal. The crisis had apparently come to an end.

"That's it," said Aubriot. "It looks like it's back to the drawing board for you."

"No!" Wilder exclaimed. "You don't get it!" Tears overflowed her eyes and her hands were fists. "We're done for. Screwed. It's hopeless." She wept and covered her face.

"What's wrong?" asked Cherry. "You said a minute ago it's all over. But everyone's okay, and you can fix the jump drive. Once you find out what went wr—"

"The jump drive worked!" Wilder choked out between sobs. "It malfunctioned, but it worked. We've jumped...somewhere different from where we were supposed to be. The computer's still figuring it out. We must be light years off track. And now the drive's not working and we have no way of getting home or to Earth!"

TEN

A somber mood hung over the briefing room, far different from the excited, eager atmosphere of just a few hours ago.

No one had been killed in the accident, but that seemed the only upside. Cherry's heart went out to Wilder as she stood at the front giving the preliminary report. The girl's face was pale and she regularly had to pause and swallow before continuing, as if she were trying to avoid bursting into tears.

She was talking about the jump drive and what had gone wrong. Cherry didn't understand a word of what she was saying and she suspected she was far from alone.

Her guess was confirmed when a man blurted out, "Get to the point. No one gives a shit about why we're in this predicament. What we want to know is, where the hell are we and how long will it take us to get back to Concordia?"

Murmurs and grumbles of agreement came from the audience.

Wilder blinked. "I was getting to that. I'll bring up the holo to show you." She gave the command and instructed the lights to dim. In the near darkness, pinpricks of light shone in the open central area. A red line ran across the center of the holo display, from one side to the other. Four yellow dots were roughly evenly spaced along it.

Wilder's figure was shadowy in the corner. "So what you're looking at is our planned route. Concordia is to the left and Earth is to the right of the line. The yellow dot nearest Concordia is where we should have appeared after the first jump. There were four more jumps, the final one bringing us out in Earth's star—"

"Get on with it," growled the man who had interrupted before.

"As we know," Wilder continued in a trembling tone, "the jump drive malfunctioned, throwing us off course. The computer figured out our new location with the help of the star map the Fila gave us before they left. The position we actually arrived at is..." She stated a set of coordinates for the holo generator.

The stars winked out and the red line vanished. An entirely new starscape appeared.

Gasps and exclamations of dismay resounded. Cherry was shocked too. She was no astrophysicist, but even she understood the implication of the changed display. They were far, far off course. Wilder's intuition about the result of the accident had been correct. The *Sirocco* was light years from Earth and Concordia, the only two planets they knew of where humans could survive.

A single star shone out brighter than the rest.

"I've highlighted the nearest sun," said Wilder weakly.

"Are we closer to Earth or Concordia?" Aubriot asked abruptly.

Cherry jumped. She'd almost forgotten he was sitting beside her. He'd been unusually quiet throughout the meeting.

"Earth," Wilder replied.

"How far away are we? Not in distance, in time."

"Without a working jump drive, it's hard to say."

"Bullshit," said Aubriot. "It's not hard for someone like you to figure it out. How long will it take us to reach Earth using the conventional engine?"

Cherry wondered how wise he was being to push for an answer. The news had to be bad, or Wilder wouldn't be reluctant to give it, and the panic and rage in the room was already nearly palpable.

"A-assuming we can get the energy to power it..." Her voice trailed into silence.

There was a rustle as someone stood up and gave the command to raise the lights. Cherry knew the young man vaguely. His name was Niall, and he was one of the team who had created the jump drive.

"To reach Earth from here," he said, "it's going to take us nineteen years, give or t..."

The remainder of his sentence was lost in a roar of shock and outrage.

"Nineteen years!" a voice yelled. "My parents will be dead by the time I get back."

"No way!" another shouted. "I left my children behind. I'll never see them grow up. Will they even remember me?"

"Everyone on Concordia's going to think we're dead," a third person called out. "And how are they going to survive without the seeding material from Earth?"

Cherry was in shock too. She'd guessed the situation had to be dire, but even she had underestimated *how* dire. What was worse, she already knew how it felt to be gone from home for decades. When she'd returned from the Galactic Assembly to a Concordia over a hundred years further on in time, the sense of displacement, of loss and not belonging had been devastating. And the third person who had called out had been correct: without the organisms from Earth, would there even be a Concordia to return to?

Kes, who was sitting on the other side of the room, met her gaze as he hugged his little girls. He hadn't been at the first meeting, and Cherry hadn't had time to speak to him before they set out. He also knew how terrible it felt to be moved on in time and severed from the people you loved. But, perhaps more importantly, he had to be thinking of his kids. They would grow up aboard a starship, not having the freedom to run and play, not feeling the rain or the wind, not seeing a sunset.

She caught a snatch of loud conversation: "Can we even do it? We don't have nineteen years of supplies. This was only supposed to be a six-week trip!"

The protests and angry reactions were growing louder. People were getting up from their seats and moving toward Wilder, who was backing into a corner. The young woman looked frightened. Cherry flashed back to the day she'd met her outside an entrance to Sidhe, being set upon by two bullies. If someone didn't do something, she was going to get hurt.

"Oy!" Aubriot yelled, rising to his feet. "Simmer the fuck down!"

His large frame and booming voice drew the attention from Wilder. The volume in the room dropped several notches.

"I said shut up!" he roared.

Silence and stillness reigned.

"You!" He pointed at the people nearest Wilder. "Back off! Leave the kid alone, unless you want me to crack your bloody skulls together." He glared at them until they did as they'd been told.

"Right, sit down." He waited until everyone had complied. "Listen to me. We're screwed. That's clear. I just wanted Wilder to get that fact out of the way. Now we all know where we stand. No one wants it and no one predicted it, but here we are. Get over it."

He rested his hands on the back of the seat in front of him. "I'm assuming control of this mission. And before you say it, no, it's not because of my massive ego, though I'm not denying it. It's because what we need most right now isn't scientists and engineers, it's someone who can take charge and give orders. And that's me. Anyone who wants to argue about it can talk to me outside, now. Any takers?"

His stare traveled the length and breadth of the room. None met it.

"Good. First, no one touches a hair of Wilder's head or they'll answer to me about it. She tried her best, so I don't want to hear a word of blame against her or the other engineers. They're in the same predicament as us, don't forget. Second, you all need to calm the fuck down. Hysterics isn't going to help anyone. Third, we need to figure out a survival plan that'll keep us alive until we reach Earth. That means food, water, and energy, but also a rota and distractions so we don't go crazy. Luckily, you're some of the most intelligent and capable people on Concordia. Act like it. Organize yourselves. Check the supplies and fuel. Plan ahead."

He turned to Cherry. "Cherry Lindstrom is Chief Survival Coordinator. Send all your reports and suggestions to her."

She muttered, "Thanks, dear."

Eleven

As Wilder's cabin door opened, she deeply colored. Rising from her chair, she said, "Kes, I'm so s—"

"Shh! There's nothing to apologize for. You didn't mean for any of this to happen."

"Hi, Wilder." Miki skipped in. She immediately climbed onto Wilder's bunk and started bouncing. Nina toddled over and also tried to climb up, but she was too small.

"Hey, girls," Kes admonished. "Remember what I said? You have to behave yourselves. How about you play with the toys you brought?"

"It's okay," said Wilder. "They can bounce if they want. They don't exactly have a lot of space to run around." As she'd spoken, her tone had grown higher and by the time she finished she was choking on her words. She covered her face and her shoulders shook as she wept.

Miki, immediately concerned, hopped down from the bed and patted Wilder's back. "It's okay. It's okay," she soothed. "Don't be sad."

Nina sat on her bottom and began wailing too, in sympathy.

Kes wondered if this had been the best idea.

In the days following the jump drive disaster, he had wavered between despair and anger. He knew the latter was irrational. It had been his decision to join the mission and his decision to bring Miki and Nina. Wilder had pressured him, but he couldn't blame her for that. What she'd said had made perfect sense—he *was* the best person to supervise gathering the seeding material from Earth. Only it looked like he might never see Earth at all, and he might have condemned his children to a lingering death.

Yet he knew Wilder had to be hurting too. So when he'd calmed down somewhat, he comm'd her, asking to see her. "Miki, that's very kind of you. Wilder and I would like to talk now. Can you play with Nina?"

This did the trick. In another minute, his daughters were in a corner playing a make-believe game and he was comforting his friend.

How could he ever have been angry about the situation? It was just another terrible event similar to all the others that had dogged the colony since Arrival Day. No one was to blame.

Wilder's tears seemed to be lessening. He waited patiently, his arm around her shoulders. Should he say something? He decided it was better to let her cry it out. It might be the first time she'd given vent to her feelings since the accident.

Eventually, she murmured, "I keep going over everything I did, everything *we* did, trying to figure out the mistake, but I can't find it. I still don't have any idea what we did wrong. The prototype worked fine. The tests were all successful. I can't figure it out."

"You've checked the drive?"

She took her hands away from her tear-stained, blotchy face and nodded. "We've all taken a close look at it. It's damaged, though it's hard to see how it happened."

He asked softly, "So there's absolutely no way you'll be able to get it working again?"

"None that we can think of. Not unless you know of a jump drive repair shop within a few light years?" She smiled wanly.

"Sorry, I can't help you with that."

Fresh tears ran from her eyes. "Oh, Kes, I'm so—"

He held up a finger. "I won't hear it. Not a word. You understand?"

She hung her head. Quietly, she said, "There's more. Things are worse than you think."

A heavy feeling settled on his chest. He guessed what was probably coming. "Is this about the supplies?" At the meeting when they'd learned the desperation of their situation, he'd known it was impossible they had enough food and water to last them until they reached Earth.

"We only have six months' worth," said Wilder. "We thought we were probably overdoing things loading so much for what was supposed to be a six-week trip, but..."

He stopped listening. Six months. They had only six months before everyone would begin to starve. A lump rose in his throat. In six months Miki and Nina would begin to feel hungry all the time and ask him for food, and he would have nothing to give them. What would he do then? Would he be able to do the kindest thing and put them out of their misery? The sick bay had to have strong sedatives.

He cleared his throat. "What about power?" he interrupted aimlessly, his mind shying from horror.

"I just told you," said Wilder, looking at him strangely. "Didn't you hear me? Energy shouldn't be a problem. We can use the energy-gathering capability of the Parvus's weapon system to supply the regular engine. We'll have to work out how to safely divert the stored energy to the engine, but I'm confident it can be done."

"That's something at least." His words belied the image in his mind's eye: a starship of rotten corpses arriving at Earth nineteen years from now, everything in her working perfectly, every system functioning—except the life she'd once supported. "What about our friends in the Galactic Assembly? Do any of them live in these parts?"

"Not that we're aware of. We're broadcasting a general distress comm—Aubriot argued against it, saying we shouldn't announce our vulnerability to the entire galaxy—but the distances between intelligent civilizations are immense. You remember how long it took us to get to the Assembly's space station? And Concordia is in a section buzzing with life. By comparison, we're in the middle of a barren desert. If our message does happen to reach a friend, we'll have died of old age before they find us."

A bolt struck him. He gasped. Perhaps there was a way... Then his shoulders sagged as another realization hit.

"What?" Wilder asked. "Did you think of something?"

"I did, but it won't work."

"What was it? Maybe I can help."

He replied heavily, "Theoretically, if we have energy, we can have food. All the food we eat is primarily formed from light and carbon dioxide."

"CO2's no problem. We breathe it out." Wilder's features brightened. "And we can re-purpose the ship's lights."

"Plants also need macro- and micro-nutrients, but maybe we could get those from planets."

"We could convert the Ark to *grow* things rather than simply store them, using planetary dust as the growing medium. That's brilliant, Kes."

"Except..." He paused.

"What?"

"Think harder."

Her face fell. "We don't have any plants."

"No, we haven't. We don't have anything fresh in the supplies, do we?" He already knew the answer. Concordians had been surviving on stored food since the Scythian Plague. Everything to eat on the *Sirocco* would be dried, canned, frozen, or pasteurized, all potential for regrowth destroyed.

Wilder shook her head sadly. "I'm pretty certain you're right, but I'll ask Cherry to double check to be sure."

"It's definitely worth double checking. If we only had potatoes, they could keep us going a long time before malnutrition set in."

Eating nothing but potatoes for years would be a miserable existence, and he was pretty sure there was nothing else that *would* sustain them for nineteen years, yet perhaps some form of life was better than none.

"I'll look into it," said Wilder.

"How have you been?" he asked gently, worried that his question would start up her tears again.

She did blink several times before answering, "Awful. Just awful. I'm grateful to Aubriot for protecting me against revenge attacks, but most people have made it clear through their looks what they'd like to do to me."

His guilt over his anger twinged. "That's very unfair."

"Is it? If it hadn't been for me, Concordians would have left for Earth years ago. They would be right on the Scythians' tail. Now, help probably won't arrive at all. And without the seeding material, the colony is sunk. Humankind will sink back into barbarism. And it's all my fault." Her lower lip trembled.

Despite the situation, he chuckled. "Humanity brought to its knees by the actions of one young woman. That's quite the charge to lay at your own feet. Aubriot would like a word with you about who has the largest ego on the ship."

She smiled. "I guess it isn't *all* my fault."

"Not quite *all* of it."

After a pause, she said, "Thank you."

"For what?"

"For trying to make me feel better."

"What else are friends for?"

TWELVE

Cherry stared at the man. She was reminded of a time, decades ago, when she'd been in his place. She'd been the angry, bitter one, and Cariad had been the interviewer. How she'd hated Cariad at that moment. She'd hated all Woken but especially the woman Ethan loved. Their relationship had improved later, when she'd accepted Ethan was as principled and sincere in his feelings as he was in everything else, and the lines between Gens and Woken had blurred.

Time changed things.

Except maybe in this case.

"What if I refuse to tell you?" the man repeated, snapping at her. "What then?!"

She slammed the interface on the desk. "What do you expect me to say, huh? What *exactly* am I supposed to say? I'm in the same situation as you. We all are. We're just trying to make things a little more bearable. Is that a crime?"

All she wanted to know was his professional background. The ship's database didn't contain detailed information on the mission members, and Aubriot had asked her to create a profile for each of them. He wanted to know the types and range of skill sets they had aboard.

"Why?"

"Why what?" she asked irritably. She glanced down at the interface. She'd forgotten the man's name.

Bernard Garcia.

"Why bother making things more bearable?" he asked. "What's the point?

We're all going to die anyway. We might as well blow up the ship and get it over with."

There it was.

She put a tick next to his name. Garcia wasn't the first person to express suicidal thoughts. It was something else Aubriot had asked her to note.

"Everyone dies," she said. "It's just a matter of when. We're going to keep going as long as we can."

"And what if I don't want to?" His voice had softened and he broke eye contact. This was why he was being obstructive: desperation and dread.

"Then..." She paused.

What Aubriot hadn't told her was how to handle the people who wanted to end it all right now. She was no psychiatrist. Hell, she wasn't even a good listener. She was the last person people came to with their problems, needing a sympathetic ear. "You know who I am, right?"

He nodded.

"Then you know I arrived on the *Nova*. I was there at the beginning. A lot's happened since then. Terrible disasters. So many people died trying to make the colony a success. But we kept going. Looking back, I'm not even sure why. It seemed impossible we would survive." An image appeared in her mind: Ethan in Sidhe as they awaited the Scythian's return, going from section to section, bolstering confidence, focusing minds and hearts in the face of almost certain annihilation. If it hadn't been for him they would never have made it.

If only he were here now.

"I don't know what's going to happen," she continued. "Maybe this really is finally it. It's over and we're done. But we're not giving up. It's been decided. You're one of us, and we need you. So hang in there, okay?" Her words sounded hollow. She winced but tried not to show it.

Garcia appeared unmoved. "I guess so."

"Good. Now, you're a horticulturist, right? Can you explain what it is you do in your job? In detail, please." She started up the voice-to-text on the interface.

His face twisting with unspoken emotions, he said, "I propagate plants from cuttings. My role on the mission was to..."

She zoned out and let the recorder do the work. It had been a long day, and she'd spent most of it dealing with other people's anxieties and fears about what was going to happen. She'd tried to help, but she had no answers. She didn't even know what to tell herself.

———

Garcia had left and she sat alone in the small room, her only company the barely discernible hum of the ship's engine. All her strength seemed drained from her though she hadn't moved for hours. The thirty-odd faces she'd seen today passed through her mind. Would she see them change over the next nineteen years? Would they have the opportunity to grow older? Or had her day's work been a futile exercise, a distraction? Did Aubriot really think they had a chance, or was he only enjoying himself playing the big boss in his life's finale? So much for his potential immortality.

She dragged energy from somewhere and collated all the files she'd created before sending them to the database. Leaving the interface where it was, she walked out.

Aubriot wasn't in their cabin, and he hadn't left a message.

The man was so annoying. His lack of consideration was getting worse. Here she was, being his freaking *secretary* while he swanned around the ship acting like he was the Leader, and he didn't even have the decency to wait for her before he went...where? It wasn't like there were many places to go. He must have gone to dinner without her.

She comm'd him.

As soon as he answered, she barked, "You could at least have waited for me!"

"Eh? What are you talking about? I was wondering where you were."

"Where I was? I've just spent the last eight hours doing the freaking interviews you asked for. Did all my hard work slip your mind?"

"Oh, yeah. I forgot about that. Uh, thanks. Come to the Ark."

He cut the comm.

Her jaw dropped in disbelief. The arrogance of the man. Just when she thought she was used to his ways, he got worse. Maybe he was doing it on purpose, gradually loosening the restraints on his awful personality traits, turning up the heat under the pot he'd put her in, until she would finally be boiled.

Come to the Ark.

Why? What could he possibly be doing there?

She marched through the passageways, thinking up angry accusations to throw. She would let him know exactly what she thought of him, tell him all his faults, all the reasons he was unbearable to live with, and then she would tell him she was done. The *Sirocco* wasn't big, but there had to be a spare cabin somewhere. If there wasn't, she would sleep in the briefing room or the refectory. Any place that Aubriot wasn't would be just fine.

And yet here she was still doing what he'd told her.

Dammit.

She carried on walking.

The Ark was 125,000 cubic meters of refrigerators, freezers, and dry rooms. There was nothing aesthetically pleasing about it. The decks, bulkheads, and overheads were unpainted metal, and the layout was basic: passageways ran from one side to the other of the five levels, dividing the chambers, and an elevator stood at each end.

As she crossed the short linking bridge, she realized Aubriot hadn't told her where he was in the Ark. Exasperated, she was about to comm him when she spotted his tall figure at the end of the bridge. Kes and Wilder were with him.

"Huh," he remarked as she arrived. "It's us four together again. Weird, right?"

"Hi Cherry," she replied sarcastically. "Thanks for coming. How was your day?"

Kes and Wilder threw each other a look.

"Uhh…" Aubriot looked nonplussed. "So, Wilder had this idea—"

"It was Kes who thought of it," Wilder interrupted.

"Whatever. We might have found a solution to the food problem."

"You're kidding." All of Cherry's anger and frustration dissolved. "What?"

"We grow our own," Wilder replied excitedly. "Here in the Ark. We've come to see how we can convert it."

"Convert it into a greenhouse?" Cherry asked. "Put in lights and irrigation and so on? That's brilliant!"

It seemed so obvious. Why hadn't she thought of it? Out of all the mission members, she was the only farmer. As she knew well after interviewing everyone, she was the only person experienced in actually growing crops. She'd been an idiot. "Wait, do we have enough energy for lighting? And where would we get the extra water from?"

"Energy isn't a problem," said Kes, "thanks to the Parvus's weapon."

"Which *I* argued we needed to install," Aubriot added smugly.

Wilder briefly rolled her eyes. "We'll have to use some of the *Sirocco*'s lighting. Things will be a little darker over there. We didn't make lights a priority in the Ark."

Kes explained, "We wanted to keep the biological material as inert as possible for the return trip, and light stimulates growth."

"Right," Cherry said. "But it can be done?"

"We think so," Wilder replied. "We really think so. Water shouldn't be a problem. It's pretty common in space and I'm sure we can figure out a way to harvest it."

"That's fantastic!" Cherry gazed up and down the gray, dim passageway, imagining an open, bright, humid, green space, lush and rich with nutritious calories to keep everyone alive.

Something niggled. It wasn't a complete answer. They would still need to spend nearly two decades in space, Concordia wouldn't receive the seeding material as soon as needed, and who knew what they would find on Earth when they finally reached it. But at least they weren't sentenced to death by starvation.

None of those wrinkles were what was bothering her. "But where are the crops going to come from? We were supposed to be picking up the seeds. We aren't bringing them with us."

"Ah," said Wilder, her eyes twinkling, "that's what Kes and I wondered too. But then I remembered the galactic map Quinn gave us. The Fila have been roaming the galaxy for eons, finding watery planets for their ever-growing populations. Their jump drive has probably made them the most widely traveled species in existence, in our galaxy anyway. They've kept records of every planet they encountered that harbors life, regardless of whether it's habitable for them."

Aubriot said, "We're going to collect plants from other planets. Anything we can eat, we'll grow here. Simple. I knew there was a solution. We just needed time to think about it."

Cherry didn't see how he'd contributed anything to the answer, but she let it go. He *had* kept them together when everyone was about to lose their minds. She asked Kes, "Are you sure we'll find something safe for us to eat? You guys didn't find much on Concordia that wasn't poisonous to humans."

"It might be a challenge, but we can try. It's certainly worth trying."

THIRTEEN

'Auntie' Cherry's face as he left Miki and Nina with her was a picture Kes would never forget. Despite the severity and danger of the situation, he smiled to himself as the *Sirocco*'s shuttle made its way through the alien planet's atmosphere. Cherry's features had been a mixture of discomfort, confusion, and plain fear. He knew she would do a good job caring for the girls nevertheless, or he would never have entrusted them to her. She'd helped bring Nina into the world. She would protect those girls with her life. He wasn't happy about being parted from them but it was a better alternative than bringing them on the expedition.

Was it a fool's errand to try to find plants to grow as crops? Most likely.

He hadn't wanted to throw a dampener on the hopeful, excited discussions about turning the Ark into a massive greenhouse, but their chances of success were tiny. What people like Aubriot, Cherry, and Wilder didn't know was that humanity's food crops had been selectively bred over millennia. Wild plants from the planet he was about to visit weren't only unlikely to be edible, they would also be low in calories, taste terrible, and have unknown growing requirements, making them difficult to cultivate.

But it was the only chance they had. At the very least, making the attempt would give the mission members hope for a little while longer.

Additional weight had been settling on his shoulders as the shuttle descended. At 1.5 g, the planet's gravity would make for a tiring trip, though its atmosphere's 30 percent oxygen would alleviate the effects somewhat.

The vessel suddenly dipped, sending his stomach somewhere above his head. He gripped the armrests.

"Sorry about that," said the pilot, Zapata, over the intercom. "We've hit turbulence. It's gonna be a rocky ride for about twenty minutes."

He wasn't kidding. The shuttle rose and fell like a boat tossed in a storm. Kes gripped his armrests tighter as bile rose in his throat. He swallowed and focused on not being sick. Just when he thought he couldn't hold out any longer, the disordered motion stopped.

He relaxed and wiped sweat from his forehead.

Aubriot, who was seated in front of him, leaned around his seat back and winked. "The fairground ride is complementary. No need to thank me."

Kes didn't even attempt to react to the weak joke.

Aubriot raised his eyebrows before facing front again.

Zapata was the best pilot in the colony, as Kes understood. He hated to think what might have happened if they'd been in less-skilled hands.

The planet's surface was rising rapidly toward them. A sea of green spread out to the encircling horizon. The scant information the Fila had gathered on the alien world before concluding it wouldn't suit their species was that, while there was plenty of the water they needed, it was spread out in lakes and marshes and dispersed through massive archipelagos and shallow reefs. There were no deep, wide oceans to support their large metropolises.

From a human perspective the information was mostly useless. They needed to know about the planet's land masses, which were irrelevant to the Fila. From what Kes could see, there was plenty of plant life. What fauna might lurk among the vegetation, they had no idea. Again, the Fila hadn't bothered to investigate, apart from commenting the planet appeared to host no intelligent life forms. The lack of built structures seemed to confirm the deduction.

Zapata requested his and Aubriot's presence in his cabin.

Kes unfastened his seat belt and followed Aubriot down the narrow aisle. As well as the pilot, seven people were accompanying them on the trip: three men and two women Kes had picked for their skills with plants, one of whom was an old work colleague, Trish, and two burly men Aubriot had wanted to bring along in case of difficulties. Everyone was armed.

When Kes and Aubriot entered the cramped cabin, Zapata told them to close the door before saying, "I don't know where to land. Take a look."

Kes peered at the bird's eye view through the shuttle window. It was the same green expanse he'd seen earlier.

"Just find a bit of solid ground," said Aubriot. "What are you expecting? A spaceport?"

"That's the problem," Zapata replied evenly, "there isn't any solid ground. The scanners haven't picked up any dense rock since we entered the atmosphere. Nothing except marshland for hundreds of kilometers. So unless you're planning on finding these plants five meters under the surface, we need an alternative plan."

"Shit," Aubriot muttered.

"What about nearer the poles?" Kes suggested. "Does the planet have an equivalent of the Earth's tundra? If we can't find rock, maybe we can find permafrost."

"Nice idea," Zapata replied, "but the shuttle's thrusters will melt any ice we land on."

Kes frowned. "You said the scanners haven't identified solid rock, but what about sand? The Fila reported lots of shallow oceans. Perhaps we could land on a seashore."

"Ah, yeah," Zapata said. "Didn't think of that. Let me take another look."

The Fila's record of the planet's topography was like a negative of a regular map. The river and lake beds and ocean floors were represented in detail, but the land masses were empty and featureless, only their outlines showing. Nevertheless, the three men were able to locate the nearest beach. Kes and Aubriot returned to their seats, and then the shuttle banked and turned.

Time passed, and a turquoise watery expanse came into view. As they flew nearer, a thin black line demarcated it from the vegetation. It was a beach of a kind, though not the color Kes was expecting. Perhaps the sand was volcanic in origin. The flatness of the planet implied it was young, though the Fila hadn't mentioned an estimate of its age. A youthful planet was a good thing—hopefully no large predatory life forms had evolved. Kes still remembered the days of the sluglimpets, before his team had developed a repellent.

The black line grew wider until the shuttle was directly above it and began to descend. The vertical takeoff and descent capability she'd been given in preparation for predicted conditions on Earth had certainly come in useful.

White-capped waves rode a blue-green sea on his right, and green branches reached toward the sky beyond the window on his left. The branches were interesting. They lacked any stems or large leaves. Perhaps the plants were a kind of gigantic moss.

Inedible, no doubt.

He shifted in his seat uncomfortably. Carrying half his body weight again was already becoming a drain. With a small bump, the shuttle settled on the sand. Zapata asked the passengers to remain sitting. He stepped out of his cabin and opened the hatch. Warm, humid air gusted in, carrying a strange, earthy scent. "Seems safe enough. Hot, though. It's forty C out there, but the sun's going down in a couple of hours."

Aubriot's men checked the immediate area and gave the all clear. Next came the grueling process of unloading the equipment and setting up camp. The task would have been arduous in normal circumstances, but at 50 percent extra gravity it was taxing in the extreme. Sweat soon bathed Kes's brow and soaked through his clothes.

Aubriot, however, seemed to be in his element. He strode over the loose, powdery, black sand, carrying item after item from the hold and dumping them in the spot chosen for the camp, leaving the unpacking and constructing to others. He was naturally muscular and strong and appeared unaffected by the additional mass.

While Kes was trying to extract a pop-up tent from a bag, Aubriot arrived, reached down, and hauled the tent out one-handed. Telling Kes to step back, he released the catch, and the tent sprang into shape.

He put his hands on his hips. "Not bad eh?"

"What?" Kes asked irritably. "What isn't bad? The tent? The planet? The whole twenty years from human civilization thing?"

"What's got *your* goat? Hey, do you remember that night we met in the bar before the Third Scythian Attack?"

"No, I don't." He actually did, but he was too hot, tired, and worried to admit it. He recalled the night too well, not only because of the attack but also because it was directly after Izzy had left him for being a terrible husband and father. He knew exactly what Aubriot was going to say and he hated him for it, because he was right.

"'Course you do. We were saying how we hadn't expected things on Concordia to turn out so normal. You had your office job, working for the government. I was pissing my life away, bored out of my mind. We'd come all that way to a new world, spent nearly a couple of centuries in cryo, only to end up living in suburbia and doing the same old same old." He turned to survey the landscape. "I don't know about you, but I'd imagined deep space coloniza-tion would be something like this. Adventure. Living on the edge. Fun."

Kes squinted at him. "A – we didn't 'meet' in the bar, you cornered me. B – I thought you were too drunk to recall anything we said, and C – how you can call this fun is beyond me. *Some* of us have people we care about whose lives have been irrevocably affected by these circumstances we find ourselves in. Maybe that's the difference."

All Aubriot replied was, "Huh. I knew you remembered."

Kes watched the man march back to the shuttle's open hold, stepping over the electric guard wire someone had just finished setting up.

He looked over the sea, taking a deep breath. Each lungful of oxygen-rich air renewed his vigor, but the effect was short-lived. A bone-weary ache had invaded his back, neck, and all his limbs, reminding him of anxiety dreams where he would feel as though he was walking through treacle.

The sun was going down. The camp would be set up just in time in the failing light. Stars twinkled to life In the darkening sky. Slow, lazy waves dragged themselves up the shore before collapsing and disappearing into ebony sand. The strange forest whispered.

FOURTEEN

While waiting for Aubriot and his goons—as Kes had come to think of them—to put the finishing touches to the rafts, he decided to give his team a few final tips about what they were looking for.

"Obviously," he said, "anything edible is better than nothing, but ideally we want plants that yield a high amount of calories preferably without taking up a lot of space. Plants that produce grains, tubers, nuts…that kind of thing. Potential food that's dense in starches or oils."

"But surely we'll need leafy plants too?" asked a horticulturalist called Garcia. Cherry had warned against bringing him, saying their dire situation had made him mentally unstable, but the man had the exact skills required for the trip. "I mean, we'll need the range of nutrients over the long term, not only calories."

"Honestly," Kes replied, his gaze roaming the landscape, "we don't have a clue what approximations to the vitamins and minerals humans need we might find here. On Concordia, our digestive systems absorbed some of the local nutritional chemicals and not others. We'll certainly turn our attention to leaves—or what passes for leaves—but for now it's best to focus on calories. We need energy to keep us going. Without it we'll quickly become weak and stop thinking straight. It'll take a while for malnutrition from lack of micro-nutrients to set in."

His comment sparked another idea, but he filed it away to bring up with Cherry, Wilder, and Aubriot later. "You have your field testing devices to check for known poisonous compounds. If a sample passes the test, log the exact location you found it, take plenty of pictures, and bring a piece back."

"How much do you want us to collect?" Trish asked.

"A sample about as big as your finger is fine for starters. After we've carried out more checks we can take seeds, roots, whatever makes sense."

"What about the local fauna?" asked Trish. "Should we collect insects too?"

"I'm more worried about the fauna *attacking* us," Garcia muttered.

"That's why we'll be working in threes," said Kes. "You're with me, by the way," he added.

Garcia snapped his mouth shut and nodded.

To Trish, he said, "Good question. Well done for thinking outside the box." Concordians ate very little animal protein, only a sea creature similar to Earth shrimps. Some people wouldn't even eat those. The *Nova Fortuna* generational colonists had eaten locusts bred aboard the ship but that was ancient history to these people. "I'm certainly open to the proposal of growing insects as well as plants in the Ark. However, we have to bear in mind that we'll also have to grow the plants to feed them. I would need to do some calculations about whether devoting the required space would be worth it."

"The rafts are ready for boarding," called Aubriot, standing on one of the two structures and holding a long pole sticking up from the water. "Please show your ticket on entry."

They had decided to build rafts because traveling on foot through the marshy jungle would be laborious, hot, and dangerous. A short scouting mission at daybreak had revealed that, once under the odd, skeletal canopy, the ground was treacherously boggy and visibility extended only as far as the thick stems of the next 'tree'. If something wanted to attack them it could get close before they spotted it, and then they would have a hard time running away or killing it without risking shooting each other.

Faced with the prospect of a challenging, risky trek, Zapata had come to their rescue by suggesting this wide estuary farther up the beach after studying the Fila map. The slack movement of the water indicated the current was slow. It seemed feasible to move upstream to conduct their investigations.

Carrying their equipment bags, Kes and Garcia waded out the short distance to Aubriot's raft accompanied by Trish and her partner, a man called Ryan. Aubriot's men were to take turns poling the other raft, with two more of the scientific team as passengers. Zapata remained at the camp.

Aubriot drove his pole into the water, and, bobbing and wobbling, the raft eased away from the shore.

It had taken all morning to construct the vessels from dead 'wood' that had washed up from the ocean. It was fortunate they had suitable tools for the task, originally intended for use on Earth. The sun was high overhead and Kes had unbuttoned his shirt in an attempt to cool down. As they moved out onto the water, a soft breeze lifted it, drying his sweat.

"That's better," Garcia commented, wiping his neck with a cloth.

Kes pulled his hat low over his brow. He would burn to a crisp in the brilliant sunlight.

Aubriot had stripped to the waist while building the rafts. He gazed ahead as he guided his vessel inland, looking pleased with himself. It was clear he was seeing himself in his mind's eye: tall, well-muscled, good-looking, performing his manly task in a manly manner. He was loving this whole experience.

Kes rolled his eyes, sighed, and wondered how Cherry was getting along looking after Miki and Nina.

The darkness of the sand on the estuary bed made it hard to see anything in the water, but he looked into it nevertheless while they went along. He vaguely remembered some aquatic plants on Earth that produced edible, nutritious corms. Growing crops in water wasn't the most obvious solution to their problems, and if the a-grav went out it would be a disaster, but he was worried that air-breathing plants might not thrive in the comparatively lower oxygen levels on the ship.

He spotted some trailing, dark green fronds but nothing promising. Holes in the sand indicated creatures living beneath the surface, but that was to be expected. Every ecological niche would be filled. The question was, were they filled by anything not poisonous to humans?

Thick vegetation grew along the banks and overhung the water, seemingly impenetrable. Whenever he looked up, everything was unchanged except the banks drew in more closely.

After an hour and a half of slow progress, conversation on both rafts had dried to silence and Aubriot had mentioned a couple of times that the current was growing stronger and hard to move against. Kes was about to suggest attempting to get ashore by pushing through the greenery. But before he could speak, one of Aubriot's men called out, "There's some dry ground."

The piece of land wasn't easily visible because it was covered in very low-growing plants curling into the water, but it seemed solid.

Without waiting for a discussion, Aubriot propelled his raft toward it. The edge bumped against a firm surface within the vegetation, and he leapt out, calling to Kes to toss him the rope. In another couple of minutes, he'd tied up around the thick, tough stem of one of the tree-like plants. The second raft came to shore.

They split into three parties of three. Aubriot accompanied Kes and Garcia. Their group was to explore inland while the other two parties would head up and down respectively of the banks of what had become a wide, shallow, slow river. Each team would move forward for two hours, searching, and then return to the rafts. There was no chance of getting lost. With the *Sirocco* in geostationary orbit, she would track them via their ear comms and relay the information to hand-sized interfaces everyone carried. The planet's rotation was slower than Concordia's. At this latitude and longitude the days currently lasted twenty hours and the nights seventeen, but at 1.5 g four hours of locomotion would be about all most of them could manage.

Aubriot strode ahead, leaving Kes and Garcia lagging. The ground was drier here than near the coast, and it had risen marginally higher as they'd journeyed, the vegetation growing less thickly. They were able to walk more or less in a straight line.

"Slow down," Kes called out to Aubriot. "It's not a race." He stopped to examine the base of a plant composed of long, soft leaves sprouting in clump directly from the black soil. He pushed his trowel into the ground and levered the plant up. Its roots were thin and straggly, not tuberous as he'd hoped.

"This looks promising." Garcia was pointing at dry, brown pods hanging from the branches of a shrub.

"Break one open," said Kes.

Aubriot had walked back to join them. "I'll do it. Could be dangerous."

Kes bit his lip as he stifled a laugh. Aubriot was taking his he-man role very seriously.

He grabbed one of the pods. There was a loud report, and suddenly the air was filled with flying beans and pieces of pod casing. Several hit Kes in the face.

"Wow," Garcia remarked. "Excellent seed-spreading strategy."

"Yes," said Kes. "Impressive."

Aubriot stood as if stupefied, holding the remains of one of the pods.

"See if you can find one of the beans to test," Kes told Garcia. "I'll continue looking."

"What *was* that?" asked Aubriot. "Is it safe?"

Kes replied, "Just a plant trying to give its babies the best start in life. Nothing to worry about."

"Oh, right."

A few meters away a vine coiled up a tree. Its tendrils appeared particularly thick and fleshy. Were they nutritious?

As Kes walked toward it, Aubriot said, "Going to answer a call of nature. I'll be back in a bit."

Kes heard but didn't reply, his interest taken by the vine.

He cut off a small piece and popped it into his analyzer. While he was waiting for the results, Garcia came over to him. "Those beans are full of toxic alkaloids."

"Damn. Never mind. It's early days. We have an entire planet to search."

"Are we going to carry on looking until we find something edible?" Garcia asked. "That could take years."

"We don't have a lot of choice. We don't have enough food to last us until we reach Earth." The reason they were searching for plants to grow as crops wasn't any secret but, aware he was straying into dangerous territory in terms of the man's mental health, Kes didn't say any more.

"What if we don't find anything?"

Kes patted Garcia's back. "We're bound to find something. We did on Concordia. You found those beans within twenty minutes of—"

"*Arghhh! Shit! Fuck!*"

It was Aubriot.

Kes and Garcia sped in the direction of his voice.

They found him on the ground, curled up on his side, his pants pulled up but open at the front.

"I-I wiped my-my..." He let out a groan.

Kes and Garcia shared a look of dismay and disgust. It was clear no one had warned Aubriot to never trust any unknown leaf for toilet purposes.

"He's *your* friend," said Garcia.

'Friend' implied a far more amicable relationship than was the case, but Kes had to admit he had been Aubriot's acquaintance for many long years. "All right. I'll do it."

Garcia left the scene.

Kes fished in his bag for a soothing ointment.

Fifteen

Aubriot's demeanor was different during the return journey from the river. The bravado and pride were gone, replaced by a subdued, reflective air. The trip had also been unsuccessful in research terms. None of the three teams had discovered any vegetative material that passed the initial poisons check. The only sample they brought back was the thick, starchy stem of a plant that did contain poisons but they were all soluble. The stems could be made edible, though the process would require lots of water.

The sun had sunk below the forest canopy, and the shadows of the thin, contorted branches stretched out over the water like a crone's grasping fingers. Everyone was hot and tired after their hours of searching but as they were now traveling downstream, poling the rafts was easy and everyone took turns.

Kes removed his hat and lay down, putting it over his face. It was too dark to see the surrounding vegetation properly anymore and his eyes ached from hours of constant searching. The movement of the water was so gentle it was barely perceptible. He could have been at home in bed or floating in space.

He began to drift off.

"What's that?" someone said.

The voice had come from another raft but it was loud with excitement.

He grabbed his hat and sat up.

Trish was standing, raft pole in one hand, pointing at something in the water. Following her gaze, he saw small, dark brown lumps breaking the surface. The more he looked, the more of them he saw. A field of the things spread out far and wide. They must have risen up since the rafts had passed this area earlier. There were so many, they were unmissable.

"We'll check them out," said Trish eagerly, driving the pole down. Her raft moved toward the nearest lumps.

Kes was excited too. Maybe this was the aquatic plant he'd been hoping to find. But something made him uneasy. The brown lumps seemed tempting somehow, and if they were tempting to humans...

Trish's raft had stopped. She held it steady against the trivial current while another one of her team reached out with a knife.

Kes said, "Wait a min—"

The water erupted.

The torrent hit Kes's raft and upended it, dumping all the passengers in the water. He was swept away by the force, pushed toward the bank. Then it tugged him under.

Stirred-up sediment had turned everything murky and dark. Which way was up? Flailing, he tried to reach a firm surface. He needed to find where the riverbed lay and so how to reach air.

Something hit his back. He extended an arm behind him, wondering if he'd bumped against someone. His hand brushed some hard, thin things.

Claws?!

He tried to get away, but water pressure pushed him into them. Soon, he was right in among them. The claws gripped his clothes, his legs, neck, hair, dragging at him. A scream tried to force itself from his aching lungs. He grappled with them, fighting against them, writhing and turning to free himself.

Then the force that had pushed him underwater and into the grasp of the clawed creature turned. Now he was being pulled in the opposite direction. Bubbles and muted murmurs of sound were all he could hear. He could see nothing in the opaque water.

The water's movement hauled him from the creature's hold. The claws opened, releasing him. His head broke the surface. He whooped in air, filling his lungs. In the dim light, he spotted gray, tangled roots rising up to plant stems. *That's* what had held him? Not claws. Not a predator, wanting to eat him.

He swiveled, treading water, toe tips brushing the muddy bottom. What had happened to everyone else?

Two rafts bobbed nearby, empty. Where was the third? And what had happened to Trish and her companions, who had been closest to the eruption?

What had happened to everyone else?

The rafts were moving, slipping toward the center of the river. He was moving in that direction too. He kicked against the drag, beat his arms like wings, craning to see the cause.

His heart froze.

The water was

idly turning, spinning. As he watched, the spin grew faster.

Whatever the plant—or animal—Trish had spotted was, it had a strategy: entice the prey with tasty pods and, when the quarry got close enough, explode the water with such fury the victims were forced under and drowned. Then, to mop up any survivors, create a whirlpool to drag them in.

He kicked harder.

He turned onto his front and drove his arms powerfully through the water. The roots he'd become entangled in were about five meters away. He swam like crazy toward them. Soon, he was gasping, his muscles protesting. But the river bank wasn't getting any closer. He wasn't making any headway. If anything, the bank was moving farther away.

He tried to redouble his efforts but he was already exhausted. The long, hard day in 1.5 g, the oxygen deprivation of long submersion, the horror that his companions were probably dead, all took their toll. No matter how hard he tried he couldn't extract any more power from his arms and legs.

The roots edged away from him, darkening in the dusk. The whirlpool pulled him in inexorably. The sound of rushing water became louder.

A cry of despair blurted from his lips.

What would Miki and Nina do without him? They'd already lost their mother. If he died they would be orphans. Cherry, Wilder, and the other mission members would be kind, but they needed their parents. No one would love them like he did. No one else would take the same care of them. And they were stuck on a starship in a galactic wilderness. Would they even survive?

His thoughts on his children, he slipped under.

Sixteen

Wilder's comm chirruped.

"Hi, Ch—"

"Get here, now," Cherry said.

"Sure, but where are you?"

"Kes's cabin. I need help." There was the sound of wailing in the background and an out-of-tune song.

It had to be the kids. Kes had asked Cherry to look after them while he was gone. Wilder wasn't sure why. Cherry didn't have the first idea how to handle children. Wilder knew *that* too well from personal experience. Her intentions were good but her execution was terrible.

Kes's cabin door opened on a chaotic scene. Miki was bouncing on the bed where Cherry was sitting, bashing her on the head and singing to the beat of a song. Nina sat on the floor, legs splayed, screaming.

Cherry looked at her pleadingly. "I've tried doing everything they asked but it isn't working. Nothing I do pleases them. They won't shut up."

"Well, Miki seems to be having a good time," Wilder commented as she picked Nina up. She cuddled the little girl and soothed her, rubbing her back. Nina's sobs quietened.

"Why didn't I think of that?" Cherry asked.

"To be fair, it isn't easy to do with one arm. I think she's just tired."

"I thought she might be. I asked her if she wanted to sleep but she said no."

"Hm," said Wilder. "I don't know much about kids but I think they always say that." She'd spent some time with Tycho and Stephie and their grandchildren and picked up some second-hand knowledge. A twinge of sadness hit her.

Tycho had died not long after he'd heroically offered himself as a test subject for the Scythian Plague vaccine. He'd been a good friend and yet she'd rarely made time to visit him. "The trick is not to ask them, just go by the clues they give out and decide when it's bedtime yourself."

"Oh, really?" Cherry asked, frowning. "If they're tired, why don't they just go to sleep?"

"I don't think they know tiredness is what's making them feel grumpy."

Cherry's frown deepened. "That doesn't make a lot of sense."

"They aren't logical like adults."

"Adults aren't very logical either, but at least they know to go to bed when they're tired."

Nina's head flopped onto Wilder's chest and her eyelids drooped.

"Miki," Wilder said, "could you draw me a picture of your house? I don't remember what it looks like."

"Okay," she replied happily, leaping from the bed and landing with a thump. She skipped to the table interface and turned it on.

"I asked her if she wanted to do some drawing!" Cherry protested, her eyes round. "She said she wanted to sing instead. She didn't mention anything about the bouncing."

"Most kids like to feel useful, valued. Miki likes helping people, don't you?"

The little girl nodded, her gaze intent on the interface.

Cherry sighed heavily. "I'm not cut out for this. I hope the expedition to the surface returns soon. I don't know how much more I can take, or how much longer the girls can put up with my terrible babysitting skills."

Nina's little body had gone limp and her breathing was regular and heavy. Wilder placed her carefully in the small cot in the corner and put her stuffed Fila toy under her arm before covering her with a blanket. "You'll be fine."

Cherry looked skeptical.

"I can help out a little if you want," said Wilder, somewhat reluctantly. She had plenty to do already. Though she didn't want to tell anyone and raise false hopes, she hadn't entirely given up on fixing the jump drive. And work had already begun on transforming the Ark.

Cherry's expression brightened. "You wouldn't mind? It would be great if I could get a break every now and then."

"No problem. You know, it isn't fair that this job's been left only to you. We have a ship full of people who could help."

"Kes wouldn't like just anybody looking after his kids, but I know he trusts you."

"Okay." She sat next to Miki. "They might like to play with Piddle and Puddle. I wonder how Kes and the others are getting on."

"Will Daddy be back soon?" asked Miki, naturally fully aware of the conversation.

"Probably not for another few days," Wilder replied, "but Auntie Cherry and I have lots of fun things for you to do while you're waiting."

"We do?" Cherry asked.

———

Nina had woken from her nap. Wilder balanced her on one hip and held Miki's hand as she walked into the Ark to see how Niall was getting on with the remodeling. He was bent over, looking into a conduit. His eyebrows lifted and he stood up as she arrived.

"I've taken over from Cherry for a few hours," she explained, "so she can get some sleep."

"Right." He squatted down again. "Good luck with that."

"What's been happening? Have you made much progress?"

"I think it can be done," he replied into the opening. "We'll have to strip circuitry from the *Sirocco* and remove every other light from the passageways, but I think we can do it. Dragan's figuring out what isn't essential on the main ship."

Miki released Wilder's hand and ran to the conduit.

"Hey!" Niall exclaimed, pushing her away. "Stay back. It's dangerous."

"Come here." Wilder took Miki's hand. "Sorry," she said to Niall.

"You shouldn't have brought them in here. You know that."

"You're right. Come on, girls, let's leave Niall to—"

"But that's typical of you, isn't it?"

Wilder had half-turned away. She turned back. "Huh?"

"You're so irresponsible. Everything you do is slapdash."

She could only stare at him.

"The first time you made a-grav you nearly killed yourself. That's why you needed me to give you the parts, remember? Before you went to the *Opportunity*."

"Of course I remember."

Niall had been a scrawny little kid when she'd met him face-to-face for the first time. He'd changed, and not only physically.

"You always rush ahead. Everything has to be done yesterday. And look at where that attitude has got us."

"That isn't fair! You're blaming me for what happened to the jump drive?" She only recently been able to convince herself it wasn't all her fault. Niall's words were blowing all her hard work away. "The Leader said, at the meeting, we had to..." She swallowed as tears flooded her eyes.

"We should have waited. We should have done things properly. Completed all the tests."

"You think I don't know that? You were on the team too, don't forget. You could have spoken up. Why are you making this all about me?"

Nina wriggled uncomfortably. Miki had been staring, open-mouthed, at each speaker for the duration of the spat.

"I did say we needed to slow down," Niall argued. "Dragan and I both argued we should delay the launch."

"You did?"

"We did, but you didn't listen."

"I don't remember." It was the truth. The weeks leading up to the departure of the *Sirocco* were a blur of exhaustion. Many things had been said. She'd thought that, reservations aside, they'd been in agreement to push forward regardless. She wasn't sure how much Niall's memory had been influenced by the catastrophe and perhaps his own feelings of regret and self-blame.

"We can talk about this later," she said, "when we have some free time." It wasn't an appropriate conversation to be having in front of Miki, who seemed to absorb everything going on around her whether or not she appeared to be paying attention.

"Fine," Niall said bitterly. "Enjoy your time with the kids, considering it'll be the only chance you'll have."

"What?!"

What was he on about now?

He returned his attention to the interior of the conduit. "Figure it out. By the time we reach Earth your child-bearing days will be nearly over. Factor in the time we spend there, the journey back—assuming we *can* ever go back— you'll be old when we get home. I don't know if you ever wanted to have kids, but unless you think it's a good idea to bring new life into our hopeless situation here, you can forget it."

SEVENTEEN

As he was going under, Kes heard something slap the water. The noise came from near his head. Reflexively, he reached up and grabbed. A line or rope of some kind lay in his fist. The line moved. Either it was alive or someone or something was on the end of it. Was it part of the predatory creature's ensnaring tactic? Whatever it was, it was his last chance. He held on.

The line dragged him through the water, just under the surface. He seemed to be moving in the direction of the bank. He began to struggle for air again. His legs aching, he kicked, propelling himself upward a few centimeters until his head was no longer submerged. A blurry scene greeted his tired eyes: a dusky sky, a shadowy river bank, the line in his hand black and stretching out toward...Aubriot.

The man was hauling him in, hand over hand, like a fisherman lifting an exhausted marlin from the ocean after hours of battle.

Kes hit vegetation. His face was full of wet leaves and stems. Roots like the ones he'd mistaken for claws earlier—only a few minutes ago—were entangling his clothes.

But he was saved.

The rafts were gone. Remnants of one were scattered on the bank, shattered to pieces by the explosion. The others had disappeared into the whirlpool.

Trish was gone too, along with the men with her. Aubriot, Kes, and Garcia still lived because their vessel had been farthest from the plant or creature when the water erupted. Aubriot's man had survived too, and the woman accompanying him, but the third passenger on their raft hadn't.

The way Aubriot told it, he'd swum to shore after the torrent hit, avoiding the whirlpool pulling everyone else to the center of the river. Then he'd pulled down a vine to use as a rope to rescue people.

He *had* saved them. Kes had to give him that. But he didn't have to be so smug about it. Four members of their party had died. Trish had been a work colleague and long acquaintance.

Where the forest was impassable, they were forced to wade along the river margins, despite the danger. In some places the water was deep and they'd had to swim.

Kes waded through the shallows to the shore, last of the party to reach it, weariness dragging at his every step. By some miracle Aubriot's ear comm hadn't been washed out in the disaster. He'd comm'd Zapata about their situation and the pilot had offered to fly them the rest of the way to the camp. Zapata was waiting, as he'd promised. Before climbing aboard the shuttle, Kes took a final look at the dark, silent expanse of water.

———

He was sharing a tent with Garcia. He would have preferred to sleep alone, especially after the ordeal they'd endured, but he wanted to keep an eye on the man following Cherry's warning. The way he felt at the moment, he sympathized with Garcia's feelings. If it weren't for Miki and Nina, he might also be tempted to simply give up. The trip was a disaster and their chances for survival were so slim it hardly seemed worth going to any effort. The seeding material wouldn't reach Concordia in time even if they did make it to Earth. And what would they find there? The Scythians would have reached it before them and the planet would be under alien control.

What was the point?

He'd eaten and washed and settled down in his sleeping bag when Garcia arrived. The man uttered a brief greeting and climbed into his own bag.

"Is it okay if I turn out the light?" Kes asked.

"Sure. I'm dead beat after today."

Kes reached out and pressed the button. "We'll have a rest day tomorrow. I think it would be nice to hold a ceremony for the people we lost."

"We're continuing with the mission?"

"Of course. Did you think we'd be returning to the ship?"

"But four people died today! It's far too dangerous to continue."

There was a shuffling sound, as if Garcia was turning onto his side to stare at Kes, though the tent's interior was pitch black.

"We have to find food we can grow on th—"

"I *know* why we're here!"

Kes couldn't answer him. He was too tired and heartsore. He'd known Trish for years. She'd been instrumental in creating the Scythian Plague vaccine.

Garcia was right. The deaths had shown the danger of the mission. Only the mad or desperate would carry on. He wasn't sure which of the two they were.

"How many more of us have to die before we give up?" Garcia asked.

"We'll take every precaution we can, but the day after tomorrow we have to set out again. We don't have a choice about it."

"Why not? Didn't you guys find this planet on the Fila map? Can't you find another one? Maybe there's somewhere safer than this."

In fact, there wasn't. Planets harboring life were rare in the galaxy. They were extremely lucky this one was only a couple of months' flight from the spot where the faulty jump drive had flung them. The next world where they might find crop plants was years away, and it was 2.3 g, a gravity humans would struggle to move in.

Kes replied, "We don't have sufficient information to know we'll find better or safer conditions somewhere else. We have to thoroughly explore this world. It could be our best option and we won't be coming back."

Another rustle issued from Garcia's side of the tent. Perhaps he was turning onto his back. "Maybe we should try to settle here rather than continuing on. What about it? The gravity isn't too bad once you get used to it. We could bring down the supplies from the ship, and there's plenty of water. If we had a permanent base we could take our time about finding local food we can eat. We wouldn't have to rush and take risks. We could at least live out the rest of our lives in the sun and fresh air, not stuck in an artificial environment, breathing each other's stinky breath and drinking recycled piss."

"There aren't enough of us to build a sustainable colony. You know that."

"I suppose so. Just thinking aloud."

He sounded sad and wistful. Kes wished he could think of something to say to make the man feel better, but Garcia's words had conjured a dreadful vision in his mind: Miki and Nina, fully grown, everyone else long dead, the only surviving humans on an entire planet, utterly alone. And then, one day, one of them would die...

"It's out of the question," he reiterated. "We're going to continue to Earth."

Garcia didn't say anything for a long while. Kes thought he'd fallen asleep and he was drifting off himself when he heard, "Have you ever wondered if we're being punished?"

He opened his eyes. "What?"

"I learned all about what happened in the early days of the colony when I was at school. About the Guardians, the Natural Movement saboteurs, and the first Scythian attacks. I learned a bit about Earth too, how humans had ruined their own civilization. It's like someone is telling us we destroyed one civilization so we shouldn't be allowed to have another. Every attempt we make to build ourselves up, something comes along to beat us down again."

He had a point.

Kes said, "It's true that, when we were working on the *Nova Fortuna* Project, the worst challenges we imagined were things like engine problems and crop failures. No one ever thought the destination planet might be claimed by another species, or the Natural Movement had infiltrated our ranks. So much was unknowable. We couldn't ever have predicted what happened. But I don't think we need to look to the supernatural for an explanation of the disasters that have dogged us. The range of variables is so wide, the experiment is bound to throw up highly unpredictable outcomes."

After a pause, he went on, "Besides, you're only looking at the bad things that happened, not the good. Humankind has befriended other intelligent species, and for many years the Concordia Colony was very successful. It kept the flame of human civilization burning when it had gone out on Earth, in spite of the enormous odds against us, or, if you like, the terrible hardships fate has thrown at us. That says something, don't you think? Something about our endurance, adaptability, and sheer determination. This time will pass. Things will get better. I'm sure of it."

His words had lifted his own mood, though he didn't know if they'd had the same effect on his companion. Garcia only grunted "Good night" and was silent.

As Kes fell asleep, he was calm and hopeful. Losing Trish and the others was awful, but what he'd said was correct. Concordia had clung to existence for decades. He was confident that, somehow, it would continue to do so.

When he woke in the morning, Garcia's sleeping bag was empty and the tent flap was open. Kes climbed out and stood up, sucking in lungfuls of the heady air. Though he'd slept many hours, the sun was only just coming up and the camp was quiet.

He looked around for Garcia but the man was nowhere to be seen. Guessing he must have gone to freshen up or get something to eat or drink, Kes returned to his sleeping bag. But he was fully rested and didn't need any more sleep. After fifteen minutes, he exited the tent again. There was still no sign of Garcia.

Concerned, he woke up Aubriot.

They searched everywhere, all the tents, even the supply ones, the shuttle, the forest fringes, and up and down the beach, calling Garcia's name. Soon, everyone joined in the search.

Yet it was hours before Kes spotted the footprints of bare feet in untrammeled wet sand leading down to the water's edge. The sand's dark color had made them hard to see.

The footprints led into the ocean, but none could be found emerging from it.

Eighteen

The Fila map showed an island a couple of kilometers off shore. They hadn't spotted it due to its being so low-lying and nearly the same color as the ocean. Aubriot felt confident he could swim out to it but, considering the incident on the river, he wasn't willing to risk it. Plus, he needed the scientists to go too. He didn't have a clue what an edible plant might look like and he didn't want to know. Plants were boring—when they weren't trying to kill you. Though, he had to concede, they were necessary for survival.

Zapata said, "I'm willing to give it a try. It won't hurt to take a look."

The map was, predictably, free of any information relating to the ground above the waterline and the island was small. If there was a beach, it was likely to be narrow, perhaps too narrow to land the shuttle.

"Let's do it," said Aubriot.

Kes seemed hesitant but he didn't say anything. Aubriot would have overridden any objection anyway. The expedition needed a strong leader and sense of purpose more than ever. That idiot walking into the ocean and offing himself had thrown even more of a downer over everything. Some people were so selfish.

The others standing around the interface in the supply tent hadn't moved.

"Come on," he said, snapping his fingers. "Wakey wakey. Let's go."

Like mannequins slowly coming to life, his companions moved away.

"Get your equipment," Kes said to them tonelessly. "We'll meet at the shuttle in ten minutes."

As he was about to leave the tent, Aubriot grabbed his shoulder. "Can I have a word?"

They waited until the tent was empty.

"You need to smile more," Aubriot said.

"I need to..." Kes narrowed his eyes. "We've lost five people, one of whom killed himself, and you're telling me I need to *smile*?"

"Yeah, because, for better or worse, you're a de facto leader on this expedition too. The rest of them aren't only taking their cue from me, they're taking it from you. And if you go around like your mum's died, it affects everyone. So get your nose out of your navel and put on a brave face. Get it?"

Kes slowly nodded. "You're right. It's hard though. When I think about what I've brought Miki and Nina into, it's difficult to be upbeat."

"Your kids are probably better off on the *Sirocco* than on Concordia right now."

"Maybe. I feel bad about Garcia too. Cherry warned me about him. If I'd woken up when he left the tent, or if I hadn't brought him along in the first place, he would still be alive."

"Bah, he would have walked out an airlock instead. There's no stopping some people. We've got a job to do, so let's do it, all right?"

"Okay." Kes inhaled deeply before stepping out into the sunshine.

———

Zapata landed on a tiny strip of beach not much wider than the shuttle. As his passengers disembarked, waves slapped against the landing pads nearest the ocean.

"I'm taking her back to the mainland," he comm'd Aubriot.

"You don't want to wait?"

"I'm not taking any chances. I know there are no moons and supposedly no tides, but this bird is our only way of getting back to the ship. She'll be safer at the original landing site."

"Fair enough. I'll comm when we want to be picked up."

"Copy. If we lose contact I'll be back at sunset. Tell everyone to move away from the shuttle, at least thirty meters. I'll wait for your all clear."

Aubriot chivied the others, telling them to hurry up with collecting their equipment from the hold. When everyone was at a safe distance, he comm'd Zapata. The little party watched as the shuttle engines fired and the vessel flew the short distance to the farther shore.

"Right," Aubriot said when the small flare from the shuttle's engine vanished. "Time to start work. This island's pretty small. I reckon we should split into pairs and search half each. We can cover it all in one day."

"Agreed," said Kes. "I'll take Marcus with me, and Goslin, you go with Aubriot."

Goslin didn't look too pleased with the proposal but if that was the case she was too polite to say anything about it. Splitting up the scientists made sense so Aubriot also didn't voice any objection. Most of the ear comms had been lost in yesterday's disaster. They were down to two. Kes wore one and Aubriot had the other.

"We'll take this side." Aubriot pointed left. "Meet you back here when we're done. Ah, wait a minute." He'd spotted a largish rock near the water's edge. He dragged it up to the center of the beach. "This marks our starting spot. You ready?" he asked Goslin.

When she nodded, he said to Kes and Marcus, "See you later, you two."

Goslin was medium height and black-haired like most of the Gens, and not bad-looking. She hadn't said much so far. Like most cerebral types, she was quiet. That didn't matter. Most people didn't have anything interesting to say.

That was one good thing about Kes. If he was in the mood, he could hold a conversation. And his red hair made him easy to spot. If his ginger mop hadn't been so visible disappearing in the river, they might be six people down, not five.

Goslin had wandered closer to the shallow waves.

"Hey!" he called out. "Maybe you shouldn't go there. Remember what happened at the river?"

She threw him an annoyed glance. "As if I could forget! I want to look for seaweed. There isn't any near the campsite but there might be some here."

"What's the point? Who wants to eat seaweed?"

Her shoulders lifted and sank and she turned fully to face him. "All the seaweed on Concordia is edible, and it's highly nutritious. It's just that people aren't used to eating it. It would also be easy to grow on the ship. Now if I can *please* do my work? You stick to fighting off ravening beasts and whatever else it is you're good for."

"All right, don't get your..." He was about to say *knickers in a twist*, but Cherry had told him off too many times for using Earth English.

"Don't get my what?" Goslin asked irritably.

"Never mind." He folded his arms. "I'll keep an eye out for ravening beasts."

———

"Aubriot," Kes comm'd, "where are you?"

"What do you mean, where am I? I'm on the flipping island, the same as you. Do you want latitude and longitude?"

"Get over here. Hurry, please."

Shit.

He checked Kes and Marcus's position on his small interface. Goslin was in a clump of trees, scraping at something growing on their trunks. "We're leaving," he called out. "Gotta help the other two. They're in some kind of trouble."

It took twenty-five minutes to reach Kes after returning to the beach and running around the coastline. There was no telling what might stand in their way in the island's interior. Some areas had proven impenetrable.

In all the time it took, Kes never answered his comm again.

Aubriot hoped it had only fallen out.

He spotted Kes's back first. For some reason, he was coated in black dirt, head to toe, though his signature hair color was still visible. He was squatting down and his back was curved as he appeared to be pulling at something.

He was.

Aubriot sprinted to reach him.

Kes was pulling on a vine, in the same way Aubriot had hauled the man from the river yesterday. Only Marcus wasn't in water, he was up to his shoulders in mud.

"Can't...get...him..." Kes gasped.

His ear comm *had* popped out. The small, white device lay on the ground. Kes looked to be at the end of his strength. He must have been pulling on the vine the entire time it had taken them to reach him.

Aubriot took it, and Kes collapsed onto his side.

"Don't move," Aubriot shouted to Marcus. "Don't struggle. It'll only suck you in more."

"We already figured that out," Marcus replied dryly.

"Goslin?" Aubriot looked over his shoulder. He'd gone ahead of the scientist in his rush to get to Kes. She had just caught up. "Give me a hand. Grab this vine."

They pulled.

Together, they slowly managed to reverse Marcus's gradual descent into the quicksand. Following Aubriot's instructions, he went limp except for his grasp on the vine, and Aubriot and Goslin's combined strength gradually eased him out to his waist. When Kes had recovered, he joined them. Eventually, when everyone was near exhaustion, Marcus crawled from the mire and collapsed onto solid ground.

"See?" Aubriot said to Kes as he rubbed his tired arms. "It isn't all bad. Just need to be on our toes."

"You're right. In fact, it's better than you think." He pulled a plastic bag from his pocket. A piece of white root about the size of a finger lay inside. "I'd asked Marcus to dig up a plant similar to the one I took this from. That was how he got into trouble. This tuber passed all the toxicity screens. I may have found one of our future crops."

NINETEEN

FIVE YEARS AFTER LEAVING CONCORDIA

The Ark was a restful place to go when things got heated on the ship, and things had been more and more heated lately. Wilder liked to sit in one of the growing rooms, where brilliant lights overhung the lush beds, lighting the rest of the space in a soft glow. The atmosphere was warm, humid, and enriched with additional oxygen to meet the needs of the plants. Most importantly, the growing rooms were quiet.

In the *Sirocco*, it was hard to escape other people and their noise. There was always someone shouting down a passageway, playing their music too loud, or arguing with a neighbor. The conditions reminded her of Sidhe and its surfeit of screaming babies as the colony struggled to rebuild its numbers. Only then she'd been able to escape by building her own hamlet among the trees and inviting her friends to live with her.

It seemed like another life. She'd spent so much time aboard the ship, sometimes it was hard to remember living another way. More than one-fifth of her years had been spent traveling in space and yet she was only one-quarter into the journey to Earth. She would be in her late thirties when they arrived, assuming they arrived at all.

The door opened.

"I thought I would find you here," Kes said.

If it had been anyone else, with the possible exception of Cherry, she would have been annoyed at being disturbed, but her dejection lifted a little at his appearance.

"Is it okay if I come in?" he asked.

"Sure."

"Is everything okay? I heard about the argument."

She sniffed. "Puddle died this morning."

"I'm so sorry. I didn't know."

"It's okay. He was lonely after Piddle died. Only lasted a few weeks."

Kes sat next to her but didn't say anything. The sad but comfortable silence stretched out.

"I like to come here too sometimes," he eventually said, "to hide from Miki and Nina."

She chuckled. "You hide from your kids? I thought it was supposed to be the other way around."

"As you know, they're inquisitive and lively. There are only so many questions I can answer and only so much squealing and giggling a man can tolerate." He sighed. "Izzy would have had more patience, or she would have known how to quieten them down."

"Don't feel bad. You're a great parent."

"Thanks. I don't think I am, but thanks anyway."

It suddenly struck her: this was why he was here. He was parenting *her* too, as he had all her life, right from the time he'd brought her the sluglimpet repellent spray for her settlement. Or maybe he wasn't being a parent exactly, more like a big brother.

"I had to get away," she blurted.

"I know, and, for what it's worth, I think you did the right thing."

The argument with Niall had been getting out of hand. She couldn't even remember what it had been about. Their yelling must have been heard all over the ship. Everyone was in everyone's business as always. It was suffocating. She'd had to get away. "You mean walking out of there?"

"Sometimes, arguments aren't about what they seem to be about, and they can't be resolved by settling the issue at hand. Sometimes, it's better if both parties take time to cool down and think about what's really bothering them."

"That's the problem. Nothing *is* bothering me, except sadness about Puddle, and the usual anxiety about this position we're in. It's Niall. He's the problem. He's hated me for years, from even before we set out. I don't know why. We used to be friends. He was one of the team working on the a-grav machine."

"He *hates* you?"

"From what I can tell, yes." Her vision became blurry and she struggled to keep her voice steady. "He'd been cold toward me for years. Then, after we left, for the first few months he would verbally attack me, blaming me for the jump drive failure. Then after that he took to ignoring me, like I didn't exist to him. Lately, he's started up with the verbal attacks again."

"I've noticed."

"You have?" It felt good to know it wasn't her imagination. "Could I be doing something to annoy him?"

Kes smiled. "You aren't annoying. It isn't that."

"Is he... Is he losing it, do you think?"

Since the expedition that had succeeded in discovering seven plants they could grow as crops, two mission members had nevertheless given up hope. They had spaced themselves, one in a dramatic fashion involving an armed fight at the airlock, the other quietly when no one was looking. Their deaths made three suicides so far, including Garcia's. If Niall was about to give up too, it would devastate the already fragile ship's morale, and break her heart. Though sometimes he seemed to hate her, she couldn't help feeling close to him after their years of working together.

Kes replied, "If, as you say, this has been going on since before we left Concordia, his feelings are only tangentially related to our circumstances. I would say it's something to do with his relationship with you."

"We don't have a relationship, unless you would call constant arguing a relationship."

"It can be, yes."

"I try to avoid him as much as I can, but it's hard."

Kes was silent, looking down as he seemed to think over her problem.

She turned her attention to the rows of plants in their beds. *How much easier life would be if all you had to do was grow.*

"You know," Kes said, "when Izzy left me, it wasn't because she didn't love me. It was because she couldn't stand to be around me anymore. She couldn't take the constant disappointment and frustration my behavior caused."

"I'm sorr—"

"It was a long time ago," he said dismissively, though his expression told another tale. "My point is, she *could* get away. She went to stay with one of her sisters, the one who had always disliked me. Here on the ship, there's no real getting away from anyone. We're forced to live cheek by jowl whether we like it or not."

"Isn't it horrible?" She would have to return to the *Sirocco* to sleep, and then she would see Niall at meal times or pass him in the passageways. "But I don't understand. You and Isobel were married. Niall and I only know each other because we're colleagues."

"I remember him from the time of the plague. He'd taken charge of a group of vulnerable people and kept them safe until the vaccination reached them. He was and is an intelligent and caring young man. I find that hard to square with his attitude to you."

"Me too." She wondered what his point was.

"What happened to him when the biocide hit?"

"Uh…" She frowned as she thought back. "His home was destroyed in the Oceanside attack and a biocide capsule landed nearby. He and his mother ran from it, but he ran faster. It caught up to his mom and she died. He said he looked back and she was gone. It must have been terrible."

"What about his father?"

"I can't remember exactly. I don't think he knew him."

Another silence commenced. She relaxed into it. There didn't seem to be any explanation for Niall's baffling dislike of her, but it felt good to talk to someone with a sympathetic ear.

"Wilder," Kes said, "is it possible your friend has deeper feelings for you than you think?"

"Deep feelings of hatred, you mean?" she asked sarcastically.

"No, I don't mean that. You know what I mean."

"You think he actually *likes* me, and that's why he's so mean to me?"

"Listen. Imagine you lost the closest person in the world to you when you were just a child, that you saw her die an awful death. How would you feel about being close to someone else in a similarly dangerous situation? Imagine how scared you would be of having that person taken from you. And you have absolutely no control over what happens. You can't help how you feel, and you can't get away from the person. You have to see them day after day, feeling how you feel, knowing they could be torn from you any minute."

"But isn't that how it is with you and your kids?" she asked quietly. "Yet you aren't nasty to them."

His face tightened in pain. "We're talking about you, remember? Anyway, it's different for me. I'm older and, dare I say, somewhat wiser than Niall. I've learned to cherish and be grateful for every moment I have with the people I love."

She recalled something Niall had said to her once when she'd been babysitting Miki and Nina. He'd cruelly pointed out that having her own children was now off the table. Had that been because he'd been mourning the life they could have had if disaster hadn't struck?

Kes's explanation of his behavior seemed far-fetched, but it was *an* explanation and Kes was a man too, so maybe he would know.

She hugged him.

"This is nice," he said, hugging her back, "though I'm not sure what I've done to deserve it."

TWENTY

Spending time on the planet surface was mandatory for all mission members for mental health purposes. Cherry would have done it anyway, as would, she guessed, absolutely everyone else on the *Sirocco*. She hadn't set foot on soil in years, not since visiting the world where Kes and the other scientist, Goslin, had discovered the crop plants. That had been a hot, high-g place. The *Sirocco*'s scanners told them this planet was cooler and its gravity was also closer to Concordia's. As well as hopefully improving their mental health status, they would also take the opportunity to boost their vitamin D levels, supplementing the mandated sessions under a UVB lamp. Kes had been the instigator of that requirement. To avoid being cold when they stripped off and give their skins a chance to harness the sunlight, the shuttle was to drop them near the equator.

"Got your bikini?" Aubriot asked, lifting his eyebrows suggestively in the neighboring shuttle seat.

She rolled her eyes. "You know I don't have a bikini. Why would I have packed a bikini for a mission to Earth?"

"I know. I just like thinking about it." He grinned.

"What are you? Fifteen?"

"I'm young at heart, that's all."

He was young in body too. Aubriot hadn't aged in all the time she'd known him, whereas she was becoming painfully conscious of her fine wrinkles and gray hairs. Kes was aging too, and Wilder was now a woman in her early twenties. Yet they weren't even halfway to Earth.

"What are we going to do when I'm an old woman and you're still in your prime?" she asked.

His playful expression faded and he looked into the middle distance. "Hadn't really thought about it." His tone implied the opposite. He clearly had thought about it. A lot.

She winced. She hadn't guessed he was already one step ahead of her. But of course he was. That was Aubriot all over—calculating, planning, scheming, thinking about how the future looked *for him*.

"Has anyone noticed, do you think?" she asked quietly, diverting the subject from their relationship.

"I've had a few funny looks from time to time," he replied, grimacing.

"It's going to come out eventually. People aren't stupid, especially not the people on this trip. Maybe you should just tell them and get it out in the open."

"Make an announcement? *By the way, everyone. I could be immortal. In other news...*" He shook his head. "I'd be lynched."

"Lynched? What does that mean?"

He tugged at an imaginary rope around his neck.

"You think you'd be murdered?! Why would anyone want to kill you?"

"Think about it. You said yourself you're worried about growing old before we reach Earth. How do you think people are going to feel when they realize I won't? I'm not exactly Mr Popular already. That's not my style. They would hate me even more."

She tutted. "They don't hate you."

Aubriot wasn't far wrong when he said he wasn't popular, but would the rest of the mission members really turn on him?

"You don't feel it, do you?" he asked.

"Feel what?"

"The tension. The pressure everyone's been under ever since we knew we wouldn't die of starvation. It's been building for years. All it needs is a trigger to set it off. Something like hearing one person has it better than them. People hate a tall poppy. They'll cut me down."

"You're being paranoid."

"I hope so."

She kissed his cheek. "Don't worry. If they come for you, I'll protect you."

He put an arm around her. "I know you will, Bandit."

She rested her head on his shoulder. "Why do you call me that?"

"Too hard to explain, and you don't like Earth English. Do you know what Cherry means?"

"Isn't it just a name?"

"It's a fruit. Small, sweet, and beautiful."

———

A crystalline surface spread out as far as the eye could see, white and glinting in the sunlight. Zapata had set them down on a dried-up salt lake bed. They unloaded the equipment and then the shuttle left. The pilot's next task was to collect fresh water ice from a colder region of the planet.

They began to set up tents. The plan was to expose themselves to sunlight for short periods only at first, to avoid burning. Even the darkest-skinned Concordian was pasty after the years aboard ship, and pale-skinned Kes wouldn't be able to tolerate more than a few minutes' exposure at a time.

"It would have been nice to have a break like this on our trip to the Galactic Assembly," he commented to Cherry as they worked.

"Stars, yes." She recalled the months of utter boredom. "But then it would have taken us even longer to get home." *And I would have missed Ethan's last moments.*

She drove a peg into the crusty soil and straightened up. Miki and Nina were playing a chasing game that involved a lot of screaming. She marveled at their adaptability. Neither of them had been off the starship for five years, yet here they were acting like playing outside in the fresh air was the most natural thing in the world.

It was so good to feel the sun on her back again, even if it wasn't Concordia's sun. "Kes, I've never asked you—which do you miss most, Concordia or Earth?"

"Ah, that's a hard one. Hmm." He frowned. "I'm afraid I would have to say Earth. I grew up there, you see. It's hard to let go of the place you grew up."

"Well, I grew up on the *Nova*. I don't get homesick for her."

"I suppose a starship doesn't inspire as much of an attachment as a land-scape. We tried our best to make the ship a nice place to live, and to prepare you all for the reality of living on a planet surface. But, when I think about it, we were clueless. It's a miracle you survived and established a successful colony."

Cherry still sometimes had to remind herself Kes was one the people behind her existence. So was Aubriot, but he had always seemed different from everyone, neither a Woken nor a Gen.

"You did your best," she said. "Are you ready for some sun-bathing?"

"Actually, I'm going to sit in the shade. The reflected light will be enough for my skin."

"Just the reflected light? You must be a vit D-generating machine."

He smiled. "One of my many talents."

She joined Aubriot, who was already lying in the sun wearing nothing but shorts. The rest of the group was doing the same. She began to strip. "What do I do with this?" She took out her sidearm.

"I put mine with my clothes. I mean, what are the chances of something attacking us here?" He gestured at the surrounding emptiness.

The place did appear entirely devoid of life. Dragan had found the old, dried-up skull of a three-eyed animal when they'd first arrived, but there were no tracks or other signs of habitation or activity.

Following Aubriot's lead, she put the gun on her piled garments after stripping down to her shortest shorts and a halter top. She lay down on her front and pulled her hair out of the way to expose her back.

"Cook yourself fifteen minutes on one side," said Aubriot. "Then turn over and cook the other side. That's enough for today, according to the doc."

"Only half an hour?" She basked in the warm rays. "I could get used to this."

"Gotta build up tolerance, and we're collecting salt today too, don't forget. That'll give us more exposure."

She *had* forgotten. She and Aubriot were tasked with replenishing the ship's supply of sodium chloride. They had to dig up quantities of the salty soil, rinse water through it, collect and filter the water, and then leave it to evaporate.

"Ugh," she remarked. "Never a day of rest."

Aubriot softly chuckled. Their days aboard the *Sirocco* were mostly filled with nothing but rest.

Miki and Nina, in their sundresses, had finally given up chasing each other and were building a den out of odds and ends they'd scrounged from the equipment stores. Cherry's heart twinged a little as she watched them. She'd never thought of herself as a mother. Yet at certain times, such as when when she watched Kes braiding their hair, she could see the appeal. Not that it would have been a possibility with Aubriot anyway.

She sighed and turned onto her back. Her feelings were undoubtedly an effect of long years spent in unstimulating, claustrophobic conditions. The two little girls had become a focus for everyone. They were doted on, though it hadn't seemed to make them spoiled.

The strains of an argument drifted from the tent she and Kes had erected.

She lifted her head to peer over Aubriot's torso. Kes was sitting under the awning, alone. He wasn't the source of the argument. He'd turned and was gazing into the interior.

Aubriot sat up, blocking her view.

The voices grew louder.

She sat up too and leaned forward to look around him.

"I knew it!" a man shouted. "You bitch! I knew you'd been screwing someone else."

Aubriot met Cherry's gaze. Her eyes widened.

Miki and Nina had stopped what they were doing and were looking at the tent. Kes rose to his feet and moved to the opening.

"It isn't how it looks," came a woman's voice. "Let me explain. Oh!"

The sound of a hard slap accompanied the exclamation.

"Hey!" Kes darted inside.

Cherry stood up and beckoned to Miki and Nina. "Girls, come with me."

Their gazes flicked to her and back to the tent.

"And you," the man's voice continued, "you're as bad as her! You knew she was with me."

There was the sound of a scuffle.

"Come on," Cherry repeated, but the children were transfixed. "Girls! Go in your house!" They finally listened and crawled into their flimsy construction. Cherry parked herself in front of it. "Don't come out until I say so."

"I'd better sort this out," said Aubriot.

But before he could move closer, a woman stumbled into the light, as if pushed, clutching her face. It was Maddox, one of the soil specialists.

"No!" Kes hollered. "Stop!"

A man emerged too, followed by another and Kes, who was wrestling him. The second man was armed and trying to aim at Maddox. The sun-bathers began to get up and move away.

"Cut it out!" Aubriot dodged from the line of fire.

A pulse round hissed.

Maddox screamed and ducked. The shot missed.

Kes got the armed man on the ground. They tussled. "NO!" Kes screamed. There was a second hiss. "Shit! *Shit*."

He rolled back on his heels. The man he'd been fighting lay motionless, smoke drifting up from his head.

TWENTY-ONE

All was still, the only sound stunned silence, every person frozen. The entire event had taken moments. From the beginning of the argument until the man's suicide, a handful of seconds had passed.

The spell broke.

Maddox ran to the dead man's side and collapsed, sobbing, onto his chest. "I'm sorry! I didn't mean for this to happen. I'm sorry. I'm so sorry."

The onlookers regarded the scene uncomfortably.

Maddox lifted her head and said to Kes, "I didn't know he would... I really didn't mean..."

Kes ran a hand through his hair, his features stricken with sadness and horror.

Cherry was also at a total loss as to what to say or do. The only saving grace in the situation was Nina and Miki hadn't witnessed the suicide. She peeked into their den. "Are you okay playing in here for a little while? We're having some problems and Daddy's busy."

"Sure, Auntie Cherry," Miki replied.

"Good girls. I'll sit out here."

"Is there something we can cover the body with?" Aubriot asked. "Can't have everyone looking at it."

Kes nodded and disappeared into the tent.

Aubriot's words seemed to ease the tension. People began to move and talk.

"This is your fault," someone muttered, addressing the other man in the love triangle. It was Clarkson, one of the two doctors on the mission.

Clarkson looked at his feet.

Maddox got to her knees, her face a red and shiny mess of tears and mucus. She croaked, "We were only having a fling. Just a bit of fun. Brian was never supposed to find out. If he hadn't caught us kissing... Oh, stars!" She thrust her face into her hands and began sobbing again. "What have I done?"

Cherry expected Clarkson to comfort her but he didn't. Maybe he feared the judgment of the crowd.

Kes reappeared with a couple of towels and Aubriot helped him cover up the body.

Another suicide.

At this rate, would anyone make it to Earth, or would the *Sirocco* arrive at her destination empty?

Clarkson finally responded, growling through his teeth, "It isn't my fault. It's that damned engineer, Wilder. She's the one who built the jump drive. *She's* the one who got us all in this mess."

"That's right." Maddox wiped her eyes. "We're all bored out of our minds. I was just looking for a bit of excitement. Something different to do. Something to look forward to. Can anyone really blame us for trying to have some fun?"

"Hold on," said Cherry. "You're seriously blaming Wilder for your affair?"

"She's right though," someone said. "If it wasn't for those stupid engineers, none of us would be here. The four people who've killed themselves would still be alive. Those people who drowned, they would be alive too. Wilder's the head of the team. The buck has to stop somewhere."

Dragan studied the skull he'd found. Did the speaker even know he was here?

Cherry retorted, "A lot of things would be different if the jump drive hadn't failed. That doesn't make any of this Wilder's fault." She looked to Kes and Aubriot for support, but they'd apparently decided to move the body out of sight. She couldn't see either of them and the body was gone.

Wilder and Niall weren't here to defend themselves. They were in the group who would come to the surface next week.

"Who *is* to blame, then?" asked Clarkson angrily.

"No one's to blame," Cherry retorted. "It was an accident. They happen."

"Especially around incompetent people," Maddox spat.

What she and Clarkson were doing was clear. Everyone present was witness to the fact that her infidelity had driven her partner to suicide. The conditions everyone was living under had contributed to the act, no doubt, but the two were at high risk of being censured and ostracized. Trapped aboard a starship for many years to come, their lives could become even more miserable. They were trying to shift the focus onto someone else. Wilder was an easy scapegoat.

"Wilder is not incompetent," said Cherry, "and neither are the other engineers. She's the smartest person you'll ever meet. They were under time pressure. You know that. You know we had to try to get the seeding material from Earth as fast as we could."

"And look how that turned out," Clarkson responded. "It isn't only *us* down the drain, it's the entire colony. Is anyone even still alive back home? Or have they all starved to death, waiting and wondering what happened to us?"

"Don't bring Concordia into it!" Cherry exclaimed. "This is unbelievable. A man has killed himself because *you* couldn't keep it in your pants!"

"What's going on?" Aubriot was back. "What's all the shouting about? A man's dead for stars' sake. Have some fucking respect."

Chagrined quiet fell. Maddox went to Clarkson's side but he turned away. He was smart. The two couldn't be seen together or everyone would associate them a tragic death. Her shoulders slumped and she dropped listlessly to the ground, softly weeping.

"Kes is making a report for the ship's log," Aubriot said to Cherry. "Then we'll bury the body. Best to get it over with quickly."

"Can I talk to you?" She took his arm and led him out of earshot of the others before filling him in on the guilty couple's tactical response.

"Damn," he said. "Bad news for Wilder."

"I know. I thought we'd seen the last of the recriminations and complaints against the engineering team. And why are they singling *her* out? She wasn't the only one involved in building the jump drive."

"No, but it was her invention. And she's young, female, and not good at sticking up for herself. She's vulnerable, someone to pick on. It's like I said before, there's a lot of fear, anger, and resentment simmering under the surface. What's happened today has turned up the heat."

Twenty-Two

The first sign that something was wrong was the water shutting off as Wilder was brushing her teeth. She pressed the faucet again to rinse her mouth but nothing came out. They'd run out of toothpaste years ago, so it was no big deal in that sense—she just spat into the washbasin regardless—but in every other sense the sputtering pipe was worrying.

She comm'd Dragan.

"Your water's out too?" was the first thing he said.

"Uh huh. Has someone else contacted you about it?"

Was the problem localized or shipwide?

"Not yet. I wanted a drink, but, nothing."

"Okay, can you tell Niall? I'll see if I can find out what the problem is."

It was better to leave informing Niall to Dragan. Maybe Kes was right that his animosity came from a deep-seated affection for her, but it was animosity, nonetheless.

She quickly pulled on a shirt and pants and opened her cabin's interface, from which she could access all the ship's data. If they had a blockage or a leak, internal sensors should have picked it up and activated an alert.

Nothing showed up.

Ugh.

Something was wrong. There was no doubt about it. The fact that the ship wasn't identifying the issue meant the relevant sensors were malfunctioning too. She, Dragan, Niall, and whoever else they could rope in would have to search for the leak or blockage manually, going over the plumbing system inch by inch.

She wrinkled her nose, hoping the fault was in the clean, not dirty, water pipes. People thought building starships was exciting and glamorous. But in fact, in many ways you were just constructing a giant house that happened to be flying through space. The passengers had the same bodily needs and functions as they had everywhere else. They pooped, peed, shed skin, and sweated just the same, and it was the engineers' job to deal with it all.

Maintaining the *Sirocco* had become more and more challenging over the years. The ship was aging. Her structure and systems were wearing out. Every month, it seemed, they had to dip into the small stock of spare parts. One day, the stock would be used up, and then what would they do? There were no handy suppliers to contact for replenishment. Neither would there be any on Earth.

They had begun to resort to greater levels of ingenuity to fix things. Nothing was ever thrown away. Where they could repurpose materials they did, and they avoided replacing a worn-out or broken part whenever they could, choosing rather to mend it or rejig the system to function without it. In the beginning, she'd relished the challenge. It broke the endless days of monotony. Now, every time she was reminded that the *Sirocco*'s working life was playing out, it only added to her stress level.

The complaints about the lack of water began to come in. First, the cook comm'd her, saying breakfast wouldn't arrive until the water in the galley did. Next came a flurry of personal messages, asking why the bathrooms weren't working.

Her comm chirruped again. "I know, I know!" she exclaimed. "We're doing everything we can. Please be patient."

"Uh, I guess you already know about the problem with the water," said Cherry.

She closed her eyes. "Yes, sorry. I didn't mean to snap. You're about the twentieth person to tell me."

"Okay, as long as you know. I guess I should just mop it up as best I can until you get here."

"Huh? You have a leak? Why didn't you say?"

"I just did. I said—"

"Never mind. Where are you?"

"The Ark. Deck Two. I wanted to check the water potatoes."

"I'm on my way." She rushed out of her cabin. "What's it like? How bad is it?"

"Bad. I wish I was taller. I'm in danger of being... *Whoa!*"

The comm cut out. Wilder tried to raise Cherry several times but she didn't answer.

After telling Dragan and Niall where to meet her, she sped toward the Ark.

She got there first.

The lowest deck was awash and water was flooding from the elevator shaft.

"Holy shit!"

The ceiling lights were shining down on the mess.

Why was the power still on?

She ran back into the bridging passageway, gingerly stepping on the dry deck between tongues of water. Where had they put the isolator?

Niall and Dragan appeared at the farther end of the bridge.

"Don't come down here," she called out. "It isn't safe."

Where was it?

Thin lines marked the edges of a square panel shoulder height in the bulkhead. She slammed it with a fist, popping it open. Inside was a lever. As she pulled it down, the lights shining from the Ark side of the passage went dark.

"Cherry? Cherry?" she comm'd desperately. "Are you okay?"

Niall approached. "Is it that bad you had to cut off the entire section? Without heat, the plants will begin to die."

"Yes, it's that bad," she hissed. "Look!" She pointed at the water snaking out of the Ark.

Niall's eyebrows popped up. "Holy shit."

"That's what *I* said. Cherry? Are you there? Can you hear me?"

No answer came.

She bit her lip as a lump swelled in her throat.

"Cherry's in there?" Niall asked.

"Are you competing in the stupid question of the day contest?!"

Dragan arrived. "It must be the supply to the flooded beds."

"Yes," said Wilder. "Cherry said she was in the water potatoes room."

Niall commented, "I said we should have put them on Deck One."

"Stars," Wilder exclaimed, "if you don't have anything useful to say, can you please shut up? I need to think."

Meanwhile, Dragan was running back into the main ship.

"Where are you going?" she called.

"To get flashlights."

———

They shut off the water supply to the Ark and then climbed the service shaft to Deck Two. The water was ankle-deep. As they waded through it, ripples and splashes hit the walls, the noise echoing around the metal-walled chambers. The air was moist and rich with the scent of wet soil.

"Which way is the water potatoes section?" Dragan asked.

"I can't remember," Wilder replied, annoyed. The question was reasonable, but she'd been fielding numerous complaints and questions from personnel on the *Sirocco*, demanding to know when the water supply would be reinstated. She'd taken her comm device out of her ear, turned it off, and put it in her pocket. Dragan had comm'd Captain Vessey, to let her know the situation was being investigated and things would return to normal soon.

"You're sure that's where Cherry said she was?" Niall asked.

She rolled her eyes and didn't reply.

"I'll start looking for the leak." Dragan sloshed away.

Wilder and Niall continued in silence. The light from their flashlights danced on the water, sending shimmering reflections over the bulkheads and overhead.

Though her duties didn't include any agricultural tasks, she came to the Ark often. It had become a sanctuary to her, an escape. She knew the place well. Yet the darkness was disorienting. Everything looked different. Which way were the flooded beds?

"I think..." She turned in a circle, running her flashlight's beam over the surfaces. The conversion of the Ark to growing beds had involved removing many of the inner walls, opening out the rooms. The result was a mixture of large sections for main crops and smaller nooks for seed germination and propagation of cuttings.

"I think the water potatoes area is over there." She moved forward. "Cherry! Cherry! Can you hear me?"

Her friend hadn't responded to a single comm since she'd reported the leak. There were so many electrics around. Lights, heating, sensors. Wilder's grip on her flashlight tightened.

"We should never have run the two supplies together," said Niall. "We should have kept the main ship's water entirely separate from the Ark's. If the bridge was ever severed, that would be it. We would lose every drop we have into space."

"If we get cut off from the Ark we'll have a helluva lot more to worry about than not having any water. Any more helpful comments? I mean, this is really helping us find Cherry."

A beat later, her light brushed the tops of water potato plants. In truth, the foliage was nothing like an actual potato plant's, but the white, starchy corms the plant produced vaguely resembled the vegetable when cut open. They would only grow when their roots were submerged in about half a meter of slowly circulating water.

The tank was empty, the leaves collapsed and soggy at the bottom.

"She has to be somewhere around here." Wilder ran around the edge of the tank.

"Take it easy," Niall warned, "or you'll—"

She slipped and fell heavily, landing on her backside. Her pants were soaked through. But it didn't matter. As she'd fallen, the beam from her flashlight had skimmed something she recognized. "She's here! Cherry's here."

She crawled forward, shining the light in the right direction.

There was the familiar sight again: the soles of a pair of boots.

Cherry was on her back, motionless with her eyes closed.

TWENTY-THREE

An unfamiliar ceiling appeared in Cherry's vision. She moved, but a thousand hammers pounded in her head. She gave up and lay down.

"Ah, you're awake at last," said a voice.

She turned and squinted in the speaker's direction.

Clarkson. **Doctor** *Clarkson.*

She was in sick bay.

"Try not to move around too much," he said.

"Don't worry. I wasn't planning on it."

He approached, smiling. "Glad to see you still have a sense of humor. That's a good sign."

If she could have shrunk away from him, she would have. The man's presence evoked feelings of disgust. It wasn't that he'd been having an affair—she was in no position to criticize in that regard—but the way he'd turned the spotlight onto Wilder to save himself made her sick.

"You have a severe concussion," he went on. "Gave yourself a real good whack on the head when you slipped."

Ah, yes. Her memory was returning. She'd gone to check on the water potatoes. They were nearly ready for harvesting. But then water had spurted from a bulkhead and begun to flood the deck. She'd comm'd Wilder, and...that was the last thing she remembered. "How long until I'm better?"

"Two weeks, minimum, until your symptoms resolve, and you could be suffering from long term effects for months, I'm afraid. Like I said, your fall did a number on your brain. If it's any consolation, it could have been a lot worse. People have died in similar accidents."

"I have to lie here for two weeks?"

"I doubt you'll have a lot of choice. Watch my finger."

He held his forefinger over her face and moved it to the left and right. "Not bad. How's your vision? Any ringing in your ears?"

He *did* appear out of focus, and she realized she'd been hearing a high-pitched background noise ever since she'd woken up. She gave him her answers.

"You see?" he said. "It's going to take a while for your brain to recover. The best thing you can do to speed up healing is to take it easy, remain as still as you can, and rest."

"Okay, I get it. Could you tell Aubriot I'm awake?"

"Will do. Anything else you need?"

"What happened in the Ark? Did they find the leak?"

"It's fixed. They're recovering the lost water now. They'll filter and clean it and return it to the system."

That was a relief. She'd been worried they would have to return to the last planet they'd visited to restock with water. Not only would the trip delay them even more, it would remind everyone of the altercation and suicide, and perhaps of Clarkson's blame-casting.

It was better for morale to move on, literally and figuratively.

———

"Hey." Aubriot leaned down and kissed her forehead. "Thank fuck you're all right. I was worried about you."

"How long was I out? I forgot to ask Clarkson."

"A couple of hours. Have you seen the lump on your head?"

She reached up and her fingers touched a large bump under a cold poultice. "I'm only just beginning to remember what happened. My foot caught on something floating in the water, maybe a lead or hose? I recall falling, but I couldn't save myself. The nearest thing I could grab was a growing tank on my left, and..." She shrugged, waggling the small stump that was all that remained of her left arm.

"Ah well. You're okay now. That's all that matters."

Over the course of the day, Wilder visited her too, and Kes. But Clarkson only allowed each visitor to stay for ten minutes before asking them to leave and let her rest. She was secretly grateful. She couldn't concentrate on a conversation for long, and she kept dozing off.

The next day, however, she began to get bored. She hated inactivity. It was one of the reasons she enjoyed farming. There was always something to do. Yet she didn't want to risk further injury to her brain so she followed doctor's orders, staying put for fifteen days. On the sixteenth day, Clarkson discharged her with a list of dos and don'ts to aid her long-term recovery.

The doctor hadn't given her any notice she was nearly ready to leave. He waited until the day itself, perhaps not wanting to get her hopes up, so the news came as a pleasant surprise. She packed her small bag of belongings and stepped out into the passageway. She hadn't set eyes on anything outside sick bay in over two weeks. The experience was disorienting, as if she was seeing the ship for the first time. She was thrown back to the moment she'd boarded the *Sirocco* more than five years ago.

Had so much time really passed?

Yet her life on Concordia seemed a distant memory. Arrival Day, the sluglimpets, the Scythian Attacks, the shuttle explosion, the Guardians, Ethan, Cariad, Garwin...the events of her past melded together in her mind.

Extreme dizziness and nausea were assaulting her. She reached for the bulkhead to steady herself, swallowing the saliva pouring into her mouth. Should she return to sick bay? Clarkson would want to know about her symptoms.

No.

She'd lingered in that tedious place long enough. If she could just make it to her and Aubriot's cabin, she could rest. She would probably be fine if she lay down for half an hour. All she could do to recover was rest, the doctor had said. She could do that in her 'home' as well as anywhere else.

The cabin was a few minutes' walk away. She made her way slowly along the strangely unfamiliar passageways, taking care to stay near a bulkhead in case the dizziness hit again. She managed to reach the cabin without collapsing.

Relieved, she put her hand on the security panel.

She'd made it.

The door slid open.

Aubriot was lying on his back in bed, naked, the sheets crumpled around his feet.

Maddox, also naked, sat astride him.

Twenty-Four

Maddox turned to Cherry, her face a picture of surprise and embarrassment. Then her expression shifted to a smirk.

Aubriot grinned sheepishly. "Well, this is awkward."

Cherry took a step backward in shock.

The door slid closed.

She staggered down the passageway, numb and confused, not sure where she was going.

She didn't know what to think. She'd always known about Aubriot's womanizing. There had been a time when he was at a low ebb that she'd wondered if he was planning on sleeping with every available woman in the colony.

But she'd thought those days were over. They'd never discussed it, but she'd thought they were exclusive, a couple.

She shook her head. She hadn't imagined it. They *were* partners. He knew that.

"Cherry!"

Footsteps sounded behind her.

"Cherry, stop. Wait a minute."

She couldn't get away from him. After her long bed-rest she was too weak, and the dizziness had returned.

His hand fell on her shoulder. He was barefoot and bare-chested, wearing only shorts.

"Leave me alone!"

"Come back to the cabin. Maddox has left. We can talk."

"I don't want to talk. Don't touch me."

She pulled his hand off her and continued down the passageway, leaning on the bulkhead to steady herself.

"Cherry, don't be stupid. You aren't well. Let me help you."

She ignored him. The shock was wearing off. Tears overfilled her eyes. She kept her head turned away from him so he wouldn't see them. She wouldn't allow him to see her weakness, how much she was hurting, what he'd done to her.

He kept pace with her. "Where are you going? Back to the sick bay? Is your concussion bad?"

She had no strength to answer him. It was all she could do not to drop to her knees and let her rage and sorrow overwhelm her.

"Where are you going?" he repeated. "I'll carry you. I don't mind if you don't want to be in our place for a while. You need time to think. I understand."

Something between a sob and gasp of outrage at his condescension escaped her lips. She halted momentarily. "Fuck off," she hissed. "*Fuck...off!*"

"All right, all right!" He backed away, hands raised. "Whatever you say."

But he didn't leave her alone. He stayed by her side until she reached the place she'd been unconsciously heading for: Kes's cabin.

She thumped the door with her fist. It would have made more sense to press the buzzer, but she badly needed to hit something.

"Why have you come here?" Aubriot demanded. "Why him?"

Kes's immediate look of concern when the door opened cut to her soul. It was the look Aubriot should have been wearing when he'd seen her a moment ago—concern, or happiness that she was finally discharged from sick bay. Not that abashed smile, like a little boy caught stealing cake. His expression would be burned into her memory forever.

"What's wrong?" Kes asked. "Are you okay?"

Her chest heaving with the effort to not cry, she could only look at him.

He asked Aubriot, "What's happening?"

"Nothing," he replied sullenly. "Cherry, come with me. This is stupid."

Kes seemed to guess something was off. "I'm pretty sure she doesn't want to go with you. That's right, isn't it?" he asked her.

She looked down and shook her head.

"Come inside." He moved out of her way.

"No," said Aubriot. "She needs to come with me." He reached for her shoulder again.

Kes stepped between them. "Cherry's made it clear she doesn't want to speak to you right now. Respect that and leave."

"She isn't in her right mind. She's had a shock, that's all."

"Hmpf. I think I know exactly what kind of shock you mean. In which case, she's *completely* in her right mind. Go away."

"I'm not going without her. I know what you'll do. You're going to turn her against me. Poison her mind."

"From what I've heard you've already done a fantastic job of that yourself. Now piss off."

Kes moved into his cabin, but Aubriot followed him.

"I said..." Kes raised his tone "...*leave!*" He put his hands on the larger man's chest and pushed him into the passageway.

Aubriot swung for him. Kes swerved but not quite in time. Aubriot's fist grazed his jaw. Kes attempted to punch him back but his opponent brought up his forearm to block the blow. Aubriot hit him again, and this time his fist landed squarely on Kes's cheek, flooring him.

"Stop it!" Cherry screamed. "If you hit him one more time I will never, ever forgive you and I will never speak to you again!"

With a thunderous look, Aubriot unfolded his clenched hand and his arm dropped to his side. He stomped off without another word.

She helped Kes to his feet. "Are you hurt? He's such an asshole."

"I'm fine." A reddish-purple bruise was already forming on Kes's cheekbone and around his eye.

"Do you want to go to sick bay?"

"No, I'll just put some cold water on it. Not much of a knight in shining armor, am I? Falling at the first blow."

"Oh Kes, don't say that." She didn't know what a knight was but she knew what he meant.

She was glad to see Miki and Nina weren't home. She would have felt terrible if they'd witnessed the fight.

Kes sat on his bed as she wet a cloth with cold water.

"Thanks, I can do it." He took the cloth from her. "You sit down too. You look in a worse state than me. Were you discharged today?"

She nodded. "About ten minutes ago. I didn't tell Aubriot, just went straight to our cabin, and I found him..." That awful knot of pain fastened around her chest and throat again and she couldn't go on.

Kes put his hand over hers. "You don't have to tell me. You know what things are like around here. It's impossible to keep a secret."

"So everyone knew except me? How long has he been seeing her? Do you know?"

"I'm afraid it's been going on at least a week."

Aubriot had visited her in sick bay every day ever since her accident. She wondered if he'd hooked up with Maddox before or afterward. Or was it both?

The emotions she'd been battening down rose up. She put her head on Kes's shoulder and wept. Huge, wracking sobs consumed her. He hugged her tight. She hadn't cried so much since Ethan died, and that time it had been Aubriot who had comforted her. How ironic.

"I don't even know what I'm so torn up about," she said when her feelings were a little more under her control. "I've always known what he's like. This shouldn't have been a big surprise."

"You're making it sound like this is your fault. It isn't. His behavior is inexcusable. You don't deserve any of this."

"Don't I?" She sniffed and wiped her sleeve over her eyes.

"Of course not."

"I'm not so sure. I was in Maddox's shoes once. Maybe you don't know, but I was one of Garwin's affair partners, a long time ago. Is this payback, I wonder? It sure hurts to be on the receiving end."

"I didn't know that, but I do know it was rumored Twyla was aware of her husband's habits and didn't have a problem with them. And you were much younger then."

She smiled sadly. "I think I was only doing it to make Ethan jealous. Or I was screwed up."

Kes put the cloth against his face again. "Did you ever read the colony records from the decades we missed?"

"No, I didn't. Too depressing."

"There were a lot of problems with family relationships. Lots of divorces, poor parenting. The colonists really struggled with living in nuclear families and raising children. You remember Wilder building her forest settlement?"

"How could I forget?"

"The couple she was assigned to as a child in Sidhe never gelled with her. From what I can tell, she was basically neglected."

"Maybe she was, but she didn't go around having affairs, if that's what you're getting at."

"No, but she couldn't get used to living with two 'parents' and the parents couldn't get used to being responsible for her upbringing. They didn't know what to do. We *Nova Fortuna* Project creators made a huge error in assuming that the Gens would simply pick up relationship skills that hadn't been practiced on the ship for six generations."

"That was dumb," said Cherry, "but it doesn't excuse Aubriot, does it? He wasn't a Gen."

"You're right, it doesn't. Aubriot's a prick. Always has been and always will be. And I say that as someone whose life he saved. I was thinking more in terms of what it did to you. So, please don't blame yourself for your life choices. You were dealt a shitty hand."

She heaved a heavy sigh. "Thanks for saying that. I'm not sure I completely believe you, but it's a nice thing to say."

"Something else to bear in mind is what Aubriot told me once. In a rare moment of camaraderie, he said he, you, Wilder, and me were all screwed up. He and I in particular."

"Huh? Why?"

"We were the ones who went to the Galactic Assembly. We missed decades on Concordia, and he and I had also missed nearly two centuries while in cryosleep. He said we were out of our natural time and therefore fundamentally broken. Not in those words, of course."

She gave a short laugh. "He said something like..." she put on his accent *"We're fucked in the head."*

Kes chuckled. "Actually, I think that's exactly what he said."

She closed her eyes.

Since she'd surprised Aubriot in bed with Maddox, while he'd followed her to Kes's cabin, and during the argument when he'd tried to get her to go back, he'd never once said he was sorry.

TWENTY-FIVE

People would often say, as if sympathizing, it must be hard growing up on a starship, but it was the only life Miki knew. She vaguely remembered the place she'd been born, and she had even fainter memories of Mom—she wasn't sure how real they were, or if her mind had only created them from what Dad had told her—but nearly all her childhood had been spent on the *Sirocco*. The ship was her home and the people aboard were her family even though they weren't related.

Her favorite people, after Dad, were Auntie Cherry and Auntie Wilder. That was what she used to call them. These days, she called them just Cherry and Wilder. It was more grown up. Nina had copied her, like she always did.

Miki sighed and rolled her eyes.

"What's wrong?" asked Nina.

They were in the middle of their homework assignment: an essay on how to manage a starship, what roles were involved and how they contributed to the successful running of the ship.

It was a tedious task. Miki suspected Dad hadn't thought very hard to come up with it. He seemed to be in a dreamworld a lot of the time.

"Nothing," she replied. "This is boring. Let's write something else."

"No, we have to do this one."

"I bet if we wrote something different, Dad wouldn't even notice. He would think whatever we gave him was the work he'd set us. Especially if we back each other up."

"But that would be lying!"

"I suppose so, but it wouldn't be a serious lie. It would be fun, and if he finds out, we can pretend it was a joke. Yes! That's it. Let's do it as a joke."

Nina looked uncertain.

"Dad won't mind. You know he never gets mad."

"Hm, okay. What should we write about?"

Miki drummed her fingertips on the table. Her eyes widened. "I know. We could write about the Final Day Five."

"What?" Nina's mouth opened wide in horror. "We're not supposed to know about them."

"That's what makes them the perfect thing to write about. We can show Dad he doesn't need to sneak around anymore trying to 'protect' us." She made quote marks in the air with her fingers. "It'll tell him we already know all about it and that we're grown up enough to handle the truth."

Nina folded her arms over her chest. "But then he would *definitely* know we haven't written the assignment."

"It doesn't matter. This is a much better idea."

When her sister didn't answer, Miki continued, "You do what you like. *I'm* writing about the Final Day Five."

Nina shook her head "You're going to get in So Much Trouble."

"I don't care." Miki wasn't sure where her determination was coming from, but it felt exciting and good to write about the rumored group and to show her father she wasn't a little girl anymore. She deleted what she'd written so far and started again.

What is the Final Day Five?

The Final Day Five is a mysterious organization said to exist aboard the starship Sirocco. *When exactly the group came into being, no one knows for sure, except its members, naturally. Some say it began soon after the disaster that befell plant-hunters on an expedition to an alien planet, when four souls were lost to a fresh-water predatory organism.*

She paused and re-read her words, nodding approvingly to herself. For an opening paragraph it wasn't bad, clearly introducing the subject and hinting at the information to come. She particularly liked the fact she'd used 'souls' rather than 'lives'. Her choice was more interesting and poetic.

Another person died on the trip, a man named Bernard Garcia. One of the last things he said before his disappearance and presumed death by drowning, was he believed the Concordia colony was being punished by some sort of higher power. Garcia proposed the idea that everything bad that had happened was a result of humanity's destruction of its home planet. He suggested there was some-thing supernatural preventing humans from ever succeeding in re-creating a thriving civilization because it did not deserve the reward.

She frowned, unsure she was expressing exactly what she wanted to say. Reminding herself she had plenty of time for edits, she plowed on.

It is rumored that Garcia was not alone in thinking this way, and a small subset of the Sirocco's personnel have continued to hold this opinion or belief. These people are known as the Final Day Five. Their title is self-explanatory...

Miki mentally patted herself on the back at the neatness of 'self-explanatory', which captured so much meaning in one word.

... but for the purposes of this essay it is best to be clear: the group is supposed to consist of five people who think an apocalypse approaches. They've concluded that Concordia has followed Earth in its demise and our starship is the last remnant of human civilization. The Five say a cataclysm will strike before the Sirocco reaches her destination, destroying everyone aboard and putting out the flame of humanity forever.

Who are the people with this...

She couldn't think of exactly the right word. She switched from her assignment to a thesaurus and looked it up.

...nihilistic conviction?

That is the great mystery. On the one hand, no one has ever proclaimed the belief aloud (to the writer's knowledge). On the other hand, whispers about the group continue. The only conclusion to be drawn is that one or more members of the Five began the rumors themselves, hoping to draw others to their cause while at the same time not showing their hand.

What is the purpose of the Final Day Five?

The most chilling aspect of the existence of the group isn't what they think, but what they might do. Without hope for the future, why should they continue with tasks essential to the ship's maintenance and passenger survival? And if their predicted apocalypse doesn't arrive, will they create their own?

The implication of what she was writing hit her. She shivered. Maybe the change of assignment subject wasn't such a good idea after all.

"How are you getting on?" Nina peered at her interface. Her eyes moved from side to side as she scanned the text. She looked at her sister. "Are you sure—"

The cabin door opened.

"How are you getting on, girls?" asked Dad. "Nearly finished? The assignment was a bit mediocre, wasn't it? I'll try to think of something more interesting for your next one."

"I'm done." Nina proudly gave him her interface.

"Excellent. How about you, Miki?"

"Um..."

Her fingertip rested on the Delete icon. But if she wiped her essay, she wouldn't have anything to show for all the time she'd spent.

"Miki didn't do the work you set," said Nina innocently.

"Nina!"

Nina kept her attention on Dad, refusing to look at her. She could be a real bitch sometimes.

"Really?" Dad asked. "Is that right? That isn't like you, Miki."

"I did write *something*, only..."

"Oh well, that isn't too bad. Can I read what you've written so far?" He handed Nina's interface back to her, saying, "This looks good. I'll take a closer look later."

Tendrils of apprehension creeping over Miki, she handed him her assignment.

As Dad read, his already pale skin turned paler and his mildly interested expression became aghast. He murmured, "I had no idea..." His eyes leaden, he gave the screen back. "I see we have some talking to do."

TWENTY-SIX

Another nine years.

Wilder stared at the overhead. She'd turned on the light, but she couldn't get out of bed.

It would be another nine years before the *Sirocco* would arrive at her destination—assuming she didn't irretrievably break down on the way—and then what? What was there on Earth to look forward to? The Scythians would have already arrived. They had numerous ships, equipped and armed. What should have been a simple trip to gather living resources had turned into a last, desperate attempt to rescue humanity from domination and slavery.

It was hopeless.

Yet no one wanted to mention the fact. Most people, herself included, put on a mask of determination and optimism. Deep inside, they had to feel the same way as her. It was the great *unmentionable.*

Each day she had to drag herself out of bed. Each day, the effort became harder. She worked in the Ark mostly, and her route led her past an airlock. Twice per active shift, once on her way to work and once on her return, she struggled with the temptation to step out of it.

And the bullying made everything so much worse. It had been going on for years. A snide remark just within her hearing here, a subtle push as she passed someone in a passageway there. Once, when she'd been sitting at a refectory table alone eating her dinner, a gob of spit had landed on her plate. She'd looked up to see Goslin's retreating back.

She'd told none of her friends what was going on. Not Cherry, Kes, Dragan, or Niall, though the latter was more of an acquaintance than a friend.

She might have told Aubriot, who'd stuck up for her when the jump drive had malfunctioned, but what was the point? It would only make things worse. Her persecutors would find new, more cunning ways to hurt her, and Aubriot couldn't protect her around the clock. She could go to Captain Vessey, but the captain rarely left her cabin, spending most of her time drinking the ship's rotgut.

Her comm chirruped. She reached out and slipped it into her ear, forcing an upbeat note into her tone as she said, "Hi."

It was Cherry. "Glad you're awake. Are you on your way?"

Wilder checked the time and mentally cursed. She'd agreed to help with a harvest today. "I overslept, sorry. I'll be there as soon as I can."

"Great. See you soon."

She hopped out of bed, willing her limbs to move. After quickly changing from pajamas into her working clothes, she trotted to the Ark. "Which deck are you on?" she comm'd Cherry when she arrived.

"Four. Don't you remember? It's Fat Grains today."

Fat Grains. What a name. She'd forgotten who'd thought it up. Definitely not Kes. He would have given them a double-barreled Latin name no one understood. He probably had, in fact, and not bothered to tell anyone.

The common name was perfectly descriptive.

The plant had been discovered on a planet they'd visited two and a half years ago, only the second planet on their journey that supported a diverse range of plant life. The first world they'd visited, where so many lives had been tragically lost, had been the source of the majority of their crops, but it hadn't yielded a cereal grain. The addition of Fat Grains to their diet had been transforming. They could now eat bread of a sort, though it was unleavened and somewhat oily due to the fat in the seeds. But the readily obtained starch had seemed to boost everyone's energy and spirits—for a while, until the shroud of apathy and sense of just-hanging-on descended once more.

She exited the elevator.

An entire deck was devoted to the cultivation of Fat Grains.

A coppery-orange sea spread out before her. The plant used a red-hued chemical to gather energy from sunlight. As its seeds ripened and the plant began to die, the color intensified and deepened.

The sight was beautiful, she knew intellectually. But she couldn't feel it.

"Hey," Cherry called out, "over here."

She was standing in a group of five. Dragan was here too, as well as Kes, Aubriot, and Miki. Cherry and Aubriot seemed to be getting along better these days. She guessed Cherry had learned how to ignore his arrogance and assholery. She had not.

"We waited for you," Cherry said as she approached.

"Sorry I'm late."

"Don't worry about it."

"Let's get started," said Aubriot tetchily, as if *he* didn't forgive her tardiness.

"Yeah, we haven't got all day," said Dragan dryly.

They did have all day, and the next, and the next. Fat Grains dried on the stalk and remained good for weeks.

Due to the fact the crop grew in a room only three meters high, with banks of lights hanging a half a meter below the overhead, there was no room to wield complex harvesting equipment even if they'd been able to build it. They were forced to cut and gather the stalks manually. She and Dragan had fashioned long, two-handled blades to scythe through the crop, and the person walking behind would scoop the cut stalks into a hopper.

As the two weakest harvesters, she and Miki would be the scoopers.

"Can you work with Aubriot and Dragan?" Cherry asked. The two men were a similar height, so it made sense they would be partners for the task.

"Actually," said Kes, "I'd prefer if Wilder worked with us, if it's all the same to you."

Cherry lifted her eyebrows. "Sure. It doesn't really matter."

Wilder was surprised Kes preferred to not work with his daughter too, but she was relieved she wouldn't have to spend time in Aubriot's company.

"I know," said Aubriot. "Let's make a competition of it. Whoever reaches the middle first—"

"Let's not," Cherry interrupted. "One, the blades are damned sharp and I don't want to lose my other arm or use up what's left of our medical supplies. Two, we should be focusing on doing a good job, not a fast one."

Aubriot curled his lip. "Whatever. Just trying to make things a bit more interesting."

"Thanks for your suggestion," Cherry replied sarcastically.

Maybe she hadn't forgiven him after all.

They set up at diagonally opposite corners of the room. Cherry's small stature implied she was weak, but her right arm was surprisingly strong, or perhaps not surprisingly considering she had to use it for everything.

The razor edge of the blade sliced the stalks as if moving through air. A fresh scent that always reminded Wilder of rust or blood rose up. She bent and cupped her hand around the fallen heads of grain before sweeping them into the wheeled hopper.

"I want to talk to you both about something," said Kes quietly.

"Something to do with Miki I'm guessing," Cherry replied. "That's why you wanted Wilder to work with us."

"Is she okay?" Wilder loved Kes's daughters like sisters.

Kes answered, "She's fine. Too fine, in a sense. Stars, that girl's smart. She's found out about the Final Day Five."

Cherry halted. "How?"

"That's what I'd like to know," said Kes.

Wilder said, "But I thought everyone knows they mustn't mention anything about the Five to them."

"They do." Kes moved forward. "Let's not stop. I don't want her to guess we're talking about her."

"How do you think she found out?" asked Cherry.

"How did any of us find out?" asked Kes bitterly. "Do you remember? I know I don't."

Cherry sighed. "It was a long time ago. You're right. I can't remember who told me. I recall you telling me about Garcia, what he said in the tent that night he disappeared. And then people began talking about how bad things always happened to the colony, that we could never seem to catch a break. The usual bellyaching."

"Was it Vessey who mentioned the Five?" Wilder seemed to remember the captain talking about apocalypse believers during one of her drunken rants.

"I don't think so," Cherry replied. "I haven't got any sense out of her in years. All I can remember is suddenly everyone was talking about them. Then discussions moved on to other things. But the FDF has always stuck in the back of my mind. Every so often someone will mention them or slip them into a not-so-funny joke."

Wilder gave the hopper a shake to create room for more stalks. "Does it matter? Miki's fifteen, right? Maybe she's old enough to know about these things."

"Don't you think she has enough to contend with already?" Kes demanded. "Does she really need to worry about someone with a death wish blowing up the ship? She's just a kid."

"I was fifteen when I built my tree settlement and went with you to the Galactic Assembly."

"That was different! That was about living, not dying."

Kes appeared to be losing his temper, so she dropped it. He wasn't the same calm, kind man she'd known for so long. He was nearing the end of his tether, as they all were.

Another nine years.

How would they ever make it?

TWENTY-SEVEN

ubriot leaned his forehead against the shower stall as the hot water streamed over his shoulders and down his back. His muscles ached from the day's work, but not too badly. Others like that weakling, Kes, would be in worse shape. He smiled, recalling the punch he'd given him when Cherry had run off to his cabin. It was a few years ago, but the memory was fresh and he relished it.

He would have liked to punch him some more. It would have taken the edge off his anger and frustration, but Cherry had made him stop, threatening to give him the silent treatment forever. He'd done as she wanted yet she'd barely spoken to him for ages afterward.

So much for giving in. He should have carried on punching while he had the chance. It wasn't like he could hit Kes now for no reason.

She'd been unreasonable. Why couldn't she see that? She'd been in sick bay for weeks.

A man has needs.

Sure, it had been awkward and uncomfortable for everyone when she'd walked in on him and Maddox. He hadn't intended for that to happen. He did have a sense of decorum. It would have been better if she'd never found out. He'd planned on keeping it a secret. No knowledge, no harm.

Closing his eyes, he tipped his head back and gathered water in his mouth. After sloshing it around, he dropped his head forward and spat it out.

Women.

They were nothing but trouble. He and Cherry had had it good for a long time. Why did she have to go and spoil everything with her jealousy? If she'd wanted to screw Kes, or...

Painful anger rose in his gut. He pushed away the thought of Cherry with someone else, turned off the water, and stepped out onto the mat.

The evening lay ahead. He dried himself off and put on pants and a shirt, the best he had. Everyone's clothes were wearing out. How long had it been since they'd run out of printer supplies? He couldn't remember. The printer probably no longer worked anyway. The engineers had scavenged all non-essential equipment for materials and parts.

Checking himself in the mirror, he wondered who might be interested in returning with him to his cabin tonight. Maddox? Goslin? Durbin? He'd bedded all the single women and several married ones too. Cherry had never slept with him again, and he'd never tried anything with Wilder. He had an intuition Kes would put a stop to it. She'd also made her dislike of him obvious.

Wilder was off limits, that was clear. She was out of bounds in the same way Cherry had been, emotionally, when she'd been in love with Ethan. Her feelings seemed to have changed over time. He'd had a sense he'd grown to mean more to her, but then...

He walked to the refectory where most people met at the beginning of the quiet shift. The atmosphere was convivial by the time he arrived. Vessey was propped in a corner, already off her face. Goslin, Maddox, and Durbin were sitting together. That was a bad sign. Would he manage to separate one from the rest, like a lion singling out the weakest member of a herd? He had a sour taste in his mouth. He was growing tired of the hunt. Cherry, Kes, and Wilder were absent as always. The three had formed their own little happy family.

Dragan and Niall were here. He decided to join them. It would be good to be brought up to speed on the state of the ship.

He helped himself to a cup of ship-made alcohol from the jug and walked over. The two men acknowledged him with a nod as he sat down, though they didn't seem overjoyed to see him. *Never mind*. He'd never cared about being the flavor of the month.

"What is it tonight?" He sniffed his drink.

"Purple Carrot Top brandy," Dragan replied. "Last year's. A fine vintage." He swirled the liquor in his cup before taking a sip and grimacing.

Niall snorted a laugh. "It might be nearly undrinkable, but can you imagine what this place would be like without booze? Personally, I thank the stars every day I was stranded on a lost ship with a bunch of biologists."

"Come on," said Dragan. "Are you trying to tell me you couldn't have made your own alcohol? It isn't hard. And who says we're lost?"

"Not me," said Aubriot. "We're on a direct heading. In my case, going straight home."

"Huh, home." Niall stared into the bottom of his glass, swirled the remains of his drink, and downed the dregs. "Not sure where that is anymore. By the time we reach the end of this voyage, I will have lived on this ship longer than I did on Concordia."

"And I'll be knocking on old age," Dragan commented.

Niall rose to his feet. "That's enough for me tonight."

"Leaving already?" said Aubriot. "The night's young yet." He'd been hoping to spend time with drinking buddies. Pulling women was losing its allure, and most of the men would have little to do with him. To be fair, it was understandable considering he'd screwed their girlfriends or wives. Neither Niall nor Dragan seemed to have any romantic interest in the women. Dragan had left a spouse behind on Concordia. What Niall's story was, he didn't know.

"Yeah, I'm done," Niall replied. "A man can only stomach so much hooch. And we have a long day ahead tomorrow."

"What are you doing?" Aubriot couldn't imagine any time-hungry tasks remained on the ship. Time was the one thing they had in plenty.

Dragan gave Niall a look, and the latter winced as if he'd said too much. Dragan leaned closer to Aubriot and said softly, "Keep it to yourself, but the man here had a brainwave about the jump drive. We're going to try something out, but we want to get the work done in a day. If we take longer, people will notice, and we don't want to get anyone's hopes up."

Aubriot got it. Morale was low and extremely fragile. It might only take one more disappointment to push certain people over the edge. "Don't worry. Won't say a thing. But what are the chances it'll work? Seems odd to think of something after all these years."

Niall shrugged. "Honestly? Virtually no chance. It's just something I noticed as I was re-reading the Fila's original engine plans for the millionth time."

Aubriot lifted his glass. "I'll toast to your success." Swallowing a mouthful of the liquor, he shuddered as the fiery sensation burned down his throat into his stomach. "*Shit.*"

The younger engineer was making his way through the tables, somewhat unsteadily.

"Is Wilder in on it too?" Aubriot asked Dragan.

"Yeah, she—"

A shout of outrage broke into their conversation.

Aubriot looked toward the source. Niall was tumbling backward. Someone must have pushed him. The doc, Clarkson, was on his feet, hands clenched, face beetroot red and sweaty. All the cups around him were overturned and the table was awash with spilled alcohol. Niall must have stumbled into it. A minor offense, yet Clarkson was furious.

He reached for Niall, his other hand bunched into a fist, apparently about to haul him upright and hit him.

"Hey!" Dragan yelled. "Leave him alone!" He raced to Niall's aid.

The fist intended for the younger man swung around and connected with Dragan's jaw.

Aubriot shouted at Clarkson, "You! Put a lid on it."

Niall launched himself at Clarkson, and the two men went tumbling to the deck. Dragan was bent over shaking his head as if to clear his brain. Aubriot sped to the tussling fighters and tried to pull them apart.

Someone leapt on his back and pummeled his skull, screaming incoherently into his ear. He overbalanced and fell backward, crushing the person beneath him. He felt the softness of a female figure but that was all he knew before someone else jumped him.

He was in a melee of wrestling bodies. A blow landed on his ear. Pain exploded in his head. He punched and kicked, not even knowing who he was hitting. It could have been Niall and Dragan. It was impossible to tell. All he knew was he had to fight. He had to get to his feet or risk being crushed.

He took a punt to the eye. An elbow struck his nose. Hot blood coursed from his nostrils and down the back of his throat. He choked, coughed, and yelled, still fighting to get up, but the sheer weight of bodies pinned him down.

Somewhere in a remote corner of his mind, he saw the brawl from afar. He couldn't see himself, but he witnessed the battling mob, writhing like mating snakes. A decade of anger, deprivation, misery, and fear was erupting. Where it would lead, he couldn't guess.

Twenty-Eight

Cherry pressed Kes's door chime.

When the door slid open, Kes said, "You don't need to do that. Just come right in. You're one of the family."

"Aww, thanks." She was glad he didn't mind her coming over so much. Aside from the farming, she had little to do, and she loved spending time with the girls. As they'd grown older, they'd become easier to handle and more interesting. "Miki and Nina not home?"

"They wanted to help out in sick bay."

"They did? They're kinder than me."

"And me," said Kes. "I don't have time for those blockheads. Let them suffer. It might make them think twice next time. Bunch of animals."

Cherry was disgusted by the behavior of the people involved in last night's fight too. "Do you know who took part?" She sat at the desk.

"More than half the ship from what I can tell. I popped my head around the sick bay door earlier. The place is full, but the patients seem mostly walking wounded. Miki and Nina wanted to play medic, so I let them. It'll keep them occupied for a while. I saw Aubriot in there."

"*That's* no surprise."

"And Dragan and Niall."

"That is. I can't imagine them in a drunken brawl. How did they look?"

"They weren't too badly off. They were on their way out, saying they had something to do."

"Wilder wasn't there, I hope?"

"Of course not. You know she doesn't join in the drinking sessions. She told me this morning she's busy today. I suppose she must be working with Niall and Dragan. Would you like some tea?"

It wasn't Concordian tea. They'd run out of that within months. But the foliage of one of the crop plants was aromatic and made an acceptable substitute.

Without waiting for an answer, he began a brew, inserting an element into a heatproof container and adding two spoonfuls of dried leaves.

While waiting for the water to boil, he sat next to Cherry. "I'm glad we have a little time alone. I want to thank you for all your help with the girls over the years. It isn't easy being a single dad. You've been my savior on more than one occasion."

"You don't need to thank me. It's been a pleasure. And Wilder's helped too. I can't take all the credit. She was better than me with Miki and Nina when they were younger."

"You've both been tremendous," said Kes. "I couldn't have wished for better aunties. Izzy would have been relieved to know the girls had two amazing female role models in their lives."

The sound of bubbling water came from the container. He got up, turned off the element, and poured two cups of tea.

"You must miss her." Cherry accepted her cup.

"Yes, even now."

Cherry gazed into the rising steam. Kes had never asked her about his wife's last moments and she'd never offered to tell him, except to pass on Isobel's message of love. "I'm sorry if this is insensitive, but I think you were lucky to have the time you did."

"I know, and it isn't insensitive. I only wish I'd appreciated her more at the time, but there's no point in living with regrets. She gave me Miki and Nina, and for that I'm forever thankful."

Cherry took a sip of tea, and a comfortable pause in their chat developed. She enjoyed these quiet moments with friends best of anything she could do on the ship. They made life bearable. What would she have done if Kes and Wilder hadn't come along on the mission?

She looked up at Kes and found his gaze resting on her.

They held eye contact while seconds ticked past.

Slowly, he leaned forward. She remained still, not calling a halt to what was about to happen.

He kissed her, his hands resting on her shoulders.

Her pulse quickened. Kes had been a friend so long. She'd never consciously thought of him like this, and yet he was kissing her exactly as somehow she'd known he would.

He drew away and asked huskily, "Should I lock the door?"

She nodded.

———

She lay next to him, shoulder to shoulder on the narrow bed.

Her passion spent, the cold reality of what had happened was hitting, hard.

Kes seemed to feel the same. He was focused on the overhead, not speaking.

Compelled to break the silence, she said, "That was...good."

"Yes," he replied dully.

She quietly added, "But..."

He turned and gazed at her earnestly. "But a-a mistake, right?"

Relief hit her like a wave. "*Big* mistake."

"I'm so glad you feel the same. I got carried away and—"

"So did I. I don't know what came over me."

Kes turned onto his back again. "I do. We're only human. Evolution drives us to procreate."

"Is that all it was? We need closeness as well. Intimacy."

"Yes, that too."

"Besides, I think I'm passed procreating now."

Kes's eyes snapped wide. "Stars, I hope so!" He sucked in a breath. "I mean, if you were to...I mean, it wouldn't be..." He faltered to silence.

"Don't worry. I really doubt anything will come of it. This voyage is sending us all crazy. If we aren't beating each other up we're falling into bed with the nearest warm body." This time, it was she who gasped at the implication of what she'd just said.

"It's okay," said Kes. "I know I'm not just a warm body to you." He wrapped an arm around her. "You know, I'm surprised there haven't been any pregnancies on the ship. I don't have to concern myself with contraceptives, but we must have run out of them a long time ago."

"There have been pregnancies." Cherry wasn't especially close to any other women except Wilder, but gossip was about the only interesting thing to talk about. "People try their best to avoid them but the doctors have had to deal with some accidents."

"I'm glad no one has been tempted to bring new life into this hellhole. I bet Aubriot has been responsible for a few of the accidents. You're well rid of him. You deserve better."

"I know. You don't need to tell me. But Aubriot hasn't fathered any babies. I know that for a fact. He's infertile."

"He is?" Kes's tone was shocked. "His gene editors really screwed up. Did his parents ever find out? They would have sued the company into bankruptcy."

"It wasn't a mistake exactly. It's a side effect of..." Cherry hesitated. Did she have any right to be telling others Aubriot's secrets?

She recalled seeing him and Maddox together.

Screw him.

"The genetic engineering his parents arranged when they conceived him was ground-breaking and illegal. It was supposed to give him extreme longevity. It seems to have worked, but the downside was it made him sterile."

"Damn," Kes breathed. "That makes sense. Now I think about it, he hasn't aged a day since we left Earth. It's like he reached his late thirties and then just stopped. I don't know why I didn't notice. I must have been used to him looking like a male model and didn't think anymore of it. Poor Aubriot."

"Poor Aubriot?"

"Doomed to being an utter arsehole for all eternity."

Cherry chuckled.

They cuddled until she said, "We'd better get dressed before the girls come back."

TWENTY-NINE

"I'm against it." Shadowed bags hung under Captain Vessey's eyes and she looked old, but she appeared sober for once. How old was she? She'd been middle-aged when they'd set out and she seemed to have aged even more than the decade they had been traveling. Aubriot had stepped back from taking a leading role once the personnel's survival was secure, leaving the tedious everyday running of the ship to the captain.

Kes didn't envy Vessey. She hadn't done a terrible job, but neither had she been the type of leader to inspire the crew or maintain morale. She'd been barely adequate, listening to specialists in their fields and following their advice. She reminded him a lot of Ethan's daughter, Meredith, who had ended up committing suicide. At least Vessey didn't have the pressure of being measured against the greatest Leader in the colony's history.

"Me too," said Niall.

All gazes turned to him.

"Huh?" said Wilder. "The fix was your idea!"

"That doesn't mean I trust it. In fact, if anyone has the final say on whether we try again, it should be me."

Vessey coughed. "We all remember very well what happened the last time we tried to jump. As I understand it, the result could have been much worse. And, actually, as captain, I have the final say."

Aubriot murmured something inaudible.

Everyone had to know what *that* was about. He was itching to be boss again.

Zapata said gently, "Perhaps this is one of the few things we should put to a vote. Considering what happened with the jump drive before, I mean. A second attempt could be putting everyone's lives at risk."

Kes was surprised to hear the pilot speak up. He'd kept mostly to himself ever since the jump accident. His only tasks aside from maintaining the *Sirocco* on her heading had been flying the shuttle on detours to harvest a sun's energy or visit a planet. He'd been laconic on those trips.

"It will be putting all our lives at risk," said Dragan. "No question."

"But continuing as we are, that's just as risky," Wilder protested. "If we don't do something, there's no guarantee we'll ever reach Earth. We're down to our last supplies of equipment and materials, and that's with eking out everything. I swear some systems are surviving on spite alone. What if we lose the CO_2 scrubbers, or the water treatment bacteria die, or the Parvus's energy-harvesting system fails? You know what's worse than spending the next nine years traveling? Spending the rest of your life stranded in deep space."

"Nevertheless," said Vessey evenly, "these scenarios are hypothetical, whereas making another jump attempt will be a reality. We've survived so far, due to the resourcefulness, hard work, and positivity of everyone aboard. I'm not willing to put all our lives in jeopardy to avoid something that might not happen."

"Then you don't understand the situation," Wilder snapped, "and you have no imagination."

Kes studied her. She was under tremendous pressure like everyone else, but there was something additional underlying her words, something personal and emotional. She had an investment in activating the jump drive she wasn't stating.

"Maybe Zapata's right," said Cherry. "Maybe we should have a shipwide vote on it."

Vessey retorted heavily, "Out of the question. Are you forgetting what happened a couple of days ago? What if opinions are split down the middle? What do you think will be the result if a large minority don't get their way?"

It was a good point. Niall, Dragan, and Aubriot bore physical reminders of the brawl. After Miki and Nina had returned from helping out in sick bay, Kes had discovered he'd under-estimated the damage wreaked. There had been broken bones, deep lacerations, and dislocations. The least fortunate were still recovering.

Vessey's comment seemed to subdue Wilder at first, but then she blurted, "If we don't do it now, when the time comes that we have no choice it could be too late. In an emergency situation we might not have a chance to get everyone into capsules. We can't keep a jump as a fallback option. It's insanity. And we're forgetting Concordia and Earth. We've forgotten the reasons for our mission. If the jump drive works, we might not be too late to save the colony and help Earth prepare for the Scythians' arrival. There might still be time to do both, but only if we act now."

"Wilder's right," said Cherry. "We've been focusing on saving our own lives. That was never the point. It doesn't matter if we stay alive long enough to reach Earth if we're too late to make a difference. Who cares if we bring back material to seed Concordia if the colony's dead? What makes our lives so important compared to all the ones we could save?"

A lead weight settled in Kes's chest. "Cherry, I..." He couldn't say it. His own life wasn't important. It hadn't been since Izzy had died, except that he hadn't wanted to leave his children orphans. But when it came to Miki and Nina, his basic instinct was to keep them alive at all costs.

Cherry looked at him, her eyes wet. "I'm sorry. You know how much I love the girls, but it's true."

Niall said, "Speaking as the person who suggested the fix, I say we—"

"I know what your problem is," said Wilder. "You don't want to take responsibility if the drive malfunctions again. Whether it means everyone dying or only being crushed by disappointment, you don't want that on your shoulders."

Vessey commented, "The disappointment from trying and failing is another thing I have to take into consideration. I don't need to explain how hard everyone's finding the situation psychologically. My own struggles are no secret." She glanced from face to face, reddening. "There are plenty of people who won't be able to take another setback. They're barely holding themselves together as it is."

But Wilder didn't seem to hear. She rose to her feet and jabbed a finger at Niall. "Your problem is you'd rather live in an unhappy little bubble than step outside and risk *feeling* something. This ship is like your life. Cut off from everything that matters. You don't want to activate the jump drive because you don't *want* to get to Earth. You don't *want* to face up to what might be there, or what we might find on Concordia if we make it back. You're a coward!"

"Christ on a bike!" Aubriot exclaimed, also standing. "Sit down and shut up. This isn't a therapy session or couples counseling."

"*You* sit down!" Wilder marched up to him, put two hands on his chest, and shoved him.

His jaw dropped and he sank into his seat.

"You're the last person to be telling me what to do," she went on. "*I'm* the one who invented the jump drive, and a-grav, and I'm the one who master-minded converting the Ark into growing rooms to keep every last person on this ship alive. What have you done except try to get into the pants of everyone with tits? Everyone knows you wanted to be captain. Everyone knows you want to run the show. But what kind of example have you set? What have *you* done to boost morale?"

Kes could only watch in admiration. Wilder was on a roll. It was good to see her knocking heads and taking names. It was good to see her finally standing up for herself.

She turned to Vessey. "I hear what you're saying about divided opinions, but it isn't fair to keep the knowledge of the possible jump drive fix to ourselves. Every person on this ship has the right to decide whether they want to take the risk. We must take a vote, but only when Niall, Dragan, and I have explained everything as well as we can. Then everybody will be voting in full knowledge. It's the only way."

Dragan said, "I'm happy to do my share of explaining."

Niall gave Wilder a surly look before adding, "Okay. Me too."

"You already have my vote," said Cherry. "I'd hate to carry on living like this knowing I could be on Earth."

"Or dead," muttered Aubriot.

"If I'm dead I won't know it."

Kes sighed. "I suppose you have my vote too. I want Miki and Nina to live, but what kind of life is this? It's no life at all." He winced internally. His daughters were enduring almost exactly the same existence all the Gens had aboard the *Nova Fortuna*, except the generational colonists had enjoyed considerably more comfort. As one of the project's scientists, he'd condemned those thousands of nameless people to never walk on soil, breathe fresh air, or feel the rain.

Mere existence was not enough. He wanted his children to really *live*, if they were to live at all.

————

Wilder was true to her word. She spent the next days talking to the *Sirocco's* personnel, outlining Niall's fix and the possible outcomes if it failed. If anything, she over-explained. Kes saw a couple of people tell her they didn't need to hear any more, that they didn't care. They were willing to take any chance to escape this purgatory, no matter how small.

Niall and Dragan did the same. Kes also witnessed a softening in Niall's demeanor toward Wilder, and he wondered if he'd been right about the young man all along.

After three days, the vote was taken.

When the results came in, they were unanimous.

Every single person had voted to attempt the jump.

THIRTY

As Wilder passed Niall in the jump room, he caught her hand. She halted, surprised at the friendly touch.

"Can I talk to you outside?" he asked.

She followed him to a quiet section of passageway.

They'd been working on the jump capsules, repairing the broken casings and jammed emergency releases. Sadly, they didn't have to fix many. Several people who had begun the voyage were no longer alive. But the capsules that were to be used had to be completely up to scratch. They had no wiggle room when it came to safety.

As Niall paused, seeming to struggle for words, she frowned. "What is it?"

He'd been acting weird for days. He was usually quiet but lately he'd become almost silent, not even saying much to Dragan. Was he regretting suggesting the fix for the jump drive? If it didn't work, the failure would be a heavy load to bear. People were not forgiving about such things, as she knew too well.

He sucked in a deep breath. "I have an apology to make."

"You have? To me?"

This was new. She could probably count on the fingers of one hand the times she'd heard Niall say sorry about anything, least of all to her.

"Yes, of course to you," he replied irritably. "Unless there's someone else here?"

"Ugh, if you're going to be like that, I don't want to hear it."

"Wait, okay? Just wait and hear me out."

She leaned against the bulkhead and folded her arms across her chest. "If this is about what I think it's about, it had better be good."

"You're not going to make this easy for me, are you?"

"Why should I?"

He sighed. "Fair point." His gaze focused on the deck, he continued, "What you said in the briefing room...It was true."

"Damn right it was." She paused. "Which part do you mean?"

"You're going to make me say it?"

"I swear, Niall, after everything you've put me through for the last twelve years—"

"All right!" he exclaimed, lifting his hands. "Okay, I get it. I've been an asshole."

"And then some."

He tipped back his head and turned his gaze upward.

He was looking everywhere except at her.

In a strangled tone he said, "You're right. I was—am—a coward. I don't want to attempt the jump. I saw how people blamed you, and I didn't want that to happen to me. When I thought of the fix, I was excited. You know, in that way you feel when you think of a solution and it's just perfect? When everything slots together in your head and you can't understand how you didn't see it before?"

She nodded. This was the level at which they really understood each other. There were no words to adequately describe the feeling he was alluding to, but, between them, no words were needed.

"And then when we did the work and managed to complete it, I was riding on a high. I could have solved the problem that had dogged us for a decade. I could have found the solution that would allow us to escape this living hell. But, after, I had time to really think about the implications. What if I was wrong? What if my 'fix' ends up killing everyone?"

She replied, "Like Cherry said, no one will be alive to care about it. Anyone surviving on Concordia must already think we died, and the people on Earth don't know we exist. So it cancels out. It doesn't matter. Unless you're bothered about what people here are thinking in their last few seconds of life. That would be pretty dumb."

"Thanks. If I ever need a boost, I know where to come."

"What do you want from me?" she asked. "A pat on the head? A cuddle? You want me to kiss it better? Is that it?"

"Gee, you're a hard woman."

She shrugged. He was wrong. She wasn't hard. She was only hard toward him. "Life made me this way. Is your apology done? Can we go back to work now?"

"I haven't finished."

His face twisted in discomfort. She was simmering with anger and felt no sympathy. She likened his expression to being badly constipated and stifled a laugh. Her ire faded, leaving only fatigue and anxiety over the coming jump attempt. "Just get it over with. Tell me."

His eyes finally met hers, and she saw the pain behind them. She reached out and touched his shoulder, compassion welling up.

"I need to apologize to you, too," he said, "personally. When the Scythian Plague was over, everything had changed. Our old lives were gone forever. I was only a kid and I'd been forced to grow up fast. I think that did something to me. I don't know what, but it was like I was scared to be happy. I couldn't allow it in case it was taken away from me again. I couldn't relax, couldn't enjoy myself. All the time, I felt like another disaster was around the corner and there was no point in taking pleasure in anything. I'm not sure if I'm making any sense."

"I understand. And you were right, about the next disaster looming, I mean."

"I took it out on you. I don't even know why. But you became my target. Just seeing you around brought out the worst in me. I should have left you alone, stayed out of your way, but building the *Sirocco* was the best thing I could do with the skill set I have."

"Dragan and I couldn't have done it without you."

"And you...you were a saint. I don't know how you've put up with me for so long."

"Some days, I don't know either."

He sighed. "I'm not good with words. I'd rather work with an engine any day than try to explain myself."

"You've done a pretty good job." She held out her arms.

As they hugged, he said, "I thought I didn't deserve a cuddle."

"You don't, but you're getting one anyway." Moments passed, and then she said, "You know what? Jamie Bond is a stupid name."

"So is Deadly After Midnight."

"True."

When they parted, he asked, "Now that's over, are *you* okay?"

"What do you mean?"

"Lately you've been...I don't know...preoccupied."

She gave him a tight smile. "It's nothing important. I'm looking forward to getting to Earth. Aren't you?"

"You say it like it's a given. I'm glad I got my apology out of the way. I'd hate to die knowing I haven't set things right between us."

"That's what I love about you. You're such an optimist."

THIRTY-ONE

Cherry lowered herself into her capsule. The last time she'd done this she'd been trapped in the awful gel that was supposed to protect them from the effects of the jump.

If they did jump.

Wilder and the other engineers did seem confident about their fix, but they'd been confident last time. She guessed they knew what they were doing.

She'd made sure to hug Wilder, Kes, and the girls and tell them she loved them. Similar potentially 'forever' goodbyes were taking place around the chamber. Tension thickened the atmosphere like the gel about to pump into her capsule. She'd caught Aubriot watching her as the goodbyes were going on. She'd quickly averted her gaze. He'd made his bed—with Maddox and most of the women on the ship—so he could lie in it.

She was aging much faster than him anyway. He would have moved on to younger prey soon enough, whether or not she'd spent a couple of weeks in sick bay.

Pretending the ache in her chest didn't exist, she closed her capsule's lid and mentally sought pleasant thoughts to occupy her while ensconced in the gel. Her mind immediately flew to her dalliance with Kes. She smiled and blushed. What a pair of middle-aged fools they'd been. She was glad he was on the same page as her regarding his feelings. He meant a lot to her, just not like that.

What a pity. He was a good man, but it was not to be. She seemed destined to be attracted only to unobtainable or unsuitable men, while he was in love with a ghost.

The last few capsule lids were closing. Once Vessey gave the command, the nozzles supplying the gel would open, the capsules would fill, and the *Sirocco* would jump—hopefully.

Try as she might to stay calm, her heart would not obey. Memories of the last attempt rushed into her head. The choking and fear were vivid. She sucked in air through her mask, staring out, the scene distorted by the transparent lid. Were others feeling the same? Any minute, she expected someone to leap from their capsule, screaming and crying. It wouldn't have surprised her. The pressure they were all under, had been under for years, was immense.

Soft clicking sounds came from every side of her capsule. The nozzles were opening. She braced herself, preparing to be swamped by the horrible, tepid gel.

She waited.

Nothing happened.

She raised her head and peered into other capsules. Confused looks were passing between the occupants.

Reclining her head again, she continued to wait.

Had something gone wrong?

Were they about to jump without the benefit of the gel as protection?

She looked out again.

A capsule was opening. Wilder stepped out and walked over to Vessey. A moment later, the captain's voice came over the comm: "Sorry, everyone. There's been a delay due to a problem with the gel emitters. You can exit your capsules but don't stray too far for now. As soon as I have an update, I'll let you know."

Angry chatter quickly filled the room as people climbed out again. Cherry looked for Wilder but she'd already left. Dragan and Niall were inspecting the capsules, telling annoyed enquirers to leave them alone and let them work.

Cherry went to find Wilder, expecting she was avoiding being accosted once more as a scapegoat. The passageway was empty. Wherever she'd gone, she'd gone there fast.

She comm'd her. "Where are you? Are you okay?"

"Yeah, I'm okay," the younger woman replied, her tone flat with what sounded like disappointment.

"Don't worry," Cherry said. "If it's only a problem with the nozzles, I'm sure it can be fixed."

"That isn't the problem. It's something else. Something I suspected as soon as the gel failed to appear."

"What is it?"

"Come to the gel tank and I'll show you."

Cherry didn't know where it was. She had to ask Wilder for directions. When she arrived, she couldn't see the problem. She'd expected there might be a leak similar to the one that had flooded the Ark. But instead Wilder pointed at a section of the tank wall. On closer inspection, Cherry saw a hairline crack running from the base to the top of the unit.

"I checked inside," Wilder said resignedly. "It's empty. There's nothing left except a thick, tacky residue. The original jump malfunction must have caused the crack, and the water content of the gel evaporated through it over the years. There's nothing to fill the capsules."

———

"We're so close," said Aubriot. "Too close to back out now."

"Absolutely not," Vessey argued. "As I said before, we have a perfectly viable alternative. A much safer alternative, which is to continue as we are."

"We've been over this," Wilder groaned, her head in her hands. "The chances we'll survive until we reach Earth aren't as good as you think. We have huge obstacles in our way, probably some we haven't even thought of yet."

"My duty is to protect the lives of the people on this ship," Vessey replied, her voice growing louder, "and that means not subjecting them to risks. *Real* and *present* risks, like jumping without the protection of the gel, not hypothetical what-might-happens."

"That's about the stupidest thing I've ever heard!" Wilder exclaimed, leaping to her feet. "Just because there's a danger here and now, it doesn't mean a worse one isn't around the corner. You have to weigh up *all* possibilities. The gel was only ever a safeguard. The jump drive was specifically modified from the Fila's version to account for differences in our anatomy and physiology. It's designed to be safe for humans."

"Was the drive ever tested without the subject encased in gel?" Vessey asked.

"No, but that was only because we didn't have time and we could only use people for the experiments. If we'd had animal subjects and a few more months..."

"Wilder's right," said Niall. "The gel was precautionary only, exerting a body-wide pressure to counteract the stresses of the jump. I'm not a biologist, but I expect the worst we'll see if we jump without it are burst capillaries, maybe some bad headaches, that kind of thing."

Vessey pursed her lips. "I suppose we could do the same as before. If you explain to everyone—"

"The result's gonna be the same," said Aubriot. "Everyone wants this. Everyone will want to take the risk. Our people are mostly scientists. They're smart. If they have questions they can ask the engineers, but I guarantee they'll do whatever they can for a chance to end to this nightmare."

The captain closed her eyes and murmured, "I've tried. I've done my best. It wasn't enough. I wasn't good enough. But I tried." She opened her eyes. "Go ahead. Do what you want."

Thirty-Two

They had come for her during the quiet shift after the big fight in the refectory, which Wilder hadn't even been aware of at the time. When the fight fizzled out, these brawlers had come to find her. Goslin, Marcus, Durbin, and Ryan. She didn't know any of them well. She only ever mixed with the people she trusted: Cherry, Kes, his daughters, Dragan, and Niall. Though Niall had expressed his dislike for her endlessly over the years, she'd known he would never hurt her.

Unlike the rest of them.

Goslin and Durbin were botanists, Marcus was one of Aubriot's muscle men, and she wasn't sure what Ryan did. All she knew was Ryan's partner, Trish, had died on the first plant-hunting expedition.

When her door chime had sounded, she hadn't suspected anything. No one she didn't know very well had ever been to her cabin before. No one had approached her on her home territory, so to speak. In her cabin, she'd assumed she was safe.

As soon as she opened her door, she knew her mistake.

They were clearly drunk. Goslin held onto the frame for support. Marcus leered, his expression lopsided and pupils dilated. Ryan and Durbin were flushed and sweaty and looped arms around each other's shoulders like twisted versions of fairy tale characters. All four bore bruises and scratches.

"Glad to find you home," Goslin slurred. "C'n we come in?"

Wilder stepped back. "No, I..."

Marcus caught the edge of the closing door and the four 'visitors' surged through the gap.

The door closed.

Four additional bodies had quickly filled the small cabin. The air seemed to turn thick with their exhalations.

"Wh-what do you want?" Wilder eyed the exit. It was impossible for her to reach it without pushing through the group.

"Simple." Goslin's eyes narrowed. "We want justice." The woman leaned in until her face was only centimeters from Wilder's, who could smell the alcohol on her breath. "We want to put things right."

"Yeah," Durbin chimed in, "after what you did to us."

"I didn't do anything to you. I don't know what you're talking about." Wilder edged to one side. Her ear comm was on her bedside table.

Goslin placed a heavy hand on her upper arm and pushed her back to her original position.

"Where're you going?" Marcus asked. "The night..." he gestured expansively "...is young."

Ryan and Durbin giggled. Goslin wasn't amused. She leaned even closer until all Wilder could see was her face with its open pores and bloodshot, crazed eyes. "Y' know exactly what we're talking about. You're the one who made that faulty drive. You're the one who told us it was okay. You're the one who got us in this mess. And now you're going to pay."

"That isn't true," Wilder protested. "I wasn't the only person who built the drive, and you chose to come on this voyage of your own free will. Do you think if I knew it was faulty I would have given the go ahead? I'm here too! I'm stuck here the same as you. Do you think this was all planned?"

"She didn't say it was planned," said Ryan. "She's only saying you're an idiot."

"Right," Wilder retorted. "The idiot who converted the Ark so you could all eat. I'm *that* idiot, am I?" Despite her clear danger, the senselessness of Goslin and the others' thinking frustrated her beyond belief. How could they be so stupid? They weren't fools—a fact that had probably kept her safe until now. Deep down, they knew they weren't being logical, that their hatred of her came solely from a need to blame someone for their predicament. It was the alcohol talking, and whatever these people did to her tonight they would probably feel remorseful for in the morning. But that wouldn't save her now.

Her appeal to their rationality seemed to have made a small impact. She could almost see the cogs of Goslin's mind whirring as she tried to think up a suitable response.

"Doesn't matter," said Durbin. "Doesn't matter what you did after. Y' can't make up for landing us here in the firs' place."

"S' right," Marcus agreed. "There's no taking that back."

"Well then." Wilder's pitch rose tremulously. "Is hurting me going to get you to Earth? What difference is it going to make?"

"Nothing's gonna get us to Earth," Goslin said sadly. "Too late. Never gonna reach it now."

Wilder's ears pricked up. Was Goslin one of the rumored Final Day Five? Were her companions too? If so, who was the fifth member?

"It's about balance," Goslin went on. "Justice. Why should you be allowed to get away with what you've done?"

"I haven't done—" Wilder gurgled.

Goslin's hand had fastened around her throat. "Shut y' stupid mouth."

"That's it," Marcus said gleefully. "Let's get her to the airlock!" He bent down and grabbed her around the waist.

Ryan grasped her knees.

Before she knew it, she was being carried out of her cabin.

A hand—she wasn't sure whose—was clamped so tightly over her face she could barely breathe, let alone cry out for help. She fought violently, her muffled screams loud in her ears, but her skinny frame was no match for the strength of four people, even drunk.

The lights overhead passed by, bright panels alternating with dark where they'd removed them to use in the growing rooms.

She knew the way to the airlock well. In the early days, she'd often been tempted to take that route for a final time, like everyone else on the ship, no doubt. The end would be painful but it would be brief compared to the everlasting death of the voyage. But she hadn't taken that path. She'd turned away, trying her best to find small pleasures in day-to-day life, focusing on the present, not thinking of what the future held. She'd gotten by, and now these drunken morons were about to make all her efforts pointless.

Rage consumed her. She writhed like a mad thing. Opening her mouth, she bit down hard on the fingers that slid into it. A single scream got out, cut off immediately as the hand fastened down again. This time, its grip was so tight she really could not breathe at all. Her chest bucked as her lungs struggled for air.

Blackness closed in. The last thing she heard was laughter.

When she woke up, she was on her side on the deck. Confused, she stared at the smooth tiles. Someone was cursing. It was a male voice, and the person sounded drunk.

She gasped, remembering what had just happened. She must have passed out, and they'd put her down when they reached the airlock. She couldn't see her captors. They had to be behind her, at the hatch, and they were cursing because...

Of course! They couldn't get it open.

After the suicides during the first year of the mission, airlock security had been upgraded. The systems required the biodata of two people before they would open: the captain's and one other high-ranking member of the ship's personnel. It had been so long she'd forgotten, and so had Goslin, Marcus, and their friends.

Huh, it won't be so easy to get rid of me and get your 'justice'. I only have to...

Slowly, she turned onto her front and moved her hands and knees under her body.

"She's getting away!"

Wilder leapt to her feet and ran. Fingertips snatched at her jersey, but she pulled away. She might not have much muscle compared to most people, but her lightness made her faster than most too, especially compared to these lumbering drunks.

Their thudding footsteps echoed behind her. A gasp of effort sounded. Hands closed around her knees. Her legs dragged from underneath her, she slammed into the deck.

She looked back. It was Goslin. The woman was grinning maniacally at her success. The other three were coming up fast.

Wilder bent her knee and drove her heel into Goslin's face. At the thud of impact, the woman shouted in pain and her grip broke. In an instant, Wilder was on her feet again and running. Had she broken Goslin's nose? Hopefully.

She swerved around a corner. Another long passageway lay ahead. When she looked back again, Goslin was nowhere to be seen and she'd put distance between her and her pursuers. They would never catch her now.

She hadn't returned to her cabin. She'd found a place to sleep in the Ark, on a pile of dry Fat Grain stalks. It had been like the days at Sidhe, when she'd slept in out-of-the-way places to avoid going home to her fake parents. As her heart rate and breathing slowed, tiredness had overcome her.

What would happen tomorrow? Would Goslin and the other attackers even remember what they'd done? Probably not. They'd all been very drunk. But one thing was clear: feelings were reaching fever pitch. She wasn't safe anymore. What was worse, she couldn't tell anyone about it. What could the few friends she had realistically do to protect her? She couldn't live under lock and key for the next nine years. It was bad enough to be trapped on the *Sirocco*.

She really hoped Niall's proposed fix for the jump drive worked.

THIRTY-THREE

Settling into her capsule, Miki peeked at Nina and saw her sister peeking at her. Miki smiled and gave her a little wave. Nina was a pretty nice sister, though she could be a pain in the ass sometimes.

This capsule was way bigger than the one she'd used in the first jump. She could see it from here. It looked so tiny, but Nina's old one looked tinier. They must have been specially made for them. She hadn't known that at the time. She remembered that first jump. It had been exciting to go on a big adventure. The gel covering her face hadn't been much fun, but that part was soon over.

This time there wouldn't be any gel, which was great.

What was taking so long?

She lifted her head again to look around the room. Dad wasn't in his capsule yet and neither was Cherry. They were chatting.

She guessed it didn't really matter when they jumped. They'd been aboard the *Sirocco* more than ten years. Another few minutes wouldn't make any difference. But it was annoying to wait.

There was that big man, Aubriot. She didn't like him, but he ignored her, so that was fine. He was in his capsule now. Who else? Captain Vessey was getting into hers, and the pilot, Zapata. As soon as the jump was over, he would have to go to the bridge to fly the ship the rest of the way to Earth.

Earth.

What would it be like? She'd seen pics and vids, but it wasn't the same as actually being there. She'd been on the surface of two planets and spent her early childhood on Concordia, so she wasn't a complete newbie, but she still found it hard to imagine. It was weird to think she was going back to the place

Dad had been born centuries ago. Dad was *really, really* old. She giggled as she recalled teasing him about it.

"I want to run again," said a voice.

The engineers had arrived. It was Dragan, the older one, who had spoken.

"Actually run," he went on, "for kilometers."

"You already do that on the treadmill," said the other guy, Niall.

"It isn't the same."

Wilder was with them. Wilder was about her favorite person ever. She loved Dad, but Wilder was more fun. Wilder knew how to make things interesting. *She* would never have set an assignment on the ship's personnel.

Miki sighed and rolled her eyes. She hoped the days of boring schoolwork were over. On Earth, there would be too much else to do. She also hoped the adults would calm down. They'd been getting crazier and crazier. That fight they'd had! Some of the patients in sick bay had been badly hurt. Even now, days later, they wore arm slings and casts. She'd had no idea people who were supposed to be friends could inflict so much damage on each other. *Nina* was more mature than some of them.

What's taking so long?

All the capsule lids were closed now except one. Wilder was at the control panel. She would start the countdown and get into place before the jump activated.

Miki caught her eye. Wilder gave her a quick smile and a thumbs up before climbing into her capsule. The lid swung closed, and Miki lost sight of her as she lay down.

The decreasing numbers of the countdown sounded out. They had a whole thirty seconds to wait.

Dad had explained there was a small risk in doing it without gel but it should be fine. She believed him. He would never put her or Nina in danger if he could help it.

Twenty seconds to go.

She hummed a tune, her latest favorite song. She'd found it last week on an old file deep in the ship's database.

Come into my arms, baby
And I'll never let you go
I'll take you all the way, baby
All the way to Arrival Day

All the way to Arrival Day. *Arrival Day!* She hadn't thought about what the words meant until now. The song had to be ancient, written around the time of the arrival of the *Nova Fortuna*.

How cool was that? Here she was singing a song about—

"Five."

"Four."

"Three."

"Two."

Earth, here I come!

"One."

She braced for...something. Would a shudder pass through the ship like last time? Would the jump drive make a noise?

No movement or sound came.

Would the Scythians attack them when they arrived? Dad had said it was unlikely they would have reached Earth before them, but not impossible.

She waited expectantly, listening and looking for a signal it was okay to leave her capsule. Craning her neck, she saw puzzled faces exchanging looks.

What had happened?

Wilder's capsule opened. She climbed out and crossed to the control panel. Her voice came over Miki's comm. "Please remain where you are, everyone. I'm checking our status. I'll update you as soon as I can."

She must have comm'd Niall and Dragan separately. Their capsules opened too. The three engineers left the room.

Nina's head was up and she was looking at her. Miki pulled a funny face, making her sister laugh. They mimed and gesticulated at each other to ease the boredom. By the time Wilder returned, Miki was breathless with laughter and her stomach muscles ached.

Wilder opened a general comm again. In a quiet voice, she said, "I'm very sorry to report the jump attempt failed."

Instantly, capsule lids flew open. Shouting and wailing echoed around the room.

Wilder was saying something else, something about the engineering team and the problem, but the noise drowned her words. Figures were moving toward her. Aubriot climbed from his capsule, and so did Cherry. The large man waded through the crowd, heading for Wilder.

Dad's voice came over the comm. "Stay where you are, girls. Don't get out until I say so, and try not to look."

THIRTY-FOUR

A heaviness had settled over the ship worse than any Kes had known in the decade-long voyage. The nightly drinking sessions had ended. When people weren't working they mostly kept to their cabins, coming out only to collect food. In the passageways, no one made eye contact, keeping their heads down and their gazes focused on the deck. The place was eerily quiet. No sound of conversation was to be heard, no strains of music or vid audio tracks leaked from cabins or communal rooms, only the far-distant thrum of the engine as it carried them steadily and faithfully across abyssal space.

He tried to pretend to Miki and Nina that everything was okay, but they'd grown too big to fool. Too big and too smart. Initially, they'd been disappointed the ship hadn't reached Earth, but life on the *Sirocco* was normality to them. They'd accepted that things would go on as always and they'd bounced back from their disappointment with youthful resilience. Yet they were sensitive girls. They picked up on the despair and melancholy. It began to affect them, firstly as concern for the other passengers, and then the mood invaded them. The spark left their eyes and their bickering and banter stopped. They spent their time together quietly, helping each other and showing consideration for each other's feelings. It was then he knew something was seriously wrong.

He was also deeply concerned about Wilder. Now more than ever, she was under threat of an attack from a disgruntled crew member looking for someone to blame. If it hadn't been for Aubriot defending her, she might have been seriously hurt in the jump room when the most recent attempt failed.

Yet Wilder was acting as though nothing was wrong, that she wasn't in danger. He couldn't let the situation continue. If something happened to her he would never forgive himself.

Cherry was first to arrive. She sat next to him. "Thanks for doing this. I should have done it myself days ago but I was preoccupied with work in the Ark."

"No problem. I was thinking I should have done it a long time ago too. Thank the stars nothing's happened yet."

"Nothing we know of."

He looked at her quizzically.

"Wilder's solitary and private. She also loves us and wants to protect us. She wouldn't want us to worry about her. If something has happened already, she might not say so."

"Hm, you're right. I didn't think of that."

Aubriot entered the briefing room. His gaze slid across Cherry as if she didn't exist. Then he gave Kes a nod before sitting opposite them.

It had been with great reluctance Kes had invited him. The less he had to do with Aubriot the better, but he couldn't deny the man would be useful for what he had planned.

Niall and Dragan appeared.

"Wilder not here yet?" asked Niall.

Kes replied, "The time I gave her is ten minutes from now. I wanted to discuss our approach before she arrives. I think we can all agree she isn't going to like any kind of intervention into how she lives her life."

Niall snorted a laugh. "No kidding."

Kes went on, "But I think we can also agree something needs to be done."

"Absolutely," said Dragan.

They quickly hashed out a plan. It wasn't hard. Just simple, rational precautions to keep Wilder safe.

"The stupid thing is," Niall said when they'd finished, "the jump drive fix was *my* idea, not hers. That's common knowledge. I don't understand why everyone seems to have it in for her."

"Simple," Aubriot retorted. "She's a born victim."

"Do you *have* to be so mean all the time?" Cherry asked.

"Just saying it how it is." Aubriot turned to Niall, "You and Dragan socialize, have a drink with the rest. You're one of the crowd."

"Not intentionally," said Dragan.

"Intentionally or not, that's what you do." Aubriot faced Cherry. "You're disabled so people feel sorry for you."

She spluttered, "I am *not*—"

"And Kes has kids," he continued, ignoring her, "making him a bit of a father figure. He's older than most too."

"Thanks," Kes muttered.

"Wilder's an oddball. Doesn't fit in. And physically she's no threat. The worst she could do is poke someone in the eye with one of her bony elbows. If anyone on this ship is going to get picked on, it's her. That's obvious."

"Well, thanks for pointing all that out," said Kes. "I just remembered I invited Vessey. It looks like she's a no-show."

Wilder stepped into the room.

Five pairs of eyes turned to her as an awkward silence fell.

She halted. "Sooo...you've been talking about me. Nice."

"Please come and sit down," said Kes.

From the look on her face, he had a feeling that if it hadn't been he who had invited her, she would have turned right around and left. As it was, she moved slowly and warily as she took a seat.

"I'm going to be completely honest," he said. "We have been talking about you, and this meeting isn't about the running of the ship. I lied when I told you that because I had a feeling you wouldn't come if you knew the real reason."

"The real reason is me. *Great*."

Niall said, "We're only looking out for you."

"And what if I don't want you to look out for me? Do I get a say in this?"

"Christ," Aubriot said, "you haven't even heard any suggestions before shooting us down. Remind me to never do you any more favors."

"I didn't ask you to—"

"That's it!" he exclaimed. "I'm out." He rose to his feet.

"Sit down," said Cherry. "We've put Wilder on the spot and she's upset."

To Kes's surprise, Aubriot did as Cherry requested, though his lips moved as he murmured something under his breath. Kes caught the words *Ungrateful bitch*.

Cherry leaned over the table and put her hand on Wilder's. "Please listen to us. I can't stand the thought of you getting hurt. After what happened in the jump room, you can't deny you're in danger."

Wilder's face bore no expression but she didn't move. Her gaze flicked from person to person around the table. "I'm not staying in my cabin. I can't live like that."

"No one's saying you must," said Kes.

"And I don't want someone acting as my guard, trailing after me wherever I go."

"That isn't what we had in mind."

Her shoulders lifted and fell, and some of her tension seemed to leave her. "Tell me your ideas and I'll see what I think."

"Good," said Kes. "Thanks for listening at least."

He outlined their plan. They would arrange their sleep schedules so someone would always be awake and contactable in an emergency. Cameras were to be placed over her door. She was to carry an alert button around her neck. The list went on.

After some quibbling, she agreed to everything they proposed. Kes was relieved his long-time friend would be safe.

THIRTY-FIVE

The alert button dangled from Wilder's neck as she leaned through the open maintenance hatch. It clunked against a water pipe. She shone a flashlight around the interior. No drips were visible at the pipe joints and the areas beneath them were dry. Ever since the flood, she'd carried out regular visual inspections of the plumbing that supplied the growing beds, refusing to trust the sensors again. Everything seemed in order.

As she leaned back, the button caught between two pipes and tugged at her neck.

Softly cursing, she put down the flashlight to free it.

It was then they grabbed her.

Hands seized her arms, waist, and legs, lifting her bodily off the deck and dragging her backward. But the alert button remained at an angle, stuck between the pipes. She was trapped by the lanyard, her head inside the bulkhead cavity.

She yelled.

Trying to wrench a hand free to press the alarm, she writhed and fought.

A finger roughly pushed into her ear, flicking out her comm.

"Something's round her neck," someone said.

Another hand appeared. There was a soft *snick*, and the tightness around her neck disappeared. They'd cut the lanyard.

They pulled her out.

It was the same four who had attacked her in her cabin: Goslin, Marcus, Ryan, and Durbin. They'd snuck up on her quietly while she was distracted.

So the other time had been no mistake. Drunk as they'd been, they'd known exactly what they were doing. They'd remembered, and this time they were stone cold sober.

She gathered a breath to scream for help. Goslin shoved balled-up cloth into her mouth. Marcus fastened a gag.

They'd come prepared.

This time, she was going to die.

They picked her up, lifting her horizontal so each could wrap their arms around her and prevent her from struggling. Still, she continued to fight and resist, summoning every ounce of strength she had to break free.

They carried her from the growing room and through the silent Ark. It was the quiet shift. She'd come here now purposefully in order to avoid encountering other people. It was hard being the most hated person on the ship. They must have been watching her movements, perhaps following her from her cabin, waiting for a moment like this, when she was alone and vulnerable.

They didn't want to make any more mistakes.

Goslin was trying to slip something over her head one-handed, but Wilder was squirming too much, turning and jerking her head and shoulders. Whatever that thing was, she didn't want it on her.

"Wait until we get there," said Marcus. "It'll be easier."

Goslin heeded his advice. The pressure of her arm around Wilder's shoulders strengthened.

Where were they taking her? What had Goslin been trying to do?

"When we do it, that's the end, right?" asked Durbin.

"The beginning of the end," Marcus corrected. "This will be the trigger."

The 'trigger' was her death, no doubt.

"I can't wait for it all to be over," said Ryan. "We've been punished enough."

They had to be the apocalypse believers. They thought by killing her they were hastening the Final Day for humankind.

"What'll happen?" Durbin asked. "Will it be fast?"

"It doesn't matter," Goslin replied. "Fast or slow. As long as it's finished at last."

You're a bunch of morons!

Didn't they understand what they were saying? How could they be so deluded? Had the pressure and isolation turned them psychotic?

They put her down in a passageway deep within the Ark. She sat on the deck, knees drawn up, as the four stood around her. She wasn't tied up but there was no sense in trying to run. They would be on her in a second.

What were they going to do?

Goslin fished in a bag she'd slung over her shoulder and brought out a rope.

For a moment, Wilder was confused. Were they going to tie her? What was the point? It was four against one and they had her surrounded. They were also not inebriated like last time.

The end of the rope swung free.

A noose.

Her gut contracted. Her heart threatened to force its way out of her chest.

Dread oozing from every pore, she lifted her gaze upward.

This section hadn't been properly finished. Where there should have been overhead tiles were structural beams.

The Final Day believers had planned everything to the last detail, including the exact spot they would hang her.

A sense of crazed hysteria filled her. She almost giggled.

Why hanging? Why not strangle her, here and now?

Why not cut her throat?

Did hanging her have some kind of ritual significance? These people were out of their minds. They'd moved on from simply spacing her. Their insanity had become more elaborate.

Goslin moved to lift the rope over her head.

Wilder had a brief vision of herself hanging by her neck, gagged, eyes popping and face filling with blood as she slowly strangled.

She hadn't endured all the torments of her life, worked so hard for all she'd achieved, to die like this at the hands of deranged clowns.

She dropped onto her side and, feet together, kicked Ryan's knees.

The joints bent sideways at the impact and he screamed as he toppled to the deck.

Durbin sank down beside him, wailing in distress. Goslin gasped. Marcus snatched the noose from her and reached out with it, trying to slip it over Wilder's neck. Wilder also reached out. She grabbed Marcus's head and dug her thumbs into his eyes with all her might. Blood and gore erupted from the sockets.

Inhuman shrieks issued from his throat as he blindly clutched at his face, fingers scrambling to remove her thumbs.

"What..." Goslin's features were pale and painted with horror. "What are you...?"

Wilder leapt up, slammed a fist into Goslin's face and then took off. When the two women overcame their shock they could still easily overpower her, and now their impulse to hurt her would be even stronger.

She only had to reach the *Sirocco.* If she could just alert one of her friends she would be safe. She couldn't risk going to anyone else in the ship. She didn't know who to trust and who might side with the apocalypse believers.

She sped down the passageway. Goslin was already on her tail and so was Durbin, judging by the sound of the pursuing footsteps. She ripped off her gag and wrenched the sodden cloth from her mouth before throwing both down.

She turned a corner, turned another. There it was!

Racing across the bridge, she calculated which of her friends' cabins was closest. One was only a minute away. She risked a glance over her shoulder. Goslin's face was now a picture of fury. Durbin looked anguished as she labored beside her, gasping and panting.

One minute.

She was over the bridge.

She swerved to the left and then immediately right, hoping to confuse her pursuers. But Goslin guessed correctly. She was gaining. No alcohol slowed her down this time. She seemed determined not only to get her 'justice' but also to enact revenge for what Wilder had done to her pals.

A second right turn, and then a left.

How many times had she walked these passageways in the last ten years? Thousands. Tens of thousands. She could have gone anywhere in the ship blindfolded.

"Bitch!" Goslin yelled. "You're done. It's over."

She'd gained on her and was only meters away, but Wilder was only meters from sanctuary.

Goslin launched herself as she had before, wrapping her arms around Wilder's knees. Wilder fell and Goslin fell with her, gripping her legs tightly.

It didn't matter.

She'd made it.

Wilder stretched out an arm and thumped Dragan's cabin door. He had to be in. It was the middle of the quiet shift. If he wasn't, she would scream and holler. Other friends were nearby. Someone would hear and come to her rescue.

The door opened.

Dragan stood in the frame in his pajama bottoms. His mouth fell open as he took in the scene. "Wilder! Come inside."

Goslin released her hold, no doubt mortified that she'd been caught trying to commit murder.

Wilder clambered to her feet. Never more relieved in her life, she stepped into the cabin.

The door closed.

"Thanks." Her chest heaved. "You saved my life. It was the Final Day Five. They were going to..." Her words petered out as she took in the cabin's interior.

She'd never been here before, never had reason to come here.

Against one wall, a bank of figures rose from the deck to the overhead, lining slim shelves. Tiny men, women, and creatures in strange poses or fighting in combat. Each model had been intricately painted. What were they made from? She couldn't guess.

She turned on her heel.

More shelves, filled with figures, occupying every wall. Dragan's bed was a mattress on the floor, the only furniture in the room.

He was watching her.

"I had no idea you were so into..." She faltered. "What are these...?" She wasn't sure how to describe them.

"People. Just people, and some animals."

"Just people? But there are so many of them. I guess I'm surprised you never talked about your hobby."

His eyelids lowered. "Famous people, from history." He stepped to a shelf and picked up a figure of a man. "Alexander the Great." Putting it down, he picked up another. "Cleopatra." He picked a third figure from a shelf. "Charlemagne." He faced her. "They're all here. Every person of significance who ever lived. Well, maybe not *everyone*. Some will have been forgotten or didn't make it into the data files for another reason."

Uneasiness began to take root in Wilder's stomach. The amount of time and effort Dragan must have put into creating the figures bordered on obsessional. And she didn't recall him ever mentioning an interest in history.

"All the important names in human civilization," said Dragan. "The first Concordian Leader, Ethan, is here somewhere. You and Niall and I have a place too."

"We do?" She would have been flattered if she hadn't suddenly become very afraid.

"History begins here..." he pointed to a low corner "and here..." he swung around to point to the opposite corner next to the overhead "is the end."

The End.

The end of human civilization.

Shit.

Dragan was the fifth member of the Final Day Five.

He crossed the cabin and opened the door.

Goslin and Durbin were waiting.

THIRTY-SIX

"Help! Help me."

Aubriot squinted groggily as he tried to focus. The chirrup of his ear comm had dragged him from a deep slumber.

"What?"

He hadn't caught the announcement of the caller's name.

"Who is this?"

"M-Marcus. It's Marcus. I can't see. I think she…God, I can't see anything! My eyes! My eyes."

Another man's groans sounded faintly in the background.

"You can't see?" Aubriot echoed. "Has there been another fight? Comm sick bay. I'm not a medic." He angrily cut the comm, took out the ear device, and put it on the nightstand. After punching his pillow into shape, taking out on it some of his annoyance at being woken up, he tried to go back to sleep.

Why had the man comm'd *him* for help? Sure, he was the one who'd invited Marcus to come on the voyage, reasoning they would need some muscle as well as brains. Who knew what they might find on Earth? And, sure, he'd been useful on the plant-hunting trip, even though he'd managed to nearly kill himself by walking into quicksand, but it wasn't like they were close. Why should *he* be the person Marcus contacted when he was in trouble? Why not go straight to professionals who could handle a medical emergency?

Aubriot turned onto his back and opened his eyes.

Maybe Marcus was too out of it to know what he was doing. He *had* sounded like he was in a lot of pain.

Muttering "*Fuck it*" he re-inserted the ear comm. "Where are you?"

"Ark," Marcus mumbled. "In the Ark."

Aubriot comm'd sick bay, waking the medic on duty. "Someone's had an accident in the Ark. Name's Marcus. And someone else might be hurt too." He listened to the reply. "No, I don't know where exactly." After listening again, he asked, "How the hell would I know what's wrong with him? Why don't you go and find out? Isn't that your job?"

When the medic mercifully stopped asking stupid questions and left him alone, Aubriot lay on his back and stared into the middle distance, silently debating with himself. Half a minute later, he cursed aloud and climbed out of bed. After quickly pulling on clothes and boots, he went to find Marcus.

He found him before the medic, coming upon what looked like a murder scene. Bloody smears coated the bulkheads, hand prints and long finger trails from where Marcus had stumbled about, apparently wandering from one side of the passageway to the other. His face was out of a horror flick. Dark holes were all that remained of his eyes, along with the red-stained material hanging from them and coating his cheeks.

Aubriot was no stranger to swearing, but words to express his reaction to the scene didn't exist.

Marcus was on his knees, moving his head from side to side as he sightlessly scanned his surroundings, hands outstretched. The other man Aubriot had heard lay on his side, his legs at strange angles. He recognized Ryan. The second man seemed to have passed out with pain.

"Holy shit!"

The medic had arrived.

"About time," Aubriot snapped. "I comm'd you five minutes ago."

Ignoring him, she went straight to work. "Help's here," she told Marcus. "Please stay calm and remain still while I check on your friend." She knelt next to Ryan and felt his wrist while watching his chest.

Deeply curious about what had caused injuries of this magnitude, Aubriot approached Marcus and bent down. "What happened? Were you two fighting?"

"Wilder," Marcus gasped. "Wilder, the bitch. What do my eyes look like? Are they bad? Will I see again?"

"Wilder?" Aubriot straightened up.

Wilder did this?!

He took another look at the scene. Why would Wilder attack two fully grown men? Had she lost her mind?

Then he noticed the rope. Dropped carelessly on the deck, it lay in loose coils, one end shaped into a noose.

Cold fear gripped him.

He opened a comm. "Kes, someone's tried to kill Wilder. See if you can comm her, but I'm guessing if she was contactable she would have called for help. I'm going to try to find her." He returned his attention to Marcus. "Where is she? Where's Wilder?"

"I don't kn—"

Aubriot's slap threw him into the bulkhead.

"Hey!" the medic yelled. "What the hell are you doing?"

"He tried to kill Wilder. He's a would-be murderer. A maniac."

"He's my patient and he's probably delusional. Leave him alone." She got on her comm, requesting help.

Aubriot thrust his face into Marcus's. "Tell me where she is."

"I really don't know." The man's tone was full of pain. "She ran off."

"Is she alone? Were there more of you?"

"Goslin and Durbin went after her. But you don't understand. The end is coming. Wilder has to go first for the end to begin."

Leaving Marcus rambling, Aubriot sped away.

———

He met up with Kes in the *Sirocco*'s briefing room. He hadn't been able to find Wilder and neither had Kes. Before they had a chance to speak, Cherry arrived.

"No sign of her?" Kes asked.

Her eyes full of tears, Cherry shook her head.

They'd decided not to put out a shipwide comm, not knowing who was a friend and who was an enemy. The last thing they wanted to do was to let others know Wilder was alone and vulnerable.

"Niall and Dragan can't have found her either," said Aubriot, "or we would have heard from them."

"Niall anyway," said Kes. "I couldn't raise Dragan."

"You couldn't raise him? Why not?"

"I don't know. Maybe he was drinking last night and he's out of it."

"He should be bloody well looking like the rest of us."

Cherry said, "It's odd he didn't wake up to his comm alert. That's pretty loud."

"It *is* strange," Kes softly agreed.

Niall ran in. After a brief scan of the room he turned his anguished face to them. "No luck?"

There was no need to give the obvious reply.

"Shit. I really hoped one of you had brought her here."

"Do you know what's happened to Dragan?" Aubriot asked.

"Isn't he searching like the rest of us?"

"No, he isn't answering his comm."

"He isn't? Why not?"

"That's what we're hoping you'll tell us," Aubriot replied through his teeth.

Niall ran a hand through his hair. "Dragan's been behaving oddly for a while, but he likes Wilder. He'd want to help her."

"What do you mean he's been behaving oddly?"

Shrugging, Niall replied, "It's hard to explain, but you know if you're friends with someone for years you can tell when they're a little...off?"

Aubriot was already on his way out of the briefing room.

"Where are you going?" Cherry called after him.

"Dragan's cabin."

Thirty-Seven

No one answered the chime. Something was happening inside. Aubriot could hear muffled shouts and the thumps of heavy things hitting the deck and walls. As Kes and Cherry came running up, Niall following at their rear, Aubriot said, "She's in there. Has to be. How can we get in? Can any of you override the lock?"

Panting, Kes replied, "Only Vessey can do that."

"Comm her then." Aubriot hammered on the door. "Wilder?! Are you in there? Dragan, you hurt a hair on her head and I'll fucking kill you!"

"Yeah," Niall commented sardonically, "that's going to make him open up." He stepped to the door. "Dragan? It's Niall. Is Wilder with you?"

A particularly heavy *thunk* reverberated, accompanied by a yell of pain.

Aubriot couldn't make out if it was a male or female voice. He pushed Niall away and leaned close to the crack. "Open the door! Vessey's on her way, so it's opening soon whether you like it or not. If Wilder's hurt, someone's going to pay. You better hope it isn't me who gets hands on you first."

"Get out of the way," Niall commanded. "Let me speak to him."

Aubriot stepped back. "Did anyone comm Vessey?"

Cherry replied, "She said she'll be here in two minutes."

A lot could happen in a couple of minutes. Aubriot found himself inexplicably anxious about what they would find when the captain opened the door. Why did he care? He didn't give a shit about the geeky girl.

Yet the thought of her dying stirred something in him. Pity? Sadness?

They would all suffer for her loss. She was smart. They needed her.

That had to be it.

Where the hell was Vessey?

Niall had continued to try to get an answer from Dragan, talking through the door, but without success.

The noises from the cabin abruptly stopped.

"Dragan?" Niall repeated. "What's happening? Are you okay? Is Wilder there with you?"

"Whatever was going on," said Kes, "it appears to be over, for better or worse."

Aubriot said, "If he's hurt her, I'll—"

"Where are Goslin and Durbin?" interrupted Cherry. "Do we know what happened to them after they left Marcus and Ryan?"

"I've comm'd them several times," replied Kes. "No answer from either of them."

"I'd bet a fortune they're in there too," said Aubriot. "Marcus, Ryan, Goslin, Durbin, and Dragan. That makes five. The Final Day Five."

"Not Dragan," Niall objected. "He's no apocalypse believer. He's an engineer."

"This trip has changed people," said Cherry. "People have done crazy, stupid things, things they wouldn't normally do."

Aubriot looked at her but she didn't make eye contact.

She went on, "None of us can say what someone is or isn't capable of."

"I still say..." Niall didn't finish his sentence. Vessey had appeared.

She jogged to reach them. "Can someone explain what's going on?"

"No time," said Aubriot. "Open the door."

"Opening doors without the cabin occupant's consent is a violation of priv—"

The door slid open.

Goslin's lifeless body slumped out. She sprawled on the deck, arms loose, mouth hanging open, face suffused red. Livid contusions ringed her neck.

She'd been strangled to death.

The cabin looked like a whirlwind had swept through it. Thousand of small figures littered the floor. Shattered shelves hung from the walls.

"What the f—"

"Wilder!" Cherry called in, leaning over Goslin's corpse. "Are you okay?"

There was another body. Female. Curled into a fetal position. Her head had been bashed in. Dark blood stained her black hair and pooled around her. The broken remains of a strangely shaped skull lay in the pool.

The dead woman wasn't Wilder.

Two people crouched in a corner.

Aubriot recognized Dragan, though only barely. It wasn't only the blood spattering his face that caused confusion—horror had contorted his features.

Wilder had to be the person crouching behind him.

"I-I couldn't let them..." said Dragan as Cherry squatted down.

"It's okay." She reached out and touched Wilder's shoulder. "It's over. Goslin and Durbin are dead."

"What about Marcus," Wilder whispered, "and Ryan?"

The implication of her question hit Aubriot. It was obvious what must have happened but he'd been too preoccupied to put two and two together. "That was *you* who did that to them? Shit, I'm impressed. Never knew you had it in you."

Cherry turned and said, "For once, will you shut your big mouth?"

THIRTY-EIGHT

For the second time in less than a week, Miki settled into her jump capsule seat. Maybe *this* attempt would work and they would actually go to Earth. She rolled her eyes. Grown-ups were so dumb. The fact they were in charge of everything was mind-blowing. She didn't know how some of them made it to adulthood, let alone did things like build starships and travel through interstellar space.

Dad hadn't told her half of what happened in the incident with Wilder, which had led to this third try of the jump drive, but she'd managed to piece the rest together by eavesdropping on gossip. She'd explained some of it to Nina, only the less gory parts. Nina was still only young and too sensitive. She didn't want to upset her.

The way Dad had explained it was there had been another fight, that some people had wanted to hurt Wilder. The people—he'd admitted when she pushed him on it they were the Final Day Five—had believed Wilder was to blame for the *Sirocco*'s predicament and she had to pay. They also believed they were on a final journey, the culmination of humanity's long path to destruction, retribution for squandering the gift of civilization. We didn't deserve to claw our way back to evolutionary success, and the universe was punishing us, thwarting each attempt to crawl out of the mire.

Given all the terrible events she'd learned about in history classes, it wasn't such a crazy idea.

What *was* crazy was the nutcases blaming Wilder for the current situation. Wilder was a nice, kind, smart person and would never hurt anyone if she could help it.

What Dad hadn't mentioned was the loonies wanted to *kill* her. Actually murder her. Just the thought of it made Miki choke up.

Thank the stars they hadn't succeeded.

From what else she could gather, Wilder might have died if one of FDF, Dragan, hadn't changed his mind at the last minute and defended her. He'd killed Wilder's attackers with a skull he'd taken as a souvenir from a visit to a planet. They were friends, so it made sense he would want to protect her. It would have been hard for him to hurt Wilder, even if he did believe she needed to die for the final apocalypse to arrive.

Miki sighed and gave her head a little shake.

Grown ups were definitely weird. Yet she was nearly one herself. She would have to remember not to be stupid just because she was an adult.

The best thing was, Dragan had admitted he'd done something to stop the jump drive from working after the last fix. He'd thought if they made it to Earth, it would only be prolonging humankind's downfall. Everyone would suffer more. It was better to accept our fate and end things here and now.

I bet Wilder figured it out. She must have guessed what her friend had done when she knew about his messed-up thinking.

When they got to Earth she would ask her.

If they got to Earth.

Surely this time they would?

Everyone had been so depressed after the last failure, if the same thing were to happen again, living on the ship would be a real downer. And the more she'd thought about it, the more interested she was in seeing Earth.

The final few people were arriving. There was a big man with bandages over his eyes and another man on crutches. They had to be helped into their capsules. Two women were missing, but she knew where *they* were. There had been a double funeral for Goslin and Durbin—another thing Dad had tried to keep a secret.

No one else had to get into their capsule except Niall. He was going to start the countdown sequence this time, probably because Wilder had been getting way too much negative attention. Did she have a plan for what to do if the attempt failed again? Miki hoped so. It must be so hard to have nearly everybody aboard hating you. They *had* to get to Earth. Then all their problems would be over. They would have some new things to eat and plenty of water. And it would be great to see the animals she'd read about in children's books.

And birds!

She'd never seen a bird. On Concordia, only insects, shuttles, and helis flew. It would be amazing to see an animal flying.

The countdown had begun. She crossed her fingers.

Please, please, let it work this time. Please!

The computer's voice droned on, stating the decreasing numbers.

Would it make a difference that they didn't have the gel to protect them?

————

Wilder shut her eyes as the countdown droned on. The past twelve hours was a haze of pain, fear, sorrow, and elation.

She'd come so close to dying. When she'd realized Dragan was one of the Final Day Five, she really thought she'd had it. Trapped in his cabin with Goslin and Durbin at the door, she could never have escaped. Three against one? She hadn't stood a chance.

And Dragan had come so close to doing it. She'd seen the intention in his eyes. He'd been hardening his resolve, forcing himself to go through with it. But in the end, something had stopped him. Had it been a dose of sanity suddenly hitting him? Or maybe he just couldn't bring himself to hurt a friend.

The events that followed were a blur she didn't want to make clear. They'd fought Goslin and Durbin together, the two women attacking like maniacs, expending every last gram of strength and venom to fulfill their mad quest. She couldn't remember who had killed them and she didn't want to. All she knew was that one minute she was in a violent storm of hitting, kicking, punching, and the next she and Dragan were in a corner, alone with two dead bodies.

Her body ached but her mind hurt more. She longed for this journey to be over, to reach Earth.

If only they could reach Earth.

Reality shifted.

Her sense of her position in space had disappeared. Opening her eyes, she saw her view fold and then stretch. A piercing sound assaulted her ears and pressure clamped down, threatening to burst her eardrums.

Then it was over.

The jump drive had worked. It had damn well worked. Niall had been right.

But that didn't mean they'd reached their destination. The drive had worked before and sent them to an entirely different place. They might not be at Earth but perhaps so far away they could never reach it before dying in space. Perhaps they were in another galaxy.

Niall and she had agreed she wouldn't be the one to check their new coordinates, not after what happened before. If they'd messed up again, this time he would take the flack. He was growing braver every day. Just a few hours ago he'd told her he loved her, that he'd loved her since she was Deadly After Midnight and he didn't even know how old she was or what she looked like.

Her capsule lid opened.

Niall was already out and walking to the console.

All around the room, lids were opening and people were sitting up. No one seemed to be hurt, thank the stars. Miki waved at her. She waved back.

Now all gazes were on Niall. Not a sound could be heard, not a whisper or breath.

His head was down as he consulted the screen.

He looked up, and his facial muscles worked as he tried to control his expression. He couldn't control himself any longer. He broke into a huge smile.

"We're in the Sol System. We made it. We finally made it."

THIRTY-NINE

"At least it's still green," Aubriot commented.

Cherry watched the holo of a blue and green globe slowly revolving in mid-air on the bridge, half its surface in darkness. The land masses moving into the light of its star were indeed mostly green.

Earth.

Humanity's home, but not *her* home. Concordia was several jumps away, only two weeks' distant, providing the jump drive didn't malfunction again. It was hard to believe after the long years of the outward journey.

"What did you expect?" asked Wilder.

"Don't know exactly," Aubriot replied. "When I left the place was a mess. Could have been a global nuclear war since, or climate change could have turned it all to desert."

"I thought the Natural Movement had taken over most political systems," Wilder countered. "Wasn't that what the scientists who built the Guardians said in their vid? That's what you said, Kes, right?"

Kes gave a nod.

"So nuclear weapons would have been banned."

Aubriot replied, "With those freaks, you never knew what was coming next. They could have done anything." He leaned closer to the globe, as if looking for something in particular. Whatever it was, he didn't mention it, only repeating. "Could have done anything."

"Well, we're here now," said Cherry. "What's the plan? Kes? You're head of the Collection Team."

"The plan hasn't changed as far as I'm concerned. I have my list of items to gather and I have a fairly good idea of where to find them. I'll have to rejig the various team roles as we've sadly lost so many people."

Cherry asked, "Is there any point? We must be too late to save Concordia." When they'd visited the Galactic Assembly, traveling at near light speed, decades passed on her home planet. The journey to Earth had taken years. How much time had passed at home while they'd been gone?

"I haven't given up hope," said Kes. "Life is a persistent phenomenon. It endures, even when all odds are stacked against it. I haven't carried out a thorough survey of Concordia, but on Earth living organisms were found in the most unlikely places, from bodies of water sealed off for millennia to the upper reaches of the stratosphere. Micro-organisms had even been found on space stations and satellites. If we complete our mission and return I don't know what we'll find, but I doubt Concordia will be barren. Even if no one has survived, perhaps we can start again."

He gave a small cough and continued, "There used to be a seed vault on Earth, designed to last thousands of years. If the Natural Movement didn't destroy it, that would be a good place to begin looking for what we need."

Aubriot's upper lip lifted into a sneer. "I know the place you mean. That'll be long gone. It was exactly the sort of place the loonies would target."

"I'm not so pessimistic," Kes replied. "As the *Nova Fortuna* Project neared completion, I noticed all mention of the vault had disappeared from the media, and when I searched for information on the net I found nothing, not even in archived pages."

"Someone was thinking ahead," said Aubriot.

"I hope so."

"That's a good sign," Wilder commented. "Maybe the vault's still there. Do you remember where it was, Kes? I agree we should try there first."

"I know the rough location and I think I recall the external features. Most of it was buried in a hillside."

"We're forgetting something," Aubriot said. "Our little delay means the mission's changed. We don't only have to collect the seeding material, we have to protect Earth from the Scythians."

Vessey, who had been watching the globe in silence ever since it appeared, said, "We can't realistically do that. It took decades to build the military defenses on Concordia. Here, from what I can tell, the same infrastructure and technology no longer exists. How can we protect an entire planet from an advanced, hostile alien species with only what we have aboard the *Sirocco*?"

"I don't know the how," Aubriot retorted. "I only know the why. We have to face the fact that Concordia's probably screwed. From up here, Earth doesn't look much better. Look at the dark side of the globe. What do you see?"

"Nothing, of course," said Wilder. "It's night time."

"If there were cities you would see lights. When I lived on Earth, the planet was lit up like a birthday cake at night. You could see all the metropolises, roadways, the lot. And look at the green parts. Where are the developed areas? Don't tell me everyone took to living underground. Are we picking up any transmissions? Radio? TV?"

There was a silence as his words sank in.

Wilder murmured, "Is anyone left, I wonder."

"Doesn't look like it," Aubriot replied harshly. "Which means the last remaining human civilization in the universe is probably us. And the Scythians know about Earth. If we're going to survive—not as animals grubbing for food in the forest—but *really* survive, without losing everything we've achieved, we have to make humanity's home safe."

Cherry hated it when he talked sense. She couldn't help agreeing with him. "If a *how* exists, we won't know what it is until we get down there. Who's going to be in the first landing party?"

Vessey grimaced. "Everyone is itching to set foot on land, naturally, but I want to be cautious. Earth might have been home to two of you, but that was thousands of years ago, and to everyone else it's unknown territory. We can't afford to lose any more personnel. I want to restrict the first landing team to five people only. When we have a better understanding of conditions, perhaps we can commit more people at a time to the many tasks."

"Five isn't a lot," said Aubriot. "It's better to have more in case things get hairy."

"The more people down there, the more we could lose. And we mustn't forget about the possibility of the Scythians turning up. If that happens, we'll need all hands on deck."

One of the first things they'd done after arriving from the jump had been to scan for other starships, but there had been no trace of any.

Kes said, "It would be extremely bad luck if the Scythians were to turn up at almost exactly the same time as us."

"Bad luck has dogged us ever since we left the Solar System," said Aubriot bitterly. Then he held up his hands. "Not that I'm saying there's anything supernatural about it." He grinned and continued, "Getting back to the point, I want to be in the first team. Kes has to come too, since he wants to look for that vault. And Wilder should be included so she can suss out what's what about planetary defense. That makes three. Who the other two are, I don't care. I don't think it matters too much."

"Seeing as I don't matter," said Cherry, "I'd like to go."

Aubriot softly tutted.

Vessey said, "I'll let the Chief Scientific Officer decide on the fifth member of the team, as beginning the seed material harvest will be the primary focus of the mission."

"Hm. " Kes flushed slightly. "In that case, I'd like to take Maddox. She's the best biologist we have left alive. Providing her inclusion won't ruffle too many feathers, that is."

Aubriot shrugged. "Fine by me."

"Me too." Cherry tried to sound nonchalant.

"That's decided then," said Vessey. "There's no time like the present. Begin your preparations. I'd like to send you down within the hour."

"Uhh, Captain..." Zapata had been sitting at the pilot controls, silently monitoring the scan data. "We've picked up a signal."

"We have? What kind of signal?"

"It's very simple. Just a single repeating tone, like an alert or warning."

"Where's it coming from?"

"Right..." he did something on his console "here."

A light appeared on the holo. It pulsed, presumably in time with the signal the *Sirocco* was receiving.

"If I remember rightly," said Kes, "that's in the same area as the seed vault. Perhaps it's a beacon, part of the original design to enable it to be found in the far distant future."

Vessey said, "I hope that's all it is."

FORTY

Aubriot stepped from the shuttle. At first glance, Earth looked nothing like the dream he'd had years ago back on Concordia. They'd landed in what used to be northern Europe. They were in the farthest reaches, on an island within the Arctic Circle. The place must have been sparsely populated even in the distant past. It made sense that the scientists had chosen it for the seed vault. Back then, the ground had probably been permanently frozen, which would have helped to preserve the seeds.

Things had changed.

Like most of the rest of the globe, the island was green. Not as lush and verdant as a jungle, but green nonetheless. When he'd left Earth the climate had already warmed significantly, and the process had clearly continued. Here, the permafrost had melted, the sea level had risen, encroaching on the land, and vegetation had grown on what must have once been barren slopes.

The rotting metropolises and overgrown roadways of his dream were not to be seen, and there was no sign of people reduced to savagery. So far, it didn't appear his mind had conjured an accurate premonition. He'd also seen Scythian ships descend from the skies. He dismissed the speculation. It must have been only a dream, sparked by the news that Wilder had figured out how to build the jump drive. None of it meant anything.

What did Kes think? The conditions on the island had to be bad news for seeds. He couldn't see the man's expression behind the visor of his EVA suit.

It would be hard to navigate the terrain suited up, but Kes had insisted they wore the protective clothing. According to the Guardians, a pandemic had ravaged the human population, sounding the final death knell for global civilization. Kes feared coming into contact with local inhabitants. Even after all the years that had passed, the deadly virus could infect them. The current population would have a natural resistance—something Concordians lacked.

Kes had insisted they were armed too.

Aubriot had no problem with that. "Sure you want to check out the vault first? Not the signal origin?"

"I'm sure," Kes replied. "That's what we're here for, to collect material to help Concordia."

It seemed a waste of time. Whatever Concordia's lack of biodiversity was going to do was done. But Aubriot was no botanist and it wouldn't hurt to let the others carry out their plan. After the disastrous voyage, people needed a hope to cling to. "All right, it's this way, yeah?"

"I think so. I'm working from memory, don't forget."

Kes had said the vault lay south of the island's airport, and Zapata discovered the airport's location on a very old educational program. Nothing remained of the structure. Woodland now grew there. Zapata had struggled to find somewhere to land. In the end, he'd set down on a flat outcrop at the base of the hillside. Whatever road might have run from the airport to the vault was long gone. They would have to trek over the natural landscape.

"The external section of the vault is small," said Kes as they set off. "There are double doors at the entrance to a tunnel that quickly sinks into the ground. But the place is solid. Unless someone blew it up, it should still be there. We only have to find it."

They were climbing rising ground, thick with undergrowth and trees. Unable to see more than a few meters, they had to use their HUDs to maintain a steady direction.

"How does it feel to be home, Kes?" Cherry asked.

"I don't think it's hit me yet. I'm focusing on the job at hand. Ask me again later."

Aubriot noted she didn't ask how *he* felt. She hadn't said more than was necessary to him in five years. Her ability to hold a grudge was phenomenal.

"I can't believe this is really Earth," said Maddox. "It didn't seem real when I was growing up. It was just somewhere mentioned in history class, somewhere I'd never been and would never go, yet it was supposed to be so important. It was almost mythical."

Wilder said, "I don't feel any connection at all."

"You don't?" Cherry asked.

"No, it's just another planet to me. What about you?"

Cherry didn't answer.

Aubriot spotted a set of boulders. "I'll climb up there and take a look around."

The boots of his suit gripped the mossy surfaces well, and the boulders were riven with cracks, probably from the freezing and thawing of ice. He was soon standing atop the tallest one. A silvery ocean lay to the north. He could see the shuttle on its outcrop. He turned a hundred and eighty degrees and scanned the trees mounting the steadily rising ground.

Something caught his eye. Activating the zoom on his visor, he closed in on the anomaly in the low canopy. A line of gray concrete broke the repetitive green. "I think I see it." He fixed the position on his HUD and climbed down. "This way." He pushed through ferns and bracken.

The team of five formed a straggling line, Aubriot at its head.

"Slow down," Kes warned. "We don't know if anyone else is around."

But there had been no signs of people. They hadn't come across any tracks, not even animal trails, and Aubriot's inspection of the landscape hadn't revealed any rooftops or other signs of habitation.

After a couple of minutes, Maddox cried out, "I found something."

She was some distance back down the slope. Aubriot hadn't realized he'd been going so fast. When he reached her she was pointing upward and the others were clustered around her, also looking up. A rusted metal mesh about a meter square hung from a tree trunk, partially embedded into the fork of a branch.

"I wonder what it is," said Cherry.

"It's definitely something from before the fall of civilization," said Kes. "It was manufactured."

"How did it get up there?" Maddox asked. "Who put it there, and why?"

"I don't think anyone put it there," Kes replied. "My guess is the tree grew through it, and as the tree grew taller, it lifted the metal up. Whatever it is, it used to be on the ground."

"Hmpf," said Aubriot. "We're not far from the concrete I saw. Let's go. We're interested in the vault, not bits of old metal."

When they reached their destination, the explanation of the metal in the tree became clear. Two or three similar panels lay on the forest floor. It was hard to tell exactly how many because they were deeply corroded, bent, and broken, their edges jutting up from the groundcover. They were the remains of a steel walkway.

A rectangular concrete facade rose from the forest, divided into three sections. Uppermost was a shattered glass panel. Below that was a mesh like the walkway remains, rusted and full of holes. Flies buzzed lazily around it. At ground level, double doors faced the explorers, one standing open, hanging from its hinges.

Kes said nothing but his shoulders sagged.

"Is there any point in going in?" Aubriot asked. The place was a joke. So much for preserving a cache of seeds to benefit all humankind.

"We should take a look around anyway," said Kes heavily. "We might find something worth collecting in the deepest regions. Seeds can remain viable for remarkable lengths of time. Even thousands of years. And they would have been stored well here. Some might have survived the warm temperatures."

They stepped into the dark interior. Their helmet lights activated, revealing a shadowy corridor sloping downward.

In the first rooms, mold grew on the walls and their feet crunched on rat droppings wherever they walked. Cockroaches had taken up residence too, quickly scurrying into the darkness whenever a beam of light hit them. Broken shelves and empty foil seed packets, ripped open, were all that remained of the vault's carefully stored contents.

The place had been ransacked.

"People must have come here during the pandemic," said Kes. "Food supply chains would have broken down."

Cherry asked, "Were they looking for food or seeds to grow their own crops?"

"Who knows? Growing the seeds would make the most sense, but if they were starving..."

The packets had been labeled with Latin names. Only Kes and Maddox understood them. They lamented as they recognized plants that would have grown on Concordia, but the packets were empty.

"We need to go deeper in," said Kes. "We might have better luck there."

They passed more ransacked rooms. The temperature reading on Aubriot's HUD dropped as they walked deeper underground. Narrower corridors branched out from the main. Kes selected one based on the sign at its entrance. He went ahead, but after only a few steps he yelled and backed up, crashing into Cherry, who was directly behind him.

Bones lay on the ground. A skull grinned. A collapsed rib cage, a pelvis... Aubriot turned away. "Let's try somewhere else."

"No," said Kes. "Grain crops for temperate regions were stored in this section." He delicately stepped over the bones and continued down the corridor.

In this colder region of the vault, no moss grew though humidity was high. How deep were they?

Kes tried a door but it was locked.

"That's a good sign," said Cherry. "Maybe no one broke in."

Aubriot said, "Or maybe someone's in there and has locked the door."

Kes slammed his shoulder into it.

"Shouldn't you be a bit more cautious?" Aubriot asked.

"Shut up and give me a hand."

"All right. Keep your hair on. Stand back."

When Kes was out of the way, Aubriot kicked the door next to its lock.

The mechanism tore away from the frame and the door flew open. He darted to the side, but nothing and no one emerged.

Kes leaned in, his helmet light illuminating the place. "Jackpot."

———

Kes's bag of seed packets felt satisfyingly heavy as he returned to the shuttle, though a long road ahead remained. He had no idea if the seeds would sprout, or if they would grow in Concordian soil depleted of micro-organisms, but the packets were sealed in triple layers of foil and the temperature in the storage room had been almost freezing. It was as much as he could have reasonably hoped for, if not more.

The light was failing. It was autumn, and in this part of the world days were only a few hours long this time of year. Zapata had turned on the shuttle lights to help them find it—perhaps unwisely. They still had no idea who lived here or how they might react to strangers.

Still, Kes was grateful. They pushed through the undergrowth, following roughly the same path they'd taken to reach the vault.

When they were at the shuttle, every face was smiling as they removed their helmets. There was a sense of elation in the air. Finally, after all their trials and tribulations, things seemed to be going their way.

Zapata appeared. "Vessey doesn't want you to investigate where the signal's coming from."

"Huh?" said Wilder. "Why not?"

"Something about it being too dangerous. She said it could be a Scythian trap."

"I suppose it's a possibility," said Kes. "They might have arrived before us and set something up."

"Like a booby trap?" asked Cherry.

"Exactly. Designed to draw us in if we return home."

"It does sound like something they would do," she said. "They can't breathe Earth's atmosphere any more than they can breathe Concordia's. They can't live here, but they still want their revenge."

Aubriot interjected, "We don't have to do what Vessey says."

"But we should," said Kes. "She *is* the captain."

The disdainful curl of Aubriot's lip showed what he thought about that.

"We have plenty to keep us occupied at the vault," said Kes. "It'll take us all day tomorrow and probably the day after to explore it thoroughly. Then we need to collect samples of soil, water, and plants from other regions. We have lots of exploring to do. The signal can wait."

FORTY-ONE

Cherry watched through the shuttle window as the North American prairie receded into the distance. The sea of deep-rooted, tall grasses was nothing like she'd ever seen on Concordia. Kes had said the area hadn't been like that when he left Earth. Vast tracts of farmland had covered this place. But the land had reverted to its former state before a colonization. Large-headed, heavy animals roamed it, living off the grass. The *Sirocco* wouldn't be taking any of *those* home, thank the stars. She couldn't imagine what their hooves would do to the soft, rubbery plants that covered most of Concordia's mainland.

Kes had talked about bringing back smaller animals and insects, like bees. These were striped, winged creatures with stings, though they were rarely dangerous. He said if Concordia had bees, they could grow a wider range of crops. Bees were needed to fertilize the flowers. He said they also produced a delicious, sweet substance called honey. He'd been vague about *how* they produced it, which wasn't like him. She guessed there might be something unsavory about the process and he didn't want to put her off.

They would need to find the right bees, however. Only a particular kind would do.

Harvesting the seeding material was going well. And horticulturalists on the *Sirocco* had already germinated some seeds from the vault. The success was a wonderful reward after the trials of their journey.

For now, they only had to concentrate on finding Kes's listed wild plants and samples. She had a box full of prairie soil containing worms and other small creatures as well as invisible micro-organisms supposedly essential to establishing diversity of life on Concordia.

Next stop was somewhere on the west coast with a warmer, wetter climate.

There were Earth people about. Of that, the *Sirocco*'s crew was certain. On their travels they'd seen evidence of agriculture and some small villages. Vessey hadn't wanted them to make contact just yet, mindful of the disease risk and the potential for conflict. Cherry understood, but she was curious to meet some true Earthers. Kes and Aubriot didn't count. They were from another time.

Kes reckoned they wouldn't be able to understand the locals. These humans spoke many different languages, not the single one everyone spoke on Concordia, and their speech would have evolved into something neither he nor Aubriot would recognize. Yet they were still people. Surely they would find a way to communicate?

"Penny for them?" Kes sat down beside her.

"What?"

"Sorry. I was asking what you're thinking about."

"Oh, the usual. Everything and nothing. How about you? Are you happy Miki and Nina will be coming down to the surface on the next trip?"

He grimaced. "*They're* definitely happy about it. Me, not so much. I'm not convinced it's safe."

"We haven't had any problems so far."

"That doesn't mean we won't have any. I'd rather they didn't come down at all, but if I insist I'll never hear the end of it. They're the only ones who haven't been here yet."

"It's their heritage, the place their father is from. You can't blame them."

"I don't. I do understand. That doesn't mean I have to like it. How about you? How do you feel about Earth now you've had a look around?"

"I think I like it. It's beautiful."

"It looks much better than it did when I left. Humans nearly annihilating themselves has done wonders for the place."

"It still isn't home, though. Concordia is where I belong."

"That's understandable. You fought so hard for it. And..." he tapped the box on her lap "...you're still fighting."

"I guess I am, but this beats going up against the Scythians."

They chatted for the remainder of the journey until Zapata announced, "Touch down in five. Found a nice little spot for you guys near the foot of a mountain."

"Excellent," Kes said. "Sounds ideal for our last expedition of the day."

———

As Cherry donned her EVA suit for the *nth* time, she noticed it was beginning to smell. Could she clean it? She peered into the open front before she secured the seal. Was it even possible? She put on her helmet and descended the ramp with the team. Maddox was a member again. So far, she'd had the decency to stay quiet.

Steep mountain slopes rose to their left, the peak out of sight. In front lay a wooded valley, deep green and thickly forested.

"It rains so much on the west coast," Kes explained, "this qualifies as rainforest, though the tree species are different from what used to grow here. I would expect to see some of these in a subtropical climate. The plants in this place would do very well in southern Lyonesse. I want to take plenty of samples." He slowed his pace. "You go ahead."

He was waiting for Maddox to catch up. He was always careful to keep her apart from Cherry when he could. She continued down the slope, glancing back every so often. Kes and Maddox were deep in conversation. The final time she looked back, Maddox was alone.

Cherry stopped. When Maddox reached her, she asked, "Where's Kes?"

"He spotted something he wanted to collect. He said he'd meet us at the bottom."

Doubtfully, Cherry scanned the vegetation up the slope. She couldn't see Kes at all. Maddox continued on, and after a few moments, Cherry followed.

When they reached a creek running through the base of the valley, they began to collect their samples. As Cherry only knew about crop plants, her task was to collect soil samples. She scooped dirt from the creek bank and placed it in a box before filling in the label. Then she straightened up and took another look up slope.

Kes still hadn't arrived.

Where was he?

In case she'd missed him she asked Maddox, "Have you seen Kes?"

"No," she replied irritably. "I told you, he's collecting something up there." She waved vaguely in the direction they'd come from.

Dissatisfied—if Kes was only collecting a plant he should be here by now—Cherry began to climb the slope. She tutted to herself. Why not comm him?

She tried.

Nothing.

She tried again.

The hush of the forest was her only reply.

She ran down to the others. "Kes is missing!"

They took some convincing. Maddox assured her he was about somewhere and probably distracted, but after Cherry comm'd him several times over without receiving a response, they were finally persuaded.

As they searched for him, Cherry alerted Zapata.

"Stay as long as you like," he replied, "though don't forget to pop back to replenish your suits' oxygen. I'll wait, and I'll let Vessey know what's happening."

They searched and searched, far and wide through the valley and up the mountainside, but they found no trace of Kes. He'd vanished into thin air.

Forty-Two

"I don't want to be the one to tell Miki and Nina their father's gone missing," said Wilder.

Cherry was comming her from the shuttle after the long search for Kes.

"You have to tell them something," said Cherry. "They must have guessed there's a problem. We should have been back hours ago."

Wilder sighed. "Okay, I'll do it. I guess it'll be better hearing it from me than a captain's announcement. What's happening? Are you leaving now?"

"I don't want to but I don't have a choice. Vessey wants us to return to the *Sirocco*. She's worried that if someone took Kes they might attack the rest of us now it's dark."

"She has a point."

"I know, but..." The comm went silent. When Cherry spoke again, her voice was charged with emotion. "I can't help feeling I'm giving up on him."

"Don't feel bad. He wouldn't want you to put yourself in danger for his sake. You know that. Besides, you can carry on the search tomorrow."

"But that means he'll be here all night. What if he's fallen and he's lying injured somewhere, unable to call for help? And I'm not so sure Vessey will agree to us coming back. You know how ultra cautious she is."

"Kes is vital to the mission. No one else has his depth of knowledge. She won't abandon him easily."

"You say that, but he was telling me the other day we have almost everything we need. And all the information is available to the other scientists. They could finish the job without his help now, I think."

"Cherry, worrying about what might happen isn't going to help find Kes. Come back to the ship, and together we'll persuade Vessey to continue the search when it's daylight there. Aubriot will help too."

"Will he? I'm not so sure. He and Kes never really got along."

"Aubriot doesn't get along with anyone. Consulting with him on planetary defenses has been damned hard work, let me tell you. It always amazed me how you put up with him. But even he knows how important Kes is, and he can be forceful when he chooses. If all else fails, he'll bully Vessey into agreeing."

With a note of sadness, Cherry said, "I guess I'll see you soon."

Wilder set off to bring the bad news to Kes's daughters.

But before she reached their cabin, Vessey comm'd her. "I need you on the bridge, immediately."

Grateful for the opportunity to put off her dreaded task a little longer, she changed direction. When she arrived on the bridge, Aubriot and Niall were there too.

"You'll never believe this," said Niall.

"Believe what?" she asked wearily. The three of them looked far too cheerful considering Kes was missing.

"Play her the recording."

Vessey hit a button.

"To the starship currently in orbit around Earth, greetings from the Global Advancement Association. We apologize for our silence. We assumed you were an alien ship. We have been delighted to discover you are human, like us. We would like to suggest a meeting at a neutral site so we may discover more about each other. As a gesture of our goodwill, we will return your crew member, who was mistakenly taken captive in a region of..." the voice stated a name Wilder didn't recognize "*...today.*"

"Holy shit," said Wilder. "When did we receive that?"

"A few minutes ago," replied Vessey. "I wanted to discuss our response before we send a formal reply."

"We're meeting with them, right?"

"Of course," said Niall. "We have to."

"I don't want to act hastily," said the captain. "The message was in English, but according to what I've heard, that should be impossible. Someone told me that language on Earth would have evolved beyond our recognition. Why is it we can understand the speaker?"

"Because," Wilder said, "because... I don't know." She desperately wanted the message to be genuine but Vessey was making sense.

"I don't know either," said Aubriot. "Doesn't mean anything fishy's going on."

"No," said the captain, "but we can't forget the fact the Scythians have their sights on Earth. It isn't a safe place for us."

Niall asked, "How could the Scythians have learned English?"

Vessey replied, "They could have been scanning transmissions on Concordia for years."

Wilder's initial elation was slowly fading but she refused to give up hope. "We have to meet this group. If there's the slightest chance we can get Kes back, we have to take it."

Vessey's brow furrowed. "You're right. I'll draft a reply and we'll meet them. But I want to urge the utmost caution."

FORTY-THREE

They'd grabbed him so quickly, Kes hadn't had the presence of mind to comm for help. He'd been bending down, easing a small plant out of the soil, when hands had seized him and thrown him on his back. All of a sudden, four faces stared down, long hair hanging. Fingers pawed at his EVA suit. Understanding what they intended, he struggled. He couldn't let them take his suit. He understood it must make him look strange and frightening, but—

Too late.

They'd figured it out. Deftly, they unfastened the suit and snapped his helmet seals open.

No, no, no!

They tore off his helmet and tossed it into the undergrowth.

As they saw his face their eyes widened. He tried to sit up, but they forced him down. A gag fastened over his mouth, and a bag descended over his head. His wrists and ankles were tied, and then someone pushed a shoulder into his stomach and lifted him up.

He was being carried away from his friends and safety. In less than a minute, modern-day humans had kidnapped him.

———

He tried to figure out which way he was being taken but it was impossible. He'd been disoriented during the attack. All he could tell was he was being carried upward. The person carrying him grunted with effort and staggered. He didn't struggle, fearing he might fall a long way if dropped.

Then his captors seemed to be walking along level ground. He counted in his head. *One, one thousand. Two, one thousand. Three, one thousand...*

He was passed to someone else like a sack of rice. The march continued.

Thirty-eight one thousand. Thirty-nine one thousand...

They grew tired of carrying him. He was placed on his feet, his ankle bindings cut, and he was pulled forward, someone tugging him by his wrist ties. He continued counting, though he lost his place several times. He estimated approximately forty-five minutes later, the ground turned significantly downward and the air grew cooler and still.

Voices burst out, loud with surprise and excitement. The man holding his wrist ties said something, and then he was unceremoniously pushed to the ground. His landing wasn't as hard as he'd been expecting. He was lying on a soft surface that rustled beneath him as he tried to sit up.

Hands pushed his chest, forcing him down again.

Someone pulled the bag off his head.

Similar faces to the ones he'd seen before gazed down, their long hair obscuring their features except for their dark, curious eyes.

"Please," he said, "can I sit up? Please untie me." Or rather, that was what he tried to say. His gag reduced his words to muffled nonsense. He lifted his bound wrists.

These people might not speak his language but communication should be possible. It would be easier with his hands free.

Nervous laughter was the only response.

He had a sense that, now they had him, they didn't know what to do with him. It wasn't every day a spaceman appeared in the neighborhood. A woman began investigating his EVA suit, pulling at the gap where it hung open. He had no idea what had happened to his helmet. She commented to a man and pushed the open suit over Kes's shoulders. The man untied his wrists and ankles, but only to allow the others to remove the suit. As soon as Kes was wearing only his normal clothes, they tied him up again.

Their activity had allowed him to get a better view of his surroundings, glimpsed in gaps between his audience of fifteen or so adults and children. He was in a cave, but these people were not cavemen. Humanity hadn't sunk so low. Electric lights hung from wires across the ceiling, and the place was furnished with plain wooden furniture. In a corner a mother nursed twins, an infant at each breast.

He was pushed down again.

A hand reached out to touch his hair. The woman who had instigated removing his suit leaned close and peered into his eyes. He guessed his coloring was unusual in these parts. In different clothes—they wore simple, homespun stuff that looked colored with vegetable dyes—these people could have been Concordians. They were uniformly black-haired and olive-skinned.

He plucked at his gag. "Please, let me talk." He lifted his wrists. "Untie my hands."

Chatter followed as the group apparently discussed his request. They came to an agreement. One of the men unfastened the gag.

"Thank you," Kes breathed. "Thank you." He lifted his wrists again. "Now my hands. Please."

The woman shook her head.

Kes held out a brief hope that the gesture didn't mean *No* in this part of the world, but he was wrong. His wrists were not untied.

No matter. He could still do a lot to make a connection with these people. He had to make them understand he wasn't a threat. Feeling like a character from a man-meets-savage vid, he said, "I'm Kes." He touched his chest. "Kes."

Several onlookers murmured, "Kes."

"Yes." He nodded. "Kes." He motioned, two-handed, at the nearest people. "You? What are you called?"

In his peripheral vision, a kid, no more than four or five years old, lifted a familiar object.

"No!" He launched himself on the child.

Lacking the use of his hands and legs, all he could do was force the girl to the floor. She lay under his chest, wriggling and yelling. If she accidentally pressed the trigger on his sidearm, they were both dead. "My gun," he tried to explain. "It's—"

Pain exploded in his head as someone kicked him. Another kick landed on the side of his stomach. Hands roughly hauled him off the girl, who was now screaming. The woman who had removed his EVA suit slapped him with a vehemence that told him she was probably the girl's mother.

"You don't understand," he protested, nearly weeping. "She could kill herself or one of you." It wasn't only concern for the child that terrified him. If anyone in the group died he was sure his own death would soon follow.

The woman seemed to understand his agitation was centered around the weapon. She took it from her daughter's hands, causing louder screaming and some stamping of feet.

As she turned the gun over in her hands to examine it, Kes said, "Please, please be careful."

The woman repeated slowly, "Careful." She lifted up the weapon. "Careful?"

"No. It's a gun. Gun. It can hurt you." He performed a very bad mime of firing a weapon, being hit, gurgling, and falling down dead.

Her eyebrows lifting, the woman stared at the gun once more. She looked down the barrel.

"No!" Kes cried out, waving his tied wrists. "Please, put it down." He mimed placing something on the floor.

A man took the gun from the woman and put it down.

"Yes, that's it." Kes sagged with relief and closed his eyes.

A hand shook his shoulder. It was the woman. Her eyes questioning, she pointed at the gun and then drew a finger across her throat.

"Yes! It can kill you." He gargled and toppled over onto his side. "Dead. You see?"

The little girl was on her hands and knees making a not-so-subtle attempt to nab the gun. She sneezed.

"No," Kes said, sitting up. He spoke sternly using his best fatherly voice and waggled a finger at her. "It's dangerous. Leave it alone."

Chagrined, the child crept backward and tried to act innocent.

Her mother admonished her and picked up the weapon.

Instinctively, Kes ducked, but this time she was holding it more carefully. As he straightened up, she said something to the group. They had a short discussion and seemed to come to an agreement. One of them untied his wrists.

He thanked them gratefully and rubbed his head where he'd been kicked. The woman took his hand, inviting him to stand.

Chatter was going on all around him. These simple folk were unsurprisingly amazed by the man in weird clothing carrying around deadly devices. They didn't seem to intend him any harm, and they'd probably been frightened by the arrival of the shuttle and team of collectors. He hoped they understood he didn't intend them any harm either.

He held out an open hand, gesturing for his gun.

The woman looked at it and then raised her gaze to him warily.

"I won't hurt you. I promise."

After a moment's hesitation, she handed the weapon over.

He scanned the room, found a bare expanse of rock, aimed, and fired.

The shock that passed through the group told him they'd never seen a pulse weapon.

Turning the gun around, he returned it to the woman grip first.

At the burst of fire, her daughter had leapt to her side and continued to cling on, arms wrapped around her mother's hips. The woman caressed her child's hair and spoke to someone Kes hadn't noticed before, sitting in a corner.

The man was crouched over a low table on which sat something resembling a ham radio.

FORTY-FOUR

The figures approached on horseback, wading through grass so tall it obscured the horses' legs. To Wilder, it was like watching a fairy tale come to life. Horses figured in old stories of Earth but she'd never seen any real ones. She peered at each rider in turn but she couldn't spot Kes.

Vessey, who remained aboard the *Sirocco*, had mandated they were not to stray more than thirty seconds from the shuttle. Zapata hadn't left the controls and was ready to take off at a moment's notice.

"Stop!" yelled Aubriot through his helmet comm. "Don't come any closer. Where's our companion?"

"He's on his way," one of the riders replied. "He should be here soon. We didn't want to meet you where he was found. We preferred an open space, where we can all see each other."

Wilder recognized the voice from the message. "How come you speak our language?"

"If you let me come over we can talk face-to-face like civilized human beings."

"All right," said Aubriot. "Just you." To Wilder and Cherry he said, "Draw your weapons."

The man climbed off his horse and began to walk closer, but then he halted. "Please, put away your...guns." He appeared to struggle to remember the word.

"It's only a precaution," Aubriot replied. "We won't cause any problems if you don't."

"I'm unarmed." The man lifted the flaps of his open coat and turned in a circle. "I know what your guns can do. You could kill me and my colleagues easily. Our intentions are entirely peaceful."

"I think he's telling the truth," Wilder told Aubriot quietly. "Look at them. They don't even have vehicles. Our technology is way superior to theirs."

"Appearances can be deceptive, but..." Aubriot said to the stranger, "We'll put our weapons away."

"I wish I knew where Kes is," Cherry remarked as she stowed her gun, "and what the hell's going on."

"You and me both," said Wilder.

The man approaching them was bearded and wore a wide-brimmed hat. When he drew close enough to converse at a normal volume, he said, "It would be good to see your faces."

"Not happening," Aubriot replied flatly. "Before we begin any negotiations, we want to see our man alive and well."

"I wasn't aware we had anything to negotiate, but please accept my assurances your companion is unharmed and will be here within a few minutes."

"Why is it you can speak English?" Wilder persisted.

"I'm a lifelong student of ancient languages. Many times I've been, er, teased about my studies. But everyone forgot their teasing when I could understand what the man from space was saying."

"You've spoken to Kes?" Cherry asked excitedly.

"I have. I'm not sure why you are so suspicious and doubtful. We are all human, it seems. We have no reason to be enemies, though we're very puzzled about where you're from."

"Maybe if you hadn't kidnapped one of our party," said Aubriot, "we might like you more."

"Ah, yes. That was an unfortunate mistake. The people who took your friend captive were scared of him, of all of you. You have to admit, you dress strangely, and your transportation is remarkable."

"But you know about starships," said Wilder, "or you wouldn't have sent your message."

"We do, through historical research and...well, that's another subject we should talk about in more depth when we know each other better."

Aubriot said, a threatening edge, "No one's getting to know anyone better until we see Kes."

"What's that?" Cherry asked.

Wilder heard it too. A high-pitched whine had started up.

"I believe that's your friend arriving."

The sound was coming from the sky. A dot appeared and quickly grew larger. Soon, Wilder could make out rotor blades. "You have helis?!"

"That isn't what we call them, but yes. We've had them for a few years but they're very expensive and difficult to manufacture. You're lucky our branch of the GAA had one on site."

The small craft approached. Like the Concordian helis, it was small, a two-seater. Both seats were filled. The heli touched down, sending undulating waves through the grass. The passenger door swung open.

"Kes!" Cherry yelled, running to him.

"Don't come near me," he shouted. "Get me an EVA suit. Throw me a suit!"

FORTY-FIVE

The *Sirocco's* sick bay quarantine rooms were small but comfortable. They included a bed, interface, comms, restroom, and a small exchange and sterilization chamber where the patient could receive meals and return the used receptacles. Medics and doctors passed through an air-sealed anteroom to take vitals and provide medical care.

Kes had been the one to insist on the installation of the ship's quarantine chambers, mindful of the pandemic that had put the final nail in the coffin of Earth civilization. Wilder hadn't thought they would be necessary for the first mission. They would only be spending a short time on the planet, collecting what was needed to replenish life on Concordia. Who would be dumb enough to expose themselves to viruses against which they had no natural protection?

Kes was in a quarantine room four days before he fell ill.

There was no telling if it was the disease that had wiped out most of Earth's population, a mutation, or another virus entirely. Something new could have crossed from animals to humans since the departure of the Guardians' ship, the *Mistral*.

All anyone knew was that on day four of Kes's return, his temperature suddenly spiked, he lost his appetite, and he began to cough and sneeze.

"It might only be a cold," he reassured Wilder over comm.

"What do you mean?" She leaned her forehead on the transparent barrier separating them. "You aren't cold, you're hot."

"It's the name of a very common virus. When I lived on Earth it was every-where w. People caught colds two or three times a year, sometimes more in a bad season. For the Project, we kept it and all other viruses off the *Nova*. The generational colonist candidates spent a month in isolation and were thoroughly screened before they could board."

"But didn't you have a vaccination for the cold virus, like you developed for Scythian Plague?"

"We had many vaccinations but not for that. It's only a mild illness, and there are so many varieties, it didn't make sense."

"So you won't get very ill?"

"Not if that's all I've got."

Miki and Nina came to visit him every day, often chatting for hours at a time. Wilder sometimes suggested they should leave and let their father rest, but he'd always argued against it, saying he wanted them to stay. They asked him what Earth was like and about the people he met. He wouldn't allow them to go to the surface without him, so they remained frustrated in that regard. But they were good girls. They had to know he was frightened for their safety because they didn't push it.

They told him what they'd been doing, which was helping out with cataloging and storing all the seeds and samples. Nina seemed to have a real flair for biology like her father. Miki didn't care for the subject much, preferring to focus on the mechanics of the storage systems. The Ark's growing rooms had been re-converted to their original purpose. The Global Advancement Association had assured them they could supply food for the return journey to Concordia.

Cherry popped in to see Kes frequently, when she could spare time from meetings with the GAA. She would give updates, new information, and progress, but in truth Wilder couldn't take much of it in. She was too focused on Kes.

On the seventh day of Kes's quarantine, his face and hands were flushed and Dr Clarkson looked worried as he examined him. Enclosed head to toe in protective gear and breathing external air through a long tube, he drew a privacy curtain around his patient's bed for a closer examination.

When, after a long time, the doctor emerged Wilder asked him how Kes was doing.

"Worse than yesterday, I'm afraid."

His voice slurring slightly, Kes asked for Miki and Nina. They came, and he told them he wanted to talk about their mother. He asked them if there was anything they wanted to know about her.

Wilder stepped away, overcome. Her eyes filling with tears, she quickly left sick bay. When she'd regained control somewhat, she returned.

Kes's daughters were listening intently as he talked about how he and Isobel had met. He described what his future wife had been wearing and the first words she'd said to him, which had been, *I know who you are, Earthman.* The girls giggled, and Wilder had to leave again. They didn't understand. They didn't know why their father was telling them the stories.

When they'd gone, Wilder went back and asked softly, "Isn't there anything to be done?"

"Hundreds of years ago, maybe. Before the Natural Movement destroyed health care, we had anti-virals, all kinds of things. But there was no need for them on Concordia and civilization here is too undeveloped. Clarkson is going to speak to the GAA but I don't hold out much hope. It's bad, Wilder. I can feel it."

"I can't believe there's nothing that can help you."

"Don't feel sorry for me. I've had an amazing life and I've known great love. There aren't many who can say that."

The ninth day, Kes spent mostly unconscious. His neck was swollen and his face was almost as red as his hair. When Clarkson came to check on him, he reported the GAA had no record of diseases with Kes's symptoms, and their standard of medical care seemed inferior to the *Sirocco's*. He spent only a short time with his patient before leaving without meeting Wilder's eye.

In a brief moment of lucidity, Kes whispered, "Hey."

She swallowed and smiled. "Hey."

"Whenever I wake up, you're always here."

"Of course I am."

"Don't you have anything better to do?"

"No, nothing."

After a pause, he said, "I'm glad. You know, I used to have a sister like you."

"I know. You've told me before."

"I have? I don't remember. I'm forgetting a lot lately."

"It's okay. I like it when you tell me."

His eyes closed and she thought he'd fallen asleep again, but then they popped open. He croaked, "I remembered something important. Tell Clarkson to take my blood. It'll contain antibodies...you understand?"

"I understand. I'll tell him."

Due to Kes's illness, they would be able to vaccinate Concordians against the virus.

On the tenth day, Dr Clarkson announced it was time for final goodbyes.

Wilder had tried to explain what was happening to Miki and Nina the previous evening, but they hadn't seemed to take in what she was saying. They arrived in sick bay looking shell-shocked. Cherry turned up at the same time. For some reason, Aubriot had come too, though little love was lost between the two men.

"Shit," Aubriot said as soon as he laid eyes on Kes. It was the first time he'd seen him since the meeting on the prairie. He folded his arms and leaned on the bulkhead, his head down.

Cherry put her open hand on the transparent barrier, her chest working, tears dripping from her cheeks.

"I want to see my Dad," Miki whispered to Wilder, her eyes pleading.

"He's right there, sweetheart. Say anything you want to him. He'll hear you." Wilder wasn't sure this was true but it would comfort the girl. Kes was lying on his side, facing them, his eyes only slits and his chest barely moving. He appeared to hover between life and death.

Miki said stubbornly, "I want to go in and *see* him. I want to-to-to hug him."

Nina was on her knees, staring at her father disbelievingly.

"You can't go in," Wilder replied gently. "It isn't safe."

"I want to see him!" Miki marched toward the anteroom.

"Miki, no!" Wilder grabbed her but she wrenched free.

She almost reached the door before Aubriot caught her. She fought him like a wild thing, biting, scratching, kicking, screaming, "I want my Daddy! I want my Daddy!" over and over.

Nina held onto her knees and rocked, quietly keening.

"Give me a hand, can't you?" Aubriot asked angrily as he took another blow to the face from a flailing elbow. But Wilder didn't know how to help him.

Dr Clarkson ran in. When he saw what was happening, he locked the anteroom door.

"Miki." Wilder tried to catch one of her waving arms. "Miki, please try to calm down. Your father wouldn't want this. Please give him peace."

Her words made it through the girl's pain and panic. Miki's struggles eased. Aubriot released his hold on her and she collapsed. She crawled to the wall and said to Kes, "I love you, Daddy."

Just above the sounds of grief came his quiet reply, "I love you too, my darlings."

His eyes closed and he was gone.

FORTY-SIX

Kes's funeral took place three days later on the wide open plains of North America, attended by everyone who could be spared from the *Sirocco*. Wilder had cried so much she was hoarse and her eyes had puffed up. She didn't know how she would carry on without her friend.

As she stood at the graveside, Niall put an arm around her shoulders. He'd been trying to comfort her, but nothing he could do would ever fill the hole left by Kes's death. She could see in her mind's eye, clear as day, her friend's face looking up at her through leaf fronds the morning he'd come to her tree settlement. He'd brought her a bottle of sluglimpet repellent to spray on the tree trunks. Since then he'd been her greatest ally, supporter, and advocate. When she needed someone he'd always been there. What would she do now he was gone?

Vessey was giving a speech, listing all the contributions Kes had made to the Concordia Colony. All the captain needed to say was, without him, the colony would not have existed. Of all his achievements, his greatest had been saving everyone from certain destruction by the Scythian Plague.

"Do you think he ever imagined he would be buried on Earth?" Cherry asked quietly as Vessey droned on.

"I don't know. I don't think so. But I think he was happy to be home. And this is a nice place to be laid to rest." Wilder gazed over the grassland as it rippled in the wind.

"Was he from around here?"

"No, another country. I can't remember its name."

Kes had rarely spoken of his life on Earth. Wilder had the impression the subject was painful for him because it triggered memories of his sister and other loved ones he'd left behind.

"I'll miss him," murmured Cherry.

"Me too. Beyond words."

Miki and Nina were weeping but otherwise they were holding up well in the circumstances. It was the first time they'd been coaxed from their cabin since their father's passing. Hopefully, their youth would give them resilience and they would heal with time.

Save for the sound of the wind in the grass, all was silent.

Vessey's speech was over.

One of the ship's crew lifted a shovelful of soil and tossed it into the grave.

"Take as long as you want to pay your last respects," said the captain. "We'll return to the *Sirocco* when everyone is ready."

Miki took Nina's hand and led her away.

Wilder noticed a significant member of the ship's personnel was missing. "Where's Aubriot? He didn't come? I don't believe it. I know they didn't get along, but that's so disrespectful. Isn't he worried what people will think?"

"Aubriot doesn't care what anyone thinks," Cherry replied. "He was there when Kes died. He probably thinks that was enough."

"He *did* help with Miki."

"Yeah. That's the thing with him. He isn't kind, hell, he isn't even likable, but when he's needed, he's there."

"I suppose we have to give him that."

They walked through the grass. To try to distract herself from her sadness, Wilder asked, "What's been happening in the meetings with the GAA? I must have a lot to catch up on."

"You do. Where to start? The good news is that civilization is more developed here than we thought."

"I guessed it was when I saw they had helis."

"They have more than helis. Communication networks, electricity, schools, industries. The people who captured Kes were country folk, poor and uneducated, scraping for survival in the mountains. They weren't representative of typical Earthers."

Something didn't sound right. "Are you sure the GAA aren't trying to impress us? We've hardly seen any evidence of development. The only transmission we picked up was that repeating signal, remember? And who are the GAA anyway?"

"They're the central group coordinating worldwide technological development. They collect and study old data, books, anything they can find, and share it. And we didn't pick up any communications because their networks are underground. Old networks they've discovered and are repairing. They don't broadcast through the air if they can help it. We told them about the signal but they didn't know what it was. They weren't aware of it, and when we mentioned it they were concerned. They're going to find out where it's coming from and close it down."

"Why don't they want to use air transmission?"

Cherry took a breath before replying, "You remember the message they sent to the *Sirocco*? They said they thought we were an enemy ship."

It took Wilder a moment to work it out. "Oh, no. This is the bad news."

"Sadly, yes."

"The Scythians got here before us."

"From the Earthers' description of their ships, it has to be them. They arrived a little over two years ago. Their ships are even faster than the Guardians' *Mistral*."

"But they left again? There's no sign of them."

"After destroying some burgeoning cities. According to all reports, their ships never landed. No actual Scythians were ever seen."

"Well, they can't breathe the air, so..." Wilder frowned. "I get it. The Earthers have gone to ground, like we did on Concordia."

"They have. We told them about the Scythian spiders and how they traced us by scent. That terrified them."

"They should be terrified. Dammit. We were beaten in the race to reach Earth despite Niall's fix for the jump drive."

"On the plus side," said Cherry, "we're here now. We made it. Things could have been a lot worse. We still have time to help the Earthers defend their planet. You were working with Aubriot on ideas about that. Did you get very far?"

"Not far at all. And now what you've told me has made all our discussions irrelevant. I'll need to consult with the GAA and find out what tech they already have before we can figure things out."

"You should get started right away. We know from past experience the Scythians will be back. They won't be happy until they've destroyed Earth like they tried to destroy Concordia."

Right away?

Kes was only just buried. She needed time to mourn. And she wasn't even sure this was their fight. "Shouldn't we go home first? We've spent the last couple of weeks collecting everything we need to reseed our planet. Helping the Earthers prepare their defenses will take months, maybe years. What about *our* world?"

"I have to admit, the same thought occurred to me. But then I thought what Kes would want, and..." Cherry's features twisted and her eyes filled with tears.

Wilder found herself suddenly weeping too. "I know. I know what you're saying. I'll think about it. It's too soon to make any decisions." The pain was too fresh.

A voice was calling faintly on the breeze. Wilder blinked as she noticed how far they'd walked from the shuttle.

Vessey was a small figure, waving. It had been her calling.

The captain's voice burst from Wilder's ear comm. "Back to the shuttle now! Everyone, back to the shuttle immediately."

"Huh?" Cherry's hand was on her ear. "What's the...oh, shit." She stared at a spot behind Wilder.

Wilder turned, and froze.

In the deep blue of the distant sky, a crescent-shaped spacecraft was descending.

REDEEMER

ONE

It was time to collect nectar from the Consort of Midnight but Cleve didn't want to go. His mother and father bustled around the cabin, preparing all the equipment they would need: grapples and ropes for climbing the cliff, soft suits made from flour sacks they would use as protection, bottles to hold the nectar—assuming they were successful—knives to release the precious fluid, drinking water and snacks for the long trek, all the usual paraphernalia. They took the same stuff every year.

This would be his fourth time. He'd begun participating in the ritual when he was ten. On his first trip he'd only been allowed to sit at the bottom of the cliff and watch as the others went up. He'd missed out on the elation of their success, feeling as though he hadn't really taken part. The following year had been better. Then, he'd climbed to the first stage, from where he'd been able to see the nectar harvested. On his third visit, when he was twelve, he'd finally been judged sufficiently mature and experienced to climb all the way to the night-blooming Consort of Midnight. After that, he'd trained often with Dad.

Tonight, he was supposed to be actually gathering nectar. It should have been an honor, an initiation into adulthood. He should have been happy and excited.

He did not want to go.

"Don't just sit there, lazybones," Mom exhorted. "Give me a hand packing these suits."

Cleve got to his feet and trudged to her side. She handed him one of the flour-sack garments and picked up another to fold and stow in a backpack.

"Is there one for me?" Temel asked.

"Of course not," Cleve snapped. "You won't need it."

At ten years old, his younger brother would be keeping vigil at the base of the cliff as Cleve had four years ago.

"But I might still be in danger," Temel said hopefully.

Cleve tutted and shook his head. They were *all* in danger, only his parents didn't want to admit it. He squashed the suit into a ball and shoved it into the base of his backpack.

"Not like that!" his mother protested. She pulled the suit out.

"What does it matter?" Cleve scowled.

"It matters. If you put tension on a seam it might break, and then where would you be? These are only loosely sewn. It isn't possible to sew them tighter. The material is too thick." When Cleve continued to scowl, she rolled her eyes. "If you're going to sulk go back to your corner. I'd rather do it myself than look at that face any longer."

He strode across the cabin and sat down, his arms folded. That was how he remained until, twenty or so minutes later, everything was ready. His father shouldered his pack and his mother did the same. Temel had a small backpack of his own. Cleve's sat next to the door.

He faced an impossible choice. He could refuse to leave the cabin, abandoning his family to whatever fate might befall them. Or he could go along, risking the nameless fate.

"It's time to go." Dad opened the door.

Cool night air flooded the cabin, accompanied by a surge in the constant background noise of singing cicadas.

His father glared from under lowered brows. "Cleve, are you coming?"

The three figures of his little family were watching him. Mom, her graying hair cropped to ease the summer's heat. Dad, a little taller than Mom, untidy stubble sprouting on his chin and cheeks. Bright-eyed Temel, puppy fat straining the buttons of his too-small shirt. The three stood in a little group. There were more people in the valley, other families, farmers, store-owners, classmates. But these three were Cleve's world. "All right, I'll come."

He joined them and picked up his backpack, slinging it over his shoulder before stepping out into the darkness.

The Consort of Midnight was half-a-day's trek away, but the journey took longer by night. The jungle trail was hard to follow in the dark, and they had to keep watch for jaguars. Dad made Cleve and Temel walk in front, where they were less likely to tempt a hungry feline into a risky attack.

When they'd been walking for an hour and Cleve's mood had evolved from resignation to rising fear, a hand landed on his shoulder, making him jump.

"Take it easy," said Dad. "I just wanted to say, I'm glad you changed your mind. It wouldn't be the same without you."

His words did little to alleviate Cleve's feelings. His father was still being too casual about the threat. Perhaps it wasn't too late to persuade him to turn back. "Would it really hurt if we missed it this year? Don't you guys have savings? We could cut down on food and supplies. I could definitely eat less, and so could Temel. Right, Temel?"

"That's not the point," Mom argued. "This isn't only for profit. If we don't collect the nectar it wouldn't only affect us, it would affect everyone who uses the stuff. How would Ma Kristophel make her scented toiletries? And what about Farmer Jake's cordial? Consort of Midnight nectar is the main ingredient. Besides, this is what our family does. It's what we've always done. If we stopped harvesting nectar, who would we be? What else could we do?"

"I'm sure Ma Kristophel, Farmer Jake, and the rest of the customers could get their nectar somewhere else. Hell, they could climb the cliffs themselves if they want it so badly."

"Don't curse," Dad admonished. "And I don't want to hear any more arguments. We're doing this, and that's final."

"What's that?" asked Temel.

A pale blue light shone through the trees, silhouetting the trunks and gilding the leaves. The light shone upward from the valley. It was clearly not starlight or moonlight. It was also too blue and shimmered in a non-astronomical fashion.

"It's nothing," Dad replied.

Cleve knew what it was, though it was the first time he'd seen it. It was the first time this year he'd been outside so late. He'd heard the rumors of the alien encampment glowing blue at night—not brightly, but enough to be noticeable in the darkest hours.

The alien presence was the great unmentionable in valley life. The creatures had arrived months ago, their crescent-shaped ship descending to the valley floor. Hundreds had landed all over the globe, it was said. Since then, they'd slowly constructed domes over each ship.

No one had done anything about it as far as he knew. News of what went on in the rest of the world was hard to come by. There was an hour-long radio broadcast every evening, but Mom and Dad had forbidden him from listening to it lately. He guessed it was because they didn't want him to worry, yet not knowing what was going on was more worrying.

People had probably tried to make contact with the aliens or even attack them, and they'd failed. Now all that could be done was to tolerate their presence and hope they didn't mean any harm. He hoped so too. There was plenty of land for them to settle if that was all they wanted. He had a horrible feeling it was not, and that it wasn't safe to roam in the area around their dome.

He walked on, first in line, Temel behind him, then Mom, then, last of all, Dad.

Why did his family have to harvest the Consort of Midnight nectar?!

Why couldn't they leave it one more year?

Why did they have to hike through uninhabited areas in the early hours of the morning when no one else was about?

"Here we are," said Mom, relief in her tone.

She was scared too. She just didn't want to admit it.

They'd arrived at the cliff base. Cleve had been so preoccupied he'd almost walked past it.

A rough, rocky surface rose above their heads, the top obscured by shadows and vegetation. In amongst the jagged, irregular shapes of plants was a soft luminescence. The Consort of Midnight was blooming, right on time. The trumpet-shaped flowers of the rare species would be heavy with nectar. The air seemed to carry their delicate scent, even here, far below.

"I can see it!" Temel exclaimed.

"You can see *them*," Dad corrected. "They're right across the cliff, see?" He pointed, moving his finger from left to right. Speaking to Mom, he continued, "It's going to be a bumper harvest. We can live all year on it. I hope we brought enough bottles."

"I packed some expandable ones," she replied.

"Good thinking." Dad rubbed his hands together gleefully. "We have a long night ahead of us. Let's get started."

Cleve glanced at the blue, spectral light in the distance and then at his little brother. "Maybe... Maybe I should stay down here with Temel, as it's his first time."

"He'll be fine," said Dad. "Won't you, son?"

"Sure, Dad. You go up, Cleve. I bet you'll harvest more than Mom or Dad."

"Not likely," said Mom. "It takes time and practice to get it right, but if you do, Cleve, I'll give you a small bonus to share with your brother. How does that sound?"

"Cool," Temel breathed.

Dad was already swinging the grapple. Foliage crowded the trail, and the sharp metal hooks bashed through the leaves. "Stand back," he warned, before slinging the grapple up the cliff face.

Dad had been harvesting Consort of Midnight nectar all his life. He knew this area like the back of his hand—as he often mentioned. But the surroundings changed every year. The cliff crumbled a little. New plants grew and old ones died. Yet Dad's throws remained true. The grapple caught on the gnarled trunk of a small tree. He tugged on the rope. When it didn't fall down he jumped onto it, dangling by his hands and wrapping his legs around it. The rope bore his full weight.

"Cleve," he said, "this one's yours. Mom and I will go farther down. Temel, you come with us."

"But, Dad..." Cleve demurred.

His father ignored him.

As his family walked away down the trail, he threw his backpack to the ground, tore the fastening open, and pulled out his suit. He swore as he put it on, using all the words he could never say in front of his parents. It didn't make him feel any better.

When he was suited up, the flour-sack material hanging loose on his body, he pulled the hood over his head and face. This was the only part of his kit his parents had purchased. The hoods were expensive. A transparent shield covered his face and a thick, closely woven cloth covered him to his shoulders. He slipped thick gloves onto his hands. Then, his heart heavy with foreboding, he lifted his backpack onto his shoulders and began to climb. Hand over hand, rope gripped between his thighs and feet, up he went.

Harvesting nectar from Consort of Midnight blooms was easy. It was the fact that the plant only grew on vertical surfaces at least fifteen meters above the ground that made it hard.

That, and the bees.

Bees loved the nectar as much as humans did, if not more. They built their hives close to the source and fiercely defended it.

The first bee smashed into Cleve's visor, almost causing him to lose his hold on the rope. He was still many meters from the Consort of Midnight plants but the bees knew his intention. Another bee arrived and landed right in front of his nose, crawling curiously across his vision. Cleve switched his attention to the rope. He didn't dare look down but, judging from the distance to the nearest flowers, he was already high up. A fall from this height could kill him.

The sounds of his mother and father climbing and talking drifted over.

"You doing all right, Cleve?" Mom called.

"Uh huh. Where's Temel?" Bees buzzed all around him, pushing their stingers toward his face and gathering thickly on his gloves and suit.

"He's right underneath me. Don't worry about him. You got your first nectar yet?"

"Not yet. Nearly there."

He wished he could see her. It would be more reassuring than hearing her. He couldn't see anything except the bees and the cliff face, faintly lit by the luminescent blooms and the distant glow of the aliens' dome.

He reached his first flower. The trumpet poked out, long and slender. Holding tightly with both hands, he kicked the cliff. Loose, sandy soil tumbled down. He pushed his foot into the hole and rested a large portion of his weight on it. Now came the really tricky part. He eased one shoulder out from the strap of his backpack, and swung the bag around to his front.

The bees were going crazy. He could barely see what he was doing.

More by touch than sight, he took a bottle out and unscrewed the lid. After stowing the lid in a pouch on the side of the bag, he felt for his knife. He took great care to avoid the blade as he pulled it out. A cut or tear in his suit would allow the bees in and he would be lucky if he only suffered a few stings. Some nectar collectors had been stung to death.

He placed the neck of the bottle at the base of the bloom and pierced the petals with the tip of the knife.

Nectar gushed out.

Dad had been right that this would be the best night for gathering. A lifetime's experience had told him down to the space of a few hours when was the perfect time to do it.

"I got some!" Cleve yelled. "Mom! Dad! I got some nectar."

The bottle was full and still the nectar poured out. Cleve hastily replaced the lid, put the bottle in his bag and retrieved another. He managed to fill it a quarter full before the nectar slowed to a dribble.

Bees swarmed over his hands, the bottle, and the flower, drinking the dregs with their long tongues.

"Mom!" Cleve called. "I got my first nectar!"

No answer came.

Somewhat annoyed, he called again, "Mom! Dad!"

The forest was silent.

"Mom?" His voice was quieter this time. Were his parents joking around? Maybe they were teasing him about his earlier worries.

"Mom, if you're there, please answer."

Nothing.

"Dad?"

Cleve fastened the lid on the quarter-full bottle and put it in his bag along with the knife. "Temel?"

Above, the vegetation rustled.

He froze.

Something was there. A creature. It couldn't be a jaguar. They didn't climb this high. Was it a monkey?

The thing was climbing down toward him. It moved awkwardly, as if unused to the environment.

Cleve tore his pack off his back and flung it at the creature. Without waiting to see the result, he launched himself from the cliff and slid down the rope so fast it grew hot under his hands.

Landing with a thump on the trail, he flew in the direction his parents and brother had taken. "Temel! Temel, where are you?"

"Here," a small voice squeaked. "I'm here, Cleve."

He tried to follow the sound but only met solid cliff face beyond the cloaking foliage. "Keep talking. I can't find you." His eyes wide, he looked over his shoulder.

A dark shape moved closer, scraping along the track. It was large and its outlines weird. It looked like nothing he'd ever seen.

"I'm here, Cleve," Temel called.

How would he ever save his brother from the animal? Maybe he shouldn't lead it to him but away from him. Had the creature killed Mom and Dad? Was it—

Something clasped his ankle. He nearly jumped out of his skin.

"Come inside," said Temel. "We can hide."

He had found an opening in the cliff. Cleve ducked down and slipped through the gap. He barely fit. Temel crouched at the end. Cleve squashed up close to his brother.

The meager light went out. The thing had found them and was covering the entrance. But it was too big. It would never be able to get in.

Cleve held his brother tightly.

Temel whispered, "If we wait long enough it'll give up and go away, won't it?"

"Yeah, for sure," Cleve replied quietly, forcing confidence into his voice. "We just have to wait."

But what had happened to Mom and Dad?

Two

It was like old times. Cherry studied Aubriot's crouching, shadowed form as he hid behind a tree trunk, peeking out, keeping watch on the Scythians. The aliens had plagued humanity since the early days of the Concordian colonization, and she and Aubriot had spent years fighting them. Only this time the Scythians had actually landed, and the planet she and her former lover were defending was not Concordia but Earth, the cradle of human civilization.

In all the years she'd known Aubriot he hadn't changed and would never change, while she'd aged and begun to grow stiff. She shifted position in the ferny undergrowth to ease her aching joints, causing the fronds to rustle.

"Shhh!" Aubriot hissed.

"They're a hundred meters away," she retorted in a harsh whisper.

"Doesn't matter. They might still hear us. We don't know what they're capable of."

She silently grumbled, though he'd made a fair point. In the past, Concordians had gone to huge lengths to hide themselves from the hostile aliens, assuming they used sight to search. But the mechanical Scythian spiders had hunted the colonists through their scent and nearly succeeded in wiping them out.

She pushed down a leaf and peered over it. The structure the aliens were building seemed nearly finished. Construction had continued day and night since they'd arrived. First, trundling robots had laid down a low wall surrounding the ship, squirting a pale, faintly lustrous liquid that hardened on contact with air. Later, machines with articulated limbs placed blocks on the base, each layer tapering slightly inward. The result was a dome roughly a hundred and fifty meters in diameter. Aubriot called it an igloo. The top was out of sight but the construction noises continued. They had to be closing off the dome by now.

She grabbed Aubriot's sleeve and tugged. When he looked over his shoulder she jerked her thumb toward the trail. He shook his head.

Why he wanted to stay, she didn't know. There was nothing more to see.

Moving as quietly as she could, she rose to her feet and walked, stooping, into the forest.

Back at the Earthers' settlement, the low houses and narrow streets were mostly quiet. Nearly all the local inhabitants had moved out soon after the Scythian ship appeared. Earthers didn't have the technology let alone firepower to defend their territory from a space-faring species, and they weren't stupid enough to try. They'd fled, getting as far from the threatening presence as they could.

Yet, according to the grapevine, Scythian ships were landing all over the planet. What would the Earthers do when there was nowhere left to hide?

Cherry went immediately to Wilder's hut. In answer to her knock, she heard a faint *Door!* through the wood.

A moment later, a flustered-looking Wilder pulled the door open. "I'm never going to get used to this ignorant tech."

"You'd better. We might not have the luxury of responsive devices ever again."

Wilder grimaced. "Don't remind me. What's happening at the construction site?"

Cherry followed her into the hut. "Nothing new. I think they're nearly finished."

"Want some tea?"

"Sure." The Earthers' drink was nothing like what Concordians called tea, but it was light and refreshing. "Where did you get it?"

"I found a house someone left in too much of a hurry. They hadn't packed up any food as far as I could tell. We can eat for days." Wilder handed over a mug of steaming liquid. "I just made this. I'll make myself another."

"Should we stick around that long?" asked Cherry. "There doesn't seem to be a lot of point. Maybe we should take our lead from the Earthers and find somewhere to hide. The Scythians must have a plan for what to do after they've finished building their domes. I'm guessing it involves destruction and slaughter."

Wilder lowered herself onto the sofa with resignation. "At the very least we should get Miki and Nina away from here. We have to look after them now Kes is gone. What does Aubriot say?"

Before answering, Cherry rested her elbows on the windowsill and gazed out into the deserted street. It was only wide enough for Earth vehicles—basic automobiles that had to be manually driven. There was no net for them to connect to, nothing to navigate by or prevent collisions. It was a wonder the Earthers managed to use them at all.

Earth also lacked good infrastructures for food supplies, medical treatment, education, and other essentials. It wasn't that the planet didn't have these things, but provision was patchy and uneven and depended entirely on local conditions.

History lessons aboard the *Nova* had told of the decline of Earth's technological development due to the rise of the Natural Movement. Nevertheless, it felt odd to return to humanity's birthplace and find it more backward than its deep space colony.

"You know Aubriot," Cherry replied. "He's all for attacking the Scythians as soon as possible, before they get a foothold. He would do it alone, only even *he* understands it would be suicide."

"Before they get a foothold? They already have one. And what would we attack them with? Our bare hands? Firing from the *Sirocco* is out of the question. That ship's our only way home."

"You don't need to convince me how stupid it would be. We do need to get away from this place. I don't think watching the Scythians is going to tell us anything. Maybe we'll leave in the morning. I would have liked to figure some things out but I've given up."

"Like what?"

"Like why there are no doors in the domes, for one thing. It was the same with the Scythian city in Suddene. No doors. Only soft, squishy material you could push through. There doesn't seem to be any of that stuff in their construction material."

"Maybe it's permeable to gases. The Scythians can't breathe Earth's atmosphere."

"Okay, but how are they planning on getting in and out? Unless they don't intend to ever leave their domes they need exits. That wall looks solid."

"Just because it looks solid, doesn't mean it is," Wilder countered. "There might be seams that are invisible to human eyes."

"Yeah, you're probably right."

A figure appeared at the end of the street. Cherry opened the door and beckoned.

A moment later Aubriot stepped through the entrance. "You disappeared in a hurry."

"I didn't have a reason to wait around. We weren't seeing anything new."

"How would you know if they did anything new if you weren't there to see it?"

"So did you notice something different?"

"That's not the point."

"Ugh, get yourself something to eat. Wilder's found a new store."

Wilder pointed toward the kitchen. "It's all in there."

Aubriot strode past them, glowering.

"One thing's for sure," Cherry went on, "if the Scythians wanted us dead we would already be checked out. There's no stopping their spiders. Once they get a whiff of a scent they follow it, slicing through everything in their paths until they..." She swallowed, recalling seeing Garwin hacked to pieces and the loss of her own left arm. "If the Scythians wanted to eradicate all humanity they would have started by now. They have something else in mind."

"You haven't figured it out?" Aubriot had emerged from the kitchen with a sausage of cured meat. He took a bite and leaned a shoulder on the wall. Somehow, he could chew and yet maintain his usual supercilious expression.

Cherry glared at him, refusing to take the bait. They'd been romantic partners, of a sort, for so many years. Of all the Concordians she'd been one of the few prepared to give this Earthman the time of day. She'd allowed him into her heart, prickly and arrogant though he was, and in return he'd betrayed her. It was a betrayal he'd never apologized for, never even appeared to see a need to apologize for, and she'd long ago moved past the point at which she could ever forgive him.

Yet circumstances forced her to be around him. Despite all his many, many faults, Aubriot was their best military tactician. If she and the people she loved were going to survive, she had to tolerate his presence.

Wilder gave in. "Are you going to enlighten us?"

Aubriot smirked. "Don't you remember the Scythians' demands you refused, Cherry? Before they launched the biocide?"

"Oh, shit." She moved from the window and slumped into a chair, putting her head in her hands.

"What?" Wilder asked. "What were the demands?"

It had been the worst moment of Cherry's life. After the Scythians had returned to Concordia and annihilated Oceanside, they'd made a proposal. The Leader at the time, Meredith, had wanted to accept but Cherry had overruled her, firing off a refusal. Her decision had resulted in countless deaths, including most of the peaceful Fila. The aliens' biocide had just about destroyed life on Concordia, and all because she hadn't wanted to give in to the Scythians' demands.

Aubriot poked her shoulder. "What's your answer going to be this time?"

"To what question?" Wilder insisted.

Cherry replied woodenly, "They want to live here. They want to colonize Earth, with human beings as their slaves."

"And they can do it," said Aubriot. "On this piss-poor planet, with its Iron Age tech and Neanderthal natives, it'll be easy. It's over. Earth's screwed."

Three

The head of the Global Advancement Association was a stooped old man. To Cherry's eyes Dakarai Buka looked even older than Ethan had when he died. Perhaps late eighties or early nineties. A strong puff of wind could blow him over. That explained why he hadn't been present when the Earthers had returned Kes. He was too frail to be riding horses, flying around in helis, or even waiting out on the prairie to meet strange humans from another world.

Naturally, he spoke no English. He relied on the Earther translator, Itai, to communicate with the Concordians, as they did with him. Itai sat next to the old man, leaning close as he listened to the quiet words. He was as silver-haired as Buka but perhaps thirty years younger, ruddy cheeks above his clipped gray beard giving the impression of vigorous middle age.

When Buka stopped speaking Itai gave a nod and turned to the room. "The GAA has received a report indicating the Scythians may have begun to attack. Two people have gone missing in the vicinity of one of the domes. A mother and father. Their sons managed to evade capture by hiding in a hole too small for the Scythian to enter."

Vessey asked, "When did this happen?"

"Two days ago."

"Why have we only just been informed?" Vessey looked nervous. She'd been all for abandoning the Earthers and returning to Concordia the minute the Scythians had appeared. It had only been Aubriot's absolute refusal and strong arguments against it that had dissuaded her.

"The region is remote," Itai replied. "We only received news of the incident ourselves a few hours ago."

"What else do you know?" asked Aubriot. "When did the attack take place? What do the Scythians look like?"

After Itai translated, the head of the GAA laid a bony hand, freckled with sunspots, on the man's arm. The translator leaned toward him again, and then said, "Mr Buka would like to know why you're asking about the appearance of the Scythians. We thought you were familiar with these aliens."

"We've never—" Aubriot began.

But Vessey talked over him. "No Scythians have ever landed on Concordia during the colony's existence. The assaults on our planet have taken place from orbit or via automated devices."

The old man smiled wryly and he spoke again.

Itai translated, "So Earth is honored by this special privilege."

"They've landed because Earth is weak," Aubriot said loudly. "It doesn't have the tech to fight back. But it's more than that. When the Scythians discovered humans living on Concordia they tried to wipe us out. You see, our planet used to be theirs a long time ago, before they ruined it and made it uninhabitable to their form of life. Finding another intelligent civilization on it upset them. Only they couldn't kill us all easily, so they changed their minds and decided they would re-colonize, with us as their personal servants. We turned down their kind offer, and they tried to sterilize the planet instead. You're lucky they didn't do that here. We survived the biocide attack with mass vaccination. You'll never manage the same thing on Earth. Concordia has a much smaller population and better transportation. If the Scythians launch their biocide on Earth, it'll destroy you and all life. They don't seem to want to do that—yet. They've switched to the colonization plan again. That attack you heard about—they must have abducted those people in order to study them. They'll need to know all about our anatomy if they want to control us."

By the time he reached the end of his short speech and Itai had translated it, a leaden silence fell in the room. No one seemed able to speak. Cherry cast her gaze around the small space. The GAA had taken over a subterranean building that had to be centuries old. The concrete walls were stained and worn shiny by the passage of bodies. What had the place been in its previous life? Offices? A prison? Aubriot had said this region had once been very cold, which explained why construction had been underground. The Earthers had figured out how to repair the ancient geothermal energy mechanism to supply power.

Buka spoke.

Itai translated, "We would like to know the Concordians' plan for helping us defend ourselves against this invasion."

Vessey spread her hands wide. "You must understand, there's very little we can do. As I've explained before, it was fortunate that the Scythians didn't attack our ship when they arrived. They seem to have recognized the weapon we carry, which is the same type used to defeat them in the past. If we fire on their ships we will inflict significant damage. That's what seems to be currently holding them back. Yet if they do attack, they will surely destroy us in the end. We're at stalemate for now. How long the situation will last, I cannot tell. My guess is that the Scythians have more ships on the way. They're only waiting for them to arrive before removing the *Sirocco* from the equation."

"So you're going to leave?" Itai demanded.

Though Buka hadn't spoken, his frown indicated the translator had expressed his sentiment accurately.

"Nothing's been decided yet."

"You're going to abandon Earth, your home planet?"

Vessey looked uncomfortable. "The expedition to colonize deep space set out from here centuries ago. Concordians have no memories of Earth. They view Concordia as their home planet. And we have plenty of problems of our own. The *Sirocco* was heavily delayed on her journey. Our planet desperately needs the material we gathered if our people are to survive."

"So now you've got what you need you will leave us to our fate? Your own kindred?"

"If we could help, we would, but I'm not sure..."

All through this exchange, Aubriot's jaw muscle had been twitching, to Cherry's amusement.

Should the *Sirocco* have departed at the first sight of the aliens? Probably. It would have been the sensible thing to do, given all the points Vessey made. But the captain wasn't expressing the majority opinion of the ship's personnel. She didn't dare give the order to leave when so many Concordians were against it. Despite what Vessey said, most of them wanted to help Earth. That was the reason the captain had stuck around. She didn't have the authority or strength of will to enforce an unpopular decision. Aubriot might have managed it without significant repercussions, but not her.

What was his take on the situation? He'd seemed hell bent on fighting the Scythians at first, in his typical antagonistic manner. But recently he'd appeared to begin to change his mind. Though combative, he was also pragmatic. Whatever stance he took in the end it would come down to one thing: it would suit him personally.

Buka said via Itai, "Where do we go from here? Must we plead or beg you to stay and help? You have so much to offer—technology, skills, and knowledge that has been lost to us. Will you really deny us your aid? Surely there must be something you can do."

"We will continue to monitor the situation," Vessey said tightly. "The news about the abduction was useful. Please keep us informed about any further details that arrive and anything else you find out about the Scyth—"

Aubriot interrupted, "You didn't answer my questions earlier. Do you have a description of the aliens? When did the attack take place?"

"It took place at night," Itai replied. "The boys who escaped could only say the creature was large, about two and a half meters tall and wide."

"Two and a half meters *wide*?" Cherry echoed.

"That's what the children said."

She couldn't imagine what the Scythians looked like. The only large aliens she'd met had been at the Galactic Assembly. But that had been half a lifetime ago, and the Assembly was half a galaxy away. It would have been nice to have their allies around, if not to offer military backup then at least to give advice. Humanity was on its own, however. The distress signal the *Sirocco* had sent out long ago when the jump drive failed had gone unanswered.

Buka made several more attempts to get Vessey to commit her ship's resources to Earth's defense, but the captain remained firm on wanting to wait and assess further developments. The meeting broke up without any decisions having been made. The old man rose unsteadily to his feet and Itai helped him from the room.

Vessey sunk her head into her hands.

Aubriot said, "You're gonna have to piss or get off the pot."

She shot him an angry look. "Thanks for your support just now."

"What did you want me to say? You know you don't have the backing of the crew."

"Well if you or anyone else has any suggestions about helping the Earthers I'm all ears."

"Cherry and I are still investigating the Scythians. Until we know their weaknesses it's hard to develop a plan to defeat them."

"I seriously doubt that's even possible."

"If we can't defeat them on Earth," Cherry interposed, "how will we defeat them on Concordia? Sooner or later they'll go back to see if anyone's still alive, and then they'll finish the job they started."

"Good point," said Aubriot. "We could learn valuable lessons here."

Vessey lifted her gaze to the ceiling. "The kind of lessons that involve a lot of bloodshed, no doubt."

"Hopefully more of the Scythians' than ours."

"If they even have blood," Cherry added.

Vessey rose to her feet. "I'm going back to the ship, providing she still exists. Keep me updated about anything you find out."

"Before you go," said Cherry, "Wilder had an idea she wanted me to run past you. She said she wants to go with Niall to find the source of the signal we detected near the seed bank."

"Why does she want to do that?"

Cherry shrugged. "It might be significant."

"I don't see how. The Earthers themselves didn't know about it. It must be something left over from before the collapse of civilization, like the seed store."

"Let her do it," said Aubriot. "It isn't like she'll be any use if it comes to a fight."

Cherry spluttered, "Wilder helped develop and maintain the armaments on Concordia!"

"Yeah, but there aren't any armaments here."

"Tell her from me," said Vessey, "that anything she can do that might contribute to Earth's independence is welcome, but she cannot use the shuttle, and only she and Niall are to go. Our resources are already stretched to their limit." She left the room.

"That went about as well as I expected," said Aubriot.

"Which part?" Cherry asked.

"All of it."

"I guess we couldn't expect anything better. I'm going to find Wilder and tell her what Vessey said."

She stood up to leave, but Aubriot grabbed her hand. Stiffening, she halted and carefully pulled it from his grip.

He rolled his eyes. "After you've talked to Wilder, have you got anything else you have to do?"

"Why?" she asked warily.

"I was wondering if you wanted to hang out."

"Are you kidding?"

"Don't look at me like that. It's a reasonable question."

"It would have been a reasonable question twenty years ago, before we knew each other properly. Before you..." She swallowed. After all this time, the memory still hurt.

"Christ, you know how to hold a grudge, don't you? That should be water under the bridge by now. Can't you let bygones be bygones?"

In answer, Cherry stalked from the room.

"You fucked Kes, didn't you?!" Aubriot's angry response rang out. "I know you did. You act like you're so superior, but you're no better than me."

FOUR

"What *is* this place?" Niall asked.

Wilder replied, "You mean, what did it used to be?"

The field of broken concrete spread out for hundreds of meters. Twisted shards, uplifted by tree roots, protruded from the ground, and thorny weeds covered the gray surface in dense patches, but it was clear the site had once been large and significant. A network of buildings had occupied a part of it, though now the walls only stood at waist height.

"Your guess is as good as mine," she went on. "It must be from Aubriot's time."

Niall shook his head. "It's hard to believe he's that old."

"He hasn't *lived* all those years. He spent the journey on the *Nova Fortuna* in cryosleep, then when we went to the Galactic Assembly time dilation hit us, and then—"

"Oh yeah, I was forgetting you went on that trip too. So you're how much older than me?" He was trying to keep his expression deadpan but a cheeky smile leaked through nonetheless.

"Do you mean chronologically or emotionally and intellectually?"

Laughter burst from Niall. "Come here, old lady." He pulled her into his arms. "You're older and better than me in every way and I don't mind admitting it."

"Huh, took you long enough."

They kissed until the roar of an approaching engine broke through their pleasant distraction. The *Sirocco's* shuttle was a bright spot of light in the blue sky.

Wilder and Niall backed off a little more. The shuttle settled on a relatively empty spot, the engine cut out, and the noise died. A moment later the hatch opened and Zapata beckoned them, calling out, "Don't hang around on the concrete. It isn't made to absorb heat."

They ran over the hot surface and climbed up to the open hatch.

"Thanks for helping us out," Wilder panted.

"No problem," the pilot replied. "But you understand I can't wait around for you, right? It'll be a while before Vessey notices the shuttle's missing but if she does I'll be in a world of shit."

"Sure, we get it. We've packed enough supplies to last us a few days."

"You think it's going to take you that long?"

Niall replied, "We don't have any idea what we might find. We might be finished in a day or a week, or we might need even more time."

"Well, comm me when you need picking up and I'll get there as soon as I can, the captain's diversions permitting."

"Thanks," said Wilder. "We appreciate it."

"I don't know what Vessey was thinking," said Zapata, returning to the pilot's cabin. "How are you supposed to go so far north on a planet with virtually no long-distance transportation?"

"We approached the GAA for one of their helis but they said they couldn't help us." Wilder settled into a seat and fastened the belt. "They said they're in too much demand. They're booked up months ahead."

Zapata halted at the cabin entrance. "Figures. It's really something to see how low Earth has sunk since our ancestors left it, right? This place used to be an airport, with hundreds of airplanes flying in and out every day."

"What's an airplane?" Niall asked.

"Like a heli but with wings and wheels."

"Huh?"

Zapata waved a hand dismissively. "Never mind. I'll explain another time."

———

It had been months since Wilder had been to the island where the ancient seed vault was located, yet nothing seemed to have changed. Zapata landed at the coast as he had when she'd been one of the party to search for the seed store. Kes had been in the team too. An ache expanded in her chest. It was still hard to believe he was gone. As she walked with Niall away from the landing site and into the forest, the noise of the shuttle's takeoff behind them, she recalled the older man's silver-streaked red hair and kind, cheerful expression.

He'd been a good friend. He'd been there for her at her lowest moments, the parent or older brother she'd never had, and she struggled to accept she would never see him again.

"Are you okay?" Niall asked, watching her.

She heaved a sigh. "Let's find this signal beacon."

She took out the locator from her pack. The signal originated in a spot beyond the seed vault, on the other side of a low mountain. Trees grew thickly up the slope and all around. With no tracks on the uninhabited island, they were in for a tough trek.

"It's that way." She pointed directly at the mountain. "Do you want to go up and over or take the long way and go around?"

Niall squinted up at the peak. "I'm not sure that up and over isn't the longest route." He peered at the screen. "Do you think the signal might be coming from the far side of the seed vault? Maybe we could go through the mountain. That would certainly be easier than trying to force a route through the forest."

"I didn't think of that." She studied the map more closely. "I suppose it's possible. When I came here before we didn't go right into the depths of the vault. We found the seeds we needed and left. I don't know how big it is. It might take up the whole mountain." She lifted her gaze to the slope. "That would make it huge."

"On the other hand, why would the people who built the vault have set up a signal beacon so far from the entrance? It doesn't make a lot of sense."

"Nothing about the signal makes any sense. That's what makes it so intriguing."

"I hope," said Niall, "after we go to all the trouble of investigating it, it's worth the effort."

"You're getting ahead of yourself. I'm just hoping we find whatever's making it."

"We won't find anything if we don't get moving. What do you think? Up and over, around, or through?"

Recalling the skeletons of desperate people she'd seen on her previous trip, Wilder didn't relish the idea of re-entering the mountain. "Let's try going around. It'll be chilly on higher ground and harder to find somewhere flat to camp."

"You don't want to go into the vault?"

"I will, but as a last resort. It isn't nice in there."

"I'll take your word for it."

They lifted their packs onto their backs and set off, pushing through dense scrub. Niall went first, using his heavier bulk to forge a path. Brambles snagged at their clothes and low branches made them stoop. Wilder didn't remember it being this hard. She guessed the original party must have been lucky, stumbling across the remains of the original track leading to the vault entrance.

They toiled on for an hour before Niall halted. "Do you know where we are?"

The higher ground was out of sight. Vegetation crowded so closely that visibility was limited to three or four meters. Wilder was scratched, sore, and tired. "I thought you did. You're the leader here."

"You're the one who's been here before."

"Not to this part. We went directly to the vault."

"Well, my question stands. Where the hell are we?"

Wilder surveyed the surroundings. "This isn't going to work. We need someone who's used to wandering around in wild places. We've barely stepped out of a lab all our lives."

"Shall we go back?"

"I don't think we have a choice."

An upside to their mistake was that their return passage was easy to find, marked by the crushed ground cover and disturbed and broken foliage. Another upside was that they arrived at their starting point in half the time of their outward journey. Soon, they were looking up at the mountain once more from the original spot.

Niall said, "Unless you fancy doing the same again, only climbing, it looks like we have to enter the vault."

"Enter the vault? You make it sound like a sim." In truth, the prospect did hold fantastical potentialities. "Just so you know, there are human remains in there. It's creepy and cold."

"The dead can't hurt us. Let's do it. Do you remember the way?"

Wilder led him in the direction she roughly remembered. When they passed the piece of metal grid suspended high on a tree branch, remnant of the ancient walkway, she knew she was on the right track. Within another few minutes, the broken double doors gaped open before them, revealing darkness.

The sun was grazing the forest canopy.

She asked, "Do you want to make camp here and go inside tomorrow? It'll be night soon."

"All the more reason to go in now. We can bed down in there if we get too tired to go on."

"Yeah, but..." She couldn't think of a rational objection. "Okay." She retrieved her headlamp and put it on.

Niall did the same. "You go first this time."

"*Thanks.*" She ventured into the dark.

The seed vault was just as chilly and lonely as she remembered it. Scattered remains of torn seed packets and the boxes that had contained them littered the floor. Animal and human scavengers had taken the seeds. The Concordian team had been scavengers too, of a kind, though they needed the seeds for planting, not eating. The intact packets they'd found were now safely aboard the *Sirocco*, only awaiting the journey to a new planet to fulfill their biological destiny.

As Wilder pushed deeper into the mountain, memories of her earlier visit flooded back. She recalled the passageway where they'd found the skeletons and wordlessly guided Niall away from it. The vault was vast. She realized the first time she'd visited her party had been extremely lucky to stumble across the cache of undisturbed seeds. Everywhere else seemed ransacked.

After an hour or longer of wandering, a smooth wall confronted them and a set of stairs led straight down. It seemed obvious to descend. If there was a way through to the signal site it was here, though for some unknown reason her guts tightened at the notion. Perhaps it was only that they'd walked in the dark for so long and so deep into the mountain, under tens of thousands of tonnes of rock. She stepped down the stairs and Niall followed unquestioningly. He didn't know this area was new territory to her.

The metal treads resounded with their footsteps, perhaps the first human footfalls that had hit them in centuries.

"Are you sure this is safe?" Niall asked.

"Absolutely not. Hold onto the handrail in case the treads collapse."

The concrete shaft was square and the stairs ran around the edges. The light from their headlamps didn't penetrate the central well.

"This is odd," Niall commented.

"I know. Where are the storage rooms? Where are the seeds? What was the point of this part of the vault? Why would the builders make it hard for people to reach whatever's down there?"

They continued to descend. The place had the feeling of something secret, an area deliberately hidden. Perhaps the seeds stored at the bottom were precious. Or were they dangerous?

The beam from Wilder's headlamp hit a concrete floor.

They'd reached the bottom of the stairs. Stepping from the final tread brought them to a plain, square landing with a single, unadorned metal door, tightly shut.

"*Shit*," Niall breathed. White bones draped in dusty rags gleamed in the rays from his lamp. "These are the remains you told me about?"

"They're *different* ones. Yuck." Wilder tried the door but it resisted her.

"He or she must have been trying to get in."

"So it seems. We don't have a way in either. This is a dead end. We should go back."

"Don't give up so easily." Niall stepped to the door and also tried the handle.

Unsurprisingly, the door didn't open.

"What's this?" As Wilder had moved out of his way, her headlamp lit up a section of wall displaying a series of numbers. Some numbers were set in grids, others were in lines. Beneath them all rows of bumps protruded from the surface.

"A puzzle!" Niall exclaimed. "They're all puzzles." He pushed one of the buttons. "It's mechanical. I bet if we put in the correct answers the door opens."

"Cool." Wilder assessed the first puzzle, her feelings of fear and foreboding dropping away.

Niall leaned his head close to hers as he also took in the details of the problem.

3 2 1 0
1 9 2 0
0 8 1 ?
7 5 2 4

Wilder got it first. "The missing number is two. Add together the first two digits then multiply by two. The answer's six." Without waiting for Niall's agreement she pressed the relevant key.

The next puzzle consisted of two rows of numbers.

? 7 2 7 3 7
? 7 5 7 6 7

Niall said, "Seventeen, twenty-seven, thirty-seven... It's one and four." He pressed the keys.

Wilder was already working on the third problem.

So they continued all the way down.

"These are too easy," Wilder complained.

"I don't know how that dead person couldn't figure them out," Niall agreed.

They reached the bumps.

"Were these for blind people?" Wilder ran her fingertips over them. Next to the rows of bumps was a single, plain button. "How can we show our answer? We can only either press the button or not press it."

While they'd been working no sound had come from the door so she'd assumed it hadn't opened. She tried the handle again in case she was wrong. The door remained locked.

Niall had closed his eyes and was touching the buttons. "Can't feel anything unusual."

"Let me try."

The bumps were shaped as an irregular pyramid. One bump sat at the top and another sat beneath it. Below those were two bumps in a row. Three bumps were in the third row, then five, then eight, then...

"Ugh," Wilder said, annoyed at herself for taking so long to understand. "It's the Fibonacci sequence."

"Of course. How many are in the last row?"

"Thirteen."

Niall pressed the plain key twenty-one times.
With a click, the door unlocked.

FIVE

The idea was for the Concordians to grab a Scythian of their own. The aliens were increasing their abductions. All over the globe, people were disappearing. The attacks always took place at night and targeted individuals out alone or in small groups, usually in remote, rural places.

Since the aliens' brief visit two years ago, the majority of Earthers had moved their activities underground wherever possible. The situation was similar to how it had been on Concordia: with little to no defensive capability, the best strategy was to hide. Yet a subterranean lifestyle was impossible for many. Topography, lack of digging and construction equipment or the necessary skills prevented it. Other communities had underestimated the threat, and though the vanishing of their members had raised their awareness, their efforts were last-minute. Plenty of Earthers remained vulnerable to attacks.

When yet another report of an abduction arrived from the GAA, Aubriot's response had been *Two can play at that game.* It would send the message that Earth wasn't going to roll over and accept defeat without a fight. It would also give the Earthers vital information about exactly what they were up against.

As well as Cherry and Aubriot, the Concordian team to execute the mission, leaving from a wood half a klick from a Scythian dome, consisted of Maddox, Dragan, Maura, and Acton.

Cherry watched Maddox turning over a pulse rifle in her hands. Even after all these years, she found it hard to look at the woman without a certain image popping into her mind. Maddox had never spoken to her about the incident. She hadn't apologized, but nor had she tried to rub it in Cherry's face, though the sly smile she'd given at the time was also something Cherry had never been able to erase from her memory.

Maddox looked up, and her gaze drifted to the space where Cherry's left arm should have been. "Are you *sure* you're coming too?"

"Why wouldn't I?" Cherry retorted hotly.

"Cherry's one of our best fighters," said Aubriot. "She was at the Battle of Sidhe, defending it against the Scythian spiders. Of course she's coming."

Like Maddox, none of the other team members had received extensive military training. Maura and Acton were fellow scientists, and Dragan was an engineer. Cherry had tried to dissuade him from volunteering. As one of the people to design and build the *Sirocco*, she'd felt his skills were too valuable to put at risk. But he'd insisted and, after registering the desperation in his eyes, she'd relented.

She guessed he wanted to atone for what he'd done. Or rather, what he'd nearly done. As one of the Final Day Five—the apocalypse cult that had formed during their long space voyage—he'd come close to killing Wilder. At the last minute he'd come to his senses, protecting her from his deluded associates. Wilder had forgiven him and they were friends again, but maybe playing an active role in Earth's defense was his way of forgiving himself.

Aubriot said, "We have time for some training before we set off. Maddox and Dragan, come with me. Maura and Acton, you're with Cherry."

Cherry took her pair to the edge of the woods and proceeded to deliver a severely truncated version of the basic training she and Aubriot had developed years ago on Concordia. At the time, she had never imagined she would be repeating herself on Earth.

They had three hours before they set off. The plan was to reach the Scythian dome at midday. They hoped the night-time abductions meant the aliens were nocturnal, so most would be resting at that time. If they couldn't grab one, they should at least be able to get a good look at the creatures and the interior of a dome. The purpose of the structures was clearly to provide the aliens with a breathable atmosphere, but other than that no one knew what went on inside them.

Was it crazy to launch an attack in broad daylight? Perhaps. It went against the grain. Dangerous activities were usually safer done in darkness. But maybe it wouldn't make any difference. The Scythians had developed interstellar space travel. The idea that they wouldn't have systems to detect movements around their domes day *and* night wasn't feasible.

Cherry spent most of the available time in target practice and familiarizing her pair with their armored EVA suits. There had not been much time to develop and manufacture the suits during the rush to leave Concordia, so the *Sirocco* only carried a handful, but they would be essential for the attack.

Too soon, the preparation time was up.

Aubriot approached through the trees, asking, "You guys ready?"

"As we'll ever be," Maura replied.

"Cool. Let's get to the heli."

The Earthers' heli was larger than their usual ones, large enough to hold six passengers. It would drop them close to a dome. There seemed little danger of the Scythians firing upon it on its approach. The aliens had ignored air vessels passing over them. What would happen after humans attempted to break into a dome was another matter.

The pilot only nodded as they boarded. The language barrier remained a problem. Itai, the Earthers' translator, had said he was teaching others the Concordians' ancient version of English, but it would take time until they were proficient. For now, everyone was confined to hand gestures and facial expressions to communicate. Cherry hoped the pilot truly understood that if the mission was successful and the Concordians emerged with a Scythian, he might have to risk fire to land and collect them.

As was the case with all the Scythian domes, this one sat on open land, far from any human habitation. The ivory dome was a blister on the green landscape, strangely incongruous. For the first time, Cherry saw the upper surface, which was smooth and complete.

How did the aliens leave it? They had to have a way. No one was in any doubt they were responsible for the disappearances.

"You sure that stuff's gonna work?" Acton asked Aubriot nervously.

Aubriot shrugged and lifted the package on his lap. "I've been told it's an effective explosive. Whether it'll punch a hole in the side of the dome, who knows?"

The Earther pilot said something and then the heli plummeted from the sky, eliciting gasps from the passengers.

"Visors down," Cherry ordered. "This is it."

As soon as the landing skids touched ground the Concordians piled out. The pilot had set them down roughly fifty meters from the dome, as instructed. Aubriot raced toward the structure, carrying the explosive. The heli whined as the pilot took off. Cherry tightly gripped the detonator.

The others seemed frozen. Had they forgotten the plan already?

"Get down!" she urged.

Snapped from their trance, the four Concordians squatted and turned their backs to the dome.

Cherry scanned the structure. The smooth surface remained whole.

She comm'd Aubriot. "Not seeing any response so far. You're good to go."

He reached the dome.

Still, the aliens didn't react.

Aubriot slapped the package against the wall so hard Cherry winced. Intellectually, she knew the explosive wouldn't go off without a detonator, but that didn't stop her from *feeling* it would.

Then he was on his way back. "Blow it."

"Not yet. It isn't safe. You'll get hit by the shockwave."

"Do it. We don't know how long we have."

She set her jaw, refusing to answer. Damn the man and his stupid heroics.

"Cherry! Bloody well do as you're told."

He'd almost reached her.

"Shut up and get down." She swiveled, crouched, and pressed the button.

At the same time as she heard the *Boom*, a force knocked her on her face. The sharp-edged trigger box was underneath her belly. She scrambled onto her knees and tossed it to one side before turning around for a look at the dome.

A dark, jagged-edged hole gaped in the wall. Dusty haze filled the air, and shards of white material were spread far and wide.

They'd done it.

"My suit's leaking," said Acton. "I think a piece of the dome hit me."

"You know what to do." Cherry leapt to her feet.

Acton would run back to the cover of the forest and wait to be picked up.

One man down already, she sped with the others toward the hole. Nothing was visible within. The Scythians didn't appear to light their dwellings. So they were definitely nocturnal?

Something appeared at the hole. At first, Cherry couldn't make it out. Its form was so odd, so unlike anything she'd ever seen, she couldn't take it in. Its skin was bronze and papery and stretched tightly over a skeletal frame. Two large, white eyes, bisected by a vertical black line, stared out.

A pulse round flashed. Aubriot had fired.

The creature was gone.

A beat later, Aubriot was at the hole. He halted, waiting for the others to catch up. In another second Cherry was at his side. Together, rifles lifted, they peered in.

The interior was pitch black. It seemed to absorb sunlight, reflecting nothing. Cherry switched her visor to night vision. Now, she could see a little, but it was only another wall a couple of meters away. It appeared to ring the dome— an inner layer of protection.

"It's full of CO2," Aubriot remarked.

She hadn't noticed, but her HUD agreed. Gas was pouring from the breach.

"Dragan's with me," said Aubriot. "We'll go right. Cherry, you go left with Maddox and Maura."

"No, Maddox is with you."

"Not since you lost Acton."

There was no time for arguing. Cherry roughly gestured for the woman to follow her and stepped into the dome. Taking point, she walked into the dark passageway. No aliens were in sight but she couldn't see far due to the curvature of the dome.

Maura asked, "Did anyone get a good look at that thing?"

"Not me," replied Maddox. "I only saw—"

"Stay focused," Cherry snapped. "If anything moves, shoot, remember? And if it's near enough and hurt enough, grab it."

"Yeah, we remember," Maddox replied sarcastically.

The CO_2 increased as they walked farther from the breach. Everything else stayed the same. The white outer walls were a rich, light-absorbing black on the inside, mirrored by the interior wall, which extended overhead, running parallel as it curved beyond view.

One minute. That was the agreed period of time they would spend trying to capture an alien. Even so short a time was highly risky considering that the hole they'd blown was their only exit.

Forty-five seconds had passed. How far had they come? Perhaps only thirty meters. They'd been walking slowly.

"See anything?" Aubriot comm'd.

"Not a thing. You?"

"Zilch."

"Get ready to leave in ten seconds."

"I might just—"

"No. That's not what we agreed."

"But we might not get—"

A shriek, quickly cut off, broke through his words.

"What was that?" Aubriot asked.

"I thought it was from your end."

"Maddox!" Maura yelled. "Where's Maddox gone?"

Cherry swung around. Maura was alone. The passageway was empty.

"She was right behind me," Maura gasped, "and then she wasn't."

"Maddox has gone missing?" asked Aubriot.

Cherry ignored him.

It didn't seem possible that an alien could have snuck up behind them silently, snatched Maddox, and retreated out of sight without Maura noticing. She would have turned immediately she heard the other woman cry out. The Scythian would have to be lightning fast to do it.

"We're on our way," said Aubriot. "Get out of there before they take someone else."

So quick to abandon your girlfriend?

Cherry pushed the spiteful thought aside.

How had the Scythians taken Maddox?

The answer niggled at the edges of her mind. It was something to do with the Scythian city on Concordia.

She had it.

"Maura, go back. When you meet Aubriot, tell him... Never mind. Just go back. Now."

There was no time to check Maura had followed her order. Cherry punched the interior wall. As she'd predicted, her fist sank in, followed by her arm up to her elbow. She leaned her shoulder against it and pressed with her right knee. Slowly but surely her body sank into the spongy substance. Then she was through it.

Maddox was vigorously struggling with one of the bronze-skinned creatures. It held her around the waist with its... Whatever they were, they were not arms. And it didn't have hands but long claws. The thing bent over her and tugged at her suit. The claws scythed through the armor and the suit split like overripe fruit. Cherry's mind flew to the Scythian spiders and Garwin's horrific death. Maddox's struggles became more frantic. Without oxygen, in a couple of minutes she would be dead.

The creature didn't seem to have noticed Cherry. It was too preoccupied with killing Maddox.

Where was its head, its brain? Near the eyes, presumably.

Cherry took aim. She was in grave danger of hitting Maddox too, but if she delayed the woman was dead anyhow.

She fired.

The Scythian fell, but it didn't die. It writhed on the floor like a mad thing, bucking, jerking, whirling.

Maddox took a step past it and its claws raked the leg of her suit. She screamed as blood ran from the gashes, but she didn't stop until she reached Cherry's side. "Where did you come from? How do we get out of here?"

"This way," Cherry replied.

The Scythian seemed to be weakening. Its movements had slowed to twitches but it crawled. Cherry shoved Maddox into the wall face first and pushed with all her might. The sponge absorbed her until she was gone.

Cherry faced the alien for a good look at it.

She finally understood about the Scythian city on Concordia.

The creature was dying. Its eyes slowly opened and closed.

She fired off another shot.

It was still.

As she emerged on the other side of the wall, she found herself suddenly grabbed. Aubriot lifted her onto his shoulder and began to pound down the passageway.

"Put me down!" she yelled. "Put me down! Stars, I can run, you moron."

Maddox must have gone ahead. Cherry's night vision picked up the residual heat of splashes of blood on the floor.

They were outside, and still Aubriot didn't set her on her feet. She was forced to let him carry her all the way back to the waiting heli. He threw her into a seat and then climbed aboard, slamming the door. Instantly, the heli lifted into the air. Cherry was thrown to the side as it banked.

They were all here.

Acton sat at the back of the craft, Dragan beside him. Maura and Maddox sat in front. Maddox's visor was up and her face deathly pale as blood ran from her wounds. Aubriot was beside Cherry, staring out the window. They hadn't managed to capture an alien, but they'd made it into and out of one of their domes and—

"Shit," Aubriot said, "would you look at that!"

Before even following the direction of his gaze, Cherry knew what must be happening. Her close look at a Scythian had revealed a key fact. It explained the weird configuration of their ancient city, all walls and no doors. It explained a lot of things.

A circular opening had appeared at the top of the dome, and the aliens were emerging from it. Tinted transparent spheres over their heads and tanks on their backs—no doubt supplying the CO_2 they breathed—they beat their thin-skinned wings and flew.

Six

The purpose of the puzzles at the door remained unclear to Wilder as she walked with Niall down the tunnel beyond it. What was clear was the puzzles were part of an intricate mechanical lock but why they'd been placed there was a mystery. "I still can't believe that person at the entrance couldn't figure them out."

"You aren't *still* thinking about that?"

"I can't understand it. It's bugging me."

"Really? I couldn't tell. You've only been talking about nothing else for the last five minutes. How about thinking about something different? Like where this tunnel is taking us."

She poked her elbow into his side. "One problem at a time. I'll work on the door lock, you concentrate on the cryptic destination."

"Seriously," said Niall, suddenly grave, "we could be walking into danger. That was probably the reason for the puzzles you're obsessing about. They must have been designed to keep people out. They were a safety measure."

"Then they weren't a very good one. We made it through without too much difficulty."

"That skeleton didn't."

"No. But why?"

"Because he or she couldn't solve them. That's obvious."

Wilder chewed her lip. "Do you think there was something wrong with that person? Like they had low cognitive function?"

"What's the point of speculating?" Niall added, after a pause, "Not everyone would be able to solve those puzzles so easily. And if you didn't know the Fibonacci sequence, it might be hard to figure out."

"Yeah, but that person *died* trying to solve it. They took however long they had left and still didn't understand it."

"They might not have had very long left. Hey, look!"

Wilder swept her headlamp in the direction Niall's was pointing. The monotonous concrete of the dusty tunnel was broken by a door.

"And this one doesn't have anything to solve to open it." Niall grasped the doorknob and turned it.

"You shouldn't just open a door like that," Wilder chided. "Wasn't it you who was saying we could be walking into danger?"

The interior reminded her of a starship cabin. A single bunk stood against the wall, the bedclothes neatly made. There was a desk and chair and a small cupboard, presumably for personal items and clothes. Above the cupboard was an empty shelf. Despite its tidiness, the room had an abandoned, forgotten air.

"Well," said Niall, "at least we have somewhere comfortable to sleep tonight."

Wilder gave a shiver. "I think I'd rather sleep on the floor in a sleeping bag." She crossed the room to the bed and touched the covers. The fibers parted under her fingertips. Experimentally, she pushed both hands down on the mattress. It sank beneath her touch and she found herself pressing against the bed frame. "This place is incredibly old."

"Is that so surprising? The seed vault was built in the days before the appearance of the Natural Movement, right?"

"It was, but something gave me the impression this area is newer, an add-on, you know? At a later date."

"Maybe you're wrong."

"Maybe." Wilder bent down to open the cupboard door, but it was jammed shut with rust. "I bet there's nothing inside it anyway." She stood up. "This was someone's room once, but apart from the bedding there's no sign of their things. The shelf and desk are empty. There are no pictures on the walls. Whoever lived here packed up their stuff and left."

"Let's carry on looking around," Niall said. "If the rest of it is as neglected as this room there hasn't been anyone here for a long time, so it's completely safe."

As they walked down the corridor they encountered similar rooms, all containing single bunks and minimal furniture, all in a state of extreme age. Unlike the seed vault, the place was so far underground no rodents or bugs had colonized it. It was lifeless.

Wilder began to long for the surface. "How big do you think this is?"

"We've walked a long way. Farther than the diameter of the mountain at its base, I would say. We're now under the surface on the other side, which means it's impossible to guess how big this place is. It could extend the width of the island."

"Have we passed the signal beacon yet?"

"I don't know. I lost the signal not long after we entered the vault."

A pair of doors appeared in their way. Accordion-style, they encompassed the entire width of the tunnel. A small rectangular window glinted in the light from Wilder's headlamp.

"Interesting," she murmured, stepping closer. She peered through the window but saw nothing but empty space. "That's a big room. Way bigger than anything we've come across so far."

"Let me look," said Niall.

Wilder moved away from the window and inspected the doors. A simple handle was set into one of them halfway up. She grasped it and tugged. With a metallic screech, the doors parted, folding up as they opened.

She sensed, rather than saw, a vast space. The light from her lamp faded into darkness, and the air felt different. While the tunnel had felt close and stuffy, here currents wafted against her skin. She called out, "Hello?"

Her voice echoed back three or four times.

"Shhh!" Niall hissed.

"Why? A few minutes ago you said this place is completely safe."

"There's no point in taking unnecessary risks."

"I just wanted to confirm my suspicion, and I was right. This room is huge. It must reach as high as the surface. I wonder if it's a natural cavern." She set off to explore.

"Slow down," Niall urged. "You have no idea what's ahead. Oh."

"Oh, what?"

"The signal. It's reappeared. I can see it now."

"Then let's find it! Lead the way."

Holding his interface in two hands, Niall swiveled to get his bearings. "This way." He moved off, checking the screen and the ground in front of him alternately.

Wilder followed, glancing from side to side, but she saw only concreted ground.

Niall proceeded on a diagonal from the double doors, crossing the wide area in silence.

After a couple of minutes, Wilder asked, "Are we close yet?"

"Nearly. Uhhh..." He veered to the left.

"Wait, there's something ahead of you." Her light had reflected from glass and she'd caught a glimpse of their two figures, shadowy under the bright spots of their headlamps.

It was another set of double doors. Two large windows were set into them.

"Look!" Wilder exclaimed. "It's a control booth."

The walls of the room were crammed with equipment. Screens, dials, gauges, buttons, and sliders on panels festooned it. Ropes of wires ran between them, bound with tape.

Wilder's heart raced. "What's it for? And what's it doing down here?" She felt as though they'd stumbled across something significant, though she had no idea what it could be. "Can we get inside?"

Niall's hands were already on the handles. He pulled cautiously but they didn't budge. "It's locked."

"Maybe there's another set of puzzles."

But the walls to each side of the doors were blank.

"They must have locked them for a reason," said Niall. "The equipment must be dangerous."

"Not after all this time." She tried the handles, but she didn't pull. She pushed, and the doors opened. Light filled the room and a holo flashed to life in the center. Wilder gave a little jump and grabbed the edge of the door.

The translucent holo was of a man wearing old, patched clothes, little more than rags. He was speaking but not in English.

After a few moments, Niall asked, "Can you understand anything he's saying?"

"Not a word."

One thing was clear, however. The man was not giving a friendly greeting to the visitors from the future. His eyes were narrow and spittle flew from his mouth as he spoke.

He was angry.

SEVEN

Cherry cradled the man's head. Blood from his chest wound welled up with each breath he took. As he exhaled, it coated his lips and face in a fine spray. So much blood. She could feel it, wet and warm.

He was saying something, murmuring words she couldn't catch. She leaned down, bending her body over his, turning her head so her ear was closer to his mouth. She could hear him now, but she couldn't understand him. Of course. He was an Earther, speaking their language. Of course she couldn't understand.

He was saying his last words, probably giving her messages to pass on, messages of love, perhaps apologies. Who knew what he was saying? None of them could understand and no one would know what he said with his last breaths.

She nodded anyway.

He was too out of it, too far gone to remember that she was from another planet light years distant, that she spoke another language and had a different history. She gave another nod. "I understand. I'll tell them."

Relief lit his fading eyes. Then they lost focus and his body relaxed.

Cherry held onto the slumped form. She was back on Suddene inside Chimera, the chamber built to house Concordia's fifth armaments silo. She was holding Isobel, Kes's wife. Inside the dark tent the iron smell of blood had been strong. Little Nina had been quiet and still as her mother died.

"Cherry."

What would she tell Kes? How would she explain that Isobel was gone?

"Cherry, he's had it. It's over."

How would she tell Kes?

"Give him to me."

As Aubriot tugged the body from her grasp, she looked up, confused. What was he doing here in the tent?

But she wasn't in the tent. Trees surrounded them and she was sitting within ferny undergrowth.

"Are you all right?" Aubriot had laid the pilot's body out.

She blinked. "Yeah, I'm fine."

"You don't look fine. You're covered in blood, for one thing. Not a lot we can do about it now. Come on, we need to get moving." He reached down as if to lift her to her feet.

"I told you I'm okay," she snapped, standing up. "And, while I remember, you didn't need to carry me out of the dome. I'm not a kid you can haul around."

"Pardon me for wanting to save your life. Don't worry, the next time you're in trouble I won't make the same mistake. We'd better get moving."

"*I* wouldn't mind a little support," said Maddox.

The rest of them were here: Acton, Dragan, and Maura. Cherry wondered how she hadn't seen them.

Maddox did look as though she would need help with walking. The gouges the Scythian had inflicted on her leg looked painful, though she wasn't bleeding heavily anymore. Yet there had been a coquettish tone in her remark. Cherry scowled. Wouldn't the woman ever give it a rest?

"We should head west to get back to base," said Acton.

"I agree." Aubriot swiveled as he looked at the sky. "Sun's over there and it's the afternoon, so we go that way." He held out a hand to Maddox, who limped over to him. "If we can manage without any rests, we should make it back before sunset." He set off, an arm supporting Maddox. The others followed in a line.

Cherry took a final look at the pilot and the crashed heli before joining them.

———

Twenty or thirty Scythians had erupted from the dome. She would never forget the sight of the creatures bursting out in such numbers, climbing aloft on their wide wings. They'd been out to get revenge for their murdered comrade. At least, that was how it seemed as they flew after the heli. Or perhaps they didn't care about the Scythian she'd killed. Perhaps they were only angry about the hole in their precious dome, still leaking CO_2.

The Earther pilot wrenched his vessel's engine up to maximum output and angled the nose-tip down to maximize acceleration. The passengers hung forward in their harnesses.

Aubriot opened a window and the wind howled in.

"What are you doing?" Cherry yelled.

"What do you think?" He shifted in his seat and leaned out, pulse rifle under his arm.

"Stars, don't hit the rotors!"

But he had the right idea. She did the same. Luckily, from her position she could shoot with her right arm. Aubriot was forced to shoot left-handed.

The Scythians swarmed after them in a bunch, making an easy target. She got off two rounds. One hit a Scythian's wing. Through the tint of the creature's visor she glimpsed its mouth opening, but any sound it made was blocked off. It separated from the rest, its flight erratic. It began to whirl and tumble over and over, losing altitude. What happened to it next Cherry didn't see. She'd hit another Scythian in its midriff. The creature clasped at the wound in agony. The movement caused it to drop down. It beat its wings to regain height, but it stopped flying again, reaching for its wound.

A window shattered. There was a zing accompanied by a metallic ping.

"What was that?" Maddox yelled.

Aubriot replied, "They're firing back."

At first, Cherry didn't understand. She hadn't seen any flashes of pulse fire, yet it was undeniable that the Scythians were attacking. How? They weren't holding anything in their claws. They wouldn't have been able to fly.

Another zing.

The round must have passed close by her head but there was no ping. Where had it gone? After checking no one was hurt, she returned her attention to the Scythians and fired again. They'd spread out now, probably to be harder to hit.

She saw their weapons. Within each pair of prehensile feet was a metal object somewhat like a pulse rifle only smaller. All pointed at the heli.

Aubriot hit an alien, the pulse round exploding against its scrawny neck. The wings folded and it plummeted from the sky, the wind turning it lazily as it fell.

The heli was maintaining distance from the pursuers. If anything it was pulling away, but not fast enough. All the Scythians had to do was hit the engine or a rotor and it would crash. They'd reached the forest. Would crashing into trees be safer or more dangerous than crashing on open land?

Cherry fired again, letting loose a stream of rounds. But aiming backward was hard and both she and her targets were moving. She couldn't hit a thing.

The heli swerved. Her stomach lurched as it sank. They were losing speed.

Had the heli taken a hit?

She faced forward. The pilot hunched over his controls and blood oozed from his back. It was only then she noticed the hole in his seat. The zing she'd heard earlier had been a round hitting it. The projectile had passed through it and into the pilot. He'd been hit and hadn't said a thing.

Aubriot reached over seats and grabbed the man's shoulder. He moved. He was conscious, but barely. He pushed himself upright and gripped his controls again. The heli swooped upward. But its flight was erratic. The pilot couldn't maintain control. They began to fall again.

Acton blurted, "We're gonna crash!"

What followed was hard to recall exactly. Cherry remembered the jerking of the heli as the pilot, seeming to lapse in and out of consciousness, grabbed and let go of the controls. Aubriot unfastened his harness and tried to get to them. Cherry yelled, telling him fasten his harness.

The forest canopy loomed upward and swung from side to side, matching the motion of the aircraft. A peek over her shoulder revealed the Scythians hovering, beating their wings impossibly fast as they watched, their bronze forms bizarrely out of place in the deepening blue sky.

The scene seemed to freeze in silence.

Then the forest rushed toward her, the crash of breaking branches and battering of foliage burst in her ears... Everything cut out.

When she woke she was hanging upside down and her head felt thick with blood. She groped for her harness catch and released it, the understanding of what would happen dawning too late. She hit the ceiling of the heli and crumpled, groaning in pain.

Others were moving around her, dragging themselves free.

Where was Aubriot?

What had happened to the Earther pilot?

Somehow, she got out.

The heli was a bashed-in mess. The rotor blades had torn free, and the cabin was bent and deformed. She sat marveling at it. How had she managed to extract herself from that disaster?

"Hey," said Aubriot. "You okay?"

"Nothing broken, I don't think."

"Can you help me with the pilot?"

———

"We should hurry up," said Maura. "Maddox, can you go any faster? Maybe we can carry you."

"I'm doing the best I can."

"I know what you're thinking," said Aubriot, "but the Scythians won't come after us in here."

"He's right," said Dragan. "There's no way they can maneuver through the trees. Not with those massive wings. And they can't shoot at us if they're walking."

"But they could fire on us while they're flying," said Maura.

"Canopy's too dense," Dragan replied shortly.

Cherry walked on in silence. They had learned a lot. They now knew the Scythians were primarily fliers, not walkers. They also knew their weapons fired projectiles, not pulse rounds. And that their domes were vulnerable to regular explosives. They had other vulnerabilities. Sunlight was too bright for their eyes. Their visors had been tinted. And they couldn't breathe Earth's atmosphere.

The knowledge had come at the cost of the Earther pilot's life, but it was invaluable. Surely there was a way to defeat these creatures. If the Earthers mounted a sustained attack, perhaps they could drive them off the globe.

Cherry's shoulders slumped. How could she have forgotten? Aubriot had talked about it at the meeting with the GAA, but he hadn't followed his train of thought to its natural conclusion.

The Scythians had a deadly weapon in their arsenal: the biocide.

Even if they could be persuaded to give up on their plan of colonizing Earth and enslaving humanity, they would never leave peacefully. They would do the same as they had on Concordia. They would release their deadliest weapon.

Everything that had been learned didn't matter. It didn't matter what anyone knew or did. The situation was hopeless.

EIGHT

s Wilder watched the man's holo talk and wondered what to do next, a second voice spoke from the darkness behind her.

"Whoa!" She started and swung around. Her headlamp caught another man's face in its beams.

"He's armed!" Niall blurted and clutched her, attempting to drag her away. His light had flashed against the muzzle of the rifle.

Wilder resisted. "He isn't aiming at us. I think it's safe."

The man had continued to talk, and he raised a hand as if attempting to reassure them. But, like the holo, his words were unintelligible.

Niall leaned closer. "This one's real, right?"

"I think so, but I'm sure as hell not going to touch him to make sure."

"Where did he come from? Did he follow us in here?"

"He must have, but..." An odd feeling was nagging at her. She knew it couldn't be right no matter what her gut was saying. "Let's go into the room. I want to get a proper look at him."

As she'd hoped, when they went into the place the holo was playing, the stranger followed. He seemed to be appraising them as much as they were appraising him.

He was tall, taller than most Earthers she'd seen, and he wore unusual clothes. A neatly fitting pin-striped suit clothed him from his neck to his knees, and he didn't wear pants but closely wrapped strips of cloth around his calves. His boots were black and looked new, except for the fact they were coated in thick dust. His hair was the oddest part of his appearance. It was long but it had been gathered into a bun on the top of his head. For an Earther he was impressively clean shaven.

But was he an Earther? Could her feeling be correct, and, if so, how? How could it be possible?

He appeared to conclude his assessment. Lifting a hand, he gestured toward the interface Niall was carrying.

"Does he want me to give it to him?" Niall asked.

"Try it and see what he does."

The stranger took the interface, said something she assumed meant 'thanks', and carried it to a console, where he sat down.

Wilder joined him and peered over his shoulder. The man didn't object. He placed the interface on a smooth black pad and then touched another with his fingertips.

"What's he doing?" Niall asked.

"How would *I* know?"

The man inclined his head and was still. Was he concentrating? It was hard to tell. His eyes remained open though unfocused.

"Niall, look at his chest. Is he even—"

Light burst from the chamber they'd just left.

Niall returned to the open door. "Look at that place!"

It was even larger than Wilder had guessed. The ceiling hung thirty meters above and the floor was a hundred and fifty meters in diameter. A seam circled it seven meters in from the wall. The outer edge of the floor was ordinary tile while the inner was metallic. Long tubular lights were suspended from the ceiling.

"Look," said Wilder, "he's shut off the holo too. I didn't notice at first."

"I wonder if he owns this whole setup. Maybe he was broadcasting the signal so someone would come and rescue him."

"He doesn't look in need of rescuing." The more Wilder had seen of the man and his behavior, the greater was her conviction that her gut reaction had been correct. "This is going to sound crazy, but I think I know him."

"That does sound crazy. You can't possibly know him. He's an Earther, and this is our first visit to this place. Unless you think you saw him somewhere else?"

"I did see him somewhere else. Somewhere not on Earth and a long time ago. I remember him from when I was a little girl."

"That's insane. Are you feeling okay?"

"I'm fine, and I know I'm right."

"I suppose it's possible he had a doppelganger, or maybe you're misremembering."

There was no point in trying to convince Niall. Besides, she was sure she would be proven right soon.

The man straightened up, turned, and smiled. "I'm pleased to make your acquaintance. Could you please tell me your names?"

Niall's wide eyes turned to Wilder and then back to the man. "H-How come you're speaking English?"

"He learned it," Wilder explained. "He learned it just now, from our interface. That's right, isn't it?" she asked the man. Except he was not a man.

"That is correct. I have analyzed the data on your device. I may mispronounce some of your words at first. I would appreciate it if you would inform me of the correct pronunciation."

"Happy to." Wilder introduced herself and Niall. "Do you mind if I try to guess your name?"

"If that's your wish, I will comply."

"Huh?" Niall touched her shoulder. "What are you doing? We're going to be here a long time if you try to do that."

"I don't think so." She frowned. The name had been on the tip of her tongue, but it had slipped away. Concentrating, she searched her memory again. She'd been young when she'd learned it, and she'd been on the periphery of everything going on in the colony.

She had it. "Are you called Strongquist?"

He smiled. "You have met my counterpart. Many things are becoming clear to me. You must be from the colony the other Strongquist set out to help."

Niall breathed, "What the hell?"

"We named the planet Concordia," she said.

"So the mission succeeded. That is gratifying to know."

"It did succeed, only... A lot's happened since then."

"I would be interested to hear about it. Your interface only contains recent information."

"I can tell you everything. I was there from the start."

"You were? I don't understand. Even if you were one of the scientists suspended in cryosleep on the ship, you should have died of old age many years ago. Unless perhaps you were only recently revived?"

"That's another long story."

"I would also like to know why you have returned to Earth."

"I get it," Niall announced. "He's a Guardian."

"Finally," Wilder replied sarcastically.

"Hey, I never saw one." He stepped closer to the android, who regarded him with a questioning look. "So he looks like one of the androids who arrived on the *Mistral*?"

"As far as I can remember he's the original Strongquist's twin. It must have been easier to reuse his design."

"Actually," the android demurred, "the second Strongquist is a copy of me. Not that it really matters. Is he among your party?"

"He died," replied Wilder. "I'm sorry. They all died defending the colony."

"I see. So they followed their programming. Steen would have been pleased."

"Steen?" asked Wilder.

"One of the Makers. The holo that was activated when you entered this room was a recording Steen made before the team shut everything down."

"He didn't seem too happy in it," Niall remarked.

"He grew very bitter toward the end of the project. He would rail about the sacrifice he'd made for people he had no connection to and would never meet. I think in the beginning his focus was on the project's scientific challenge. It was only as its completion drew near he saw beyond it to the dull, unsatisfying, and dangerous remaining years of his life. He saw more clearly what he'd given up—the chance of escaping Earth. His message is full of anger and does not contain useful content. It is probably not beneficial to watch it, though I am able to translate it if you wish."

Niall had wandered to the doorway and was leaning out, resting one hand on the frame. He whistled. "They built a starship in here?"

"That is correct. It was a truly magnificent feat, considering the state of Earth at the time. The materials and parts had to be sourced from all over the globe or manufactured here in unfavorable conditions. And it all had to be completed in secrecy. The Natural Movement as an entity had disintegrated during the collapse of civilization, but the general anti-scientific sentiment continued. Plus, anyone with a supply of food or still-functioning equipment was a target. That is why the scientists came to Svalbard, where they would be safe from marauders and scavengers."

Wilder asked, "Do you know what happened to them after they launched the *Mistral*?"

"My knowledge of the past stops at the moment I shut down. The logical answer is they all died many years ago."

Niall turned his attention away from the chamber. "Why did they create the signal beacon?"

"I was not aware of it until your arrival triggered my reactivation. I perceive it now but don't know its purpose. When I was ordered to shut myself down, all I knew was that my assistance might be required again. I didn't anticipate ever meeting anyone from the colony, but the team might have hoped a delegation would arrive on Earth one day. Or perhaps they simply hoped their work would not be forgotten."

Wilder mentally added, *Not forgotten by people who understood.*

The android's story made sense of the puzzles at the entrance. Only someone with an understanding of arithmetic and a basic interest in mathematics would be able to open the door. To anyone else, the site would remain an enigma.

NINE

Cherry stuffed the remainder of her belongings into a bag. She hadn't brought much down from the *Sirocco*, and in her brief time on Earth she'd only acquired a few additional items. Everything fitted into a couple of bags. She took a last look at the small room she'd occupied for the previous few weeks, and then walked to the door.

Itai was on the other side of it.

They each took a moment to get over their surprise, and then the Earther looked her up and down, taking in the bags. "So it's true."

"I'm sorry, but I'm in a hurry." She tried to move around him, but Itai stepped sideways to block her exit.

"You're really leaving? All of you?"

"Nothing's been decided yet. But we are returning to the ship for now."

"How long will you be gone?"

"I don't know. We have things we need to discuss."

"You could do that here, with us. Buka is open to more discussion."

"I'm sure he is. Look, would you move out of my way? The shuttle is scheduled to depart in fifteen minutes."

Itai rested a hand on the door frame. "They'll wait for you. You're too important to leave behind."

Cherry sighed. Even two-handed she was no match for a fully grown man, and the last thing she wanted was a fight. She felt guilty enough as it was. This might be the last time she spoke to an Earther, and she didn't want to depart the planet on bad terms.

"Can't we talk about this?" Itai asked. "There's still a lot to talk about."

"Maybe there is, but we have things to talk about too. So if you wouldn't mind...?"

"Please, hear me out."

She put down her bags. "You have one minute."

"You say 'you' have things to talk about too as if you're different from us, but we're both human. Concordians are the same as us. If you leave you'll be abandoning your own kind. How will you be able to live with yourselves knowing you refused to help your cousins when they were in need?"

"We have helped you. We risked our lives breaking into a Scythian dome. We drew them out into the open in broad daylight. Now you know what they look like and what they can do, you're in a better position to fight them. We've done a lot already. You seem to be forgetting we could have left at the first sight of them."

"I know, and we do appreciate the fact that you stayed. Only..." He was out of arguments yet he still didn't want to let her go.

She said gently, "We understand what you're up against. Believe me, we really do. But we have others to think about. Our people are waiting for us. They desperately need the seeding material. If we don't return soon we could be too late." The last point was speculation though she wasn't about to admit it. The *Sirocco* had been absent from Concordia for so long, no one knew what they might find upon their return. The colony might not have survived, or the Scythians might have dealt a second dose of biocide, rendering the planet entirely sterile.

Lifting her bags, she pushed past Itai. He didn't resist. As she reached the end of the passageway, Buka hobbled into view, leaning heavily on a walking stick.

He raised a hand and said something she didn't understand. She hurried away. Word had gotten out that the Concordians were leaving. She didn't want to wait around for more Earthers to accost her. Things could turn nasty.

When she made it to the shuttle she was the last to board.

As Zapata flew them up to the *Sirocco*, the mood in the passenger cabin was somber. Everyone seemed to be wrestling with their feelings. Cherry's were mixed too. Since her realization that, regardless of aid the Earthers received, their future was doomed, she'd battled with her conscience. Kes would have probably wanted to stay. Aubriot had the same attachment to the planet of his birth. For her, Concordia was her home and her first allegiance, yet she also felt a duty to the Earthers.

She wished Ethan were here. Not only would he have known in his heart the right thing to do, he would have confidently and decisively led the Concordians to do it.

Aubriot slid into the next seat. "I bet you're glad you got your way."

"What?" She squeezed herself up against the window. Aubriot was not particularly bulky but he was strong and, for the first time since she'd known him, his presence felt physically threatening.

"Don't play innocent. You got what you wanted all along."

"You mean leaving Earth? Nothing's been decided yet."

"And yet here we are *leaving Earth*. Seems to me the decision's been taken. Only no one's told the Earthers. Vessey's recalled us all to the ship so no one gets lynched when she gives Buka the bad news."

Lynched. He'd used that word before. It was something to do with hanging.

"If you really think the Earthers will kill us if we don't help them, maybe it's better that we leave, and soon. We've already done a lot for them and they aren't the least bit grateful. They seem to expect us to sacrifice everything we have, even our lives, to protect them, as if we don't have our own planet to protect."

"So that's what you've been telling everyone. It's no wonder the mood changed." He was clenching and unclenching his fists as they lay on his knees.

"You really think I orchestrated this whole thing?" It was true that, following the mission to break into the dome, she'd expressed her worries to other Concordians. She'd explained her realization that Earth was in an impossible bind, faced with the choice between enslavement and destruction. The people she'd talked to might have discussed her thoughts with others, but none of it had been deliberate. If other Concordians had come to the same conclusion as her and related their change of heart to Vessey, it wasn't her fault.

When Aubriot didn't answer, she went on, "You said it yourself—Earth's screwed. It doesn't take a genius to figure it out. Anyone who lived through the biocide would come to the same conclusion eventually, so save your blame for the ones who are actually responsible for this situation—the Scythians."

Aubriot still didn't answer. He only stared at the back of the seat in front of him, continuing to clench his fists. He seemed to be undergoing some kind of mental crisis.

"What I don't get is," she said, "you *know* Earth can't be saved. You saw it first, right? That day we got back from spying on the Scythians building their dome. You saw it then. You said as much. Why can't you accept it's over for the Earthers and it's time for us to move on?"

He jerked his head around to face her, his features rigid. "Because I can't," he spat. "Cherry, you never saw Earth in its heyday. There were billions of people. The night sky lit up from vast cities. Roads and railways traveling thousands of miles. Planes and shuttles filling the skies. Container ships sailing across the oceans, transporting food and products between continents. Art, music, books, vids, sims, dancing, circuses, restaurants, sports, clubs, societies..." He caught his breath before continuing, his tone softened, "Medicine, manufacturing, construction, technology, research, finances, law courts..." He paused again. "Then the Natural Movement shit on everything and now it's gone." He added quietly, "It's like a bloody country town in the arse end of nowhere. Everything's gone. *Everything*."

She hadn't realized the changed Earth had affected him so badly, but it was hard to be sympathetic toward someone who never sympathized with anyone except himself. "What did you expect? The Guardians told us things had gone downhill after the *Nova* left. I don't know what you thought you would find."

"*Something*," he muttered. "A sign of what went before. There were paintings, Cherry. Already hundreds of years old in my lifetime, worth millions, billions, even. Beautiful works of art. Where are they now? If they still survive they'll be rotting in a basement somewhere with no one to appreciate them. There were buildings, ancient monuments, surviving from great civilizations. You could go and see them, walk around them and imagine the famous people who lived and died there. Where are they? Who remembers those people?"

"Just you, I guess."

Was he finally grieving Kes, his remaining link to his past? Aubriot hadn't shown any emotion regarding his fellow Earther's death. It was hard to imagine Aubriot feeling anything for anyone, but it was possible. More likely, he was missing the one person who remembered how important he'd been in Earth's former incarnation.

Aubriot nodded, saying, as if to himself, "Just me."

TEN

Vessey looked better than she had in a while. The rumor was she hadn't touched a drop of alcohol since the *Sirocco* entered Earth orbit. Her skin was clearer, the bags under her eyes less heavy, and her demeanor was more assured. More key to her improvement than going teetotal, Cherry guessed, was the fact that the captain felt the ship's personnel was finally behind her.

She greeted the shuttle passengers brightly as they disembarked and chatted to a few who were her personal friends. Perhaps spurred by the responses they gave, she announced an immediate meeting.

It was a little too soon. It would have been better to give people time to settle in and get used to being aboard the ship again. But, with some grumbling, the Concordians left to put their luggage in their cabins before going to the meeting room.

In particular, it would have been a good idea to give Aubriot time and space to accept they'd done all they could for their Earther cousins, and that now they were going to put their own needs first. Cherry watched as he stomped off angrily. She contemplated saying something to Vessey but the damage was done. Canceling the meeting the minute she called it would make her look indecisive and weak. They still had a journey ahead, assuming the jump drive worked.

Cherry decided to go straight to the meeting. The cabin she now shared with Miki and Nina after taking on the girls as—she felt—an inadequate adoptive parent, was on the other side of the ship, and her minimal luggage wouldn't get in the way. Several others had the same idea and when she arrived the room already had some occupants. Vessey arrived and nodded at her. She walked to the front of the room to wait, clutching the back of a seat nervously.

When everyone had arrived, she gave a cough to quieten the murmuring. "Thank you for coming at such short notice. I think we all know why we're here. The situation on Earth has become untenable. The Scythians have constructed domes all over the planet and hundreds of Earthers have gone missing. It's clear that the aliens have embarked on a program of subjugation of the human population and colonization of the planet."

She gave a voice command and the lighting dimmed. "Also, I would like you to look at this."

A holo lit up the room. It was a spacescape, showing Earth with its thin layer of blue, luminous atmosphere.

Vessey said, "Display Scythian vessels."

Brilliant spots appeared, high above the atmosphere in orbit.

"There are more," Vessey said. "What you can see is only what the computer can display on the holo. Scythian vessels surround the planet."

"How many?" someone asked.

"Twenty."

There was a whistle and several gasps.

"We've known the number for a while, but now I can tell you the scan data indicates that many are transports. They brought the colonization vessels after discovering Earth was undefended a couple of years ago. The *Sirocco* must have come as quite the surprise upon their return."

"And her gun," came a comment from the audience.

"Exactly," said Vessey. "We've been lucky. If the Scythians had attacked us with the same ships they used to attack Concordia, we couldn't have defeated them. The Parvus's weapon has bought us time, but it's my belief that time will shortly run out. The aliens must have called for military backup. We need to leave, and soon, if we're to make it home."

A hand rose. It was Maura's. "But the Parvus's weapon deterred the Scythians before. Why wouldn't it work now?"

Cherry replied, "The Scythians had already released their biocide when the Parvus started attacking them. They had no reason to stick around and risk their ships. They thought the biocide would kill us anyway. If they really want Earth, the Parvus's weapon won't be a deterrent, especially not in this part of the galaxy where there are no Assembly members to come to our aid."

"But the Scythians must know where we're from," Maura argued. "What's to stop them going to our planet and attacking us again?"

"Nothing at all," said Vessey, "but Concordia is easier to defend. We've done it before and we can do it again. Maybe we can convince the Scythians to leave us alone if they already have Earth as their prize."

Maura asked, "Give up our origin planet in return for being allowed to live on theirs?"

"The Scythians might accept the tit for tat. It's impossible to know, but, regardless, we can't protect Earth with our one ship, and Earth's population is too large and spread out and their infrastructure is too weak for it to protect itself." Vessey took a breath. "It's a lost cause. It's time we accepted that and moved on. We've gathered everything we need to re-seed Concordia so there's no reason for us to wait any longer. We're going home. We'll make the first jump in forty-eight hours."

"When are you going to tell Buka?" asked Aubriot. "He's gonna kick off."

"Naturally, I expect Mr Buka will be extremely disappointed. I hope he can understand and accept my decision with grace. Regardless, we leave in forty-eight hours."

"What about Niall and Wilder?" Zapata asked.

Vessey replied, "What about them?" Before the pilot could answer, she quickly scanned the room and added, "Shit. I'd forgotten about their plan to investigate the signal. Does anyone know how far they got?"

"They, er..." Zapata squared his shoulders. "I flew them to the island."

"You what?! I gave you express orders not to—"

"I'm sorry, but I thought it was less dangerous than letting them attempt to reach it on an Earther ship."

"Ugh. You're probably right. But this direct contravention of my order will not be forgotten. As you flew them there you can damned well fly back and pick them up. Comm them to let them know you're coming so they're ready to leave as soon as you arrive."

The meeting broke up. As the attendees left, Cherry realized she couldn't see Miki or Nina. Maybe they'd missed the notification. The girls had been shadows of their former, cheerful selves ever since their father's death, and their mood hadn't been lightened by the fact that they hadn't been allowed to return to the surface since his funeral.

How would they feel about returning to Concordia? They would be leaving Kes's grave behind and would never be able to visit it. And when they arrived home, what would they find? Did the house they'd shared with their father even exist anymore?

Similar prospects applied to everyone on the ship. Many had left loved ones behind who must have died, and no one knew the truth about the current state of their planet, but the girls were young and they'd loved Kes so much, they would be even more traumatized.

Cherry steeled herself as she walked to their cabin, preparing to break the bad news.

The atmosphere on the ship had changed. Enthusiastic chatter floated along the passageways as the Concordians discussed Vessey's decision. In the long years of the journey, the mood had not been so upbeat. It was understandable. Though they would be flying to an unknown fate, they would also be flying from known danger and a hopeless cause.

Now the decision had been made, and the right decision, guilt began to eat at Cherry. It felt bad to abandon their cousins in their hour of need. She was glad she wasn't the one who had to break it to Buka.

When she arrived at the cabin, it was empty.

She comm'd Miki, guessing the girls were probably working in the Ark. Its re-conversion to a storage facility wasn't quite complete, and they had been helping out as a welcome distraction.

Miki didn't answer the comm, so she tried Nina.

The result was the same.

It was odd. Wherever they were on the ship they should be reachable, and as their bunks were empty they obviously weren't asleep.

Why weren't they answering?

Then she saw their ear comms on their bedside tables.

What the hell?

She strode to Miki's table and picked hers up. Why in all the galaxy had she taken it out?

Cherry scanned the cabin. The light on her interface was flashing. A message was waiting.

Cherry, please don't be mad, but we decided we want to live on Earth. Nina overheard the captain talking about the plan to go back to Concordia really soon. We don't want to go. We know it's dangerous, but we want to be on Earth, near Dad. We don't want to leave him all alone down there. So we're going to stow away on the shuttle. Don't try to find us. We hope you have a safe journey home. Thanks for everything you've done. You were like another Mom. We love you. Have a good life.

Love, Miki and Nina.

ELEVEN

It was surreal to sit with a Guardian and tell it all that had happened on Concordia since the arrival of the *Nova Fortuna*. Wilder had never imagined she would meet another one so long after all the others had been destroyed. She'd certainly never imagined she would meet one on Earth. It was a lot to take in.

She told Strongquist about the First Night Attack, when saboteurs had turned off the electric fencing and sluglimpets had invaded the camp, killing colonists horribly by dissolving their flesh. And she told him how Ethan and Cariad had saved many lives with their calmness and quick-thinking.

"That was the night the *Mistral* arrived," she said. "It was a lucky coincidence. If it hadn't been for the Guardians many more people would have died, possibly everyone. The sluglimpets were relentless in those days. We found out later that the Fila had eradicated their food source in that area, so they were starving."

"The Fila?" Strongquist asked.

"Sorry, I'm getting ahead of myself. I'll explain about them in a minute."

"Before you go on, I heard Niall refer to me as a Guardian earlier, and you used the same word again just now. This was the name the colonists gave us?"

"The other Strongquist explained... Can I call you Strongquist II? It's confusing."

"Call me whatever you like. I can be known by another name if it helps."

"Strongquist II is fine, I think. Though..." She vaguely recalled Cherry had an antipathy toward the Guardians and had probably disliked the original Strongquist. But changing his name wouldn't make anything better. The resemblance to the first Strongquist was an unmistakable reminder. "Never mind. Where was I? Oh, yes. Strongquist explained they were there to protect the colony from descendants of the Natural Movement members who had infiltrated the project. That was how they got the name Guardians." She paused. "You have to understand, I was young when all this happened. I wasn't there for the First Night Attack, thank the stars. I didn't go to the surface until later. What I'm telling you is secondhand."

"I only need to know the gist."

"Well, there were lots of problems in the beginning, and not only due to the saboteurs. The scientists—they called them the Woken—and the generational colonists, the Gens, both thought they should be in control of the colonization. There was a *lot* of anger, a lot of fighting. Between the Natural Movement saboteurs, sluglimpet attacks, and the vying for control, it was a miracle the colony succeeded. To be honest, the presence of the Guardians made things worse in some ways. They were armed, you see, and the Woken turned them into a militia to subdue the Gens. You can imagine how well that went down."

Strongquist II nodded. "An unfortunate and unforeseen consequence. The Makers did not anticipate that result. They thought they were helping the colony, and that without their intervention it was doomed."

Niall commented, "Their intentions were good. And this..." he gestured at the vast chamber outside the office "...this monumental effort shows the lengths they went to in order to safeguard the survival of human civilization. And it worked, right? I have a question, Wilder. When was it the colonists realized the Guardians were androids?"

"That was after the cave settlement was sabotaged, I think."

Strongquist II asked, "So they managed to maintain the subterfuge for some time?"

"Oh, months, if not a year."

"The Makers were conflicted about whether to divulge our true nature to the colonists. Some felt it would cause distrust if it was known we were not human."

"It did, as I remember. Most Gens hated the Guardians." Wilder thought of Cherry again. "Though, to be fair, that was mostly the Woken's fault. Who likes the person aiming a gun at them? Uhh, where was I?"

"The sabotage of the cave settlement," said Niall.

"Right. You know, it's funny but the revelation about the Guardians seemed to bring everyone together."

"A common enemy," said Strongquist II.

"Perhaps. Anyway, it was around that time we discovered the Fila. They're an intelligent alien species who had colonized Concordia decades before the *Nova* arrived. But we didn't know about them because they're aquatic. They were living in the seas, oceans, rivers, and lakes, and we didn't even know they existed. They also didn't know about us at first, not until we started living and working near water."

"So humanity has made first contact with an extra-terrestrial species? How interesting. Do the two sets of colonists coexist peacefully?"

"The Fila have left Concordia," Wilder said sadly, thinking of Quinn, who she would probably never see again. "The ones who survived the biocide, that is."

As Strongquist II opened his mouth, clearly about to ask for further explanation, she held up her hands. "This is going to take all day. I have an idea. How about you return with us to the *Sirocco*? Concordia's history is bound to be somewhere in her data banks. You can learn all about it there. And I'm sure everyone will be fascinated to meet you."

"I'd be delighted to accept your invitation. Shall we leave now? How did you come to Svalbard?"

"What?!" Niall exclaimed. "No way. We can't leave without having a look around. Right, Wilder?"

"I guess so." She frowned. "Yeah, of course." This might be the only chance she had to see the place where the famous *Mistral* and Guardians had been built. She asked Strongquist II, "What's left to see? What's the power source for the lighting, for instance?"

"A fusion reactor."

"Holy shit," breathed Wilder. "You have a freaking fusion reactor on site?"

"Only a small one. I recall the team planned to shut it down. It must have re-started as you entered the outer door. It's pleasing that it still works after all this time."

"Show us," said Niall. "I want to see everything."

The site put anything Wilder had ever seen on Concordia to shame. It extended far deeper into the mountain and surrounding land than she'd thought. Many workrooms contained equipment she didn't recognize, but that was clearly highly sophisticated. Strongquist II explained these were the areas where the Makers had constructed the androids. In other places the purpose of the machinery was to create the many parts that made up a starship, including the a-grav. It was astounding to think that humans had invented the precious drive centuries ago, only for the knowledge to be nearly lost.

It *was* lost here on Earth.

"I'm blown away," Niall remarked as they left yet another work site. "Just when I think I've got my head around the scope of all the scientists and engineers did, I see something else amazing. It was hard enough building a starship on Concordia, where we had the entire colony behind us and priority for all its resources. How the hell did the people here manage to do everything they did, in secret, and scrounging materials or making things from scratch?"

Strongquist replied, "You're forgetting they had a much larger population and longer history to draw upon. As I understand it, the scientists had developed an underground network in response to the rise of the Natural Movement."

"They were *driven* underground from the sound of it," said Wilder.

"That may be a more accurate description. They had technical knowledge and skills to maintain effective channels of communication. While the world was falling apart around them, they used their intelligence and training to survive, building communities of like-minded people. The resources of earlier generations remained available to those who understood how to use them. There were abandoned space programs and myriad other scientific endeavors all over the globe."

"That makes sense," said Niall. "Earth's population must have still been in the billions then. What I don't get is, why didn't the scientists and engineers use their advantages to try to re-establish an advanced civilization? I mean, I'm grateful that they built the *Mistral* and you androids. If they hadn't I might not exist. But wouldn't it have been easier for them to put their skills to use on Earth, trying to rebuild civilization where they could be more certain of the outcome, rather than trying to save a colony light years across the galaxy?"

"Do you think they didn't?" Strongquist II asked. "If you search the archives you will find many instances of attempts to do exactly that. All failed, often with much loss of life and permanent injury, not to mention the destruction of irreplaceable equipment. Eventually, the consensus was that once civilization passes a certain point in a downward trajectory, recovery is impossible, in the short term at least. Therefore the scientists faced the choice of saving a space colony they knew was well-planned and heavily resourced, or making their own colonization attempt on another planet. In truth, despite Steen's ravings, the latter option was not viable. The team managed to build the *Mistral*, but a ship the size of the *Nova Fortuna* was beyond its capabilities. Moreover, there were far more people wanting to leave the planet than the two thousand the original colony ship carried. Who would have chosen who was to go or stay, and based on what criteria?"

Wilder gazed around the workroom, with its dusty benches and tall stools, its dry sinks and rusted faucets, its silent machines and dark corners filled with items left behind. She saw shadows of the men and women who had worked here, laboring for a purpose from which they would personally derive no benefit, striving for a cause to benefit humanity, not themselves.

She imagined the camaraderie of the united endeavor, the thrill of the intense work and the anxiety that something might go wrong, that they might not achieve their goal, or the willfully ignorant majority of humankind might attack. And they did it all knowing they would never find out if they'd succeeded, whether all their effort would be worth it.

Perhaps it didn't really matter to them. Perhaps it was enough to simply try.

"You've seen the main work areas," said Strongquist II. "Would you like to see the residential accommodation?"

"I think we passed through a section on our way in," Niall replied. "I'm not interested. Are you, Wilder?"

She shook her head. Rooms where people relaxed and slept were predictably similar across the ages, but that wasn't what put her off. She felt a strong connection to the people who had lived and worked at the site. Now they were gone, lost in time. "I'm glad we came here. Especially glad we met you, Strongquist II, but I think we should report in and tell our captain what we've found. It feels important, though I'm not sure how just yet."

"Let's go up to the surface and comm Vessey," said Niall.

The android said, "I will show you the way."

TWELVE

The stairs wound up and up. Every five meters or so motion-activated lights would blink on, revealing another section with no apparent exit. At the same time, lights below would turn off, plunging the lower levels into darkness.

"How much farther is the door?" Niall asked.

"Only ninety-eight meters," replied Strongquist II.

"Ninety-eight meters? I thought you said this was the quickest way back."

"It is, by five point zero five meters."

Niall grumbled something Wilder didn't catch, but she could guess at his complaint. His thighs and calves had to be aching as much as hers. The android might have chosen the shortest route but it was also the most strenuous. Naturally, as a machine it hadn't factored physical exertion into its choice of exit.

She was puzzled. The stairs they'd descended at the far end of the seed vault hadn't been anywhere near so tall. The corridors had sloped downward, accounting for some of the additional height they were now scaling, but it couldn't be all of it. "Where exactly are you taking us? You know we have to go back to the coast, right?"

"There's a gully running across the lower slope of the mountain. That's the quickest way to the place where your shuttle landed, if I understood your description correctly."

"Why didn't the Makers enter via the seed vault? Why did they create this entrance?"

"In the early years the vault was the only entrance. This stair was constructed in later years, for safety. People would turn up at the vault from time to time, following a rumor of a massive storehouse from the old days, stuffed to the rafters with grain and dried and preserved food supplies. Often, they were starving when they arrived. Hunger made them desperate and violent, and chance encounters with the scientists resulted in some deaths. So this shaft was sunk at the far end of the gully. Only those who knew the way were able to find the entrance. If, by chance, a stranger who had heard about the project arrived, they could still enter via the vault by solving a few puzzles. It was a basic safeguard and yet surprisingly effective."

Another set of lights flicked on. Still, no door appeared.

"There is a third exit," said Strongquist II, "a much larger one, for equipment and materials. A dirt road ran from it to a hidden harbor on the far side of the island. The forest must have overgrown the road by now."

The last comment had sounded wistful. Wilder glanced over her shoulder at the android. Its head was down. She hadn't had much to do with the machines in the early years of the founding of Concordia. Mostly all she knew about them was from Cherry, who had described them as creepy. This one didn't seem creepy. In fact, if she hadn't known what it was, she would have been surprised to discover it wasn't human. Were its emotions programmed in order to fool the colonists or did it really feel them?

Just when she thought she had to take a rest before climbing farther, and perhaps abandon her backpack, the next set of lights revealed a metal door set into the rough-hewn wall.

"At last," said Niall.

He was the first to reach it. He turned the knob but it didn't move. "It's rusted." He tried again to no effect. "Don't tell me we have to go all the way back down."

"Allow me." Strongquist II had reached the landing. "It's a simple mechanism." He gave the knob several blows with his fist. Flakes of rust fell from the door and frame. Gently, Strongquist II grasped the knob and turned it. A loud creak resounded. The door opened and sunlight burst from the gap, drowning out the meager interior lights.

"We've been in here all night," said Wilder. "I can't believe it."

"I can." Niall stepped through the opening, raising a hand to shield his eyes. "Come and take a look."

They were high up on a rocky crag protruding from the mountainside. A forested vista spread out and beyond it lay the ocean, the beams of the rising sun gilding the waves.

"It's so beautiful," Wilder said. "It could be Concordia."

Strongquist II joined them. "Your planet must be very Earth-like. I heard it was supposed to be. That's why it was chosen."

It was odd to hear him describe her home planet as Earth-like when to her it was the other way around.

"How long will it take us to reach the airstrip?" Niall asked.

"Approximately two and a half hours," replied Strongquist II, "depending on how fast you walk."

"Then we should comm Zapata to pick us up."

"I'll do it," said Wilder. "Boy, do we have a surprise for everyone."

But before she could comm the pilot, his agitated voice sounded in her ear. "Wilder, Niall, can you hear me? Please respond."

"We're here," she said. "What's up?"

"Thank the stars. I've been trying to contact you for hours. Vessey's hopping mad."

"She found out you brought us here? Shit." Wilder pulled a face at Niall. "Sorry about that. We'll tell her we insisted or something."

"That isn't the problem. We're leaving for Concordia soon. She wants everyone aboard pronto."

"We're leaving? But what about the Earthers? What happened to the plan to help them fight off the Scythians?"

"The plan's changed. Are you at the pick-up site?"

"Not yet. We should be there in under three hours. And we have another passenger for you."

"No, absolutely not. We're not taking any Earthers with us. Vessey's strict orders."

"Um..." Wilder looked at Strongquist II, who had been listening to her end of the conversation. "I think she might change her mind about this one."

"I doubt it, but I guess that's on you. I'm gonna be making at least one more trip to the surface, so I can take him or her back down when Vessey says no."

"It isn't a him or a her, technically," Wilder replied.

"Huh?"

"Never mind. See you in a few hours." She cut the comm.

"We didn't discuss my accompanying you to Concordia," Strongquist II said mildly.

"Ugh, you're right. I just assumed you would. It seemed logical. You're a Guardian, and I associate them with my home planet."

"Do you want to stay here on Earth?" Niall asked. "What would you do?"

"I would like to apprise myself of all facts pertaining to the current state of affairs before making my decision, in particular regarding these Scythians you mention."

"Makes absolute sense," said Niall. "Let's go. I don't want to keep Vessey waiting. She's already pissed off."

Strongquist II walked to the side of the crag and stepped down. Niall followed, and Wilder was about to do the same when something in the distance caught her attention. Two large birds had flown into view. The pair circled and she watched, fascinated. Before coming to Earth she'd only ever seen birds in educational vids at school. Roughly guessing their position, which was in the area of the pickup point, she concluded they had to be very large indeed. The birds disappeared behind the mountain.

"Wilder," Niall called, "what are you doing?"

"I'm on my way."

She climbed down from the crag.

———

Strongquist II led them on a tough march through the forest. As Wilder watched the android effortlessly navigating the dried stream bed, often stopping to allow them to catch up, she wondered why the Makers had left him at the *Mistral*'s construction site. He had said that the Strongquist sent to Concordia was his copy. Did that mean Strongquist II was a prototype? Could he be defective? Was that why they hadn't sent him? And if he was defective, did he know?

Or was there another reason for the android's presence? The Makers had activated the signal before they left, so they clearly expected or hoped that one day someone would detect it and come looking. As she and Niall entered the site Strongquist II was triggered to turn on, yet he didn't know why. Or did he know and he just wasn't telling them? Could the androids lie? She couldn't remember, but Cherry might. She'd been involved with them from the start. Making a mental note to ask her friend when she got back to the ship, Wilder hurried on, scrambling through the undergrowth.

By the time they neared the rendezvous point, she was hot and sweaty despite the cool temperature. She was also panting and tired, as well as sore from thorns that had caught in her skin. The Makers were either hardier than her or they rarely left their site.

Strongquist II was waiting. Beyond him lay the wind-churned ocean.

"I thought we'd never make it," said Wilder. "I can't wait to get aboard the shuttle and relax."

"Yeah," Niall replied, "I'll happily take an angry Captain Vessey over another trek through the wilderness."

As they neared the android, however, he held up a hand, warning them to stay back.

"What's wrong?" Wilder asked.

"An aircraft is at the site. I don't recognize the design."

"Oh, that's just Zapata and the shuttle. He must have arrived early and he's waiting for us."

She walked around Strongquist II and out into the open. The vegetation petered out as it neared the shoreline, where slabs of rock stepped down to the water. She turned, expecting to see the familiar lines of the shuttle and perhaps the friendly pilot getting some fresh air before the return journey.

Zapata was not there and neither was the shuttle.

Two slim points faced her, joined by a silver crescent covered in intricate yet chaotic swirls.

A Scythian ship!

With a sharp intake of breath, she tried to run back to the forest.

A shadow descended, and there was a burst of downward, fetid air. Something fastened tightly around her waist and lifted her from her feet. Suddenly, she was meters from the ground, looking down at the upturned face of Strongquist II, who quickly disappeared into the trees.

The Scythian ship slipped from her mind as her immediate impulse was to tear at the things gripping her. They were feet, covered in knobbly skin and oddly prehensile. She fought her instinct. She was already so high that falling would kill her. All she could hope was that the bird would set her down somewhere and not drop her.

It had to be one of the two birds she'd seen before. She hadn't known some Earth birds attacked humans. Why hadn't anyone warned her?

She craned her neck to get a look at the creature. Close up, she wasn't even sure it was a bird. It didn't have feathers but pale brown skin, stretched out over a skeletal frame to form its wings. She looked up for a view of its head...

She screamed.

The thing wore a transparent helmet. It was looking at her. Round white eyes, each with a central, vertical black line stared into her face. A lipless mouth opened. She caught a glimpse of layered jagged scales, and then it spoke. It was talking. There seemed no other word for it, though she couldn't hear what it said. Even if sound had permeated its helmet, the wind at this height was too noisy to hear anything else.

Understanding hit like a lightning bolt.

She looked down at the ship, now little more than a silver crescent on a distant shore. She looked at the creature.

It was a Scythian.

The Scythians could fly.

And it would kill her. There was no doubt about it. They hated humans. No one they'd kidnapped had ever been seen again.

All strength left her. With shaking fingers, she plucked feebly at the feet around her middle. Better to drop to a quick death in the ocean than face whatever fate awaited her inside a Scythian dome.

She hoped Niall was safe, hiding among the trees. She'd seen two of the creatures. Where was the other one? The skies were empty. The island was far below. The alien ship was a sliver of bright metal on a thread of rocky shore. They were higher than the mountain peak. She struggled to breathe.

Why was the alien flying so high? What was it planning to do?

The great wings beat hard and the Scythian banked to the left, sending her legs trailing.

Let me go! Let me go, you disgusting creature.

Even at this height and in the freezing gale she could smell it. A rank odor emanated from its feet and skin.

What was it doing here? The island was uninhabited. Had the Scythians detected the signal too? Had they come here to investigate?

It was descending. Its banking had turned into a spiraling downward glide. Slowly, the ocean drew nearer. Cringing, she looked up into its face again. It continued to talk, but it was no longer looking at her. Its focus was on the shore or perhaps its aircraft.

She followed its gaze.

There was the other one. The massive wings were unmistakable. But it wasn't flying. The wings were only partially outspread as it crouched on the rocks. What was it doing?

A terrifying image of the other Scythian feasting on Niall flashed into her head, gnawing at him with the gray, scale-like teeth.

But that couldn't be right. The aliens would suffocate if they took off their helmets.

There was Strongquist II!

The android stood at the alien's head, one hand on its long neck, the other arm holding the pulse rifle against its helmet.

That was why the creature that had captured her was descending. Strongquist II was threatening to kill its partner if it didn't bring her back.

She could breathe easily again and the roaring of the wind had lessened. They were about three hundred meters high and dropping lower every second. The white tips of the waves were clear, the hull pattern of the alien vessel defined.

What would her captor do? Would it put her down gently on the rocks? Did it understand she would be hurt if it dropped her more than a few meters?

She couldn't see Niall, which was a good thing. Strongquist II must have told him to hide in the forest. The android really was a Guardian. It was protecting them.

A hundred meters.

Fifty meters.

Strongquist II watched carefully. She made eye contact and gave a small wave to show she was okay.

Below, the water surged.

The Scythian had to fly closer to the shore if it was to set her down safely.

Another gliding circle. They were thirty meters up.

Closer to the shore. You have to fly...

The feet opened.

She shrieked.

Perversely, she flailed for the open, taloned 'fingers', clutching at them. But the alien was already swooping out of reach.

The ocean rushed up at her impossibly fast. She plunged into icy water. Just before it closed over her head she managed to take a breath. Then she was in the frigid ocean. Bubbles resounded in her ears. Water pressure crushed her eardrums and lungs. Her eyes opened on darkness. How deep had she gone? Which way was up?

She kicked and pushed down with her arms. Was she going in the right direction? It was cold, so cold. Where was the sunlight? It should be above but she couldn't see a thing.

She needed to breathe. The coldness made her want to gasp. Her chest worked as she fought the desperation for air. Was she swimming correctly or was she only thrashing around?

Quinn, where are you when I need you?

The Fila had tried to teach her to swim on one of the rare occasions she'd taken a break from her work, but she hadn't been very good at it. Her arms and legs refused to coordinate.

Quinn, I need you. Where in the wide galaxy are you, my old, dear friend?

Her thoughts were turning fuzzy. The darkness seemed to grow. It closed in.

I have to breathe.

Sorry, Quinn.

Sorry, Niall.

I must breathe.

Something touched her head. Snapped back to alertness, she swept it away. What was it? Was it one of those predatory fish she'd heard about? The thing touched her arm, but before she could hit it, a claw fastened around her biceps. She tried to prise it off with her free hand, only to realize it wasn't a claw but another hand. Someone had grabbed her. She was being saved!

Relaxing her body, she allowed herself to be towed. Moments later, her head broke the surface and she inhaled air in a great whoop.

Strongquist II bobbed next to her. "Are you hurt?"

"No, I don't think so," she panted. "Thank you! Thank you for saving me."

A wave lifted them closer to shore. Along with it came the body of a Scythian. The massive wings were spread out but the rest of it hung out of sight.

On land, another alien lay on a slab of rock, dead.

THIRTEEN

As they journeyed back to the *Sirocco* Niall was quiet and pensive. He stared out of the shuttle window, brooding. When Wilder reached to take his hand he didn't resist but his grip was limp and apathetic. Bewildered by his attitude, she didn't know what to say. He seemed angry but she didn't know why.

Zapata had arrived while Strongquist II had been helping her from the water, and there hadn't been time to talk about what had happened. The pilot had insisted they left as soon as possible, reasonably speculating there might be more Scythians in the area or on their way. As everyone had been getting ready to leave, she'd changed from her wet clothes into one of his spare flight suits. The garment swamped her but at least she was dry and warm.

She didn't know exactly what had gone on between the time the Scythian had snatched her and the moment she'd seen Strongquist threatening to kill the other one. Perhaps something else had happened that had upset Niall.

Or was he annoyed because she'd stepped out into the open, ignoring the android's warning about the strange ship? How could she have known it was a Scythian craft and not the *Sirocco*'s shuttle? It was an easy mistake to make. Niall might have done the same.

"Is something wrong?" she asked.

"No, why?"

"Uhh, no reason."

I nearly died. Don't you care?

She released his hand. He didn't react.

She turned away from him. Two could play the ignoring game.

"Strongquist, what happened while I was up in the air? How did you manage to catch the other Scythian?"

"It was not difficult. The alien landed just beyond the trees. It clearly suspected there was more than one human in the vicinity. I asked Niall to show himself—we were both hiding by then—in order to entice it under the canopy. It took the bait, and I pounced on it from behind. The hard part was dragging it out onto the rocks. I am stronger than humans but my strength has its limits. And, of course, I had to prevent it from flying off. So I shot its wings, disabling it. The creature became more passive after that."

"I bet it did."

"I had several concerns. The alien who captured you might not have cared about a threat to its partner's life. Or they may have been unable to communicate. Or the one I captured might not have told yours that it was in danger. Any number of things might not have gone according to plan. As it was, the event that surprised me was your captor dropping you into the ocean. That decision was its undoing, for it allowed me a clear shot at it without any danger of hitting you. The obvious next step was to dispatch the alien in my control."

"Why do you think my one dropped me instead of handing me over?"

"I cannot answer with any certainty. I am only familiar with human psychology. If I were to speculate, I would say it may have never intended to participate in an exchange and was only stalling until it was sufficiently close to attack me. Perhaps, according to their culture, the one I injured had lost honor and its life was forfeit, so its partner did not care if I killed it. Who knows? It's impossible to say without further information."

"I hope we never find out." Wilder shivered though she was no longer cold. She didn't want any more close encounters with Scythians. Her first sight of them had been a shock. After the attacks in Concordia's early years, living under the threat of their return most of her life, and the later decimation of the colony, she'd given a lot of thought to what they were like. Yet she'd never imagined anything so horrible as the creature that had carried her high into the air. Why had it done *that*? Strongquist was right. It was impossible to say.

———

Disembarking at the *Sirocco* took longer than usual. Before taking them to the bay, Zapata had to deliver their cargo to the hold, which turned out to be a tricky process. If it hadn't been so precious, Wilder suspected he might have been tempted to abandon it. But after half an hour or so of maneuvering he managed it and they could finally fly around to the bay.

It seemed like the entire ship's personnel had turned up to greet them. The news of their adventure must have spread. Wilder was first to exit the hatch.

Cherry stepped forward from the group to give her a hug. "Thank the stars you're okay. I was worried about you." Stepping back, she added, "Why the heck are you wearing *that*? Thinking of training to be a pilot?"

Before Wilder could answer, however, Cherry turned white and her mouth fell open. Her gaze was fixed on something over Wilder's shoulder.

Niall and Strongquist had left the shuttle.

"Bloody hell!"

The exclamation had come from Aubriot.

"It can't be," Cherry breathed.

Aubriot stepped forward. "*This* is the Earther?" he asked Vessey.

"Who else could it be?" the captain snapped. "I assume you're already familiar with Niall and Wilder."

Zapata said, "Got everything into the hold, Captain. I didn't think I'd manage it but I did in the end."

"Thank you. I'll take a look at it all right away. Cherry, would you mind taking our guest to the mission room and making him comfortable? Dragan, could you come with me? And I'll need a couple of biologists."

Niall said, "I'd like to take a look too, if you don't mind."

"I thought you might want to recuperate after your ordeal, but the more the merrier."

"I'm fine. It was Wilder who got put through the mill."

They left and the group began to break up. Today's show was over.

Cherry hadn't moved a muscle.

Strongquist's features were impassive as he watched Aubriot walk up. His gaze followed Aubriot while he inspected him from the toes of his boots to the top of his head.

"Fuck me." Aubriot turned to Cherry. "It's really him."

"It isn't a he," she replied icily, "it's an *it*."

Wilder mentally checked herself. Cherry was right. Strongquist II wasn't a person. It was a thing. Yet since he had saved her life her attitude toward him had changed. It was hard not to see him as human. Even if he hadn't been her savior, he looked like a person, sounded like a person and even mostly behaved like one.

"It isn't the Strongquist we knew," Cherry continued. "I saw him cut to pieces with my own eyes."

"*Pftt*," said Aubriot. "You know what I mean. It's his twin or whatever."

"I don't know what Vessey's told you," Wilder said, "but this Strongquist saved me from the Scythians."

"Yeahhh," Cherry drawled, her expression not changing, "they have a habit of doing that."

"You found him at the seed vault?" Aubriot asked Wilder. "I thought we searched that place pretty thoroughly."

"We didn't see half of it. We left after we found what we were looking for, remember? But he wasn't in the vault. Didn't Vessey explain? The signal was coming from the place the Makers built the *Mistral* and the Guardians."

"She didn't explain shit." Aubriot tutted and shook his head. "The woman's not fit to lead. So you found the construction site? What was there? I mean in terms of equipment. Did you have a look around?"

While Wilder listed what she could recall, Cherry continued to stare at the android. He appeared unperturbed by her scrutiny. Eventually, Wilder became uncomfortable on his behalf. "Someone should take Strongquist to the mission room. I can do it."

"I am happy to answer any questions," the android said. "It appears my arrival has caused some agitation."

"Oh, I've got plenty of questions for you," said Aubriot, "and I want to hear more about the place the *Mistral* was built."

"Why are you so interested?" Cherry asked. "What difference does it make? Don't tell me you're still thinking about protecting Earth."

"It's a whole new discovery. Throws a new light on things."

"It doesn't throw a light on anything. One android and some starship-building equipment isn't going to save the Earthers."

"Why the pessimism? Oh, that's right. You don't give a shit about Earth."

"Why should I care about *your* home planet? You'd happily sacrifice everyone on this ship for a war we can't win."

Wilder interjected, "I thought Vessey had decided we're leaving?"

But neither of them heard her. They continued to bicker.

They hadn't gotten along since breaking up years ago, but lately their animosity seemed to have intensified. It didn't help that, as two of the most experienced and competent people on the ship, they often had to work together.

"Come with me," Wilder told Strongquist.

"Wait." Cherry had noticed they were leaving. "You haven't heard the news. Miki and Nina have gone down to the surface. No one knows where they are."

Fourteen

Wrinkling her nose, Cherry squatted down and grasped the edge of the Scythian's wing. When she lifted it a noxious smell escaped and she wrinkled her nose more. "Gross!"

"They aren't the most pleasant life form I've encountered," Maura commented.

"That's putting it mildly," said Acton. "I've seen quite a few odd species since arriving on Earth but nothing compares. These creatures are abominable."

Cherry straightened up. "What can you say about them?"

"Apart from the obvious," Maura replied, "that they're aerial, CO_2-breathing, and predatory, it's hard to say anything just yet. We're taking samples to analyze in the lab, and then someone will perform a full autopsy."

"Did you say predatory? Do you think they're here to prey on humans?"

"I haven't seen anything to indicate it. The one that snatched Wilder didn't try to take a bite out of her as far as I'm aware. What I meant is their forward-facing eyes, sharp teeth, and grasping and slashing appendages tell us they evolved to catch and eat prey, that's all. Humans have some aspects of predator anatomy too but Concordians are vegetarian."

"Yeah," said Acton, "let's not jump to that particular nightmare scenario just yet, if you don't mind."

The dead Scythians only took up a small portion of the hold. Most of the rest of it was occupied by the vessel Zapata had towed back. Though it followed the alien ships' usual design, it was the smallest Cherry had ever seen. Niall and Dragan were attempting to open a humped section at the widest part of the crescent. It was easy to guess why: it had to be where the aliens sat while flying it. The hump probably contained the control center, though what the engineers would be able to discern from inspecting it was uncertain. So far, they hadn't even gained access to the strangely marked vessel.

Vessey stood to one side, watching.

Cherry approached the captain. "Aubriot and I are ready to go planetside as soon as Zapata's rested."

"I'm not sure what you mean."

"What?" she spluttered. "You know exactly what I mean. We have to find Miki and Nina and bring them back."

"I told you the matter is still under consideration. I've been consulting with Buka about exactly how to handle it. Luckily, I haven't given him formal notice of our plans to leave, so there's still room for negotiations."

"*Negotiations*! These are two teenage girls we're talking about. Kes's daughters. What's there to negotiate? We have to get them back. We've delayed long enough waiting to pick up Wilder and Niall."

"What you're forgetting is that Wilder and Niall are essential crew. Miki and Nina went to the surface of their own free—"

"They're kids! They don't have any idea what they're doing or the danger they're in."

Her tone stubborn, Vessey continued, "They have as much information at their disposal as everyone else aboard this ship, and though they might not be quite adults yet, they are intelligent and capable individuals. If they don't want to leave their father's grave site, that's up to them. I have a responsibility to *all* the *Sirocco*'s personnel, not just those two. If it were only a matter of picking them up it would be different. But I can't risk more of my people searching an entire planet to find them, delaying our departure for who knows how long." As she'd spoken, the captain's voice had grown louder and more strident. By the time she finished she had the attention of everyone in the hold.

"Are you talking about Miki and Nina?" Niall asked.

Cherry replied quickly, depriving Vessey of the chance to spin the facts to fit her agenda. "They got it into their heads they need to stay on Earth and not return to Concordia. They don't want to leave Kes." She choked up. *She* didn't want to leave Kes either. But he was dead. He had no knowledge of and didn't care who might visit his remains.

"You have to understand," said Vessey, "Buka suspects we plan to leave. Miki and Nina's actions have given him bargaining power and he's using it. Whereas before we could come and go as we pleased, now he's saying we need to request permission to land, that the 'increased use of air space' must be managed for safety. It's complete nonsense, of course. All they have is a few helis. We'd be in more danger of colliding with a flock of birds than hitting one of their aircraft."

She swallowed before continuing, "Painful as it would be to leave the girls behind, the simplest solution would be to do just that, which, after all, is exactly what they want."

"You don't know that," Cherry protested. "They could have changed their minds already and be looking for a way to come back. We don't know where they are or who they're with. They could be wandering around the countryside trying to find where their father is buried. Or Buka could be holding them against their will, refusing to allow them to comm us. We don't know anything, and the only way to discover the truth is to go down there and find them, speak to them face to face, and hopefully persuade them to come back."

"What about these?" Maura touched a dead Scythian with the toe of her boot. "The latest development changes things, doesn't it? The aliens have been snatching humans, presumably to study, but now we have two specimens of our own, plus one of their ships."

"So?" Vessey asked.

"So we can offer the Earthers information about the enemy in exchange for returning Miki and Nina."

"You clearly don't know the first thing about diplomacy. As soon as Buka knows we're prepared to offer something valuable for the girls he will up the stakes, demanding more and more concessions and delaying the process in order to squeeze as much out of us as he can, while also getting us to stick around as long as possible. I'm not prepared to accept further delay. We need to leave soon, before it's too late."

Cherry had a horrible feeling it was already too late, that there was no hope of saving Concordia. She was also not persuaded by Vessey's reasoning, though she had to concede that diplomacy was not a personal strength. Maybe the captain was right. "Do you mean we should pretend Miki and Nina aren't that important to us?"

The captain replied resignedly, "*If* there is a way to get them back quickly and simply I'm happy to hear about it. But what Maura is suggesting would take weeks, firstly to gather data and then to bargain with Buka."

The discussion had captured Dragan's attention. "What if we offer to give them the bodies and the ship in return for Miki and Nina? Straight exchange. If Buka doesn't know where they are, that would light a fire under him to find them. The whole thing could be over in a day or so."

Vessey shook her head emphatically. "*We* need these bodies and the ship. We can use the information we glean to protect Concordia when the Scythians inevitably return."

Cherry had another reservation. If Miki and Nina had to be dragged, screaming, back to the *Sirocco* they might never get over it. It could damage them forever. They stood a better chance of staying alive, but at what cost? She had learned the hard way, while caring for Wilder when she was a teenager, that forcing them to do what *you* thought was best rarely brought good results.

There had to be a better way. She just didn't know what.

"I have an idea." Niall walked to the alien nearest the ship and grabbed its wing tip.

"An idea about what?" Cherry asked.

"Uhh, sorry. I meant about opening the ship. Could someone give me a hand?"

Niall and Dragan pulled the corpse over to the small vessel and up onto it. The helmeted head flopped and bounced, the lax features sagging. Niall pressed the tip of a claw against the hull.

"I get it," said Dragan. "There's no patterning on that spot. Maybe it's a sensor."

"That was my guess," Niall agreed, "but it didn't work."

"We could try another claw or another part of its body."

"Try its foot," Cherry offered.

"Its foot?" asked Dragan.

"They hold stuff with their lower limbs and use their wing claws for cutting and slicing. You're forgetting they fly. They would fly onto the ship and open it, not climb onto it like a human."

"Makes sense," said Niall. "The one that snatched Wilder held her with its feet."

"Whatever you say." Dragan hauled the creature around until its feet were nearest the bare patch on the hull. It didn't seem to take much effort, though the Scythian had to be three times his mass.

Niall tried each toe of one foot in turn. At the third try, the humped section split from the rest of the ship. "We're in!"

FIFTEEN

It was hard for Wilder to pay attention as Aubriot questioned Strongquist II. The news about Miki and Nina was extremely worrying. The girls were smart and resourceful but they'd spent most of their lives on a starship. They would have struggled to survive by themselves on Concordia, let alone on a planet with a poor infrastructure and where the inhabitants had gone into hiding.

She itched to ask Aubriot what was being done to find the missing children and if there had been any news of them. Had her and Niall's trip delayed the search? She would feel terrible if it had.

But Aubriot was busy drilling the android for information.

"Did these Makers, as you call them, give any indication of where they were going when they left?"

"As I've already told you," Strongquist II replied patiently, "all I know is that after the *Mistral's* departure they planned to abandon the site. There was no reason for them to stay, and they feared the launch of the starship would attract unwelcome attention. Though few of Earth's inhabitants possessed significant military capability then, the number of intruders had increased and there was a realistic threat of a sustained attack. Furthermore, the Makers had no reason to stay once their work was done."

"All right," Aubriot said tetchily. "Where do you *think* they might have gone? Where would it have been logical for them to go?"

Wilder asked, "Why do you want to know? What difference does it make? The *Mistral* left Earth centuries ago. The Makers are all dead and it's a different place now."

He turned to face her sharply. "Because those people were the last of the peak of scientific and engineering achievement in human civilization. They weren't the country bumpkins messing around with ancient artifacts they don't understand living down there today. You think you're smart, right?"

"Well…"

"You are. You're a freaking genius. Niall and Dragan aren't far behind you. Imagine a hundred of you. A thousand. The cream of human intelligence. Do you think people like that would fade away, living out their lives tilling the soil and brewing their own beer? If you lived on Earth now, if you'd grown up there, is that what *you* would do? Would you be satisfied with that kind of life?"

Wilder recalled the long years on the *Sirocco*, with little more to do than keep the ship running and maintain the growing systems. "I would be bored out of my head."

"I know you would. So would the Makers. Wherever they went, whatever they did, there's a chance they left stuff behind that we can still use."

"That we can take back to Concordia? The Ark's already full and the Scythian ship takes up most of the hold. We don't have space to stow anything big."

"Use to defend Earth!" Aubriot spat, glaring.

If a man could be said to be beautiful he was it, but when he got angry he turned ugly fast.

Wilder leaned slightly away from him. "But I thought we were leaving—as soon as we get Miki and Nina back."

"That might be what Vessey thinks, but that woman doesn't have her head screwed on straight. If we give up on Earth, what's the point? We might as well throw in the towel." He continued more softly and as if partly speaking to himself, "The kids aren't so important. We have bigger issues at stake. Much bigger." Narrowing his eyes, he returned his attention to Strongquist II. "Do you have a list of all the equipment at the construction site?"

"Not an exhaustive one, I'm afraid, only a general understanding. And as I was showing Wilder and Niall around I noticed some things were missing."

Aubriot swiveled aggressively toward Wilder again. "You toured the site? Why didn't you tell me?"

"You didn't ask. What did you think I would do? Just leave?"

"I want to know what you remember. Everything. Write it down and send it to me." He swiveled back to Strongquist II. "One more thing. What's in your programming about the Concordia colony?"

"Nothing at all. I was not constructed for the same purpose as my counterparts."

"You don't have any protocols to follow about assessing personality types and their fitness to lead?"

What a strange question. Why was he asking that? Wilder vaguely recalled a run-in between Aubriot and the Guardians.

"I do not."

Aubriot regarded the android suspiciously, as if he suspected him of lying.

She asked, "Do you know what purpose you were constructed for?"

"I believe I am a prototype. Perhaps the first successful model. The history of my manufacture was never explained to me."

"But you are programmed to protect humans," she said. It seemed obvious from the android's behavior when the Scythian snatched her.

"That function overrides all others, including self-preservation."

Aubriot rose to his feet and slapped Strongquist II on his back. "Useful bloke to have around. Just remember, you don't need to interfere in the ship's politics. Got it?"

"I don't anticipate doing anything in that regard."

She watched Aubriot leave. As was his habit, he hadn't said he would see her later or anything like that, and it wasn't only because he didn't do platitudes. He knew she disliked him and that was unlikely to change. There was no point in social niceties between them.

She had a bad feeling about his mention of 'ship's politics'? He clearly disagreed with Vessey's decision to return to Concordia. What exactly did he have in mind?

Strongquist II was watching her expectantly. She didn't know what to do with him. Apart from Aubriot, everyone else seemed to have forgotten about the android's existence in all the excitement over the Scythian bodies and their ship.

"Um, you should wait here until Captain Vessey decides what to do with you."

"As you wish." Strongquist II rested his hands on his knees.

Wilder walked to the door. She desperately wanted to shower and change into her own, clean, clothes, but something occurred to her. "If you had to choose between defending Earth and returning to Concordia, which would you pick?"

"I am reluctant to give a reply. I don't believe I have sufficient knowledge of the situation on the respective planets to make an informed decision."

"Fair point. What if you had access to all the available information? Would you tell us then?"

"I will give my opinion, for what it may be worth."

"I'll ask Vessey to give you access to the ship's database. You can find every—"

"What?!" Cherry had arrived. "What did you just say?"

"I was telling Strongquist II I'll get him access to the *Sirocco*'s data."

"Are you out of your mind? Have you gone crazy? Why the hell would you think it's a good idea to allow that thing access to our data?"

"He has a high level of computing power."

"*It*, not he."

"Okay, *it*. It's difficult to not think of it as a man."

"Try harder. Have you forgotten all about Faina?"

Wilder put a hand over her mouth. "*Shit.*"

She hadn't exactly forgotten. She'd been present when the Guardian had appeared on Concordia decades after it was supposed to have destroyed itself smashing the *Mistral* into a Scythian ship. Hell, she'd gone with Kes to the site where the escape capsule had crashed. After that, she hadn't had much to do with Faina because she'd gone to live with Quinn on the *Opportunity*. It had been Cherry who had followed the android into the ancient Scythian city.

Faina's programming had been compromised by the aliens. They'd sent her to the planet to re-activate the defense systems that would destroy approaching starships. The android had been turned against the colony, her functions subverted.

"What do you know about that thing?" Cherry demanded. "You don't have a clue about it, do you? All you know is that it was at the *Mistral*'s construction site. That's it."

Wilder stared at her.

"And now it's here, with us, on the only ship with the only people who stand the tiniest chance of putting up a fight against the Scythians. You think that's a coincidence?"

Strongquist II hadn't moved while they talked. He sat still with his hands on his knees, facing the bulkhead. Cherry strode up to the android and peered behind his ear.

"May I ask what you're looking for?" he remarked mildly.

She peered behind his other ear and then inspected his neck, pulling at his collar to look down it. "Where is it?"

"Where is what?"

"You know what I mean. Where's your off switch?"

"My... *off switch*? I'm not mechanical per se. I have an inbuilt power pack and—"

"How can we turn you off?" Cherry demanded. "All the Guardians had a mole or a freckle somewhere on their neck that could be pressed to turn them off. Where's yours?"

"I understand what you mean. That was a feature of the later model. I can only be deactivated and activated remotely. I have no external controls."

"Figures. How do we deactivate you remotely?"

"The computer on Svalbard can emit the signal."

"Double figures. Stars, you're a liability."

"I had anticipated being an asset."

Cherry turned to Wilder. "I'm going to tell Vessey we need to return it to the surface, fast. It's too much of a security risk. We can look for Miki and Nina at the same time. Are you up for that?"

"Absolutely. I just need to get changed."

"Be quick. I'll stay here with it to make sure it doesn't do anything shady. If Vessey won't let us take it back to the surface I'll try to persuade her to destroy it. Actually, maybe it would be better to destroy it right now."

Strongquist II's eyebrows rose.

Sixteen

Dakarai Buka stared mournfully out from the interface. He seemed to have aged in the brief interval since Cherry had seen him. Captain Vessey stood to one side of the screen, her arms folded tightly over her chest. She looked furious, perhaps understandably. As she'd explained after summoning all the ship's personnel to the bridge, Buka had told her he had important news to convey but he would only give it with all the Concordians present.

"It's as if he doesn't trust me to relay news from Earth to you truthfully," she'd concluded.

Maybe the suspicion of the GAA's leader was correct. The captain's eagerness to leave Earth and all its problems far behind was no secret. Cherry suspected that if Miki and Nina hadn't pulled their stunt Vessey might not have agreed to his demand.

The old man's eyes drooped and his lips sagged as he spoke. From off screen came Itai's translation. "I received a report half an hour ago from a distant province in South America. You may remember the incident where Scythians snatched a mother and father while they were out in the jungle with their two sons? Thankfully, the children were unharmed, though their parents have never been found. This report comes from the same area."

Buka took a deep breath before continuing, via translation, "Last night, the aliens emerged from their dome, flew to the nearest village, and murdered every man, woman, and child. Only one young woman managed to escape. She walked through the night and the morning to reach the nearest habitation and tell others of the massacre. I say she managed to escape, but it would be more accurate to say the Scythians let her go, for she...she..." he wiped his eyes and breathed in deeply again "...she has what I believe to be a message carved into the skin of her back. I won't show you it. It is too distressing. But after a doctor cleaned up the wound I had a copy drawn."

He held up a sheet of paper. "Can any of you tell me what this might mean?"

The paper was covered with short, vertical lines. Cherry winced, imagining the many cuts they represented. At the top of the paper—presumably in the area of the woman's neck—were two lines standing alone. Below them were eight rows of eight lines.

"Sixty-six," said Vessey. "Sixty-six in total."

"Yes, we can count too," Buka snapped.

Wilder asked, "Is that how many people were killed?"

"Sixty-nine people died, seventy if you include an unborn child, so the numbers only roughly correspond."

Niall said, "The Scythians have four toes on each foot. It would make sense they use base-eight for their number system."

"What's base-eight?" Itai asked, not waiting for Buka's response.

"It's just a different way of counting, from zero to seven instead of—"

Wilder gasped and clapped her hand over her mouth. Tears started into her eyes.

"What's wrong?" Cherry asked. "Have you figured out what it means?"

"It's not complicated," she replied in a strangled tone. "It's a simple representation. Two equals sixty-four."

"Two what?"

"Mr Buka," Vessey said, "we'll discuss this matter and get back to you." She cut the comm. "Wilder, explain."

"It's easy," Niall said heavily. "Two Scythians equals sixty-four humans, give or take."

"I see," Vessey said. "The two Scythians you killed. The massacre was retaliation for their deaths."

"Well, technically it was Strongquist who killed them, but..."

The aliens had implemented a brutal deterrent against further attacks.

A pall settled over the bridge.

Aubriot asked, "Does Buka know about the Scythians Strongquist killed?"

Vessey replied, "Not unless someone has gone behind my back to tell him. He doesn't know anything about the trip to investigate the signal and neither do any other Earthers."

"So he doesn't know we have one of their ships either. We need to keep it that way."

"That was my plan, for now."

The screen flashed. Buka was hailing the ship.

"He didn't wait long," someone muttered.

"You'd better answer," said Wilder.

"I'd better?" retorted Vessey. "Why?"

"We need to maintain a dialogue. Miki and Nina are down there!"

"Yes," said Cherry. "We have to get them back."

Vessey bit her lip and studied the assembled Concordians from under hooded eyes, as if trying to get the measure of their feelings about the missing girls.

Cherry repeated forcefully, "We have to get them back. They're just kids, and they're the children of a highly valued and respected member of this team. I can't believe you're contemplating leaving them behind, not after everything Kes did. If it weren't for him we would have starved to death. The least we can do to honor his memory is to not abandon his children."

"She's right," Aubriot said. "Can't ditch the nippers."

Cherry rolled her eyes. He didn't care about Miki and Nina. He was only jumping on the opportunity to keep the *Sirocco* in orbit, hoping there might be a way to protect his beloved Earth.

"They are half-Earthers..." someone mumbled.

Cherry stared at the crowd but couldn't figure out who had spoken. It might have been Marcus, blinded by Wilder when he attacked her. The man seemed to seethe with silent hatred for everyone and everything. Judging from other expressions, the sentiment of the Concordians was mixed. No one else spoke, probably not wanting to commit themselves.

Vessey said, "Every day, the possibility of Scythian military backup arriving grows greater. The longer we delay our departure the more likely it is we'll *never* depart. Is that what we want?"

Silently, the interface blinked.

"Aren't our hands tied anyway?" Maura asked. "Any attack on the Scythians will be avenged on the local population thirty-two fold. Many Earthers are in hiding but some have nowhere safe to go. We have to consider them."

"We do," Vessey agreed, "but let's not get our priorities mixed up. Are we for the Earthers or our own kind? Do we try to save someone else's planet or our own?"

"Now, hold on," Aubriot said. "Don't turn this into them and us. We're all human beings. And you're lining up the situation here with some airy fairy notion of what might happen somewhere else. For all we know Concordia could be dead. Like it or not, Earth might be our only chance for survival. Seems to me that after all this time, that's the real situation."

"I wish Kes were here," Wilder murmured. "He would know what to do."

"If Kes was here," Cherry said, "we would already be planetside searching for the girls."

"All right," Aubriot announced, slapping his knee before standing up. "Vessey, you're not a bad person, but you're no leader. There. I said what's been obvious to anyone with eyes to see right from the start. All through this mission you've been shilly-shallying, dithering, going backward and forward, and it's getting us nowhere. It's clear what's needed here is a firm hand."

A voice called out, "And we can guess who you mean."

Aubriot shrugged. "There's no point denying it. I *do* think I could do a better job. But don't forget, I could have gone around—"

"Sit down!" Vessey blurted, turning pale.

"I could have gone around behind the captain's back rallying support," Aubriot repeated, speaking over her, "but I haven't. At heart, I believe in democracy."

Cherry snorted.

"I said, sit down!" Vessey's gaze roamed the room but no one was looking at her. All attention was on Aubriot. She slumped into a seat.

"I propose a vote of no confidence in our captain. If the majority thinks she's competent to lead, fair enough. I'll shut up and let her get on with it. If she loses the vote, we'll elect a new captain. Someone who'll make a decisive plan about what we do next. Maybe that'll be me, maybe it won't. What do you say?"

Chaos erupted as everyone started shouting at once.

"Who are you to tell us what to do, you freak?" someone yelled above the rest. "What's wrong with you?"

"Yeah," a second voice added, "how come you never seem to get any older? Everyone's aged on this trip except you. What's that about?"

Aubriot looked taken aback. His gaze flicked to Cherry, the only person who knew his secret. She stared back at him blankly.

Before the thread could be followed, however, someone else exclaimed, "You can't have a vote of confidence about the captain of a starship! That's mutiny."

"But he's right," came the reply. "We need someone to make a concrete decision, someone who can think of the best way out of this mess."

"I say we vote!"

"No, he's only doing this because he knows Vessey wants to leave, and she's right. Concordians for Concordia. What did the Earthers ever do for us? They killed Kes with their nasty disease."

Cherry tried to figure out who had spoken. It had sounded like Maura but she wasn't sure. It wasn't possible to tell in the sea of flushed, angry, and agitated, faces. The volume of voices rose.

Aubriot was looking at her, a peculiarly intense expression on his face. As soon as he caught her gaze he nodded toward the corner of the room. She followed his direction. Zapata stood there, leaning his back against the bulkhead, arms folded over his chest, head down, like he was fed up with all the arguing. She felt the same.

Still, what was Aubriot trying to signal?

She looked back at him. He nodded in the direction of the pilot again, more emphatically. Then he said to the crowd, "I'm just stating my opinion. Everyone's entitled to their opinion." He made a subtle gesture, flicking his fingers at her.

He wanted her to leave? With Zapata?

He wanted her to leave with Zapata.

She grabbed Wilder's arm. "Let's go."

"Where?"

She stood on her tiptoes to whisper, "To get the girls."

Understanding dawned in the younger woman's eyes. They quickly eased through the mob of over-excited Concordians.

"Zapata," said Cherry. "Can I speak to you outside?"

"Sure, anything to get out of here."

It was quieter in the passageway. When she explained her proposal to the pilot, he hesitated but only for a few seconds. "Vessey's gonna kill me, but what the hell. This mission's turned into a free for all, and I hate the thought of those girls down there by themselves."

Cherry was partly elated, partly furious. She finally had a chance to find Miki and Nina and bring them back. On the other hand, she was playing right into Aubriot's schemes. He didn't really care about the girls. He was only using them to undermine Vessey's authority and force her to keep the ship in Earth orbit a while longer.

Everything was about him and what he wanted, as usual.

SEVENTEEN

As Wilder stepped down from the shuttle, she surveyed the surroundings. It was here that Miki and Nina would have snuck away from the vessel, probably the instant Zapata had left it. By the time the Concordians had boarded, the girls would have been long gone.

Where?

It was a bleak place. The site the Global Advancement Association had picked for their headquarters was in the north of a large continent, not as northerly as the seed vault, but sufficiently high latitude to give a distinct chill to the air. Unlike the island of the seed vault, this area wasn't forested. A small settlement stood a kilometer or so away, and a few low buildings huddled beyond the landing pads. Flat plains stretched out in all directions to the featureless horizon.

No, it wasn't featureless.

Wilder squinted and shielded her eyes with her hand. To the east a small bump broke the monotonous view. Light from the low sun glinted on the structure.

"Is that what I think it is?" she asked. Cherry and Zapata were chatting as they exited the shuttle.

Cherry checked and replied heavily, "Yeah. It's one of their domes."

"So close to the GAA?"

"They're all over the place."

"But why didn't the group move after the aliens arrived?"

"There can't be many underground complexes. The association probably didn't have a lot of choice except to stay here. It's this way." Cherry headed for the buildings.

They didn't get far before several figures emerged.

The shuttle's arrival had been noticed.

Cherry said, "Now we find out how serious Buka was about asking permission to land." She halted. "I don't think it's a good idea to leave our only method of getting back to the *Sirocco* unattended."

"You think they'll try to steal the shuttle?" asked Zapata. "They'd have a hard time piloting it."

"That wouldn't stop them from taking it." She glanced at the vessel and then the small delegation approaching. "Are there weapons aboard?"

"Always."

"Then I suggest you go back and lock yourself in."

"What about you guys?"

The danger of what they were doing was beginning to dawn on Wilder too. She'd been focused on finding Miki and Nina, who were like sisters to her. But now that Dakarai Buka suspected the Concordians were about to abandon Earth, who knew what he might do? And here they were, walking right into his hands. "Maybe we should get a couple of those rifles."

"I thought about it," Cherry replied, "but no. If we act too aggressively it's only going to inflame the situation. Let's tread carefully for now."

"I'll be waiting for your comm," said Zapata. "Good luck."

While the pilot retreated, Wilder said, "Tread softly? That doesn't sound like you."

"I guess I'm getting old."

One of the men arriving to greet them was Itai, the translator. "We're delighted you decided to pay us a visit, though it's somewhat unexpected."

Cherry replied, "I apologize on behalf of our captain for not seeking permission to land. We're here on an urgent matter that couldn't wait for formalities."

"I see. I'm sure Mr Buka will be eager to hear about it and do all he can to help. Please come with me. Your, er..." he glanced at the shuttle "...pilot won't be joining us?"

"He's busy running flight checks. We don't expect to be here long."

It was Wilder's first time at the GAA headquarters. From the bare, utilitarian style of the place it seemed to be a former military bunker or some other governmental building. Someone had mentioned that the GAA had resurrected its ancient geothermal energy system.

They descended with Itai to the lower level, and he took them immediately to a small room. The leader of the GAA was waiting.

The old man didn't get to his feet. He gestured for them to sit down, murmuring something Itai didn't bother to translate, probably a greeting. He continued, "We appreciate your quick response to this terrible tragedy, and we understand why you didn't follow protocol and request permission before landing."

Terrible tragedy?

For a heartbeat, horror seized Wilder as she inferred he was talking about Miki and Nina. Then she realized he meant the massacre at the Earther village. Vessey had cut the comm after he delivered the news. He hadn't heard from the ship since.

"We, uhh..." Cherry stumbled over her words as she also took a second to catch his meaning. "We were so sorry to hear about it. I don't think you've met my colleague. This is Wilder, one of our engineers."

The old man nodded at her then returned his expectant gaze to Cherry.

Wilder said, "We were all devastated to hear what happened. Is there any more news?"

"The location of the attack is very remote and the government has few resources. We haven't received any updates yet but I expect more information will reach us in the coming days. I'm eager to hear about your plans to help us now the Scythians have taken this next, horrific step. Did any of you make sense of the markings on the girl's back?"

"We're still working on it," Cherry said. "We're actually here for another reason. We want to retrieve two Concordian girls who arrived when the shuttle came to collect us the other day."

"Two girls?"

"They were supposed to stay on the ship but they stowed away and snuck out while no one was watching. We're here to take them back."

"Their names are Miki and Nina," Wilder added. "They're teenagers." Buka and Itai seemed genuinely puzzled, though she was wary of trusting her impression. She wasn't good at reading people.

The two Earthers spoke for a while. Itai left the room. Buka, Cherry, and Wilder sat in awkward silence, the language barrier a gulf between them, until Itai returned a few minutes later.

"There are no girls from your ship here," he announced.

"But they have to be," said Cherry. "Where else could they go?"

"I can assure you, no Concordians are present in this base."

"They must be hiding. They're intelligent, and one of them is strong-headed. They must have found somewhere—"

"It isn't possible. We've recently taken in about fifty refugees and we're packed to the rafters. There's only one way in and out. They couldn't have entered without someone noticing."

"Could someone be helping them?"

"Why would anyone do that? We're living on rations. Why would anyone give up their food to a pair of strangers?"

Wilder said to Cherry, "They must have gone to the settlement out on the plain."

"That's deserted," Itai responded quickly.

"That doesn't mean they aren't there," Wilder retorted.

Cherry said, "I'm still not convinced they aren't here, somewhere."

Buka spoke. He seemed agitated.

Itai listened and appeared to weigh his words before translating, "We're naturally concerned for the welfare of the adolescents, but we have weightier matters at hand than two runaways. Mr Buka would like to know what you're going to do in defense of Earth."

"As I said—" Cherry's words were cut off as Buka spoke again. She waited.

"We believe your ship to be armed," Itai said. "Otherwise the Scythians would have attacked it. You could destroy the Scythian domes, or fire upon their ships. The aliens should receive a clear message that their invasion will not be tolerated."

Cherry snapped, "If it was as easy as that don't you think we would have already done it?"

"I don't know," Itai translated. "Would you? Wouldn't it be easier to avoid any risk to yourselves and leave us to our fate?"

"Avoid any risk to ourselves?!" She rose to her feet. "You realize you're talking to one of the people who broke into a Scythian dome? Someone on our team nearly died."

Buka also stood up, leaning on his cane. Spittle flew from his mouth as he spoke.

Itai said woodenly, "Our pilot on that mission *did* die, one of the very few we have. Hundreds more of us have been snatched. An entire village was annihilated. And you expect sympathy because a few of you put yourselves in danger?"

Wilder touched Cherry's arm. "We aren't getting anywhere. We should go take a look at that settlement."

"I apologize for Mr Buka's anger," Itai said. "He is under a lot of pressure. The GAA is one of the few organizations with the reach to mount a response to the invasion, but even we lack equipment and skills to act effectively."

"Look," Cherry said, "what you don't understand is..." She hesitated.

Wilder squeezed her arm, fearful she was about to spill the beans about the Earthers' hopeless predicament and the *Sirocco*'s imminent departure. "Sit down."

As Cherry took her advice, Itai said, "What don't we understand?"

Wilder replied, "The situation is complex. It's going to take us a while to figure out a strategy for helping you. We need time to work on it." She felt like shit for lying to them. Despite Aubriot's challenge to Vessey's leadership, it seemed a foregone conclusion that the Earthers were on their own. Realistically, there wasn't anything the Concordians could do. Everyone would realize that eventually, even Aubriot.

"And in the meantime," Itai said, "you want us to find these girls?"

"That's right," Cherry replied.

"I will speak with Mr Buka and we'll see what we can do."

The men talked. Buka appeared to calm down. He glanced at Cherry and Wilder. After a little more discussion, he nodded.

"Phew," Wilder murmured. "I think he's agreed to help us."

Cherry was watching the men suspiciously. "I'm not so sure."

Buka addressed them as if he was taking his leave, and then hobbled out.

Itai said, "We will arrange a team to search the base top to bottom."

Cherry replied, "I thought you said it wasn't possible they're here."

"I, er, may have been wrong. Please wait. If we find them I'll let you know immediately."

Itai stepped toward the door.

Cherry got up and followed him. "Can we search too?"

"I'm afraid not."

He shut the door.

Cherry turned to face Wilder. "I don't trust—"

A noise had interrupted her.

It was the sound of a lock snicking shut.

Eighteen

Cherry closed the comm to Zapata.

"Did he say where he's gone?" Wilder asked.

"Not exactly. He's found somewhere in the middle of nowhere with no visible habitations. He'll wait there."

"For how long?"

"As long as it takes for us to get out of this mess."

"You're sure he won't just go back to the ship?"

Cherry shrugged. "What can I do? It's up to him what he does." She had abandoned her chair and was sitting on the floor, leaning on the wall. She rested the back of her head against it. "I've known Zapata a long time. He's usually pretty reliable. Did you know he flew me to Suddene once, in the middle of a storm?"

"I didn't. When was that?"

"During the Biocide Attack. I had to get there to..." She sighed. "Never mind. It was when Isobel died." She closed her eyes and rubbed them.

"Are you okay?"

When she opened her eyes she found Wilder watching her with concern.

"I'm just pissed at myself," she explained. "Coming down here was dumb. How could we have been so stupid? Now Buka has four bargaining chips—us and the girls. We've played right into his hands. Vessey's going to be furious." She slapped her forehead. "And I went and told him you're an engineer. He knows how valuable you are. He knows our captain won't want to leave without you."

"We didn't get a chance to think this through."

"It was Aubriot's fault, pushing me to go right there and then, to sneak out while Vessey was distracted. If it hadn't been for him we wouldn't be here. Damn that man. I hate him."

"What *is* it with Aubriot?" Wilder asked. "Someone at the meeting said about him not getting any older. I've noticed it too. It's weird."

"Everyone must have noticed by now. He won't get away with it much longer."

"Get away with what?"

"I suppose it won't hurt to tell you. It'll come out in the end, one way or another. You know Earthers used to genetically engineer their embryos?"

"I'd read about it, yeah. They used to remove abnormalities and congenital diseases, then progressed to enhancing intelligence, physical attributes, etcetera."

"Well, you can imagine the level of engineering Aubriot's parents could afford. They used an experimental treatment on him, designed to eradicate aging."

"*Eradicate* aging?! I mean, I can understand they could maybe delay it. You're telling me he's immortal?"

Cherry gave another shrug. "Even he doesn't know how long he'll live, but, for now, the treatment's working. As far as I can tell, he hasn't aged a day since he was revived on the *Nova*."

Wilder whistled.

"If only being immortal compensated for being an asshole," Cherry continued. "I honestly don't know what I ever saw in him."

"Apart from his perfect body and devastating good looks."

Cherry gave a sly smile. "There is that. But even they don't count for much in the end."

"He really likes you, though. I can see it in the way he looks at you."

"*Likes* isn't the right word. I don't think he likes anyone, at least not more than he likes himself. I'm a challenge to him. He knows I loved someone else, preferred another man over him, and he can't stand it. So he spent years with me, hoping I would grow to love him as deeply."

Wilder didn't ask who it was she'd loved so much, and Cherry was grateful. She continued, "And he can't take rejection. It wounds his massive, fragile ego. When I left him it was the greatest insult, even though he deserved it. He thinks he should be able to do whatever he wants and still have me hanging on his elbow. He can't get over the fact *I* broke up with *him*. *That's* what you see when you see him looking at me."

The door opened. Two armed men stood outside. One entered and roughly searched them. He seemed to be looking for something. When he came up with nothing he inspected them more closely. Cherry wondered if he was going to make them strip. But when he checked her ears he found what he was looking for. He flicked out her comm and put it in his pocket. Then he did the same with Wilder's. The Earthers had figured out they must have told their shuttle pilot to leave.

The other guard gestured with his rifle.

"Looks like we're going somewhere," Wilder said.

"And I liked it here so much." Cherry joined her as they were forced from the room.

The guards took them deeper into the complex and down another level. They passed Earthers, who eyed them curiously. The place was indeed packed as Itai had said. Things were getting desperate. Two years of living in hiding, watching the skies for the Scythians' return, and now doubling down on their restricted movements, had had a disastrous effect on the Earthers' already fragile infrastructures.

On the lower level they were taken to a dead-end corridor and put in a room with two bunks, a reinforced steel door, and toilet in the corner.

"They plan on keeping us here a while," said Wilder.

Cherry noted the dismay in her tone. "Don't worry. It won't be much different from the time we went to the Galactic Assembly. We'll get through this."

The door closed with a clang.

"Do you think the others might leave without us?" Wilder asked.

"Not a chance," Cherry replied, with more confidence than she felt. In fact, they were both expendable. Vessey was desperate to leave, Niall and Dragan could operate the jump drive, and Aubriot... Aubriot would be Aubriot, looking out for number one. "We'll be fine."

———

Their share of the Earthers' rations at dinner time featured salty porridge, crackers, pickled vegetables, and water.

"We ate better on the *Sirocco*," Wilder muttered.

Cherry stoically chewed a cracker. She'd spent the last few hours going over their options. All seemed bleak. Their chances of escape were minimal. She couldn't take on the guards one-armed, and though Wilder could fight if backed into a corner she was no warrior. Plus, the guards had weapons. Not pulse rifles—they appeared to be similar to the projectile-firing devices the Scythians used—but deadly nonetheless.

Their only hope lay in persuading Buka to let them go, but the old man would never do that without a massive incentive, and she couldn't think of anything to offer him. Would he even believe her if she did? He knew the decisions lay with Vessey. What had he told the captain?

When their meals were finished, she told Wilder they should sleep.

"I don't think I can."

"Then lie down and rest at least. It's going to be a hard few days until this is sorted out. We need to stay focused."

"What's the point?" Despite her words, Wilder lay down. "Do you think they're going to turn out the light?"

They didn't turn out the light.

Long after Wilder had fallen asleep, the cell remained illuminated. Cherry rested on her back, her hand behind her head. She'd given up on trying to figure out what to do. Her mind had traveled back to the early years of the Concordian Colony, to Ethan and Cariad, to Garwin and Twyla, to the arrival of the Guardians, the destruction of the *Nova Fortuna*, and to the building of Sidhe.

The remainder of her missing arm ached as she recalled the moment a Scythian spider had sliced it from her body. She didn't remember anything after that until she woke up in the infirmary. She'd learned later that Aubriot and Ethan had saved her, and that Aubriot had put her over his shoulder and run with her to safety.

Just like he had inside the Scythian dome.

In his own way, he cared about her. But even if she could forgive his infidelity, which she didn't think she could, she could never be with him again.

What time is it?

The minimal sounds of activity had died away a while ago. Deciding to take her own advice and try to get some sleep, she turned onto her side and closed her eyes.

Footsteps approached along the corridor. It was an odd time of night for visitors. Perhaps someone had come to retrieve their dinner trays. But there seemed to be two sets of footsteps.

When the door opened, Itai stood outside with a guard.

Cherry sat up.

"Please wake your companion and come with me."

"Huh? Does Buka want to speak to us?"

"Quickly, please." Itai glanced at the guard.

Cherry shook Wilder's shoulder. "We have to go."

Wilder groaned. "What?" She blinked and sat up. "Where? What's happening?"

"I don't know." Something about the situation seemed odd. "Get up."

Itai took them to the stairs leading to the upper level. He told guard something. The man shook his head. Itai spoke again, more forcefully. After some back and forth, the guard appeared to relent.

"This way." Itai ascended the steps and the guard remained at the bottom.

"He isn't coming with us?" Cherry's suspicions were growing.

"I will explain everything soon. For now, it would be extremely helpful if you don't ask any questions and do exactly as I say."

Was he breaking them out of the place? It was one explanation for his shady behavior. As the only person who could communicate with the Concordians, Itai must have achieved a measure of trust and authority in the GAA. If anyone could convince the guards that Buka had asked him to collect the prisoners and that accompanying them was unnecessary, it was him.

But why?

Why was he doing this?

The translator had nothing to gain from helping them and a whole lot to lose. If things didn't go according to plan they could end up cell neighbors.

On the next level the corridors were quiet and empty. Itai took them at a fast walking speed to an area that was new to Cherry. "Are you going to tell us where we're going?"

He replied quietly, "Contrary to what I said earlier, there is a second exit. It's kept locked and therefore unguarded. I managed to get the key."

"Thanks," Wilder breathed. "Thanks so much."

"Wait until we're outside. You can thank me then."

The other exit was at the top of a second set of stairs and dusty with disuse. When Itai tried to open the door the key wouldn't turn in the lock. He tried again, twisting sharply. Somewhere distant, a baby began to cry. Itai looked over his shoulder. His attempts to open the door became more frantic.

"It's probably just rust," said Wilder.

"Rust? What's that?"

It was a simple word, but he was speaking a second language. Cherry told him, "You need to hit the lock with something. Do you have anything heavy?"

"Would this work?" He pulled a hand weapon from his waistband.

They took a step back.

"You could try," said Wilder, "but be careful."

Itai banged the grip sharply against the lock three times. The noise echoed up the corridor. He shoved the weapon into his pants, and gave the key another sharp twist.

The lock opened.

They ran out.

It was deep night, and frost sparkled on the land under the starlight. The black, blocky shapes of the bunker's surface buildings stood two hundred meters away.

"Can I thank you now?" Wilder asked.

"You're welcome." Itai smiled. "But I have something to ask in return."

Now his actions made sense.

Cherry said, "You want to come with us to Concordia."

His smile widened. "Naturally."

NINETEEN

"We shouldn't be doing this," Nina whispered.

Miki rolled her eyes. It was so typical of her sister to change her mind at the last minute. Not even at the last minute. It was too late to leave their hiding place now. If they did, the pilot was bound to notice. Then he would tell Captain Vessey and they would be in deep trouble.

"We *are* doing it," Miki replied. "So be quiet, or Zapata might hear us."

She did *not* want to get found out. This was their only chance to go to Earth. The captain had ordered an immediate recall of all personnel to the ship, and Zapata was going to collect them. That had to mean the *Sirocco* would be returning to Concordia very soon. It was now or never.

She had to get to Earth. The idea of leaving Dad behind filled her with so much sadness she couldn't bear it. Losing him had been hard enough. Never being able to visit his grave was a prospect she couldn't even consider. He wouldn't be a few kilometers away, he would be light years from them, alone in the dark.

It didn't make sense. She knew that. She knew he wasn't conscious of anything anymore. But knowing it didn't change the way she felt.

A gentle hum permeated the storage locker they were hiding in.

"That's the a-grav field," she said. "This is it. The shuttle's about to leave. We can't back out now anyway." The only light penetrating the locker came through the slim gap around the door, so she sensed rather than saw Nina's frown. Miki added, filling her voice with confidence, "Don't worry. It'll be fine. The Earthers will look after us."

The entire trip down to the surface her heart beat hard in her chest. The source of her fear had changed from the threat of discovery. Now, she feared what might happen to them after they arrived. She hadn't thought that part through carefully. All she knew was they had to remain hidden until after the *Sirocco* left, so there was no chance the Earthers would give them back.

She didn't know how long the Concordians would search for them before they gave up, nor how she and Nina would survive while they waited.

Surely it wouldn't be that hard.

The sensation of flying came to an end as the shuttle's drive cut out and the vessel landed with a small bump. Miki clutched Nina's arm and whispered, "We have to wait until Zapata leaves. Then we slip out."

Nina didn't reply. She must still be having second thoughts. It didn't matter. They were committed.

The clunk and whoosh of the hatch opening followed. There was a click from the pilot's cabin door and then heavy footsteps passed by right outside the locker.

Miki softly counted to ten before taking a peek. The passenger cabin was empty. She climbed out, stood to her full height and stretched. Nina climbed out too.

"Don't forget the bag," Miki reminded her.

Nina reached into the locker for it.

"Hurry up."

Zapata had sealed the hatch but there was an emergency release. Miki twisted the handle and the hatch split from the hull. Cold air swept in. Outside, gray cloud blanketed the sky. The shuttle sat on a concrete pad. There was a group of low buildings, and a narrow road led to a small town. Both places seemed deserted.

So far, so good.

She'd been worried they would be seen by Earthers immediately and reported, but there was no one around. It had to be something to do with everyone hiding from the Scythians. That was what Cherry had said. They'd all gone underground.

Luckily for us.

Nina said, "Maybe we should—"

"Come on!" Miki trotted down the steps. When her sister remained at the top, she said, "Give me the bag."

Nina was forced to come down to comply. As soon as Miki had their few belongings and supplies, she walked quickly away from the shuttle. She didn't want to run in case someone noticed and thought they looked suspicious.

There was Zapata!

She hadn't left enough time. He had his back toward them, heading for the buildings. If he looked behind he would spot them.

She turned in the opposite direction.

Two of the Earthers' helis were parked on pads. Beyond them was open countryside. Wide open. The area had once been farmers' fields but weeds covered the ground.

Miki checked over her shoulder. Nina was following, and Zapata had nearly reached a building. He hadn't seen them. When he returned to the shuttle he would find the hatch open, but maybe he would think he'd forgotten to close it.

"We'll go there." She indicated the town.

They waded through waist-high vegetation, moving directly across country. Prickly seed heads caught on their clothes as they brushed past the plants. Soon, they were covered in them. Insects buzzed all around. Something crawled up Miki's sleeve. She flicked it off.

She vaguely remembered a time on Concordia when a cloud of flying pests had descended on her and Dad. He'd carried her into their house, shielding her from the attack. But she couldn't remember any other life forms on her home planet. Only humans and the biting insects. Earth was so full of life. There had been a time when Concordia had been like this, but now it was barren. Earth was better. Once the Earthers had fought off the Scythians, it would be good to live here.

When they reached the first house, she looked back at the shuttle. The landing area remained empty. Her tension eased. Her plan had succeeded. No one knew they'd left the *Sirocco*. Now all they had to do was find somewhere to stay for a few days and wait for the Concordians to leave.

At first glance, their new dwelling didn't appear promising. The little town had clearly been abandoned ages ago. Doors and windows stood ajar, revealing empty interiors. Weeds from the fields encroached the streets. An overturned stroller lay at a corner, rusted and grimy. If she remembered rightly, it had been two years since the aliens paid their first visit to Earth. The people who had lived in this place might have gone into hiding soon after, judging by the state of things.

"*Don't* tell me we're going to live here," said Nina.

"Only for a little while."

"What will we eat? Is there even any clean water to drink?"

"Stop complaining. Do you want to be near Dad or not? You didn't have to come with me if you didn't want to."

"You didn't tell me we would be living in a dump."

"What did you expect? Did you think we would be living in a palace? Life on Earth is different from how things were on the ship. A lot different. Things are harder here, but they're...richer. Life is more fulfilling." There was only so much she could make up to try to appease her sister. She sought a distraction. "Let's look in there."

The door to one of the houses was closed, as if someone had taken the time to lock it. Useful things might be inside—things like food, bedding, and warm clothes. She was already feeling cold despite their exercise crossing the fields.

"Is Dad even buried near here?" Nina asked as Miki tried the door.

It opened.

"I don't recognize this area," Nina said. "Do you know where we are? Dad might even be buried in another country. Did you consider that?"

Miki was looking at a cramped but comfortable living space. "Hello? Is anyone home?"

The closed door had prevented dust from blowing in from the street. Two small sofas faced a fireplace. It was the first fireplace she'd ever seen, but the ashes and grate told her its purpose. Painted pictures of flowers and landscapes hung on the walls. A rug covered most of the wooden floorboards.

A strange feeling crept over her. She had the impression she'd stepped back in time.

"Hello?"

Was someone living here?

The remains of the fire could be days or years old. She simply couldn't tell.

"There's a kitchen," said Nina excitedly, all her misgivings apparently forgotten. She'd always been like that. Her mood could change in an instant.

"Check the cupboards." Miki followed her sister. "The previous owners might have left someth—"

"There's lots of food!" Nina stood in front of an open cupboard filled with packets of dried basic supplies.

Miki recognized flour, noodles, beans, and peas.

"And here." Nina had triumphantly opened another door. "And here! There's enough to last us weeks."

A rifle stood propped against a wall.

Miki's relief and elation rapidly sank. "No."

"No what?"

"We can't stay here." She glanced into the living room, half-expecting to see it occupied.

"Why not? This is the perfect—"

"Someone already lives here. We have to leave, now."

"But—"

"Now!" She grabbed her sister's arm and tugged her toward the exit.

"Ow, you're hurting me. I thought we were going to live with the Earthers. That's the whole point. What are you frightened of?"

"We're going to live with the Earthers after the *Sirocco* leaves. If they find us now they might send us back to the ship. We need to..."

A noise had come from somewhere in the house.

"What was that? Did you hear something?"

Her sister shook her head. "What did it sound like?"

"Shhh! There it is again."

The noise had been louder. It had been human. A human voice, but not speaking.

The third time the voice sounded, Nina's eyes widened. "I heard it. It's coming from over there." She pointed at the open door leading into a hall, adding, "It sounds like someone's hurt."

Miki silently nodded. The noise the person was making was the groan or cry of someone in pain.

"We should help them," said Nina.

Miki clenched her hands into fists. She didn't know what to do. They *should* help the person, but that would mean revealing their presence.

Nina said, "Dad would want us to help them."

Put like that, the answer was simple. "You're right."

While they'd been talking, the person had groaned again. They walked toward the sound. Miki went first. Beyond one door was an empty bathroom. The other door was closed.

She knocked. "Are you okay? Can we come in?"

The person answered in a language she didn't understand. She looked at Nina, who shrugged.

"We're coming in."

A man lay in a double bed, the covers pulled up to his chin. Closed curtains blocked the daylight, so it was hard to make out much more. The man's hair was straggly and greasy, and long stubble clothed his face nearly to his eyes.

"Are you sick?" Miki asked. "Do you need something?"

The man replied in a quiet, grating tone.

She couldn't understand a word or even guess at his meaning. She stepped closer. "My name's Miki, and this is my sister, Nina. We did knock at your front door but no one answered." It was a lie but he couldn't understand her anyway, and pretending made her feel less guilty. "We can go if you don't want us here, only..." She looked around the room. Her eyes were becoming accustomed to the low light.

A dresser stood open, clothes spilling out. She returned her attention to the man. "Are you ill?"

He didn't seem ill. His eyes were bright and his skin looked healthy, if rather dirty.

As they held each other's gaze, she began to see something in his expression she didn't like. Something hungry and mean.

"If you don't need us, we'll go." She turned to her sister. "We're leaving."

She took a step away from the bed.

The man threw back the covers and leapt out. He was fully clothed. He'd never been ill. He'd been pretending.

Miki tried to run.

A large hand caught her forearm and clamped tight.

"Nina, go! Run!"

Her sister froze.

In another instant Nina broke from her trance and moved, but the man was ahead of her, hauling Miki with him as he strode closer. He shoved Miki into her sister so they tumbled to the floor, stepped out of the room, and slammed the door shut. A key rattled in the lock.

Disentangling herself from Nina, Miki yelled, "The window!"

She raced to it and tore open the curtains. It was locked too.

"Smash it!" Nina exclaimed.

They looked around for something hard, but the only things that might break the glass were the bed and the dresser, both too large and heavy to lift.

"I'll punch it out," Miki announced.

"Be careful."

She snatched a shirt from the floor and wrapped it around her fist.

But as she drew back her arm, the man appeared outside.

He was aiming his rifle at them.

They backed away.

He yelled and gesticulated. He wanted them to sit on the bed.

Would he really shoot unarmed girls? Miki couldn't believe it, but she had Nina to consider. She could not put her sister in even more danger.

She sat down.

TWENTY

The man came for them not long after it turned dark. It was hard to tell night had fallen. The man had hammered planks onto the outside of the window, blocking out most of the light. Miki thought he had come to bring them food or at least some water, or maybe he would allow them to go to the bathroom, but he didn't do any of that. He pointed the rifle at them, tucked under the crook of one arm. He was holding something in his other hand.

When Miki saw what it was she quailed.

Two lengths of cord dangled from his fist.

"What does he want?" Nina whispered.

"I-I think he wants to tie us up." Miki hoped she was right, and that he didn't want to do the other, unmentionable thing that sprang to mind.

He thrust the cords at Nina and then pointed at the door.

"He wants you to go into the hall with him," said Miki.

"I don't want to." Nina was clearly on the edge of tears.

"I don't want you to either, but I think you must." *Why, oh why did I bring her here?*

If something bad happened to her sister she would never forgive herself. What was she talking about? Something bad was already happening to her. "Nina, I'm so sorry."

"It isn't your fault. I'll do what he says. Maybe we'll find a way to escape." Nina went to the door and gave Miki a single, wet-eyed glance before stepping into the hall.

As soon as the man shut the door Miki flew at it. She thumped it with her fists and screamed, "If you hurt my sister I'll kill you! I swear I'll kill you!" She continued to thump it until it jerked open again so forcefully she was knocked to the floor.

The man kicked her, first in her ribs and then in her head. The second kick dazed her. She lay still, confused and not resisting as he bound her wrists. Then he picked up his rifle. He gestured for her to stand up.

Nina's hands were also tied. Jabbing them with the muzzle of the rifle, the man forced them out of the house. No lights were on in the town. All was still. The place was as quiet as it had been when they'd arrived. The man had to be living here alone. For some reason, he'd remained after everyone else had left.

He indicated the direction he wanted them to go.

Starlight glittered in an obsidian sky. Space looked different down here on Earth than from a starship. Here, the stars seemed to move ever so slightly. Looking out from the *Sirocco* they were steady pinpricks of light. Their appearance from Earth should have been more friendly, but it wasn't.

They passed the last houses, standing each side of the road, and then they were out in open countryside.

Where could the man be taking them? Was he taking them away from his house to...to...? Miki shook her head. She couldn't contemplate the threatening thought. She focused instead on looking around for possible ways to escape. Vegetation grew tall on the borders of the road. If they could run into it he might not find them. But he would have time to get one or two shots off before they were hidden. However, he couldn't shoot at both of them at once.

"Nina," she whispered, "we can't let him take us to wherever he's planning to go. We need to get away. When I give the signal, you run into the weeds, okay?"

"No way."

"You have to!"

"I know what you're going to do. You're going to try to distract him so he doesn't shoot me."

"No, I—"

"Yes, you are. And then what happens?" Nina asked quietly but fiercely. "What if he doesn't catch me but you're dead? What do you think I'm going to do all alone with my wrists tied? How am I supposed to go on without you?"

Miki didn't have an answer. For what felt like the millionth time she regretted not bringing ear comms. She'd been so determined they weren't ever going back to the *Sirocco* she'd left hers behind and made Nina leave hers too. She'd been so, so stupid. "Maybe you can find some other Earthers who—ow!"

The man had jabbed his rifle in her back, in the exact same place he'd kicked her. She got the message and stopped speaking. Her burgeoning bruise throbbed and her head ached in sympathy.

They trudged on through the night. The dirt road split off to a narrower, more overgrown track to the left, but the man didn't take it. He kept them going straight another few hundred meters, until suddenly he jabbed Miki again. She cried out, not understanding what she'd done wrong.

Nina said, "I think he wants us to go that way."

There was a gap in the vegetation, barely one person wide, where the plants had been trodden down. Miki stepped off the road, Nina followed, and the man continued walking behind them. The little path was hard to see in the dark, and a couple of times the man shouted when she veered off it.

Then she saw where they were heading.

How she hadn't managed to spot it before, she didn't know. Perhaps it was because she'd kept her head down, focusing on following the trail. The structure was still some distance away, but it stood out plainly as it glowed gently in the night. A pale silver dome protruded from the surrounding shadowy scrub. It had to be one of the Scythian domes she'd heard people talking about on the ship.

"Oh!" Nina exclaimed softly. She'd seen it too.

He was going to give them to the aliens?!

Why would he do that? He had to be mad. The Scythians were the Earthers' enemies. They'd been abducting people all over the globe. Why would he hand over two girls he didn't even know and for no reason?

That was *it*. There was no debating any longer. They had to escape. They might die in the attempt but at least it would be quick. Who knew what horrors lay in wait for them inside a Scythian dome?

"Nina, when I count to three, run."

"No!"

"Don't argue. One, two, thr— arghhh!" The rifle dug into her ribs. "Now!"

She whirled and kicked the muzzle. Not hard enough. It flicked up but the man held onto it. She ran at him head down, and drove into his chest. He stumbled backward. Her momentum kept her going and, unable to use her arms for balance, she began to fall forward. Her forehead smacked against the man's knee as she went down. It hurt but didn't stun her. The impact seemed to complete the man's stumbling because suddenly he was under her.

Where was Nina?

She had no time to check that her sister had done as she'd asked. The man was squirming under her, trying to get both hands on his rifle. She bit his arm. The man grunted. He was heavier and stronger than her. She had to do something to knock him out, fast.

She thrust the top of her head into his jaw and heard his teeth snap closed.

A yell of pain erupted from him.

Had he bitten his tongue?

She leapt to her feet and kicked his head once, twice. For the third kick she recalled him kicking *her* head and kicked even harder. He groaned and rolled. Still, his eyes didn't close and his grip on his rifle remained firm. Liquid oozed from his lips, black in the low light. She aimed a fourth kick, but before it landed his hand shot out and fastened around her ankle.

He tugged sharply and she fell on her backside. She tried to scramble upright but he was faster. A boot thudded down on her middle. The man was standing over her, the weight on his right foot crushing her. She couldn't move. She couldn't breathe. She brought up her knees and squirmed, trying get out from underneath him but it was no use.

Wavering slightly, the man lifted his rifle.

He'd given up on his plan of taking her to the Scythians.

He was going to shoot her.

Thick drops of blood dripped from his chin and spattered on his boot as he took aim.

Her vision narrowed to the gaping hole of the barrel, through which would come her destruction. She turned her head and shoulders away. Her muscles became rigid as she prepared for death.

Would she see Dad again?

She hoped so, though it was sooner than she'd wished.

There was a cry—a female cry, then a yell of rage. Quick footsteps followed and a thump of impact.

The weight on her chest was gone.

The man hit the ground. His rifle was knocked from his grasp. Nina kicked it further away.

"Run!" she shouted. "Miki, run!"

She turned onto her front and managed to get her knees under her. In another second she was up and running. Vegetation flashed past, snatching at her clothes. She didn't know where she was going or where Nina was. All she knew was she had to put as much distance between herself and the Earther as possible, before he could get his rifle and come after her.

If they could both hide so long he gave up looking for them, they could find each other in the morning. Maybe they would even be able to untie their wrists.

A tremendous crack exploded.

She gave an involuntary jerk.

He'd fired.

The noise was far louder than a pulse rifle.

Had he hit Nina?

There was another shot.

Please, don't let him hit Nina.

She crouched as she ran and glanced from side to side. She couldn't see the Scythian dome. It had to be behind her.

Where's the man?
Where's Nina?

When Miki had run for a few minutes, she slowed and took a look over her shoulder. It was hard to see much in the darkness, but the Earther didn't seem to be in sight. She slowed down some more. Then, panting, she stopped and dropped low. Peeking over the foliage, all she saw was a sea of dark gray leaves, stalks, and dry seed heads. She ducked down.

Where was her sister? Was she okay?

She rested for a moment, catching her breath, and then took another look. Stillness and silence confronted her.

No.

Over to the left the plants gently rustled and swayed.

Praying she was heading for Nina and not their attacker, Miki crawled toward the movement. The rough ground scraped and scratched her knees. Rarely daring to raise her head, she trusted she wasn't going too far off course as she continued on.

As soon as she found Nina they could hide together and wait out the night. The man would have to give up searching for them eventually.

The vegetation crackled and swished. Something was coming toward her.

She held her breath.

It was impossible to get away without making a noise. She could only wait, frozen between fear and hope, unable to see farther than a meter all around.

A head burst into view.

Nina!

"Miki! I found you! I thought I saw—"

"Shhh!" Miki urged. "He might be listening."

They huddled close, gently sobbing. They were together again. That was something. Miki didn't know what they should do next, whether they should go back to the place where the shuttle had landed and try to find some friendly, not-crazy, Earthers to help them, or if they should find another way out of their predicament. Whatever they did, at least they would not be alone.

A draft of stinky air hit her nostrils. At the same time, something hit the ground behind her.

Nina's features turned rigid with fear as she focused on something over Miki's shoulder.

"Wh—" Before she could get a word out, steely hands fastened around her waist and she was swept up into the air.

Twenty-One

"What does that mean?" Itai demanded.

"It means," Cherry retorted hotly, "we can't contact our pilot."

She'd just explained about the guards removing their ear comms. She wasn't sure how Itai had imagined Concordians communicated with each other. Had he thought they had some kind of inbuilt system? But the information was obviously news to him. He must have anticipated the shuttle arriving soon after they escaped. But without a way of comming Zapata, that wasn't going to happen in the short term, perhaps never.

Itai swung wildly around, recklessly waving his gun. "But it won't be long before your absence is noticed. Buka will figure out how we left and he'll send men after us."

"No, really?" Cherry asked sarcastically.

"Maybe we should go back," Wilder suggested. "If we return immediately, we might make it before anyone notices we're missing."

"That can't happen." Itai said. "I must leave with you. You haven't stated it outright, but it's clear that you think Earth is doomed. I agree, but *I'm* not. *I* still have a chance." He muttered something else to himself in his own language as he peered into the night.

"What other option do we have?" Wilder asked. "It sounds like we're going back in that cell whether we like it or not. There's nowhere to hide in this wilderness, and even if there were Buka's guards would soon find us."

Cherry said, "I'm not in love with the idea of going back in there." Her gaze was on the weapon Itai was carelessly moving around. She made eye contact with Wilder. If they could coordinate they could get it from him. She might have tried alone if she had two arms. But Wilder didn't seem to understand her look. "We should leave. Let's not make it easy for them."

"I agree," Itai replied. "There's a small township not far away. We can hide there and wait for your pilot to return. It's that way." He indicated a direction and waited expectantly. When they didn't move, he added, "You two walk ahead of me."

So the fact he hadn't put his gun away wasn't accidental.

They had no choice except to comply. He guided them through the darkness across long-abandoned fields. Cherry wondered why the Earthers around here had given up farming after the Scythian attack of two years ago. Concordians had continued to grow crops despite the ongoing threat of the aliens' return. On the other hand, the Concordians would have starved if they hadn't. Earthers had survived by farming for a long time after the fall of civilization. They must have had plenty of stores to rely on. But the food wouldn't last forever. What was their long-term plan? They didn't seem to have one. It was no wonder they were desperate for the humans from outer space to save them.

She and Wilder walked in front of Itai for about half an hour across the semi-wild landscape until they hit a road. They followed the cracked, weedy surface for another fifteen minutes before they reached the outer buildings of the settlement. The houses had been empty for a long time.

"What happened to the people who lived here?" Wilder asked.

"They're in the bunker," replied Itai, "or they went elsewhere, or they're dead."

"The Scythians took them?"

"They killed themselves." Itai's tone was flat. "There were a lot of suicides in the months after the bombardments. Many people had lost everything, or feared a second attack, or refused to live in hiding."

The sky had lightened in the east. If Buka didn't already know they were gone, he would soon.

"Where are you taking us?" asked Wilder. "It won't be hard to search this place top to bottom. Hiding seems futile."

"I know somewhere. Turn to the left. It's down this street, I believe. It's been a while since I was here and the place has changed somewhat, but I think I'm right."

As they turned, Cherry got a look at Itai. He was glancing from side to side as if he expected someone to step out from the shadows.

She asked, "Do you think Buka's men are here already?"

"They would seize us immediately if they were. There's a rumor about someone still living here—someone gone mad from fear of the aliens. I don't know if the rumor is true but I'm not taking any chances."

The madman didn't appear. Itai took them to what had once been a shop.

The wide glass window was smashed in and the sign hung at a crazy angle. Inside, shelving ran the length of the place, all picked clean, whether by humans or animals.

"This was a grocery," said Itai. "There's a cellar out the back. We can hide in there."

"That's dumb," said Cherry. "If you know about the cellar so do others. We would stand a better chance of not being found out in the fields."

"It isn't safe out in the fields."

"Why not?"

"The Scythians regularly comb them for humans."

She had no argument against that.

They waded through debris to reach the rear of the store. Torn and gnawed packaging, dust, and plant matter blown in from the street littered it. As Itai had predicted, an open hatch in the back room revealed stairs leading down to a cellar.

"It's dark in there," said Wilder, peering in.

"Go down," said Itai. "I will find some lamps."

"But..." Wilder's protest dried on her lips as he lifted his gun.

"Please don't argue," he said. "I only need one of you alive."

Cherry said, "If you think you'll be allowed aboard the *Sirocco* after murdering one of us, you're deluded."

"Perhaps, but it's a chance I'm willing to take. I know your captain will be anxious to have her engineer back."

"This is insane." Wilder stepped down the stairs.

When Cherry had descended and her head was below floor level, Itai shut the hatch, plunging them into near-complete darkness. Only a faint ray of light escaped the edges of the opening.

"I can't see a thing!" Wilder complained.

Cherry's glimpse of the cellar before Itai shut them in had shown her a small room about four meters square. Shelves adorned the walls, all empty. As before, the floor was littered with the leavings of looters. "Just sit down somewhere. If you blunder about you'll hurt yourself."

She descended the remaining steps carefully, until Wilder's hand brushed her. "There are only a couple more steps."

They sat down together.

"Do you think he'll be back?" Wilder asked.

There were sounds of Itai moving around overhead. The idea that he might just shut them in and leave them here—bargaining for passage on the ship in return for revealing their location—had occurred to Cherry too. "I don't know. But don't worry. We'll be okay, I'm sure."

Wilder's arm snaked around her shoulders and hugged her. "You're not my mom. You don't have to reassure me."

Cherry chuckled. "I never was the greatest mom to you, was I?"

"You mean after my incident with the a-grav machine? Forget about it. I was a bratty kid."

"I'm not going to argue about it. Look, as soon as Itai's distracted, we have to—"

The hatch opened. Despite the short interval it had been closed, the light was blinding.

"I found a lamp," said Itai. "We don't have to sit in darkness." He walked down several steps and put down the lamp. Then he pulled the hatch almost completely closed and fiddled at the edge of it. "I've put a rug over the opening."

Cherry rolled her eyes. His tactic was an exercise in futility.

The lamp burned some kind of oil and gave off an unpleasant vapor. If Buka's people didn't find them soon they might die of smoke inhalation.

Settling down opposite them, Itai rested his gun in his lap, his hand loose on the grip. The lamplight cast up-shadows on his face, lending him a sinister look. Cherry hadn't managed to fully convey to Wilder her intention to overpower him, but she'd said enough to get her point across. Now all they had to do was wait for an opportune moment, when he was lulled into inattention.

"Something I've been wondering," she said. "You told us a group of refugees had arrived at the GAA's bunker. How did they get there? This place seems in the middle of nowhere, and I haven't seen any transportation except helis."

"They walked and rode horses. One family had a truck to transport children and the elderly."

"I didn't see any horses or a truck."

"The truck is in a barn. We ate the horses."

"Gross," Wilder muttered.

"So you have mechanized transportation?" Cherry asked.

"It was one of the first innovations of the GAA, along with roads, of course."

"What do your vehicles run on?"

"Alcohol. How is your planet's transportation powered?"

"Electricity."

"Ah, yes. That's right. I've seen it in old books. Unfortunately, we haven't managed to create the infrastructure for battery-powered vehicles. Before the Scythians came we had some power plants, but they were the first things they attacked."

"They knew what they were doing," Wilder said. "Destroying the frameworks of civilization."

Itai's mouth turned down and his shoulders sagged. "It was a terrible time. I lost my wife and children. I was away from home, in another city, organizing the foundation of a technology education center. It was the beginning of a new, bright future for humanity. From that school we would have sent out people trained in the old skills, possessing the knowledge of past generations. We would have sent them all over the world to teach others. Eventually, humankind would have regained everything we'd lost. But the Scythians came. They razed every major metropolis, blasted the roads, destroyed factories, manufacturing plants, apartment blocks."

He swallowed and continued, "By the time I made it home, my family had been dead for days, killed by falling rubble."

"I'm sorry." Wilder reached out to touch his free hand.

That should have been the moment. They should have jumped him and grabbed the gun. But Cherry didn't move, trapped by her thoughts.

In a sense, what had happened to Earth was Concordia's fault. If she wanted to be particularly egocentric it was *her* fault. The aliens had offered Concordia a choice: to submit to slavery or die. She'd overruled the Leader and defied the Scythians. As a consequence, they'd launched the biocide, killing hundreds of thousands of Fila and most other life. It had taken her a long time to come to terms with what she'd done, if in fact she ever had.

After leaving their home planet to die—as they thought—the Scythians had come to Earth. They'd found the coordinates from the Guardian, Faina, and they wanted to complete their revenge on humanity.

It was simple. If she hadn't refused the Scythians' proposition, if she'd accepted life under Scythian rule, they might never have come to Earth. The family of this man sitting opposite her might not have died. Civilization might have advanced here.

Heavy footsteps sounded overhead. Dust sprinkled down lightly, the motes shining in the lamp's glow.

Itai lifted his gun and put a finger to his lips.

The ceiling reverberated as something heavy was dragged across the floor. More footsteps resounded. There was a scraping noise and the shuffle of textile. The hatch flew open.

Itai lifted his weapon.

Cherry leapt on him. "Grab his gun, Wilder! Grab it."

He threw her off. She landed in a pile of trash. In the time it took her to struggle upright, it was all over. Guards had run down the stairs and Itai was on his face, a boot on his back. Another guard had his gun. Wilder was on her feet, staring slack-jawed at the open hatch.

Aubriot stood there, looking in, and next to him was Strongquist.

TWENTY-TWO

The flight to the Scythian dome was a nightmare Miki would not soon forget. Her stomach grasped painfully tight, she'd been carried aloft so fast it had taken her a minute to figure out what was happening. She recalled Nina's upturned face receding, pale in the starlight. Then a second creature had descended to snatch her sister, and it all made sense.

Pure terror had followed. Would the alien drop her, leaving her to plunge to her death? Or would it take her to its dwelling place, and what would happen then? Perhaps the first possibility was better than what else might happen.

And Nina. Poor Nina.

She couldn't bear the thought of what might happen to her sister.

The alien had flown with her to the dome. All the while a horrible smell had wafted down from its wings. The center of the dome's roof had spiraled open, and they had descended through the opening. Inside, a second portal had opened, barely visible in the scarce light. From then on everything was hazy. She recalled being unable to breathe, or rather, choking on the air. She must have passed out because the next thing she knew she was on solid ground and the pressure around her middle had gone.

A warm body lay next to her. She turned onto her side. It was Nina.

Thank the stars!

Nina was coming around.

"It's all right," Miki whispered. "We're safe."

For now.

She looked around. Others were here. Other people.

She sat up.

Earthers of all ages were staring at them, from little children to a woman so old she only had a few wisps of white hair clinging to her scalp. The group numbered about twenty, and they crowded together in one corner of the room.

It was a strange place. The walls were dark gray and made from a material she didn't recognize. It was smooth, matt, and featureless. Above, high above, was what seemed to be the ceiling of the dome, glowing softly like the sky at dusk. The walls didn't reach anywhere near it, at only about four meters tall. Atop the walls, forming a barrier over the room, was a layer of barely discernible, transparent sheeting.

An Earther spoke. A man addressed her and Nina.

Miki shook her head. How to convey she didn't speak their language?

"We can't understand you," Nina replied loudly, as if shouting might make her meaning clear.

The man spoke again.

Miki replied, "We aren't from Earth. We're Concordians." She cupped her ear as if trying to listen, and then gave an exaggerated shrug.

The man turned to talk to his companions. After a short discussion, he faced them again. The group stared at them once more in silence.

"What is this place?" Nina asked.

"Some kind of holding pen, I guess."

"How long will they keep us here? Are they going to let us go?"

"I don't know." In fact, Miki doubted very much that the Scythians had any plans to set them free. What did they plan on doing with them? She'd heard snatches of conversation aboard the *Sirocco* about the aliens kidnapping people, but as soon as the speakers noticed she was listening they shut up. If anyone knew what happened to the humans taken into captivity, she hadn't heard anything about it.

Nina said softly, her voice full of fear, "They're never going to let us go, are they? Do you think they're gonna...gonna..."

"Shhh!" Miki hugged her. She knew what her sister had been about to say. The same idea had occurred to her—that the Scythians might feed on humans. But the notion was too terrible to state out loud. "Everyone on the *Sirocco* knows we're missing. They'll be searching for us. They'll find us and rescue us."

"Are you sure?"

"I'm sure. Cherry and Wilder won't leave without us." As soon as the words were out, she knew they were true. What a stupid thing she'd done. Instead of talking to Dad's friends about how she felt, she'd run off and messed up their plans. They would either delay the ship's departure or they would stay on Earth to try to find them, missing their chance to go home.

A shadow crossed the pale light and the Earthers reacted with frightened murmurs. A Scythian was descending, holding something in its feet. It landed on the transparent barrier, which dipped under the additional weight. With one wing claw, it cut a slit and then emptied its burden through the gap. Something fell and hit the ground with wet splashes.

Instantly, the Earthers fell upon it, grabbing handfuls of the material and shoving them in their mouths. The man who had spoken before thrust a cupped, full hand in the girls' direction. He seemed to be holding a kind of cereal mash. Miki wrinkled her nose and shook her head. She was not *that* hungry.

"Is that all there is to eat?" asked Nina.

The question seemed rhetorical. "You should try some if you want." Miki looked up. The Scythian had gone and the cut it had made was no longer visible.

The Earthers cleared the food in under five minutes. They didn't exactly fight over it. They made sure the old and young were fed. But it was clear they were hungry. The aliens weren't supplying enough sustenance, either through ignorance or deliberately. If they didn't give more, eventually everyone would die.

"What do we do now?" Nina asked.

"We should try to get some sleep." It had been night when the crazy Earther had forced them out of his house and over the fields. They needed to conserve their energy for whatever lay ahead.

They moved to a corner of the room. Miki lay behind Nina and wrapped an arm around her, using her other arm as a pillow. The Earthers were settling down too.

"I don't think I *can* sleep," Nina whispered.

"Just try."

All thoughts of slumber were driven from Miki's mind, however, when another foreboding shadow crossed overhead. This time, two Scythians had arrived.

The Earthers reacted with terror, screaming and wailing as they crowded together.

One of the aliens slashed the ceiling open. The Earthers' screams became muffled. They had clapped their hands over their mouths.

It took Miki a couple of seconds to figure out why. "Nina, cover your mouth. Don't breathe."

Her sister's wide, frightened eyes stared out as she did as she was told.

The aliens descended, flapping lazily down. As soon as the first one alighted, it walked awkwardly across to the huddled Earthers and spread its wings threateningly. They were so wide they almost touched the walls.

The other Scythian waddled toward Miki and Nina. Though her hand covered her nose, Miki could smell its stench. She choked and coughed, accidentally breathing in the room's new atmosphere, which made her choke harder.

The alien hopped into the air and reached for Nina.

"No!" Miki thrust a hand against its midriff, pushing it away. The alien's skin had a horrible, greasy feel.

It landed and focused its strange eyes on her. One wing swept smoothly around, the claw catching her cheek and slicing it open. She shrieked and grabbed it. Hot liquid spilled from between her fingers.

"Don't!" Nina yelled. "I'll go with it." She pushed Miki out of the way.

"No!" Miki shouted. "Not my sister! You're not taking her." She tried to fight off the alien, and in return received two more gashes, one to her arm and another to her hand.

The creature wrested Nina from her grasp and carried her aloft.

"Noooo!" Miki screamed.

TWENTY-THREE

Cherry gazed sourly at Aubriot across the table. He was so full of himself, cocky with the knowledge that he'd 'saved' her again. Yet Buka's guards would have found them anyway, regardless of his and Strongquist's help. The fact clearly didn't stop him from being smug.

Itai's expression was a marked contrast. He stood handcuffed, flanked by armed men, his head down.

Buka trembled with rage as he spoke to him. Cherry was concerned for the old man, fearing he might have a heart attack or stroke. When Itai replied he seemed contrite. Was he apologizing? If he was, Buka didn't accept it. He barked an order at the guards, who grabbed Itai's arms to take him away.

Itai protested and struggled. When Buka ignored him, he turned to the Concordians. "He wants to lock me up but you need me, right? You need me to translate for you."

"Nope," Aubriot replied flatly.

"Your presence won't be necessary," said Strongquist. "I am able to perform translation duties. I have familiarized myself with the local language."

Were they aware he was a machine? Cherry didn't know who she trusted least. She gave Wilder a look, but the younger woman only shrugged. She wasn't familiar with Guardians. She'd only been a kid during the early years of colonization. And Aubriot had turned a hundred and eighty degrees in his attitude. At one time he'd seemed to hate and fear the androids even more than her, if that were possible. Now, because it suited him, Strongquist was his best buddy.

Itai was taken away.

Buka spoke to Cherry and Wilder and Strongquist related his words.

"Please accept my apologies for incarcerating you. I hope you understand we're in a desperate position and as leader of the GAA it's my responsibility to do everything I can to help my fellow human beings in this crisis. I hope you can forgive my actions and move on." He handed them their ear comms.

"I can't speak for Wilder," Cherry replied, "but I don't accept your apology. As far as I'm concerned what you did was unforgivable, and your apology makes no sense anyway. *I'm* one of your fellow human beings and you threw me in a cell. What had I done to deserve that? I came here to find two girls. That's it. And you took advantage of us for your own ends. So don't tell me you're sorry. I don't want to hear it."

There was a soft *tsk* from someone. Aubriot. He gave her a slight shake of his head, as if chiding her. She wanted to punch him.

"It really isn't excusable," Wilder added, though with less vigor. "You can't talk about helping humanity while at the same time incarcerating the innocent. Doesn't make a lot of sense."

"Your responses are noted," said Buka. "I will endeavor to be less hasty in the future. Can we discuss the plan for helping Earth now?"

Cherry was about to answer that there was no plan, that as soon as they found Miki and Nina they would leave the system and Earthers could go screw themselves, but Aubriot got his reply in first.

"The way I see it, there has to be a campaign of mass resistance. Everywhere, all over the planet, you guys have got to stand up for yourselves. Up until now, you've allowed the Scythians to walk all over you, like doormats. You've got to fight back, hard, with everything you've got. Blow up the domes, wage guerrilla warfare, attack, attack, attack. Show the bastards you're not going to be their slaves. If you want your planet back, it's the only way."

Cherry's jaw fell open. What was he talking about? Had he forgotten about the biocide? Did he want Earth turned into another Concordia? "But..."

He turned toward her, hard-faced, and repeated, "It's the only way."

Buka said, "There's no guarantee we will win."

"Right," said Aubriot, "but what you don't get is, it's been like this through most of Earth's history. Go back far enough and you'll discover everyone was at each other's throats for thousands of years. Millions died in wars. Billions, probably, as one leader or another fought for land, or money, or just the love of a beautiful woman. For humans, it's normal. It's what we do. The Scythians are just another catalyst for the same old same old."

Cherry couldn't find the words to respond. Wilder appeared similarly flummoxed.

"History's come full circle," he concluded. "We're back at the beginning."

Wilder spluttered, "I-I don't think that's right. There has to be a different way."

Cherry finally got her brain in gear. She leaned over the table to talk directly to Buka. "What he *isn't* mentioning, and what you have to take into account, is the Scythians' biocide. He told you about it in the early discussions you had with Captain Vessey. Do you remember? The biocide is the reason we're here. It destroyed most life on Concordia. If the Scythians change their minds about enslaving you, if you make their lives too difficult, they'll just kill every living organism here. Not only all humans. *Everything*. And there won't be anything you can do to stop it. Believe me, you do *not* want to see that stuff spreading over the land, through the water, destroying everything it touches. You do not want that."

Aubriot threw her a dark look. She smiled facetiously.

"I do remember you mentioning a devastating pesticide," said Buka.

"It isn't a pesticide as such," Wilder explained. "It's a virus. A virus that targets all living things, multiplying as it spreads. That's how it's so destructive."

"On Concordia," said Cherry, "we managed to vaccinate everyone. You'll never do that here."

"But you have the vaccine?" Buka asked.

"We..." They didn't have the vaccine but they could manufacture it, the same as they'd used Kes's blood to manufacture a vaccine against the Earth virus that had killed him. They had people who knew how to do it. "No, we don't."

"But we could make it," said Aubriot.

"Not in sufficient quantities," Wilder protested. "What's the population of Earth? A billion? Two billion? Do you even know?"

"The number is irrelevant if we can get the information out." Buka knitted his fingers and rested his hands on the table. "Ever since you came here, you've had a habit of acting...how can I put it?...superior? It's clear you think your society is far in advance of ours. But what have you really seen of Earth? When you arrived we'd already suffered one attack, an attack that caught us unawares. You didn't see the level of development we'd achieved before then. You also don't understand the GAA or our workings. This association exists to disseminate information. That's its primary purpose. We delve into the past—old data bases, ancient machinery, archaic books, even—strive to understand and reverse engineer, and then we spread what we know all over the world. We are already aware of how vaccination works. Give us the necessary—"

"You don't get it!" Cherry exclaimed. "Even if you manage to protect every human being, the biocide will kill everything else. How are you going to survive on a barren planet?"

"How did the Concordians survive?"

"We had stores, but—"

"So do we."

She groaned and put her face in her hand.

"You don't understand," said Buka. "People are already rising up. We've been receiving reports from all over the globe of attacks on the domes. Most are unsuccessful, but people are trying. They've had their loved ones taken away from them and they know what's coming next. They know the Scythians are preparing to subjugate all humanity. Many won't tolerate it. With or without your help, there will be a war. Without your help, we don't stand a chance."

"*You* don't understand," said Wilder gently, "Concordia is barely clinging on. That's why we're here—to collect the material we need to revitalize our planet."

"I do understand that very well," Buka replied. "And if you succeed in your endeavor, Concordia could return the favor to Earth. It could be the repository from which we draw in order to re-seed our planet."

"I'm no biologist, but even I know you're underestimating the amount of biodiversity here. It's built up over a billion years. What we've taken from Earth will only recreate a shadow of it on my home planet. I hope it'll be enough to kick start ecological development, then evolution can take over."

"Exactly as it can here."

"He's got a point," said Aubriot. "There's been plenty of mass extinctions on Earth. Each time, life started up again, spreading out, diversifying. If conditions are right, that's what happens, over and over. Scythians might try to kill everything but a few things will survive, the same as they did on Concordia."

"But...Earth is beautiful," Wilder said helplessly.

Then she was silent.

Cherry had no words either. Aubriot and Buka were set on their course, and she didn't have the inclination or willpower anymore to force them off it. But there was something else to discuss. "What about Miki and Nina? We have to find them."

"Now *that*," Aubriot said, "we do agree on. What's happened to the little tykes, Buka? Any ideas?"

"It seems clear they must have gone to the abandoned settlement where we found you, but I'm afraid they aren't there any longer. When my people were trying to find you and Itai, they searched the settlement thoroughly. There was no sign of anyone."

"They would have been hiding," said Cherry. "We need to search it again."

"There's something you don't know." The GAA leader looked uncomfortable, and Strongquist paused as he waited for him to continue. "The settlement was not entirely abandoned. One individual couldn't be persuaded to leave. He is mentally ill, and he was convinced the Scythians were gods who had come to punish humanity for its sins. It seems likely that, according to what the searchers found, the girls from your ship encountered him."

"So?" Cherry asked. "Then you just need to find where he's gone, and Miki and Nina will be with him."

"When I said no one was found at the settlement I was speaking the truth. However, the mentally ill man *was* found, wandering in the fields. From what could be gleaned from his babble, it seems likely that he took the girls to the Scythian dome and—"

"No!" Cherry yelled, leaping to her feet. "No, don't tell me that. It isn't true."

Strongquist continued his translation in an even tone, "...the aliens have them."

Twenty-Four

"Are you out of your mind?!" Cherry demanded after Buka had left the meeting room. She was boiling with rage, and she needed a diversion from the news that the girls had been taken by the Scythians and were probably dead.

There was no doubt who was the object of her question.

Aubriot replied, "Save it for the cowards on the ship."

"*Cowards*? It isn't cowardice to not want to die in a pointless war—a war that has nothing to do with us. Let the Earthers fight their own battles. We have our own problems to worry about. Does Vessey know what you're doing?" She had a suspicion he was acting unilaterally, that the captain hadn't agreed to the message he'd given the GAA. She might not even know about it.

"After you snuck off..." Aubriot began.

She restrained herself from hitting him. He'd all but *told* her to sneak away and go to the surface to find Miki and Nina.

"...I reminded the *Sirocco*'s personnel about their heritage, their duty, and what they owed to the people of this fine planet. I also made the very good point that what we learn here fighting the Scythians we will be able to apply on Concordia, when the time inevitably comes."

Her jaw set, Cherry replied, "So you persuaded them to stay."

"In a word, yes."

"You did it on purpose, didn't you?"

He raised his eyebrows innocently. "Did what?"

"If you're going to make me spell it out—you orchestrated everything so I was off the ship while you were giving your little speech, changing people's minds, because you knew I would argue against you. Like you, I've been around since the early years and people listen to me. You wanted a powerful opposition out of the way. You never gave a shit about Kes's kids. You wanted me gone. I'm right, aren't I?"

"That's not nice, Cherry. Of course I care about the girls. I'm not a monster."

"Huh. Maybe. But you care more about yourself and what you want."

Wilder said, "What about the *Sirocco*? If we help the Earthers wage this war, the minute the Scythian backup arrives they'll blast her out of the sky."

"Ah, I thought of a solution to that problem. Wouldn't have got Vessey on my side otherwise. The *Sirocco* only has to make a little jump to be out of danger." He lifted a hand and placed his fingertips on the table. "She starts here..." he moved his hand to one side "...and jumps here. At the right time, she jumps back again..." he moved his hand to its original position "...and picks us up. The Scythians don't have jump tech or they would be here by now."

"*At the right time*?" Cherry asked. "When's that going to be? This war will last years. It'll never be over."

"Millions will die," said Wilder.

"Everyone dies," Aubriot retorted.

"Not everyone. Not according to what I've heard."

Aubriot looked sharply at Cherry. She glared back.

"And what's going to happen to Concordia while we're gone?" Wilder continued. "We desperately need to begin the re-seeding process if it's going to be saved."

"Concordia's an open question," said Aubriot. "We've been gone so long, we don't know what we'll find when we get back. The colony might have died out. That's what Kes seemed to think would happen. In which case, what would be the point of restarting it? We can live here just as well."

"Not if the Scythians do the same here as they did on Concordia! Then we'll have *two* dead planets and nowhere to live."

Cherry said, "You don't want to go back, do you? You've decided you want to stay on Earth. You're home now and you don't want to leave. That's fine. But don't drag all of us into it. You stay here. We'll go."

"He wants us," said Wilder. "He wants me, Niall, and Dragan. We can help wage this hopeless war against the Scythians. And he wants all the scientists. They're the ones with the knowledge to help humanity survive a biocide attack. He wants the *Sirocco*, too, for everything she can offer. Maybe he plans on taking out as many Scythian ships and domes as he can before she jumps."

Aubriot gave a supercilious grin. "I always said you were smart, didn't I?"

"You're sick," said Cherry.

"And him." Wilder jabbed a finger at Strongquist. "You want him too."

"*It*!" Cherry said.

While they argued, the android had remained quiet. Now the attention was on him, he said, "I will fulfill my programmed purpose and defend humans wherever possible."

Wilder asked Aubriot, "Are you taking *it* to the Makers' place to look over the equipment?"

"You read my mind."

"Stars," said Cherry. "Is there anything you haven't thought of?"

"Something will come up. I'm not perfect." Aubriot knitted his fingers, turned his hands palm outward, and stretched his arms. He stood up. "Sorry, ladies. Lots of work to do. Strongquist, with me."

He left, the android in tow.

"That man's unbelievable," said Cherry. "Blithely committing millions of people to their deaths, like it was just another Tuesday."

"He's in his element. There's no stopping him."

"There is. There has to be. We just need to think of it. In the meantime..." She got to her feet. "We have to do what we came here for. We have to find Miki and Nina."

"But Buka said they must have been taken into the dome. It seems a solid explanation for their disappearance. It's devastating, but—"

"I'm not giving up on them and neither should you. They might still be alive. But before we do anything let's see what we can find out about what's happening on the ship."

They left the bunker and walked to the shuttle, where Zapata was lounging.

He straightened up as they approached. "I-I had to tell Vessey—"

"It's okay," Cherry interrupted. "You couldn't hang around forever, hoping we might comm you one day."

He seemed relieved.

"But," she continued, "if you feel like you owe us one..."

He sighed. "You want me to fly you somewhere? I mean, why not? It's not like Vessey could get any more furious at me."

"No, actually. I was wondering if you were there while Aubriot was turning everyone to his side."

"It was all over by the time I got back. I only got the chance to talk to a few people. Niall and Dragan were telling me they're making progress with the Scythian vessel we captured when Aubriot nabbed me and asked me to bring him and the android down."

"Did anyone tell you what happened after we left?"

"They didn't say a lot, and I didn't push. I try not to get involved, you know?"

Cherry did know. The pilot was notorious for never having an opinion on anything. He was one of those people who just did his job, which would have been fine in ordinary circumstances, but in situations like this, opinions mattered. "Do you know if they had the vote of confidence in the captain while we were gone?"

"I'm pretty sure they didn't. Vessey's still in charge as far as I can tell."

Maybe even Aubriot had concluded that was a step too far.

"Do you think the others really agree with Aubriot about helping the Earthers wage a war, or did he just browbeat them into it?"

"Honestly, I don't know."

Wilder asked Cherry, "Are you thinking you can get them to change their minds?"

"Maybe, but..." Thousands of dead Fila bodies, floating on the ocean surface, filled Cherry's inner vision. The decision to make a stand against the Scythians had been her greatest regret. The guilt she'd felt had been enormous, unbearable. Yet she could also understand the objection to living in thrall to another species. It was all too much to think about. Better to focus on the things within her control. "It's going to take Aubriot time to set things up. If we want to try to stop him, we still have days—days we can spend looking for Miki and Nina. We should get all the help we can to do that." A realization struck and her eyes widened. "I've had an idea." She asked Zapata, "You're confident Vessey's still captain?"

"As confident as I can be."

"Great. Wait here."

She found the android with Aubriot. The latter was in the midst of setting up an operations room within the GAA bunker. He was energized, barking orders via translation to the Earthers.

"Strongquist, can I talk to you a moment?" Cherry asked.

"Certainly."

"Don't keep him too long," said Aubriot. "I need my translator."

Ignoring him, Cherry said, "I want you to come with me."

"Uhh..." The android's gaze switched to Aubriot, who was overseeing the setup of interface screens. "For what purpose?"

"I need you to help us find the girls who have gone missing. You remember they've most likely been taken into a Scythian dome? I want you to help us get them out."

"In that case, I will go with you."

"Hey," Aubriot yelled as they reached the door, "Strongquist, where are you going?"

Cherry replied, "He's coming with me. He's going to help—"

"No, no, no." Aubriot strode closer, hands on hips, shaking his head. "Not happening. The android stays with me. Like I said, I'm worried about the kids too, but billions of Earthers take priority."

"Billions of Earthers you're committing to slaughter. Anyway, you can't overrule me. You don't have superior status. You're just another member of the crew."

"Oh, I see. Very clever, Cherry. Very clever. You remembered the Guardians have to obey whoever's highest in command."

"I did. I have a good memory, don't you think?"

"When it comes to hard feelings it's fucking excellent. Strongquist, you're programmed to protect humans, right? So you should stay here and help me plan Earth's defense."

"Defense isn't the same as launching a war," Cherry retorted. "*That's* what you're actually doing. Strongquist, there are two adolescent girls in immediate and present danger. I order you to help me rescue them."

"I...I..." The android looked from Aubriot to Cherry and back again. "I must go with this woman. When the girls are safe I will return and continue my translation duties."

"You can't leave! How the hell am I going to talk to these people?"

"Try sign language," Cherry said.

TWENTY-FIVE

The Scythians came for Miki later. When the ceiling had self-repaired and the room had filled with breathable atmosphere once more, some of the Earthers tried to tend to her wounds. There was little they could do. Though they wrapped the cuts in rags torn from their clothing she continued to bleed. The gashes were too long and deep, and the cloths were soon sodden with her blood.

She'd been lying down for hours, helpless and hopeless, paralyzed with fear for Nina and regretting everything she'd ever done, when two of the aliens arrived. Whether it was the same ones she couldn't tell. They did the same thing as before—one of them corralled the Earthers into a corner while the other tottered to her side in its ungainly gait.

She did not resist.

Not only was fighting back pointless, she *wanted* to experience whatever happened because that was what had happened to Nina. She'd persuaded her sweet sister to come to Earth. She'd taken her from the safety of the *Sirocco* and risked her life. Now it looked like both of them would die.

Dad would not have wanted this. He would have wanted them to stay safe. He would have wanted her to look after her sister.

Tears streaming down her face stung her cut terribly as the alien took her in its feet. She hung from it loosely, not fighting as it beat upward. She saw only the dome's ceiling as she was flown across the space, her chest heaving as her lungs fought to draw in oxygen. She could have turned her head for a sight of the aliens' dwelling but she had no will to do it, convinced she was going to a dire fate.

The alien landed. There was the sound of something ripping, and then it unceremoniously pushed her with one of its feet. She fell and hit a soft surface.

She could breathe again.

The ceiling of this room was opaque. Something at the edge of her vision caught her attention. A set of straps dangled from the center of the ceiling. The sight was so odd it made her turn her head.

A Scythian was suspended within the straps, its wings folded tightly and neatly along its back. A transparent globe enclosed its head, a tube leading to the wall hanging from the rear.

The creature was looking at her.

It moved toward her, tiptoeing on its long-toed feet. She understood the purpose of the harness. It allowed the creature to walk lightly and easily, not in the gawky, lumbering manner of the other Scythians she'd seen.

She was lying on a padded mat, raised about a meter off the floor. As the alien approached, she shrank to the edge and lifted her head for a better look at her surroundings.

Another purpose for the harness emerged. Low structures dotted the place. Some were flat, bare screens with displays, others held receptacles and equipment items, a few seemed to be for storage. The floor wasn't the bare earth of the humans' enclosure—metallic tiles covered the surface. It seemed to be some kind of laboratory, like the ones on the *Sirocco* where the scientists worked.

The Scythian had reached her. She couldn't escape. There were no doors, and the walls were too smooth and high to scale. Even if she could reach the ceiling, she lacked the aliens' sharp claws to cut through it.

"Leave me alone!"

The alien moved around the mat to her side. She scooted away again, but it must have activated something or issued a command. A web of threads erupted from all sides and pinned her down flat. As she struggled, the webbing tightened.

"What have you done with my sister?! Where's Nina? What have you done to her? If you've hurt her I'll kill you all! Every last one of you." Her threat was empty and ridiculous, considering her position, but it felt good to yell it out.

The Scythian hopped lightly up. It was so close its odor filled her nostrils and she gagged. A foot neared her face. She tried to turn away but the threads held her fast. She had a close-up of the bronze skin before shutting her eyes.

Was this it? Was it the end? Would it be quick, or would the creature cut her open alive?

There was a repetitive pinging sound, and the tension of the webbing on her face disappeared. As she opened her eyes the tip of a claw filled her view. She would have reared backward if she'd been able to move.

The expected slash didn't arrive. The claw moved out of her vision and was replaced by the creature's toe. The pinging sound must have been the noise of it severing threads over her face. The Scythian prodded the cut on her cheek and she sucked in a breath as pain knifed from it.

"Don't touch me! It hurts. Leave me alone. I want to see my sister! Where is she?"

The creature bent down until its globe-encased head was only a short distance away. Its eyes were round and white. A black line running down their middle widened as they drew closer.

Miki held her breath. Not only was the alien's smell horrible, the *otherness* of the thing was too awful to bear.

A cold, wet sensation hit her cheek. She flinched.

It must have applied something to her face.

The ache from her wound began to ease.

The alien inspected her other cuts. One wing opened out and it reached down delicately to slice the webbing over her injuries before smoothing an ointment over them.

She stopped struggling, transfixed. The Scythian was actually treating her. It seemed impossible, yet she couldn't imagine another explanation. When it had finished its claw swooped close to her face again and she gave a little scream, but it only touched her mouth.

She clenched her teeth and hissed, "Leave me alone! I want to see my sister. Let us go!"

The creature angled its head and tapped her mouth again.

"What do you want? Stop doing that."

The Scythian hopped down. She watched it as it tippy-toed over to a flat screen. The long toes swiped the surface, causing the display to change. She rested her head. She had no idea what it was doing. When would the ordeal be over? The fact that she hadn't been killed immediately gave her a small hope that Nina might be okay.

There was a hiss to her right. Her head snapped around. A robotic arm had appeared, sporting a long needle. The needle descended. She couldn't move away. She couldn't move a thing. As it pierced her she yelped. Several long seconds passed, and then it withdrew.

The Scythian was back. For a third time, its great wing unfolded and the claw drew close to her face. She was not quite so frightened as before when the tip poked her mouth.

"What the hell are you doing? Why do you keep doing that?"

The large eyes watched.

Her rage suddenly dissipated. She was weak and alone, far from her friends. She didn't know where Nina was or if she was alive. She didn't know if either of them would ever get out of this place or even live another day. "Please, please let us go. If you aren't going to kill us, let us leave. We'll go back to our ship and leave the system. I promise. I promise we'll go back to Concordia."

Dad would never have wanted this.

The alien moved away again.

She didn't bother watching it. She was exhausted and heartsick. She missed Nina already, and she missed Cherry and Wilder. She hated herself for making them worry.

The ceiling opened and a Scythian flew down. It slashed the netting, grasped her around her middle, and carried her up. When it descended she expected to go back to the room with the Earthers, but it had taken her to a different place. The alien dropped her before she reached floor level. She landed awkwardly and fell to her knees.

"Miki!"

It was Nina! She was here.

She was alive.

TWENTY-SIX

Aubriot's face was a picture as he strode out of the bunker and across to the landing area. Cherry could imagine what he must have been like as a toddler, screaming himself into a fit whenever he didn't get his way. She could have been the bigger person and resisted the urge to chuckle, but she did not, despite her fears about Kes's daughters. Aubriot's rage-filled expression was welcome light relief.

Her reaction didn't improve his temper.

"Funny, is it?" he spat. "All right, you win."

"It's very gracious of you to come all the way out here to tell me," she replied, "but I already know. So you might as well go back inside and twiddle your thumbs while we try to find Miki and Nina."

Wilder asked, "Can't you use Itai to talk to the Earthers? Buka won't mind, surely."

"Tried that," Aubriot replied shortly. "Buka was all for it, but Itai won't play ball unless I get a cast-iron guarantee from Vessey he has a berth on the *Sirocco* to Concordia. Man's not stupid."

"And the captain won't allow it?" Wilder asked.

"She says if she does that they'll all want to come."

"She's right," said Cherry. "She can't set a precedent. *She's* not stupid either."

"Short story is, you've got me. That's why I'm here. Not to offer my congratulations."

Cherry blinked. "We've got you?"

"I'm gonna help you in your useless effort. Then, when you finally realize it's a wild goose chase and those kids are sadly departed, I can have the android back and get on with the real business of fighting back against the invasion."

"They're not *sadly departed*," Cherry retorted, her voice trembling. "Don't say that."

"Whatever. What's your plan?"

"Who agreed to you joining us?"

"So you don't have one. No surprise there. But I have. You wanna hear it?"

"*I* want to hear it." Wilder interposed herself between them. "Have you thought of a way of getting the girls out of the dome?"

"Like I said, I think it's too late, but I know a way to get in and search it if that's what you want to do."

"How?"

"Slice the lid off it. Open it up like a boiled egg. We know the explosive we used before can crack the shell. You remember the Scythian city on Suddene, Cherry?"

How could she forget? Aubriot was the only other Concordian who had ever entered the place, when he'd destroyed the ancient planetary defense system—the system the compromised android Faina had been sent to reactivate.

He continued without waiting for an answer, "The rooms didn't have any ceilings, right? Didn't make any sense at the time, but now we know why. Flying's easier than walking for them. My guess is, the set up inside the domes is the same. And they must be filled with CO2. If we blast the top off, all their sweet carbon dioxide will escape, Earth's poisonous atmosphere will flood in, and pandemonium will ensue. Exactly the kind of chaos we need to look for the kids."

Cherry had to concede his idea made sense.

Wilder said, "A lot of Scythians will suffocate and die."

"All the better," said Aubriot.

"I'm not saying it's a bad thing, but what about the two equals sixty-four warning? For every Scythian killed in the attack they'll execute thirty-two humans. Does Buka know about that? Has anyone told him?"

Aubriot grimaced. "*They'll* execute them, not us. There are always casualties in a war."

"I don't like it either," said Cherry, "but what are we supposed to do? Let them walk all over us? People are going to die regardless, and we have to get Miki and Nina back. What the Scythians do in retaliation isn't our responsibility. We aren't the aggressors here."

"Now there's the woman I remember," said Aubriot condescendingly. "I was wondering when she would show her face again."

She gave him a withering look. "How do you plan on blowing the top off the dome?"

———

They approached at midday. The sky was clear, the sunlight strong and hot. Buka had given them plenty of the explosive substance. It was safe to drop it onto a hard surface. There was no danger it would explode on impact. A thick layer of adhesive coated each lump except for two spots where it could be held.

The GAA leader had allotted a large proportion of the group's military arm, created after the first Scythian attack. With Strongquist's help, Aubriot had outlined the plan. After that, the troops would mostly be acting alone. The android would take part in the mission, but real-time translation of orders would be difficult in a time-critical scenario. Buka had also loaned them five of the GAA's helis. The *Sirocco*'s shuttle lacked the maneuverability required for the first part of the mission. Zapata's role would come later—if they managed to break the shell of the dome.

"Cherry," yelled Aubriot, "I'm telling you for the last time, wait outside with Wilder. You can come in and search for the girls when we've secured the place."

She could barely hear him over the whine of the heli's rotors as it rose into the air.

"I don't take orders from you," she yelled back.

"It's not safe dropping into the dome unarmed."

She tapped the muzzle of the rifle she had strapped to her back.

"You know what I mean. You can't hold onto your rifle *and* the line. You'll be a sitting duck."

She didn't know what a duck was but she got the idea. "It'll only take a few seconds. I'll be fine."

"Then at least let me go below you."

She shrugged.

The ground troops and Wilder had set out earlier and were currently waiting, hidden in the vegetation around the dome. Cherry hoped they were well hidden. If the Scythians understood they were about to be attacked it would make the mission all the harder. They might even kill their prisoners, assuming they had prisoners.

The helis crossed the distance in less than a minute. The aircraft circled the space above the dome. In the bright sunlight, the opaque blister glowed soft and shimmering, shining out in the drab grayish green of the surrounding landscape. Cherry was reminded of the opalescent interior of the shell of a Concordian sea creature. How could the horrifying aliens create something so beautiful?

She hoped with all her heart the stunning structure contained an exceptional prize.

The troops dropped the lumps of explosive.

A hole spiraled open at the top of the dome. The Scythians were coming out.

All the helis swept away. Cherry was thrust into her seat and her stomach lurched.

Aubriot pressed the detonator.

A loud report erupted from the dome and smoke drifted up.

She craned her neck to see the result.

Scythians were pouring from their airlock and beating into the sky on their wide, leathery wings. The GAA's ground troops rose from their cover and began firing.

"Did it work?" she asked Aubriot.

He was leaning out of the side of the heli, aiming at Scythians flying their way. "Can't tell yet."

Cracks radiated from the explosion sites on the dome. At the distance, without a full view of the structure, it was impossible to tell if the fault lines joined up.

She squinted in the direction of the bunker. The shuttle had already taken off.

In the years of journeying through deep space after the accident with the jump drive, water had been their number one need for survival. Though the *Sirocco* had the usual water-recycling system, it wasn't leak-proof, and they'd needed additional water to grow crops. Luckily, water hadn't been hard to find in the asteroids and comets of planetary systems. What had been a challenge at first was harvesting it.

The engineers had built a device for this purpose and fitted it into the base of the shuttle. The mechanism fired bolts fitted with backward-facing spikes and attached to thick metal ropes wound around drums. Zapata would fire the bolts into the water-bearing space object and tow it to the ship. It was this device the pilot had used to bring the Scythian vessel to the *Sirocco*, and it was this Aubriot had proposed to remove the 'lid' from the aliens' dome.

It was a terrible risk. If they lost the shuttle they had no way of returning to the ship. They couldn't use it routinely in the war against the Scythians, but for this purpose, the risk was worth it. If they didn't get Miki and Nina back, Cherry didn't know if she even wanted to return to Concordia.

Aliens continued to stream from the dome. Whatever effect the explosions had caused, they hadn't damaged the Scythians' exit. GAA troops were picking some off from below, but many shots were missing their mark. A few holes in the aliens' wings didn't seem to impact their ability to fly. Only hitting their body or their heads had any effect.

A bunch of Scythians were converging on a heli, hammering the occupants with shots. Aubriot turned his attention to the group and pulse rounds flew from his rifle. But it was too late. The heli's nose tipped downward and it whirled erratically. In another second it had plummeted into the scrub and exploded.

The shuttle arrived. Lines shot from its base and the bolts disappeared, sinking deep into the surface of the dome. The helis flew closer in an effort to shield the shuttle from attack. Many aliens who had emerged were concentrating their fire on the ground troops, and the flow of aliens from the dome had slowed.

The shuttle heaved upward. The lines tightened.

The dome remained whole.

"C'mon, Zapata," Cherry muttered. "You can do it."

The Scythians understood what their attackers intended. Every single one aimed its fire at the shuttle's underbelly. The vessel must have lost its spaceworthiness, but it could be repaired. What couldn't be repaired was the pilot, at least not immediately. If Zapata got hit and the shuttle crashed it was goodbye Concordia.

The GAA troops sharing Cherry's heli were yelling.

"What are they saying?" she asked Strongquist.

"They are anxious that the dome won't break open."

Stupid question.

Time crawled as the shuttle strained.

"Come *on*!"

A roar split the air.

Flame flared from the shuttle's rear.

Of course! As he had ever since he'd been flying it, Zapata had been using the vessel's a-grav drive to power it, but the engineers had also built in an outdated thruster system as a backup. At the last minute the pilot had remembered and activated it, doubling the pulling force.

A mighty *crack* resounded.

The dome was splitting apart. The top was lifting off. The shuttle pulled away, dragging the fractured part.

Inside their habitation, Scythians would be suffocating, choking, dying.

It was time to go in.

TWENTY-SEVEN

Aubriot's head was beneath her as Cherry dropped into the Scythian dome. He clung to the line with one hand and sprayed fire from his rifle with the other. She could only hold on.

The removed lid had revealed a honeycomb of rooms. At the center sat the vessel the aliens had arrived in. Radiating from it were sections of various sizes, some containing equipment, others empty. Aliens flew between them. In the haze of flapping wings it was hard to see what they were doing, but presumably they were rushing to get breathing apparatus now the structure was exposed to Earth's atmosphere.

She had explained to the troops—via Strongquist—that the walls separating the rooms might be soft enough to push through. Otherwise, they would have to blast their way in. A ground team was already making its way to the outer wall to blow a hole in it for the drop team to exit.

Aubriot was only a few meters from the ground. The heli was lowering them into an empty room. That was no good.

"Try to get into the next one," she yelled to Aubriot. The neighboring room contained equipment and perhaps Scythians. It was better than nothing at all.

"What?" His aim and focus remained downward. "What did you say?"

"The next room!"

"All right. I'll try."

They continued on the same downward trajectory, but then the heli swept sideways, bringing his feet level with the upper edge of the wall. He stretched out a leg and hooked his toes over it. When the heli dropped lower, he slid down into the room with the equipment. He took a leap from the line, making it swing. She was twisted around. The next sight she had of him, he was reaching out. He grabbed the line, drawing her close.

She jumped.

Her boots hit dirt.

She looked up. The heli was gone. All troops dropped, its mission was accomplished.

This room seemed empty of Scythians. She had no idea what the devices it held did, but maybe Wilder could investigate them if they succeeded in taking the dome.

No. The room wasn't empty. There was movement in a corner. Bronze-skinned wings opened out and a figure rose up. The alien's head was bare. It wouldn't be able to breathe, but in the time it took to die it was still dangerous.

She aimed and fired.

A hole opened up in its middle, smoking and oozing blood.

The wings folded and the Scythian crumpled to the ground, twitching.

A reeking haze hit her—the odor of the burning wound. She swallowed saliva.

Aubriot was probing the wall. "It's soft. I think we can push through."

"Be careful."

The danger with forcing a passage into a room was that it took time. You couldn't leap out and surprise the occupants. With a little observation they would know you were coming.

"I'll go through here." She moved to the opposite end of the wall. With two of them emerging at once they might reduce their likelihood of being hit.

From all around came the loud bangs of the GAA troops' fire, interspersed with shouts and the occasional scream. Strongquist was with them, helping to coordinate the attack.

She went low, hoping to avoid attracting attention, and pushed the muzzle of her rifle in first, following it up with her shoulder. When her head was through, a strange sight struck her and she smelled food. It wasn't exactly an enticing smell but neither was it unpleasant.

Aubriot had arrived just ahead of her. He scanned the place.

Nothing moved.

She had emerged next to a large steel container. She peeked over the edge and was surprised to see grain.

Aubriot had straightened up and was striding around, poking into corners. "No one's here. Time to move on." He pressed another wall experimentally.

"Wait." A second device seemed to be for cooking. "What's all this for?"

"Doesn't matter. We can figure it out later."

The second item was a small tank, also containing grain, but it was partially cooked and steaming. The cooker continued to operate, heating its contents.

"Do you think the Scythians eat cereals?"

He joined her. "Who cares what they eat? As long as it isn't us."

"These are Earth crops. I'd swear it. I used to grow these on Concordia. What are the chances that Scythians can eat our food? Their anatomy is entirely different."

"You think this is to feed humans?"

She hardly dared to hope she was right. Her belief that Miki and Nina were still alive had been nebulous—a dream built on guilt that she hadn't done enough to comfort the girls in their grief and fear, and that she would never have the opportunity to correct her mistake. She nodded.

"That's not a stupid guess, but if they are here we still need to find them. Let's try over there." He marched to the wall diagonally opposite and thrust it with his fist.

He cursed.

The wall was solid.

"They're inside that room!" Cherry exclaimed. "They have to be. The wall's hard because it's impermeable to gases. The Scythians must keep it supplied with oxygen for humans to breathe."

Aubriot took a step backward. "I'll comm Strongquist. Ask him to bring explosives."

"And kill anyone in the blast range?"

"Good point." His brow wrinkled. "Gotta get in somehow."

She checked the room again. "I know. Drag that cooker over." It was the tallest piece of equipment in the place.

Aubriot hauled the machinery over and pushed it up against the wall before climbing onto it. Standing on his tiptoes, he reached upward. Another meter remained between his fingertips and the top of the wall. "Can't reach. I'll have to jump for it."

"Don't do that. This thing could fall over. Give me a hand up." She slung her rifle onto her back.

He squatted and held out his hand, pulling her up beside him.

"And the rest," she said.

"I should go first."

"I don't have two hands. Now shut up and help me."

He knitted his fingers and made a cradle for her foot. With his boost, she easily reached the top.

When she looked over the wall, her heart leapt. "There are people in here!"

Human figures huddled in a corner, their fearful faces turned upward. She couldn't see Miki or Nina, but there were about twenty people. The girls had to be here but out of sight.

A transparent barrier covered the upper area of the room. She'd been right.

The Scythians supplied it with an atmosphere humans could breathe. She pressed on the barrier. It gave but seemed tough.

"Can you see the kids?" Aubriot asked.

"Not yet." She pulled her knife from its sheath and pushed it into the transparent sheet. It split easily.

Booooom!

A shock ran through the wall.

It had to be ground troops blasting a hole in the dome.

The captives flinched.

"Don't worry," she called to them. "We'll have you out soon."

She tucked her knife into its sheath and pulled at a cut edge. Like all Scythian materials she'd encountered, it was odd. Soft and slightly sticky, it clung to her hand.

"Push me up," she told Aubriot. "I'm going in."

"Wait for Strongquist to get here. I've comm'd him."

"*Push me up*!"

Muttering, he did as she asked. She got one knee onto the wall and then the other. As she climbed onto the barrier it sagged. She lowered herself through the gap she'd cut. When halfway through, she gripped the edge as tight as she could and dropped the rest of the way. Swinging by one hand, she looked down. A few of the men had gathered beneath her.

She let go.

The men caught her and set her on her feet.

"Miki! Nina!" She searched the unfamiliar faces.

They were pale and gaunt. They looked half-starved. How long had these people been here?

Where were Miki and Nina?

"I'm looking for two girls." No one answered, naturally. They couldn't understand. She pushed through the crowd.

Where were they?

She spun around to the captives and held up two fingers. "Two girls." She touched her hair. "They look like me."

Unlike Concordians, Earthers came in all colors. Some had very pale skin and blue eyes, some were very dark-skinned and their eyes and hair were black.

"Two girls," she repeated with desperation. "Have you seen two young girls?"

But the captives only answered her with uncomprehending looks.

"Cherry!" Aubriot shouted from outside. "Did you find them?"

"They're not here. They must be somewhere else."

"Get the people away from the opposite wall. Strongquist's gonna blow it."

Her mind a whirl, she pushed the captives away from the area. They might not understand English but they seemed to understand what she was trying to do and why. All of them quickly moved to the other side of their cell.

She covered her ear with one hand and the other ear with her shoulder.

Just in time.

The wall exploded, showering them with lumps, shards, and dust.

Strongquist leaned in. "We must leave, quickly." He beckoned to the humans.

"Have you found Miki and Nina?"

"No, but the Scythians are successfully repelling the attack." He stepped aside to allow the people to pass and then stuck his head in again. "There's a safe passage to the outer wall but I don't know how much longer we can hold it."

"We have to find the girls. We can't leave yet."

"We must, Cherry. The dome has been searched. This is the only place humans have been found."

The captives had gone. The room was empty. But she was sure Miki and Nina had been here. They must have been. The Scythians hadn't killed the people they'd snatched. They were keeping them alive. Miki and Nina weren't dead, but where were they?

Aubriot ran in. "It's time to go."

"I know, but..." Her desperate gaze roved the bare room.

Where are they?

"No more heroics," Aubriot said. "We've done our job. There's nothing more to do. We have to get out of here."

Reluctantly, she had to agree.

TWENTY-EIGHT

After the Scythian had brought Miki from the examination room to Nina, her sister had shown her how to wear a respirator. Under the watchful eyes of the guard, Nina had put on her own, demonstrating how to place it over the face and tighten the straps. The devices were awkward things, poorly made. The aliens were still learning about human anatomy. Miki hoped it worked. She'd had enough of choking while being transported within the dome. But Nina had assured her it did and that the tasks they had to perform weren't too bad.

"At least they aren't going to kill us," she'd said.

Not yet.

When Miki took an experimental breath she heard the click of a valve opening. Air tainted with an odor she couldn't place filled her lungs. When she exhaled, the valve clicked again.

Nina gave her a questioning thumbs up.

Miki had been exhausted. She hadn't slept since arriving in the dome, not since they'd left the Sirocco, in fact. They'd had the long walk to the settlement and then across the fields. They'd been terrified so many times, she'd been cut, and now they had who knew how many hours of work ahead. And then to eat they would have to fight the other humans for the horrible mash. She marveled at Nina's resilience.

She adjusted the tank on her back to a more comfortable position and returned the thumbs up.

Her sister beckoned her to follow.

They passed through an airlock into a round tunnel, leading down. There were lights but, like everywhere else in the Scythian areas, they were turned down so low it was difficult to see where she was going.

She guessed they'd walked for ten minutes or so, steadily downward, when the tunnel opened out into a large chamber. It was so big it had to be outside the dome. The Scythians were spreading out underground.

Long, narrow vats occupied the space. Each vat held a liquid. The light reflected in it, creating ripple effects on the ceiling. Grids divided the liquid into sections, and running along one of the longer sides of each vat was a tray filled with a dark substance.

Nina took her hand and guided her through the vats to the far end of the chamber. Two other workers were here but they ignored them, perhaps due to the Scythian sitting in a corner, watching.

Nina picked a pair of tweezers from a pile and handed them over before taking a pair for herself. Then she showed her what to do. She leaned over the vat to reach the tray and dug around in the dark material. After searching for a few seconds, she retrieved a little worm-like creature. She dropped it into one of the sections in the vat.

Miki peered at it. The creature squirmed, as if shocked by the sudden transformation in its environment, but then its movements became less urgent. It relaxed and swam downward. Miki peered more closely, squinting, but she couldn't see it anymore. She checked another of the sections. In this one a larger version of the worm undulated languidly.

Nina poked her and gestured with her tweezers, glancing pointedly at the Scythian.

"I get it," Miki said, though she doubted Nina would be able to make out her words.

She'd spent time with the scientists on the *Sirocco*, learning about living organisms. She'd guessed they felt sorry for her after Dad's death, and maybe they thought she might become a biologist like him. She'd learned how animals went through growth stages. She guessed what she and Nina were supposed to do was to help these alien organisms move from one growth stage to the next, from a soil-based environment to an aquatic one. These creatures probably ended up as Scythian food.

So she and Nina were factory farmers now?

Like her sister had said, it was better than dying.

During that session with the tanks, Miki observed several growth stages of the farmed animals. They appeared in the trays—perhaps hatching from tiny eggs. When they were a couple of centimeters long they were large enough to go in the liquid. She hesitated to call it water, though that was what it looked like. She couldn't smell it through her mask so it might have had an odor. The Scythians breathed carbon dioxide. Maybe other things about their planet were different too. On the other hand, Concordia had water and that was their origin planet, so...

Pondering questions like these helped to pass the time, though they also reminded her of Dad, and the familiar painful knot would form in her stomach.

The creatures grew larger in the liquid medium. In the hours she spent working she didn't see anyone feeding them, and she wondered if they absorbed nutrients through their skin. At around four centimeters, they moulted. The shed skin would float to the surface and had to be removed. Then the worker had to find the creature, often submerging their arm up to the armpit to feel for it in a corner. The new version had pincers and being nipped seemed unavoidable. Miki's fingers were soon sore and bleeding while performing the task.

She had to transfer these secondary stage creatures to another, communal tank. There, the food was others of their own kind. They cannibalized each other. Despite her own difficulties, she felt sorry for the latest additions she dropped into the tank. They would be immediately set upon by older, larger rivals. It seemed odd to allow the produce to destroy itself, but she guessed the Scythians saw it as a necessary part of the life cycle.

The 'winners' in the group tank moulted several times, growing as big as her hand and fearsome. The Scythians provided a scoop with a lid for getting them out, which was just as well. The workers would have been quickly rendered incapable of working otherwise. After a final moult, the creatures spent their last growth stage breathing the atmosphere. They were housed in individual cages under the tanks, fed meal, and grew about thirty centimeters long. By this time they were vicious. They would throw themselves at everyone who passed by, pushing their heads between the bars and snapping their teeth.

She imagined the animals growing in their natural surroundings. She guessed they started life on a river bank or shoreline. When a seasonal flood came or there was a particularly high tide, the wriggling first-stage creatures would be swept into the water—or other liquid. While growing larger, they would encounter others of their kind and fight and eat each other. Then, when they'd reached maturity, they would haul themselves out onto dry land, find a partner, and mate.

Only what happened here was the Scythians ate them.

How did they eat them? Did they consume them raw, biting off their heads and spitting them out before feasting on their bodies, breaking apart the carapaces to reach the flesh? Or did they neatly dispatch them, chop them up and put them in a stew? Or maybe they barbecued them on sunny days, sprinkled with a little salt, and ate them with friends they'd invited over, sharing beers.

She giggled.

Nina gave her a questioning look.

She was so tired. She wished she could rub her aching eyes. How long did they have to work? Until they dropped?

A piercing whistle sounded.

The other workers put down their tools and walked to the exit.

It was finally over.

They should be able to sleep now, at last. She wasn't hungry, and she didn't know if the aliens would give more of the cereal mash anyway. But her stomach pangs would return eventually. She and Nina would either have to eat slop or starve. Or, rather, they could eat slop and starve more slowly.

How long would they last? Cherry and Wilder would never find them, and the *Sirocco* would depart.

When she'd told Nina they should live on Earth to be near Dad, this wasn't what she meant.

———

Inside the dome it was impossible to tell if it was day or night. Miki had a feeling they'd worked through the day and it was now nighttime. Not long after they were returned to the cell with the Earthers, another allotment of cereal mash arrived. This time, she ate it. It was as if her stomach had woken up. She found she was suddenly famished. Nina ate too. Their cellmates were fair in portioning out the food, and they were given two handfuls. It was not enough. As Miki settled down to sleep, her stomach rumbled.

She curled up with her sister in a corner. The Earthers no longer stared at them, and the atmosphere was friendlier. They were all in this dreadful situation together, united in their imprisonment and suffering.

"What happened to your face?" Nina asked quietly.

Miki had forgotten about the cut she'd received from a Scythian's claw. She touched the spot. The ointment had dried and as it flaked away the skin beneath it felt tender but whole. The bleeding had stopped and her injury seemed to be healing.

"Do I have a scar?" she asked.

Nina nodded. "It's not bad. It's a little bit cool, in fact."

Miki smiled, straining the damaged skin. "Let's sleep."

The Earthers were also settling down. What did *they* do in this place? She didn't remember seeing any of them in the animal nursery, though she wasn't sure. It was hard to make out people's faces behind the respirators. Maybe there were more underground chambers where the Scythians grew different types of food.

As her imagination took over, it conjured scenes of aliens waddling in their strange gait through golden fields of wheat, cracking whips on toiling humans.

An inescapable heaviness descended on her eyelids and she slipped into a deep slumber.

Seconds later, it seemed, something grabbed her.

Snapped to alertness she flailed, slapping and kicking the thing gripping her. As she recognized the feeling of Scythian skin, she froze.

Why couldn't the aliens leave them alone? Where were they taking them now? She felt as though she'd only slept an hour or so. Surely they didn't have to work again already?

Where was Nina?

Another alien was here. It had her sister in its grasp and was flying upward.

As Miki was also carried aloft the Earthers huddled and watched.

She held her breath.

The Scythian holding her flew out of the cell and continued to the top of the dome. A portal spiraled open and the alien flapped through it. The creature was wearing a transparent globe over its head.

They were going outside.

The hatch closed. They were inside a chamber. Above, through a round hole, stars twinkled in a deep blue sky. The night air was fresh, cold, and moist. Miki inhaled deeply.

The alien didn't fly out with her as she'd anticipated. It flew across the chamber to a small vessel, dropped her into it and then climbed in too. The seat reclined so far she was almost lying flat. It was much too large for her and protrusions from it dug into her back and legs.

Straps snaked out and closed over her, holding her tightly against the ridges. Next to her, the Scythian had folded its wings into a receptacle behind its seat. Similar straps held its body in place and its legs were angled forward. With its long, prehensile toes it gripped the flight controls.

The vessel started up and lifted into the darkness.

TWENTY-NINE

Are you from another planet?

Miki stared at the interface screen, almost unable to take in the words, though they were written in plain English.

How did the Scythians know that? How did they know her language?

Had they seized the *Sirocco* and taken everyone captive?

She lifted her gaze to the alien. It stared back at her unblinkingly, the black slits of its eyes narrowed to slivers. The light in the room was too bright for it, she guessed. To her it was a normal level, though stronger than the usual light levels in Scythian domes. They must have turned it up to help her read the text. The room was like the one in the other dome, where she'd been examined, only this time she wasn't restrained by webbing.

How was she supposed to answer? If she nodded, would it understand the gesture? Should she speak?

Should she answer truthfully?

If she answered correctly, would that mean she was collaborating with the aliens? What would the knowledge she was from Concordia mean to them? She didn't know if it was meant to be a secret.

The Scythian reached out with a claw and tapped the screen, as if to redirect her attention to it.

"Y-es?" she replied doubtfully.

It tapped the screen again. When she didn't understand it moved its claw toward her hand.

She snatched it away, drawing it to her stomach.

The alien touched the back of it so lightly she barely felt the contact, and then tapped the screen again.

"Oh!" It wanted her to touch the interface.

When she did, a keyboard appeared. She hesitated and then typed Yes.

The Scythian didn't look at the screen. Did it have another way of understanding what she'd written?

The question disappeared and another took its place.

What is the name of your planet?

Suddenly, she understood what must have happened. At the other dome, the alien that had healed her wounds had also touched her mouth a few times. She'd been shouting, demanding to know what had happened to Nina. It must have realized her words were different from the other humans'. It had gone to a console. Had it recorded her?

And yet, things still didn't make complete sense. On Earth, people living in different places spoke different languages. Why did the Scythians think she was from another planet and not just another country?

The alien tapped the screen.

She clutched her hand to her stomach again and shook her head. She would not answer any more questions. Why should she? How would it benefit her to tell them anything?

"Let me go. Let me and Nina go. You have no right to keep us here."

It tapped the screen.

It was horrible. They all were.

On the flight from the previous dome the small vessel had filled with the pilot's odor. She'd nearly vomited several times. They'd flown for hours, through the night and into the morning. When the sun rose the cover over the cabin had darkened and the sun became a glowing ball in a dark blue haze.

What was the Scythians' planet like?

Was it covered in a layer of thick cloud? Or perhaps it was so far distant from its star that daylight was like dusk on Concordia? And what were the landscapes like? She imagined many seas and shorelines where the creatures in the vats wriggled and crawled. Did plants grow there? And if they did, were they green? Could their plants photosynthesize in the low light? Dad had told her about plants and animals that derived their energy from chemicals. Was that how things worked on the Scythian world?

Her questioner tapped the interface again, more forcefully.

"I'm not telling you anything else. I demand to be released, along with my sister." She tilted her chin upward and looked down her nose at the creature. It was a haughty stare she'd practiced and used when she wanted to get her way. It had worked on Dad sometimes. Other times he'd only chuckled.

The Scythian's claw approached her cheek. She stiffened. The tip traced the line of her scar.

What did it mean? If she didn't answer would it cut her?

Her eyes became wet and she sniffed. Drawing her chin into her chest, she gave a little shake of her head. The Scythian didn't withdraw its claw. The tip remained resting against her cheek. The pressure increased.

She moved her head but the claw followed. She felt a sharp sting and the tip sank into her skin. "Ow!" She batted at it. "Leave me alone!"

The alien moved away.

Tiptoeing on its long toes, it swung in its harness to a console.

Blood trickled down her cheek and she wiped it. She lay down on the pad and stared morosely at the ceiling. Through the transparent barrier she could see the underside of this new dome. It was much bigger than the other one and very, very far from it. She hadn't been able to see the landscape she'd passed over on her flight, but she'd flown for so long she supposed she might be in a different country.

At least Nina was here too. She'd been brought in another vessel. It had been such a relief to see her waiting when she arrived. But they had to be thousands of kilometers from Dad's grave now. The whole point of them coming to Earth was lost. They would probably never escape from the Scythians. Along with the other humans being held captive, they would spend their days growing the aliens' food while slowly starving to death themselves.

But she would not answer any more questions. She regretted saying she came from another planet. Why should she tell them anything?

A Scythian approached overhead. At first, she didn't take any notice. Several had flown over while she'd been in the examining room. Then she noticed it was carrying something and it was descending.

Nina!

It held her sister in its feet, hanging limply like a doll.

Their gazes met.

Miki leapt to her feet. "What are you doing with my sister? Don't bring her here. Take her back."

The alien at the console watched.

The Scythian above landed with a thump, depressing the barrier. It put Nina down but it didn't cut a slit to push her through into the room.

"What are you doing?" Miki demanded. "She can't breathe out there."

Nina was spreadeagled, her mouth open and eyes staring. She clutched at the barrier, trying to tear it.

"Let her in!" Miki screamed. She tried to jump to reach her sister but the distance was too great.

Nina was coughing and clutching at her throat. She scrabbled at the surface, her movements growing weaker.

"All right," Miki said. "All right! I'll tell you the answer. I'm from Concordia. That's the name of my planet." She picked up the interface and began to type.

The Scythian above took Nina in its feet and lazily flapped away.

"I'll tell you everything."

THIRTY

The last of the Earthers who took part in the raid—the walking wounded—were arriving at the bunker. Cherry stood to one side as they staggered in. Some would never make it back. They'd died in the fight or afterward during the mad dash to safety. The helis had been reserved for the badly injured. Everyone else had been forced to return on foot, making the best use of the vegetation as cover while the Scythians took pot shots from above.

The aliens might have several disadvantages here on Earth, unable to breathe the atmosphere or go face to face with humans on the ground, but in the air their capabilities were vastly superior. It was lucky so many had died of suffocation when their dome had been ripped open. Otherwise, no one would have stood a chance of getting away.

"Thinking of helping?" Aubriot asked, finding her at the bunker entrance. "Leave it to the medics."

"I'm watching the sky."

He peered into the clouds. "Any sign of anything?"

"No, but they must have noticed where we went. It won't be long before they come for us."

"If they do attack, it won't be from space. Vessey's parked the *Sirocco* right overhead. Won't be a Scythian starship dares come within a thousand klicks of her."

"Yet."

He shrugged. "Best enjoy the respite while we can."

"I don't get why we had to leave so soon. I thought we'd defeated them."

"A second wave of Scythians arrived, all togged up with respirators."

"A second wave? From where?"

"Don't know. Strongquist reckons they might have dug out more space underground."

"But maybe Miki and Nina are there! We have to go back."

"Is that a joke? They're already repairing the dome, we lost two helis and half the troops are dead or wounded."

"But they could be—"

"Forget it. The kids aren't there. Either they never were or they're dead. End of. It's time to move on."

"Huh, for you maybe. I'm not giving up on them."

"Let's leave it for now, okay? We need to debrief, go over what we learned."

"Later."

"Suit yourself."

He disappeared inside the bunker. Stragglers from the raid continued to limp in. Wilder approached from the heli landing area. "I'm glad you got out of there in one piece. Was it bad?"

"Not as bad as it could have been."

"No sign of the girls?" she asked, her tone softer.

Cherry shook her head. "Can you repair the shuttle?"

"It shouldn't be a problem. Buka has the materials and Zapata's already on it. Should take a couple of hours. Are you planning on going up to the *Sirocco*?"

Cherry gave a huff of exasperation. "I don't know what I have planned. I don't know what we do from here. There might be areas beneath the dome we didn't get to search, and I don't know how we will now. If only we had the equipment we have on Concordia. We could blow that place open."

"Well that wouldn't exactly be safe for Miki and Nina, would it?"

"I know, I know..." Cherry rubbed her forehead.

Wilder touched her arm. "You look exhausted. Go inside. Get some rest. I'll fix the shuttle, and then we'll talk with Buka and Aubriot and see where we go from here."

Strongquist walked up the stairs. "Mr Buka would like to speak with you, Cherry."

"What about?" She wasn't in the mood to be pushed for promises on how the Concordians were going to help protect Earth.

"He has some news about the missing adolescents."

———

Two Earthers sat with the leader of the GAA in the meeting room. From the state of their garments and the gauntness of their faces, Cherry guessed they'd been rescued from the dome.

Of course. In her despair over failing to rescue Miki and Nina, she'd forgotten the possibility that other captives might have seen them.

Aubriot was here too, pretending he gave a shit.

"Please, sit down," Buka said via Strongquist. "I would like to thank you for helping to free our people."

"I heard you know something about the girls from our ship?"

"I have some information, yes. As soon as I discovered you hadn't found them, I enquired among the former captives. These men say they remember two girls who didn't seem to be local. They spoke a foreign language and wore strange clothes. One was about fifteen and the other perhaps twelve or so."

"That sounds like them!" Cherry gripped the arm of her chair. Would the news be good or bad? "Do they know what happened to them? Are they okay?"

Strongquist translated the question. Buka spoke to the men. They replied, their gazes on her. Strongquist translated, "The girls were alive the last time they were seen, but they were taken away. These men don't know where, and they're sure no one else in their group knows."

"Is it possible they were taken underground?"

The frustrating chain of dialogue repeated.

"There is an underground chamber, but it's unlikely the girls were there. They had just returned from there when they were taken."

"But if they weren't in the other chamber and they weren't in the cell with the others, where else could they have been?"

A short conversation took place.

"That seems to be a puzzle. These men say the only way for anyone to escape—prior to their rescue—was by dying, yet the girls appeared healthy the last time they were seen."

The stark reality of what life must have been like in the dome hit Cherry forcefully. She swallowed. "They're sure they were okay?"

Buka said something in a tone that didn't require translating. "They were well the last time they were seen."

"When was that?"

"Not long ago. The captives had no way of measuring time, but it appears the girls were taken away recently, perhaps only yesterday."

"How long were they in the dome?"

"Only a short time."

She asked, bitterly, "So if you hadn't locked me and Wilder up we might have found them?"

Strongquist translated the question but Buka didn't answer. The Earther men's attention traveled from Cherry to the GAA leader, and they shifted uneasily.

Aubriot said, "There's no point in getting on your high horse now. What's done is done."

"Your concern for Miki and Nina is touching. Really touching."

"Don't start that bullshit, Cherry. I'm just saying there's no point crying over spilt milk."

"Or anyone's life except your own."

Buka raised a hand. "I will make further inquiries. I may be able to discover more information. Please wait here." He got to his feet and shuffled from the room, leaning heavily on his cane.

"This war had better be over soon," Aubriot remarked, "or he won't be around to see the end of it."

Cherry ignored him. The war would not be over for a very long time, if ever.

She asked Strongquist to ask the men for more details about Miki and Nina, what they looked like, how they acted, and so on. It was clear from their answers there could be no mistake. Kes's daughters had been in the dome, and they'd only just missed them.

Buka returned. He lowered himself carefully to his seat and propped his cane against it before saying, "You may not be aware, but the GAA has a network of observers tracking the Scythians' movements. Yesterday night, two vessels departed the dome you attacked. I asked our network if they'd picked them up, and the answer came back immediately. They traveled south."

Two vessels?

If the ships in question were two-seaters like the one brought back to the *Sirocco*, they could have been carrying a girl each and a pilot.

"Do you know where they went?"

"We are still working that out. Our observers are all over the globe. If the girls were aboard the vessels, we should be able to discover where they were taken."

THIRTY-ONE

This chamber for growing the Scythians' food was much larger than the other one. The vats stretched out so far it was hard to see where they ended, and tens of human workers tended to the creatures living in and under them. The walls echoed with the scrapings and scratchings of the mature animals in their cages.

The respirators were just the same. Miki tightened the straps on hers a little more and lifted a set of tweezers. Nina was already at work a few rows away, but she dared not go over to her. Here, three Scythians watched them, stationed on platforms spaced out across the chamber. Besides, she couldn't talk to her sister. Communication was nearly impossible through the masks covering their faces.

Also, what could she say to her?

That she'd told the aliens everything about Concordia, and the *Sirocco*, and why Concordians had come to Earth?

That she was a traitor?

It was bad enough that she'd dragged her sister into this mess. Now she'd doomed everyone else too.

She dug in the soft, brown substance, looking for a worm to transfer to the liquid. Tears blurred her view and she blinked hard, unable to wipe them away. Maybe she should take her mask off and suffocate herself. Maybe she should stick her head in a vat.

One of the wriggling creatures appeared. She spitefully snipped it in two. It was the smallest revenge for what the Scythians had made her do, but it felt good. Yet the creature seemed unaffected by its bisection. Each half continued to wriggle. She heaved a sigh, fogging her visor. When the mask cleared, the severed animal remained alive.

Something sharp poked her arm. A Scythian was at her side. The slits of its horrible eyes were wide in the dim light as it inspected her. She'd lingered too long. Hastily, she picked up a half of a worm and dropped it in a section of the vat, quickly following with the other half in another section.

The Scythian moved away. She exhaled.

She moved to another area. There were no worms here, but some of the older creatures were sufficiently large to face battle with their rivals in the communal tank. With distaste, she transferred them to their almost-certain deaths.

Then something new happened.

A large hatch opened at the side of the chamber. A Scythian stood each side of the opening, and two humans were dragging a cage full of snapping animals toward it. Something emerged—a questing foot. One of the watching Scythians thrust it back, and then the humans arrived with the cage. They pushed it against the hole and pulled up a section. The creatures inside raced out and were gone. The hatch closed, and the event was over. The humans hauled the cage back to its original position.

So what she'd thought was the final growth stage wasn't? The leg that had emerged was much bigger than those of the creatures in the cages.

There was no point in speculating. She couldn't ask anyone for information, and what did it matter anyway? Who cared about the life cycle of the livestock?

By the time she reached the end of her shift she was sore, tired, and hungry. The cereal mash was the same as in the other place and her stomach rebelled as she ate it, but she forced it down. She couldn't look at Nina as they ate, let alone speak to her. Shame filled every fiber of her being.

When they'd finished, they sat away from the others. Their cell companions had quickly established they couldn't communicate and left them alone.

Nina put an arm around her and rested her head on her shoulder. "What happened to you before you came to work? Was that Scythian examining you again?"

She meant the interrogation.

Miki hugged her sister back. "Did you get hurt when they brought you over? Did you pass out?"

"It was horrible, but I was okay. Why did they do that?"

"They were trying to make me..." She couldn't say it. How to confess what she'd done? "They know we're from Concordia. I don't know what difference it might make, but you should know that. They know we're from the *Sirocco* and we're different from the Earthers."

Nina sat up and faced her, her eyes wide. "Do you think the Scythians will use us as hostages? They might threaten to kill us if the captain doesn't do what they say."

Miki hadn't even thought of that particular disastrous scenario. "I think the ship's probably left by now anyway."

Nina gave a sigh and returned her head to Miki's shoulder. "That's something, I suppose." But she sounded disappointed, as if she hadn't imagined they would be abandoned so easily.

The knowledge that her sister was withholding entirely justified blame was a painful knot in the depths of Miki's chest. "I-I'm sorry," she whispered. "I'm sorry for everything."

"It's all right, Sis." Nina softly stroked her hair. "It's all right."

Their cellmates were settling down to sleep. Above, the dim light inside the dome remained unchanging. Miki had already lost track of whether it might be day or night. The briefest of glimpses of their surroundings before she'd been brought inside had revealed a vast jungle landscape, such as she'd only ever seen on ancient vids of Earth. Nothing similar existed on Concordia, certainly not now but also before the devastation caused by the biocide.

It had been her last sight of freedom.

"What are we going to do to get out?" Nina asked.

Get out? "I don't think we can."

"But maybe there's a way. We only need to think of it."

"If it was possible to get out, do you think all these people would still be here?" There were double the number of humans in this room as in the other dome, and she'd noticed another room containing people adjacent to theirs.

"Just because they didn't manage it," Nina replied, "that doesn't mean we can't."

"They're older than us, bigger and stronger. We're small and weak. If they can't do it, how can we?"

"Maybe you don't need to be big and strong. Maybe it helps to be small. I don't know. I just don't think we should give up."

"If there's a way..." Miki's chin trembled and her shoulders shook.

Nina grabbed her arms and peered into her face. "What's wrong?"

"Oh, Nina. I told them everything. *Everything*! All about the *Sirocco*, and the long journey we took to come here, and...and..." Sobs overcame her.

"How? How could they ask you all that?"

"They know English. The questions were on a screen."

"But how could they know our language?"

"I don't know. It isn't important. But now, even if the ship's left, the Scythians know the biocide didn't work and that people survived on Concordia. Now they'll go back there to finish them off. What have I done, Nina? What have I done?"

Her sister wrapped her arms around her. "You couldn't help it. It isn't your fault. If you hadn't answered them they would have let me die."

It was true, but somehow the fact didn't make things any better. She felt as though there must have been a third option.

"We have to escape now," said Nina. "If the ship's still here, we might be able to warn them."

"But we can't escape!" Miki exclaimed wretchedly.

"Miki." Nina's tone was serious. She sounded ten years older than she was.

Miki stopped crying and looked at her.

"What would Dad say?" Nina asked.

"I don't know. What do you mean?"

"Do you remember when the jump drive failed?"

Miki did, though only vaguely. "Do you?"

"No, of course not. I was too young. But I do remember Dad talking about it. He said it was the worst moment, when everyone realized they'd been thrown years off course, and that even if they did try to make it to Earth they would starve long before they arrived."

Miki recalled her father speaking about that time occasionally too, but she still didn't understand Nina's meaning.

"Don't you remember that time he told us they could have given up? He said some people did. They just gave up on life. But most of them didn't. They kept on trying. They looked on planets for plants they could grow for food, they converted the Ark into a farm, and they *kept on trying*. And they made it. After all those years as we were growing up, they made it here. He told us, when he was..." Nina wiped her eyes "...when he was dying, that we must remember that and never give up. We have to keep on trying. Always. Don't you remember?"

Miki did not. Their father's death was almost a blank in her mind, and it wasn't something she wanted to dwell on.

"I know it looks hopeless," Nina said, "but we have to do what Dad told us. Right?"

Miki nodded numbly. "Right."

Thirty-Two

"No," Cherry said firmly. "We go directly to the dome. Now."

"I never heard anything so stupid," Aubriot replied. "And what do you propose we do when we get there? Walk up to the dome and knock, asking to be let in? Or if the Scythians aren't accepting visitors, ask if we could please have the kids back?" He made a dismissive *pfft*.

"If we don't go there right away who knows what might happen?" she argued. "We could be too late. If Buka had let me and Wilder search for the girls as soon as we arrived we might have found them. A little bit of time can make all the difference. We have to act immediately."

"And if we go off half-cocked we could ruin everything. I know you care about the kids. We all do. That's why we have to plan this carefully. I'm sure they're safe for now. The Scythians must think they're important, otherwise why transfer them somewhere else?"

According to Buka's sources, Miki and Nina had been taken to a Scythian dome far in the south. It was the largest alien structure of all and the site of one of the first abductions. It was also the place where the massacre of the villagers had occurred. Cherry agreed that it did seem the aliens valued the girls, though she didn't know why.

"Another thing," Aubriot added. "They'll know all about the earlier attack by now. They'll be prepared. We can't try the same trick again. Besides, from the sound of it, it wouldn't work anyway. Zapata struggled to lift the lid off an ordinary-sized dome. This one's bigger. The biggest. We need different tactics, different equipment."

Strongquist said, "If you would like my opinion—"

"We wouldn't," Cherry retorted.

"I would also advise returning to Svalbard."

"We can work out different tactics right here," Cherry said. "Everything else is speculation. Am I right, Wilder?"

Their friend hadn't said a word. She folded her arms over her thin chest. "Actually, Aubriot has a p—"

"Fine!" Cherry snapped. "Fine. Let's waste some more time. Why not? I'll be outside." She stomped out of the room and slammed the door.

That was one thing to be said for the Earthers' old-fashioned, low tech portals. They were certainly useful for something to take out your temper on.

She marched up the stairs and out into the sunshine, where a migration was underway.

Buka had decided to evacuate the bunker. Revenge for the dome attack was expected by the hour. A small military contingent would remain to keep the communications hub going as long as possible, but everyone else was moving out. The remaining helis would take the worst-injured. Nearly every vehicle was being utilized to transport the rest.

She watched the activity. Itai walked past with guards, his hands secured behind his back. He glanced at her and then looked down.

What a fool.

She checked the skies. If it were not for the *Sirocco*'s protection the bunker would be a smoking ruin by now. That was for sure. How much longer could the Earthers rely on the presence of the starship?

Zapata approached, wiping his hands on a rag. "Is Wilder around? I finished the repairs."

"She's inside," Cherry replied woodenly.

"Something wrong?"

"Nope."

He looked bemused at this clear denial of the truth. "Where are we off to next? Back to the ship?"

"We have a few detours to make first."

"So where are we going?"

"To the Makers' site."

———

A wave of sadness hit Cherry as the shuttle touched down. On one side was the ocean, on the other the forested mountain she remembered from her last visit. When she'd come here with Kes he'd been healthy and happy, keen to find the seeds to re-green Concordia. He'd been his usual positive, energetic, courageous self. She missed him so much.

"Wakey, wakey," Aubriot chided, snapping her from her memories. "Are you coming or not? We haven't got all day. Weren't you the one saying we have to hurry?"

Throwing a dark look at his retreating back as he made his way off the shuttle, she followed him wordlessly.

"It's quite a walk," Wilder said once they were outside, "whichever route we take."

"There's more than one?" asked Aubriot.

"There are two."

"There are actually three," Strongquist corrected. "But the third route isn't important for our purposes."

Wilder said, "We either go through the seed vault or over the mountain. The distance is the same." When Strongquist opened his lips as if to speak, she added, "Give or take."

"Over the mountain," Aubriot and Cherry said simultaneously. After sharing a mutual glance, he continued, "I'm no fan of that vault. Too many skeletons."

Cherry didn't want to go in because the place would remind her too strongly of Kes.

Everyone was armed. The possibility that the Scythians might have found the place had been discussed on the trip over. Wilder thought it was unlikely. The Makers' beacon had deactivated, and if the aliens had managed to find an entrance anyway, they would find getting inside difficult if not impossible. But it wouldn't hurt to bring rifles just in case.

Strongquist led them under the trees and along the narrow, rocky bed of a dried-up stream. The path soon began to climb, and Cherry quickly found herself out of breath. She began to lag the others, struggling upward. Her rifle seemed unusually heavy. After some time, Wilder noticed her and halted to wait for her to catch up.

"It's hard work, isn't it?" she asked when Cherry reached her.

"It's been a while since I got any real exercise. Spent too long sitting on my ass aboard that ship."

"I can carry your rifle if you like."

Cherry hesitated but then handed her weapon over. "Thanks. That would be a big help." They continued to climb. "The raid on the dome took its toll on me too, I guess."

In truth, she'd been feeling tired for a while. Bone tired. And not just physically, mentally too. The struggle to survive never seemed to end. She'd known it all her life, ever since disembarking the *Nova*. First it had been the sluglimpets, the Woken, and the Guardians, then it had been the Scythians. And running through all of it was the effort to build a civilization. She had conjured life from the soil. She had fed the colony with crops teased from almost nothing. Food for the hungry.

And she hadn't even chosen her destiny. It had been chosen for her, many generations ago, somewhere on this planet, by her forebears. They had elected to spend the rest of their lives aboard a colony ship and assign their far-off descendants, willing or not, the task of creating a new home for humankind.

She felt as though she'd lived several lifetimes already. How did Aubriot manage it?

She'd had enough. Her will to battle on was finite. She would use her remaining energy on rescuing the girls. She owed Kes that much. But then she reckoned she would be done.

The entrance to the Makers' site was a small door tucked behind a protrusion of bare rock, almost impossible to see unless you knew where it was. Strongquist took them through it and down many steps before they reached the cavern where the *Mistral* had been crafted.

The sight of the massive underground space took Cherry's breath away. She paused at the entrance, taking it all in. It was as if she'd stepped back in time to the early days of the Concordia Colony.

"You all right?" Aubriot asked, noticing she'd stopped.

"Doesn't it make you feel weird, knowing this is where they built everything? The Guardians, their ship, *everything*?"

"It's impressive, I'll give it that. But we don't have time for being awestruck. We've got a job to do. We need to find something to help us get into that dome and get the kids out."

"I still think it's a waste of time. What could be here that would help us? Even if we do find armaments or a bomb—which, let's face it, is very unlikely because the Makers have zero reason to leave something like that here—what good is it going to do? We can't blow the dome up with Miki and Nina inside. And other humans will be with them."

"If there's any high tech on this planet, it's here. Until we search the place thoroughly we don't know there's nothing we can use, if not to rescue the kids, then in the war."

She had been walking with him across the main chamber, but at his comment she halted, her fist clenched. "That's what this is about, isn't it? You aren't interested in saving Miki and Nina, you're looking for stuff to use in your war."

"Keep your hair on. Anything we find to help us get the kids out will be useful in other ways too. Stands to reason. We're just killing two birds with one stone."

Wilder had gone ahead with Strongquist to a small room adjoining the chamber. Through the open door, Cherry spotted another figure and she froze. But then she relaxed as she realized it was only a holo. She recalled Wilder saying the Makers had left a message for later generations who might stumble across the site, but she hadn't listened to it.

Curious to see one of the builders of the *Mistral* Cherry walked over to the room. Aubriot went in another direction.

Strongquist was working at a control panel and Wilder was idly watching the holo.

She explained, "Strongquist is uploading the language Buka and his people speak and creating a database we can use for translation."

"I suppose it'll save us having to use him all the time."

"Exactly. He says he can do it for all Earth languages eventually if we want him to."

"I hope we won't be here that long."

"Itching to get home?"

"Yes, but not without Miki and Nina."

The android turned to face them. "It's done. Now all I need to do is build some simple translators. I'm sure I can find the materials around here somewhere. If you wouldn't mind waiting?" He moved toward the door.

"Actually," Cherry retorted, "I *do* mind. This excursion is a waste of time, but I'm overruled, so..."

Wilder winced.

Strongquist said, "Would you like me to unmute the holo and translate his speech to English?"

"I'm interested to hear what he has to say," said Wilder. "I had a look around in here before but I didn't understand what the equipment is for. The holo's message might give us a clue."

Judging from the man's expression, Cherry was doubtful he would tell them anything useful. He looked livid.

"Hm," Strongquist murmured. "This is interesting."

"Can't you do the translation?" Wilder asked.

"No, that isn't a problem. There's a later message, recorded after this one."

"Oh, in that case, can we have the later one? That's probably more relevant."

The holo disappeared and another appeared in its place. The man was the same but his clothes were different. His expression was different too. He seemed much happier.

When he spoke, his first words were unintelligible before an artificial voice cut in.

"... did you find us, I wonder? I hope you didn't break in via one of the hidden entrances, and that you figured out our little puzzles at the bottom of the seed vault. If you did, that means civilization has returned to a reasonable level of development. If you broke in, well, you probably won't understand a word of what I'm saying and it doesn't matter anyway."

He waved a hand as if dismissing his audience. "Go away, and don't come back until you've figured out how to understand me." He chuckled. "If you *do* understand me, that makes me very happy. It means our time has come. Science and technology are no longer feared and hated. People like me and my friends aren't despised and persecuted. The world has become a better place. It's safe for us to wake up and rejoin society."

The holo continued to speak, but Cherry didn't hear it. She and Wilder were staring at each other, open-mouthed.

Wake up?!

She flew to the door, leaned out of it and screamed, "Aubriot, get in here!"

Wilder said mildly, "You have your comm, you know."

"Oh, yeah."

While Cherry comm'd Aubriot, Wilder asked Strongquist to halt the recording and take it back to the beginning. When Aubriot arrived, they watched the message the whole way through and then watched it a second time.

The Makers hadn't left the site, or at least not all of them. Some had elected to return to the world and live out their lives the best they could, but forty engineers and scientists had entrusted their bodies to the same cryosleep used aboard the *Nova Fortuna*. They had set a date for the system to revive them or it could be triggered externally. The man in the holo, whose name was Steen, explained that if the visitors could understand him and human society was no longer hostile to science, they were invited to start the process.

At the end of the second viewing, the three watchers were silent.

"Holy *shit*," Wilder breathed.

"No kidding," said Cherry.

She'd thought Aubriot was the last of the obnoxious Woken.

THIRTY-THREE

One thing that puzzled Miki was where the other Earthers went. Several of their fellow captives also worked with the odd worm-turned-carapaced creatures, but the others went elsewhere. When they returned they looked tired, so they'd clearly been working, but doing what? Like in the other dome, it was impossible to find out because they didn't speak the same language.

"What are you thinking?" Nina asked as they settled down to sleep after another day's labor at the vats.

"Just wondering what else humans do around here. What do you think?"

Nina covered her mouth with the back of her hand as she stifled a yawn. "I don't know. Who cares? Have you had any ideas about how we can escape?"

The question dragged Miki back from the realms of speculation to harsh reality. "I haven't. Have you?" Nina had been the one talking about never giving up. Why couldn't *she* think of something?

As soon as the thought popped into her mind, Miki chided herself. She was the older sibling. It was her job to look after her sister, especially now Dad was gone. "I mean, if you have any suggestions, I'd love to hear them."

Their conversation was interrupted. A woman had walked over. She was gesticulating, as if she wanted to talk. Miki paid her more attention. The woman rubbed her stomach and said something.

"I think she's asking if we're hungry," Nina said.

Miki thought so too. "No, we're fine. Thank you." She smiled and gave a thumbs up.

The woman looked questioningly at her hand. She didn't understand thumbs up?

Miki pointed at her and rubbed her own stomach. "Are you hungry?"

This appeared to be understood. The woman grinned before reaching forward and grabbing Miki and Nina into a hug.

It was nice to be welcomed into the group.

A shadow passed overhead. A Scythian had flown over. The woman had noticed too. She pointed to where the creature had been a moment ago and then performed a series of actions. Miki and Nina watched closely.

At the third repetition, Miki got it. The woman had been miming picking out worms with tweezers and putting them in the vat. "Yes! That's what we do." She nodded vigorously. "We grow the Scythians' food. What about you? What do you do?" She opened her hands in an inquiring gesture.

But their new companion didn't seem inclined to answer. She pointed above again and then, chuckling, drew her finger across her throat.

"Wh-what?" Miki asked.

The woman laughed wickedly, mimed cutting her throat again, and pointed upward. Then she nodded, her eyebrows raised.

Nina said hesitantly, "She...wants us to kill the Scythians?"

"I think so. But that's dumb. How could we ever kill one? They're much bigger than us and they have those horrible claws on their wings."

"I think she might be crazy," Nina said, "like that man who took us to the dome."

"You could be right. There certainly seem to be a lot of crazy Earthers."

The woman was making her way back to the other side of the cell. She said something to her group and they laughed, throwing appreciative glances at Miki and Nina.

"Did we agree to something?" Nina asked.

"I have no idea."

———

The following day they were back at the vats, performing their tasks. Miki hadn't slept well, not only due to worrying about their troubles, but also over concern she and Nina were living with someone who was mentally unstable. As if things weren't bad enough. They didn't need threats from within their prison too.

Neither Miki nor Nina had been allotted the chore of dragging a cage of snapping animals to the hatch in the wall yet, but it was an inevitability. It was the most hated job—Miki could tell from the demeanor of workers who had to do it—and there was no reason she or her sister would be excused. It turned out today was the day.

A Scythian came up behind her and made her jump. It poked her and waved its claw at a cage full of particularly large creatures. Her shoulders slumped and she looked around for someone to help. She couldn't possibly drag the cage by herself.

Everyone promptly looked away.

Except one person.

A young man caught her gaze and gave a short nod.

She breathed a silent *Thank you*.

As she reached for the cage, the animals grew more agitated, as if they guessed what was about to happen. Did they have the same fight to the death they faced in their earlier growth cycle? A closer view of what was through the hatch might tell her—not that she really wanted to know.

Shell-encased, articulated limbs flashed out from between the bars, trying to grab her. The creatures' jaws clicked and ground. She kept her legs and feet as far from the cage as she could as she and the young man hauled it over the sandy floor. When they reached the wall they shoved it tightly up against the hatch. If one of the creatures escaped it could do serious damage. Miki had already seen cuts and slashes on the legs of workmates who got too close.

The hatch jerked open. One hand on the back of the cage, while keeping a safe distance from it, Miki crouched to see what lay on the other side. The young man tapped her shoulder and gave a small shake of his head. But she wanted to see. It couldn't be that bad, could it?

The caged creatures were slowly crawling through the portal, exploring the newly opened space. A loud bustling and rustling leaked out. One creature remained at the back of the cage, sitting on its scaly behind, hesitating to take advantage of the new freedom.

A Scythian waddled over and gave the cage a kick, and the reluctant straggler moved.

Still, Miki couldn't see what awaited the animals. The light level on the other side of the hatch was even lower than usual.

Almost before she could register the action, something darted into the cage, grabbed the remaining creature, and disappeared.

The hatch slid shut. The spectacle was over. What had she learned?

As she returned the empty cage to its former spot, she mentally replayed the sight that had flashed before her eyes.

What had she seen?

An arm or leg had reached out to take the animal into the other room. But *had* it been an arm or a leg? She didn't recall seeing anything resembling grasping fingers or toes. What kind of appendage had it been?

Now, in her mind's eye, she could see it.

It had been a claw. A small one, but a claw nonetheless. It must have hooked the creature rather than grasped it. What had made her take so long to figure it out was the fact that the claw had been surrounded by webbed material, like...

As she'd been musing over the memory, she'd picked up some tweezers and was absent-mindedly transferring a worm to liquid. When understanding hit, the tweezers and the worm fell from her frozen fingers. Both sank out of sight, but she barely noticed.

What she'd seen was a Scythian wing and claw. It had been a smaller version, but now she thought about it, she was sure. The room beyond the hatch held young Scythians in the final growth stage, feeding on the younger stages and fighting over them. The animals she'd thought were Scythian food were Scythians.

THIRTY-FOUR

Strongquist had known all along. He'd been truthful when he'd said Wilder and Niall had triggered his activation when they'd entered the site, but ever since then he'd been following instructions to not divulge the presence of the sleeping Makers until he'd assessed the state of things on Earth. If a certain level of human civilization had been reached again, he could —with or without the visitors' knowledge or approval—trigger the process that would bring the engineers and scientists back to life.

If his assessment was that Earth remained uncivilized and unfriendly to their kind, he was to return to Svalbard, close up the site, and deactivate, ready for when another opportunity might arise. If no visitors ever found their way in, the Makers would awaken at the time they'd set. Strongquist would have been waiting.

The Makers could not have anticipated the current situation. They hadn't even known that other intelligent species existed in the galaxy when they entered their sleep, let alone imagined they would have invaded Earth. Of that, Wilder was sure. She wasn't as knowledgeable about the history of the creators of the Guardians as Aubriot or Cherry, but she could guess that much.

What would they make of everything when they woke up? It would take days to find out. The cryosleep revival procedure took a long time and couldn't be hurried. Even if followed correctly to the last detail, problems could still result. Some Woken had been affected by blindness and paraplegia. Some had not survived.

It was lucky they had Strongquist to oversee the process. On the *Nova* trained personnel had performed the revivals. Wilder had no clue what to do, and neither did Aubriot or Cherry. Not that Cherry would have cared. She'd been in an even more foul mood than usual.

"The first stage has initiated," said Strongquist. "All the capsules are operating within normal parameters."

The cryosleep chamber was beneath the vast cavern. The android had opened an invisible door and led them down to it. Twenty capsules stood each side of a steel-lined room, looking as pristine as the day it had been finished. The capsules were solid boxes reminiscent of coffins, and each had functioned perfectly according to the data reports. The fusion reactor had been put to good use.

"How long until we can talk to them?" asked Aubriot.

"A week at least," the android replied. "Some may take longer to return to consciousness."

"A week? That's a long time."

"It will take longer for the Makers to return to normal functionality."

Aubriot stretched his arms out to each side. "Yeah, I remember that feeling. Stiff and cold, like you'd fallen into a freezing sea. But, still, great news. Fantastic. I came here thinking we might find something we could turn into a devastating weapon. The last thing I expected was the weapon would be human."

"Huh?" Cherry lifted a lip scornfully. "What makes you think they'll agree to fight? They're expecting to wake up to a fairly normal world."

"What choice will they have? It'll be either fight or die. Of course they'll help their fellow humans."

Strongquist said, "This was a question I asked myself when I was debating whether to reveal the Makers' existence. It's my belief that, knowing them as I do, they would want to participate in the effort to save Earth from the aliens' exploitation. Not least because a world in servitude is not one they would want to encounter when they awoke at their chosen revival date."

"See?" Aubriot sneered. "They will want to fight. And what a difference they'll make. These people built a *starship*, from scratch."

"So did Wilder," Cherry said.

He opened his mouth but nothing came out. Finally, he said, "Yeah, well, that was different." He lifted a finger. "And the Makers created the Guardians too."

"You say that like it's a good thing. Don't you remember all the trouble they caused? And didn't they sedate you because they thought you were a danger to the colony?"

He tutted and shook his head as if she was crazy, but he also didn't come up with an answer.

"Someone needs to tell Vessey what's happening," Cherry announced. "I volunteer to climb those damned stairs and comm the ship. Unless someone else wants to do it?"

"Be my guest," Aubriot said.

"I'll come with you," said Wilder. "It'll be a lot harder going up than coming down, but I'd like to speak to Niall and Dragan. I want to find out what they've discovered about the Scythian ship."

They returned to the main chamber and then began the long climb.

"Unbelievable," Wilder commented. "Who would have thought the Makers were still alive?"

"More's the pity."

"You don't think it's a good thing?"

"Do you remember the Woken?"

"Sure. A few of them, anyway. Cariad…Anahi…and Kes, of course."

"He was about the only decent one. Cariad was okay once you got to know her. The rest were a bunch of stuck-up egomaniacs. Like Aubriot."

"Surely not *that* bad?"

"No, not as bad as him, but not much better. They all thought *they* should be running the colony, not us Gens."

They continued to climb for several minutes until Cherry halted. "Can we take a breather?"

"I don't remember that time very well," Wilder said, stopping on the step below. "I was just a kid. But I'm sure the Makers won't be the same as the Woken. The situation here's entirely different."

"The situation might be different. Doesn't mean the people will be." When Cherry's panting eased, she said, "Come on, let's go."

They climbed all the way to the top and stepped out into bright sunshine and a strong, cool breeze.

"That's nice." Cherry rested her hand on her knee as she caught her breath. The view over the forest canopy as it spread down the mountainside was beautiful. In a cleft sat the neat triangle of the distant ocean and above it a clear blue sky.

Wilder was looking in the same direction. "I spotted the Scythians that attacked us from here. I didn't realize what they were. I thought they were two huge birds."

Cherry chuckled. "Two huge, very ugly birds."

"How was I to know? I hadn't seen a single bird before coming to Earth. I didn't know their normal appearance. I still don't. And I only got a glimpse of the Scythians. I wish I *had* recognized them. It would have saved us a world of trouble, and," she added sadly, "that village wouldn't have been massacred."

"You mustn't blame yourself. The Scythians are going to do a lot more damage before their time on Earth is over. Shit. I sound like Aubriot. Ugh." Cherry put a finger to her ear. "Time to update Vessey." After a pause she said, "That's weird."

"What's up?"

"She's not answering."

"She's probably asleep. Try the ship."

Watching Cherry's face after she sent the comm, Wilder asked, "Still nothing?"

Cherry slowly shook her head. "You try Niall."

"I'll try Dragan. Niall's been off with me lately." Wilder comm'd her workmate. When Dragan didn't respond she comm'd Niall.

Nothing.

Their gazes met.

"You don't think...?" Cherry asked.

"No, it can't be. I know—Zapata." Wilder sent a comm request to the pilot, who was waiting for them on the other side of the mountain.

Her request melted into the ether, unanswered.

"No reply." She added, hopefully, "But he would never just abandon us."

"Not deliberately," Cherry agreed, "but who knows what Vessey's told him? She could have tricked him somehow."

"Look," said Cherry, "we're going to be here days waiting for the Makers to wake up. Why don't we walk back to the shuttle? We can use its comm."

As they trekked the same route along the stream bed, daylight began to fade. If they didn't hurry they would be journeying back in darkness, but that was the least of Wilder's worries.

The view of the landing site was obscured the entire way. Her fears were not confirmed until they stepped out of the forest and onto the flat land leading down to the water. Here, they could see clearly the spot where the shuttle should be.

It was empty. Their ride home was gone. Zapata must have returned to the *Sirocco* under some pretense of Vessey's.

The shuttle was absent, and no one on the ship was answering comms. The two facts could mean only one thing: Vessey had ordered a jump.

The Concordians had abandoned them.

THIRTY-FIVE

L ife in the Scythian dome had become a monotonous, boring routine consisting of long hours of work and short rest periods, mostly spent sleeping. Meager meals punctuated the days twice only—once before work and once afterward—when the humans would portion out the scant amount of tasteless mash as fairly as they could. No one was so self-sacrificing as to refuse their allotment, yet no one demanded more, not even the biggest men.

It was a sad testament to the altruism people could show, Miki thought, in these extreme circumstances. The sadness came from the fact that no one on the outside would ever know of the kindness humans had shown each other within the domes.

She'd tried to count the sleeping periods as they passed, but she'd become muddled. She wasn't sure, but she estimated they'd been brought to this dome ten or eleven days ago. Judging from the gauntness of her cellmates' bodies, they'd been here longer. They tried to communicate with her and Nina sometimes, but their efforts were generally no more successful than the first time, when the woman had pointed at the Scythian overhead and mimed cutting her throat.

What had *that* been about?

One of her points was clear: Miki and Nina were either growing Scythian food or the aliens themselves. That part she hadn't quite figured out. Not that it mattered. She might want them dead too, as the woman had, but what could anyone do about it?

Then, on the twelfth or thirteenth night, when she was deeply asleep curled up next to her sister, someone shook her shoulder. A figure crouched over her, softly silhouetted in the dull lighting.

She sat up.

No Scythians were around and the dome seemed particularly quiet. If any of her fellow prisoners were awake they didn't look it, none except this one, an adult man.

Now he had her attention, he dipped a hand into his shirt and drew two things out. In another second the objects were in her hands and he was on his way back to his side of the cell.

She lay down, tucking the things under her. Clearly, neither he nor she was supposed to have them. What had he given her and why? Surreptitiously, she ran her fingers over the objects. They were made from metal, a little shorter than her forearm, curved, long and narrow, finishing in a point. She took a peek. It was hard to make them out in the near darkness, but in the end she saw they were implements for digging, similar to tools used in the *Sirocco*'s Ark.

They must have come from another section where the workers had to dig small holes. How odd that the man had given them to her. What was his intention? As there were two tools, she guessed one was meant for Nina. She would give it to her later when she woke up. They would have to find a place to secrete them. Nothing could be taken from the work sites. The Scythians made sure they put all the tweezers back at the end of their shifts, and they conducted random searches, though rarely of Miki or Nina, perhaps because they were young and weak.

———

Miki had tucked the digging implement under her top and down the back of her pants. It made bending difficult but it was the best she could do. It was important to keep it hidden, she just didn't know why she had it. Nina had done the same. As they put on their respirators, she hoped she wasn't about to get her little sister into trouble yet again. What would the Scythians do to them if they were found out?

They walked down the tunnel to the room full of vats. Inside, everything seemed normal. Three Scythians sat on podiums, the creatures in the cages rustled and gnashed their scaly teeth, and within their earthy substrate the worms would be wriggling. It seemed to be just another working day.

Miki took Nina's elbow as they walked to the far end of the vats. She wanted to keep Nina close. They began work, transferring half-grown specimens to their almost-certain deaths, victims of older members of their species. As they worked, Miki watched the room from the corners of her eyes. She kept her head low and her movements steady, though her heart raced. The other humans must have something planned, but what? And when?

Hours passed. The skin on her hands and arms grew wrinkled from constant dipping in the liquid. Her fingers grew sore from the nips of the livestock.

A soft *thunk* came from the other side of the vat. Miki looked up and met Nina's eyes, wide with panic. Nina's gaze flicked to the nearest Scythian and back to Miki, pleading written in her look.

What was wrong?

Nina had stopped moving.

Keeping her pace slow and nonchalant, Miki walked around the tank to join her sister. Before she reached her, she saw the problem. Poking out from the leg of Nina's pants was the end of the metal tool. It had slipped to the bottom. Nina would have a hard time retrieving it and returning it to her waist unnoticed.

Miki reached for a pair of tweezers, pretended to fumble them, and dropped them. She stooped, tugged the tool from the leg of Nina's pants, and stood up behind her, quickly lifting her shirt and shoving the tool into her waistband. Then she dug into the soil with the tweezers.

Nina's hidden contraband was a problem. She'd lost weight since coming to the dome and her pants hung loose on her hips. The tool could easily drop out again. She must have been moving carefully all this time to try to prevent it.

But, the next second, that was the least of their concerns.

All the workers nearest the Scythians suddenly jumped on them. Instantly, the podiums became a whirl of human and alien limbs, thrashing, slashing, battering, stabbing. Other workers had brought in the digging tools too and were using them to attack the watchers. Screams and yells filled the air.

Miki watched in horrified fascination. Would they manage to kill them? But what did it matter? They were—

A woman grabbed her. She motioned to the vat and shouted something.

"I-I don't understand."

Shaking her head in frustration, the woman climbed onto the vat, balancing on the section separators, and held out a hand.

"You want me to come up there?"

Still confused, she allowed the woman to help her up. The woman pointed at the ceiling.

It was low, only just above her head. Miki hadn't taken much notice before. Between supporting metal beams, the soil was bare and crumbly and the roots of plants hung from it. Now she saw it more closely, she realized how unstable it looked. They were lucky there hadn't been...

"You want me to dig!" She turned to her sister. "They want us to—"

"I know! I know." Nina was already climbing up and pulling out her tool.

The woman ran off, heading for one of the groups tackling the Scythians.

Together, Miki and Nina hacked at the soil. Miki worked with all her strength, driving the point into the surface over and over again. Clumps of dirt rained down, battering her visor.

The Earthers must have guessed this area was not far underground, and like at the other dome, it lay outside the above-ground structure. If they could just break through, they might escape.

But was she tall enough to reach the surface? What would she do when she'd dug as high as she could?

The sounds of fighting continued. For the first time, she heard what she guessed was a Scythian voice. Amongst the pants and gasps of the humans there was a noise between a whistle and a grunt. Were they killing it? She hoped so. She hoped they killed them all.

She and Nina quickly excavated what seemed like a tonne of soil. It cascaded into the tank, turning the liquid into mud. It began to pile up around their feet.

Her arms and back ached with the effort. The visor of her respirator steamed up with her heavy panting. But she didn't slacken her pace, not for a millisecond. The Scythians would crack down hard after a failed escape attempt. They would probably execute everyone. She and Nina were digging for their lives.

But she couldn't reach high enough! She was on her tiptoes, extending her arms as far as they went, and the point of her tool was only scratching the soil. Nina had given up digging upward and was digging outward in an apparently desperate effort to do *something*, even something that didn't help. Yet there was no sign of daylight.

Hands grabbed Miki's thighs. She looked down in shock. Men, their arms and hands cut, their hair slick with blood, were holding her legs.

They lifted her up.

In a frenzy, she drove her tool into the soil with power she didn't know she possessed.

She had to break through. She had to. If she didn't Nina would die.

She—

The point of the tool met no resistance.

A ray of sunshine shone into her eyes. She blinked, unbelieving.

She believed.

She threw the tool down and tore at the earth with her bare hands. Plants filled her fingers. Green, fresh plants, and the light blinded her.

The hands on her legs lifted her higher.

She was looking at a sea of vegetation. It was alive with insects, and above was the dear, sweet, blue sky.

Grasping the nearest stalks, kicking and squirming, she hauled herself out. The soil was unstable close to the hole. After turning around she lay flat on her stomach and peered in. Nina was on her way up, lifted by the men. She grabbed the back of her sister's shirt and dragged her the rest of the way.

A smooth, pale white wall rose in a curve over to the right: the Scythians' dome. It was as the Earthers had guessed. The room with the vats lay outside the dome's perimeter.

To the left was jungle.

She ripped off her respirator. "Nina, we have to run!"

An Earther man appeared in the hole, dripping blood.

She hoped he made it out. She hoped they all made it out, but she couldn't wait around to see.

She took her sister's hand, and they raced for the trees.

THIRTY-SIX

The man lay on his side, covered in a blanket, shivering. Cherry pulled the blanket higher over his shoulders and tucked it in. His skin was so pale it was almost translucent, and his hair was auburn tinged silver. Cherry was reminded of Kes. Was this how he'd appeared when he was revived? She'd never witnessed someone undergoing the final stage of the process, alive yet not quite aware, not completely conscious. She'd only ever seen the Woken when they were up and walking around. The man hovered, drifting in and out of dreams, murmuring indistinctly. She didn't speak his language so couldn't understand his meaning. It didn't matter. He was talking about a time centuries past and, aside from his cryo companions, about people long dead.

"How's this one doing?" Wilder asked, sitting down beside her.

"Not too bad. Of them all, I'd say he's recovering the best. Do you recognize him?"

"Huh?" Wilder peered closer. "Holy shit. It's the holo."

"Took me a while. He looks different, right? Older."

"Yeah. Do you think they waited a while before entering cryo?"

"Maybe there was a problem that took a few years to fix but he didn't bother re-recording the message. We'll soon find out. He should be coherent in a day or so, according to Strongquist."

"And then what will we tell him?"

"Everything. We'll have plenty of time to do it."

Wilder nodded her agreement sadly.

They were stuck on the island. Now that Zapata had flown away in the shuttle and the *Sirocco* had apparently jumped from the system, they had no way of leaving. Not unless Strongquist built them a boat. Which, going by his —*its*—performance so far, might not be impossible.

If it hadn't been for the android they would already be feeling the effects of starvation. Thinking they would only be here a few hours they hadn't brought any supplies. Zapata had taken away the shuttle's emergency rations, and the seed vault no longer held anything edible.

But they were surrounded by an ocean, and the water was full of life. Through various ingenious methods, Strongquist had supplied them with seaweed, shellfish, and fish. In truth, with its indefatigable efforts, they could probably live out their natural lives here, though for Aubriot that would be a very long time.

The man muttered something.

"Did you catch that?" Wilder asked.

"How could I?"

"Uh, I forgot." She pulled out a lanyard with a small device attached and handed it over. "Strongquist gave me two a minute ago. I'm wearing mine already. I came here to give you yours."

"He made translators?" Cherry slipped the lanyard over her head.

"Yes, *he* did. It transmits to your ear comm. So you're finally thinking of him like a person?"

She didn't answer.

"Look, I get it. You had a bad time with the Guardians in the early days. But Strongquist's done nothing except help us in every way possible. I think you should be nicer."

"Why? It doesn't have feelings," Cherry said stubbornly.

"I'm not so sure about that. He kind of grows on you. When I first met him I asked if I could call him Strongquist II, but now he's just Strongquist."

"Who are you?"

The man from the holo had spoken. The translator repeated his words in English, clear as day, in Cherry's ear.

He'd turned onto his back while they'd been chatting, and now he was staring at them, looking a little frightened.

"It's okay," Wilder replied. "We're friends."

His eyes widened and he tried to get up.

"Take it easy." Cherry placed a gentle hand on his chest.

He pushed it away and looked around wildly.

"He can't understand us," Wilder said.

"Get Strongquist."

Cherry managed to restrain the man while waiting for the android to arrive. He was weak anyway, as well as obviously disoriented. As he took in his surroundings his struggles eased.

"Steen," Strongquist said, striding between the rows of revived Makers.

At his arrival, Steen visibly relaxed. His head sank into his pillow. "It's good to see you again. What year is this? And who the hell are these people?"

———

The following days were what Cherry could only describe as 'interesting'. The Makers continued to slowly come to full consciousness. The cryosleep chambers turned out to be a superior design to the ones on the *Nova*. All forty men and women survived the process physically and mentally unharmed.

As they began to walk around, eat, and talk, Cherry was struck by their deep camaraderie. Then, as time went on, she upgraded her description of their relationship to love. They bickered, teased, and nagged, but their deep familiarity and affection was clear. How couldn't it be so? These people had suffered the same persecution, they'd toiled to find each other, and they'd undertaken a massive endeavor, an endeavor spanning years and requiring every gram of their cooperation, intellect, and ingenuity.

She understood at last what had bound the Woken on Concordia, the scientists who had created the *Nova Fortuna* Project. At the time she'd only seen that they kept themselves separate and seemed aloof. Perhaps that was so, but what she hadn't taken into account was their long history of laboring as a group toward a common goal.

What also made the days interesting was bringing the Makers up to speed on all that had happened since they entered their chambers. When they heard that the *Mistral* and Guardians had made it to Concordia they'd been giddy with relief and joy. When they learned that Cherry and Wilder were among the first Gens to set foot on the planet, they gasped in wonderment and touched them as if to make sure they were real. When they were told that Aubriot was *the* Aubriot, the Project's founder and main backer, they laughed, some saying, "No way!" and "It can't be true!"

When all was explained, it was time to tell them about the Scythians. Cherry started with the attacks on Concordia and the trip to the Galactic Assembly. Then she explained about the biocide. The Makers listened in silence. Eventually, she grew tired of talking and asked Wilder to take over. Wilder told them about the *Sirocco* and the reason for the voyage. Then she told them about the state of things on Earth.

She concluded with the purpose of the return to Svalbard and Strongquist's revelation about their existence. "It was quite the surprise," she said finally. "I never imagined I would ever meet you guys."

"Likewise," said Steen.

Aubriot hadn't said a thing for hours. He'd stood, hands on hips, watching and listening, as the details were explained. "So now you're all compos mentis and up to speed, do you have any ideas about fighting off the invasion?"

"Stars," said Cherry, "give them a minute. They only just woke up."

"We've been here weeks. The time to fight back is long past due. If we don't do something soon Earth's never going to be free."

"I haven't told them the last bit," Wilder said.

"What's that?" Steen asked.

"The shuttle that brought us here has left, and we think the *Sirocco* has jumped from the system. It's just Cherry, Aubriot, and I here, and we have no way of leaving this island."

"No transportation?" Steen asked, eyebrows lifting. "That shouldn't be a problem."

"You're gonna build a boat?" Aubriot asked. "That'll take weeks. We need something now. I was thinking we could reactivate your signal beacon and rig it to comm the GAA."

"No need." Steen rose to his feet. His pallor had improved and he looked more like the holo he'd recorded. "Come this way, ladies and gentlemen."

He led them to the exit leading up to the cavern and then crossed the vast chamber. When he reached the opposite side, he asked Strongquist to deactivate the security system. After waiting a moment, he pressed a panel. A section of wall popped out.

Wilder said, "You guys and your hidden compartments. What's in here?"

"What's in here," Steen announced, sliding the section to one side, "is our way off the island."

Within the newly revealed room stood six vehicles. They were not the most streamlined or attractive Cherry had seen. They were simple and blocky, though large. Each could hold around ten or fifteen people. They reminded her of something.

They had no wheels.

"Hey," she blurted, "are these—"

"I believe you called them flitters."

THIRTY-SEVEN

The reality that she wouldn't be returning to Concordia didn't begin to hit Wilder until she was traveling over the plains of Earth on one of the Makers' flitters. Up until then, all the time she'd spent at their site on the island, waiting for them to recover from cryo sleep, the fact that the *Sirocco* was gone and wouldn't be coming back hadn't seemed real. But looking out over the flat, grassy landscape stretching to the horizon really brought the fact home. Maybe it was because Kes was buried out here somewhere. Like her, he would never go back.

She couldn't quite believe that Niall and Dragan would desert her. She'd been with them through thick and thin, racing to build the *Sirocco* to the Leader's insane deadline. Dragan, in the depths of his madness and affiliation with the Final Day cult, hadn't been able to bring himself to hurt her—because they were friends. Niall had blown hot and cold in his affection, but she'd counted him as a friend too. How could they do this?

She grasped the handrail of the flitter and told herself the wind was stinging her eyes.

"I hear you build starships too," said a voice.

Steen had appeared beside her. She still found it hard to reconcile the physical presence of the man with the holo. "Who told you that?"

"Your little friend."

"Cherry? You'd better not call her 'little' to her face."

"I thought it was better than 'one-armed'."

Wilder chuckled.

"It's good to see you laugh."

Huh? Was he getting fresh with her? She guessed several centuries in cryosleep might do that. "I haven't had much to laugh about lately. Sorry if my glum face brings you down."

"Not at all. It would take a lot more than a frown to bring me down. When I got in that cryo capsule I didn't know if I would ever wake up, or what I would find if I did. I used to be an angry, bitter man. I loved life. I was *not* happy about the group decision to expend our remaining resources and years of our finite lives on the hope of saving a colony on a far-off planet, on complete strangers who might not even have made it there." He smiled. "But my opinion didn't count. I was overruled, and so if I wanted to stay at the site I had to do what everyone else wanted. We didn't even think of building cryosleep capsules until after the *Mistral* had departed. I had a chance at a new lease of life, the opportunity to live in a new world right here on Earth. A world of the future. It's a pretty amazing one, don't you think?" He gazed out across the plain.

"From what I hear it's a better place for you," Wilder said, "and it *is* beautiful, but it isn't home. My home is that far-off planet you helped to save."

"I'm sorry your ship left without you. Maybe one day we'll build a new starship, together, and journey out into the stars." His hand moved to slide over hers.

She quickly moved hers away.

He shrugged, smiled again, and returned to his seat.

She cringed. Steen was a little creepy. But maybe his flirtatious comment wasn't only wishful thinking. If the Makers had built the *Mistral* here, maybe she could build a starship. But, she realized sadly, that had been a long time ago, when Earth was rich with the leftovers from the peak of technological development. All that was gone now. Getting back to Concordia might take a lifetime.

Several hours later, they arrived at the new headquarters of the GAA, which had set up in the heart of a bombed-out, deserted town. The people Buka had tasked with disguising the site had done a great job. Wilder didn't see it until they were right in front of it. The garage door of a destroyed department store rolled up, and the flitters glided in.

All the Makers insisted on being at the meeting with the head of the GAA. They had no single representative, not even a small group of people. Everything was decided democratically after long—sometimes very long—discussions. Sometimes the discussions dissolved into arguments, and then they would agree to go away and cool off before returning to talk.

The room was crowded. There weren't enough chairs, so half the participants stood at the back and sides or sat on the floor in the middle.

Buka arrived and hobbled to his seat. His rheumy-eyed gaze traveled from one intelligent, alert face to another, as if he couldn't believe his luck. He *was* lucky. Everyone on Earth was. The planet had just received an injection of humanity's brightest and best, the cream of the crop.

The Makers chattered noisily, apparently unaware of Buka's arrival.

Aubriot stood up and raised his hands. "All right, shut up everyone. Shut up," he repeated, louder. As the noise quietened, he swept a hand toward Buka. "May I introduce Mr Dakarai Buka, Head of the Global Advancement Association. Over to you, Mr Buka." He flopped into his seat and rested his elbow on the table and his chin in his hand, as if he expected to be in for a long, boring meeting.

His prediction came true, for the most part anyway. The Makers had to hear the details of the Scythian invasion, details Wilder already knew. She zoned out. A while later, when the topic moved on to a plan of action to repel the aliens, things became more interesting. Aubriot rose to his feet again. "If we talk about this bit by bit with everyone having their say, we're gonna be here all day. I propose we split into teams. Maybe you can organize yourselves according to your expertise. I'll coordinate."

The Makers stared at him in silence.

"Come on, chop chop." He motioned with his hands, chivvying them.

Steen said, "That isn't how we, er..."

Someone opened the door, hitting a Maker in the back. After apologizing, the newcomer walked to Buka and whispered in his ear.

The old man nodded and spoke to him. When the messenger had left, he said, "Two people of great importance have arrived. What they can tell us may have a large bearing on what we decide today. I have asked that they be brought here immediately. I would like to ask for your patience for a few moments."

Wilder wondered who it could be. She didn't know of any Earthers of influence except Buka. She wasn't aware there even were any.

Quick footsteps sounded outside and the door opened again.

In stepped Miki and Nina.

A shriek went up from Cherry. She flew across the room and grabbed the girls, weeping with joy and relief. Wilder was simply dumbfounded. She couldn't believe they were here, alive and well.

"I apologize for not telling you sooner," Buka said. "I couldn't be absolutely certain they were safe until the heli bringing them up from the south arrived."

It took Cherry about fifteen minutes to calm down. The two Makers who had been sitting next to her gave up their seats for the girls, and though she stopped crying she couldn't take her eyes off them.

Miki told their story.

What a story it was. Wilder listened intently as the girl described the interior of the domes, the trapped people, and the work they had done tending to the alien creatures. Miki explained how she suspected the creatures were actually baby Scythians and the aliens were growing their young in underground chambers outside the domes.

The Makers seized on this fact, and Miki lapsed into silence as they ran with it. She caught Wilder's gaze and looked away. Something was bothering her. Was there something she hadn't said?

But Miki was young and probably overly concerned with unimportant things. Perhaps she felt bad about absconding from the ship. Wilder decided to reassure her later that she was completely forgiven.

The chatter in the room was rising. A Maker was proposing blowing up the 'alien nursery' Miki and Nina had escaped from. She asked the girls, "Did most of the people get out?"

"Uh huh," Miki replied softly. "Most of them."

"Then it's perfect," the woman went on. "We want to minimize collateral damage. A successful attack on the aliens' young will send a firm message. And if they don't leave, we'll blow up another nursery, and another."

Cherry shot to her feet. "You can't do that. The minute the Scythians think they might not win this war, they'll launch their biocide and destroy the whole planet. We told you about that back on Svalbard, remember?"

Buka cleared his throat. "We have begun a vaccination program, based on the vaccine your captain gave us before your ship left."

"Oh, she did, did she?" Cherry asked icily. "That was so kind of her. But it's beside the point. You can't vaccinate all living things. I've seen the biocide effects on Concordia. You do not want that here on Earth."

The Maker said, "We might be able to find a way to neutralize the virus before it spreads."

"You won't. It works too fast. Depending on the conditions, it can travel faster than a man can run." Cherry made eye contact with Wilder and held it.

"She's right," Wilder said. "You should listen to her."

"I am listening," said the Maker tetchily, "but there's more than one opinion here."

"I'm not stating my opinion," Cherry retorted through her teeth, "I'm stating a fact."

More Makers spoke out, others responded. Aubriot had plenty to say too. The noise began to overwhelm Wilder. The consensus seemed to be moving toward blowing up the Scythians' nursery, but she didn't want to stick around for the final agreement. She crossed the room to where Cherry, Miki, and Nina sat, picking her way through the Makers sitting on the floor. "How about we get out of here?"

They heartily agreed.

THIRTY-EIGHT

"We're lucky to have you guys here, with all your experience of fighting the Scythians. We would be clueless otherwise." The woman who had argued with Cherry at the meeting seemed to be speaking sincerely, but Wilder had the impression her words were only a sop to Cherry's feelings.

Cherry seemed to think the same. "Lucky for you, maybe," she replied in a neutral tone, though her eyes displayed her dislike, "not for us. We have our own home to protect."

"I'm sorry you feel that way," said the Maker stiffly. "We're all human after all."

Cherry was being a little churlish, considering the efforts the Makers had gone to in order to help the Concordians, but Wilder didn't blame her friend. She was down about being abandoned too, though Miki and Nina's safe return mitigated her sadness.

Aubriot strode in. "You guys ready?"

"Very ready," Cherry replied, as if she couldn't wait to get out of the place, or more particularly, away from the Maker and her fake compliments.

They were setting off for the south and the Scythian dome where the girls had been held captive. From other things Miki had said, it seemed the place was central to the aliens' activity. Buka had confirmed it was the largest dome on Earth, and large numbers of people had been abducted from the surrounding area. Fortunately, many had escaped at the same time as Miki and Nina.

The fact that the dome was important had fueled everyone's determination to make it the first strike in the coming war—everyone except Cherry. She feared what the Scythians might do as a counterstrike. The voice of one person counted for little, however, despite her 'experience of fighting the Scythians'.

As they got up to leave, the Maker said, "You know, in a funny way the Scythians' arrival might be good for humanity as a whole."

Cherry froze and stared at her. "How the hell do you figure that?"

"I know it must sound strange but, well, my specialism is human psychology, so I am speaking from a place of knowledge. I was the person responsible for programming the androids you called Guardians for their interactions with the colonists."

"Oh," said Aubriot, an edge in his tone, "that was you, was it?"

"You see," the Maker went on, "the common person needs someone to hate, an enemy or 'other'. That's how they form a favorable picture of themselves, by comparison with a group they dislike, and for some it's how they understand society, by dividing it into acceptable and unacceptable people. Their relationships are based on this worldview. When the Natural Movement started up, the world was divided according to a new paradigm—or perhaps a very old one, depending on how you look at it—those who accepted a scientific understanding of life and those who didn't. Scientists, engineers, technicians, doctors, physicists, mathematicians, all these and similar people became the 'other'."

She looked at Aubriot. "You were around to see the first effects."

He grimaced. "It wasn't pretty."

"It was the beginning of the end. My friends and I were the remnants of the remnants, clinging on to rationality and the scientific process. Civilization was in full collapse, and it appears to have only just begun to recover. But now the Scythians are here—"

"They will be a common enemy," Wilder interrupted.

"Exactly. Humans will stop fighting among themselves, killing each other in endless wars. They will band together, unite against the alien invaders. Ideally, they should also have a figure to follow, a leader, dead or alive, to worship. A redeemer who takes on their sins."

"People will die," Cherry said.

"Sadly, yes. It's an age-old question: is it better to die than to live as a slave? I can't speak for everyone, but for me the answer is yes. I will do all I can to defeat the Scythians, even at the cost of my life."

They were brave words, but *she* was not going south. Along with the rest of the Makers, she would remain far from the fighting. The GAA wanted to preserve humanity's new and greatest assets.

Would her opinion be different if she were to see agony, terror, and death close up? Wilder didn't know.

"We have many more ideas on what we can do to fight back," the Maker said. "With time and effort, we will rid Earth of their presence."

"Time's getting on," said Aubriot.

————

Miki and Nina came with them on the journey. They would stay well away from the action zone, but they could help advise on the placement of the explosives. Cherry also didn't want to let them out of her sight and Wilder felt the same. Strongquist would be with them as well as a group of locals.

They landed in a clearing in a hot, steamy jungle. The local people were waiting to meet them. A man and woman greeted Miki and Nina warmly. Miki explained they were former captives of the Scythians who had taken part in the escape. The couple had two boys with them, but they left them behind for the trek down to the dome. The pale hemisphere glowed in the valley, an easy-to-spot navigation beacon.

The attack team walked down the trail between tall trees, each person carrying an item of equipment needed to blow up the Scythians' nursery. Sweat soon covered every inch of Wilder's body and her palms grew slippery. Insects buzzed in her ears.

Then Aubriot and Cherry began to bicker. Perhaps he'd tried to be friendly again and she'd rejected him—again. He alternated between being sarcastic and nice to her. Neither tactic worked. Wilder didn't know why he kept on trying. Cherry was never going to forgive him for what he'd done all those years ago. At least, maybe not unless he begged, and he was not the type to beg.

Suddenly, he exploded. "I'm sorry! All right? Is that what you want to hear?! I'm fucking sorry. Now, for fuck's sake, forget about it and move on."

Wilder winced with second-hand embarrassment. Everyone in the group was pretending to not hear the argument, though, naturally, everyone could. The local people wouldn't understand what was being said but it didn't really matter.

"I don't give a shit," Cherry yelled back. "Why are you even telling me? I haven't cared about you in a very long time. Why can't you understand that and leave me alone?"

"That's a lie and you know it. If you didn't give a shit about me why treat me like a pariah?"

"Because you deserve it! Because you're an asshole who only ever thinks about himself. You know what? I *did* sleep with Kes."

Oh, stars! Wilder glanced up the trail. Had Miki and Nina heard? She hoped not. If Cherry wanted Aubriot to stop bugging her this wasn't the right time for it.

"You know what else?" Cherry continued, raging. "He was better than you. He was a better person than you in every way. The wrong man died!"

Holy shit. Wilder halted. She had to say something to make them stop fighting.

But Cherry stomped past, her mouth tightly shut. She seemed to be done.

Aubriot passed by too, head down. Cherry's words had been harsh but perhaps he needed to hear them. Maybe she'd succeeded where everyone else had failed, bringing his ego down a notch.

Thirty-Nine

Cherry dug a hole in the dark soil. She was helping to place the explosives according to the Makers' instructions. The devices had to be buried just below the surface and facing in a certain direction.

Twilight was falling. If any humans the Scythians had captured remained alive they would be returning to their cells, according to Miki's estimates. It was also the time the aliens would be leaving the dome. Local intel said they had stepped up their efforts to seize people since the escape.

Luckily, there was plenty of cover at the edge of the clearing, and the explosives didn't need to be right up against the Scythian nursery to destroy it and everything inside.

When she'd dug a hole sufficiently deep to submerge the device she slipped it in and covered it up so only a short antenna protruded. Crawling backward, she returned to the trees. The dome glimmered in the half light, fifty or so meters away. The spot where the captives had made their escape was no longer visible. The Scythians must have filled it in.

How were the rest of the team doing?

Stooping low, she made her way through the jungle to the rendezvous point. Most of the locals had returned already. Miki and Nina were retreating with Wilder to the top of the rise, moving out of sight. Cherry was conflicted about having the girls close by, even though they would be far from the explosion zone. But Miki's help had been invaluable in estimating the location of the nursery. The local couple had gotten it wrong at first until she had corrected them with pointing and gestures.

A dark shape swept overhead.

Damn.

The Scythians were coming out for their night patrols.

Leaves in the undergrowth rustled and another local man appeared. He gave a nod. His device had been placed. Cherry counted ten men and women. That was nearly everyone. Only Aubriot was missing. He'd volunteered to undertake the placement farthest from cover, but he should be back by now. Of all of them, he needed to make it. He was carrying the detonator.

She peered into the deepening gloom. Where the hell was he? If they didn't blow the place soon the Scythians were bound to spot the humans lurking beneath the forest canopy.

Guilt nagged at her over what she'd said to him. She'd been overheated, tired, despairing of never seeing Concordia again, worried about being responsible for Miki and Nina now Kes was gone. What she'd told Aubriot was true, all of it. But he didn't need to hear it right now, and especially not in front of everyone. As he'd stated a few times, he was not an actual monster, annoying though he was.

He was coming.

The tall man was nearly doubled over as he crept stealthily through long grass.

A shadow blocked the light of the rising moon.

Another Scythian!

That was two in less than a minute. They had to be stepping up reconnaissance.

Aubriot had sunk into the vegetation. He must have spotted the threat too. He had about thirty meters to go to reach cover and be a safe distance from the explosion. Just thirty meters. She peered at the top of the dome. A winged shape rose from it, gray in the failing light. Another alien, so soon.

Aubriot, hurry up.

The creature swept a wide circle, cutting out the light of the first stars, and flew away.

Now's your chance.

Where was he?

There he was.

Aubriot had risen and was heading for them. His gaze met Cherry's across the open space. Despite all his self-aggrandizement, he was actually quite brave, braver than he'd been in the early years of the colony. And she couldn't deny he'd protected her from danger more than once. She decided to cut him some slack from now on.

A Scythian swooped.

She hadn't seen it coming and neither had Aubriot. The creature descended from his rear, wings opened wide, legs outstretched.

"Aubriot!" she screamed.

It was as much warning as he got before the Scythian's feet fastened on him. But it was enough to foil the creature's attempt to drag him into the air.

He swung around and punched the alien in the throat. The creature was stunned and its grip slipped. Aubriot tried to wrestle free, but then the taloned toes tightened once more. The great wings beat, lifting upward. Aubriot kicked and punched, hitting its stomach, chest, legs, anything he could reach. He grasped its neck and squeezed, bending it. The Scythian faltered, wobbled, and toppled to the ground.

Cherry had her rifle out and was aiming, but she couldn't get off a shot without risking hitting Aubriot. As he grappled with the creature, cuts opened up on his back, welling blood. The alien was attacking him with the claws on its wings.

And still she couldn't get a clear shot.

He'd got it underneath him, a knee on its neck, while the dreadful claws did their work. He was trying to get the globe off its head, but the claws were tearing into him.

The sky filled with shapes. More Scythians were coming.

Aubriot!

She ran out. She had to kill the thing.

He saw her. "Get back!"

It was like Garwin's death all over again, sliced to shreds by the Scythian spiders.

"Get back," he gasped. "I'm gonna blow it."

He reached into his pocket.

The Scythian's claw cut across his face.

With a final, despairing look, she ran back into the trees.

The others had gone, and so should she, but she couldn't. She couldn't leave him.

Aubriot and his attacker had morphed into one struggling shadow, a writhing heap of darkness in the grass. Scythians were alighting all around and waddling closer to witness the spectacle.

A *whoompf* resounded, a shockwave traveling through the ground and air. Cherry's legs jerked from the impact and the wave passed up her body. Soil and vegetation erupted in a gigantic fountain and rained down, filling her hair and mouth, spattering against her hastily closed eyes.

When she opened them again, devastation spread out before her. The Scythians in the blast zone were prone, motionless or twitching. What had been a simple forest clearing was a mess of earth, roots, and shredded foliage.

And something else.

Here and there within the devastated space lay smaller Scythians and weird animals with carapaces. None moved.

The nursery was destroyed. Humanity's counterattack had begun.

She heard a groan. A very human groan.

Aubriot was alive.

The sound had come from somewhere nearby.

She saw him.

The blast had blown him toward the forest, and now he lay only a few meters away. Closer to the dome, Scythians were landing, but they were distracted, inspecting the corpses of their dead offspring.

She crawled out on her stomach.

He was barely recognizable. His face was a mask of blood and his limbs were bent at strange angles.

"You did it," she whispered. "We've begun to fight back."

His chest labored and his eyes were turning glassy. She wasn't sure he'd heard her.

"I love you," he said.

"I know." Her tears dropped onto his face. "I hated you, but I love you too."

This seemed to register.

He swallowed. "See ya, Bandit."

FORTY

s Wilder reached the spot where the Earthers' heli was waiting, a familiar but very unexpected voice sounded in her ear.

"Wilder, are you guys ready for pickup? I have your location. ETA seven minutes."

"Zapata?! What the hell? You're back? What happened?"

"It's a long story. Is there a clear landing site nearby? Get to it ASAP. I hope the girls are with you."

"Uhh..." The only available open space was occupied by the GAA's heli. For the *Sirocco*'s shuttle to land the heli would have to leave. Even so, she wasn't sure the shuttle would fit. "They are, but we're in the middle of a jungle."

"Listen. I don't have wiggle room. Either I pick you up in seven—six—minutes, or I don't, ever. I repeat, is there room for me to land?"

"Yeah," she replied hastily. "There will be. We'll be waiting."

Miki and Nina were staring at her.

"The *Sirocco*'s back," she announced. "We're going home."

"Good news," said Strongquist. "Would you like me to instruct the heli pilot to move his vessel?"

"Yes, but..." A black hole had opened up on top of the dome. "The Scythians are coming out. Tell the pilot he needs to get far away." She told the girls to get deeper into the trees and went with them. The local people helping with the attack were already melting into the forest.

She saw the expression on Miki's face. "You want to go back to Concordia, right?"

Miki looked doubtful.

"Yes," Nina replied, "we do." She nudged her sister.

"I guess so," Miki murmured, "but I'm gonna miss Dad."

"You'll miss him just as bad here as there," Nina said. "It's time to go home, Sis. Dad wouldn't want us to stay on Earth just for him."

Miki didn't answer.

Wilder said, "You have six minutes to decide. If you don't leave now you'll never have another chance. Understand?"

Miki nodded, biting her lip.

Scythians were flying from the dome. Surely it was past time to detonate the explosives. What was Aubriot waiting for? Wilder peered into the valley, but all she could see was the tops of trees and the semi-luminous dome. Another creature swept into the air. Recalling the time a Scythian had carried her aloft, she shivered. She'd come so close to death, and many had already died. The aliens had to be stopped somehow. Maybe tonight's effort would begin to turn the tide.

So she would get to see Niall and Dragan again? And everyone else on the *Sirocco*. They *hadn't* left after all. She couldn't imagine what had happened, but there would be plenty of time to hear about it later between jumps back to Concordia. They should be there in only a few weeks, finally bringing the seeding material her world so desperately needed.

Or perhaps not. Everything hinged on Zapata being able to land the shuttle, and they had to board it without being killed.

Wilder scanned the tree-filled slopes. Where the hell were Cherry and Aubriot? If they weren't here in five minutes, Zapata wouldn't wait. Why hadn't the explosives gone off? Had the mission failed?

She was about to comm Cherry when a dull roar resounded and the ground trembled. Between overhanging leaves, she glimpsed a fountain of dirt and dust rising into the dusky sky.

They'd blown up the Scythians' nursery!

Yes!

Humanity had finally hit back at the aliens.

But she wouldn't be around to see the fallout. She had work to do elsewhere. Cherry and Aubriot should finally be on their way back. Strongquist appeared, and the noise of heli rotors briefly rose and faded.

"Are you coming with us?" she asked.

"Coming with you to Concordia? I hadn't considered it as an option."

"You could be useful there. We have a lot to do."

"There is much to do on Earth too."

"Do you *have* free will?" It was a question that had only just occurred to her. "Can you come and go as you please?"

"Within the restraints of my programming, I can choose my own path."

"So you aren't programmed to serve the Makers?"

"I am not. In the remaining time, I will consider your offer."

Wilder trotted to the head of the trail.

It was empty.

She comm'd, "Cherry, where are you?"

"I-I'm on my way."

Cherry sounded out of breath.

"And Aubriot?" Wilder asked. "He's with you, right? Only—"

"He's...he's..."

Shit. She'd been mistaken. Cherry wasn't panting, she was crying.

"You have to hurry," Wilder said. "Zapata's on his way."

"What?! How?"

"I don't know yet. We only have a few minutes."

Cherry's head appeared, bobbing as she trotted up the trail.

"This way," Wilder called out, heading back to the girls and Strongquist.

There was a distant sound—the whine of the shuttle's a-grav drive.

Cherry ran up. Her face was grimy except for tear tracks running from her eyes. She gasped, "The *Sirocco* came back?"

"I can't believe it either. Zapata says he can't wait around. We have to leave as soon as he lands."

Cherry's chest heaved. "Aubriot didn't make it."

"I got that. It's a shame he's gone." Wilder didn't feel a hypocrite saying it. She meant it, even though she hadn't liked the man.

"Maybe he'll turn into that person the Maker was talking about." Cherry wiped her eyes on her sleeve.

"What person?"

"Someone for the Earthers to rally around, a figurehead. His story might grow over time, you know, how the stories of famous people do. He would have liked that."

"Yeah, he would."

The shuttle's whine increased.

Zapata comm'd, "I see the landing site. Coming in. Be ready."

The imposing vessel appeared in the night sky. Scythians flew straight for it.

"He'll never touch down," said Wilder, dismayed. "It's too dangerous."

Cherry marched toward the clearing. "Bring the girls." She hefted her rifle to her shoulder.

"Nina, Miki, you're coming?" Wilder asked.

Miki nodded, her gaze on her sister. "We're coming."

Pulse rounds lit the night, but not from Cherry's rifle. She hadn't begun firing yet. It was Strongquist. He was aiming through the canopy, picking off the aliens, laying cover for the descending shuttle. "I have decided to decline your offer," he called out. "I wish you luck in all your endeavors."

Wilder grabbed Miki and Nina's hands, and they ran.

Cherry began shooting. She was on the very edge of the clearing, firing round after round at the whirling Scythians. The aliens swooped and soared, trying to get closer while avoiding being shot. Strongquist and Cherry's efforts kept them too busy to shoot at the shuttle.

The vessel was down, its hatch opening.

Wilder reached it and helped the girls to board before turning back to her friend, who hadn't changed position. "Cherry," she yelled, "Come on! It's time to go!"

"I'm not coming."

"What? You have to come back to Concordia!"

"I'm going to stay here and help the Earthers. Good luck."

"But—"

"Take off in ten seconds," Zapata comm'd.

"Wilder!" Nina called. "Come inside. Close the hatch."

With a sense of unreality, Wilder climbed into the shuttle, and the hatch closed. Before she reached a seat, the vessel rose into the air. She was forced to the deck, where she sat numbly. After several minutes, the upward acceleration eased and she summoned the willpower to find a seat and strap in.

She comm'd Cherry, her voice trembling. "What are you doing? I don't understand."

"I'm sorry, but the Makers need someone to advise them about the Scythians."

"But we need you on Concordia too."

"You'll be fine without me, and you'll be great for Miki and Nina. I was never the motherly type."

"None of those things is true." Wilder's tears flowed freely.

"I'm done," Cherry said. "I'm tired, and I'm done. Maybe the GAA will give me a room somewhere far from the fighting, and I can annoy the Makers by telling them they're wrong."

"I don't get it."

"I'm not sure I do either. Tell the girls I'll visit Kes's grave for them. You take care. You'll be the last of the first Concordians. You have a reputation to uphold. It was good knowing you, Wilder."

The comm went dead.

FORTY-ONE

The shuttle landed in the *Sirocco*'s bay. Heavy clunks echoed through the cabin as the clamps snapped into place.

"Stay right where you are," Zapata ordered. "It's the safest place."

"What's going on?" Wilder asked.

"When we jumped back into the system we found the Scythians' military ships had arrived. Unlike the transports, the battleships weren't shy about attacking us."

The entire shuttle shuddered.

"That's the Parvus's weapon firing," Zapata explained. "We've taken a couple of hits, but we're giving as good as we're getting. It won't be long until the ship runs out of juice, though, hence the deadline for picking you up. If we waited too long we wouldn't have the energy to jump."

"We're going to jump?"

"Imminently."

"With us in the shuttle?"

"You're welcome to try and run for a capsule if you think you can make it."

"I'll take my chances here."

Miki and Nina had only heard Wilder's half of the conversation, so she told them the bits they'd missed.

"What about Cherry?" Miki asked.

"She isn't coming back to Concordia." It was blunt, but Wilder didn't know a gentler way of explaining it.

"Will we ever see her again?" Nina asked.

"Maybe one day. She said she'll visit your Dad's grave from time to time."

"That's good," said Miki. "It's good he won't be alone."

And then the *Sirocco* jumped.

———

Vessey had tricked them. Or, rather, most of them.

Over the course of the next few hours, Wilder learned from Niall and Dragan all that had happened since the shuttle had disappeared from Svalbard.

The captain had comm'd Zapata, instructing him to fly her to the GAA's headquarters to hand over vaccine samples. That had been no lie. She did take the samples to Buka. But after the pilot had flown her back to the *Sirocco*, she'd ordered him into his cabin and locked him in as a punishment for disobeying orders previously.

A handful of the ship's personnel had been in the know about exactly what she was doing and why.

Vessey's cronies knew she planned to abandon Cherry, Wilder, Aubriot and Kes's daughters and take the ship home. Her reasoning was that time had run out, and a few had to be sacrificed for the sake of the majority.

But she told the rest of the crew something different. She announced that the ship would make one jump out of the system, purely as a safety precaution. Later, when Aubriot, Cherry, and Wilder had had time to retrieve Miki and Nina, the *Sirocco* would return and pick them up. But the waiting period stretched out, and in the meantime Vessey's allies tried to persuade the others that it wouldn't be safe to go back, that the might of the Scythian military must have arrived, and if the ship returned to Earth everyone would be going to their certain deaths.

The tactic worked on some, and opinion began to turn in favor of continuing the journey home. They had everything they needed to re-start ecosystems on Concordia. Abandoning crewmates was hard, but, after all, two of them were half-Earthers anyway, and one of them was generally disliked.

But the persuasion hadn't worked on everyone. Niall and Dragan had figured out Vessey's scheme. They broke Zapata out and, with the help of the personnel who hadn't been turned, they mutinied.

The former Captain Vessey was now the one confined to her cabin. Her erstwhile supporters had faded away, and the *Sirocco* jumped back to the Sol System, only to meet a nasty Scythian surprise.

The journey home began. The days sped past and sense of normality returned, somewhat. Each jump was coordinated to land the ship in the vicinity of a star. Then it was just a matter of waiting to build sufficient power to move on again.

And so they continued, leaping across the galaxy, taking a single second to traverse a distance that, on the outward journey, had taken years.

The trip to Earth had cost many lives: suicides of those who had given up hope, accidental deaths of plant-hunters who had searched alien planets for crops to keep everyone alive, the tragic loss of Kes, and, finally, Aubriot—perhaps immortal yet not indestructible. But they had completed their mission. The Ark was full from decks to overheads with material to rejuvenate their ravaged planet. If anyone still lived on Concordia, the *Sirocco*'s return would seem like a myth made real, history come alive, replete with riches.

When the day came for the final jump, which would take them home, Miki approached Wilder. The girl had been subdued and quiet the entire journey. It wasn't surprising. She had to be grieving for her father and missing Cherry. But this time Wilder read something new in her eyes.

"Miki, what's wrong?"

She collapsed into Wilder's arms. "I'm so sorry. I've messed everything up. We're all going to die!"

Wilder almost laughed. It was such a ridiculous thing to say. But the girl was only fifteen and had a taste for the dramatic. Wilder swallowed her chuckle. "I'm sure we aren't all going to die. Tell me what's bothering you. I'm sure we can put it right."

Her head pressed against Wilder's chest, Miki replied in muffled tones, "They knew I was from Concordia, and they interrogated me, and I spilled my guts. I told the Scythians everything."

Wilder was still. Then she gently pulled Miki away and looked into her downcast eyes. Miki wouldn't meet her gaze. "I don't understand. How could the Scythians possibly know you were from Concordia?"

"I don't know for sure, but I think they analyzed my speech, and, somehow, they knew. They asked me lots of questions, and I had to answer or they would have killed Nina. I told them all I knew. I couldn't let them kill her."

Miki seemed completely sincere. Wilder was confident she thought she was telling the truth, but it didn't add up...

Except it did.

The Scythians had investigated the Guardian, Faina's database. They would have learned about the language spoken on Concordia.

Miki's guess was probably correct. The aliens had matched her speech with the information from Faina and put two and two together. Their finding would explain the presence of a high-tech ship with jump capabilities in orbit around humanity's low-tech origin planet.

The Scythians knew the Concordian colony had survived the biocide. They knew Concordians were returning to re-seed the planet. They knew the humans would be arriving soon.

After one more jump the *Sirocco* would be home, but what would her crew find there?

REPRISAL

These soldiers had done what they had done, and been done unto in
return. This was how it went.

In the cycle of slaughter, reprisal begat reprisal, forever.

— Laini Taylor

ONE

Seeds, tubers, corms, bulbs, spores, rhizomes, cuttings—everything needed to replenish Concordia's biome was stacked deck to overhead in the Ark. Wilder walked the aisles, past refrigerator units, shelves full of boxes and thick packets neatly filed, and glasshouse areas sectioned off by transparent plastic curtains moist with condensation. The growing tanks that had kept the crew fed on their long voyage had been dismantled months ago, yet she could still remember where they'd been and the crops that had grown in them. She'd worked the 'fields' for years, after all, along with everyone else.

The scientists said the seeding material also carried fungal spores, bacteria, and other micro-organisms that subtly promoted growth. These were missing from Concordia, as well as all the other species the Scythians' biocide had destroyed. Their absence was the reason plants struggled to grow. Wilder didn't doubt the scientists were correct. Her crewmates weren't exactly her best buddies, not after all that had happened, but they knew their stuff. Kes had picked only the best for the trip.

She halted.

Tall shelving units stacked with containers flanked her. A faulty light flickered above, casting the space into chaotic darkness.

She checked her surroundings again. Everything was different now, but she was sure it was here she'd found Cherry, flat on her back on a deck swimming with water. Her friend had slipped and sustained a severe concussion. She'd been lucky she hadn't been electrocuted.

Cherry.

"It was good knowing you, Wilder."

Those had been her parting words. Now she was on Earth fighting the Scythians, and it was up to the remaining personnel of the *Sirocco* to continue the fight on Concordia.

For the aliens would return one day, perhaps soon. They knew that their biocide hadn't wiped out the humans. They knew the colony had survived, and they knew of its plan to restock the planet with life from Earth.

She walked on.

A comm arrived.

"Where are you?" Niall asked. "It's time to jump."

"Already? Sorry, I got distracted. I'm on the Ark."

"What are you doing there?" His tone was cold, impersonal, irritated.

"Just reminiscing."

"Right." A touch of scorn. "Vessey's going to blow her lid if you don't get over to the jump chamber in the next five minutes." The captain had been reinstated to her position for the brief time it had taken to jump home. If there was one thing she could be relied upon for, it was to coordinate the journey back.

"All right. Tell her I'm coming."

"Tell her yourself."

The comm cut out.

Swallowing her anger, Wilder sent a message to Vessey, saying she was on her way. Then she stomped toward the exit.

Niall had been cantankerous and distant ever since a Scythian had snatched her on the Makers' island on Earth. She hadn't pushed him about his attitude. She knew what his problem was. Kes had given her an insight into what was probably going on with Niall, and she thought the older man had been right. She was sympathetic, but it was no excuse to treat her so badly.

When she reached the jump chamber, a few people remained outside their capsules, chatting. They side-eyed her as she walked in. She ignored them and walked to the nearest empty capsule. There was no point in placating them. Her rep had never recovered from the failed jump that had taken them years off course, and it never would. Everyone had expected to be away for only a few weeks. Instead, with the effects of time dilation, they had been absent for decades. Even if their loved ones had survived to old age on the crippled planet, they were probably long dead. It was hard to forgive something like that.

"Jumping in two minutes," Vessey announced.

Wilder stepped into her capsule and lay down, sinking into the spongy seat. She fastened her harness.

What would Concordia be like? Was anyone still alive? If the colony had failed, was there any point in re-seeding the planet, especially considering the Scythians were bound to return? Maybe it would make more sense to go back to Earth and try to make a life there.

Her stomach sank at the idea. Earth was beautiful, but it wasn't home.

"One minute," Vessey announced.

The shell of Wilder's capsule closed.

A voice sounded in her ear. "Wilder?"

"Hey, Miki. Everything okay?"

"Yeahhhh…" Silence.

"Are you worried about what we might find when we arrive? You're not alone. But don't be too concerned. The Scythians don't have jump drive. It will take them years to reach Concordia."

The young girl's breathy sigh came down the line. "I feel bad for telling them everything."

"You didn't have a choice. If you hadn't they would have killed Nina. No one blames you. Besides, the Scythians would have returned to Concordia anyway, sooner or later. It's their origin planet. They have a sentimental attachment to it. It doesn't matter that they can't live there anymore."

"I guess so," Miki replied doubtfully. "I just can't help feeling that Dad would be disappointed in me."

"No, he wouldn't. He would have been proud of you for protecting your sister. And, anyway, he loved you so much I don't think anything you did could have disappointed him. You don't need to concern yourself about that."

A pause.

"Thanks, Wilder."

The computer countdown began.

"See you in Concordia orbit," Wilder said.

The numbers counted down. She'd endured many jumps now, journeying to Earth and returning home. She should have become accustomed to the sensation, yet she still tensed as the countdown neared its end. Traversing spacetime in a manner at odds with the natural movements of the human body was something that could never feel familiar.

Three.

Two.

One.

Zero.

Reality shifted.

She could no longer feel where she was in space. Her view beyond the transparent shell of her capsule stretched wide and then squashed in, folding in many pleats. At the same time a piercing whistle assaulted her ears.

Then it was all over.

Her capsule opened.

Excited voices filled the chamber.

"Home," someone said. "Finally!"

"I can't believe it," said another. "It doesn't feel real."

"I wonder what we'll find down there," said a third. "I wonder what's left."

The tone turned somber and the voices quietened.

Vessey cut through the conversations. "At your stations, everyone. You all know what you should be doing. Zapata, where are you?"

After a preliminary check of the state of things on the planet surface, the captain would go down with a small team. Everyone else would follow later. The *Sirocco* was not to be abandoned entirely. A skeleton crew would remain on duty, but on a regular rotation. It would not be right to condemn anyone to spending long periods of time aboard the vessel.

Wilder sat up. People were climbing out of their capsules. She gave Miki and Nina a wave, trying to look positive, though inside she felt quite different. She was all the girls had left in terms of a parent and she felt utterly unequipped. She barely had her own life in order. How was she supposed to be a mother to two orphans?

"No!" Niall was at the wall interface, staring at the screen. "Dammit! Captain, you have to see this."

"Is it what we thought?"

"Yes."

Vessey's features tightened. "Right. Then I don't need to see it. Plan B, everyone. Back in your capsules. Niall, do the honors."

Wilder's heart sank deeper than her body into her seat as she resumed her position in her capsule. The shell closed over her again, and the countdown started up. It would be shorter this time, the minimum the engines needed. They could only make a small jump, using up the remainder of their power.

The question was, would it happen fast enough?

An alarm blared out. A split second later, the ship shuddered.

They'd been hit.

She prayed the jump drive hadn't sustained any damage. If it had, they were screwed.

This time, the countdown seemed agonizingly slow. She willed the numbers to decrease faster. The alarm continued to sound, loud and urgent, as if the ship was begging her crew to do something, fast, before it was too late. But there was nothing they could do. They'd used most of their power getting here. There was too little left to operate the Parvus's weapon *and* jump. It was one or the other, and until they understood the situation better, getting the hell out of Concordia's system was the safer option.

The *Sirocco* lurched, and Wilder was pressed tight up against the side of her seat.

The assault seemed to have come from the port side this time.

Not the jump drive. Not the drive!

The countdown was only just audible over the alarm. It whispered tantalizingly.

Two.
One.
She held her breath.

Two

"Someone turn off that damned alarm," Vessey ordered.

The cover of Wilder's capsule opened, but this time she didn't sit up. Though they'd only completed two jumps and she was fully rested, exhaustion had settled on her. Lifting her head felt like too much effort. Or was it only dread of what she was about to discover?

They'd known it was a possibility. The alternative scenario to what everyone had been anticipating had been the great unmentionable subject of the return voyage.

She lay still, waiting for the motivation to rise. Others were moving around and talking. The earlier excitement had disappeared and been replaced by grim resignation.

"Any ships within range?" Vessey asked.

"The scanners aren't picking anything up," Niall replied. "We're safe for now."

For now.

A face appeared in Wilder's vision, long red-black hair hanging down.

"Why aren't you getting up?" Miki asked.

Wilder smiled thinly. "Just taking a minute. Want to give me a hand?" She unfastened her harness, and Miki helped her climb out.

"The jumps make me feel sick too," said Miki. "What's going on? Vessey said something about Plan B. Have we left Concordia?"

"Yes, but we've only gone a little way. We're at its closest neighboring star."

"How come?"

"Uh..."

Miki really didn't know? Wilder hated to be the one to break the news. "Didn't you feel the hits?"

"Hits?" Miki's eyes widened. "I thought there was something wrong with the ship. We were under attack?!"

"Where's Nina?"

"She's gone back to our cabin. She always needs an hour to recover from a jump."

"In that case, come with me. Let's see what the scanners picked up."

Miki was going to have to deal with what faced the returning Concordians, despite her young years. It was better that she knew what they were up against. It wouldn't be fair—or even possible—to keep her in the dark.

They walked to the bridge. Zapata was already at the pilot's controls, probably moving the ship to the optimum spot within the new system to avoid detection. They couldn't be too cautious. Vessey stood with Niall, assessing the scan data. They looked up as Wilder and Miki walked over.

Vessey frowned. "Miki, I'm not sure this is the right place for you at the moment."

"She needs to know what's going on," Wilder retorted. "She's a member of this crew the same as everyone else. Hell, she and Nina grew up on this ship. And their father sacrificed his life—"

"Okay, I get it. Take a seat. Niall, put the images up for us all to see."

While the captain was sitting down, Wilder asked, "Did you get the damage report yet?"

Vessey grimaced. "The Ark took a hit that breached the hull. I've sent in a team. Hopefully, we haven't lost too much."

"I felt two impacts. Where was the second one?"

"Just above the jump drive. We had a lucky escape. My guess is they don't know its exact location in the ship. Otherwise we wouldn't be here."

"The data has rendered," Niall announced. "I'll put up the images of Concordia first, followed by what's in orbit."

The bridge lights dimmed and the center brightened with a holo of the planet surface.

Miki gasped.

Wilder's hands tightened on her armrests. She'd been expecting to see something like this, but the extent of it was shocking.

Scythian domes dotted a dusty plain under a clear blue sky. It was hard to estimate the area the scanners had captured, but if the domes were the same size as the ones on Earth, they stood only a few kilometers apart. The surface of Concordia was thick with aliens.

"But I thought they didn't have jump tech," Miki blurted. She turned to Wilder, eyes wide. "How could they have got here so fast?"

Niall tutted irritably. "They were already here, of course."

Wilder studied the holo more closely. It showed a Scythian in mid-air between the domes—unusually, considering it was daylight—wearing the same breathing apparatus they'd used on Earth. That was somewhat of a relief. At least they hadn't managed to reverse the 'poisoning' of Concordia's atmosphere with oxygen.

Miki asked quietly, "Is anyone still alive down there?"

Vessey got to her feet and strode into the holo. "These look like human figures, don't you think?" She pointed to a patch of land greener than the rest. Small, upright shapes could be spotted among the vegetation. Were they people? It was hard to tell but it seemed likely. Other macro-organisms had been wiped out by the biocide.

"What are they doing?" asked Miki.

"Tending crops, I'd say," Niall offered, "probably to feed themselves and perhaps the Scythians too."

"I think that vegetation must be crops," Wilder said. "It looks homogeneous and there's precious little else around. I can't see any trees or scrub. The place doesn't look much better than how we left it."

"But I still don't understand how the Scythians..." Miki paused. "I get it. They didn't come here due to what I told them on Earth. They'd already returned to Concordia anyway. What I said didn't matter." Tension seemed to leave her body. "That's a relief, though this is still a...a..."

"Disaster?" Vessey suggested. "What do they have in orbit, Niall?"

The landscape vanished and black space took up the central position on the bridge. Within the star-speckled darkness hung three crescent-shaped ships.

"The largest is the one that fired on us," Niall said, consulting his screen. "It was quick off the mark. I don't know about the other two, whether they aren't armed or if they didn't manage to fire before we jumped."

"They're all Scythian military," Vessey said grimly, "not transports. I'd lay money on it. We got a good look at their colonization vessels while we were on Earth."

"I can make a detailed comparison," Wilder offered. "We have plenty of information on both types of vessel."

Vessey waved dismissively. "Depressurization in the Ark and a damaged hull near the jump drive tell us all we need to know for now. There's no question in my mind that, A, Scythians arrived at Concordia many years ago and, B, they know a starship carrying humans had departed the system and was expected to return. Those ships were waiting for us."

"But how could they know that?" asked Miki.

"Probably the same way they found out you were from Concordia."

The young girl put her head in her hands.

"The colonization attempt succeeded here," Niall said. "Unsurprisingly. The place was in a weakened state when we left. The Scythian attack had destroyed its defenses, their biocide had wiped out most living organisms, the colony was on its knees. We thought Earth was in a bad position to defend itself, but compared to Concordia it's a well-stocked fortress. Those poor bastards."

"Maybe it isn't such a bad thing," said Wilder.

Niall stared. "How the hell do you figure that?"

"It might have been the Scythians' return that saved the colony. You remember what things were like when we left—food stores were running out, crops would barely grow, and insect swarms were making being outdoors intolerable. If there are people down there, it might only be because the Scythians enslaved them. They need human labor on a planet where they can't breathe the atmosphere. They would have had to fix the environment sufficiently for humans to survive."

Vessey gave a snort. "The Concordia Colony only continues to exist because it has alien overlords? That's rich. I wonder what Aubriot would have said."

"He must be spinning in his grave," Niall muttered. "But wondering about what happened isn't going to change anything."

"Exactly," said Vessey. "I have some thinking to do. We need a way forward, but at the moment I'm not seeing it."

The minimal data the *Sirocco*'s scanners had gleaned in the short time the vessel had been in orbit painted a dire scene. If colonists remained on the planet they were in thrall to Scythian masters. The aliens were somehow aware that an armed vessel belonging to the humans could appear one day, and they were on guard against it. And, aside from crop plants, the environment didn't seem to have recovered. The planet still desperately needed the seeding material in the Ark to replenish its ecosystem.

But how were they to get it there? How could they defeat the military vessels? Any small element of surprise they'd had previously was now entirely gone. How could they help the colonists, descendants of the people they'd left behind?

Miki lifted her head from her hands. "Things might be even worse than we think."

"I'm not sure that's possible," said Vessey, "but I guess I need to hear it. Fire away."

"Dad told me and Nina lots about Concordia while we were growing up. I could only just remember the place, and Nina couldn't remember it at all. He told us all the good stuff—how determined, brave, and hardworking all the colonists were, what they'd endured and come through, despite the challenges. But he also told us something else, something I...I think you might have forgotten." She looked up at Vessey timidly.

"Forgotten? Well, I've certainly had a lot on my plate during this mission.

Don't worry. I'm not Aubriot. I don't think I'm perfect and I'm not going to bite your head off for pointing out a flaw."

"Umm..." Miki glanced around the group on the bridge.

Zapata looked over his shoulder.

"Dad said the colony needed fresh genetic input. Otherwise, over the long term it was doomed. He said we needed to bring people from—"

"Holy shit!" Wilder clapped a hand over her mouth. "Miki, you're right! I'd forgotten. We've all forgotten. The original mission was to bring back the seeding material, but we were also supposed to be introducing new human DNA to the colony eventually. If not people, then donated eggs and sperm. Or else inherited diseases would start to appear and the population would weaken. In the end it would die out. Kes mentioned it at the meeting in the Town Hall, but that was so long ago."

"We were fixated on the main task," said Niall. "The delay pushed everything else to the backs of our minds."

Vessey shook her head. "And to think I was set on not taking any Earthers with us."

Miki said, "If I hadn't gone to the surface with Nina I might have remembered in time and been around to remind you. I'm sorry."

"Don't worry about it," Vessey reassured her. "This mission has been crazy for all of us. We've made plenty of mistakes. I'm certainly not blameless in that regard. But it's time to move on and look ahead. Zapata, have you brought us within range of the star to begin energy harvesting?"

"In another few minutes."

"Niall or Wilder, could you please do the usual? I'll be in my office. I have a lot to think about. If anyone has any suggestions, feel free to disturb me."

THREE

When Miki arrived at her cabin Nina had woken from her nap.

She sat up in bed. "What's happening? When are we going down to Concordia? I'm so excited to see it. I know it won't be for the first time but that's how it feels. I was only a baby when we left. I don't remember home at all." Her lips twisted downward. "I wish Dad was here. He could have taken us back to our old house. Only maybe it isn't there anymore."

Miki sat next to her sister and put an arm around her shoulders. "We won't be going to the planet surface any time soon, sorry." She gave her sister the news.

Nina gasped. "We were being *fired* on?!"

"I didn't realize either. I felt the hits and heard people's reactions, but it was all over so quickly I didn't get much time to think about it."

"I thought the jump drive might have gone wrong again." Nina rested her head on Miki's shoulder. "Are they going to force the Scythians to leave? How long will we have to stay on the ship?"

"Captain Vessey is trying to figure out a plan. I'm sure she or one of the others will think of something." Miki was trying to reassure herself as much as Nina, but the impression she had from the discussion on the bridge was that going home was going to be very difficult and dangerous.

Nina asked in a soft whisper, "Should we have stayed on Earth?"

The same idea had occurred to Miki. They'd left Dad behind, and Cherry too, and for what? She'd thought Concordia would be safe, that she was taking Nina away from the Scythians, but it had sounded like the aliens were more established on Concordia. Their defenses would be stronger, and the *Sirocco* was alone, without anyone to help. On Earth there had been helis, weapons, and a big population. Here, there was none of that.

A heavy feeling settled in her stomach. Dad was gone, and it was down to her to protect Nina. She'd done a terrible job so far. "I don't know. Maybe."

"But Concordia's our home, right?"

"It is, but..." In truth, if any place was their home it was the *Sirocco*. They'd spent most of their lives on the ship, growing up aboard her, and for a very long time her crew were the only people they'd known. They'd met some Earthers in the Scythian domes and after escaping, but they spoke a different language, making it nearly impossible to communicate. "I think Dad would say Concordia is where we belong. That's where we were born, and that's where Mom is. I was dumb when I pulled that stunt and we snuck off to Earth."

"You're not dumb."

Nina was being kind, but Miki felt dumb. Dumb and powerless.

"Did they say if there's anything we can do?" asked Nina.

"Nope. I think we can be most helpful by staying out of everyone's way." Miki bit her lip. "Or maybe not. The Ark took a hit and depressurized. We lost some of the seeding material. We could help by figuring out what we lost. I'll ask if that's okay."

"Sure. I'll get ready."

Nina climbed out of bed while Miki comm'd the captain. She felt a little bad bothering her when she had a lot on her mind, but Vessey's response was positive. She only asked to double check the Ark was completely safe before they went over.

———

The place was a mess. The crew had fixed the hull, but only roughly. Thick lines of solder ran over the plain metal surface like barely healed scars. They had fixed the interior first and were now working on the hull. An acrid scent remained. Circulation fans whined as they sensed the contaminating particles and strained to draw them into the filters.

The crew had done nothing to address the devastation to the seeding material. The hit from the Scythian ship had penetrated an area a few centimeters in diameter and whatever was gone had squeezed through the gap. The shelves nearest the breach were empty, naturally, their contents had exploded into space.

Miki read the labels. Seeds of alpine plants had been stored here. She'd hoped that some of the material might not be entirely lost, but there was no hope of recovering these. The cold and vacuum of space wouldn't harm them in the short term, but the seed packets were tiny, smaller than the palm of her hand. Locating them would be impossible.

"Oh well," Nina said. "Concordia's mountains are going to stay bare for a while."

"Or overrun by one species. Dad said some things had grown rampantly, covering hundreds of square kilometers because nothing that used to eat them or compete with them had survived." Miki had a faint memory of a swarm of insects biting her, but she didn't tell Nina about it. The image of the humans toiling in the fields on Concordia sprang to her mind. What were those people enduring?

The effect of the breach outside its immediate vicinity was less calamitous. Plenty had been dragged from storage, smashed against shelving units, thrown against bulkheads, torn apart, shredded, and jumbled up, but it hadn't been lost.

The situation seemed salvageable. She and Nina had spent long hours cataloging and storing the collected samples. They were familiar with many of the items, so identifying them shouldn't be too hard, and they could confirm with DNA analysis. Then it would only be a matter of re-packing them. The task would be lengthy and painstaking, but it would help to take Nina's mind off everything else.

"What a mess!" Nina exclaimed.

"It isn't as bad as it looks." Miki stooped to pick up a tuber. "This is one of the roots Earthers eat, remember? Wilder said it tastes floury and sweet." They hadn't tried it. Everything gathered had gone straight into the Ark.

Nina's brow wrinkled. "Yeah, I think I remember."

Miki pushed up her sleeves to her elbows. "Let's get started. First, we need to separate it all out. We can use the empty area next to the site of the breach."

"Ugh, this is going to take *forever*," Nina complained, but she squatted down and began to scoop up detritus.

Miki joined her, relieved to be doing something useful. The last thing she wanted was to cause more trouble.

Four

The Scythian vessel lay in pieces over the holding bay deck. Wilder, Niall, and Dragan had recently spent every spare moment investigating the alien spacecraft, while the *Sirocco* had leapfrogged across the galaxy. What they'd discovered didn't seem helpful for tackling the current crisis, but Wilder had returned to the bay nonetheless, hoping to find something they'd missed.

The major disappointment had been that the small, two-seater ship appeared to be only for traveling within a planetary atmosphere. As far as they could tell it didn't possess a-grav—though, to be fair, that had been a recent introduction to intelligent galactic species in this sector, courtesy of herself. More pertinently, the craft wasn't airtight. They'd guessed the Scythians who flew them must have worn breathing apparatus, and Miki and Nina had confirmed.

The Scythian planetary craft was driven by a compact engine core and battery powered turbines. The remaining components comprised predictable devices: an altimeter, gyros, a compass, and so on. Some items remained a mystery, but most differences between the alien vessel and a heli were superficial. The crescent shape Scythians favored seemed to be only a style preference. The oddly shaped seating and flight controls were suited to Scythian anatomy. The aliens clearly reclined, their wings folded to their sides, and operated the controls with their prehensile feet.

Overall, the ship's technology was surprisingly similar to something humans might invent. Or perhaps not so surprisingly. There had to be a limited number of ways to achieve and maintain flight.

Wilder gazed at the heavily studied parts of the dismantled ship, feeling she was at a dead end. Even if they managed to figure out the functions of the remaining mysterious parts, she didn't think the revelations would help.

Maybe it was time to try a different avenue of exploration. She should leave her comfort zone and venture into that cryptic discipline—biology.

She comm'd Vessey.

"Wilder," the captain answered with a note of hope, "what can I do for you?"

"Can you tell me who's been working on the Scythian cadaver?"

"Ryan mostly. Why?"

Ugh.

"Has he sent in a report?"

"Yes, but..." the captain sighed "...it's mostly gibberish. I'm no scientist. Perhaps you could understand it better?"

"I doubt it, but I'm willing to give it a try."

"Anything you can suggest that might help us—*anything*—I'd be happy to hear it. I'll send you the report."

"Thanks."

The report arrived and Wilder began to listen to it, but many of the terms were unfamiliar. She found a wall interface and opened the file on the screen. Reading the information made it more understandable, but it was quickly apparent that she needed to speak to the author himself.

This was going to be tricky. Ever since the incident where they'd tried to kill her, she'd avoided members of the Final Day Five, except for Dragan, who had ended up saving her life. Avoiding Marcus, whom she'd blinded, was easy. He rarely left his cabin. Durbin and Goslin kept out of her way. Ryan, on the other hand, seemed to cope with his embarrassment over what he'd done by pretending it had never happened. After recovering from the injuries she'd inflicted to his knees, he'd tried to interact as if she was just another member of the crew. He'd never apologized or even acknowledged the attack.

She wasn't sure she wanted him to, but she'd wished he would read the room and leave her alone. The memory of nearly being hanged by her ship-mates wasn't something she wanted to dwell on. She tried to never bring it to mind, though the event invaded her dreams. In some, she didn't manage to get away. In others, she made it to Dragan's cabin but he didn't experience his epiphany and defend her.

If Ryan appeared in her vicinity she would leave, and if he was someplace she needed to be she would delay going in until he left, whenever possible. What made it worse was the fact that everyone else seemed to want to move on from the attempted murder, too, like it was just one of the many crazy things that had happened on the ill-fated voyage. She understood how that was the most convenient reaction. Trying her would-be assassins for their crime would have been difficult, considering the circumstances, and it would have deprived the mission of desperately needed specialists.

But how was *she* supposed to 'move on'?

She reached Ryan's cabin and hesitated, her hand halfway to his door chime. Did she really want to do this? She set her jaw and pressed.

"Wilder! Great to see you. It's been a while."

"I want to talk to you about—"

"Take a seat. Can I get you something to drink?"

Ryan's cabin was neat and bare, almost pathologically so. His bed was made, his desk empty, the walls unadorned. It looked like he'd only just moved in, not lived here for years. The only sign of occupation was a faint scent of antiseptic. What had he been doing before she arrived?

"This won't take long," she said. "You've been working on the Scythian corpse, right? I was wondering what you could tell me about what you found. I read the report, but..."

He lifted an eyebrow. "Gobbledygook, right? Don't worry, I feel the same when I look at anything to do with engineering or physics. I tell you what— why don't you come with me to have a look at it? I can give you an illustrated explanation."

"Uhh..." She hadn't anticipated viewing one of the creatures up close, but when she woke up this morning neither had she anticipated a chat with the man who'd tried to kill her. She might as well go all in. "Sure."

"Actually, I'm glad you came to see me," said Ryan as they stepped out. "We haven't had a chance to talk about what happened when...you know..."

"We haven't had a chance to talk about it?" she echoed. *I haven't given you a chance, asshole.*

"I just wanted to tell you, I forgive you."

She halted, hard, as if she'd walked into a wall. "You *what*?"

"I understand you were scared and reacted in a panic. I know if you'd been in your right mind you would never have done what you did. You wouldn't have hurt me." From the mild expression on his face he didn't seem to be registering her shocked reaction.

"We...we are talking about the same incident, right?" she spluttered. "You do mean the time you, Marcus, Goslin, and Durbin tried to string me up? You mean *that* time, right?!" Her tone had reached almost screeching pitch.

This wasn't how she'd wanted things to go. The last thing she'd wanted was to get distracted by past events. They needed to focus on present problems. But she couldn't let this twisting of the truth slide. Her entire body rebelled at the notion.

"I believe you might have misinterpreted our intentions," he said.

"Oh, I don't think so," she snapped, setting off down the passageway at a speedy pace. "Take me to see the Scythian. Let's get this over with."

He trotted to catch up to her. "If you would just let me explain..."

"What you did doesn't need explaining. I don't know what's gone on in your head since then—what mental gymnastics you've performed to convince yourself you didn't do anything wrong—but *my* memory is clear. And, frankly, attempting to persuade me I misunderstood what you intended is disgusting."

"But—"

"Not another word. Show me the Scythian."

"If I could just—"

"Show me the Scythian!" She glared at him until he could no longer meet her gaze.

His shoulders slumped. "It's this way."

Understanding her fellow humans had never been her strong suit, and the effort got harder day by day. People could excuse anything to themselves, even the most abhorrent behavior. Ryan obviously had some weird psychological thing going on, with his surgically clean cabin and rewriting his heinous act in his mind. Niall was another weirdo. He was mean to her because he liked her. How stupid was that?

Maybe she would have better luck understanding the aliens.

––––––

"I put it back together, kind of." Ryan dragged a body bag out of a freezer.

A mortuary hadn't featured in the *Sirocco*'s plans. In the rush to design and build the vessel, there simply hadn't been time to include non-essential facilities. It was one of the reasons they had buried Kes on Earth rather than bringing his body back to Concordia. People who died during the voyage had been given a space burial. But the Scythian's remains could provide crucial information, and so the post-autopsy corpse had been placed in a food freezer —to many grumbles from the crew. Storing food alongside an alien cadaver was far too dangerous a risk to take, which meant fewer supplies.

"Want to help me lift it up onto the table?" Ryan asked.

"Are you sure it's safe to open it up again? Maybe you could show me slides instead."

"It's been tested for all known toxins and pathogens, I didn't come to any harm dissecting it, and it's frozen solid. There's nothing in here to concern you."

He probably knew what he was talking about. She took one end of the bag while he took the other and, together, they lifted it.

"It's so light," she commented.

"Typical of an aerial species. The bones are thin for its size and mostly hollow, like a bird's." Ryan pulled on surgical gloves. "Just a precaution." He pulled the zipper the length of the bag and pushed down the sides.

Compared to her memory of the Scythian who had grabbed her and carried her aloft, the creature was almost unrecognizable. (This was not that one—this was its partner that Strongquist had killed on the rocks, but the aliens looked extremely alike.) A stiff, frosted, dull, cut-up mess lay within the bag's folds.

Ryan chuckled. "I thought I did a better reconstruction job." He prodded a convex structure. "That's the skull." His fingers traced a line along thin, translucent membranes. "Those are its wings. The superficial features are already familiar and somewhat predictable, given what we already know about the Scythians. The skin is sensitive to ultraviolet light. No surprise there. We know they prefer to move about at night. My guess is, when they lived on Concordia they were either nocturnal or the planet was heavily swathed in cloud cover. We know the climate was very different in the past. CO2 was the main atmospheric gas. So either conjecture could be correct."

He dug around deep within the anatomical mess. Meat grated against bone and, despite the frozen state of the corpse, a faint whiff of the creature's nauseating odor wafted upward.

Wilder put a hand over her mouth and nose. "What *is* that smell?"

"It's quite something, right? I got used to it in the end. It comes from glands either side of the creature's anus. Possibly a territory-marking or sexual advertising hangover from its evolutionary past." He grinned. "The Scythians must either tolerate or enjoy their scent, otherwise they would go to greater lengths to cover it up." He dug deeper. "The most interesting part for me was its insides." He lifted a set of dry, deflated bags, like shrunken balloons.

It was the most repugnant thing she had ever seen.

"Can you guess what these are?" Ryan asked.

"Surprise me."

"Stomachs."

"Stomachs, plural?"

"Plural. It has three, possibly four. One of the attached structures was hard to identify. I knew these had to be stomachs because they were filled with partially digested material, and they led to the afore-mentioned scent-producing anus."

"And because a tube leads to them from the mouth?"

"You would think so, but, no. As far as I can tell, they only use the mouth in their heads for breathing and speaking. They have another mouth in their abdomen for ingestion. It's covered by a flap and has only rudimentary grinding structures that look like modified scales. Hence the three stomachs."

Her confusion must have shown in her face.

He replaced the stomachs within the cadaver. "In human digestion, food is ground up in the mouth, mixed with saliva, and swallowed. In the stomach, acids mix with it, breaking it down further—"

"I studied human biology at school."

"I'm sorry. I don't mean to be patronizing..."

Like you didn't mean to try to kill me.

"...I'm only giving you a comparison to make my point. Scythians employ an entirely different digestion method. First, the food is somewhat broken down by grinding within the mouth cavity. Then it passes into the first stomach, where small stones get to work on it."

"Stones?"

"That isn't so strange. That's typical of a bird's digestive system, as I discovered on Earth. In the second and third stomach, bacteria complete the process. I haven't managed to identify any of them, which indicates they're all from the Scythian planet. It could be that Earth bacteria wouldn't work for them and would give them an upset stomach."

The feeling of being at a dead end rose up in Wilder again. Finding out about the details of Scythian anatomy seemed to be a waste of time. "I'm sure this is all very interesting for you, but did you discover any information that we might be able to use to defeat them?"

"Nothing springs to mind, I'm afraid, but the news about their digestive process was reassuring in a way."

"What way?"

"Well, I believe it's long been speculated that the Scythians might want to not only use humans as their slaves, but also to farm them, so to speak."

"You mean eat us?" Wilder asked bluntly.

"If you insist on not putting a fine point on it. My investigations revealed that's extremely unlikely."

"Why?" She couldn't see what was stopping the aliens from putting pieces of people into their mouth flaps.

"Because they're vegetarian."

"They're...?" She paused. "That can't be right. Miki said she saw immature Scythians eating each other."

"I'm aware of Kes's daughters' reports. I can only tell you what I discovered. There was no animal DNA within the subject's stomachs, and everything about its digestive system screams vegetarian."

"But the rest of their anatomy is like a predator's, isn't it? Forward-facing eyes, grasping appendages, claws for cutting and slicing..."

"That's correct. Yet their digestive structure tells a different story. I agree it's counter-intuitive, knowing what we know, but it isn't impossible. Life forms can pass through several apparently mutually exclusive stages before achieving maturity. It's feasible that Scythians begin life as carnivores, preying on each other as Miki suggested, but end up as plant-eaters."

"Peaceful, docile, passive vegetarians?"

"As we know, unfortunately not."

FIVE

Miki surveyed the section of the Ark, realizing only a small amount of mess remained. Their work was running out. She needed to think of something else to do, especially since no one seemed to be coming up with a plan to return to Concordia. As far as she could tell, the *Sirocco* would remain where she was for the foreseeable future. It was like the journey to Earth all over again.

Miki needed a distraction, something focused far from the ship and the current circumstances. She wondered what Dad would have suggested, and immediately the answer came. "Nina, I have an idea. When we get back to the cabin, we can re-start our history research."

Her sister, who was crouching to reach under a shelving unit, straightened up. "No, thanks. I'm tired. I'm going to watch a vid."

"You must have watched all the vids in the database by now. Aren't you bored of them?"

"Not as bored as I would be studying *history*." Nina emphasized the final word as if it was the most ridiculous suggestion she'd ever heard.

"But we were interrupted in our studies when we jumped to Earth, and we never went back to them. Dad would have wanted us to finish." Miki felt guilty using Nina's feelings about their father as leverage, but it was for a good cause.

"I suppose you're right," Nina replied resignedly. "Do you remember where we were when we stopped?"

"The Second Scythian Attack, I think."

"All right, let's start there. But can we skim the stuff about the bombardment? It's too sad and I don't feel like being sad right now."

"Sure, we can do that."

———

They were in their cabin, reading about the early days of the Concordia Colony, when the door chime rang. It was Wilder.

Miki hugged her. It had been days since she'd seen their friend, who felt like an older sister.

"I want to give you a heads up," Wilder said, "so the general announcement isn't going to be the first you hear about it."

"Oh." Miki sat down. "What's it about?"

"We're going to jump back to Concordia and attack the Scythian ships."

Nina sucked in air. "But that's really dangerous! Last time, they fired on us first."

"I know. There's more to it than that, but you're right, it is very risky. That's why I wanted to come here and tell you myself. We'll do everything we can to keep you and the ship safe."

"Can't we go back to Earth?" Nina asked.

"It's been discussed. The decision was made to stay on mission. Captain Vessey will make the announcement at 0700 tomorrow, and the jump will take place at 0900. Needless to say, you must be in your jump seats well before 0900."

Miki nodded and said with more confidence than she felt, "Thanks for telling us. We'll be there. Right, Nina?"

Nina didn't reply. Her head was down and her hands lay listlessly in her lap.

"While the battle's in progress," Wilder continued, "you must remain in your capsules. That'll be the safest place. We'll jump again with little or no notice. You might not have time to get back to them if you leave."

"Isn't there anything we can do to help?" asked Miki.

"The best help you can give is to stay where you are so no one has to worry about you."

"All right." Miki sighed, but then she said brightly in an effort to take her sister's mind off the upcoming battle, "Wilder, you were around in the colony's early days, weren't you?"

"I was, but I was quite young. About your age, in fact."

"Did you know Leader Ethan? We were just reading about him."

"Only by sight, mostly. I did meet him face-to-face once or twice." Wilder smiled, and the worry etched into her features faded. "I had to ask his permission to build a tree village outside Sidhe."

"A *tree* village!" Miki lifted her eyebrows.

"You never told us about that," said Nina.

"I never had any reason to. So much stuff went on in those early times, it wouldn't surprise me if little of it was recorded. Ethan seemed nice when I met him, but distracted. He must have had a lot on his mind. Cherry knew him much better than me. They were friends."

"Cool," said Miki. "It's hard to imagine you guys were around all those years ago, right at the beginning."

"Did Dad know Ethan too?" asked Nina.

"He must have. They were all together at the start. But I don't think Kes was close with him like Cherry was. Ethan and Cherry were Gens, while your Dad was a Woken, one of the scientists. There was hostility between the two groups back then."

"We've been reading about that," said Miki. "Ethan brought everyone together and gave them hope to carry on."

"Yeah," Wilder said wistfully, "he really did. I can't tell you much more. I wish I'd known him better. He was a great man. But I didn't see him much after I built the tree village, and then he died very soon after I returned from the Galactic Assembly." Her expression turned thoughtful, but then she focused on Miki and Nina again. She rose to her feet. "I'm sorry, but I have to go. I have things to do before tomorrow."

"We understand," said Miki. "Thanks for taking the time to come and see us."

"It's a pleasure. I wish I had the leisure to do it more often. Maybe when this war is over we can spend more time together. I could teach you physics," she added, her tone brightening.

"Uhh, okay," said Nina, giving Miki a look. "That would be great."

Wilder chuckled and leaned down to give them a hug in turn. "See you in the jump chamber."

Six

Wilder swallowed and gazed at the overhead above her capsule. The countdown had begun but it barely registered. Should she have argued harder with Vessey when the captain announced her decision? The attack seemed rash, hasty, and desperate. Should they have taken the time to think things through better? They had plenty of supplies. They could last months in this uninhabited system.

On the other hand, the Scythians knew the *Sirocco* was back. They might have already dispatched reinforcements. The longer the delay, the stronger and better prepared the aliens would become.

Perhaps it wasn't such a bad decision. Perhaps it was the only one possible.

Yet she couldn't help feeling it was wrong.

At least this time the Ark was protected. They had detached it from the main ship and would leave it behind when they jumped. Naturally, that meant they had to make it back to collect it, or their entire journey to Earth would be wasted. Concordia would never be reseeded.

She had never liked Aubriot. At times, her feelings about him had bordered on hate and disgust. He'd been arrogant, obnoxious, callous, and overbearing. But when it came to battle strategies he'd known his stuff. If it hadn't been for his insistence that the *Sirocco* be fitted with its devastating weapon, they would be helpless against the Scythians. He'd been their best military tactician, and his death had left a vacuum Vessey was in no position to fill.

The overhead stretched wide, multiplied into myriad versions of itself, and was instantly normal again. The shell of Wilder's capsule popped open. The jump was over.

She and Niall had programmed the ship's scanners to determine the largest vessel in Concordia's orbit and transmit the coordinates to the *Parvus*'s weapon, which would lock onto them and fire. Everything would happen at computing speed, orders of magnitude faster than human capability.

As she sat up, the ship shuddered. The weapon had discharged.

A cheer rose from the surrounding capsules. She understood the sentiment. They were finally fighting back, striking a blow for humanity, getting revenge for the countless deaths and injuries humankind had suffered.

She climbed swiftly out. Though none of the crew could work as fast as scanners and armaments, they could perform in ways chips and circuits could not. Breach teams had to be at the ready to seal the hull against depressurization, medics were needed to treat injuries, Zapata had to pilot the ship through regular space, she and Niall had to interpret scanner data to inform the captain, and Vessey had to make decisions on the fly.

A second shudder passed through the ship. The *Sirocco* had either locked onto a second target and fired, or she had repeated fire on the first after concluding it remained in action. The battle had taken place without human input so far. That situation couldn't continue.

Wilder sprinted to the bridge, dodging the rest of the crew running to their stations. Niall beat her there and was already assessing the stream of information pouring in. Vessey was pale and her facial muscles were rigid as she sat in the captain's chair.

"Looks like four ships," Niall said as Wilder reached his side.

"One more than before?"

"It might have been around the other side of the planet. We scored a hit on the biggest, but it's still—"

His words were drowned out by the alarm. He might have said *Shit*!

They'd been hit.

Vessey silenced the alarm.

Wilder read the data. "Deck Two port side dorsal," she told Vessey. "No indication of a breach."

"The biggest Scythian ship is still moving," Niall said, "but that wasn't the one that fired."

"Return fire on the one targeting us," said Vessey. "Maybe we took out the other's pulse cannon."

"On it, Captain," said Niall.

The *Parvus*'s weapon could be devastating, but it was not particularly maneuverable. It would take precious seconds to reorient to the new target and lock on.

Data flooded Wilder's screen. "Another hit. Deck One, port side."

"Bring us around, Zapata," Vessey ordered.

She was presenting the other side of the *Sirocco* to their attackers, reducing the chance the same place would be hit twice, causing a breach. The ship's dorsal faced toward Concordia, protecting the jump drive.

"Firing," said Niall, quickly followed by "They're coming for us, Captain. Three ships. The other one's staying in orbit."

Wilder had seen the alert too. The Scythians were speeding toward them, trying to close the distance separating the vessels to increase the impact of their pulse cannon. Why had one remained behind? Did the aliens anticipate the arrival of more hostile ships? The idea that had occurred to her while she was talking to Kes's daughters resurfaced.

"Take us away, Zapata," Vessey said, "but remain within our weapon's range."

The pilot had already begun to sweep the ship around in response to her first order. Now, the *Sirocco* jerked forward.

Wilder gripped her panel, hoping Miki and Nina had obeyed her instruction to remain in their jump capsules. "We've been hit again."

As she spoke, Niall said, "We got that ship. It's dead in the water." He consulted his screen. "But they're gaining on us."

"Zapata!" Vessey urged.

"She can't go any faster."

The Scythian ships' engines would beat the *Sirocco*'s regular drive.

"Is the biggest one heading toward us, Niall?" asked Vessey.

"It is. I don't know why. I'm pretty sure we took out its cannon."

"Focus on the dangerous one. Wilder?"

"The hit was on the starboard dorsal, ten meters from our gun."

Vessey uttered a curse. Protecting the already damaged areas of the ship had exposed their weapon to attack.

More data arrived. "Hull breach," Wilder reported.

"I know," said the captain. Her expression was strained as she listened to her ear comm. There must have been casualties. She dispatched another breach team.

Meanwhile, Niall had fired on the second Scythian spacecraft that had operational cannon.

Wilder tightened her grip on the panel. Zapata was flying them from the Scythians at maximum speed. She managed to squeeze out, "Maybe they intend to capture and board our ship. They don't have jump tech, but they know about ours."

"*That's* why their biggest vessel is coming for us," said Niall.

"Holy shit," murmured Wilder. "Imagine what they might do if their ships could jump."

"We're running out of juice," Niall said.

Wilder checked her screen. Firing the Parvus's weapon had heavily depleted their energy stores. Zapata's maneuvering was also draining them. They had to return to the other system, and soon.

"Another hit!" Wilder exclaimed. Their attack on the second Scythian ship had been ineffective. "Hull breach, Deck—"

"Fire again, Niall," Vessey ordered.

"No. We won't be able to jump."

"If we destroy the second ship and the biggest one's cannon are dead—"

"It could be a ploy. Wilder's right. They must be slavering for the jump drive, prepared to sacrifice a lot. And they still have a vessel in orbit."

"We have to jump," Wilder urged. "We can't out-fly them and another hit could take out our regular engines. Then if we don't have power to jump we'll be paralyzed. When the Scythians get here they'll slaughter us." The crew had pulse rifles, brought along in case of problems with Earthers, but it was not military. The scientists would fall like flies under determined assault.

"But the breaches..." said Vessey. "What will happen if we jump when the hull isn't intact?"

Wilder's throat constricted. "I don't know."

She and Niall shared a glance. He shook his head. He didn't know either, and there was no time to contact Dragan, the only other person who might have a valid idea.

Vessey's lips drew to a thin line. She opened a general comm. "Jumping in fifteen seconds. If you won't make it to a capsule in time, secure yourselves as safely as possible."

Wilder was already activating the drive. She checked the energy stores. The ship would only be traveling a short distance in galactic terms, but it would be close.

Very close.

As well as not knowing what would happen if they jumped with a breached hull, she also didn't know what might occur if the jump drive lacked power to complete its function. Would it only stall, or do something else?

Niall said, "Shutting everything down except essential life support."

The lights died, replaced by an eerie red glow, and a sudden force threw Wilder against her panel. The loss of power to the regular engine had halted their acceleration, and the inertia dampeners hadn't quite managed to deaden the effect. She groaned from the impact, square in her middle.

The emotionless computer voice began the countdown.

"Are you okay?" Niall asked.

Swallowing hard to force down vomit, she shook her head.

He pulled her to the deck, and they crouched together under the console. Wrapping his arms around her, he held her tightly. The computer voice droned on.

She closed her eyes and tensed.

SEVEN

Wilder's gut was a ball of pain, eclipsing all other sensations. She opened her eyes. The bridge remained intact. Vessey was gripping the armrests of her seat. She looked how Wilder felt—about to throw up.

"We made it?" Wilder whispered.

"I think so." Niall released her and stood up before awkwardly looking away. "Are you hurt?" His gaze remained averted.

"Yes." Now was not the time for heroics. The ship was no longer under attack, and her stomach hurt like a bitch.

"I'll comm a medic."

Wilder gently lowered herself to her side to wait. From her new vantage point, she noticed the deck was grimy. She also had an excellent view of Vessey's shoes.

The captain walked over. Squatting down, she put a hand on Wilder's shoulder. "Someone should be here soon, but there have been several casualties. You might need to wait a while."

"Okay." She couldn't say anything more. Lacking anything to distract her, the pain seemed to be growing. Or maybe it really was growing. Maybe whatever the blow to her stomach had done, it was getting worse.

"I'm sorry," Vessey said, "I would wait with you but I have things to do."

Wilder squeezed her eyelids closed and nodded.

The captain left.

Where was Niall? Had he gone too? She gingerly scanned around.

He was sitting near her feet, head down, elbows on raised knees.

Willing the pain away, she managed to utter a few words. "You don't need to stay."

He shook his head and placed a hand on her ankle. His hair had grown out while they were on Earth, and it hung down, obscuring his features.

Miki ran in. "What happened to you? I came as soon as I heard you were injured."

Wilder wanted to reassure her that it wasn't that bad, but she actually couldn't speak.

"She needs a medic," Niall said tetchily. "Don't bother her."

"I *am* a medic." Miki held up a medical scanner. "For now, anyway. I'm supposed to be triaging the injured. What happened to her?"

After Niall explained about the accident, Miki asked Wilder to lie on her back. It was all she could do not to cry out as she complied. Miki ran the scanner over her stomach and transmitted the results to the sick bay. The answer that returned within a few seconds caused Miki's mouth to drop open and her eyes to fill with tears. "You need urgent care. Someone is on their way." She held Wilder's hand. "You're going to be all right."

Wilder vaguely heard footsteps.

Niall was leaving.

———

They had lost one crew member, Wilder discovered when she woke up from her operation. When the *Sirocco* had jumped a member of a breach team hadn't managed to secure himself, or at least that was what everyone supposed had happened. On the other side of the jump he was found to be missing. The only possible conclusion was that he'd been forced out of the ship. Whether he was torn to pieces during the evacuation or he died of asphyxiation when his suit ran out of oxygen, it would have been a horrible death.

When Wilder found out the missing person was Ryan, even *she* felt a twinge of pity.

Otherwise, the ship's personnel had survived the battle mostly unscathed. Wilder had only one companion in sick bay: Maddox, Aubriot's partner when Cherry had found out he was cheating. Maddox had broken her leg during the abrupt deceleration. Wilder didn't have a lot to say to her and Maddox seemed to feel the same.

Wilder read Vessey's report again. The ship was in a worse state than her crew. She had sustained two major hull breaches and severe damage to her exterior from other hits. However, the Parvus's weapon remained operational and the jump drive and regular engines were intact. Her bones were strong even if her skin wasn't in the best shape. And they'd inflicted significant harm to the Scythian fleet. All in all—Ryan's death aside—the attack had been a success.

What was more, the Ark had never been at risk. Their plan to reseed Concordia could still go ahead, if only they could drive the aliens from the planet.

The sick bay door opened, and two flashes of color darted in and ran to her side. Wilder found herself in the grip of a fierce hug.

"Let her go!" Miki remonstrated. "You'll hurt her."

Nina relinquished her grip. "I'm so glad you're okay, Wilder. You *are* okay, right?" Her eyes were watery as she stared anxiously.

"I'm fine. Really. Don't worry. I'm not going anywhere."

The girls had lost their father and Cherry, who had become somewhat of a mother to them, as Wilder had herself. She understood Nina's fear. The loss of their remaining parental figure would be devastating.

Miki perched on the edge of the bed. "What was wrong with you? The only thing I understood from the scanner was that you were bleeding internally."

"Ruptured spleen."

"That sounds serious!" Nina exclaimed.

"It was, but it's been fixed. I won't have any lasting side-effects, according to the doctor. I only need to rest for a few days to give it time to heal."

The sick bay door opened again. Niall appeared, took a quick look at the girls, and ducked out before Wilder even had time to say hi.

"Who was that?" Nina asked, regarding the closing door.

"It doesn't matter. I'm glad you two didn't come to any harm during the battle. You stayed in your seats, right?"

"Of course we did," Nina replied petulantly. "We always do what we're..." Her words trailed to silence and she flushed deep red.

She was thinking of the time they'd stowed away on the shuttle to sneak off to Earth.

"We always do what we're told *now*," Miki corrected.

"Speaking as someone who rarely did what she was told at your age," Wilder said, "all I can say is sometimes you have to follow your heart, right or wrong. It's just what you have to do. You don't have anything to be ashamed about. And, don't forget, if you hadn't gone to Earth and been captured by the Scythians, no one would have known how they raise their offspring. That's valuable intel."

Nina's features brightened.

"What's going to happen now the battle's over?" Miki asked. "I heard we didn't get all their ships."

"We didn't, but we got some."

"Are we going back to finish them off?" Nina's tone was hopeful and excited.

"It isn't as simple as that. We did inflict some damage, but the *Sirocco* didn't come off unscathed. And we lost a member of the crew."

"And you were hurt!"

Wilder smiled. "And I was hurt. Captain Vessey will have to do some thinking before deciding what to do next. We can't keep exposing our ship to attack. We were lucky last time. We might not have the same luck again. One thing..." She hesitated, reluctant to reveal too much and give the girls more to worry about.

"You can tell us," Miki said. "Whatever it is. We want to know what's going on and no one ever tells us anything."

Though her years of adolescence were long past, Wilder recalled vividly the feeling of being excluded from vital knowledge due to her youth. She wouldn't inflict the same experience on Kes's daughters. "One thing in our favor is the fact that the Scythians probably want to capture the *Sirocco* with her jump drive undamaged. Aside from us, the only other species who can jump across galactic space is the Fila, who are aquatic. Their anatomy has properties that allow them to survive the effects of jumping. Niall and I invented a new system that mitigates those effects to a level human bodies can tolerate. As far as we know, every other atmosphere-breathing intelligent species still uses regular interstellar engines."

Miki said, "So now the Scythians know we have jump tech they want it too."

"You got it. And that means they won't go all out to destroy our ship. I suspect that might be one of the reasons we survived the battle. The Scythians were holding back."

"They will be waiting for us to return," said Nina. "They'll be preparing to take the *Sirocco* away from us."

Without any regard for the human life aboard. "You see why Captain Vessey has a lot to think about? I expect we'll hear from her in the next few days."

Miki and Nina stayed with Wilder for an hour or so, chatting about more pleasant subjects, such as the work they'd done in the Ark and what they'd learned in their studies of the history of Concordia. Miki in particular seemed fascinated by Ethan, and Wilder regretted she couldn't tell her much more than she already had about the great man. She'd been a teenager when she'd known him, and not part of the inner circle of decision-makers in the colony. To her, he'd mostly been a remote and imposing figure, even though he'd been friendly and down-to-earth when she'd met him.

"Is it true he was a farmer at first?" Miki asked.

"I don't know. If that's what the history files say..."

"If he was only a farmer, how did he become Leader?"

"In those days anyone could be Leader. You just had to stand for election."

"I wonder who's Leader now?" Nina mused.

Wilder very much doubted the surviving Concordians had a Leader at all. She yawned.

"You're tired," Miki said. "We should go."

"You don't have to. It's nice to chat."

"No, you need to rest." Miki got up from the bed. "Come on, Nina. Let's see if we can be useful somewhere." She added, to Wilder, "The ship's a mess. And we're going to rejoin the Ark soon. I want to check over the reseeding material."

Wilder relaxed on her pillows after they'd gone. Maddox was asleep. Not that she had anything to say to the woman anyway. Wilder turned over an idea in her mind, an idea that had been niggling at her for days. It was hopeless, stupid, and desperate. But she couldn't see how it could do any harm, and ideas to help them in their predicament were scarce.

She comm'd Vessey.

EIGHT

"It's a waste of time." Niall had that look on his face he frequently wore when Wilder suggested something out of the ordinary. She knew from long experience it was only the beginning of his typical mental process: skepticism, doubt, a closer examination, analysis, acceptance. Nevertheless, his initial reaction irritated her more than usual.

"What's the harm?" she snapped. "It's minimal effort. We might as well try, and if nothing comes of it, so what? At least we'll know we did everything we could."

"I'm sure that'll be a major solace as we're being eaten by Scythians. *Oh well, at least we did everything.*"

"They don't eat people. They're vegetarian. Or...herbivores? I don't know. Anyway, they don't eat meat."

"What makes you so sure? Just because Miki and Nina didn't see them eating meat, it doesn't mean—"

"Ryan told me, before he...you know."

"Got sucked out of the ship."

"Couldn't have happened to a better person," said Dragan.

"Uhhh," said Vessey. "If we could stick to the subject? I can't see a reason not to try Wilder's idea."

They were in the captain's office, debriefing post-battle. They'd gone over the breakdown of the engagement, ship's damage report, and casualties. After assessing the scan data, no one had been able to determine with any certainty the status of the enemy's largest ship. It had taken a hit, but they had no detailed knowledge of Scythian military vessels. It was impossible to say if its armaments had been destroyed.

The *Sirocco* could have been in a worse state. The jump drive and regular engines remained fully operational. But it was clear that she might not survive a repeat battle. What was more, materials to effect hull repairs were in short supply. It wouldn't take many more breaches before they couldn't patch her up anymore.

"I can see two very good reasons," said Niall. "One: morale is already at an all-time low. When we don't hear anything back—I say *when* not *if* because, seriously, what's the likelihood of getting a response after all this time?—it will tip the crew over into despair. Or, two, it will stop people from trying. They will give up, imagining some great galactic power is going to come to our rescue. We need to find a solution ourselves. We need to figure out a way to get to Concordia without being blown to pieces, and we need to do it soon, before the Scythian defenses grow stronger."

"You think we should fight back at them from the surface?" Dragan asked. "Not try to destroy their ships?"

"In order to reach the surface we have to destroy their ships. I thought that's what we were attempting as a means to an end. Destroying their ships isn't an end in itself because they will just send more ships. But if we can mobilize the existing human population, attack the Scythians from within, make Concordia an uninviting place to live—"

"They give up and blast the place with biocide," Wilder interjected. Two could play at shooting down others' ideas.

Niall faced her, eyes ablaze. "Then what to you suggest we do? Give up? Kill ourselves?"

"I already made my suggestion. I haven't heard you offering up anything concrete lately. Unless I missed something?"

"Please," said Vessey, rubbing her temples, "let's not argue among ourselves. I have enough to do keeping the peace among the rest of the crew. Wilder, what form exactly would this message take?"

"It would be similar to the Mayday we sent out not long after the first jump failed, when we were decades from Earth. Do you remember?"

"Vaguely. That seems a long time ago now."

Wilder suspected the captain had also begun her descent into alcoholism. "We have to send it in English. The only other galactic language we know even remotely is the one the Fila speak, though 'speak' isn't the right word." The aquatic aliens communicated via water movement, thus their language was virtually impossible for humans to learn or use.

"They must have used electronic communication too," said Dragan. "Otherwise how could they comm the Galactic Assembly? It was the Fila who arranged for Concordians to go there, right?"

"It was, and you're right, they spoke to us using electronics. That must have been how they contacted the Assembly. But if anyone discovered exactly what they did and how, I certainly never heard about it." A sudden pang of wistfulness hit as she recalled her Fila friend, Quinn, who she'd considered one of her closest friends. "We don't have any other option except to broadcast high energy transmissions and hope someone picks them up. I know it's a long shot, but we don't know what receivers the Assembly might have, where they are, or how they work. We didn't ever learn anything about how Assembly members communicate. The Fila always took care of that kind of thing for us."

"What's the point?" Niall asked. "It didn't work before, when we were delayed. It won't work now. We need to focus on ideas that are likely to bring results. The Galactic Assembly isn't going to come to our rescue at the last minute like it did before. That's ancient history. If by some miracle our message is picked up and the Assembly still exists, it will have forgotten all about Concordia and humans."

"The *Sirocco* was in an area of galactic space that isn't inhabited by Assembly members," Wilder retorted. "That's why our Mayday wasn't picked up."

"You don't have any evidence to support that assertion! You can't possibly know that."

"You can't prove I'm wrong!"

"Guys," said Dragan, lifting his hands, "cool it."

Wilder folded her arms over her chest, fighting her growing anger. Niall was correct, of course. She had no idea why the Mayday hadn't been picked up. She hated it when his stubbornness made her irrational.

In a more moderate tone, Niall continued, "My major doubt isn't that sending a message would be pointless—though it is—it's that it will give the crew false hope. Everyone knows or remembers the Assembly arriving to head off a Scythian attack. If we give the crew even a hint the same thing might happen again, everyone will want to down tools and wait indefinitely to be rescued. We've been through significant hardship since we departed Concordia. People don't need much of an excuse to hand responsibility over to someone else and relax."

"Then the answer is simple," Vessey said. "We don't tell them."

Niall opened his mouth as if to speak but then closed it again.

As his frustration at being unable to think up an objection filtered over his features, Wilder smirked. "I think that's a great idea, Captain. We send the message as a repeat transmission, but we keep it between ourselves. I don't think anyone else has access to systems that would allow them to detect it except we four. How does that sound, Niall?"

He glared at her.

"Glad you agree. I'll draft a message and submit it for approval before sending it out."

"Now that's decided," said Vessey, "I want to turn to more pressing issues. As Niall was saying, the key to driving the Scythians from Concordia lies on the planet surface, not in space. That's what I've come to accept. We can't defeat them in orbit but there's a chance we can change their minds about living there."

Dragan said, "If they can't live there they don't want us to either. They've made that clear. Humans must serve them or be annihilated."

"I don't know what the answer is, but if we can make it to the surface we can understand the situation better. Maybe a solution will present itself. That's all I'm saying."

"So our new goal is to land the shuttle planetside?" Wilder asked. "Kind of...sneak it in? Nothing springs to mind, but I can work on some ideas."

"We all can," said Dragan.

Vessey's features relaxed into relief but instantly tensed again as she lifted a hand to her ear. "What? Say that again." The comm, silent to everyone except her, must have repeated. "Slow down! I can't understand you." Another pause. "*Ugh*! Okay, don't interfere. I don't want anyone else getting hurt. I'll be there in a few minutes."

Her attention returned to Wilder and the others. "I have to go and break up a fight. Who knew a captain's duties would be so varied and entertaining?"

"A fight?" asked Wilder. "Who's fighting?"

"Marcus and Belvedere. It's something to do with Maddox." The captain slowly rose to her feet. She didn't seem in much of a hurry.

"Maddox?" Dragan gave a short laugh. "I think we all know what *that's* about."

"We do?" Niall asked.

Wilder also didn't have a clue. Neither she nor Niall got involved in ship scuttlebutt.

"Oh, you know. Marcus must have found out Maddox is cheating on him."

"With Belvedere, presumably," Niall said.

Wilder frowned. "I thought Maddox had a thing with Aubriot. She moved on fast."

"He was never exclusive with her," Dragan explained. "It used to drive her crazy."

As well as telling them the ship's gossip, he was revealing a whole new side of his character. Despite their years of friendship, Wilder hadn't known he was so deeply enmeshed in the goings-on aboard the ship. It explained how he'd been drawn into the Final Day Five cult.

"This is fascinating," Vessey said dryly, "but I have to go."

As the captain departed, Wilder said, "But Marcus is blind and spends ninety-five percent of his time in his cabin."

"Makes him easy to find," Niall quipped.

Wilder continued, "And Maddox has a *broken leg*." A horrible image leapt into her mind. "Do you think Marcus caught her and Belvedere..."

"Doing it?" Niall asked. "Who knows? At least he would only have heard rather than seen them."

"I'm not sure that's better," said Wilder.

The three engineers chuckled.

NINE

Aside from the stories about Ethan and the battles, the history of Concordia's founding was boring. It was all about construction, farming, food supplies, the developing health care infrastructure, setting up schools and so on, and on, and on. There was a bit about the difficulties the first colonists had faced transitioning from communal child rearing to nuclear families that was mildly interesting, but not much else. Miki sighed, rested her elbow on the table and her chin on her upturned palm.

"I'm tired of this too," said Nina. "Shall we do something else?"

Miki was loath to agree. As the older of two orphans, it was her responsibility to do the hard stuff—to set the tasks a parent would have set, the tasks she also would have complained about doing. Yet she didn't think *she* could take another data set of harvest statistics from the colony's first five years. "Maybe just another fifteen minutes? Then we can stop for lunch."

It was way too early for lunch, but it was a convenient excuse.

"All right," Nina agreed, though in a grumbling tone.

Miki blinked and refocused her attention on the brain-numbing figures. No patterns or meaning emerged, and the numbers seemed to dance and meld as if they were alive and confusing her deliberately. She yawned and stretched her arms and back. "I'll tidy up the cabin while you finish."

"Hey! If I have to do this, so do you."

"Just another fifteen minutes."

Nina rolled her eyes as Miki stood up, but she bent over her work again. She'd always been ridiculously obedient.

Miki fussed around the room, moving items from one place to another, putting things that seemed vaguely related into groups, hiding stuff behind the sofa. She heard a soft *tut* and turned to see Nina giving a little shake of her head. In order to escape scrutiny, she walked into their shared bedroom. Here, she discovered something useful to do. Their bedding hadn't been changed in weeks. Neither of them bothered making their beds when they got up. Without Dad around to chide them there didn't seem much point, and no adults ever came into the inner rooms. The grubby, wrinkled sheets and covers seemed to reproach her for her slovenliness.

She pulled the bedclothes off her bed and pushed them into the laundry chute. She would have to remember to collect fresh ones from the laundry room after lunch.

"What are you doing?" Nina called out.

"I told you. I'm tidying up." She stepped to her sister's bed and picked up her pillow, and gasped.

"Don't touch my—" Nina was standing in the doorway, flushed. She strode to Miki and snatched the pillow from her hands. "Leave my bed alone! I didn't tell you to change it. I can do it myself." She put the pillow on the bed and pulled up the cover, roughly straightening everything.

"Nina..." Her sister might have hidden the evidence, but the image remained clear in Miki's mind. A pile of long, black hairs had been secreted under the pillow. Nina's hair, unmistakably, and far too much to have fallen out naturally.

"I'm going to finish my work," Nina declared. "Then we can go and eat. I'll change my bed later."

Miki's gaze followed her as she left the bedroom. What was wrong with her sister? Was her hair falling out? If it was only a medical problem, why was she hiding it? Why hadn't she told someone?

Miki watched Nina from the doorway as she bent over her interface once more. "Nina, is something wrong? You can tell me. You know I won't judge you."

"Nothing's wrong."

But fat tear drops landed on the screen, and Nina was only staring downward, not working.

Miki realized her sister had recently begun to always wear her hair in a ponytail whereas before she'd worn it down. And she used to take great care with it while now she only brushed it quickly before putting it up.

"Can I look at your hair?" Miki gently asked.

Nina gave a firm shake of her head.

Her reaction told Miki all she needed to know. Without seeing them, she could guess Nina's head had bald patches where she'd pulled out her hair. Why was she doing it? It had to be a reaction to the stress they were under. A lead weight settled in the pit of Miki's stomach. Though logically she knew the current situation wasn't her fault, she couldn't help feeling it was. At the very least, she'd failed in her primary duty to keep her sister safe and happy. Nina certainly didn't feel safe and happy if, in the quiet of the night, she was wrenching out her hair.

Miki moved to her sister's side and tried to hug her, but Nina pushed her away. "Leave me alone! I don't know what you're making such a big fuss about."

Miki hesitated. How could she help if Nina wouldn't accept it? But maybe she was right. A hug wouldn't make anything better. What Nina needed was for this whole, torturous experience to be over. She needed a home and a life free from fear. How could she give her that? They were both powerless, over-looked, a burden on the *Sirocco*'s crew. They were an additional complication in an impossible situation.

She had to *do* something. She had to make a positive difference. She had to *act*. How else was she supposed to live with herself? How could she live with the knowledge that she'd let Dad down and his confidence in her was misplaced?

She marched to the outer door.

"Where are you going?" Nina asked.

But Miki didn't answer as she left.

———

The captain's office was on the other side of the ship. By the time she reached it Miki's determination had weakened and she was muddled about what she wanted to say. Then the imagined image of Nina's head flashed into her mind. She gathered her resolve and walked in.

Captain Vessey had always employed an 'open door' policy, saying any crew member was free to come and see her at any time, to talk to her about anything. So Miki had been expecting she might see someone else in the room when the door automatically slid to the side.

What she hadn't been expecting was a dead man.

Aubriot?!

The man's deep, voluminous voice burst out at her as she walked in. He was standing in his usual arrogant pose, hands on hips, chest prominent, jaw slightly upturned so he looked down his nose at whoever he was addressing.

She screamed and clutched the door frame as her legs lost their strength.

Wilder—who she hadn't even noticed—was instantly at her side. "It's a holo, Miki. It's just a holo."

Aubriot disappeared. Captain Vessey, sitting at her desk, must have turned it off. Wilder led her to a chair.

Sitting down, Miki gasped, "I'm sorry. I thought—"

"We know what you thought," said Wilder. "Are you okay?"

"I think so." The tingles of shock were beginning to dissipate. "What was he saying? I didn't catch it. How come we have a holo of Aubriot?"

"It isn't important," the captain replied.

It clearly was important. Otherwise why would she and Wilder be watching it? What Vessey meant was *Miki* wasn't important. Not important enough to be told what was going on anyway.

"How can I help you?" Vessey asked impatiently.

Miki sat up straight. "I heard there's going to be an attempt to land the shuttle on Concordia. Is that right?"

"What if it is?"

"I want to go along."

"You want to...?" Vessey chuckled uneasily.

"I want to be one of the away team."

The captain's features grew serious. "Absolutely not. The mission is insanely dangerous. It's the last place for a young girl. You're only fifteen!"

She'd been anticipating the refusal. On her way over she'd thought up the reasoning to back up her proposal, but then forgotten it. Now it all came flooding back. "I might be almost the youngest person on the ship, but I'm also one of only two people who have had close contact with the Scythians. Unless you're suggesting Nina should go in my place?"

"That's even more preposterous."

"Nina and I fought our way out of a Scythian dome. Do you have anyone else who has done that?"

"You know I haven't but that's beside the p—"

"Who else on this ship has had conversations with Scythians?" The 'conversations' had actually been interrogations, but stretching the truth made her sound more convincing.

Vessey glowered.

Wilder was watching, arms folded over her chest, smiling.

Miki continued, "Can you name a single person under your command who is better suited to going to Concordia and figuring out a way to get the aliens to leave?" She arched an eyebrow. "Hm?"

"Your argument might have some weight," Vessey replied, "if you weren't a child. More than anyone on this ship, you have been entrusted to my care. I have a responsibility to your late father to keep you from harm. Assigning you to the mission to land on Concordia would be the very antithesis of that. I'm sorry. I admire your bravery and I can't deny you make some very good points, but the answer is no. However, if you can offer the away team any suggestions or advice, you would be very wel—"

Miki sprang to her feet. "But you aren't keeping us from harm! We aren't safe here. Not in the long run. We could have died in the last battle. And no one tells us anything. We don't know what's going on. We're slowly going crazy, living in this make-believe world where everyone pretends everything is normal, while in reality we're one wrong step away from death. Every day, the inevitable creeps closer but no one acknowledges it, not to our faces."

She swung around to stare at Wilder and turned back to Vessey. "You all pretend to care but you don't. Not really. No one knows what really goes on with us. You want us to stay quiet and keep out of the way, to be good, and as long as we do that everything will be all right. But it isn't all right. Nothing is all right. Nina's..." Her emotions choked away her words and she thrust her face into her hands.

An arm descended over her shoulders, but she shrugged it away. Talking into her hands, she said, "I want to help. You have to let me help. And I *am* the best person. I really am. If you don't recognize that then you're a pair of idiots."

TEN

No one knows what really goes on with us.

Miki had left Vessey's office but her words continued to echo in Wilder's mind. The girl had been distraught, almost hysterical. *No one knows what really goes on with us.*

What had she meant? Wilder had thought she knew Kes's daughters pretty well, but the surprise trip to Earth had blindsided her. She hoped she'd helped to fill the hole left when their father died. Had she really done any good at all? She had no idea how to parent adolescents. She'd never been parented herself. The attempts of the couple she'd been assigned to in Sidhe had been farcical. Kes's friendship had come close but he'd been more like an older brother.

Was that why Miki had been so fascinated by stories of Ethan lately? Did she crave a father figure, or maybe only someone who had known her father?

"Are you ready to continue watching?" Vessey asked.

Wilder snapped back to the present. "Yeah, sorry."

Aubriot reappeared.

The recording had barely begun when Miki had burst in. Vessey had returned it to the beginning.

Wilder's customary, visceral reaction to Aubriot flared up: dislike, bordering on hatred. She'd never forgotten the months she'd spent in close confinement with the disagreeable man aboard the *Opportunity* on the journey to the Galactic Assembly. What had Cherry ever seen in him?

Vessey had said she discovered the holo while going through his files. The file was entitled 'To be played in the event of my death' so Wilder hadn't had any qualms about invasion of privacy when Vessey had invited her to watch it.

However, why the captain had been going through the man's data at all was a question that remained unanswered. Wilder guessed she'd been looking for inspiration and guidance.

Good luck with that.

Aubriot glared at the camera as if angry about his potential demise. Wilder was reminded of the holo of the Maker, Steen, full of bitterness and rage. The men's desire to live had been strong.

"So I'm dead," Aubriot spat. "I hope I went down fighting. I'm guessing it was the Scythians. If it wasn't, if some stupid accident killed me or a disease got me like Kes, that's a crying shame, and I'm glad I don't know about it."

His arms fell to his sides and he strode a couple of paces before turning to the camera again and jabbing a finger at it. "You're all going to be worse off now I'm gone. You might not think so. A fair few of you hate my guts and you aren't afraid to show it. But I'm right. You need me. You need someone to tell you what's what and make the hard decisions. That's why I'm recording this— so you get the benefit of my wisdom and experience even though I'm no longer around. I might be dead, but I still want the colony to succeed. It's my legacy, my gift to humanity."

Wilder rolled her eyes. Aubriot was even managing to annoy her from the grave. She signaled to Vessey to pause the holo. "Have you watched this already? You could give me a summary."

"It's my first time too. I find him just as irritating as you, but perhaps he says something useful." Vessey started up the recording again.

"Right. I'm going to make this simple. I have one message for you. Just one thing for you to remember." He said two more words slowly and with emphasis: "Never compromise. There are to be no half measures, no negotiation. Cherry, I know you beat yourself up about rejecting the Scythians' proposal when they wanted to enslave the colony. Even now, you think it was a big mistake because it caused them to launch the biocide. But you were right."

His hands returned to his hips. "If there's one thing I learned running my businesses, it's this: the minute you show weakness, your enemy will go for your throat. Believe me, I saw it again and again. So you have to stay strong and never back down. Remember that, Vessey. As soon as you start to give ground it's the beginning of the end. You've lost." He paused and his expression turned pensive.

"Better no future at all for humanity than a future where we've been brought low. Who wants to live in shame? That isn't the way of humans. That isn't the spirit of the people who left Africa hundreds of thousands of years ago, leaving behind everything they knew, journeying into unknown lands without knowing what dangers lay ahead." He jabbed a finger at the camera again. "You *cannot* give in to the Scythians, not on anything, or before you know it, it will be all over. Don't give up who we are. A human being controlled by another species isn't human anymore."

His rigid posture softened. "That's it. I could say more but it would only confuse you, so that's all I have to say. It's a pity I'm dead, but I've lived an amazing life. I was there at the founding of humanity's first deep space colony. I've flown on starships. I've fought battles in space. I've loved. I've hated. I've *lived*. At the end of the day, I suppose I can't complain. Good luck, you lucky bastards. Don't let me down."

He disappeared, but his final look before the recording ended struck Wilder's core. The sadness and yearning in his eyes were emotions she'd never seen in him before. His lust for life and sorrow as he imagined his death were almost palpable. Maybe his drive and vitality were what had attracted Cherry.

"Well, that was disappointing," said Vessey.

"I'm not sure what you expected. It was Aubriot, after all."

"A revelation or tactical advice would have been nice, something to help us defeat the Scythians. Something other than telling me not to negotiate with them. As if I have the opportunity! Their go-to response at any encounter is to try to kill us. And the situation is similar to how it was at Earth—more of their ships must be on their way, if not due to Miki informing them she was from Concordia, then in response to our arrival at the system. They might have guessed where we're hiding too. Their reinforcements might stop to check around here on their way over."

The captain's spewing of her worries was clearly rhetorical. She needed a friendly listener while she got it all off her chest. Wilder was sympathetic but she had no answers. "It isn't Miki's fault she—"

"I know, I know. I'm not saying it was. She's just a kid. She couldn't be expected to stand up to the Scythians. I can't imagine what she endured in that interrogation."

Wilder recalled the sensation of long, scaled Scythians toes gripping her tightly around her middle. She shuddered. What must it have been like for the girls living in those domes, not knowing if they would ever get out alive, surrounded day and night by the nauseating Scythian stench?

Yet Miki and Nina had escaped, albeit with the help of other captives. When it came down to it and their courage was put to the test, neither had quailed.

"What are you thinking?" Vessey asked. "Have you thought of a way of getting the shuttle to Concordia in one piece?"

Wilder smiled sardonically. "Still working on it. I was thinking about Miki's request."

"Request? It was more like a demand. An outrageous one, I might add. Just the thought of how Kes would have reacted to even the mention of endangering his daughters' lives strikes terror into my heart."

"As Miki pointed out, they're already in danger. Dire danger if, as you guess, the Scythians are on their way to this system. I mean, we could jump at the first sign of approach, but where to and for how long? Unless we figure out a way to free Concordia we're screwed. As Aubriot would have put it, we need to piss or get off the pot."

"You think you're telling me something I don't already know?"

"What I'm saying is, Miki's request isn't so outrageous. She and her sister do have the most experience of Scythians of anyone on this ship. And they've demonstrated they can be brave and resourceful."

Vessey's mouth fell open. "You aren't seriously suggesting...?"

"It's worth thinking about."

"No. Absolutely not. What would everyone say if I assign a teenager to the mission? They would think I was either crazy or desperate, or both."

"Maybe it's time you stopped caring about what people say. Aubriot didn't."

"And look where that got him."

Vessey's retort didn't make any sense. Aubriot's death hadn't had anything to do with his indifference to others' opinions of him. The captain was being defensive, grasping at straws in an effort to win the argument. Few things annoyed Wilder more than irrationality. Through a clenched jaw, she replied, "Dislike him or hate him, Aubriot knew how to command."

"And I don't, I suppose?" Vessey looked about to rise from her seat with indignation.

Wilder allowed silence to be her answer. After a pause, she added, "Miki should go on the mission, along with me and Niall. You need resourceful people, not only brawn, on the surface. Shall I give her the good news?"

"Do I have a choice?"

Another rhetorical question. Wilder got to her feet, somewhat giddy from what had just transpired. "I'll let you know when we figure out a plan."

She made her way through the *Sirocco*'s passageways, heading for Miki and Nina's cabin. Vessey's face had been a picture as she left—partly shocked, partly outraged. But something needed to be done, and though the captain meant well, she lacked the brains and decisiveness to pull them out of the deep, dark hole they were in.

Wilder's understanding of the truth of the situation had seemed sudden initially, but she realized it had simmered below the surface for weeks, perhaps months. Her preference was to remain on the sidelines, working on interesting projects. She wasn't comfortable with ignoring the captain's seniority but it was necessary. She would have to take a more active, assertive role in the future.

When she arrived at Miki and Nina's cabin, Nina was hastily scraping her hair into a ponytail and Miki stood behind her with a brush. The girls seemed to have been doing some kind of hairdressing, which was utterly unlike them.

Even Wilder, who seldom noticed such things, had observed the two girls' hair resembled the nests of Earth birds lately.

Nina was flushed and wouldn't make eye contact.

"Is something wrong?" Wilder asked.

"No," replied Miki, adding bitterly, "Have you come to tell me off for getting angry at the captain?"

"Stars, I'd hoped you knew me better than that. When I was your age..." Wilder paused, realizing she sounded like an old-timer. "I'm not here to tell you off. I'm here to let you know Vessey agreed to you joining the mission."

"She did?!"

"What mission?" Nina asked.

"To go to Concordia. I'm going on the shuttle to fight the Scythians on Concordia!"

"You can't!" Nina leapt to her feet and faced her sister. "You'll die."

"I won't. I'll figure out a way to make the Scythians leave. You'll see."

"You'll be killed, and I'll be all alone." Nina collapsed into her seat and began to sob.

Wilder watched awkwardly. She'd thought she would be the bearer of good news. She hadn't anticipated Nina's reaction, even though it was entirely predictable.

Miki was comforting her sister, whispering, "I'll be fine. The Scythians will leave, and then you can go home. Maybe we can find our old house."

Wilder watched on, feeling like an outsider. The two girls were enclosed in their own small world of despair.

ELEVEN

"Holy shit!" Wilder exclaimed. "We're morons. Morons!"

She was with Niall and Dragan, eating dinner. They'd spent the day trying to figure out a way to get the shuttle to the surface of Concordia without everyone aboard being killed. The *Sirocco* might survive the brief time she would have to spend in Concordian orbit before she could jump out again, but the shuttle would be a clear and obvious target for Scythian attack. They hadn't managed to come up with anything concrete, and now that Miki was coming along the imperative for caution was even stronger.

Niall eyed her irritably. "Interesting that you include me and Dragan in your character critique."

Raising her voice had attracted the attention of their crew mates in the refectory. The chattering had paused and heads turned toward them. Wilder waited until the audience grew bored and returned to their conversations before leaning over the table to speak to her companions more quietly. "The answer has been staring us in the face. Hell, we've been *working* on the answer for weeks."

When Niall and Dragan looked back at her blankly, she asked, "Have you finished eating?"

Dragan nodded.

Niall put down his knife and fork. "I'm so keen to hear your suggestion I've lost my appetite."

"I'm not going to tell you. I'm going to show you, and then you'll agree we're all dumb as a sack of rocks." She got up from the table and, without waiting to see if Niall and Dragan were following, walked out of the refectory.

She marched to the holding bay, the only place sufficiently large for the work they'd been focused on for so long. If anything, her fellow engineers had spent longer on it than she had. They'd started while she'd been on Earth, trapped by Vessey's cowardly attempt to leave her behind along with Cherry, Aubriot, Miki, and Nina.

The bay doors slid apart, revealing the items lying on the deck in their various groups: sections of hull, engine, controls, interior, and so on. The dismantling had been meticulous. Even the nuts, bolts, and rivets had been removed and carefully examined. Reconstruction would take time and concentration, but it would be worth it. In fact, now she'd thought about it, she believed it was the only sane option.

"Yeah," Dragan conceded. "We're morons."

Niall's gaze roved the dismantled Scythian ship. "You're seriously suggesting we fly *that* to Concordia?"

"You're seriously suggesting we fly the *Sirocco*'s shuttle, a human-built vessel, into airspace controlled by the Scythians? It wouldn't last a second."

Dragan said, "I have to admit that's our biggest problem. Even if we're lucky enough that they haven't created air traffic monitoring systems, the shuttle is so easy to distinguish by sight—"

"Yes," Niall snapped. "That point has been made several times today. There's no need to repeat it."

"This does seem the obvious answer," Dragan said mildly, gesturing at the aircraft parts.

"It gives us our best chance," Wilder urged. "The vessels the Scythians used on Earth were pretty much identical, and they weren't designed for an oxygen-rich atmosphere. The aliens had brought them directly from their planet without bothering to refit them. It stands to reason they've done the same on Concordia, which means this aircraft won't be distinguishable from the others they're already using. All we have to do is strengthen the hull and make it airtight. If the Scythians miss its launch from the *Sirocco*, we'll be home free. And if they notice it, well, they might lose it among their regular air traffic."

"But the cabin will only accommodate two people," Niall countered. "We planned on sending more on the mission."

"The cabin fits two *Scythians*. We don't need the internal fittings except for the controls. We can leave them out and the aircraft will look the same from the outside. I reckon it would fit four people, five at a squeeze."

Niall's expression remained doubtful. "No one knows how to fly it."

"Zapata can figure it out, I'm sure. We know the design isn't that different from an aircraft built by humans."

"But we discovered it needs a Scythian's skin print to open it. The same is probably true for operating the controls."

"We have the Scythian cadaver in cold storage. We can take an imprint from its skin and make some gloves."

"It will take forever to put it back together again."

"We itemized everything when we took it apart. It shouldn't be too hard to reconstruct it, and it won't take *that* long, considering we're only rebuilding the bare bones of it." She folded her arms over her chest and tilted her head. "Any more objections?"

Niall was silent.

"Go on, admit it. You know I'm right."

He glared at her, turned, and strode down the passageway.

She watched his retreating back with amusement. When she saw Dragan's look, however, her smile faded. "What's wrong? Don't tell me you're having doubts too."

"Not about your idea, no. You're right. It's the only way anyone stands a chance of making it to Concordia alive, and it's ridiculous it took us so long to think of it."

Wilder was about to remind him that *she* thought of it, not them, but it seemed churlish.

"I just think you could be gentler with Niall," he continued.

She blinked. "*Me* be gentler with *him*?! Are you sure you've got that the right way around?"

"I know he's being even more combative than usual, but he's suffering. He wouldn't want me to tell you this, but he was nearly demented with worry while you were on Earth. He was the one who figured out what Vessey was up to and forced her to go back to pick you up."

She hadn't known that, not exactly. She hadn't made many inquiries about what had gone on during her absence from the ship. She'd been too sad about leaving Cherry behind and concerned about Miki and Nina and what the future held. "I guess I should thank him," she muttered.

"He doesn't want your thanks. Rescuing you is sufficient reward, I'm sure."

"I know he cares, but he's so relentlessly negative toward me. So prickly. It's hard to tolerate."

"I know. I honestly don't think he can help it. It's just how he is. But maybe you could try..." Dragan struggled to finish his sentence. He seemed embarrassed.

"I could try what? Tell me. I'm a big girl. I can take it."

"You could try being more understanding. I hate to say it, but you're often...cold. I mean, I get it. With the stuff we do, we're in our heads a lot of the time, not aware of other people's emotions or reactions. We can get into a certain way of thinking where everything has to make sense, and we apply the same expectation to people. We find it frustrating if they aren't logical. But people aren't logical, not even us. You have to allow for that. You have to allow other people to be flawed, irrational, inconsistent, whatever."

Dragan's gaze drifted to the bulkhead. "It wasn't until I accepted I'd lost my wife forever that I realized she'd been doing that for me, for years, and I hadn't reciprocated. I'd always made out I was the logical one and she was ruled by her emotions. I didn't know, then, that it wasn't a difference of intellect or rationality, but a difference in compassion. Not comprehending that until it was too late is one of my greatest regrets."

Wilder inhaled sharply. She'd vaguely known that Dragan had left his partner behind on Concordia but she'd never asked him about her. Not even once. She reached out and touched his arm. "I'm so sor—"

"It was a long time ago. I can't say I'm over it, but it is what it is. Talking about it won't make it better. All I wanted to say is, don't make my mistake."

She looked down.

When she didn't answer, Dragan said, "I'll talk to Niall. We can begin work on the Scythian ship tonight."

TWELVE

It had taken way longer to rebuild the Scythian ship than anyone had expected. Miki had spent weeks in grueling anticipation, the ache in her stomach and insomnia growing greater, waiting to hear from Wilder that they were finally ready to attempt landing on Concordia. At the end of every active shift, Wilder had come to see her and Nina, her hair an unkempt halo, shadows under her eyes, looking thinner than ever, only to announce again and again that the ship wasn't quite finished.

The snags the engineers had encountered while reconstructing the vessel weren't the only source of delay. The man most familiar with the frozen Scythian cadaver had died the last time they'd jumped to the planet. Someone else had been tasked with making the gloves the pilot would wear to fly the ship. Miki heard down the grapevine that their early attempts were unsuccessful. It had taken a while to figure out that it wasn't only the print of the creature's skin that was required to activate the controls, but the underlying bone structure too.

All the while the preparations had been taking place, her doubts had grown. Who was she to think she would be anything other than a hindrance and liability in the mission? What did *she* have to contribute? She wasn't a scientist or an engineer. She didn't possess a fraction of the knowledge or skills of the rest of the crew. She'd grown up on a starship without even a proper education.

When she'd gone to see Captain Vessey to demand to be included, it had been a spur-of-the-moment decision, a knee-jerk reaction to discovering that Nina was so anxious she was pulling out her hair. In the captain's office, she'd exaggerated her knowledge of the Scythians to try to persuade Vessey to agree. In reality, she knew hardly anything about them, very little more than anyone else. The captain had either been kind or desperate to allow her to join the mission.

She was an imposter. A fraud. She'd done something stupid, and Nina was right—she was going to get herself killed.

Yet she hadn't been able to bring herself to back out. Was she too embarrassed to admit her mistake? Was she simply ashamed of being a coward? She didn't know, but day after day, when Wilder had arrived to give an update, her mouth stubbornly refused to utter the words *Sorry, but I changed my mind.*

Now it was too late.

Wilder sat across from her in the cramped interior of the Scythian vessel, knees drawn up, her features obscured by the reflective visor of her EVA suit. Niall crouched by her side. The other engineer would remain on the *Sirocco*. Someone was needed to oversee the jumps. Next to Miki, so close they were squashed up against each other, was someone she didn't know very well—a woman called Maddox. She'd taken part in the first attack on a Scythian dome on Earth, with Cherry and Aubriot, so she had a little experience of the aliens. Between the four mission members was Zapata, the pilot, wearing his outlandish gloves.

The tiny space would have been claustrophobic in the best circumstances. As it was, with five people in bulky suits crammed in, about to embark on what amounted to a suicide mission, it felt stifling. What was more, though the seats had been removed, the interior reminded Miki of the time she'd flown with a Scythian for hours, not knowing whether her sister was alive or what lay ahead. It was as much as she could do not to panic, thrash, and scream, begging to be let out.

The countdown to jump was comm'd into their helmets. As it neared zero, Wilder gave Miki a thumbs up. She couldn't return the gesture. She couldn't move. Her breathing was loud in her ears, louder than the countdown, louder than the thrum of her racing heart. She was painfully aware she was depleting her suit's oxygen at a dangerous rate but she couldn't help it.

The *Sirocco* jumped.

The too-familiar blending of reality shifted back to normality.

"One good thing about being jammed in here," Maddox remarked over helmet comm, "we can't get thrown about."

As if defying her words, the ship lurched violently. Naturally, the second the *Sirocco* had arrived in Concordia orbit, she would have come under attack. But she might not have been hit. The plan, as Miki understood it, was to create as much of a distraction as possible so the Scythians might not notice the tiny craft launching into the upper atmosphere. Captain Vessey intended the aliens to think the *Sirocco* had returned to attack their ships again. Also, without Zapata at her controls, the stand-in pilot might be flying erratically anyway.

Even in the small space, the *Sirocco*'s movements threw them into each other. Except it wasn't the *Sirocco*'s movements. Zapata was flying the Scythian vessel out of the bay. The overhead, visible before through the overhanging transparent shell, had switched to black faintly speckled with stars. They'd left the ship and she hadn't even noticed.

Then the sky exploded.

Maddox's screams echoed around Miki's helmet, but she was silent, dumbstruck by the spectacle. Her retinas retained an imprint of a blinding flash, now faded to dull red. Brilliant stars zoomed past, almost too fast to register. Except they could not be stars. What were they?

Maddox continued with her deafening screams. The world upended. Miki caught a glimpse of a curving planet surface—yellow land and cobalt ocean—before space appeared again. The background stars had gone. Ebony had lightened to glimmering, dark blue-gray. Fiery objects rained down.

Clang!

A shock ran through the deck and shook Miki's bones. Something had hit the wing. The craft shuddered, drooped to the right, somersaulted again. Another scene of yellow and blue flew by above.

Miki shut her eyes. She couldn't look anymore. She was about to throw up, and ensconced in her suit that would be very nasty. Feeling for the straps of her safety harness, she clung to them for all she was worth. The sickening maneuvers went on, or perhaps they were not maneuvers. Perhaps Zapata was no longer flying them but was also trapped in the awful descent, helpless.

What had the explosion been? Had the *Sirocco* blown up? Had the Scythians destroyed her? Was everyone else dead?

The sensations were chaotic, but then they began to repeat. The ship was spinning, and the pull of gravity came from above. Miki risked a peek. A horizon raced around them, blurred due to speed. They were falling, whirling hopelessly out of control. They would plummet nose first into the ground, and that would be it. She would never see Nina again. Was Nina even alive? She'd left her aboard the *Sirocco*, which must have blown up.

Black misery and grief descended. She should never have left her sister. They should have been together at the end.

Above Maddox's screams, someone was shouting. Miki couldn't stand it. She turned off her comm, bent her head, and waited.

There was jostling, agitation. The whirling converted to a swoop. Her stomach rebelled and she couldn't control herself any longer. Bitter, acid vomit spurted up her throat and out of her mouth. She didn't care. She retched again and more vomit came up, soaking her front and smelling vile.

An impact threw her into Maddox. Another impact threw her the opposite way. *Thunk! Bang!* The Scythian vessel was turning over and over, each time it came down sending a teeth-rattling judder through the cabin. She was going to be killed, but it didn't matter. If Nina was dead she didn't want to live on.

Something slammed into them, and all movement stopped.

Something hadn't slammed into them. Their vessel had hit something and finally come to rest.

She was still alive.

She took no joy from the realization. Dispiritedly, she took a look at her surroundings, revealed through the veil of vomit on the inside of her helmet. An EVA suit filled the area immediately in front of her. It moved slightly. Whoever was inside it hadn't been killed in the crash, but their weak motion indicated they were injured.

Miki prodded her belly until she felt the lock of her harness and unsnapped it. The effort did little to increase her freedom of movement. Something was crushing her side, forcing her against the bulkhead, and before her was the injured person. She squirmed, pushing up, but her hands met something solid. She tried moving sideways, easing Maddox—she presumed—out of her way.

Breaking through, she came up against the shattered remains of the transparent shell, mixed with rocks and sand. She backed up, but the two mission mates had closed in behind her, blocking her exit. The stench of her own vomit thick in her nostrils, she felt the urge to throw up again but managed to ignore it. There had to be a way out. She was hesitant to move the people blocking her in case she hurt them, but—

A body shifted out of the way and sunshine poured in. Sand stretched to the edge of her view, broken only by the legs of someone in an EVA suit, hauling the second person from the crashed vessel. When he or she reached in to grab her too, she waved the hands away and crawled out.

What a mess.

Twisted, crumpled sections of hull lay scattered on the desert. She looked back at the vessel and was amazed she'd exited it alive. Only a smashed-in shell remained, driven into the sand. How had anyone survived?

Knuckles rapped her helmet. She looked up. The person gestured at their head. She didn't understand. Had she hurt her head? Had they hurt their head? She'd barely begun to accept she hadn't died.

The person thrust their helmet against hers.

"Have you turned off your comm?" Wilder asked, her words muffled but intelligible.

"Oh, yeah." Miki turned it on. "Sorry."

"My helmet's jammed," Wilder said. "Can't remove it. Are you hurt anywhere?"

"I don't think so."

"Take off your suit. We need your help."

Miki got to her feet, hastily removed her helmet, pulled apart the EVA suit straps, unzipped, and stepped out. Hot, dry air hit her, sucking the moisture from her skin, and the rays of a merciless sun bore down.

Two figures lay on the ground, one with a leg at a strange angle. Wilder and someone else were getting them out of their suits. The wreckage of the Scythian craft dotted the immediate area but otherwise the landscape was bare and lifeless.

Miki was finally back in the place she could hardly remember, the place she'd left so many years before. She was on Concordia.

She was home.

THIRTEEN

Niall approached with a knife.

"About time," Wilder said, though she knew he couldn't hear her.

Miki must have found it among the survival equipment they'd stowed in the Scythian vessel's curved wings. She'd been a real trooper, rising to the occasion after the crash. Initially, Wilder had the impression the girl was nearly comatose with shock. She'd been white as a ghost when she'd taken off her helmet—and yellow with dried vomit—and her gaze had been unfocused, but she'd quickly snapped into action as soon as she was given a task. She'd been searching the desert for the remains of the aircraft's wings and come up trumps.

Niall was saying something.

Wilder cupped a hand to the side of her helmet and shrugged. He'd taken off his suit. Unless someone spoke to her via comm she was locked in a world of silence. "Hurry up. It's getting hot in here."

He slipped the knife inside her suit near her neck and began sawing.

As well as jamming her helmet into the neck ring, a crash impact had damaged her suit's cooling system. Its insulating material protected her from external temperatures but it also trapped her body heat, and she'd been growing steadily warmer ever since crawling from the wreckage. She'd managed to open the front of the suit but it didn't make a whole lot of difference. If things got really bad she supposed she could take off the suit but her head would remain inside the helmet, and what good would that do? She could hardly travel around Concordia like that.

Niall didn't seem to be making much progress. It wasn't surprising. The suit was designed to protect against penetration by sharp objects.

"Let me try." She gestured to him to hand over the knife.

He said something.

"I can't hear you!" She gave an exaggerated shrug and held out her hand.

Scowling, he gave her the blade.

She groped for the opening. Wearing gloves didn't help. Which way around was the knife? She didn't want to hold the sharp edge against her skin. She lifted it to check. After turning it over, she felt for the gap in her suit again. She pushed the knife in.

"Ow!" She'd poked her chest with the tip.

Giving up, she handed the knife back. Niall snatched it angrily and spoke to her again, no doubt telling her off.

"Yeah? Well let's see if you can do any better."

It was going to take him forever to cut through sufficient material to allow her to pull off the suit and slide her head out of the helmet. She hoped she *could* slide her head out of the helmet. EVA suits fit pretty snugly around the neck.

When she was finally free, what then? Zapata was in a bad way. His broken leg looked nasty, jagged bone protruding through his calf. He wasn't shouting about it, but he had to be in agony. How would he go anywhere? They would have to leave him here in the middle of nowhere. At least, she guessed they were in the middle of nowhere. She had no idea where they'd flown—looped and spiraled—after the impact. Their plan was already severely awry.

Maddox was in better shape though also injured. She seemed have broken some ribs and, in contrast to Zapata, was whining about it plenty. Not that anyone was paying any attention to her. Zapata was in too much pain, Niall was concentrating on getting her out of her suit, and Miki had set off again to search for more wreckage.

Wilder had been against bringing Maddox along, and now she was regretting the decision even more. But Vessey and Niall had overruled her and that had been that. Her objection wasn't only over loyalty to Cherry, though she suspected they thought it was, she also didn't understand what Maddox added to the team except for being an extra person. More wasn't always necessarily better, and someone could be more of a liability than an aide. Maddox's attitude so far seemed to be proving she was the former.

A burst of fresh air hit Wilder's collarbones. At last, Niall was having some success. She couldn't see the area he was working on but he must have sliced through some material.

She tapped his shoulder. "Can I take it off yet?"

He held up a hand. *Wait*. His head bent down as he continued to work.

"*Come on!*" There was so much to do and they were under threat of being captured by Scythians.

As if sensing her agitation, Niall looked up. He mouthed something that looked like *Nearly there* before continuing to work. A few minutes later he put the knife down and pulled the front of her suit apart, allowing more air to rush in.

"All right. I can do it." She felt for the cut edges and tugged at them.

Together, they forced the material over her shoulders. At the same time, she stepped out of the suit's legs. Though the desert air had to be hot, its movement on her sweaty skin was a wonderful relief. She'd been soaking in a sauna of her own sweat for ages.

She pushed upward on the edges of her helmet. Her head slid through the stretchy material of the neck ring's interior, and finally she was free. "Phew!" She dropped the suit to the ground. There was a thunk as the helmet she'd come to despise hit the desert sand. "Thanks. I thought I was going to boil alive."

"You're drenched," said Niall. "Was your cooling system out too?"

"Uh huh. Where's Miki?" She scanned their surroundings.

The area they'd crashed in wasn't entirely devoid of life but it came close. Spine-covered shrubs and a lone, twisted tree with needle-like leaves clung to life in the harsh environment. The remains of the Scythian vessel's cabin lay close by, barely recognizable, and shattered fragments of the strange hull with its whirling, irregular pattern could be spotted here and there.

"She's looking for the other wing," Niall replied.

"The one with the rations? Gee, I hope she finds it. I'm parched already. It was a mistake to split the equipment up like we did. We should have put the same things in each wing, not all the food and water in one of them."

"No one anticipated this scenario."

"We should have anticipated all possible scenarios. Still, no point in wasting time on regrets."

Maddox cursed as she turned onto her side. "I hope the girl finds the water too. Zapata and I will need extra shares as we're injured. I wish I'd never come on this mission."

"You're not that badly injured," Wilder snapped, "and you could have always said no." *I wish you had.*

"You don't know how I feel. I'm in agony."

Her comment as she lay next to Zapata, who really was in agony, was so outrageous Wilder couldn't think of a reply.

"You might be lucky," Niall said. "We all might be the lucky ones."

He didn't say more. There was no need. All present knew what he meant.

What had been the explosion that occurred soon after they'd launched from the *Sirocco*? Had the ship blown up, destroyed by the Scythians? It seemed the only logical explanation but if it were true the implications were too enormous to grasp. Was everyone else dead? All the people they'd lived with, suffered with, and toiled with to survive for years, were they all gone?

Not only was the concept hard to bear, it also meant there was no going back. There was no way off the planet. They were doomed to live like the rest of the Concordians, enslaved to alien masters unless they could think of a way to overthrow them.

"There she is," Niall said.

In the distance a small figure could be seen slowly dragging something through the sand. She disappeared into the shade of the tree momentarily and then appeared again, blurred by the heat haze.

Wilder and Niall set out to meet her.

———

The ragged metal was hot in Miki's hands. It had been baking in the sun until she'd found it, and the strong rays had continued to warm it as she hauled it over the ground. Should she stop and leave the boxes here, returning to the crash site to tell the others about her discovery? In this lifeless place, nothing seemed likely to take them or disturb them while she was gone. But the supplies were precious, their only source of water and sustenance. Leaving them out in the open even for a short time was too risky.

Grasping the torn piece of wing tighter, she walked on. The scrape of the metal on the sand and stones was the only sound. No animals seemed to live here, not even insects. Where was she? Captain Vessey had explained they would be going to a country called Suddene, but that didn't mean anything to her. This wasn't how she remembered Concordia. Where she'd lived there had been houses and fields. She couldn't remember much else, but she could remember that much.

She hoped Wilder had managed to get out of her suit, and that she and Niall had been able to do something for poor Zapata. The pilot's face had been rigid and wet with sweat when she left the site for the second time. But what could anyone do? They had no medics.

The sound of water sloshing in its container brought her a little comfort. Now Zapata could at least have a drink.

Edging out her fears for the pilot was a black, thick cloud of worry ballooning from the back of her mind. She forced the thought away, blinked back tears, and trudged on.

"Miki!"

She looked up. Wilder and Niall were walking toward her.

"Wait there," Wilder shouted. "We'll help you."

She was out of her suit, thank the stars.

Miki released the piece of wing and sank to the ground. Her shoulders ached from hauling the supplies. She'd found the other wing about a kilometer away. She wasn't sure how it had ended up so far from the rest of the vessel. It must have broken off when they were still high up.

"You're an absolute star," said Wilder as she arrived.

"There's more. This was all I could fit on the wing."

"Fantastic." Wilder squatted down and began going through the packages.

"I didn't drink any of the water."

"Why not?" asked Niall, joining Wilder. "You must be thirsty."

"I thought we should ration it, save it for Zapata and Maddox."

Wilder huffed with contempt. "Maddox is fine, but you're right, we need to make sure Zapata has everything he needs, even if we have to go without."

Niall straightened up. "We should all drink when we need to. Dehydration makes people confused and disoriented. Did you spot any medical supplies?"

"There *is* more stuff there," Miki replied. "I'm not sure what it is. I thought it was important to bring back water and food first of all."

"You were right," said Niall. "You did a good job. Wilder and I will pull this the rest of the way."

"Should I go back and get the other stuff?"

"No, come with us."

As Wilder grabbed the edge of the metal, she asked, "Did you see any Scythian domes?"

"I don't think so. Nothing that looked like a dome to me anyway, but the air is hazy. It's hard to see well into the distance."

"Maybe we have something in our favor at last and we were right in thinking the Scythians aren't interested in Suddene. It's too barren for them."

"We can't be sure of that," said Niall. "Let's not get ahead of ourselves. First, we need to try to make Zapata comfortable. Then we figure out what to do next."

Fourteen

"I don't want to stay here," Zapata said. "I'd rather take my chances with you." He spoke through gritted teeth, his face a mask of pain despite the medication Wilder had given him. "I'm sorry. I'll slow you down, but if those things find me..."

Underlying his physical discomfort, Miki read another discomfort in his features. He hated being a burden but his fear of the Scythians and what they might do to him was greater.

What *would* they do to an injured human? None of the people she'd seen in the Scythian domes had been injured. They'd all been put to work by the aliens, tending their young or performing other tasks. Zapata was no use to them in his condition, except perhaps as a subject for anatomical study. If they found him they would either leave him, kill him, or experiment on him.

Wilder and Niall exchanged an enigmatic look.

Maddox said, "You'll be safer here than trekking through the desert with us, out in the open."

"For how long?" Zapata asked. "We only have limited supplies of food and water. How much can you leave me? Three days' worth? Four days? Then what? I guess you could give me a gun to finish myself off before I die of thirst," he added bitterly, immediately followed by, "I know I'm asking a lot."

"You're not asking a lot," Miki murmured, touching the man's shoulder.

"No, you're not," Wilder echoed.

Niall said, "You've been there for us since the beginning, man. If you don't want to stay here you're not staying, and that's it."

"That's right," said Wilder. "We'll figure it out somehow."

The sun was going down. They'd been at the crash site four or five hours, and they'd found just about everything they were ever going to find in terms of the supplies they'd brought along. There had been a medical kit in with the rations and water. Maddox's chest was strapped and Zapata had received a dose of painkillers, but Miki didn't know what else they could do for him. She couldn't see how he could walk, and he wasn't a small man. He was the largest and heaviest of all of them. If they had to pull him on the piece of wing she'd used to transport the food and water, they would travel very slowly.

"We need to start moving soon," said Wilder. "The Scythians will be leaving their domes. Some might fly overhead and spot us by chance. Or they could be looking for debris from the...incident...after we left the ship."

"In the dark?" Maddox asked.

"Especially in the dark. They see infrared. It was one of the things Ryan discovered from examining the cadaver."

"*Shit*." Maddox's shoulders slumped. Instantly, she winced.

"What does that mean?" Miki asked. "That they see infrared?"

"They can see the heat from our bodies," Niall explained.

"Oh." Miki looked up into the twilit sky, suddenly feeling naked and exposed. It was strange to imagine that the coming night wouldn't hide them, yet at the same time she could see through Scythian eyes five figures crouched next to twisted wreckage, glowing in the dark. Her gaze turned to the shattered remains of the cabin. "Could we hide in there?"

"We won't fit," Wilder replied, "and even if we did our body heat would radiate out of the holes. We could cover them up but then we would swelter all night." She glanced at the pilot. "Our best chance is to keep moving."

Niall grimaced. "I'm sorry, Zapata, but we have to set your broken bone. It's the only way you'll be able to move at all."

"I know," he replied quietly.

Again, Miki was unsure what they were talking about but from everyone's expressions it was clearly something awful.

"Count me out," said Maddox. "Not with these ribs."

"If you can find something for me to hold onto..." Zapata offered.

Niall shook his head. "Once we start pulling you're not going to be in a condition to hold onto anything."

"Then..." Zapata looked at Wilder.

She lifted her thin arms. "I'll do what I can, but..."

"Miki," Niall said. "You have to help too."

"Of course, but I don't know what you want me to do."

"You have to help Wilder hold onto Zapata while I pull his leg. We're going to straighten it."

Her jaw dropped. What they were proposing had to be incredibly painful. "I can try."

"Good," Niall said. "Let's get it over with."

Zapata's pants were cut from where Wilder and Niall had examined his wound. The man's leg was bare, the bone shard poking horribly through torn skin, bruised purple and oozing blood. Miki could hardly stand to look at it.

She moved to his right shoulder as instructed by Niall, while Wilder sat on his left.

"Hold him really tight under his arm," Wilder told her. "When Niall starts pulling, whatever you do, don't let go. Dig your heels in for traction." Her eyes said more, things like *If we don't manage to do this he's going to die.*

"I won't let go." Miki grabbed Zapata around his armpit. She began panting even though Niall hadn't started yet.

"Take it easy," said Wilder.

"Okay," she squeaked.

Niall sat at Zapata's feet. He rubbed his hands. He and Zapata held each other's gaze. "Are you ready?"

The pilot tensed under Miki's hands.

"I know it's gonna be hard," Wilder said, "but you should try to relax your muscles as much as you can. It'll make the job easier."

His shoulder softened a fraction. "Do it."

Niall grabbed Zapata's heel in one hand and the rest of his foot in the other. He pulled. The pilot screamed and slid across the ground.

"Hold on, Miki!" Wilder yelled.

She gripped the man's shoulder with all her might, thrusting her heels into the slippery sand. Zapata was wriggling, squirming, unable to control himself in his agony. She dug her fingers into his skin as she struggled to hold onto him. Every fiber of her being rebelled against what she was doing. She was hurting him, but he needed to be hurt. He had to suffer this terrible ordeal if he was going to survive.

Her chest heaving, she turned her head away. She couldn't bear to see what was happening. All she could do was focus on stopping Zapata from moving. Why was it taking so long? Did straightening a broken bone take a long time? No one had told her how long it would take. Her muscles were nearing exhaustion from the effort.

The pilot's screaming resounded in her ears. It encompassed her entire world. All she knew was the sound of the man's pain and her determination to cling on.

Zapata jerked backward and she fell down, sprawling on her back.

"You can let go," Wilder said.

Miki sat up. Zapata's eyes were closed. His skin shone wet in the failing light. Niall's hunched form remained at his feet. The jutting bone had gone. Only the open wound remained.

They'd done it.

Wilder leaned over the pilot. "I'll clean you up and make a splint."

He didn't seem to hear.

———

Niall had broken a branch from the twisted tree, and Wilder had wrapped material around the thicker end to make it into a crutch while Zapata recovered from his ordeal. As they worked, Miki stowed supplies into three of the backpacks she'd recovered from the wreckage. Maddox was adamant she couldn't carry anything and naturally no one expected the pilot to burden himself.

As she stuffed the backpacks with rations, Miki regularly checked the sky. They had guns. If one or two Scythians attacked they might be able to kill them, though no doubt more would soon be on their way.

The plan was to reach a place Wilder was confident still existed, a hidden place where they would be safe and from which they could launch an effort to turn the tide against the aliens. Miki didn't know the location of the place or how far away it was and she wasn't sure anyone else did. But at least they would be moving. That was something.

"All set?" Niall loomed up out of the dark.

"I divided the rations and water up like you said. Equal amounts in each in case we get split up."

He reached down and lifted a pack experimentally. "Are you sure you can carry one of these?"

"It's the water that's making them heavy. They'll get lighter as we drink it."

"If you're sure you can manage..." His gaze turned to Maddox, who sat alone some way off, staring into the night.

"I can manage."

Wilder arrived. She'd been helping Zapata to his feet and given him his crutch. "The sun went down over there..." she pointed "...so we have to head that way." She swiveled so she was pointing in the opposite direction.

"Toward the coast," Niall said.

"When we hit the ocean I should be able to figure out if we go north or south."

"You remember that well?"

"Well enough."

Niall stooped and picked up a backpack, handing it to her. "Maddox, we're leaving."

Miki shouldered another pack.

Wilder and Niall walked in front as they departed the crash site. Miki walked next to Zapata, who hopped along slowly on his crutch. Maddox brought up the rear.

The temperature had dropped fast after the sun went down, but the exercise staved off some of the chill. Miki's backpack straps dug in hard and she struggled along, only just able to keep pace with the injured pilot. The terrain didn't make for easy going. Her boots sank into the sand and the additional weight of her new load only made the problem worse. She kept quiet, however. Compared to the man trekking next to her she had little to complain about. His grunts of effort put her troubles to shame.

Everyone walked in silence except for Maddox. Her grumbles and curses accompanied them from a distance. After a while, Niall turned and noticed she was dropping behind. He signaled to the group to wait until she caught up.

"I can't go any faster," she whined when she reached them. "I'm in agony here."

Zapata said nothing, and Miki marveled at his restraint.

"I know you're hurt," said Niall, "but it's hard for all of us. You aren't carrying a pack, so—"

"You're not going to make me feel bad about that," she snapped. "I wish I'd never come on this goddamned mission. I must have been out of my mind to agree."

Wilder said, "You're not the only one who wishes you didn't come along."

"Cool it," said Niall. "Arguing isn't going to get us anywhere. Maddox, do your best. We have a long way to go to reach the coast."

It was hard to make out faces in the dark, but Miki caught a glimpse of Maddox's sullen glance. Niall told Zapata to lean on him, and the two men set off again. Maddox slowly followed them.

Wilder had hung back to walk with Miki. "How are you doing?"

"I'm fine. It's not too bad. Only..."

"What?"

Miki swallowed. "Do you know what happened...before?"

"You mean before the crash?"

"Uh huh. Is..." her voice dropped to a whisper "...is everyone else dead?"

Wilder didn't reply for a long while. "I'm sorry, Miki, but I don't know. I just don't know."

FIFTEEN

They walked through the night and into the dawn. As Wilder felt the sun's rays hit her back she looked behind her. Niall and Zapata walked as a three-legged pair, the taller man's arm over Niall's shoulders. At each step the pilot wobbled precariously and Niall struggled to keep him upright. Miki trudged not far behind them, her backpack incongruously large on her small body. In the distance, illuminated by the rising sun, was the slim figure of Maddox.

As the night had worn on, first Wilder and then Niall had given up on exhorting her to walk faster or calling a halt to allow her to catch up. Sure, her ribs had to be painful but she was unburdened. Zapata, who was in far worse shape, was putting in his best effort. And Miki had been a trooper, hauling a pack that didn't weigh much less than her without complaint. In the trying circumstances it was hard to not be resentful about carrying Maddox's food and water.

The place they'd crashed seemed like paradise compared to this new region. Not a stick or leaf of vegetation grew anywhere as far as the eye could see. A thin layer of sand overlay stony ground, and there was no sign that water had flowed or rain had fallen here for a very long time. The air temperature was already rising in line with the sun. The day promised to be brutal.

Wilder drew to a stop, unfastened the catch on her waist strap, slipped off her shoulder straps, and let her backpack slide to the ground.

Niall appeared to register the sound, looking up and asking, "We're taking a break?"

"We should call it a day—or a night." She gestured at a group of boulders.

"They'll give us a little cover and shade. There's nowhere else suitable in sight, and he can't go any farther." She jerked her chin toward Zapata, confident he was either past registering what was going on around him or too exhausted to care.

Niall glanced at the pilot. "No argument about that. Come on, buddy. Just a few more steps and you can lie down." He guided the exhausted man to the boulders and in among them before easing him to the ground.

Wilder waited for Miki. Her head was down and her hair obscured her face. When she reached Wilder she almost passed her by without noticing, but Wilder reached out to touch her. "We're stopping here."

Miki lifted her head, revealing drawn features and a sagging mouth. "Huh?"

"We're stopping." Wilder pointed at the boulders. "Take your pack off over there. We'll eat and drink before resting."

Without reply, Miki plodded along the new course. Wilder turned her attention to Maddox, still distant. While waiting, she scanned the sky. If any Scythians had passed overhead during the night they must have not spotted them or not bothered with a small group of humans wandering the desert. None of the aliens' domes were visible in the surrounding land.

Maddox was progressing at a painfully slow pace. Wilder gave up on waiting, hauled her pack onto one shoulder and walked to join the others at the boulders. Maddox would figure out for herself where they'd gone.

Zapata was already out of it, flat on his back in the shade.

"I got some water and rations into him," Niall explained, "and I dosed him with painkillers. He zonked out immediately after."

"I'm not surprised. It's a miracle he made it this far. He must be completely beat if he can sleep while his leg is in that state."

The wound in the pilot's calf had puffed out and turned a deeper shade of purple. They had no antibiotics. The last of the supply they'd brought on the *Sirocco* had been used up years ago and the ship lacked the facilities to create more. If the Earthers had them, Vessey's abrupt departure had put paid to any chance of a request to replenish the ship's stocks.

Miki was sucking water from her bottle.

"How are you doing?" Wilder asked.

"I'm good."

Everything about her said otherwise. From the shadows under her eyes to her limp arms and slumped posture, it was clear that Miki was at the end of her strength too.

"When you've eaten," Wilder said, "try to get some sleep."

"How long are we going to stay here?"

Wilder checked the sky again. Not a cloud was in sight. "What do you think, Niall?"

"At least until after midday. The heat will be unbearable by then, even for us let alone Zapata."

"How much farther do we have to walk?" asked Miki.

Wilder replied, "I'm not sure, but we seem to be heading in the right direction at least. Maybe only another day or two."

In truth, the topography told her they'd crashed far from their intended destination. They shouldn't have had to cross a desert to reach it, which meant they were closer to the center of Suddene than she wanted. Depending on how close, they might have two days' or two weeks' walking ahead of them. How could the pilot do it?

"I can manage another few days," Miki announced. "No problem."

"You're a great help," said Niall. "We couldn't do without you."

His comment sparked energy in her features. She reached into her pack and drew out a ration package.

Wilder gave Niall an appreciative look but he turned away to get himself some food. She rolled her eyes. Dragan had accused her of being cold. How was she supposed to be any different when Niall rebuffed every attempt to be nice?

Between mouthfuls he asked her, "When were you in Suddene?"

"A very long time ago." She took a swig of water.

"Did you live here? It's so long since we were on Concordia I can't remember."

"I visited for a short time after the biocide attack."

"You were only here a few days?!"

"How long did you think I'd been here?"

"Longer than that. Long enough to be confident this is the best place for us to go."

"Did you have a better idea?"

"If we'd gone to Lyonesse we would be sure of finding people."

"And thousands of Scythians too. You saw the images of the surface."

"Who the hell would choose to live in this desert?" Niall grumbled. "And now we've lost the aircraft we have no way of crossing the ocean."

"There are people here, people the Scythians don't know about."

"How can you be so sure?"

"I just know, okay? If Concordia had been invaded while I was here, Suddene would be the place I would go."

He didn't reply, only chewed his food forcefully.

Maddox appeared between two boulders. "Thanks for waiting for me, guys."

"We *were* waiting for you," Wilder replied. "Here."

Ignoring her, Maddox rummaged in Miki's pack. Wilder was tempted to tell her off. They had a strict schedule for using up the supplies. But the more

Miki's pack could be lightened the better. Wilder wasn't confident she could make another long trek.

———

Something had crossed the sun. Somewhere deep in the depths of Wilder's subconscious, her mind registered the fact. Very briefly, something had cut out the light blasting her skin from the hot desert sky. Blearily, she opened her eyes.

While she'd been sleeping, the shadow of the boulder she was lying next to had moved away and the high sun shone directly on her. Her exhaustion after the long night's trek had made her oblivious to the increased heat and her burning skin. Another realization had dragged her to wakefulness, a realization that something more dangerous than sunburn threatened.

What was it?

She sat up.

All her companions were sleeping. Zapata remained in the shade. Maddox was exposed to full sunlight but unaware. Niall and Miki's upper halves lay in shadow but their legs had to be roasting.

She touched her face. The skin was hot and sore, and her clothes were uncomfortably warm and sweaty.

That wasn't it.

The brilliant sunshine dimmed for a fraction of a second.

That was it.

She turned her gaze upward.

High above, two winged shapes were circling.

Scythians out in the open in the middle of the day?

"Holy shit! Wake up! Wake up!" She roughly shook Niall's shoulder. "Wake Zapata." She crawled to Miki and Maddox. "Scythians! We need to hide."

They moved deeper into the group of boulders, huddling in a central space where they only barely fit. Zapata grimaced with pain as he was forced to bend his broken leg. They gripped the three backpacks on their laps. They couldn't afford to leave any trace the aliens might notice.

Miki whispered, "Will they see our body heat?"

"I really hope not," Wilder replied.

Would it have been better to lie on the baking sand where the infrared might confuse the Scythians' sight? But the act of lying in the open in order to hide felt so counter-intuitive. Her first impulse had been to conceal themselves as if hiding from other humans. It was a mistake that had almost been the downfall of Sidhe.

But it was too late to move out from the boulders. If the aliens hadn't seen them yet, they would almost certainly discern movement in the lifeless scene.

"Where have they gone?" Maddox asked.

The sky was empty.

Wilder pulled out her gun and the others did the same except for Zapata, who was slumped against a boulder, his eyes shut tight. Wilder's gaze flicking between the narrow entrances to the cramped spot, she strained her ears for sounds of the aliens approaching. There was nothing, not even the noise of the wind. The air was utterly still. Sweat coating her palm made her weapon slippery in her hand. She gripped it tighter.

"Have they left?" Miki whispered. She had crouched into the tiniest ball and her eyes were wide.

No one answered.

How long should they wait before concluding it was safe to come out? Wilder wished they had a better view of their surroundings. If the aliens had flown away they would see them in the distance. But here the tall boulders blocked their sight of everything except the sky immediately above.

The faintest whiff of an odor crossed her nostrils. Instantly, every nerve in her body was alive, an instinctive, visceral reaction prompted by a horrifying memory. She was being carried aloft, an alien's long, scaly toes crushing her chest and stomach, its revolting stench enveloping her.

She hissed, "*They're here!*"

Miki had smelt them too. She'd turned deathly pale.

"We have to kill them before they find us," Wilder murmured, "before they get a chance to send out a comm. If the rest of them know where we are we're dead meat."

Niall nodded grimly.

Twisting to ease herself out of the packed bodies, Wilder rose to a crouching position and leaned through a gap between the nearest boulders. Their former resting site lay before her, the sand disturbed but with no sign of the aliens.

They had to be approaching from—

Miki screamed.

Wilder whirled 180 degrees. A Scythian was leaning in, its head encased in its breathing apparatus, wings outspread. Something was different about it, but she didn't have time to think more before firing. Her and Niall's pulses caught it square in the chest and it toppled backward.

"Two!" Wilder yelled. "There are two. We have to get the other one!" She darted to the opening, stepping on bodies. The Scythian lay on its back, moving weakly, the ribs of its massive wings twitching. She fired another round, aiming at its helmet. Though it was out of action they couldn't risk it comming its friends.

There was the other one!

It was running, and its wings beat. It was abandoning its partner, heading for the skies.

She aimed, fired, and missed. She leapt over the downed alien, trying to get closer, hoping for a better shot. An iron grip fastened around her ankle, and suddenly she was on top of the wounded Scythian. It had grabbed her as she jumped. Its burned flesh and noxious odor surrounded her, and the helmet she'd fired at was in her face. She'd only scored it. The thing still wasn't dead.

The other one was getting away. She had to do something before it alerted the rest of them. But the one holding her wouldn't let go and at this close range, struggling with the creature, she risked hurting herself if she fired at it.

With her free hand, she reached behind the helmet and grasped the tube that led to its CO_2 pack. She gave a hard yank. That did nothing. She fumbled at the base and felt a snap lock. She flicked it open, the tube came out, and finally the thing released its grip. She scrambled to her feet.

Where was the second one?

It was flying, but beneath it stood Niall, aiming. He got off two shots in quick succession. The first pierced the alien's wing, disrupting its flight. The second bright pulse round seemed about to go astray but the creature turned into its path and caught the round in its throat. It tumbled from the sky and landed heavily on its back.

As Niall finished it off, Wilder checked the alien that had grabbed her. It held the tube she'd pulled out in one of its feet, but it was still. Either it hadn't managed to replace it before it suffocated or it had expired from its wounds in the process.

Both the Scythians were dead, but had they managed to tell others about the humans in the desert?

SIXTEEN

In a flurry of haste, they made their departure. Niall helped Zapata to his feet, the older man grimacing and blanching in pain. Miki quickly pulled on her backpack. Maddox was already out in the desert, striding away from their useless hiding place.

Wilder called her back. She was heading in the wrong direction. As she returned, she complained loudly that no one had told her which way she was supposed to go.

They set out once more for the coast.

It was early afternoon. The sun was barely past its zenith. Wilder was already burned from her exposure to its rays while sleeping. She pulled her hat lower and rolled her sleeves down from her elbows. Better to swelter than burn.

Glancing back, she assessed the trail they were leaving. The looseness of the sand made their footsteps indistinct but they remained visible to a sharp-eyed observer. There was nothing to be done about it. No one in their party had the energy to cover their traces. All they could do was hope the two Scythians hadn't managed to get word out about their discovery, and that it would be a long while before their bodies were found.

"Wilder." Niall had Zapata's arm over his shoulder again while the pilot struggled along with his crutch. Niall's features were sweaty and strained.

She dropped back a few paces to draw level with them. "Yeah?"

"Did you think those Scythians looked different from the ones we saw on Earth?"

"You noticed that too? I thought I might have imagined it." Her only close encounter with a living Scythian had involved it nearly killing her, and the second time she'd seen one it had been cut up and frozen.

"Their visors were darker," Niall said, "and so were their bodies, right?"

"That's right. I guess it makes sense. They usually come out at night so ultraviolet light must hurt them. They're getting around it by protecting themselves."

"I wonder if it's an old practice or if they've only recently started doing it. Either way, it spells trouble for Concordians. They aren't able to escape the aliens day or night."

"I'm more worried by the fact that we saw two here on Suddene. I'd been hoping they wouldn't bother with this continent and it might be a safe haven for people who could make it over the ocean."

Zapata stumbled and Niall grunted as he struggled to keep him upright. "I think Scythians have been here a lot longer than they were on Earth. They've spread to inhospitable places and they've adapted their strategies to deal with a harsh climate—at least, it is to them. When you said that our colony could have survived only because the Scythians arrived and enslaved them, you might have been right. The aliens could have been here for decades, but if that's so, things might change soon."

"In what way?"

"They're figuring out how to travel around during daylight. Why? Why bother if they have humans to do that for them?"

"So they can capture more colonists?"

"I doubt it. They seem to have the local population under control. A few stragglers who lack the technology to hurt them won't make a difference one way or the other. No, it's more serious than that. I think they're moving to the second stage of reclaiming their home planet. They're planning to eradicate their need for humans entirely. Eradicate *humans* entirely."

Her stomach clenched and she stuttered, "You-you really think so?"

"What do you think? This is where the Scythian species originated. Why would they want a bunch of illegal immigrants living here when they could have the place to themselves?"

She was silent.

"I don't know for sure, of course," he said, as if trying to soften the blow. "It's just supposition."

"Makes sense, though."

Shit. How long did they have before the slaughter began? Had it already begun?

Zapata stumbled again, crashing all the way to the ground this time. He yelled as he hit, impacting his broken leg. He lay still, panting and cursing under his breath. Niall stooped to help him to his feet.

"Leave me," said Zapata. "Leave me here and go ahead. I'll take my chances."

"Don't be dumb," Niall admonished. "We're not leaving you. Come on, let me help you."

Zapata batted his hands away. "Leave me, goddammit. I've slowed you all down enough already."

Wilder went to his other side. "Seriously, Maddox is more trouble than you, Zapata." The woman had already dropped behind. "Niall's right. There's no way we're letting you stay here while we go on. Besides, if we find another Scythian aircraft, who's gonna fly it? We need you."

The pilot's shoulders sagged. "I can't do it. I can't go on. I thought I could make it but I was wrong."

"No," Wilder said, "you were right. You *can* make it. We'll take it one step at a time, okay? First, we get you upright. You can do that. Just focus on standing up."

As she'd been talking, Zapata's head had been down. He lifted his gaze to meet hers. Holding eye contact, he grasped her hand.

"That's it. You can do it."

Together, she and Niall hauled him up. Niall pushed the crutch under his arm and lifted the other one to put it over his shoulder.

"I'll help him this time," Wilder said.

"You're too weak. You won't manage."

"Let me try."

Let me in.

Niall looked at her uncertainly. "Okay, but the minute you get tired out tell me about it. We need to keep him on his feet. You saw what happens if he falls."

It seemed rude to talk about the pilot while he was right in front of them, but in truth he acted as if he was oblivious to anything except his pain and the question of whether he should go on.

She took over from Niall, taking Zapata's free arm. "Next step."

They moved forward.

While she was helping the pilot she had little energy for anything else. Her backpack became a leaden weight and the man's arm pressed down heavily on her shoulders. She relied on Niall to check the skies and what Maddox and Miki were doing. When Zapata had fallen Miki had continued walking. She probably hadn't noticed. And in all the time it had taken to get the pilot to his feet Maddox hadn't caught up. She was positively dawdling, like she was passively aggressively punishing them for the situation. Wilder had a silent vision of a Scythian swooping from the sky and carrying her off.

They walked on, and soon it became a matter of not only Zapata forcing himself to put one foot in front of the other—or rather one hop after another

—but her too. Yesterday night's walk seemed like a pleasant stroll compared to this forced march through the heat of the desert day, not knowing if the Scythians were already on their trail.

Time and again she was tempted to ask Niall to take over, but he had to be beyond exhausted. He'd helped Zapata all the previous night.

In the midst of another miserable internal debate, as she exhorted herself to walk just another hundred meters, a breath of cool air hit her, accompanied by a salty tang.

Was she imagining it?

Had extreme fatigue made her delirious?

"Does anyone else feel that?"

The others either didn't hear her or were too tired to reply.

Perhaps she had imagined it after all.

There it was again. Unmistakable, a waft of refreshing air had moved over her skin.

The realization energized her. "We're near the ocean! We're nearly there."

Niall looked back and then turned his gaze ahead again. His footsteps slowly drew to a halt.

The landscape rose in front of them, sandy hillocks mounting higher until cut off by a cobalt, cloudless sky. Thick clumps of tough undergrowth dotted the slopes.

Niall lifted his backpack straps and allowed it to slide to the ground.

Wilder halted. Without a word, Zapata stopped alongside her. Miki walked on, heedless of everyone else.

Niall walked ahead. Wilder watched him staggering through the low hills, disappearing beyond each and then rising into sight again.

He disappeared beyond the farthest slope.

Miki finally noticed what was going on. She stopped, dropped her pack, and turned to look at Wilder questioningly.

But Wilder was more interested in what was happening on the horizon.

"Wilder!" Miki called. "What's going on?"

Niall popped up on the ridge, waving excitedly.

"We made it!" Wilder called back. "We've made it."

SEVENTEEN

They hadn't made it.

When Niall had announced they'd reached the ocean, that it lay just another few hundred meters' march over the sandy hills, Miki had thought they'd nearly reached their destination. But it turned out that wasn't the case.

She'd trudged the remaining distance to the water and then dropped onto the beach, too tired to remove her backpack. A little later, after her legs had ceased thrumming and the sea breeze had cleared her head, she snapped the waist catch open and gingerly slid her shoulders out from under the straps. The pack fell backwards onto the sand and she left it there.

Where was the place they were supposed to be going? The shoreline ran for kilometers to the right, and though the view to the left ended in a high bluff, there were no signs of people living here. No footprints marked the beach except their own. There were no buildings or roads, nothing that indicated a human presence.

She waited.

Niall had gone back to help Wilder with Zapata. Maybe she should try to help too, but now she was sitting down she found she couldn't get up. Her legs simply refused to work. Instead, she watched the water. She'd seen Earth's oceans but only from afar. Now she was up close to one, the sheer amount of water all in one place was hard to take in. While she'd been growing up on the *Sirocco* water had been a precious commodity, to be measured out and conserved. The presence of so much of it seemed wasteful somehow.

A scuffling sound behind her, louder than the gentle waves, drew her attention. She started. She hadn't checked the sky for Scythians in a while. But it was only Niall and Wilder arriving with Zapata. Helping the man down the slope was hard. The sand gave way every step they took, but eventually they made it and lowered him to the beach. He lay down, instantly out of it. Even at a distance his leg wound looked awful.

"How are you doing?" Wilder asked, approaching.

"When you said we'd made it, I thought you meant we were at the end of our journey." Miki hated the petulant tone in her voice but she couldn't help it. "But we aren't, right?" She squinted as she looked up at Wilder, who stood over her, her back to the sun.

"Right. Sorry, I should have explained. The site we're aiming for isn't on the coast. It's—"

"Is it much farther?" She wasn't sure she could walk any more, at least not today.

"Uhhh..." Wilder took off her pack and dropped it. Then she put her hands on her skinny hips and gazed up and down the beach.

"Do you know where we are?"

"It'll take me a little while to get my bearings. It's been a long time since I was on Suddene."

"Are we going to rest for a while?"

"Yeah, I need to figure things out." Wilder looked pensive but she didn't have that look of deep concentration she wore when she had hard thinking to do. Her expression was more one of concern or worry.

Niall had splashed sea water over his head and chest and was walking over. "Got your bearings yet?"

Wilder bit her lip. "Let's rest, drink some water, and eat. I need to think."

Miki decided to follow Niall's example to refresh herself. She pulled off her boots and socks, clambered to her feet, and slowly stepped down to the ocean's edge. A wave surged close and washed up to her knees. She gasped. The ocean was colder than she'd anticipated, but it wasn't unpleasant. She waded in deeper. As another wave retreated she stooped and gathered water in her hands to splash on her face. As the water hit some of it leaked into her mouth. "Ughhh!" She spat to get rid of the taste.

"Too salty?" Wilder asked.

Miki hadn't noticed her arrive. "I wasn't expecting that. Do all oceans taste of salt?"

"All the ones I've encountered, but that isn't many."

Miki gazed into the murky waves. "I remember Dad saying that an intelligent species called the Fila lived in Concordia's waters. Did you ever meet any of them?"

"*Meet* them? Humans and Fila co-existed happily for quite a time." Wilder's expression turned sorrowful. "A few of them traveled with us to the

Galactic Assembly. I got to know one of them well. We were friends. He helped me a lot. His name was Quinn."

"What happened to him? Did he die in the biocide attack?"

"No, he survived, but then he left with the rest of the Fila survivors. They didn't have a vaccine and their anatomy was too different from ours for us to manufacture one. Concordia wasn't safe for them, so he left, and then not so long after I left too. I don't know what happened to him."

"It's been so long..." Miki said softly.

"Fila don't die of old age. Unless something else killed him he's probably on another planet, living out his life. I hope so."

The water didn't feel so cold now. Miki bent down to splash it on her upper body, taking care to keep her mouth closed. But as it soaked through her shirt sharp pain jabbed at her shoulders and she gave a small scream.

"What's wrong?" Wilder asked.

"I don't know." Miki pulled her shirt away from her collarbones. The straps of her backpack had rubbed her skin raw.

Wilder peered in too and sucked air through her teeth. "It's the salt. It makes wounds sting. I think we have some ointment in the medical kit."

———

Before they settled down to sleep, Wilder had walked to the distant bluff. She'd gone alone. A capable adult had to stay on the beach in case the Scythians spotted their party. So Wilder had made the trek by herself. Miki had watched her leave and seen her return at dusk, the dim light not disguising her troubled look.

A whispered argument between Wilder and Niall followed. Miki only caught a few phrases, all from Niall, whose voice was deeper and louder: *I thought you said* and *Then what do you propose?* and *Zapata will never make it.*

Were they lost? Or only very far from where they needed to be?

There was clearly a problem yet she found it hard to care. Every part of her body ached, especially her shoulders, waist, and feet, which had borne the brunt of the day's exertion. She wasn't sure *she* would make it to whatever destination tomorrow held in store, let alone Zapata. He looked ready to lose his leg like Ethan.

More than her physical pain, she was heartsick, dreading the possibility she might have lost the only remaining member of her family. If Nina was dead was there any point in going on?

Despite her inner and outer discomfort, despite Niall and Wilder's quarrel, despite Zapata's soft groans and Maddox's snores, Miki drifted into slumber.

Dad was here. She knew it even before she saw him. She sensed his presence, calm and strong. She felt his love.

"Miki, I've missed you." He hugged her tightly.

"I've missed you too." She had a vague memory of him being ill. "Are you better now?"

"Yes, I'm better. How are you? What have you been doing?"

Looking into his amber eyes, she found she couldn't remember. She chuckled. "It's weird. I don't know what I've been doing. But I'm fine. It's nice being here with you." She rested her head on his shoulder like she had when she was a little girl. A deep sense of peace and happiness settled over her. She wanted to stay like this forever, though something told her that wasn't possible.

"Where's Nina?" Dad asked.

"I-I'm not sure." Where *was* her sister? "Isn't she here?"

"I don't know. I'll go and look for her."

"No, stay with me a while."

"Okay." He stroked her hair. "My little red-head."

"I'm not really. Only a little, just enough for my classmates to tease me. Dad, what was Mom like?" It was a question she'd asked him a million times. She had a few misty memories of her mother but that was it.

He said what he always said. "She was kind, warm, loving, and smart. I always felt lucky to know her."

"I wish *I'd* known her."

"Me too. But it wasn't to be."

In the far distance, someone was shouting.

"What's that?" Miki asked.

But Dad didn't seem to hear. He was still, as if frozen.

"Dad? What's wrong? What's wrong with you?"

Her father was melting. His features were dissolving.

"Dad, don't go! Dad, Daddy, wait for me!" She reached out but he was gone. In his place was darkness, a starry sky, and the sigh of waves washing to shore.

"Where's he gone?!" Wilder yelled.

"He can't have got far by himself," said Niall.

"But we'll never find him in the dark." Wilder added, more quietly, "Do you think he walked into the sea?"

"What're you chattering about?" Maddox asked groggily. "Some of us are trying to sleep."

Wilder answered, "Zapata's gone. Niall, you check the beach. I'll go inland. Maddox, you—"

"I'm not doing anything. I'm still in agony."

"I can help to look for him," Miki offered, sitting up. The dregs of her dream about her father clung on in her mind like the sweet aftertaste of a dessert or the scent of a fading flower. She savored the sensation. Dad had visited her many times in her sleep, and each time she relished the memory, though it deepened her grief.

"Thanks," said Wilder. "Come with me. I don't want you searching alone. The Scythians might have found the bodies of the ones we killed and be looking for us."

"Look," Maddox said, "I don't want to sound callous, but if Zapata has gone off somewhere maybe it isn't such a bad thing. He's slowing us down and he knows it. If he wants to—"

"If anyone's slowing us down, it's *you*!" Wilder spat. "If you want to sacrifice yourself by wandering off, feel free."

Maddox gave her a black look but didn't reply.

While Niall headed up the beach, Miki walked with Wilder into the dunes. They had a tougher job than Niall. Zapata's footprints would be easy to spot in the sand on the cloudless night. As soon as she and Wilder stepped away from the beach a hilly expanse of dark clumps of vegetation and shadows confronted them. There was no sign of his passage and even at close range he would be hard to spot.

On the other hand, the man could barely walk. Niall was right. Zapata couldn't have gotten far. Perhaps he was hoping they would seize the opportunity to absolve their guilt about leaving him behind and not come after him.

Distant beams of light brightened the darkness.

"Huh?" said Wilder. "What's that?"

The light was coming from behind them, from the beach. It looked like three or four flashlights roaming the shore, as if looking for someone.

Shouts broke the quiet of the night. Miki didn't recognize the voices as belonging to Niall, Maddox, or Zapata.

"What the...?" Wilder muttered. "We should head back. Whoever those people are, they aren't Scythians, they're Concordians. We can explain about Zapata and ask them to help us search for him." As they pushed through the vegetation, she added, "This is fantastic. I don't know how they found us, but it's saved us a long, hard trek."

Miki was similarly confused but also happy. Their situation had reversed. They were no longer seekers but the sought. "Do you think someone on the *Sirocco* managed to comm the surface and told the people here about us?"

"That must be it! They told the Concordians we were coming to help them, so when we didn't arrive a search party was sent out. Thank the stars. I was worried we weren't going to make it. Zapata can get medical help now too."

There were five figures on the beach, though behind the beams from the flashlights they carried they were little more than black shadows.

Wilder approached the nearest one. "Boy are we glad to see you. I'm—"

"There's another one!" the man yelled to his companions. He rushed at her and knocked her to the ground. In one swift movement he threw her on her front, put a knee on her back, and jerked her hands behind her.

Miki stared in horror.

Wilder screamed and fought, but her protests were muffled by the sand.

Miki was frozen. She wanted to help Wilder but the man was big and strong. She would never defeat him. And she couldn't shoot at him without risking hitting Wilder. Shock and bewilderment also made her hesitate. What was going on? Why were these Concordians capturing her companions? One thing was clear: she had to get away. If she didn't, they would catch her. Wilder's captor hadn't noticed her yet but he might any minute.

Slowly, she began to back up. She hit a spiny shrub and fell into it, gasping as the spines stuck in her skin.

The man looked up. "One more! Get over here, guys. Where are you?!"

Miki tried to get up but the more she moved the more she impaled herself on the spiky bush. She whimpered. Two of the strangers ran up and hauled her from her predicament. She shrieked as the spines tore at her. There was no sympathy from the men. As soon as they'd freed her they roughly bound her wrists and gagged her.

Where was Wilder? What had happened to Niall and Maddox?

One of the men pushed her toward the waves. Dread made her legs weak. Were they going to drown her? She stumbled, her knees slapping into the hard sand at the water's edge. Another man dragged her to her feet, and then shoved his shoulder into her stomach. He lifted her up and she dangled, helpless, her legs hanging down his front and her face lying against his back as he waded into the waves.

Water surged, closing over her head. She shut her mouth but the brine exploded up her nose and she coughed and squirmed. The water was gone. The man had grabbed her middle, pulled her up, and then threw her down. She tensed, expecting to fall into the ocean, but her back met something solid. He'd thrown her into a boat.

As the vessel rocked, she twisted her head to try to see what had happened to her companions. Three more bodies were piled on the bottom of the boat.

Someone shouted a command. An engine started up. The boat swerved, rose over a wave, and sped away from the shore.

Eighteen

"We're not spies!" Wilder yelled. "I've never met such a bunch of morons in my entire life! We've given you a million reasons why we can't possibly be working for the Scythians. Now let us go so we can help you fight them."

"Reasons?" asked the man. "You mean your cover story? Pathetic. Couldn't you come up with something better?"

He was swarthy—black-haired like all Concordians, but his skin was darker than usual. He must have spent time in the Suddene sun. He was stocky and broad-shouldered, mid-thirties. None of the men who had captured them had given their names, but he seemed to be their leader.

When she didn't answer, he got up and left.

Wilder didn't know what else to say to convince him she was telling the truth. Niall was concussed from the blow he'd sustained when the Concordians subdued him, Maddox seemed speechless with rage at their new predicament, and Miki was clearly simply terrified. They weren't going to be any help, yet if Wilder didn't turn the situation around they could all be in a lot of danger. She didn't know what the Concordians did to people who sided with the enemy, but she knew it wouldn't be good.

If explaining their background and the reason they'd been in the desert wasn't going to work, she would have to think up a different tactic.

They'd brought them to Chimera. The excavation site for Concordia's fifth military silo had changed a lot from how she remembered it. When she'd come here after leaving the Immani ship, the cavernous space had been bare. Encampments of people sheltering from the biocide had dotted the ground but otherwise the area had merely been a hollowed-out chamber, cool and dimly lit by temporary lighting.

Now it was a village. Lines of low buildings formed streets, and streetlamps illuminated them. Sounds of bustling activity came from all around and the scent of humans struggling to stay clean filled the air. If it weren't for the dark roof arching high overhead, it might have been Sidhe all over again—Concordians driven underground once more by their age-old enemy.

Wilder wasn't sure what she'd expected when she'd suggested going to Chimera but it hadn't been this. She'd anticipated something more basic but, obviously, other minds had come up with her idea a long time ago. What better place to hide from the Scythians than on a continent where little grew and in a place beneath the ground, where aerial creatures couldn't venture? A number of Concordians must have fled here soon after the aliens arrived and they'd been here ever since, gradually improving their habitation, perhaps adding to their numbers with new people from Lyonesse over time.

Niall lifted his head and groaned.

She shuffled over to him on her butt. It was the most movement she could manage. Their captors had bound their ankles in addition to their wrists after dumping them at the dead end of a street. One of the four guards, standing with their backs to them, looked over his shoulder but then ignored her.

"How are you feeling?" Wilder asked. "Try not to move. It'll just make it worse."

Niall squinted up at her. "Wilder?"

"Yes, it's me."

He groaned again before murmuring, "Did you find Zapata?"

"No." Her heart heavy, she added, "He's still out there. When I've convinced these idiots we are who we say we are, I'll ask them to help us search for him. Unless he's done something stupid he should still be alive and not very far from the camp."

In a way it was fortunate that the pilot had escaped the Concordians' notice. The treatment her party had received had been rough and he was in no condition to endure it. Yet in another way things might have gone much better for all of them if Zapata had been captured too. His injury would have supported her story that their aircraft had crashed in the desert. Maddox only had bruising and a lot of complaints about the pain she was in, which their captors didn't seem to believe.

"What's going on?" Niall asked. "Why are they doing this?"

"They think we're spies, in cahoots with the Scythians. They say because we didn't have a boat that means we were dropped off, and if we were part of the rebel network we wouldn't be wandering the desert, we would know their location. We also wouldn't be armed. I guess there must be collaborators on Lyonesse."

He grimaced, turned to one side, and slowly pushed himself upright with his bound hands.

"Maybe you should stay lying down," Wilder said.

He didn't reply until he was sitting. "I'm okay." He looked around him. "This is Chimera?"

She nodded. "It's changed, but this is it. No mistake."

"So we made it in the end."

The mild joke brought a smile to her lips. "Not exactly how I imagined."

"I heard their boat while I was looking for Zapata." He squeezed his eyes shut as a wave of pain seemed to hit before continuing, "I didn't recognize the noise. Thought it must be a Scythian engine—a new kind of aircraft—so I ran."

"That must have looked suspicious."

"Uh huh." He grimaced again. "I think I will lie down."

The swarthy man returned. Jabbing a finger at her he said to the guards, "Bring the mouthy one."

Mouthy one?

A man cut the bindings around her ankles, grabbed her under her armpits, and yanked her to her feet. He gripped her biceps and forced her along the street in his commander's wake, taking her to a nearby habitation. She was led into a room and pushed onto a chair before her ankles were tied again.

The swarthy man was already waiting, sitting opposite her. He leaned forward and spread his knees, resting his elbows on them and clasping his hands. His gaze was keen and direct. "I'm going to be straight with you. You might have heard rumors about what we do with traitors. Maybe you've seen a body or two wash up on Lyonesse. Everything you've heard is probably true. When you die it'll be slow, messy, and agonizing, and to be honest my stomach turns whenever we do it, but people like you don't deserve any better and we need to set an example."

"I don't know who you think—"

He raised a hand. "Let me finish. I'm going to offer you a bargain. Give us useful information about the Scythians, and I promise I'll make it quick. Not only that, we'll let the girl live. Why you would bring someone so young along with you is beyond me, but then I never understood you guys anyway. We will keep her prisoner but she won't face execution. You have my word."

Wilder opened her mouth to speak but he raised a finger to silence her again. "Naturally, *I* will be the judge of whether the information you give about the Scythians is useful. We already know a lot. More than you think, I imagine. I'll give you five minutes to think about it." He rose to his feet.

"Please," Wilder pleaded, "listen to me. Everything I told you before is true. We're from the *Sirocco.* We've returned from our voyage to Earth and we want to help you fight the Scythians."

He sighed. "Not this again. You're wasting your own time with this nonsense. Five minutes. That's it." He moved toward the door. The guard opened it.

"Isn't there anything I can tell you that will convince you? There has to be something. My name is Wilder. I built the ship along with Niall. He's the man with us. *Please, wait!*"

He was gone.

NINETEEN

Ever since the moment she'd been tossed into the boat, Miki had been operating in a fog. She'd barely registered being lifted out of the vessel and forced into the back of a vehicle, and nor could she recall much of the journey to this new place, though she remembered the sensation of traveling downward along a long tunnel. The voices of the people around her seemed muffled or as if she was hearing them from a great distance. Physical contact felt as though she was being touched through a thick blanket.

Her companions and she were in trouble. She knew that much. But she wasn't sure why, or why their captors hated them. For hate them they did. Of all the impressions she had of what was going on, she felt the hatred of the Concordians. It didn't make any sense. *She* was Concordian and so were Wilder, Niall, and Maddox. They were here to help their fellow colonists.

Why had everything gone so badly wrong?

And now Wilder had been taken away for some reason. Niall had passed out, and Maddox appeared to be suffering a silent rage.

At least things were becoming clearer now. The fog seemed to be dissipating. She shifted her position. Blinking, she took in her surroundings as if seeing them for the first time. She was sitting on smooth, bare, dusty rock. It had been carved out by machinery. Narrow grooves covered the surface but they weren't sharp. They'd been softened by time and the passage of feet. This place had been created a long time ago.

The blank face of a building sat behind them, and on each side ran rows of more buildings, though these had windows and doors. Occasionally, people would wander down the street to peer at the prisoners or a head would poke out of a window to stare.

Why were she and the others on public show? Why didn't these people lock their prisoners away?

She became aware she was dreadfully thirsty. "Excuse me," she said timidly. "Could I have some water?"

The three guards looked uneasily over their shoulders and exchanged glances with each other. None replied.

She decided not to push it, though her throat was parched and her tongue thick in her mouth. Then one of the guards muttered something to another and walked away. A few moments later he returned with a cup of water and squatted down to give it to her.

Maddox announced, "I'll have that! I need it more than her. I'm injured. She's fine."

"We all need water," Miki explained to him. She was angry with Maddox, but it was true. "We were in the desert for two days. Niall especially needs it. Could we please have some more?"

The guard frowned, but he left again and returned with two more full cups. "Thank you," she called to the guard who had helped them, but he ignored her.

"I don't know why you're being so polite," Maddox snapped. "These assholes kidnapped us and they're treating us like shit. Ungrateful idiots! To think we wanted to help them out. We should have cut our losses and returned to Earth, or found somewhere else to live."

"It's just a misunderstanding. When Wilder explains why we're here I'm sure everything will work out fine."

"Huh! You sound like your dad. He was a naive fool too."

"Don't speak about my father like that! He was a good man." Tears of rage choked her. She wanted to slap the smug look off Maddox's face. "At least he didn't screw every woman on the ship." The rude language sounded strange as it left her lips but she meant every word. And Maddox had to know exactly who she was talking about. Maddox had adored Aubriot but the feeling hadn't been reciprocated. Aubriot had loved Cherry and everyone knew it.

"You little bitch!" Maddox hissed. "If I wasn't in agony from my ribs I'd teach you a lesson about talking back to adults that you would never forget."

One of the guards barked, "Quiet back there!"

Maddox glared.

"Cut it out," Niall muttered.

Wilder appeared in the doorway of a nearby house, her arm held tightly by a guard. He guided her over to them. Her expression was downcast. Her talk with the Concordians hadn't gone well.

"They aren't going to let us go?" Miki asked.

Wilder shook her head. She seemed very upset.

"What's wrong? What's going to happen now? Did they tell you?"

"They...they..." Wilder gulped air and looked at Niall, who remained prone though his eyes were open.

"What's up?" he murmured.

"I-I couldn't convince them. They won't listen to me, won't even entertain the possibility we're from the *Sirocco*."

Miki asked, "Did you tell them about the crash site? If they found that they might believe us."

"I tried to explain about it before, but they only said of course Scythian spies arrived in a Scythian aircraft. This time around I wasn't even given a chance to talk. They just gave me an ultimatum."

"What was it?"

Wilder swallowed and her gaze traveled across her companions. She seemed unable to speak.

"Let me guess," Maddox said sarcastically. "They aren't inviting us to live with them happily ever after."

"They're gonna *kill* us?" Niall asked, turning onto his back.

Miki's heart seemed to stop. "What?!"

"They think we're collaborators, traitors," said Wilder. "To them, we're even worse than the Scythians because we've betrayed our own kind. But, Miki, they said they would spare you due to your age."

The fog that had enveloped her before returned, enclosing her in a thick, gray shroud. What Wilder had said was impossible. It couldn't be true. Her companions were going to be executed? And Nina was probably dead too, as well as everyone else aboard the *Sirocco*. The Concordians were going to kill the only people she had left, her only friends. They were going to die.

Someone was screaming.

It was her.

———

"Someone shut that girl up!" the Concordian leader yelled.

Miki was hysterical but what did he expect?

Wilder almost regretted revealing the truth to her, but it didn't really matter. She would know sooner or later that they'd been killed. She would react like this after their deaths too. Wilder only hoped she wouldn't see or discover *how* they'd died. The leader had threatened a torturous, drawn-out process. Perhaps he hoped to extract information about the Scythians while they were at the height of their agony. A tremor passed through her. The prospect felt unreal. The reversal of her expectations felt bizarre. This wasn't how she'd imagined her first encounter with the new Concordians would play out. Never, in all her imaginings of meeting the descendants of the people she'd left behind, had she anticipated this.

Miki screamed, writhed, and kicked, and Wilder felt helpless. Nothing she could say or do would calm the girl down or make her feel better. And she couldn't think of anything to tell the Concordians that would persuade them she was speaking the truth. When they listened they had an explanation for everything, and their explanations bolstered their suspicions. Now they'd stopped listening.

Grim-faced men approached.

They were going to do it so soon?

She was hauled to her feet and force-marched down the street. Where were Niall and Maddox? Poor Niall. He could barely walk. Someone else was screaming. Maddox.

The buildings passed on each side at a breathless pace. Wilder wrenched her head around. They were bringing Miki too?! "Leave her behind! Don't let her see. Please don't let her see!" She fought and kicked, lifting herself off the ground as the men's grips on her arms tightened painfully.

People emerged and clustered at the street edges, staring, jeering, cursing.

"This is a mistake!" Wilder yelled. "It's a stupid mistake! We're here to help you."

Where was the leader? He seemed to have disappeared. Wasn't he going to witness the result of his decision? He'd said it turned his stomach. What a miserable coward.

They'd brought them to the edge of the cavern, near the tunnel leading to the surface. It had been her first sight of Chimera just a few hours ago, when she'd believed the confusion could be ironed out. The lighting was dimmer here. Rocky walls towered into darkness. It was here she'd met Kes, Cherry, and Aubriot again after her long separation from the surface, living aboard the *Opportunity* with Quinn. The past seemed surreal, the future an empty blank, formless, meaningless.

She sagged, hope leaving her. She really was about to die.

What would the torture entail? How would they hurt her?

The only thing greater than her fear of the pain that lay ahead was her horror that Miki would see it. The poor girl had suffered enough. She would never get over what was about to take place in her presence.

The hands gripping Wilder's biceps thrust her downward so her knees struck the rock floor. She sucked air before exclaiming, "Please take the girl away! *Please take her away.*"

"You have one last chance."

She looked up. The leader had reappeared.

"Confess you're in league with the Scythians. Tell us all you know about them."

"We're not spies! I can't tell you what I don't know!"

He looked sorrowful. "I hate that you make me do this, but you've sided with our oppressors. You don't deserve any better. Don't worry. We will remove the girl before your execution." Miki's screams had ceased. She was slumped on the ground, slack-jawed as she regarded her surroundings. "And we won't torture you. That was only a threat to make you speak. The tales you've heard about what we do to prisoners aren't true. They're lies generated by the Scythians." He frowned down at her. "Does that change your mind? Will you tell us about them now?"

"You've got this all wrong," Wilder wept. "We're from the *Sirocco*. If you would just listen..."

He heaved a sigh. "Even at the point of death you remain loyal to humanity's enemy. You're disgusting." Looking at one of the guards, he gave a nod and stepped back.

The guard pulled a gun from a holster.

Wilder's insides lurched.

"Wait," the leader said. "Take the girl away."

"Noooo!" screamed Miki. "It was here! It was here! I remember now." She rocked backward and forward, mumbling and sobbing.

Her words triggered a wave of bewilderment among their captors.

"It was here!" Miki cried. "It was here Mommy died!"

Wilder gasped. "Oh, stars, she's right. Her mother died here during the biocide attack. I'd forgotten." *Poor Miki.* And she'd brought the girl here. What a fool she'd been.

"More bullshit," said the leader, but his tone was uncertain.

"No," Wilder protested. "It isn't bullshit. It's the truth. You think she's faking? Look at her."

Miki was having some kind of mental breakdown. Her hair hung over her face as she rocked and wept.

Her hair.

"Look at her hair," Wilder commanded. "Do it." She felt like shit making a spectacle of the girl while she was in the throes of grief and shock, but she had to save their lives. "Look at the red in her hair. She's Kes's daughter. Kes, who left on the *Sirocco*. You must have heard of him and Aubriot, the last of the Earth-born. Kes was known for his red hair. You *must* know about it." Her heart in her mouth, she turned her pleading gaze from the leader to each guard in turn, praying that at least one of them knew that tidbit of information about the Concordians who had departed the planet decades ago.

"Bring her into the light," the leader said.

Wilder tensed.

A sobbing Miki was gently lifted to her feet and guided into a pool of light spilling from a nearby lamp. The leader peered at the crown of her lowered head and softly touched her hair, parting the strands.

His shoulders dropped. He murmured a command to the men holding Miki and they led her away. To Wilder he said, "I will listen to your story."

TWENTY

Wilder couldn't stop the tremor in her hands. She'd come within a whisker of death. They all had. She'd known it was a possibility when she'd suggested the mission, but to be confronted with the reality, to have a gun literally pointed at her head, was a different thing entirely.

She wrapped her hands tighter around the mug of a warm beverage the leader had given her before properly listening to what she had to say.

They'd been taken to the lounge of a building near the center of the habitation. This place was far more comfortable than the bare room where the leader had announced his ultimatum, yet it was still sparse and the furniture was worn and shabby. Pictures adorned the walls, simple 2D artists' sketches, some colored with pencils. She recognized a view from a cliff at Oceanside and a town that could be Annwn, the capital of Lyonesse. The images brought a flood of associations into her mind, memories of her life growing up on Concordia. So much had happened since then. The memories felt dreamlike, unreal. Yet here she was, back on her home planet.

"I offer you my most sincere and deepest apologies," said the leader.

"Oh, thanks," said Maddox. "That makes everything okay then."

Niall and Miki had been taken to receive medical treatment, Niall for his concussion and Miki for her psychological state. Wilder would have to share the introduction to the new Concordians with Maddox only. The prospect was not inviting.

Their host winced. "You must understand, it's vital that our presence here remains a secret. We cannot afford to—"

"How long has it been since the *Sirocco* left?" Wilder interjected, dragging her gaze from the pictures.

"According to our records, sixty-three years."

Sixty-three years? Considering the amount of time the ship had spent in space after the jump drive failed, plus the time dilation effects, it added up. Yet a momentary sense of disorientation hit. Wilder was thrown back to the moment she'd emerged from the Fila shuttlecraft after her trip to the Galactic Assembly, to find that Concordia had moved on five decades, the colonization had been a success, the colony had grown and developed, and nothing of her old life remained.

Maddox muttered darkly, "Everyone we left behind must be dead."

"And when did the Scythians arrive?" asked Wilder.

"Fifty-five years ago."

"Only eight years later?"

If the jump drive had worked correctly the first time, the *Sirocco*'s crew would have returned within months and begun the re-seeding of the planet. They would have been caught up in the invasion. Could their presence have affected the outcome? It was doubtful.

"The colony was on the brink of disaster," said the leader. "We didn't stand a chance." He stood up and held out his hand. "I'm Meric."

Wilder shook with him. Maddox glared at his hand and then up into his face. Resignedly, he returned to his seat. "The colony gave up hope of your ship returning a long time ago. It was generally accepted that something disastrous had happened—the jump drive exploding, a Scythian attack—or that you'd simply decided to abandon the mission and remain on Earth."

"We would never have done that," Wilder protested. "We're Concordians. This is our home."

He shrugged. "Nevertheless, you didn't return and the colony moved on, or rather, struggled on. The last thing I expected to find out in the Suddene desert was crew from the fabled *Sirocco*. We regularly sweep the coastal areas to find escapees from Lyonesse. Occasionally we discover spies sent by the Scythians. We generally know who they are from their physical state and the equipment they carry. As you can imagine, humans are not allowed to carry weapons anywhere in Concordia. The fact that you were armed was a dead giveaway. That, and the fact you had no mode of transportation."

Wilder gasped and leapt to her feet. "Zapata! Our pilot. I'd forgotten about him. He's injured. We have to search for him."

"Please, sit down," said Meric. "Tell me more."

"Our pilot's leg was broken when our aircraft crashed. He walked with us to the coast but then he left our campsite when we were asleep. We think he didn't want to slow us down anymore."

Meric grimaced. "The desert is a harsh environment, and it's been hours since we picked you up. If this man was already injured..."

"I have to go and look for him," Wilder insisted. "You have to take me back to the beach where you found us."

"That's a bad idea. You won't last long out there in the heat. You aren't used to it, and how would you find your friend? I will send out a search team, men and women experienced at tracking in the wilderness. They will find him, but if I were you I wouldn't hold out hope for them finding him alive. Give me a minute." He rose and left the room.

Wilder sank into her seat. How could she have forgotten about Zapata?

———

While searchers went out looking for the lost pilot, Wilder asked Meric to bring her up to speed on what had been happening on Concordia while she'd been gone and the current situation. Maddox demanded to be taken somewhere she could lie down.

"I'm sorry," Meric said. "I should have offered you a place to rest earlier. You need time to recover from your ordeal."

"I'm *in pain*," she replied irritably. "Not that anyone cares."

Wilder explained, "We think Maddox might have broken some ribs in the crash."

Meric's eyebrows lifted. "In that case, I double my apology. You should be checked out. I'll find someone to take you to the medical center. We only have basic equipment and medications but perhaps they can do something for you."

After Maddox had left, Meric poured Wilder a top-up of her drink. "Where to begin? I hadn't been born when the *Sirocco* left. It's history to me, and difficult to believe you're *the* Wilder, the chief engineer, yet you're younger than me."

"That's time dilation for you. It throws everything out of whack. But I was also very young when we designed and built the ship, not much older than Miki."

"And does my memory serve me correctly when it tells me you were one of the first Concordians? You were born on the *Nova Fortuna*?"

"I don't know if you would describe it as *born* exactly. I was squeezed from a gestational sac, the same as the rest of the Gens."

And, as Cherry had said, she was the last of them, on Concordia at least.

"Huh!" He shook his head in wonder. "What a day I'm having. I receive a message that the Sweep Team picked up some spies and find myself faced with the distasteful task of executing them, only to end up sitting opposite a walking relic of the past."

Wilder's disturbed reaction to his description of her must have shown for he added, "No offense."

"You said the colony struggled on for eight years after we left. What happened?" She wasn't sure she wanted to know. She still harbored a lot of guilt over the malfunctioning of the jump drive. But her curiosity overcame her hesitancy.

"They were hard times by all accounts. I'm glad I didn't live through them. There were plagues of biting insects and insects that ate the crops—crops that were already meager and poor quality. A large fraction of the population died of simple starvation. Others died of malnutrition caused by an extremely limited diet. Only certain plants would grow, you see, and that's all there was to eat. Very few children were born, either because women couldn't carry babies to full term or they chose not to become pregnant, not wanting to subject their offspring to a hopeless, short life. Some colonists gave up and walked into the sea or hanged themselves. It must have been terrible."

Wilder wondered at what point the Concordians had given up hope the *Sirocco* would return. After six months? A year? Two years? She hung her head.

"What happened when the Scythians arrived?" she asked quietly.

"First, they attacked Oceanside and after that Annwn, blasting both from space. Then the bombardments suddenly ceased. No one could understand why the Scythians had spared us from complete destruction. It would have been easy for them to send down their spiders to kill anyone still alive, but they didn't. Things were quiet, and, once more, we began to rebuild. Crops were sown, roads and bridges were repaired, and new houses were constructed from the remains of the ones that had been destroyed."

He rose to his feet and walked to the window, which looked out on the street, where the people of Chimera walked past. "By that time, there were signs the ecology was beginning to recover. The numbers of insects in the annual plagues were not quite so vast, crop plants grew more strongly, and the vegetation in the landscape had become more varied. Prior to that, single species would dominate huge tracts of land. The sluglimpets returned."

"Ugh, really?"

He turned to her and smiled sadly. "Yes, of all the creatures to survive the biocide and regenerate, it had to be them." Returning his gaze to the street, he continued, "A few of the most optimistic Concordians began to hope the colony had reversed its decline and might regrow. Their comments and articles are in the archives. But it was a fool's hope. No rational person could have believed the Scythians were finished with us. Most colonists were waiting for them to return and sure enough, three and a half years after the bombardment they were back. Their builder craft landed in droves."

"Builder craft?" Wilder asked, though as the question left her lips she knew exactly what he meant.

"Specialized transports that construct their domes. They descended all over Lyonesse. More came each night. People would wake up to a Scythian ship in a neighboring field or sitting on the main road into town. At first, they only constructed the domes. Some people weren't even sure it was the Scythians doing it because we only saw their robots. But when they started the abductions—"

"The same as on Earth."

"What?"

"The same thing happened on Earth. The Scythians followed the same colonization process. Miki was abducted and lived inside a dome for a short while."

"Earth has been taken over by Scythians?!" Meric returned to his seat. "This is sad news. Why didn't you tell me earlier?"

"You didn't believe we'd been to Earth earlier, remember?"

He rubbed his chin. "So there's no escape." He appeared to be talking to himself.

"If you were thinking we could transport Concordia's population to Earth, it would have been difficult even if Earth was safe. The *Sirocco* isn't as big as you seem to think. I don't know how many people we're talking about, but—"

"No escape! Damn." He looked her in the eyes. "I confess that as soon as I accepted you'd been telling me the truth, I'd hoped perhaps you could help out the people here in Chimera. Concordians living on Lyonesse are a lost cause, I'm afraid."

"What are conditions like there? The Scythian colonization of Earth has only just begun. I don't know what things will look like decades from now if the Earthers don't manage to fight them off."

"Conditions? I suppose it depends what you mean. In some ways they're much better than pre-colonization. There's no starvation—as far as I'm personally aware. It's been years since I was there, and the information we receive is sparse and unreliable. But generally the human population seems healthier than it was when we were alone. The Scythians understand how to replenish the depleted ecosystem and they have plants that grow well and that humans can also eat. But people are basically slaves. They only exist to serve the Scythians and if they fail in the task or stand up to them, or if a Scythian is having a bad day..." He drew a finger across his throat.

"The aliens keep adult men and women in separate living quarters and match them for breeding pairs, according to some criteria we don't fully understand. Babies are removed from mothers at birth and given to wet nurses and carers to bring up. Often, the infants are moved to another region, maybe to reduce the ability of their parents to find them. I never knew my mother or father. I have no idea who they are."

"Wow," said Wilder. "Me neither. That's how things were on the *Nova*."

"Really? I didn't know. So much information about the past has been lost, and after the Scythians arrived they confiscated all that remained. What we know now has been passed down orally. How strange that the Scythians and the Project's Founders treated the colonists the same way."

"Well, it wasn't exactly the same. I never had a mother, only an egg donor." Yet the similarity in the two processes *was* odd. The Founders' rationale had been they didn't want strong familial bonds to develop that might jeopardize the mission while the *Nova* was en route. Whereas the Scythians didn't want familial bonds to develop... The Founders had been as controlling as the aliens, though supposedly to fulfill a nobler cause. "What else is happening there?"

"Movement is extremely restricted and it's becoming more so. In the early days, when people began to escape to Chimera, it was hard but not impossible to break out and flee across the ocean. Nowadays it's virtually impossible. The Scythians figured out most of the ways their slaves were escaping. We haven't seen anyone except spies for years."

"So they know that humans are living here on Suddene?"

"They suspect it, but I doubt anyone has made it back to Lyonesse to confirm their suspicions."

"But they must know about Chimera. There's an ancient Scythian city here, right? Where they sited their planetary defense system when they left. They sent the compromised Guardian, Faina, to reactivate it." Cherry had told her Aubriot had destroyed the system after Faina led him to it.

"I'm not sure they do know about Chimera. The site was top secret even before the Scythians returned, right? And no domes have ever appeared on Suddene. The Scythians seemed to take the absence of human activity here as a sign the continent had been abandoned as the colony began to fail. They were right. No one lived here after the biocide attack. Port City and Chimera were abandoned. As far as we can tell, all the Scythians know is that the android managed to restart the planetary defense but then it ceased operation once more. Now, they have no reason to come here. Even if they did, they cannot access the control base themselves. It's buried beneath meters of sand. And they cannot trust humans to do it for them. It's far too dangerous."

They continued to discuss the situation on Concordia and what had happened on Earth. Meric was happy to hear about the Ark, replete with seeding material to re-start Concordia's biomes. But Wilder was dispirited. It seemed the efforts of the crew of the *Sirocco* had been useless. Humans on both planets faced an impossible task.

Several hours later, she was about to ask Meric where Chimera got its food and other resources when there was a knock at the door.

He opened it, and a man gave him a message she didn't catch. He thanked the man and closed the door. "Your pilot has been found. They're bringing him back. He's alive but in bad shape, dehydrated and suffering heatstroke. It's uncertain whether he'll live."

TWENTY-ONE

The sick bay was tiny. Just four beds squeezed into a small room. Niall was sleeping off his concussion in one and the other two were empty. Miki guessed space was at a premium in Chimera.

Chimera.

The place Mom died.

How could she not have known? Perhaps Dad hadn't mentioned the name. He'd told her it happened soon after Nina was born, that, due to the biocide attack, Mom had been forced to go somewhere remote, with minimal medical care. All the most vulnerable colonists had been flown to Suddene, where the progress of the biocide was slowest.

She'd thought she didn't remember Mom dying. She had fleeting, nebulous memories of times before that. She recalled Mom having a tea party with her and her dolls, and Mom waking her in the middle of the night to take her to another place. Dad wasn't there but Mom wouldn't explain why. She recalled flashes of brilliant light and sounds of thunder, and her Mom holding her tightly in the cellar of a strange house. That was her last memory. After that, Mom was gone, and it was just her, Dad, and baby Nina.

But the sight of the bare cavern walls, rising to darkness overhead, had brought it all back. Suddenly, she'd been a little girl again, waiting in a tent with a strange woman and her child while her mommy wailed and groaned next door. Miki had known it was only baby Nina coming but she'd been scared nonetheless. Then the noises had stopped. The woman she was with went out and when she returned she'd seemed worried. Her voice had been too bright and cheerful, telling Miki she should sleep and tomorrow she would see her baby sister.

Miki had only wanted to see her Mommy, but she'd never seen her again. Someone had told her Mommy had gone far away. It wasn't until later Dad had explained she'd died.

It had happened here. Right here.

And she was back here again. Dad was dead too, and she didn't know if Nina was alive.

The doctor had given her something that made her feel groggy but the effects were wearing off. She was beginning to think straight again. She wished the new memory would go away yet it continued to play over and over again in her mind, along with the recollection of the moment Wilder had announced she and the others were going to be executed.

Things had nearly gone badly wrong. Things *had* gone wrong, ever since they'd left the *Sirocco*.

She sat up. She felt strangely empty and light, as if all her emotions had been drained out.

Where was Wilder? Why hadn't she come in to see her?

The door opened and a woman backed in, guiding a bed on wheels. A man was pushing the other end and another man lay upon it, who she recognized.

"You found Zapata?!"

"Not us," the woman replied. "We just fixed him up."

Miki leapt from her bed and crossed the room in hurried steps.

"Whoa," said the woman. "Back to bed, young lady. The doc didn't give you permission to get up."

A sheet covered the pilot to his chin. His face was thin and drawn, and his skin red from sunburn. He was deeply asleep, his mouth hanging open.

"Is he going to be okay?"

"We think so. He needs to rest, and he can't do that with you gawking at him. I thought I told you to go back to bed?"

Miki didn't think the pilot was in any state to notice her. The medic was only saying that to make her obey. But she did what she was told anyway and watched as they lifted Zapata onto a bed and covered him up before leaving.

Now there were two sleeping patients, and she had nothing to do. Did they really expect her to stay here indefinitely?

She lay on her back and stared at the ceiling. The empty feeling persisted. She felt like a sodden rag that had been thoroughly wrung out and hung up to dry.

Staying here any longer was impossible. She had to get out. She had to see things and hear things or she would go mad. Her ship's clothes sat in a little pile on the table next to her bed. She hastily changed out of the hospital paja-mas. Her clothes seemed to have been washed. The grittiness of the invading desert sand was gone. The same couldn't be said for her boots. She turned them upside down and shook and hit them with the heel of her hand to shake free the remaining grains.

Taking care not to rattle the door knob, she opened the door and peeked out.

An empty corridor stretched from left to right. Sounds of voices and movement came from the left. She tiptoed along the right-side passageway until she reached the end. An open door led to the street. She had a momentary sense of guilt about leaving without permission, but she dismissed it.

Mom was dead. Dad was dead. Nina was probably dead too. The *Sirocco* was most likely lost. Earth had been invaded and so had Concordia. The future of humanity was grim.

What did anything really matter anymore?

She stepped outside.

Now she wasn't in a state of confusion and fear, she could take in her surroundings better. The last time she'd been in Chimera the only dwelling places had been tents. In the center of the cavern bright lamps had stood, the only source of light. The night Mommy died the lamps had been turned down low while people slept.

Was it nighttime or daytime outside? Lamps on poles stood every fifteen meters or so along the street joined by thick wires at their bases. The single-story houses seemed flimsy. Here and there a door or window was crooked or spaces gaped at their sides.

A man walked past, eyeing her curiously.

If she wasn't careful, someone would inquire at the medical center if she was supposed to be out and about. She walked briskly to the end of the street. Another crossed it, so she walked to the end of that one. More people passed. All of them stared. Everyone must know everyone else in Chimera.

A smell told her she was nearing latrines so she altered direction. She wasn't sure where she was going, only that she had to move. She had to act, to do something, to *feel* something. At a street corner she halted and looked up. Her gaze met only darkness. It seemed to encroach, to push down. Only the feeble light of the streetlamps kept it back.

She wanted to see daylight.

After growing up on the *Sirocco*, going planetside on Earth had been weird at first, but she'd grown to enjoy it. The apparently limitless space and open sky brought her joy. She longed to see it again.

Which way was the exit? In the maze of little streets it was impossible to tell. Instead, she looked for a wall and headed for it. When she reached the vertical surface she turned and followed it. The lines of houses ended abruptly at the edge of the cavern. There was no fence or other barrier to separate them.

It was darker here. She touched the wall as she walked alongside it. The rough rock had been worn smoother at shoulder height. No one seemed to come near the cavern boundaries, and she walked unnoticed by passersby.

Where was the exit? Would she have to circumnavigate the entire space?

The houses receded, leaving an open area. This was the place her companions and she had been brought, where she'd had her realization, the sudden familiarity smacking her in the face. It had to have been around here Mom's tent had been pitched, though she had no tangible memory of the site.

A wave of distress washed over her.

Yes, it must have been here.

A little farther on a hole yawned in the cavern wall. It had to be the exit, the opening of the tunnel that led to the surface. No one seemed to be about. She walked over, sauntering as if she was only here by accident. She guessed that leaving Chimera wasn't straightforward.

But no guards stood in the gap. The thick doors that barricaded it were open too. She slipped into the tunnel.

Walking to the top seemed to take forever. She trekked it in almost total darkness, groping along the wall for guidance. The air grew warmer and drier the higher she rose. Where the occasional light glowed overhead it revealed smooth tracks worn on the rough ground by the passage of vehicles. But then another light brightened her way—a light from up ahead.

She was nearly there, and it was daytime.

She hurried on.

"Stand back," a voice ordered. "Weapons at the ready. ETA thirty seconds."

The announcement brought her to a sudden halt.

Guards stood on each side of the tunnel and she'd nearly walked right into them. Bright, glaring sunshine had silhouetted the men and women, blending their figures with the general darkness, but at the command their shoulders had hunched and they lifted their rifles.

What was arriving in thirty seconds?

She edged closer.

A distant rumbling caught her attention. The people ahead of her collectively tensed, their postures tightening and feet adjusting their position.

Intrigue urged her on another few steps. She also longed for a glimpse of an open landscape, even though it would be dry and barren. Living underground made her feel like a worm in a hole, constantly fearing detection.

"Hey, who the hell are you?"

The commander had glanced back at the guards, perhaps checking their readiness, and spotted her.

She shrank into the shadows.

"Get out of here," the commander barked. "This is no place for a kid. Haven't you learned—" His head swiveled forward.

A dark shape blocked out the sun, and the tunnel resounded with the loud hum of an engine and the crackle of tires on concrete. A large truck was rolling in, nearly filling all available space with its bulk. Miki pressed her back to the wall. It rolled past her. A second truck passed, and then a third.

That seemed to be it.

The guards relaxed, and Miki judged it was a good time to slip away, but the commander yelled, "Who the hell *are* you?!"

She backed away as he bore down on her.

"Wait right th—"

"Scythians!"

The cry had come from the head of the tunnel. Guards were in the process of closing the doors, but they were half open. Through webbed sheeting, two shapes could be seen whirling in the upper atmosphere, their wide wings outspread.

"Shit! Seal the entrance." Cursing with worse words, the commander strode right past Miki as if forgetting her existence, and marched into the depths of the tunnel.

Twenty-Two

Meric's argument with the commander of Chimera's paramilitary had been building for half an hour. Wilder waited in an adjacent room with Miki as the two slogged it out. At first, their voices as they discussed Miki's transgression had barely penetrated the dividing door, but for the last few minutes the commander had been shouting, every sentence painfully clear.

"I don't give a shit who they are! They might have brought the Scythians right to our doorstep. And that idiot girl is a liability. She was a minute from wandering out into the open and giving us all away."

Meric's reply was soft, a murmured attempt at appeasement.

"Who cares whose daughter she is? You're seriously telling me you allowed Scythians spies to live because one of them has a bit of red in her hair? Are you insane?"

Again, the sound of Meric's response was audible but his words were not.

"They have no place here!" the commander yelled. "We don't know who they are or where they're from, and you're jeopardizing the safety of this community on a fanciful dream. The *Sirocco*'s crew died a long time ago and if they didn't they're whooping it up on Earth. You'll be telling me next the guy in bed in sick bay is Ethan and their supposed pilot is Aubriot. They're all dead, Meric. Dead and gone. The sooner you accept that and get rid of our unwelcome visitors the better. If you don't, you should reconsider your fitness as Leader."

The door slammed open, and Wilder and Miki jumped in unison.

Casting each a baleful glare, the commander thumped past them and out the exterior door.

Meric appeared, his brow furrowed and rubbing his hands. "I guess you must have heard a lot of that?"

"We got the gist," Wilder replied.

"I'm sorry. Commander Orson is hot-tempered and speaks his mind, but he isn't rash. He'll calm down eventually."

"Do we have to leave?" Miki asked. "I didn't realize I was doing anything wrong when I walked up the tunnel. I only wanted to go outside for a little bit. I wasn't thinking straight."

"You picked a bad time, unfortunately. Usually, there would be guards at the inner doors. Chimera is guarded day and night at both ends of the tunnel in case of Scythian attack. No one living here would want to go out even if it were permitted. But the moment you chose for your excursion happened to be the scheduled arrival of a supply shipment. We're at our most vulnerable when we open up to allow the trucks in, so all guards were deployed at the surface."

Wilder asked, "Isn't it incredibly risky for Chimera to be supplied in that way? The Scythians would see the vehicles from the air."

"The entire route from the port is camouflaged, and the trucks only travel by day. The Scythians seem to have poor sight in bright sunlight, and the heat from the desert seems to confuse them."

"I'm sorry for what I did," said Miki. "If it would make things better, I'll leave. I could go on one of the empty supply trucks to—"

"You're not going anywhere," Wilder interrupted. She turned to Meric. "Right?"

"Right," he replied, but his tone lacked conviction.

The commander had threatened that Meric should 'consider his fitness as Leader' if he didn't make them leave. If Meric was no longer head of Chimera, he wouldn't be able to protect them from people who didn't want them here.

They had to show they were who they said they were if they wanted to remain. They had to demonstrate their worth, but in reality Wilder wasn't sure they had any. What could they realistically do to expel the Scythians from Concordia? The second stage of their plan had been nebulous from the outset, and they'd even lost their only piece of equipment that might have helped them: the alien aircraft. Using that, they might have penetrated the heart of the Scythian presence, perhaps taken high-ranking officials hostage. But the craft was smashed to smithereens, and they were just as weak and powerless as every other Concordian.

"Tell me more about the set up in Chimera." Perhaps there was a way to leverage the 'freedom' of the Chimerites to strike back at the aliens. "The base is supplied from Lyonesse?"

"We receive shipments every two or three months, never on the same day or at the same time. People slaving for the Scythians on Lyonesse smuggle food and other supplies out to us, and the only remaining cargo ship carries them over the ocean via an ever-changing route. The ship is camouflaged too, but that part of the operation is the riskiest."

"It's kind of the Concordians over there to support you."

"They love the idea that a portion of the human population isn't controlled by their overlords. Occasionally, they smuggle people over too, people at risk of being killed as agitators. We take in whoever they send, though we are over capacity."

"You told me you hadn't seen anyone except spies for years."

He looked somewhat abashed. "You must understand, I wasn't about to tell you all Chimera's secrets at once."

"But the situation here can't continue forever. How long has Chimera been occupied?"

"This will be the fourteenth year since the first escapee arrived."

Wilder whistled. "Fourteen years! That's a helluva long time to wait before fighting back."

Meric replied defensively, "Concordians here and on Lyonesse are fighting back every day. The mere presence of Chimera would be an abomination in the minds of the Scythians if they knew it existed, and the slaves on Lyonesse resist control in hundreds of ways. People working in the hatcheries kill Scythian young—"

"I did that," said Miki.

"What?"

"I worked in a Scythian hatchery on Earth. I tended their babies, though I didn't know that was what they were at the time. It would be hard to kill them while they were worms. I cut a worm in half once, but both halves lived."

"Uhh..." Meric seemed to lose his train of thought. "I'm not sure how they do it, but that's what I've heard. Other slaves spoil the crops, which is a big self-sacrifice. Humans eat the food too, so everyone goes hungry."

Wilder asked, "Is it true that adult Scythians are vegetarian?"

"That's what has been observed. Once they're past the youngling stage, where they eat each other, they consume plant food only. There have been no reports of Scythians eating animals. Not that animals would be easy to find."

Except for the obvious ones.

"The two we killed in the desert looked different from the ones I saw on Earth," said Wilder. "Their visors were darkened and so were their bodies. We didn't stick around long enough to find out if the skin coloring was natural or applied, but both observations have me worried."

"How so?"

"I think it's an indication that they're trying out ways to survive here without human help."

"So they're going to free all the people they're keeping as slaves?" Miki asked.

"No," Wilder replied heavily. "I really doubt it."

"Oh..." Miki looked down.

"This is bad news," said Meric. "I thought it was odd when you said they approached you during daylight. These new adaptations mean their behavior makes more sense now." He asked Miki, "You escaped a hatchery? How did you manage that?"

"With the help of a lot of other prisoners. We dug our way out while most of them tackled the guards."

"That was very brave. I've heard of escape attempts but they're rarely successful. If people do manage to get away they're usually recaptured. There aren't many places to hide on Lyonesse. Then they're executed in front of their fellow slaves—as an example to the others, I presume."

"Meric." A woman had stuck her head in the exterior doorway. "The men in the clinic are awake and asking about their companions." She eyed Wilder and Miki.

"Maybe you should go and see them," Meric said, "while I approach Orson about you staying here a little longer. He might have cooled down a little. He's a reasonable man, only concerned about everyone's safety."

"Sure." Wilder got to her feet. "Come on, Miki. Let's go. Do you remember the way?"

Chimera wasn't so big it was easy to get lost in. Miki quickly figured out the direction in which the clinic lay. As they walked the narrow streets, they attracted the gazes of the Chimerites. Wilder had never been comfortable with scrutiny, and the hostility of the stares made her doubly uneasy. Attitudes toward them had changed since Miki's unfortunate escapade, though she was entirely innocent. But the people seemed to lack any compassion for the young girl. Perhaps they even doubted, as the commander did, that she was Kes's daughter.

Wilder put a protective arm around her. They needed an out, a way to disappear for a while, before their mere presence excited the suspicions and fears of their hosts to anger and violence. Yet traveling to Lyonesse on a returning supply truck seemed reckless, almost suicidal. The situation on the other continent had changed drastically since they'd left. It was now the heart of Scythian territory, and they didn't have a clue how to operate there undetected. How could they survive? What would they eat? Where could they live?

But perhaps there was somewhere else they could go...

"I didn't mean for all this to happen," said Miki. "I wish I'd never forced you to bring me on the mission. If I hadn't, I would be with Nina, wherever she is."

Wilder gave her a sideways hug. "You didn't force me or Captain Vessey to include you. What you said was true. You do know more about the Scythians than anyone else. You heard what Meric said: people don't usually escape their domes alive. You could know things that turn out to be vital to defeating them."

"I really don't think I do. I think it was only by luck that I escaped. The Scythian colony on Earth was new, while they've been living on Concordia for decades. Everything is tight and organized here."

"Don't over-estimate them. Chimera survived all this time, right?" Miki didn't answer, and in the intervening pause Wilder's idea took shape. "There's another place the Scythians haven't been for a very long time, somewhere we might learn more about them—old secrets they might have forgotten. What do you say to going into their ancient city with me?"

"An ancient city? Where is it?"

"Right here at Chimera, or nearby. I'm not sure exactly. Cherry went there during the biocide attack, and Aubriot went in with a team afterward."

"I don't know. I'll probably slow you down or do something stupid."

Wilder halted and grabbed Miki's shoulders, turning the girl to face her. "You're not slow or stupid. You were a hero out in the desert, finding our supplies, carrying a huge backpack for kilometers in the heat. And you're still a kid! Stars, no one could have done any better. I wouldn't pick anyone else to come with me. Do you hear?"

Miki nodded.

"Good. That's settled. We'll tell Niall and Zapata, and then we'll go."

TWENTY-THREE

Niall insisted on coming too.

"No way." Wilder was perched on the edge of his bed. She reached out to take his hand, and he pulled it under the covers. She heaved a sigh and they held each other's gazes.

Miki didn't know where Maddox was—maybe in another room?—but Zapata was asleep. He looked better than he had when he'd been brought in. His skin was peeling but it had filled out and his eyes were less sunken.

Wilder was right. Niall certainly wasn't in any condition to be coming with them into the Scythian city. He looked better too, but he remained somewhat pale and drawn, and the dressing over the spot where he'd been hit was raised in a bump.

From the reactions of the Chimerites when they learned of the proposed mission, it was a dangerous place to be. Miki also understood the city was very big and there was no water down there. They would have to carry a lot with them, though Meric had also loaned them an old device that supposedly condensed water from the atmosphere. He hadn't been confident that it still worked effectively or how long it would last. And they couldn't hang around to test it. Orson was agitating hard for everyone from the *Sirocco* to be kicked out, Meric had said.

The inhabitants might be persuaded to show a little sympathy for the people still receiving medical treatment, but that wouldn't extend to Wilder or her—especially her. Somehow, the story of her trip up the tunnel had transformed into an attempt to rush out into the open and signal to the Scythians flying above. It was ridiculous, of course, but such was the nature of gossip within a small population living in close quarters under constant threat of discovery, said Meric. Stories became magnified beyond the simple truth and individuals were targeted and scapegoated. The Chimerites needed someone to blame for their predicament and someone to 'sacrifice' to prevent things going wrong. It had sounded as though he spent most of his days keeping a lid on his people's fears.

"You aren't better," Wilder continued, "and you know it. It's going to be tough going in there. What happens if you have a relapse and can't go any farther? What are Miki and I supposed to do then? We can't carry you far. Do you expect us to leave you behind?"

"Then wait until I am better," said Niall. "Give it 48 hours. The doc will write me a clean bill of health by then."

"We don't have 48 hours." Wilder turned to Miki. "Could you wait outside?"

Miki walked to the end of the clinic's corridor and leaned on the outer wall, kicking her heels against it. Passersby threw her dark looks. She went back into the clinic. Sound traveled easily here. Though the door to the room with the beds was closed, she could hear a whispered argument. Wilder and Niall were going at it. She hoped they made it up before Wilder left. It would be sad if Niall's last memory of her was the exchange of harsh words.

The door opened and Wilder came out, rubbing her eyes with the heels of her hands.

So much for that.

"Are you ready?" she asked. Their equipment was packed and waiting at the opening that led to the Scythian city.

"I'm ready."

"Then let's go."

"Are we going to say goodbye to Maddox?"

"What do *you* think?"

———

They couldn't reach the city alone. The plain that surrounded it sat at the bottom of a drop that was too steep to walk down. They would have to be lowered to it, and then cross it to reach the city boundary.

"What's up there?" Miki asked, her neck craned as she tried to make out the edge of the upper expanse.

"A dome," replied Meric.

"Holy shit," said Wilder. "The biggest Scythian dome ever. They must have constructed it when oxygen levels rose so high the atmosphere became poisonous to them."

"That's where they got the idea for re-inhabiting Concordia and colonizing Earth," Miki said. "For them, it's old technology."

"You're right." Wilder gave her a smile. "Smart girl."

"Not really. I couldn't do half the things you do. I could never invent a-grav or—"

"There's more than one kind of smartness. Meric, can you lower us down now?"

"You got it." He walked to the cab of the excavating machine that had sat here next to the drop for who knew how long. The ropes from their harnesses had been wound around the machine's spiral-shaped point. Meric had managed to get the machine started but, considering its great age, Miki wasn't confident it would continue running. She had a vision of her and Wilder dangling in mid-air, halfway down the drop and out of reach of the side.

"Don't worry," said Wilder, appearing to perceive her uneasiness. "If this doesn't work we can get people from Chimera to lower us by hand and haul us up when we're done."

Or throw us into the abyss.

Wilder stepped off first. Her rope tightened. She beckoned to Miki. After some hesitation, she also took a step into darkness. Clinging onto Wilder, she felt her body sag into the restraints of her harness. *I really don't like this.*

There was a jerk, and the point of the excavator began to turn. Steadily, they dropped lower. The side of the cliff moved slowly past. The ground presumably approached, though there was no sign of it. Pitch blackness sat beneath their feet.

Wilder said something.

"Huh?" Miki piped, her voice barely making it out of her throat.

"Goggles."

"Oh. Yeah." She pulled the night vision goggles that had been sitting forgotten on her head over her eyes. Instantly, the ground appeared, ghostly green. It seemed a very long way away. She gave a squeak and clutched Wilder.

"Best not to look down."

They had begun to spin the same time their descent had started. All the while, the speed of their rotation had increased.

"Shit," Wilder muttered. She reached out to the side of the cliff but it was too far away.

The cliff appeared in Miki's view, and then the darkness—except now she had her goggles on it wasn't dark any longer. She had a glimpse of towering structures like angular mountain peaks, then they were gone, replaced by bare rock.

The city. It was surrounded by a high wall.

Rock.

Beyond the wall, the ground was strangely patterned.

Rock.

The city walls were patterned too. They looked like the hull of a Scythian aircraft.

Rock.

"I feel sick."

"I can't stop our momentum," said Wilder. "Try to hold on another minute. We're nearly there."

Their downward progress abruptly halted.

"Dammit," said Wilder.

Miki looked down. About ten meters remained between them and the ground.

"Meric!" Wilder called up.

When he replied his voice was faint. "Sorry, not sure what's wrong."

"Maybe we could jump the rest of the way?" Miki suggested.

"Are you kidding? One broken leg on the team is more than enough. Meric! Shut the entire system down and start her up again."

The quiet hum of the excavator engine ceased.

Silence.

They had continued to spin. If they didn't reach the ground soon, Miki was sure she would vomit.

Wilder muttered, "And to think Niall wanted to come with us! Can you imagine?"

The hum re-started and, with another jerk, so did their slow plunge into the unknown.

The last few meters passed surprisingly quickly and before she knew it, Miki's feet touched the ground. The ropes continued to spool out and pile onto their heads.

"We made it!" Wilder yelled up. "You can turn it off!"

Miki unfastened her harness and stepped out. "What do I do with this?" She gestured at the empty harness crumpled on the ground.

"Leave it right there. You're going to need it when we get back."

Miki looked at the harness doubtfully.

"You guys okay?" Meric called out.

"Yeah," Wilder replied. "Thanks for your help."

"Remember, if you comm me from outside the Scythian city I'll hear it, but once you're inside you're on your own. Good luck!"

"Thanks! You too. I hope Orson doesn't give you any more problems."

"Don't worry. I've got a handle on him."

The light from Meric's headlamp disappeared. The excavator's lights went out too. The plain and cliff face faintly glowed pale green.

"Cherry came here?" Miki asked.

"Aubriot too."

"What was my dad doing then?"

Wilder's expression turned sorrowful. "Miki, I haven't apologized yet for bringing you to Chimera. I'd completely forgotten your mom died here. If I'd remembered, I would never have agreed—"

Miki touched her arm. "I'd kind of forgotten too. I mean, I thought I couldn't remember it. It wasn't until I saw the place where it must have happened that the memory came back. Don't feel bad. I would rather remember than not. I don't have many memories of Mom."

"In that case, I won't feel so guilty. Are you ready?"

Miki tightened her backpack's straps. "Now I am."

"Then let's see what we can find."

They began the march to the Scythian city's walls.

Miki wondered if she would ever return. And if she didn't, would she be sad?

TWENTY-FOUR

Despite the many years they'd spent together on the *Sirocco*, Wilder could only remember Cherry talking about her trip to the Scythian city a handful of times, and she hadn't gone into detail. Aubriot had been an even worse source of information. Wilder had detested the man and only spoken to him when necessary. Had she known she would be coming here one day herself, she would have probed both of them deeply and even ignored her dislike of Aubriot to do it. Now he was dead and Cherry was many light years distant—assuming she was still alive.

Had Wilder done the right thing in bringing Miki along? Her prospects seemed no safer in the city than they had remaining with the hostile Chimerites, and at least there Niall, Zapata, and—to a lesser extent—Maddox could be her defenders. Wilder wasn't at all sure that here, in the metropolis the Scythians had abandoned millennia ago, she was equipped to protect Miki from danger.

One thing Cherry had said that had stuck in her mind was that the aliens, for some unknown reason, employed extremely soft, spongy materials in their constructions. In some places the material was sufficiently soft to allow passage through it with only a little pushing. The purpose for the odd property was unclear, and the discovery that the Scythians' main method of locomotion was aerial didn't shed any light.

Wilder scrutinized the crazy patterning of the city's boundary wall. "There should be a way through this."

"*Through* it?" Miki questioned. "I thought we were looking for a door."

"No. No doors. Cherry was very clear about that."

"I guess because they fly everywhere?"

"I guess so." Wilder poked a swirl darker than the rest. It was soft but it also resisted her touch.

"I saw doors in the domes," Miki remarked.

"You did? Then maybe Cherry was wrong."

"They might have been there for us. For humans."

"Makes sense. This place was built before they even knew humans existed."

"*Oh*!" Miki's arm had disappeared into the wall up to her elbow. "I think I found the way in." She pulled out her arm and examined it.

"Does it hurt?"

"No, and that stuff doesn't cling. My arm's clean."

They regarded the spot she'd pushed through. It had sealed up smoothly.

Miki asked, "It isn't possible there's anything on the other side, right?"

Could the Scythians have entered the city from somewhere else? "Noooo..."

Miki threw Wilder a look, and then thrust herself into the soft area of wall.

"Hey! Wait! I should go first!"

But Miki couldn't hear. Her head had already vanished.

Shit.

The kid was being far too reckless.

She'd gone.

A second later, the wall bulged and then Miki's face appeared. "It's safe. There's nothing here except a huge maze. And it stinks."

"Don't do that again. Next time, *I* go first." Wilder forced her way through to the other side. It *did* stink. Miki's description of the structure that sat in front of them had been accurate. It was a maze, except they stood on top of it. Deep channels ran in all directions, cutting through the ground.

"What the heck is this?" Wilder asked. "Did you see anything like it in the domes?"

"No, but I only went to a few places—cells for prisoners, hatcheries, and the places where I was examined. I didn't see a lot else."

Wilder couldn't remember Cherry mentioning a maze, so she presumed it wasn't important or dangerous. They only needed to figure out a way across it. "This would be a lot easier if we could fly."

"Maybe that's the point." Miki stepped along the nearest path between two channels.

Already, the air was beginning to feel arid. Wilder's eyes felt itchy and sore and her skin seemed to have had all the moisture sucked out of it. She forestalled stopping for a drink of water as they navigated the maze, however. They needed to get used to the new conditions. They could be here for days. "Is there anything you remember about the Scythians that might be useful?" She halted at the point of a channel.

"Like what kind of thing?"

"Like... Did you notice any weaknesses? We know they can't breathe our atmosphere and they prefer to go out at night. Did you notice anything else that might be a vulnerability, compared to what we can do, I mean?"

"They're stronger and bigger than us," Miki replied gravely. "And they have ready-made weapons at the edges of their wings, while we have to carry our knives and pulse rifles. But...they do have trouble getting around any place they can't fly. The two Scythians who questioned me seemed to be scientists. They were involved in gathering data about humans, and to move around, examine me, and input information into their system, they hung from a contraption attached to the ceiling. So their toes weren't encumbered, you see. I don't think the claws on their wings are particularly dexterous." She touched her cheek pensively.

"Did they..." Wilder hesitated. "Did they hurt you during your interrogation?"

"It was Nina they hurt to make me talk. They nearly suffocated her. But I fought with them before that, and one of them cut me."

"On your cheek?"

Miki nodded.

Wilder peered closer. Though she still wasn't used to the view through the night vision goggles, the definition was good. "I can't see a scar."

"The first one that examined me put something on the cut."

"It did? Why?"

"To stop me from bleeding, I suppose. It wouldn't want all that nasty human blood messing up its workplace."

Wilder smiled. "Whatever they used on you, it was good stuff."

Miki turned, surveying their surroundings. They were roughly half way across the maze. "I can't believe Cherry did this all alone. It's so lonely and dark, and if she fell, she only had one hand to save herself."

"She's a brave woman." Wilder studied the maze. The shortest route to the city became clear. "This way."

"Why did Cherry come here? Was she trying to find out stuff about the Scythians, like us?"

"She was following a Guardian. It had been picked up from the..." Wilder swallowed. She didn't want to remind Miki about her sister's probable death. The *Sirocco* had most likely gone the same path as the *Mistral*. "The Scythians managed to get hold of one of them, and they programmed it to come here and reactivate their planetary defense system. Cherry suspected it was up to no good, so she followed it."

"Did she catch it?"

"Not until after it had done its job. That was why Aubriot had to go in and deactivate the system again."

"So we might find the system too?"

"We might, but Aubriot being Aubriot, he most likely put the entire thing permanently out of action. But there could be things to learn if we can find it."

"You don't know where it is?"

"Not a clue. The Guardian showed Aubriot the way, I think."

Miki seemed to take this news stoically, for no response came from her.

Wilder walked the final paces to the edge of the maze. "We made it!"

Miki joined her, saying somewhat dourly, "The first stage, anyway."

Wilder looked up. Walls of buildings on the city outskirts towered above them, forming a facade. There were no roads into this place. There were entrances, arched, doorless—and far out of reach.

Once upon a time, Scythians had flown to and from the portals, free of their breathing apparatus, while day and night Concordia's sky had curved overhead. What color would it have been while rich in CO2 and low in oxygen? Then the atmosphere had altered, building in poisonous gases, until finally the decision had been made to enclose the metropolis in a gigantic dome to keep the citizens safe. What a feat of engineering it had been. Eventually, Concordia had become unliveable and the Scythians had built their starships and flown away, off to colonize new worlds.

"Here's a way in," Miki announced, up to her armpit in a wall.

"Stop doing that! I told you, I go first. You don't know what's on the other side."

But Miki was already forcing herself into the Scythian city.

Muttering curses, Wilder followed.

TWENTY-FIVE

Wilder could not imagine how Cherry had managed to travel through this place alone. It was hard enough for two entirely able-bodied people working together. The spongy barriers had seemed to exist only on the outskirts. Once they were past them, all the interior walls were solid and they were forced to use the same openings the Scythians had, only without the benefit of flight. The aliens had also had the option of simply flying higher and out of the ceiling-less rooms.

Fortunately, Wilder had sufficient knowledge of what lay ahead to know they had to bring knotted lines and grapples as well as plenty of water. But the weight of the precious fluid made climbing hard. She might have been able to haul herself hand over hand up a rope—mostly due to her lightness rather than upper body strength—but with a pack on her back it was impossible.

Miki was the stronger of the two of them despite being younger. After throwing up a grapple and testing the security of the rope, she would climb up first. Then Wilder would attach a pack to another line and Miki would haul it up. After she lifted the second backpack, Wilder would climb up. Then they would lower themselves into the next room, cross it to the exit, and begin the process again.

Some portals were close to the floor and they could simply throw their packs through and then follow them. If there was a choice of exits they would pick the lowest one. The climbing was their most arduous task, and going out of their way to reach their destination was a small price to pay for an easier ascent.

Strange debris filled several of the rooms they passed, flakes of a dull, dusty substance that gave no indication of what it might once have been. The first time Miki had descended into the debris she'd disappeared over her head and Wilder had quickly jumped in after her, fearing she might not be able to breathe. They'd misjudged the depth of the material, estimating it by comparing it with the placement of the floor in the room they'd just left.

Scrabbling around for Miki in the clouds of dusty wafers, she'd quickly located her and scooped the stuff from in front of her face. Again she'd thought of Cherry, who was about Miki's height, and hadn't had anyone to find her or help her.

On and on they went, deeper into the still, silent city, until Wilder was utterly exhausted. Lying on the floor of another anonymous Scythian room, she was too tired to speak, too tired to think. She'd briefly checked the pathfinder to make sure they hadn't deviated far from their intended course toward the center of the city. Then, she'd taken a deep drink of water, heedless of the necessity of conserving it. She was beyond parched. Her tongue was thick and her head pounded. Any sweat her body produced had been instantly absorbed by the bone-dry air.

"We're stopping here for the night?" Miki asked.

"Can you go any farther?"

"I could manage a little more."

"I can't."

Miki allowed her pack to fall to the floor and dropped down next to it. She took out her water bottle and shook it before taking a careful swig.

"I don't know how you have so much energy," said Wilder. "You've done the majority of the work, lifting up the packs."

"I'm younger than you."

"Are you calling me an old lady?"

Miki chuckled. "I'm going to take off my goggles and see what this place looks like without them."

"I wouldn't if I w—"

Miki pushed them to the top of her head, checked around her, and swiftly pulled them over her eyes once more.

"Pitch black?" Wilder asked.

"Uh huh," Miki replied tremulously. She tapped the goggles. "How do these work?"

"Echolocation."

"They use echoes?"

"They're constantly sending out sound waves too high pitched for us to hear. When the waves bounce back, the goggles interpret them to create a picture of our surroundings."

"So the picture isn't real?"

"It's as real as the picture your brain creates from the signals it receives from your eyes. More real, in fact. Your brain fills in a lot of what you think you're seeing. The goggles also process the information they receive, just a tiny bit slower."

A pause.

"What happens if they break or run out of power?"

"They won't," Wilder replied, though a shiver coursed through her at the scenario Miki's speculation had painted.

"You know so many things. You're so clever. I wish I was as smart as you."

"Knowledge and intelligence aren't the same, and there are many ways of being clever. Let's eat and get some sleep. We have a long way to go tomorrow."

Checking the water condenser—some had accumulated but it wasn't much, so the condenser was either faulty or the small amount really was all that could be pulled from the arid atmosphere—Wilder reflected that she didn't *feel* clever. She never had. Outside of engineering endeavors she was constantly confused, all at sea about people, about how they thought and felt. Too many times she'd assumed everyone was the same as her only to be caught out again and again.

'Clever' would have been figuring out how to deal with Niall's attitude, and she was hopeless with that. Dragan had tried to give her a clue but his insight hadn't helped. How could she be compassionate toward someone who repeatedly rejected her attempts to show affection? She suspected the problem wasn't with her at all, that Niall was entirely the one to blame for their disastrous relationship. If that were the case, there wasn't anything she could do about it. With a heavy heart, she wished they hadn't parted on bad terms.

As they settled down to sleep, Miki said, "Should I take off my goggles?"

"You'll be more comfortable without them, but put your hand on them so they aren't too hard to find when you wake up."

Wilder took hers off too, and then lay awake, staring into the dark, until long after the sounds of Miki's breathing had become deep and regular.

———

At Wilder's first movement as she woke, her arms protested violently. Her legs and stomach muscles were loud with their complaints too. It took her a few moments to remember where she was and why her surroundings were wholly dark. She patted the floor. Her bulky goggles appeared under her hand and as she sat up she put them on.

Miki was gone.

Wilder scanned the bare space. Like all the other rooms in the city it was featureless, its original purpose obscured by the passage of ages.

There was Miki's backpack. The fast beat of Wilder's pulse eased a little.

A grapple gripped in inner ledge of an opening.

Dammit.

"Miki! Miki!"

"Wilder?" Her voice sounded distant. "You're awake? I'll be there in a minute."

Wilder snatched up her water bottle and sucked. Her mouth had felt like it had been scoured by desert sand. She was tempted to squeeze out a scant handful of liquid to wipe her face, but they couldn't afford to waste even a drop. The moisture would disappear within seconds anyway.

Sounds of effort came from the direction of the opening. She walked to it and peered up. "Don't disappear like that. You nearly gave me a heart attack."

Miki didn't answer as she climbed. When she reached the ledge, she peeked over it. "You were sound asleep. I didn't want to wake you. I thought I would explore."

"We're all alone in here! What if something happened to you?"

"But it didn't, did it? Besides, I found something cool. Are you ready to go?"

"Ready? I need to eat, and so do you."

Miki climbed down.

Wilder found the girl's gung ho behavior alarming and concerning. Since her unauthorized visit to Earth with her sister, Miki had been quieter than normal, as if her experiences had chastened her, but then she'd demanded to come along on the mission to Concordia. And although she'd been subdued in Chimera, her demeanor had done an about-face again after entering the Scythian city.

Wilder stole glances at her as they ate. Something was going on with Miki but she couldn't figure out what. She berated herself for her lack of people skills. If only Kes were here, he might understand what was up with his daughter. Then again, if Kes were here she probably wouldn't behave like this. "Miki, I don't know how to put this gently so I'm just going to come right out and say it: you need to take it easy. Even if we weren't inside the ruins of our enemy's city, this would be a dangerous place. If you break a leg, how would I get you out? I would have to go for help and you would be waiting here alone in the dark for who knows how long. And how do you think the Chimerites would take it if some of them had to risk their lives for you? Assuming they would. They don't like us as it is."

"Ugh, okaaaay." Miki drawled like the archetypal surly teenager.

If the situation weren't so serious Wilder might have laughed. "Miki, I'm not kidding around. Do you hear me?"

"I hear you, *Leader Wilder*."

"Good." A memory flashed into Wilder's mind. She was at Cherry's house when Cherry had been General of the colony. She'd been confined there 'for her own safety'. She saw herself climbing out the kitchen window and inwardly groaned. If the colony was ever at peace again she would never have children.

Never.

"What was the cool thing you found?"

"Eat up, and I'll show you."

Miki refused to be drawn on the subject over the time it took to finish eating and pack up. As Wilder hauled herself up the rope to exit the room, her muscles screamed. Her hands were raw. How would she ever manage another day like this? How much farther would they go? They'd discovered nothing useful about the Scythians or anything even remotely interesting so far.

She lowered herself down the other side. It felt no easier going down than it had going up. A room similar to all the others confronted her. Miki was already on the other side, tossing up the grapple. Wilder dragged their backpacks across the intervening space while Miki ascended.

When she reached the opening, she leaned down to say conspiratorially, "I think Aubriot's team might have been here."

Wilder squinted up. "That's the big secret?"

Miki chuckled. "Bet you can't guess how I know."

"I bet I can't. And you're not going to tell me, right? You're going to make me climb up there and see for myself."

"Tie on the first backpack," Miki said, grinning.

Wilder frowned as she squatted and grabbed her pack. Miki's mood had improved but she seemed to have gone too far in the opposite direction.

After both packs were hauled up, Wilder climbed after them. As her head rose over the ledge and she got a view of what lay beyond, she sucked in air sharply, which caused her to cough. There was little else she could do except cling on while waiting for the uncontrollable fit to pass.

When she finally caught her breath, Miki was watching her with concern. "Sorry, I should have told you so it wasn't a surprise."

A long passage stretched from left to right, the walls rising high on each side, dotted with openings. As in the rest of the city, the passage had no ceiling and the dome arched high overhead. It was some kind of Scythian thorough-fare, a direct route—for once—leading deep into the city. At one time, it must have been thick with aliens, flying to and fro.

Yet that was not the most remarkable thing about it. The most astonishing feature, the one that had made Wilder gasp was around two meters up from ground level.

Words had been scratched on the wall next to an arrow pointing left.

THIS WAY, LOSERS.

TWENTY-SIX

The relief at simply walking rather than endlessly scaling and descending ropes was immeasurable. Even more important, the discovery of the passageway meant they would make faster progress. The time they were spending in the city had become a concern. Their water supply was rapidly dwindling despite their conservative consumption, and the condenser's output was pathetic.

Wilder hurried along with Miki down the passageway. After a hundred or so meters it split, forking to their right and left. Aubriot had helpfully scratched an arrow to indicate the correct direction so they took it without hesitation. Rather than wandering vaguely toward the center of the city they were finally going somewhere.

They were heading for the control room of the Scythian's planetary defenses, no doubt. It seemed as good a destination as any. Aubriot might have scuppered the controls but they might learn something from them nevertheless.

"How did Aubriot know which way to go?" Miki asked. "Did he have a map?"

"He had a Guardian guiding him. Then I guess he scratched directions on the way out, after he'd found the control room, in case anyone wanted to follow in his footsteps." It was typical of the obnoxious man to want to leave evidence of his presence to people who might come after, yet it was fortunate for them he had. Otherwise, they might have wandered uselessly until it was time to return, empty-handed, to Chimera.

The new 'road' stretched into the distance, but they hadn't gone far before they encountered another arrow, this time pointing upward. Aubriot had helpfully scratched another instruction: *UP AGAIN, WANNABES.*

Above, the widest, tallest, and highest portal they'd seen yet, opened in the expanse of wall. Climbing up to it would have been easy for the dead Earthman. He'd been powerfully built. For Wilder, the prospect was daunting. She'd developed somewhat of a technique over the previous day, employing the traction of flexible soles of her boots on the walls while hauling herself hand over hand, but she was most definitely unsuited to the task. The discovery of straight passages through the city had given her a ray of hope that the regular climbs were over.

"You can do it," said Miki, apparently reading her crestfallen expression.

"Maybe, but can you throw a grapple up there?"

It took Miki three tries but she managed it. She also managed the climb without pausing, though, agile as she was, even she was panting by the time she reached the top. She immediately turned and dropped a second rope to pull up the backpacks.

Then it was Wilder's turn. As she climbed, mentally forcing away the protestations of her exhausted body, she reminded herself that Cherry had done this with only one arm. Or perhaps she hadn't made it this far. Aubriot had completed the task for her, or something like that.

Miki's encouraging face grew slowly closer. Wilder concentrated on moving just one hand, then just one leg. The other hand. The other leg. On and on. She did not look down. She dared not.

Damn the Scythians and their wings.

Why, of all the possible enemies of humanity, did we have to have one that could fly?

The ledge was within reach.

She swung a sweaty hand at it—and missed.

Miki squeaked.

Wilder's body slapped into the wall. She was dangling by one arm, her entire body weight pulling on one hand. She was not a heavy person. Why did she seem to weigh so much?

Her arm felt as though it was being wrenched from its socket. The ground seemed very far below.

"Give me your other hand!" Miki exclaimed, leaning precariously far out from the ledge. "Give it to me!"

Wilder tried. She threw her free hand upward, but Miki couldn't reach it.

Wilder had been too hasty. She should have climbed a little higher before going for the ledge.

"Move back," she commanded, "or you'll fall."

Miki shuffled marginally backward. At the same time, Wilder grabbed the rope with her second hand and put the toes of her right boot against the wall. She hung there for several moments, catching her breath. It was time to live by her own advice. *Take it easy.*

Just one hand. Just one foot.

Miki moved closer, ready to help her.

"Stay away. I don't want to pull you down. I can do it myself."

Another hand. Another foot.

The ledge was within easy reach. She climbed onto it.

"I knew you could do it," said Miki.

Wilder waited for her panting to subside before replying, "You're a good big sister."

Instantly, Miki's features clouded and she looked like she might cry.

"Shit, I'm so sorry." Wilder reached out to touch her shoulder.

"It's okay." Miki sniffed and turned, saying, "Look!"

Beyond the large portal was the biggest space they'd ever seen inside the city. Fifty or more meters square, it was adorned with long, thick poles. Many had fallen and crumbled, but some remained in their original settings, protruding from the vertical sides. At one time, even thicker poles must have stood at intervals across the floor, smaller counterparts sticking out of them.

"Oh!" Miki exclaimed, and clapped a hand over her mouth. Giggling, she added, "They're perches."

She was right. In Concordia's deep past, this had been a gathering place for hundreds of Scythians, perhaps some kind of council or parliament. Wilder estimated they were near the center of the city, so it made sense—from a human perspective.

Aubriot had not left instructions for the next part of the journey. It was obvious. Directly opposite stood a wide opening that ran from the floor to the top of the wall.

Her immediate reaction on seeing it was delight. "Thank the stars we don't have to climb in there."

They did, however, have to descend from their current position.

———

Wilder dragged herself across the remaining distance to the opening, walking around any obstacles too large to step over. Her backpack felt like a lead weight, even though they'd drunk most of its original contents. If she hadn't been deathly curious about what lay before them, she might have called a halt so she could rest a while.

The ghostly vision of her night goggles revealed sectional spaces separated by waist-high barriers. Something was odd. She looked up.

Ceilings!

They were rutted, criss-crossed by grooves, and fractured. Some had entirely collapsed, but they were unmistakable.

"Is this like what you saw inside the domes?" she asked.

Miki drew her gaze from the horizontal surfaces overhead. "The ones in the domes were made from a flexible material. Not like these."

"They must be the original type and the Scythians invented a more versatile version later."

They followed the scratched directions.

Thanks, Aubriot.

In this place the aliens must have walked, easily surmounting the low divisions between rooms. Broken-off pedestals marked the spots controls may have sat. One area was open to the dome. An exit point? In another large section, shards of poles littered the floor.

Scrawled across the floor in front of one short barrier no different from the rest was the word *BULLSEYE*.

"What's bullseye?" Miki asked.

"No idea, but I think it means we've reached the control room."

They stepped over the wall.

Judging from the room's appearance, Wilder was right. A massive pole stuck up from the floor, thrust deep within a square hole. She stepped closer. Beneath the floor was a mess of destroyed wiring and boards. They were not rusted or decayed, only crushed and broken by the operation of the pole. It was a miracle they'd survived so long. The chamber must have been sealed when the Scythians departed.

"Are these the defense system controls?" Miki asked.

Wilder nodded thoughtfully. "The compromised Guardian must have opened this up, fixed whatever had failed, and restarted the system. It fired once, just before Aubriot arrived. Then he put it out of action." She winced. The Scythian planetary defenses had destroyed the *Opportunity*. If she hadn't already transferred to the Immani vessel she wouldn't be here now.

"Where are the armaments?" asked Miki. "I thought they would be nearby."

"We never found them. We had plenty else to do rebuilding after the attacks. They're probably somewhere on Suddene or perhaps under the ocean."

Miki knelt down and leaned over the hole. "Can you learn anything from *that*?"

Wilder didn't answer. As she'd expected, Aubriot had done a number on the Scythians' system. That man had never done anything by halves. He hadn't only put the system out of action, he'd annihilated it beyond rejigging or soldering it back to functionality. There would be no reverse engineering it.

She sank to the floor next to Miki.

"Is it bad?"

Resting her elbow on her knee and her forehead in the palm of her hand, she replied, "I don't know why I ever thought it would do any good to come here. We've trekked through half the city, climbed and descended hundreds of meters in total using those damned ropes, slept in pitch darkness, been parched with thirst... And for what? We're no better off than when we left Chimera. We haven't learned a single thing about the Scythians that we didn't already know."

Silence stretched out in the silent space.

"What do we do now?" asked Miki.

Wilder was too sunk in depression to answer. How could they force the Scythians to leave Concordia when the aliens had the upper hand—or wing— in every way? Humanity was on its knees and there was nothing to be done about it. And now the Scythians seemed to be moving to phase two of re-establishing their presence on the planet, removing the need for humans slaves entirely.

"Wilder?"

She groaned and sunk her head into her hands. "I don't know."

After a short while she heard Miki get to her feet and walk away.

Still, she didn't move. Should they go farther into the city? There seemed little point, and already she doubted they had sufficient water to make it back to Chimera while enduring extreme thirst. Worse, even with enough water she wasn't sure she could make it. She was bone-weary. If she held her hands in front of her they trembled. With a day or two to recover she might be okay, but they didn't have an extra day's water.

It was a horrible predicament. Although she'd thought of a potential solution she hesitated to voice it. She doubted Miki would either agree or have the fortitude to see it through.

"Urghhh!" Miki exclaimed. "What's this?"

Wilder looked up.

Miki was stooping. When she straightened up she was holding an object at arm's length by her fingertips. The object was ovoid, partially burned and...had tufts sticking out of it. Miki had gripped the thin strands.

"Bring it here," Wilder said.

"I'd rather put it down again. It's disgusting."

"Miki..." An idea was forming but Wilder couldn't figure out the ramifications. It might be something amazing or nothing at all. "I think I know what it is."

Miki walked over, holding the thing in front of her as if fearing contamination. "It has an *eye*?!"

"No kidding." So she was right.

Miki dropped the thing in her lap. It landed with a thump, its weight belying its size.

Looking up at Wilder with a frozen, one-eyed gaze was a Guardian's head.

TWENTY-SEVEN

Wilder said it was the head of a Guardian, the one that had led Aubriot to the control room. *A head?* Miki looked more closely. There were the remains of its hair, the partial mouth, and the eye she'd noticed a moment ago. Wilder was right. It was a head. The thing had been smashed up then burned, or burned then smashed up.

Miki shuddered. Did Guardians feel pain? No one had ever mentioned it. She'd seen one on Earth, called Strongquist. If she hadn't been told he was an android she would never have guessed. He hadn't only appeared to be completely human, he'd also seemed nice.

Wilder was turning the horrible object over in her hands.

"What's it doing here?" Miki asked.

"I don't know. Cherry never mentioned what had happened to the Guardian that showed Aubriot the way through the city. I'd assumed it had been destroyed, by her order. She hated the Guardians."

"Uhh, it *is* destroyed, isn't it? That's only its head."

"Guardians aren't animals. Decapitating them wouldn't necessarily put them out of action. Though this one is certainly not working."

"Did the power run out?"

"Maybe, or the head doesn't have its own supply, so when it was separated from the body..."

Miki scanned the room. "I can't see the body anywhere."

Wilder smiled. "This thing was *sawn* off. It would take more time than we have to fix the damage and rejoin it to the body, and I don't have the tools anyway."

"How long *do* we have?"

"I'm not sure, but we can't stay here much longer. We don't have a lot of water left."

"Sooo...this is it? This is our big find in the Scythian city?"

"This..." Wilder put the head down, balancing it on its neck "...is it."

The head toppled to the side and rolled to a stop.

"You know," Miki said, "of all the things we might have found, I never imagined it would be that."

"You're telling me."

"Can we do anything with it?"

"It's a long shot, but maybe. Let's get out of here. We aren't going to find anything else in this hellhole."

"I preferred the desert."

"Me too." Wilder opened her pack and picked up the head.

"I'll carry it."

Wilder hesitated but then passed it over.

It was a sign of her weakened state. Ordinarily, Wilder would have refused to allow her to take the greater burden. She was that kind of person, and she'd been a kind of proxy Mom for a while. But her face before she woke up this morning had shown lines of exhaustion, and she'd moved more slowly and with greater effort all day. Wilder had little muscle or fat on her. Physically, she was unsuited to feats of endurance, and she was quite old. She had to be in her mid-thirties.

Miki stowed the head and shouldered her pack. She took a drink of water before they set off for home. Or rather, not home, but Chimera, where they were generally disliked.

———

They followed Aubriot's directions in reverse order, returning to the main thoroughfare. Instead of climbing up to the opening where they'd entered it, they continued along it to its end. Aubriot had thought up several more taunts for the later generations he'd imagined might follow him. *SUCKERS, HAS-BEENS*—Wilder pointed out that they couldn't be both *WANNABES* **and** *HAS-BEENS*—and *ALSO-RANS* were the politer insults, if there was any such thing. Then the arrows directing them along the passageway ceased.

At first, they thought it was only that Aubriot had run out of put-downs or had grown bored with the exercise. The passageway continued onward, straight as an arrow, so they followed it. Their goggles only revealed open space up ahead, and though the route might be a longer way to return to Chimera, it was infinitely easier.

Miki was happy for Wilder more than she was for herself. She hadn't been sure she would ever leave the city and she'd made her peace with the prospect. But Wilder had people to live for. She had some kind of complicated thing going on with Niall. And if anyone was going to free Concordia of the Scythians it was her. But if they had to return the same way they'd come, she wasn't sure Wilder could do it.

They'd been walking in silence for a while. Even talking dried out your throat here. They'd kept the same, medium pace but Wilder softly panted. As Miki was about to suggest they stop for a drink, she reached behind her for her water bottle, taking her gaze from the road ahead.

"Miki!" Wilder grabbed her arm and pulled her so sharply backward she stumbled and fell on her backside.

"Why did you do that?!"

"Look!"

Wilder was no longer looking ahead but downward. Straight down. "Don't come too close."

Miki crawled forward.

The passageway abruptly ended. The walls continued the same as before, but the floor disappeared into empty space. On each side the walls descended deeper than they rose to the dome above. She couldn't see their end.

She wasn't sure how they'd come so close to tumbling to their deaths. Perhaps they'd been too lost in their thoughts to pay attention, or maybe the walls created an optical illusion from afar. The vision from their goggles might also have confused them.

This was not the way out. No wonder Aubriot's scratchings didn't direct people here.

"We must have missed something," Wilder said. "We have to retrace our steps."

They turned back.

A hundred meters or so along the path they hit an arrow they'd missed. It pointed upward.

SOZ NUMPTIES

Wilder tilted her head to gaze at the opening above, her dismay almost palpable.

"It's okay," Miki said. "You can do it."

Wilder gave her a sorrowful look and nodded. "You first."

TWENTY-EIGHT

Wilder woke. The first thing she did was check for Miki. This time, the girl was sitting right beside her, cross-legged and frowning.

"What's wrong?" The words came out as a croak.

"Have some water." Miki held up her water bottle to Wilder's lips.

She turned her head. "I don't need it."

"You do." Miki added accusingly, "You've been drinking less water than me, haven't you. All yesterday, as we were coming back from the control room, you didn't drink anything. It took me a while to realize. I thought about it overnight, and I don't remember seeing you drink once. Not even after we stopped for the night."

"I can manage until—"

"You can't. You're worse off than me. Now drink."

Chastened, Wilder took a sip. The liquid felt like nectar in her mouth and throat. It was all she could do to stop herself from gulping it all down. "Did the condenser make much?"

Miki picked it up and shook it. There was perhaps fifty mil in it. "This thing's a piece of shit."

"We only have a day's march. If we can just make it back to the exit to Chimera, we'll be okay."

"A day's *climbing*," Miki corrected.

The fact settled heavily in the pit of Wilder's stomach. "Yeah, climbing."

Aubriot's route was some way off the one they'd taken on their way in. Theoretically, considering his had been created according to the advice of the

Guardian, who had insider knowledge from the Scythians, it should be the most direct. Yet, if it were the most direct, it was not the easiest. The aliens would have flown it, and the android would not have felt fatigued by all the ascents and descents. If anything, their new way out had proven harder than their entry route.

The aches and pains Wilder had felt on previous days were nothing compared to how she felt now. Even her head throbbed. They were probably only a day's journey from Chimera, but it felt like the other side of the galaxy.

She had to do it.

She sat up and instantly lifted a hand to her head, as if pressing it might take the pain away.

"Drink some more," Miki urged.

"No, you need—"

"Drink."

She took another welcome sip but couldn't help eyeing the container. There was perhaps a liter in it. In other circumstances this wouldn't have been a problem, but her experience of the city was that it sucked moisture like a hull breach sucked air.

"Let's go." Miki rose to her feet. "The sooner we're out of this nightmare the better. And we have a prize to bring back." She lifted her pack, which contained the Guardian's head.

What an odd find it had been. It might be a treasure trove of information if they could get it working and delve the secrets of its electronic mind. But first they had to get it back to Chimera.

Wilder also stood up, though shakily.

Miki threw a grapple at the nearest opening high on the wall and hauled herself up the rope.

Another day within the Scythian city had begun.

———

Three hours later, Wilder was done. Her hands shook and refused to grip. Her arms, legs, and stomach were balls of fire. Her mouth was as dry as the ancient dusty flakes littering the city.

Her water was almost gone. Back in the desert, Niall had said if your water supplies were low it was still better to drink when you needed it. Otherwise dehydration would make you confused and cloud your judgment. But what were you supposed to do when your water ran out?

Miki stood at the base of a wall, watching her and waiting. "Just one more, Wilder. You can do it."

She'd said *Just one more* before the last five ascents.

"I can't." Wilder walked to the edge of the room and slumped to the floor. It was hard to talk when your mouth had zero moisture. "I'm sorry, but I really can't. You go on ahead. Take the pathfinder in case you miss one of Aubriot's arrows. I'll wait here."

"I'm not going without you."

"Unless you can fit me in one of the backpacks, you don't have a choice."

"But by the time I get to Chimera and send someone to find you, you could die of thirst."

"If you don't leave now, *you'll* die of thirst. I'll be fine as long as I don't have to climb that damned rope one more time. If I'm not exercising I won't sweat as much." Wilder had actually stopped sweating as far as she could tell.

It took more arguing than they had time for, but eventually she persuaded a very reluctant Miki to leave.

She pressed the condenser into Wilder's hands, "Promise me you'll still be alive when I get back," she choked. "Promise me."

"I promise."

Wilder rested the back of her head against the wall as she watched Miki climb the rope. She was so brave for someone so young. And it hurt like hell to force her to navigate the remainder of the Scythian city alone. Miki had lost her mother, her father, and maybe her sister too.

Turning onto her side to rest, Wilder vowed that she would not die and be the last of Miki's friends to desert her. She would keep her promise. She would remain alive if it killed her. She smiled grimly before slipping into exhausted unconsciousness.

When she woke, everything was dark.

Her dreadful thirst hit her and she remembered where she was.

Reaching out, she patted the floor for her goggles, She patted a wide circle, getting onto her hands and knees and crawling around.

Shit!

Where could they have gone?

There was nothing and no one else here. Hopefully, Miki would be reaching the city's outskirts by now. She might even have made it to Chimera and a rescue team was on its way. Miki would definitely not have snuck back and taken her goggles while she was asleep.

They had to be here somewhere. She crawled until she hit a wall, wincing at the pain from her blistered, raw hands. Then she crawled along the wall until she came up against a corner. She would search the room methodically, end to end and side to side. It was possible she might have moved in her sleep, disturbed by her predicament, and pushed the goggles far from her.

Rationality niggled at the back of her mind.

You couldn't have moved them that *far. You should have been able to find them easily.*

Desperation forced her to ignore the logical conclusions, and she began her search. Crawling painfully up and down the room, she swept it with groping hands. Keeping to a straight line was impossible now she couldn't see anything, and she arrived at the opposing walls at odd angles. Nevertheless, she completed the task fairly confident she'd covered all the floor space. The chances of missing her goggles were slim.

They simply weren't here.

She crouched into the opposite corner from where she'd started. Her thirst was a nail being hammered into her head. It was sandpaper scouring her throat. And now, somehow, her goggles were gone too.

She sank her face into her hands—and felt her goggles!

She'd been wearing them all this time. Dehydration was muddling her mind.

She slipped the goggles off, shook them, and tapped them. Feeling out the lenses by touch, she peered through them.

Darkness.

They were broken or had run out of power, as Miki had feared they might. How old were they? Maybe they dated back to the time before the departure of the *Sirocco* or even the biocide attack. Manufacturing in the colony had been devastated back then and had probably never recovered before the Scythians returned.

Even sitting up was too tiring. She lay on her back and stared up sightlessly.

"Wait! Just a couple of days." Niall had said.

"I told you, we can't."

"Can't or don't want to? You're just playing the hero again. It's always been the same, right back to when you invented the a-grav. You had to be the center of attention."

"That's not true. You know it isn't. Why are you doing this? Why are you always so mean to me?"

Niall's anger fell away. "I don't know. I'm sorry."

"Sorry isn't enough. I'm sick of your hostility and I'm sick of you. I try to be nice to you over and over again, and over and over again you push me away. I'm not trying anymore. We're done."

She had left him then, not looking back as she stalked away from his hospital bed. She hadn't seen his expression, hadn't taken a last look at him. He'd offered the opportunity to at least part on good terms and she'd scorned it, flung it back at him, just as he'd thrown her gestures of affection back at her. Only Niall had good reasons for being the way he was. What excuses did she have?

She lay in the dark silence for what seemed to be hours, though she had no way to track time. With no other living thing for kilometers around, she felt utterly alone.

Then the hallucinations began. There was the drip of water somewhere far distant. Impossible. Colors swam in her vision. *Things* touched her. Creatures scrabbled across the floor. Sluglimpets were coming to get her. They always attacked at night, and here the night was endless.

TWENTY-NINE

When Miki reached the comm station at the base of the cliff on the edge of Chimera, she couldn't speak. She opened a channel but couldn't say a word. At the other end, Meric said, "Hello? Hello? Who's this?"

There seemed to be nothing to tell him who was comming him.

"Is that you, Wilder? Are you back?"

"No, it's Miki," she said, but no words came out. It was as if the dust in the city had clogged her vocal cords. "It's me, Miki," she said voicelessly.

In frustration, she tapped the device.

"Is someone there?"

Yes!

She tapped again, forcefully. Then she picked up two rocks and smashed them together. Anything to make a noise.

"Huh, odd," Meric muttered to himself. Then the comm cut out.

She opened the channel again. *Meric, listen to me! I made it back, but Wilder needs your help.*

He took a minute to answer. "Wilder, if that's you, I'm on my way. If this is a prank, whoever you are, you're in serious trouble for wasting the Leader's time."

Miki sank to her knees.

A few minutes later, the beam from a flashlight shone down. She looked up, squinting, and waved.

"Only one of you?" Meric called. "Who is it? Where's the other one?"

How to explain without the use of her voice? All Miki could do was step into the harness and fasten it as a signal she wanted to be pulled up.

The hum of the excavator's engine started, and it was like the most wonderful music she'd ever heard. Now if they could only reach Wilder in time, everything would be okay. She drew level with the upper surface. Meric halted the excavator's tunneling spike, climbed down from the cab, and reached out for her. Swinging her to safety, he asked, "Miki? Why have you come back alone? Is Wilder injured?"

She gestured at her throat and shook her head.

"You hurt your throat and that's why you can't speak?"

She mouthed the word *water.*

"Ah, of course. I was forgetting how dry it is in there. Come with me. Can you walk?"

———

Niall had left the medical center. As Miki was brought in she looked for him, but his bed was empty. So was Zapata's. The first thing she'd said after Meric had given her water was that Wilder was still alive and she had to go back and bring her out. But he'd told her he would send in a rescue team, and that she was in no fit state to be going anywhere.

So here she was. The medic had inserted a tube into her arm to give her fluids. He was examining her hands when Niall burst in, wild-eyed.

"Where is she, Miki? Where's Wilder?"

"I'm sorry. She made me leave. I didn't want to abandon her, but she couldn't go any farther."

"I understand. I know you wouldn't leave her alone if you could help it. But do you know where she is?"

"I gave Meric the pathfinder. I marked the position I lef—"

He was gone.

The medic gave her something to help her sleep. As she was drifting off, she imagined Wilder all alone in the Scythian city. It was a horrible place, the most awful place she'd ever been. Even the interior of one of the Scythian domes was preferable. At least there you had the company of others. You had food and water, light and noise. Journeying through the ancient metropolis was like being in hell, the punishment being the requirement to climb and descend ropes, no matter how tired or thirsty you were. She could not have conceived a better place to put people sentenced for terrible crimes.

What would she do if Wilder hadn't survived? How could she live with herself knowing she'd left her there to die alone? She'd abandoned Nina, and now she'd abandoned Wilder too. How was she supposed to go on, those actions weighing her down the rest of her life?

She awoke, and the first thing she did was to check the nearby beds. They were all empty. Wilder had not been brought back yet, or she had and she was...

Miki swallowed and tears rolled from her eyes onto her pillow.

How long had she slept? If it was only a few hours it was too soon for the rescue team to have returned. She wasn't sure how long it had taken her to complete the remainder of the journey to the city's edge on her own but it had been a long time. And then she'd had to navigate the maze.

But if she'd been asleep a long time perhaps the team was already back. She listened. When she'd been in the medical center before it had been possible to roughly tell the time of day by the noises from the street. It had been the quiet time when she'd returned, when most Chimerites were asleep. The outside remained quiet. She must have only slept a short while.

Her hands were swaddled in dressings. Gingerly, she pushed herself up with her elbows until she was partially sitting up. How to find out if there was any news? She pressed the button next to her bed with the tip of her least-sore finger.

Several minutes later no one had arrived. She pressed it again with the same result.

"Hello!" she called out. "Is anyone there?"

Again, there was no answer. She would have to get out of bed and find someone. She pushed down her covers and swung her legs out. They, too, had dressings on them, at her knees and feet where she'd gripped the rope. Moving had made her woozy, so she waited for the dizziness to subside. When she felt a little better, she eased herself off the bed and balanced precariously on her bare feet.

Maybe this wasn't such a good idea.

"Hello! Can someone help me?"

Where were all the medics?

A sudden horror struck her. Had the Scythians discovered Chimera? Was there currently a battle being fought for the site? Was that why the clinic's staff was absent?

"*Hello?*"

A flurry of noise and movement came from directly outside the room. She walked, wobbling, to the door and pulled it open.

The passageway was full of medics. Niall ran in, carrying Wilder in his arms. Her head lolled and her eyes were closed. Her skin was deathly pale. She looked more dreadfully thin than ever. Miki lifted her hand to her mouth.

Niall spotted her standing in the doorway. "She's alive, Miki. She's still alive."

THIRTY

The supply trucks were ready to return to Lyonesse. They would be traveling in the second one, in the center of the convoy. There were no creature comforts in the back of the vehicle, not even a cushion. However, they would be given food and water for the journey, Meric had reassured them. His expression had been sad when he'd announced his 'decision'. It was clear it was not his decision at all. He'd bowed to pressure from Orson and the general opinion the commander had whipped up.

"It's not so bad," said Zapata, patting Miki's shoulder. "It doesn't make any sense for us to stay in Chimera. What good can we do here, skulking with the other cowards in their hideaway?"

The sharp intakes of breath and the glowering of Orson as they waited to board the truck showed Zapata's comment had hit home, as no doubt he'd intended.

The commander stepped forward. "There are no cowards here, only loyal Concordians. You should count yourselves lucky you're getting out alive. If I had my way this truck would be carrying out your corpses to be dumped at sea, like the rest of the spies." He swiveled to Meric, who also stood with them, waiting for the supplies to arrive. "You realize we could be playing right into the hands of the Scythians? If these people are who I think they are, we're sending them right back to their masters with all the information they came here for—the fact Chimera exists, how many people are living here, how we're supplied—everything except our damned location, and that's only because my men blindfolded them before bringing them in. You even let them go into the Scythian city to do who knows what."

"They're not from Lyonesse," Meric replied patiently. "They're from—"

"Yeah, you told me. A starship that flew out of the past. If they're from the *Sirocco* where is it? How did they get here? Did they float down from orbit?"

"That's all been explained to my satisfaction, as well as details about the ship, their journey, and Earth no one else could know."

"Information you're unable to verify, that could easily be made up."

"Robert, if you would just listen, there's still time to call this off."

Orson glared at Miki and the others. "And there's still time to put an end to the doubt once and for all, and avoid risking the lives of everyone in Chimera based on outlandish lies."

People arrived carrying the backpacks, now full.

"I think we'd better get on the truck," said Niall quietly.

Miki silently agreed. Things might turn nasty. Deadly, in fact, if Orson got his way.

Niall took the backpacks and slung them into the truck. He held out a hand to help Miki up. When she was inside, she pushed the backpacks to the front while the others climbed in. Wilder's weakness from her ordeal still showed, and Maddox winced as she made the effort. Her ribs were still healing. Getting Zapata aboard was even more of an exercise. His broken leg remained encased in a tough cast and he had to use a crutch to walk.

Meric moved to the end of the truck and peered in. "I'm sorry about this. If there were any other way..."

"It's fine," Niall replied tightly. "We appreciate everything you've done."

"Tensions are high, you see, after Scythians were spotted flying directly above us. People are scared, and when they're scared it makes them less hospitable."

"Don't apologize," said Wilder. "Zapata was right. Not about you being cowards, I mean. But that we need to go to Lyonesse if we're going to do any good in the fight."

Meric seemed to accept her point. "Your weapons will be returned to you when you arrive at your destination."

"Where exactly are we going?" Niall asked.

Meric glanced at Orson. "I can't tell you, but it's within inhabited regions."

Wilder said, "There has to be a Resistance organization operating over there, who supply Chimera. Are you sending us to them?"

"I'm afraid not."

"Compromising Chimera's security isn't enough for you, huh?" Orson barked. "You think we'll let you infiltrate the Resistance too?"

"Leave it!" Meric warned. He nodded to the three men who had brought their packs. "Guards are coming with you, and you'll be blindfolded for the duration of the journey."

"Fantastic," said Maddox. "I guess now's a bad time to tell everyone I get motion sickness?" As the men climbed into the back of the truck, she added, "Hope you guys don't mind vomit on your boots."

————

Blindfolded, sitting in a corner of the truck, Miki tried to figure out what to do next. She was to blame for them being evicted from Chimera and sent to Lyonesse, which was infested with Scythians. If she hadn't stupidly wandered to the top of the exit tunnel just as the supplies were arriving, if she hadn't allowed herself to be spotted by the commander, the Chimerites might have allowed them to stay. She'd put her friends' lives in danger, and she didn't know how to make it up to them.

The truck ride was smooth as it traveled upward. Wilder and Niall were talking but too quietly for her to hear. They were probably discussing the Guardian's head. They still seemed to hold out hope they could get it working, and that it would reveal useful information about the Scythians. But Niall had fiddled with it for a couple of days already, and Wilder had worked with him as soon as she was well enough to sit up. Nothing they'd tried had activated it, and they'd complained they didn't have the equipment to access its drive. So where was their optimism coming from? It had to be because they were desperate. They were ready to believe in anything that might mean the mission wasn't how it was—an absolute disaster.

Faint words were exchanged outside the truck. A rumbling started up and the vehicle's movement evened out. Miki could sit straight and didn't have to press her hand on the floor to remain upright. They had to be out of the tunnel and on the surface.

As the journey progressed and she tried to think up the best thing for her to do when they arrived in Lyonesse, the truck's interior grew warm. Despite the camouflage netting, Suddene's hot sun was reaching them, beating down. Miki grew warm, too, and lay on her side.

Maddox demanded water. At first, the guards refused, one of them announcing there would be a stop for water and food before the sea crossing. But Maddox argued, and whined, and argued some more. Eventually, they gave in.

"Do you want some, Miki?" Zapata asked, nudging her foot.

"No, I'm good."

Maddox did throw up, as she'd warned. They didn't stop the truck for her when she said she felt sick, but led her to the end and made her vomit in the road. That did *not* improve her temper, but Miki was way beyond caring. She zoned the woman out and concentrated on her own problems.

Some time later, the truck slowed to a stop and the engine was turned off. They were made to get out, still blindfolded, their wrists were bound, and they were marched a short distance. Miki could hear waves. They were forced into the water. She was in up to her hips, the waves splashing up to her shoulders, before their wrists were untied and they had to climb into a small boat.

"This is fucking ridiculous!" Maddox exclaimed. "Are you hoping we'll drown? Is that the idea? So you won't have the deaths of innocent Concordians on your conscience?"

She was ignored.

The trip to the larger boat took a few minutes. Ropes were tied under their arms, and they were hauled aboard and deposited on the deck.

"Surely we don't need to wear blindfolds now?" Maddox complained. "What are we going to see? A whole lot of water?"

A voice growled, "The first one of you who takes off their blindfold goes over the side. Got it?"

No one answered.

They were given water and food as the ship got underway. The voyage didn't register heavily on Miki. She noticed Niall, Wilder, and Zapata talking softly, and Maddox threw up again. Miki felt nauseated too but managed to hold it in.

Hours later, the steps of their arrival on the vessel were reversed, and they were deposited on a beach. Their wrists were rebound and they were forced up the sand. Miki's feet hit something different. A shock of recognition passed through her. She was walking on a rubbery groundcover plant. The sensation felt deeply familiar. She must have walked on it many times as a small child, though she didn't remember it. The plant was probably destroyed by the biocide. But now, decades later, it was back.

A hand grasped her shoulder and pushed her to her knees.

"Wait here," a voice said.

Footsteps tramped away. There came the sound of bodies pushing through vegetation, then silence.

After several minutes, Zapata asked, "Are they gone?"

"I don't think they're returning," said Wilder. "They want us to delay freeing ourselves until they're out of sight." There was the sound of movement. "They're gone."

Taking off their blindfolds was the easy part. Their wrists were secured behind their backs, and untying the knots proved much harder. They had to work by feel alone, sitting back to back. As soon as Niall was free, however, he quickly untied everyone else.

They were sitting on the groundcover Miki faintly remembered, surrounded by spiny shrubs. They were not far from the ocean—the sound of the waves hitting the shore was clear. Having no desire to alert the Chimerites to their unbound state, they remained where they were for a while longer, giving their captors plenty of time to leave.

While they waited, Niall and Wilder searched the surrounding scrub, keeping low, but came up empty-handed. When they were confident the Chimerites must be gone, they searched more widely. They were in a sandy cove, high cliffs on each side. The ocean was empty. The larger vessel must have anchored out of view.

At the place where the beach met the vegetation lay five pulse guns.

Niall stooped, picked one up, and checked it. "Fully charged."

"We have supplies too," said Wilder. "Things could be worse."

"Speak for yourself," Maddox said. "My ribs are killing me."

Niall stowed his weapon. "Meric said we would be dropped in an inhabited region. We need to find people who can introduce us to the Resistance. Then we can start to turn things in the colony's favor."

"Have you lost your mind?" Maddox asked. "Concordia has had it. The best we can do is not be killed or taken as slaves by Scythians. This mission was doomed from the start."

"Thanks," said Wilder. "We can always rely on you to cheer us up."

"I'm just saying it how it is. There's no point in sugar-coating it."

"And how does that help? If you can't think of anything positive to say, keep your mouth shut."

"Who made you Leader?"

"Shut up!" Niall ordered. "Both of you. We aren't going to get anywhere if we're constantly at each other's throats. Let's walk inland and see if we can figure out where we are."

Miki didn't recognize this place but she didn't expect to. Her memories of Concordia were hazy at best. It didn't really matter where they were anyway. Her mind was made up about what she had to do.

THIRTY-ONE

Wilder climbed with Niall to an area of high ground while the others waited in a hollow at the bottom. They'd marched a kilometer or so inland along a thin, overgrown trail between low hills. Though Meric had assured them they would be dropped in an inhabited region, they hadn't come across any human dwellings or Scythian domes. That wasn't so surprising. Concordia had always been sparsely populated compared to Earth, even during its most peaceful and productive period. Vast tracts of wilderness on Lyonesse had barely been explored, let alone settled.

They seemed to be in an area of the coastline north of Oceanside. The southern region was fairly arid, but here the few types of vegetation that had recovered from the biocide grew thick and lush. A type of short-stemmed, supple, tough groundcover plant that Wilder remembered from her days at Sidhe flourished, and the spiny shrubs they'd encountered near the beach proliferated over most of the terrain. The latter's presence made progress difficult, snagging on clothes, backpacks, and skin as they were forced to push past it.

It was horrible stuff, yet its presence and vitality lifted Wilder's heart. Life was returning to her country despite all the onslaughts it had suffered. Hope remained, no matter what pessimists like Maddox thought.

Niall stooped and put a hand on her shoulder. She followed his suggestion and crouched low as they moved higher. They were nearing the top of the rise, where the shrubs grew more sparsely and provided little cover. The wind blew stronger. As they drew closer to the top the shrubs disappeared, leaving only dirt, rocks, and patches of thin groundcover. They crouched lower until they were crawling on their bellies.

A gentler sun than Suddene's was high in the sky, peeking out between scudding clouds, but this would not stop the Scythians from patrolling, as they'd discovered. For the moment, the skies were clear.

Then they were moving along flat ground, and the land beyond slowly came into view. At first, Wilder thought they were looking at the shore and they'd turned back on themselves, but then she spotted a thin line marking a farther shore.

A vast estuary spread out before them, dotted with sand banks and water of varying colors according to its depth. In some places it was deep blue, where it had cut a channel through the bed and the river ran fast. In others it was pale and festooned with green seaweed.

She checked to her right. A mountain range rose high, its peaks dusted with snow. Before reaching the range the water narrowed to a wide river. "I know where we are. This is the mouth of the Vimur."

Ethan had famously first encountered the Fila on the other side of the range, caught and trapped by them in an underwater chamber while they investigated this strange new species that seemed to have suddenly appeared on Concordia.

"You're right," Niall said. "Has to be. But...shit. Look over there."

A little farther inland, on the nearside banks of the estuary, stood three Scythian domes, equidistant from each other. The tops were closed and no aliens appeared to be circling, but this was clearly hostile territory. Then again, as they understood it, so was most of Lyonesse.

"I'd hoped they hadn't come this far north," said Wilder.

"They've been here a long time. They will be wherever people are and, from memory, this place had been settled a while before the biocide attack."

Wilder thought back to the Concordia she remembered from before the Scythians returned. "You're right. There was the beginnings of a tourist industry. People came here to swim, sail boats, and play with the Fila. It was easier in the shallow water."

Near the domes was a patchwork of fields. As they'd seen in the images recorded from the *Sirocco*, crops were being grown, presumably for human and alien consumption. Concordians would be the farmers, though none were visible.

"I can see buildings." Niall pointed.

They were in the typical Concordian style, a throwback to the prefab colonization kits, low, simple, functional.

"The Scythians allow their slaves to live outside?" It seemed lax and overly trusting.

"They probably don't want them cluttering up their domes."

"I wonder if there are any Resistance members living among them."

"Only one way to find out," said Niall. "We can either try to approach those people or head down south. What do you think?"

"We should put it to the others, but I can't see any point in going south. It's more populated down there, and more people means more Scythians. Besides, we'll use up our supplies for no purpose. We need to find the Resistance. We stand as good a chance finding them here as anywhere else. Maybe a greater chance. This must be one of the areas that sends food to Chimera, or else how would the ship's captain know about the cove where he dropped us off?"

"All good arguments. Let's see what the others say."

———

"That's a dumb idea," said Maddox. "Those people are Scythian slaves. They aren't going to risk talking to us."

A muscle in her jaw twitching, Wilder turned to Zapata. "What do you think?"

"We don't have a choice. We have to make contact with the people living around here. How else are we going to survive when our supplies run out?"

"Easy," Maddox said. "We go north, build our own place, live off what we can find and grow."

"What would be the point of that?" Wilder asked.

"Not dying, which I happen to think is a very good point."

"That won't work," said Niall. "Aside from the fact that we came here to do a job, a job we can't do unless we interact with Concordians, the Scythians regularly patrol, looking for human activity. Sooner or later they'll spot us and we'll either be killed or made slaves, the same as everyone else."

"Not if we're careful."

"That's such bullshit," Wilder spat. "You think the rest of the people living here weren't careful? You think they didn't try to get away to safer areas and hide?"

"Maybe, for some of them, it worked. We just don't know about them."

Wilder groaned and sank her head into her hands.

"My first point still stands," said Niall. "We came here to do a job."

"An impossible job," Maddox countered. "It amazes me that two such supposedly intelligent people haven't figured that out yet. It's time to call it quits and make the best we can of a bad situation. The Scythians won, and that's that."

Wilder turned to Miki. "What do *you* think?"

She shrugged. "I'm happy to do whatever you guys think is best."

Maddox asked, "No devastating insights about Scythians to reveal that might help us with our decision?"

"Stars, that was mean," said Wilder.

"And uncalled-for," Niall added.

Maddox widened her eyes. "What? That's why she's here, isn't it? To give us the benefit of her detailed understanding of Scythian behavior. I mean, she *demanded* to come along." She turned to Miki. "How's that working out for you?"

Wilder slapped her so hard her head jerked around. Wilder drew back her hand for a second slap but Niall grabbed her wrist. "Cut it out. And Maddox..."

The woman was clutching her face and glaring at Wilder.

"...any more picking on Miki, or anyone else for that matter, and you're off the mission. You can find out how well your plan of traveling north works when you're alone."

Maddox's shoulders slumped. "Sorry. My ribs are hurting me."

Wilder didn't think that was sufficient excuse, but she said nothing.

Zapata cleared his throat. "We need to make an effort to not fight among ourselves."

"Agreed," Niall said. "The majority view is we approach the people tending the fields near the estuary, so that's what we'll do. There's no point in waiting for dark because, if anything, it'll be easier for the Scythians to spot us, and we're fairly rested, so I say there's no time like the present."

It was agreed that Zapata would stay with the backpacks. Not only would he slow them down, if Scythians spotted them he wouldn't stand a chance of running away. Maddox insisted on staying behind too, citing her injured ribs.

Wilder rolled her eyes but didn't object. She was sure the woman's reluctance to take part was driven more by fear than pain, but, in truth, she didn't want her around anyway.

The trail they'd followed through the low hills continued in the rough direction of the estuary. As they stepped along it the hills became taller but then lower again and lower still, until they were walking through open country. They stooped low.

Wilder felt naked and defenseless as they crept across the flat landscape. The memory of long, scaly, Scythian toes gripping her like a vice as she was carried aloft grew vivid. The alien stench was strong in her nostrils, and the wind in the upper atmosphere seemed to stir her hair. The sky was empty, however, and no sign of activity appeared at the three Scythian domes looming in the distance.

The scene remained serene. It was a pleasant day, and though the variety of plants in the landscape was extremely limited, it might have been any other peaceful day on Lyonesse before the Scythians returned. Wilder recalled the heli flight she'd taken with Kes to examine the crashed vessel in which the Guardian returned to Concordia. Sadness welled up.

They reached the edge of the farmed land.

"Do you recognize that crop?" Niall asked.

A purple-green plant trailed over the ground, spreading out from a central crown, leaves like fingers, long and limp.

Wilder replied, "It must be one of the plants Meric said the Scythians introduced to feed themselves and humans."

Niall's nose wrinkled. "Looks disgusting."

Miki gave a soft "*Oh!*" followed by "There are people."

She was looking in the direction of the estuary.

There *were* people, six or seven, wading thigh-deep through the water. At the distance it wasn't possible to tell what they were doing.

"We're looking for Concordians," said Wilder. "They're as good as any others."

Keeping low, they cut across the field.

The estuary was farther away than it appeared. The flatness of the landscape was confusing. As they worked their way closer, Wilder kept an eye on the domes. What should they do if a Scythian patrol emerged? If they were discovered, could they pretend they were farmers? Did the aliens keep a tally of the humans working for them?

Despite their efforts at avoiding detection, as they approached within ten meters of the men and women working in the estuary they were noticed. The people stopped work and turned to watch them. They wore wide-brimmed, woven hats and loose tops, tied at the waist with twine. They also wore shorts, wet from contact with the water. On their backs were net bags.

Their stances grew stiffer. Presumably they realized these people creeping toward them were strangers. A woman, hunched with age, flapped a hand toward Wilder and the others, gesturing at them to go away.

"They don't want to see us?" Miki asked.

"I think they might be frightened," said Wilder. "Let's try to talk to them anyway. We have to talk to *someone*."

When she saw her gesture hadn't worked, the older woman shook her head emphatically and began to sidle toward the bank. A couple of her companions glanced nervously at the domes.

"They really don't want to meet us," said Niall, slowing down. "Maybe it's dangerous for them to talk to people they don't know."

Wilder halted. "We only want to talk to you. We aren't from around here."

Following the older woman's lead, the men and women walked to the edge of the water. Their net bags streamed water as they left it. Fronds of seaweed hung from the gaps.

"We don't mean you any harm," Niall called out.

"Then go away!" the woman yelled back. She and her companions hastily waded the final steps to shore and then set off at a brisk walk, their bags bumping their thighs.

"Scythians!" Miki hollered.

Four aliens had exited a dome.

"Shit!" Niall exclaimed. "Get down!"

Wilder had already dropped, pulling Miki with her. They lay flat under the foliage.

"Do you think they saw us?" Miki whispered.

"Hard to tell. It might be a coincidence they came out or they might have spotted us crossing the field." Wilder asked Niall, who was on the other side of the row, "Can you see them?"

He peered out. "Can't see a thing."

Wilder waited, hardly daring to breathe. Just when she was beginning to think the Scythians weren't looking for them an impact sounded behind her, along with the crash of disturbed foliage. One of the aliens had landed.

She cursed. Niall met her gaze across the gap. If she'd remained still before, now she was utterly frozen, partly to avoid attracting the Scythians' attention, partly out of pure fear.

Niall was mouthing something at her.

What? she mouthed back.

His lips puckered up as if to peck someone on the cheek, opened a little, and then widened while his teeth drew together. *W... A or O... T.*

Water.

As understanding must have dawned on her face, he looked purposefully toward the estuary.

He thought they should go into the water?

But the aliens would see them.

Of course. He was right.

While this exchange had been going on, a second and a third impact had sounded in the field. The vegetation rustled as the Scythians walked through it, clearly searching. If they fired on them they might take out one or two, but there were four. And there were probably hundreds altogether in the three domes.

"Miki," she whispered, "if it looks like we're going to be found, run into the estuary."

"What? Why?"

"They can't follow us there. They can't move in water, only in the air or on land."

"Then they'll just shoot us."

"If they're using the same weapons as the Scythians on Earth, the rounds won't penetrate deeply. The water will slow them down fast. You need to swim deep and only come up for air when you absolutely must."

Miki looked at her with disbelief.

Could she even swim? She'd grown up on a starship.

"Just stick with me."

A heavy footstep hit the ground terrifyingly close by. Between the stalks of the crop plants, a scaly leg with long, prehensile toes could be seen. A horrible odor wafted down. Wilder slowly turned her head. Directly above them was the biggest Scythian she'd ever seen. A rifle slung across its midriff, it peered from side to side, its head encased in a tinted globe.

Then it directed its attention downward. The wings folded inward and with two of its claws it reached for the vegetation over their heads.

Wilder's lungs filled with air. "Run!"

She bolted.

She flew into the water and was up to her waist and about to dive before she noticed Miki was not with her.

There was a splash. Niall disappeared under the surface.

Where was Miki?!

Wilder checked over her shoulder.

Three Scythians stood in the field. Another batted its wings above, aiming its weapon at her.

Miki faced one of the aliens, her arms up, as if offering herself as a sacrifice.

Wilder hesitated, horror and incomprehension echoing through her bones.

The three in the field focused on Miki.

The zing of a bullet passed Wilder's ear accompanied by the tiny plop of it hitting the water.

She turned away and dove down to the bed.

THIRTY-TWO

By the time they made it back to Zapata and Maddox, the enormity of what had happened finally hit. Until then, Wilder had swum, sipped breaths, crawled from the water with Niall farther downstream, and returned to the hiding spot with a foggy confusion. All the while, the image of Miki holding up her arms to the aliens, as if begging to be taken, had stuck at the front of Wilder's mind.

Had Miki given herself up because she couldn't swim?

Had she thought the situation was hopeless and that they would all be captured regardless of what they did?

Had she done it as a distraction to allow her friends to get away?

Why? Why? Why?

Collapsing to the ground, Wilder buried her face in her hands.

"Where's Miki?" Zapata asked. "Is she on her way?"

"She isn't coming," Niall replied, his tone hard. "The Scythians have her."

"You let them take her?" Maddox asked accusingly. "Oh well, no big loss."

Wilder's head snapped up. "Shut up! Shut your goddamned face!"

"She went with them willingly," said Niall.

Maddox scoffed, "Why the hell would she do that? Are you sure you're telling us the truth?"

Wilder launched herself at the woman, elbow pulled back. Niall grabbed her and wrestled with her. Her body went limp and she began to weep. She'd failed Miki. She didn't know how it had happened or what she'd done wrong, but she'd failed her. She should have known the girl had something going on. She should have been able to read the signs.

"She'll be alive still," Zapata said. "I'm sure of it. They will put her to work like they did on Earth. They don't seem to be in the habit of killing people, only turning them into slaves."

Wilder sniffed. "We don't know that. Even if she is alive, we can't rip the lid off a dome like we did before. How will we get her out? The Scythians treat their slaves badly, starving them half to death." She recalled what Meric had told her about the aliens pairing humans up for breeding. Her stomach churned.

"I'm just saying, we shouldn't give up. Miki got *herself* out before. She might do it again."

"Things were different on Earth. People were resisting the colonization. Here, they seem to have given up."

Niall said, "Losing Miki is a big shock. We need to calm down and think things through. There is a Resistance here. If we can contact them they might be able to help us free her."

"How can we contact them if no one will talk to us? You saw how those people at the estuary behaved when they saw us. They don't want anything to do with outsiders."

"People at the estuary?" Zapata echoed.

Niall filled him in.

"So the Scythians allow humans to work outside the domes unsupervised? That's a good sign."

"Is it?" asked Maddox. "All it says to me is Concordians are so under their control they don't even bother watching them."

"I swear," Wilder said, "if you don't—"

"I'm allowed an opinion!"

"Keep your opinions to yourself for now," said Niall. "If we want to hear what you think, we'll ask you."

Maddox folded her arms and looked away.

"You should try the buildings near the fields," said Zapata. "*We* should try them. I'll go with you this time."

"With your leg like that?" asked Niall.

"Especially with my leg like this."

———

They went at twilight. As they'd watched and waited, people had come out to harvest the strange, leafy crop from a field. Then, when they collected the bundles from the ends of the rows and carried them in, they slipped among them. It wasn't until the farmhands drew closer together they were noticed in the half light. Zapata was the first to draw attention, hopping along on his crutch.

An uneasy stir passed through the men and women but they seemed too scared to say anything. Scythians had begun to leave their domes, flapping lazily up into the dimming sky. If they scanned their slaves for newcomers, they weren't able to spot them, for Wilder, Niall, and Zapata made it to the barn where the leaves were being taken.

Once they were under cover, a lanky man spun to face them. "You're the strangers! Get out of here before you get us all in trouble."

"We need help," said Zapata. "I've hurt my leg."

"Why should we care? The Scythians will do worse than hurt our legs if they find out we're harboring foreigners."

"Foreigner?" Wilder asked. "We're from Lyonesse like you."

"You aren't from these parts, and if you were traveling legally you wouldn't be sneaking around. I'm sorry. We can't help you."

"Surely you wouldn't turn away a fellow human being in need?" asked Zapata. "If you could just give us shelter for one night so we can rest? Then in the morning we'll be on our way."

"Maybe one night won't hurt," said a woman. "They could sleep here. If the Scythians find them we can say we didn't know about them."

"They won't believe us," the lanky man retorted, "and even if they do believe us they'll punish us anyway."

"We had a spot inspection the other day," someone else said. "They won't be back for a while."

The lanky man strode to a stack of harvested plants and dumped his bundle on the top. "Have it your way. I don't want any part of it." He marched out of the barn.

"Don't pay any attention to him," said the woman. "His son lives in a dome. Makes him extra cautious."

"Thanks for your hospitality," Niall said. "We understand we're asking a lot. I'm—"

"No names, please. It's safer that way. Make yourselves comfortable. There's a bit of space at the back you can bed down in. I'll come by later with water and food, though we can't spare much."

"You're very kind," said Wilder, feeling guilty at the offer of food when they had plenty in the backpacks they'd left with Maddox. Maybe they would find a way to give them some. They had brought only one thing with them aside from Zapata's crutch, and it wasn't supplies.

"It's no trouble. As you said, it would be wrong to turn away a fellow human being in need. We're all in this together, right?"

"Right."

As the woman and the other workers left, Wilder relaxed. Step one had been accomplished. From now on, all her efforts would be focused on getting Miki back. Defeating the Scythians could come later.

Zapata hop-stepped around the bundles of drying plants and Wilder and Niall followed. As the woman had said, a small area of bare ground lay between the plants and the barn wall.

"What about Maddox?" asked Niall. "Should I go back and get her?"

"Screw Maddox," said Wilder. "She can fend for herself for once and see how she likes it."

Niall also didn't seem to feel any sense of urgency about collecting their remaining mission member, and neither did Zapata.

The pilot eased himself to the ground, one hand on the planks of the wall for support. "They seem to think we're vagrants."

"Or escapees from another Scythian-controlled territory," said Niall. "I got the feeling we aren't the first they've seen."

"I suppose it must be a thing," Wilder said, joining Zapata on the ground. "There must be a few Concordians wandering about, keeping out of sight of the Scythians, but unable to gather in sufficient numbers to fight back. They won't have weapons either. The first thing the aliens would have done is confiscate and destroy any they found."

"Can you pass me the head?" asked Niall.

"You want to give it another go?" She reached into the bag and drew out the grisly artifact.

A figure stepped around the stacked plants, and Wilder shoved the Guardian's head behind her back.

"I brought you this," said the woman who had spoken to them earlier, holding a jug of water and a small cloth sack. "It isn't much."

Wilder was tempted to say they weren't hungry but it would appear suspicious. For the time being, it seemed better to go along with the woman's assumptions about them.

Niall accepted the jug and sack. "Would you stay a while? We only arrived today and we'd like to learn about this place."

Alarm appeared in her features. "Uhh... Maybe later. If I can slip away."

She was gone.

After waiting a moment in case of further interruptions, Wilder passed the head to Niall in exchange for the food and water. She took a drink from the jug and gave it to Zapata. Then she widened the drawstrings holding the neck of the sack. The scent of the ocean wafted up. Inside were dried strands of seaweed, the same weed they'd seen the people in the estuary gathering, presumably.

After handing some to Zapata, she chewed the salty leaf. It expanded in her mouth, quickly absorbing her saliva and turning into a gooey, chewy mess. It tasted familiar. Perhaps she'd eaten it once long ago, before the world had turned to shit.

Niall didn't eat or drink. He was busy examining, prodding, and poking the Guardian's head. Ever since they'd had it, Niall and she had been trying to activate it. During the days she'd spent recovering at Chimera, he had attempted various methods of supplying it with power while also avoiding the risk of overloading or short-circuiting it.

If the problem was a lack of energy, they hadn't solved it, and if it had power and there was another way of starting it up they hadn't found it yet. Wilder had speculated that, as neither she nor Miki had seen the Guardian's body, it must have been only its head that Aubriot had taken into the city, which meant it had operated on its own. What it *had* done, it *could* do, hypothetically. Moreover, either the head had run out of juice after Aubriot had left it behind—the idea of the AI spending decades alone down there, unable to even move, sent shivers down her spine—or he'd turned it off. And if there was a way of turning it off, there had to be a way of turning it on.

They'd looked the thing over a hundred times, trying to find the 'switch'. But the head was a burned, smashed mess. If there had been an on/off button it was no longer recognizable. And if there had never been a button, both she and Niall were flummoxed as to what else could be used to activate it.

She watched him, chewing the seaweed, as he tried again all the things they'd tried before. It was dumb but she understood his frustration. The vegetable matter in her mouth didn't seem to be getting any smaller. She forced the bolus down and held out her hand. "Let me try."

Heaving a sigh, Niall lifted the head to pass it over.

Whatever he touched as he did so, it must have been the magic spot.

The Guardian's eye blinked to life.

Thirty-Three

A woman screamed.

The person who had brought them food and water had returned unnoticed. She was staring at the head, her hands clutched to her face, her mouth an O of horror.

"It's fine," said Wilder. "It's only..."

The woman darted away.

"Shit," Niall said. "What do you think she'll do?"

"What do *you* think? Everyone within five klicks must have heard her."

"We'd better get out of here." Zapata struggled to his feet. "There's no telling what people will do when they're frightened."

Wilder shoved the awakened head into her bag. They abandoned the sack of seaweed and the jug and hurried to the door of the barn, but they were already too late. Seven or eight farmers blocked the entrance. More were running over, eager to discover the source of the commotion.

The man who had objected to their presence stood at the front of the throng gripping a short knife, probably used for harvesting. His companions held similar 'weapons'. One lifted a long-tined fork aloft, another had a thick stick with wide strips of material hanging from it.

"I knew there was something not right about you lot," said the lanky man. "Where's that thing you're carrying? Hand it over."

After spending days trying to activate the head, Wilder was damned if she was going to give it away. She clutched the bag tightly. "Let us out and we'll leave peacefully. We won't bother you anymore."

"You're not going anywhere. Someone's getting the message to the Scythians right now. They'll be here soon enough."

In the corner of her eye, Wilder noticed Niall's arm slowly moving toward the back of his pants. "If you've already betrayed us, why do you want what we have? Won't the Scythians take it anyway?"

"So you don't hurt anyone with it before they get here," the man sneered.

Zapata said, "Please, let us go. We don't mean you any harm and we never did. We're all Concordians. We should help each other, not fight among ourselves. All that does is make the Scythians' work easier."

"They won this planet a long time ago. The fight is over, and we know our place." The lanky man's knife-wielding arm dropped a notch. "Fine. If you refuse to give it to us, we can wait for the Scythians to arrive."

"We know our place?" asked Wilder. "What kind of defeatist talk is that? People died to make this planet ours. They toiled and fought and sacrificed their lives for Concordia. You know your place? You should be ashamed."

The man's face paled. He lifted his knife and took a step closer to her. "There's no shame in honest work. As long as we stick to the rules the Scythians treat us well. All we have to do is not step out of line."

Fury rose up in her. She'd been playing along, keeping the argument going, to distract from what Niall was doing, but this man's sentiment sparked rage. "Spoken like a good slave!" She turned her attention to his companions. "Look at you! If I hadn't seen it with my own eyes I would never have believed that Concordians had sunk so low. You're no better than animals, beasts of burden, working for masters who don't give a shit whether you live or die. What kind of legacy is that to leave your children? What kind of gratitude are you showing to your ancestors? Generations of people lived out their lives aboard a starship, colonists endured bombardments and floods and attacks, and every time, after each disaster they started again from scratch and rebuilt. Again and again. And all for what? So their pathetic, disgusting descendants could bow down to Scythians and 'know their place'."

Niall's gun whipped up. The farmers' rapt attention broke and their stares shifted to the weapon.

"Move aside." He stepped forward. "I don't want to hurt anyone but I will if I have to."

"I knew they were Resistance," the lanky man muttered.

Wilder took out her gun too.

The man drew back along with the rest, creating a gap. Zapata stepped through it. Niall went next and Wilder walked out last, turning to aim at the onlookers.

A loose group of thirty or forty more farmers hung around the entrance to the barn. Uncomfortable tingles ran through Wilder. For now, the guns were keeping them back, but with so many against so few the tables could turn quickly. All it would take would be for one brave person to break ranks and risk being shot, and the battle would be over.

Yet no one did. Perhaps they thought it was easier to leave the work to the Scythians, or perhaps they were too cowed, too used to being ordered around. To step out of line and do something different from everyone else felt scary and strange.

Wilder and the others walked away unimpeded and unchallenged. She scanned the dusky sky, the first stars glimmering. Whatever method the farmers had for contacting the Scythians, it was not speedy. The small settlement sat only a kilometer from the nearest dome. One of the aliens could cross the space in half a minute, but no winged shapes blotted out the stars.

A fast runner had to be on his way to a dome. As soon as the alert was given the aliens would fly out, and there was no cover anywhere nearby. With their infrared vision the Scythians would spot them easily.

They reached the end of the last building. The farmers watched, silent and still.

Niall hissed, "Run!"

Wilder sped into the dark field, the Guardian's head in a bag bouncing against her. They had no plan, no agreed place to rendezvous, no strategy for what to do if any of them was captured. Hell, at this rate, they were *all* highly likely to be captured, especially Zapata, who could barely walk, let alone run.

So much for making contact with Concordians. She didn't think she'd ever felt so disappointed, so disheartened, or so embarrassed for her people. She'd meant every word she'd said. All her efforts, all of Cherry's, Kes's, Ethan's, Cariad's, and every other person who had arrived on the *Nova* had been an utter waste. What was the point of saving such miserable cowards? Maybe Maddox's idea had some merit. The prospect of giving up on freeing Concordia was appealing. Why keep on fighting when the people you were fighting for weren't worth the effort?

"Stop!"

Someone was running after her. He'd shouted something else but she didn't catch it, her blood pounding and her gasps for air loud in her ears. So one of the farmers did have some balls after all, even if it was only to capture her for the Scythians.

She sped up.

Her lungs labored as she raced across the field, leaping clumps of plants that only became visible when she was nearly upon them.

"Stop! Wait!"

She didn't have breath to answer. If she had, she would have given the type of reply Aubriot had been in the habit of giving.

Footsteps thudded, getting closer. "Stop, dammit! I—"

Arms wrapped around her thighs. She and her pursuer smacked into the ground. She kicked and struggled, swinging for the man's head.

"I'm trying to—"

A punch connected. Bone and flesh met her knuckles with a crunch while pain exploded in her hand.

"Arghh!" He moved on top of her, crushing her with his weight and pinning her wrists to her sides. "I'm trying to help you, you stupid…" He panted, catching his breath, and repeated more quietly and urgently, "I'm trying to help."

"Help take me to the Scythians!" She lunged upward, teeth bared.

"No! Come with me. Now. They'll be here in less than a minute." He released her and rose to his feet. "Follow me, or don't. Your choice. I'm done risking my life for you." He loped off across the field.

She checked the domes. Black humps against a blacker sky, their tops were fuzzy and active. Scythians were pouring out. The alarm had been given and they were on their way.

The man was already becoming indistinct in the darkness. She couldn't see Niall or Zapata.

She ran after him.

He was moving fast. She had to force her aching legs to work harder just to keep him in sight. She had no chance of catching up.

Then he vanished.

She slowed down. Where had he gone? One second he was here, the next he'd disappeared, as if he'd melted into the night. Her run slowed to a jog. The scene was surreal. The landscape was empty save for the wide fields, the glints of the distant estuary, and the alien shapes speeding closer. Had she imagined the encounter? But her chest ached from where she'd hit the ground.

Something snagged her ankles, grasped her tightly, and dragged her down. She was falling. She smashed into a spongy surface that softened her impact. Starlight above abruptly cut out at the sound of a trap closing. Another type of light flared, and there was the man who had chased her.

He held out a hand to help her to her feet. "I'm glad you made the right choice."

She dusted herself down. "You're with the Resistance, right?"

THIRTY-FOUR

"Either remove me from this bag or de-activate me."

Wilder almost leapt out of her skin. In the flight from the angry farmers and the stranger chasing her through the fields before pulling her into a hole in the ground, she'd forgotten the Guardian's head had 'woken up.' Her savior also jumped. He stared at the cloth bag—the source of the voice.

Wilder had only just clambered to her feet. The stranger was in his twenties. His hair was long and unkempt and a few days' beard growth clothed his cheeks. His skin was pale, as if he spent much of his time out of the sun. His clothes reminded her of the state of her own when the *Sirocco* had finally reached Earth. They were little more than rags. Even the patches were patched.

The man appeared to know something about her. Otherwise why had he risked his life to try to save her from the Scythians? But she doubted he expected her to have a talking bag.

"I, er, I'd better take it out," she said apologetically. "It's scary-looking, but there's nothing to be afraid of."

He frowned. "It would take a lot more than a comm to—*Whoa!*" He stumbled backward, his pale skin turning paler.

She had lifted up the Guardian's head. Its face happened to be pointed in his direction, partial mouth, single, roving eye and all.

"What the...?" he breathed.

"My name is Faina," the android said. "My bearer is correct. You have nothing to fear from me. Please attempt to overcome your natural repugnance at my appearance. Who is holding me?"

Wilder turned the head around. The stranger rested a hand on the wall, staring at the Guardian's scant remains.

Faina studied Wilder's features. "You have aged, but I believe you are Wilder, one of the original colonists who disembarked the *Nova Fortuna*. Remarkable. I do not detect a net to connect to in this vicinity. What year is this and where am I?"

Wilder replied, "You're on Lyonesse, near the mouth of the Vimur, and the year is…" She looked at the man questioningly. Though Meric had told her the year, she'd actually forgotten.

When the stranger gasped it out, Faina said, "Interesting. I didn't expect to ever be re-activated. Did you reactivate me, Wilder? And for what reason? Why have you brought me to Lyonesse? The last thing I remember is Aubriot shutting me down. At that time, I was within the Scythian city on Suddene."

Wilder didn't want to talk in front of this man she didn't know. He might be Resistance and he might have saved her from capture, but she'd learned the harsh lesson that not all Concordians were friendly or sympathetic. She didn't know who this man might talk to. "That's a lot of questions, Faina. Maybe we should go somewhere I can sit down and we can talk. Can I put you back in the bag?"

"No."

The man opened an arm wide, inviting her to step into the passage leading from the base of the hole. It was so low she had to stoop. The walls and floor were stony subsoil, and the earth ceiling was propped with beams. It didn't look at all safe. Wilder held out the Guardian's head gingerly as they went along, like a grisly lantern.

Faina said, "I would like to take this opportunity to make something clear. Though I may not be organic, my mind was derived from a wide and numerous range of human minds. I think and, I believe, I experience my surroundings and the passing of time as a human being does. When my head was severed from my body I lost my ability to independently de-activate. If I were to be lost or left somewhere and forgotten, I will remain awake. I will be alone and unable to move until my power runs out, which won't be for a very long time. My existence would be torturous. So I ask that you take especial care to avoid this happening. If there is a chance I may be separated from you or another bearer, please pre-emptively de-activate me."

"I understand," Wilder replied. "I'll do it."

The android had made her point without a hint of self-pity, despite the horrific scenario she'd conjured.

"But," Wilder added, "I don't know how to shut you down. I don't know how we activated you in the first place. We'd been trying for days."

"There is a small area you must press. I will describe the spot to you when we reach a resting place."

As they'd talked, the Resistance man had squeezed past Wilder to walk in front. Maybe he found the talking head unnerving. He straightened up. They'd reached in a circular chamber. The floor, walls, and ceiling were made from concrete and a single lamp hung in the center. Two figures were seated in the shadows at the edge, and they stood up.

It was Niall and Zapata, who had managed to retain his crutch.

Wilder put Faina down on the bench and hugged Zapata tightly, Niall a little less so. "Guys! I was worried about you."

"You've got the head?" Niall asked. "Thank the stars. I was worried you might have dropped it."

"My *name* is Faina," said the Guardian.

"Weirdest thing I ever saw." The man shook hands with Niall and Zapata. "You can call me Steven, though that isn't my real name. I take it my friends brought you in?"

"That's right," Niall replied.

Zapata said, "They nabbed me almost as soon as I left the lights from the village."

"Your friends have gone to check on Scythian activity," said Niall.

"Please, take a seat." Steven gestured at the bench. "I'm sorry it took us so long to find you. Meric sent word you would be arriving in Lyonesse, but you didn't appear at the location he named. Did you meet Commander Orson?" After noting their nods, he explained, "We think he told the captain of the vessel that brought you over to leave you in a different place from Meric's instructions. Orson must have hoped you would never manage to connect with the Resistance. He might even have told the captain to drop you over the side of the boat. But if he did, I guess the man didn't have the stomach for cold-blooded murder of fellow Concordians."

"Sounds like we had a near miss," said Zapata. "At least we finally found you. A fourth member of our party is waiting for us in the woods in nearby hills. Could someone find her and bring her here?"

"Later," said Steven, "when things have died down a bit. It's too dangerous right now. As long as she stays where she is she should be safe. The Scythians don't maneuver too well in woodland."

Wilder's attention shifted to the room. "What is this place?"

"It's an old grain store." Steven gave a wink. "It was re-purposed not long after the Scythians arrived."

"So we're near the farm buildings?"

"Not far away, though the majority of the farmers don't know we're here. They have no idea we exist. But a handful are Resistance, like us. They told us you'd turned up, but unfortunately we didn't get time to make contact before the traitors informed on you."

"Traitors is a strong word," Zapata said mildly.

"What else would you call them?" Steven's jaw muscles tensed and he strode across the chamber, hands clenched into fists. "If we could *just* all band together and stand up for ourselves, we might make life so difficult for the Scythians they would leave us alone. But half the population is too scared and the other half is too plain lazy. As long as they have enough food in their bellies to keep them from starving they're content. Some of them even seem happy with the status quo." He faced them, glaring. "You should hear some things they say." Putting on a mewling voice he said, "*This is how it's meant to be* and *The Scythians are better than us. That's just how it is. No point in denying it. And it* is *their planet, after all.*"

He shook his head. "It makes me so angry, I want to knock some sense into them. So what if Concordia was originally someone else's? It was empty when we got here. How were we to know it had once been the home of another intelligent species? That was a long time ago, and Scythians can't live here without our help. It makes more sense for them to fuck off and leave us to it. *We're* the ones who can develop this place to its full potential, not them. They had their chance." His rant dried up and he looked at them sheepishly. "Sorry, I get carried away sometimes."

"Don't apologise," said Wilder. "Honestly, it's a relief to hear from someone with a fire in their belly. All we've heard since we arrived is excuses. And you're friendlier than most too. Half the Concordians we've met have wanted to kill us."

Steven joined them on the bench. "So you really are from the *Sirocco*? It's a little hard to take in. I learned about your ship when I was a kid and only half believed it then. But that's a stupid question, right? Considering you have a talking head."

"Faina isn't from our ship. She's one of the Guardians who arrived on the *Mistral*. She'd been left in the Scythian city near Chimera."

"This gets more fantastical by the minute. Maybe it's a sign things are finally going to change around here. Maybe the uprising we've been working toward for so many years will happen at last."

"Tell us about the Resistance," said Niall. "How many of you are there? How far does the network spread?"

"I can't answer you, I'm afraid. None of us can. Each member can't know too much information. It's too risky. If the Scythians catch us, they try to extract as many details as they can before execution. We've only been able to survive this long by limiting knowledge of our organization. Personally, I only know the people in this sector, and just one of us is in touch with the nearest branch, and so on."

"It doesn't matter," Wilder said. "We've made contact with you, and we have a new source of Scythian intel." She gestured toward Faina. "We can begin to put the wheels in motion. It's long past time Concordians fought back."

THIRTY-FIVE

A stony-faced woman was to be their guide for the journey south. She didn't give them a fake name as 'Steven' had, and she was silent as she waited with them for Maddox to be brought in. When their reluctant companion appeared—complaining loudly that she'd been woken from a deep sleep and her ribs still hurt and this could all have waited until the morning—their guide inspected the packs of provisions from Chimera too. The contents seemed to meet her approval. She didn't request anything else except water bottles, which she dispersed equally. Then she announced they would leave immediately.

Wilder guessed it had to be about four in the morning when they set out. Pre-dawn light had brightened the sky in the east but plenty of stars were still shining.

"Isn't it dangerous to travel at this time?" Wilder asked the guide. "Won't the Scythians be patrolling?"

"All times are dangerous for traveling. The Scythians constantly patrol. But here in the north there aren't many of them, not compared to down south anyway. By the way, we can't stop or rest for long at night. If we do—"

"Don't worry. We know all about sluglimpets."

Wilder had close experience of the animals, and Niall, Zapata, and Maddox knew their reputation, which had survived since the early days of colonization. Such was the horror they evoked.

The woman led them across farmed land, keeping close to hedgerows that overhung ditches. Her eyes were on the sky as much as the trail, though how she would spot Scythians in the darkness Wilder couldn't imagine. She guessed the Resistance members had honed their abilities over the years. Those who didn't grow good at it didn't survive.

When the fields petered out they crossed rougher ground. Their already slow progress due to Zapata's broken leg was slowed further, and Wilder sensed their Resistance companion's impatience and growing fear. Nevertheless, the woman said nothing as she frequently drew ahead and then stopped to wait for her charges to catch up.

When they reached the rolling, sandy hills near the coast it was mid-morning and Zapata was white-faced and sweating with effort. Yet their guide showed no sign of calling a halt.

Niall, who had been supporting the pilot on the other side of his crutch, said quietly, "We need to stop and rest for a while."

"Exactly what I was thinking," announced Maddox. "Unless you plan on making us walk non-stop to wherever the hell it is we're supposed to be going?"

All they knew about their destination was that it was the nearest Resistance cell to the south. From there, they would be taken to the next cell and the next until they ended up at the headquarters, though only their penultimate guide would know its location.

Their current one turned with a resigned expression and scrutinized Zapata. Then she scanned the surrounding landscape. She pointed to a copse of leggy plants a couple of meters tall. "Over there." Without looking back, she tramped to the place and disappeared within the foliage.

By the time Wilder and the others arrived she had her water bottle out and was munching on a snack. Plant leaves drooped over sloped ground and snaking roots. It wasn't a great spot to rest in, but it was mostly hidden from an overhead view.

Wilder sat next to guide, hoping to coax out information on a deeply concerning subject. "Does anyone know what happens to the people taken into the domes by the Vimur?"

The woman shrugged. "There are plenty of rumors. As to what's true and what isn't, who knows?"

"What kind of rumors?"

"Wilder," Niall interrupted, "if the stories are unsubstantiated, what's the point? You'll only worry yourself unnecessarily. It isn't like you can do anything to help Miki now."

The guide asked, "A friend of yours was captured?"

"More like she gave herself up," Niall muttered.

"All we know for sure is, anyone taken into a dome is never seen again, dead or alive. That's it. No one has ever escaped our local domes. So, I'm sorry but..."

Wilder hung her head. She couldn't stop thinking about the girl—thinking, wishing, hoping, and regretting.

"It's best to accept they're gone," said the guide. "Another victim of the Scythians. It makes you hate them more. Gives you the motivation to keep fighting." She stuffed her water bottle into her pack. "I'm going to sleep. Wake me when the sun shines in. Or, of course, if you spot Scythians."

"Huh?" said Maddox. "When do *we* sleep?"

"You sleep after we arrive." The guide took off her jacket, lay down, and put her jacket over her shoulders and head.

"You sleep too, Zapata, if you can," said Wilder. "We'll keep watch."

The roots made the ground uncomfortable, but the pilot was soon sleeping soundly. Maddox needed no persuasion to take advantage of their rest, but after some tossing and turning she gave up and sat morosely staring through a gap in the foliage.

"How much farther, do you think?" Niall whispered.

"No idea," Wilder replied. "Except it has to be walking distance. Can Zapata make it?"

"If willpower alone is all that's required, he'll make it. Whether his body can hold up is another question."

"I wish he could have stayed with the Resistance at the last place. This stage of the journey alone could be too much for him, and I'm guessing we'll have plenty more to make. In the old days, we would have used flitters. I think Ethan came up this way on a flitter, then headed inland. And when I traveled with Kes over the mountains it was by heli. Never thought I'd ever have to walk it."

"Staying behind didn't seem to be an option for Zapata," said Niall. "I suppose to the Resistance he's a liability, and they might not a hundred percent believe our story. It's easier to make him and the rest of us someone else's problem."

Wilder silently sipped water. She and Niall waited for the time to pass. Every so often Niall would stand for a better view and search the skies. But no Scythians passed overhead. The day grew cloudy and dull, and they had to guess when the sun would have been shining into the copse if it had been visible.

The guide went from deeply asleep to wide awake within seconds, sitting up and putting on her jacket. She jerked her chin at the still-sleeping Zapata. "Get him up. We're leaving in five minutes." After quickly checking overhead, she stepped out from among the tall plants.

Zapata took longer to wake up, and an expression of dismay descended over his features as he remembered where he was. But then his stoical look returned as Niall handed him water and something to eat.

They began at a brisk pace but it soon degenerated to a slow slog. Wilder took turns with Niall helping Zapata. When she walked alone she zoned out apart from occasional glances at the sky. The sound of ocean waves surging came from their left, though the water was obscured by dunes. It would have been far too dangerous to travel along the open beach.

They had one more short rest before the sun set, and after that the guide would not allow them to stop, saying sluglimpets were common in this place and would have picked up the scent of humans. The trek became a brutal endurance march. Wilder couldn't imagine how Zapata continued on. Recalling her time in the Scythian city, she was certain she could not have done it. Each pained pant he exhaled brought pangs of pity. Even Maddox softened and took turns to help him as he limped along.

They'd entered countryside where the vegetation was recovering well from the biocide. The ground was flatter too, making the going easier, but it also made them more vulnerable. Here, there was nowhere to hide from a Scythian patrol, and in the cloudy night and near darkness, the aliens would be hard to spot. Their guide seemed to grow more and more fearful. She craned her neck to look upward again and again, and once tripped and fell because she wasn't paying attention to what was in front of her.

Just as Wilder was thinking even she wouldn't make it to the next cell, Zapata gave out a groan and toppled from Niall's grasp, hitting the ground flat on his face.

"Shit," Wilder said. "That's it. We have to stop."

"Absolutely not," the guide said. "Get him on his feet."

"He can't do it. He has to rest."

"Either he walks or we leave him to the sluglimpets. If you stay with him they'll get you too."

"He can't go on," Niall said. "It's impossible."

"I'll come with you," Maddox told the guide. "I know it's harsh but when it comes down to it, it's everyone for themselves, right?"

Wilder squatted at Zapata's side. "Let me help you up. You can do it."

He didn't answer. He was completely out of it. Maybe he was dying. She had no way to tell. But she couldn't leave him. She'd been lucky enough to never witness a sluglimpet attack but she knew exactly what happened. She couldn't imagine a worse death.

An insect called loudly in the darkness. Wilder instantly recognised the sound. She'd heard it so much when she was growing up it had become background noise. But it came from another time. She hadn't heard the calls once after the biocide attack.

The guide put two fingers to her lips and made the same sound.

"What are you doing?" Maddox asked, incredulous.

"Shut up, idiot," Niall said. "It's a signal."

Sure enough, a few minutes later a shadowy figure emerged from the blackness. A tall, broad-shouldered man shook hands with the guide. He was swathed in dark garments. A scarf was wrapped around his head and the lower half of his face, revealing only his eyes. While he conducted a quiet conversation with their guide, he watched Wilder and the others, frowning with suspicion.

Wilder caught the words *your contact* and *sluglimpet food*.

"We're not leaving our friend." Niall had overheard the comment too.

"He's right," said Wilder. "All of us come with you or we stay with Zapata. We'll take our chances with the sluglimpets."

"Speak for yourself," Maddox said. "Besides, what happened to your grand plan of rising up against the Scythians? How are you going to do that while being slowly digested alive?"

"It's okay." The man strode to Zapata and bent over him. First, he picked up the crutch. "Someone grab this."

Wilder took it.

"Help me get him up," the man told Niall.

When Zapata was somewhat upright, the man lifted him onto his shoulder. "This way."

It was only after they began walking that Wilder realised their guide had departed without a word.

THIRTY-SIX

Massive shapes loomed in the darkness.

For a brief second, Wilder's heart froze and terror flashed in her mind as she inferred their new guide had betrayed them and brought them to the Scythians. But the shapes were not domes, they were angular and blocky. She couldn't guess what they might be. "What are those... things?"

"Mining equipment," the man gasped.

It was no wonder he could barely talk. He'd carried Zapata half a klick, and the pilot was not small. He was also out cold and therefore dead weight.

"Entrance is over there," the man continued, slowly squatting. "Knock three times, wait seven seconds, then knock twice." He gently lowered Zapata to the ground.

Wilder assumed he meant the direction he was facing, so she headed that way. The night seemed to have grown even darker, if that was possible, and she almost had to feel her way with her toes. When she arrived at a single-story building it seemed to rise up out of nowhere. She was right in front of the door. Using Zapata's crutch, she struck the code on the hard surface. It dully boomed within, as if the interior was larger than the exterior.

About a minute later, after Wilder had tried and failed to divine the murmured conversation of her companions, the door jerked open. The opener took one look at her and slammed it shut.

"It's all right," the new guide called out. "It's the visitors from outer space."

The door slowly opened again. Wilder found herself staring into the eyes of a young woman, maybe even younger than Miki. Her eyes were wide with wonder. "So it's true?"

"Uhhh..." Wilder wasn't sure how to answer. She wasn't actually from outer space, though she understood the Resistance man's quip.

The man called out again. "Fetch a couple of strong guys. I need some help."

A dim light shone from within the building. When the girl stepped away from the door, Wilder went in. An open elevator cage stood in the center of the room. Dusty consoles lined the walls, all bashed in, wires torn out and severed. The girl was speaking into the end of a tube. When she finished speaking, she tucked the tube inside a broken console, and then walked to the elevator and shut the sliding the metal door. All the while, she kept her gaze on Wilder. A moment later, the cage rattled and the elevator descended.

"This is a neat setup," Wilder said. "How long have you lived here?"

The girl gave her a wary look.

"Sorry. Dumb question. I suppose you're not allowed to talk about that kind of thing."

"All my life. I was born here."

"Wow. Don't the Scythians know about this place?"

"They came here soon after the invasion. Smashed the place up. Pumped gas underground. We still find skeletons sometimes."

"Don't they ever come back?"

There was that wary look again. Wilder guessed the aliens did return occasionally to check for signs of life, but either the Resistance had a way of knowing when an inspection was planned and would evacuate, or the inhabitants could hide and protect themselves from poisonous gases. Scythians would not be able to maneuver within a human mine. Clearly, the efforts of the Resistance to avoid detection had been successful for decades.

The elevator was ascending.

It carried two men. After briefly inspecting Wilder they went outside. Soon, Niall and Maddox came in, followed by the men carrying Zapata and, lastly, the tall guide.

The elevator only accommodated four people, so Wilder, Niall, Maddox and the girl went down into the mine first.

What Wilder saw within her first half an hour made her proud and angry. The Resistance hideout was obviously long-standing and well-established. On their way in they saw the generator, run from a mill in an underground stream. There were living quarters, recreation rooms, a kitchen and refectory, even a small schoolroom. She guessed thirty or forty people lived here, including the handful of children. It was an amazing achievement, built in secrecy with great ingenuity due to scarce resources.

So much thought and effort had gone into the place—thought and effort that might have been better spent fighting the Scythians. If Concordians could plan and execute such complex, challenging schemes like the mine hideout and the Resistance network, why hadn't they used the same skills to inflict damage on their overlords?

While Zapata was taken somewhere to rest and recuperate, Wilder, Niall, and Maddox were invited to join the group's organizers. They sat around a heater and were offered hot drinks flavored with a substance Wilder couldn't identify. It tasted yeasty. They were also offered a stew of tubers and mushrooms. Wilder ate hungrily. It was her first proper meal since leaving Chimera.

The man who had brought them here entered the room, accompanied by another man and a woman, both gray-haired and slightly stooped. After greeting the newcomers the older man said, "We cannot tell you our names, you understand?"

"We get it," said Maddox.

"May we ask you about the *Sirocco*, your voyage, and Earth?"

"Ask away," Niall replied. "We don't have anything to hide."

What followed was similar to the conversations they'd had with Meric. The Resistance leaders were fascinated by all that had happened since the *Sirocco* had departed Concordia. They appeared to regard what they heard as not quite believable. Though Wilder answered the questions willingly, she grew bored. She was tired from the day's walk, and she had the feeling that she would be facing the same questions over and over again as they journeyed south. The Resistance would only be sharing basic information about the newcomers, not the detailed history of the *Sirocco*'s voyage.

The night wore on and she was unable to suppress several yawns. Eventually, the tall man said, "We should let you rest. You may stay here one day and one more night, and then I will be your guide to the next cell."

"I would like to sleep," Wilder replied, "but I have some questions too. We know very little about the invasion and what's happened since. Frankly, I don't understand why it's taking you so long to stand up to the Scythians. The man we spoke to at the last place said the Resistance has been planning an uprising for years. You obviously weren't waiting for us to return. You didn't even believe we were real. So what's been stopping you?"

The old man's face twisted with shame and regret. "I was only a baby at the time, but I learned from my parents that, in the beginning, we did fight back. Despite the weakened state of the colony, we fought the Scythians viciously and desperately, throwing everything we had at them, risking our lives again and again. Many died. The death toll and destruction were devastating. The aliens had all the advantages, you see—technology, numbers, firepower, and maneuverability—whereas the colony had already been on its knees before the attackers even arrived.

"Finally, the Leader was faced with the choice of allowing the hopeless war to continue, ensuring the deaths of yet more thousands, or to surrender and save the remaining lives. He decided that enslavement and the hope of one day turning the tables and breaking free was a better alternative to continued slaughter." He took a sip of water and set down his cup before rubbing his hands in front of the heater.

"Plenty did not agree, and they were the genesis of the Resistance. Cells formed across the land, hideouts were built and supply lines created. Some members had never been enslaved, others were escapees from the domes, the towns now patrolled by Scythians, and the fields, though the aliens steadily tightened their control, inflicting savage punishments on dissenters.

"Over the years things settled down. The domes proliferated and, ironically, the human population increased too. Now we had a steady food source from the plants the aliens had introduced, and the destroyed ecosystem began to re-establish a modicum of balance, life became easier."

Sorrow suffused the old man's features. "The Resistance has disrupted this new 'normal' when it could. But we face a difficult problem. Scythians generally lived in close proximity to humans. Large numbers of Concordians inhabit their domes and the surrounding areas. Towns like Annwn and Oceanside are shadows of their former busy states but, though people still live there, so do Scythians. They've taken over the largest buildings still standing after the war, sealed off the main sections for their own living quarters, and arranged for live-in servants. No matter where the aliens are, any attack is guaranteed to result in human deaths and casualties.

"We have been hamstrung from the start, but we have done what we could, targeting patrols, blowing up domes under construction, organizing breakouts, and committing other acts to subvert Scythian domination. Chimera was established, one of three safe sites. The Resistance has done much over the years to work against the invaders but, you're right, it has not even approached the goal of returning Concordia to human ownership."

Beneath his bushy gray eyebrows, the old man's eyes brightened. "I believe the arrival of your group may be just the catalyst we need to galvanize us into decisive, significant action. This may be the beginning of the end for the Scythians."

THIRTY-SEVEN

It had taken weeks to reach the Resistance headquarters, and it wasn't until Wilder drew near, late one evening, that she'd recognised the place. The first thought that entered her head when the realization struck had been *How fitting*.

It was the cave complex near Oceanside. The honeycombed cliffs had once been the site of another rebellion many, many years ago. In a schism during the first months of the colony, Gens had created their own settlement here, free from Woken control. But, not long after, an act of sabotage had flooded the system with millions of cubic meters of water. Scores of people had died, very nearly including Cherry. Now the caves were dry once more though, as far as Wilder was aware, they had never been re-occupied before the Resistance moved in.

Its members had dug, tunneled, and blasted connections between the various caves within the soft limestone. They couldn't take the risk of traversing the cliff face as the Gens had. The danger of losing one's grip and tumbling into the ocean was obvious, but there was also the possibility a passing Scythian patrol would notice the stray human.

After brief introductions, Wilder, Niall, Maddox, and Zapata had been assigned living quarters. The next day, the process of drawing together the threads of the planned uprising had begun.

Wilder's small space was at the dead end of a narrow passage, which meant no traffic passed her door. Not that she had an actual door, only a curtain on a rail. She relished the solitude, and she'd settled in quickly, relieved to finally be able to rest and recuperate, though fear and regret over what had happened to Miki still plagued her along with anxiety over the fate of the *Sirocco*.

Roughly a month after her arrival, she was in her room one afternoon when someone beyond the curtain door said, "Knock, knock." It was the standard method of announcing your visit and saved hurting your knuckles on the bare rock.

"Hi, Niall."

He pulled back the curtain and poked his head in. "Got a minute?"

"For you? I don't know. I'll have to think about it."

He smiled and stepped in. "I was wondering if you'd got any further with the head."

"My *name* is Faina."

The android was facing out to sea. Wilder had put her in her usual place on the floor near the cliff-side opening. Not *too* close, in case a strong gust of wind should blow her from her perch. The Guardian might survive submersion in water but they would likely never find her again.

"We've been going through some things," Wilder replied. "I don't think we came up with anything new."

The problem with plumbing Faina's memory was that the Scythians had tampered with her, inserting new pathways and removing others in order to re-program her. Some of the damage had been undone but not all of it. She was unable to confirm whether what she recalled was real or fictional, uploaded by the Scythians in case their machinations were discovered. Her ability to run self-diagnostics had also been compromised.

Faina had told of a vast starship, apparently larger than any Scythian ship Concordians had ever seen, where the alien technicians had worked on her. It had taken years to travel to the vessel, and she didn't recall going to any of the aliens' planets. This last item of information had been a disappointment. If the Resistance knew of something vital to Scythian survival, something not easily created or obtained, it could have been the key to eliminating their presence from Concordia. But Faina hadn't come up with anything like that.

Much of what else she could tell them they already knew. Once upon a time, the aliens' main method of locomotion would have been a revelation. Now, humanity was as familiar with Scythians as Faina had become, if not more so. Nevertheless, Wilder had continued to question the android in the hopes of prompting the recollection of something useful.

"Shame." Niall sat next to Wilder on her low cot, the only place to sit.

"Any updates on the plans?"

"That was what I came to talk to you about. We've set a date. Two weeks from today, Operation Rebirth begins."

"So soon? Are they ready?"

"They obviously think they are. It's a little hard to tell, but I guess they know what they're doing. They've been anticipating this moment for decades, remember. All they needed was a push to set things in motion."

Wilder's impression had been the same. The return of a few members of the *Sirocco*'s crew had been a reminder of the good old days, when Concordia was under human control despite the Scythians' many attacks. Yet Wilder harbored doubts, which apparently showed on her face.

Niall put an arm over her shoulders. "You're not sure about this, are you?"

She looked at his hand on her shoulder and then into his eyes, lifting an eyebrow.

He didn't remove his arm.

"Are you sure?" she asked. "Do you get the impression they're ready?"

"Well, Chimera has confirmed. Teams of Chimerites will be crossing the ocean over the next few days and moving into position. I think, in a certain way, the Resistance has been ready for a long time. Whether they're adequately prepared and equipped is another question."

It had been hard to assess the true scope of Concordia's Resistance. The leaders had given the newcomers detailed information, and they were privy to much more intelligence than rank and file members, but they hadn't spent years at the top as the leaders had. They didn't know everything, not by a long stretch.

Wilder's gut told her the planned uprising was at best hopeful, rather than a confident endeavor. At worst, it was a desperate, final gasp for freedom, an act of defiance for those who would die rather than accept alien rule. "What worries me is the Scythian space fleet. Assuming everything goes according to plan and the Resistance manages to kill or imprison most of the enemy and free the slaves. What then? There's at least one fully operational military starship in orbit. And it's been weeks since the *Sirocco*'s attacks. The Scythian ships could be repaired and/or more could have arrived. So what if the Resistance wins the day on the planet surface? The Scythian reprisal from space will be fast and devastating." She sighed. "I take it there's still no sign of our ship?"

"You know I would have told you."

No Concordians appeared to have even noticed the battles the *Sirocco* had fought in the sky. They didn't have access to satellite data, telescopes or anything else that would have told them what was happening in the heavens. If any flashes or streaks had been spotted they must had been dismissed as shooting stars. The lack of evidence must have been one reason the Chimerites were suspicious of the newcomers' tale.

On the other hand, no starship wreckage had been found, which gave Wilder hope the *Sirocco* hadn't been destroyed. It was a tenuous hope, however. Oceans covered two-thirds of Concordia's surface. It was more likely than not the ship would have fallen into the sea or the uninhabited deserts of Suddene.

She said, "I feel like we've been living a dream ever since we got back. A hopeless delusion that this planet could ever be truly ours again. We would have been better off turning around and heading straight back to Earth. We would have stood a better chance of survival."

"We've been over this. Everyone from the *Sirocco* has. Concordia's our home."

"For how much longer?" Wilder didn't mean before the Scythians took over the planet entirely. She was wondering how much time Niall and she had, considering their role in the uprising. "Hey, I was talking to Zapata today and he mentioned it was you who got me out of the Scythian city. Why didn't you tell me?"

"There didn't seem much point, but why would you think it was anyone else? You know I would risk my life for you in a heartbeat."

She didn't answer. She *did* know that. She didn't even have to think about it. "Well, thanks."

"You don't have to thank me. You would do the same for me."

He was right.

"Uhh..." said Faina.

Wilder started. She'd forgotten about the android. "Yes?"

"Could you please deactivate me? This view is pleasant but it grows boring eventually. You may wake me first thing tomorrow."

Wilder pressed the tiny nubbin on Faina's neck that was her 'switch'.

"How is Zapata?" Niall asked.

"He's doing great. He's walking well now, as good as ever. Maddox is still complaining about her ribs though." Wilder avoided the woman as much as humanly possible. "Any news about Miki?"

Niall shook his head. The Resistance had put out feelers to locate the fifth mission member, but no word had come back. It was presumed that, if she was alive, she was inside one of the three domes near the Vimur estuary. The human population in that area was especially under the Scythians' sway and so intel on alien activity was hard to come by.

Wilder looked out over the ocean. The sun was going down and, despite Faina's complaint, the scene was breathtakingly beautiful. The lowering rays were kissing the tops of the waves, gilding them red-gold. But Wilder's mind flew far away, to the depths of the Scythian city. She had been beyond exhausted. Her palms were open, bleeding blisters, each movement was excruciating, and her throat had closed up with dehydration. A young girl was saying softly, *Just one more. You can do it.*

Wilder rested her head on Niall's shoulder and they didn't speak. After a while he left to attend to Resistance business.

Later, when the cave complex was quiet and the stars were bright over the dark ocean, she heard another, quieter, "Knock, knock."

She opened the curtain to let him in.

Niall didn't leave until morning.

THIRTY-EIGHT

Returning to the Vimur Estuary in time for the launch of Operation Rebirth had been a hard trek for Wilder and Niall, but it was here the Resistance felt their talents would be best put to use. The area was one of the Scythians' most secure strongholds due to the human population's extreme obedience and docility. The Resistance couldn't count on the majority of locals for support when things kicked off. They might even turn against the fighters and defend the aliens. Their reaction was an unknown factor in the battle plan. Wilder and Niall were to bolster the local branch's numbers and fighting ability.

Wilder had tried to explain that neither she nor Niall had combat skills, but her efforts had been to no avail. They'd acquired a mythical status. They'd stepped out of history, arrived to put right all the wrongs inflicted on Concordia. They would replenish the planet with new species from the old world and free its people. Both beliefs were true in a sense, but Wilder had anticipated a more advisory role. She was no fighter and neither was Niall.

Yet she was glad to be back at the estuary. If Miki was alive she was in one of the domes. Even if Operation Rebirth failed and the Scythians didn't leave, if she could just free Miki, it would be enough. Perhaps they could find a secluded place to live as Maddox had suggested. However, she wouldn't be telling Maddox about it.

'Steven' greeted them warmly when they reached the old underground grain store, shaking their hands. "I never thought I would see you back here again. You guys certainly lit a fire under us."

"That was our intention, I guess," Niall replied. "What's the plan for tomorrow?"

"You need to be in position by 2 a.m. That's when most patrols are taking place and the domes are at their emptiest. You're leading the attack on Dome Three, the one nearest the mountains."

"Leading?" Wilder asked. "We've never even been in a dome."

"They're all pretty much the same inside. I'll show you a model. You'll blow open the shell where it faces the river. That's smack in the middle of the area pressurized with CO2 and unlikely to contain many humans. Scythians will pour out and you'll pick them off as they come. Give it a couple of minutes for the gas to escape, then you go in."

"Do we have breathing masks?" asked Wilder.

"You shouldn't need them."

She looked doubtfully at Niall. They wouldn't be able to tell if they were breathing an atmosphere rich in carbon dioxide. If they were it would kill them fast. The gas was odorless and colorless, and it was also heavier than air. It might take longer than a couple of minutes for the CO2 to dissipate.

"The Scythians will call their patrols back immediately," Steven went on, "but we will be waiting to take them out as they arrive. Once you're inside Dome Three, your goal is to kill every alien on sight. We don't have anywhere to put prisoners and they're dangerous even unarmed. When the fighting dies down you can get the people out. They don't know you're coming. We couldn't risk warning them in case a traitor informed on us. You'll be able to tell where the people are by the doors in the walls."

He smiled. "That's the short version. We can go into more detail over dinner. Then you'll have a few hours to sleep before you leave."

Wilder didn't think she would be sleeping at all tonight, despite her tiredness from her trek. Niall seemed to have reservations too. But this was what they'd come here for, and once they were out in the field they would be able to call the shots. If they needed to amend the plan the local Resistance had made they would.

Before they ate they took a look at the model of the Scythian dome. Then they talked business over dinner, preparing for the big attack. When it came time to sleep Wilder was feeling a little more optimistic. She'd talked to the other team leaders and given them a description of Miki, emphasizing her most memorable characteristic: the red in her hair.

Finally, it was time to snatch some sleep if they could. Wilder lay next to Niall in a room near the grain store. Dug out of subsoil, the floor was hard and stony and deeply uncomfortable. Even if she hadn't been about to risk her life she would have struggled to nod off, and the snores of other Resistance fighters sharing the room didn't help.

Niall was trying but, though his eyes were closed, she could tell he was awake. She leaned close and kissed his cheek. His eyes opened.

"If things get dicey tomorrow," she whispered. "What am I talking about? *When* things get dicey, and assuming we both survive, don't be mean to me, okay?"

Her request clearly troubled him. "I'll try. I might need to stay away from you for a while."

"I can live with that." She kissed him again.

Later, to her surprise, she found herself being shaken awake. She had fallen asleep after all. Steven was kneeling over her. Everyone else was sleeping, including Niall.

She blinked. "Time to get up?"

He didn't answer, only stood up and beckoned.

She tiptoed out, following him into the low passageway.

"What's going on?" She was growing more puzzled by the second.

"Something very weird. A capsule has been found on the estuary shoreline."

"Capsule?"

"I don't know how else to describe it. It's like a coffin, only a bit longer and wider and it's oblong, not rectangular."

"Right."

He looked at her expectantly.

"I have no idea what you're talking about."

"Well, that's even stranger. I thought you would know what it is because it has your name on it."

"*My name?*"

"There aren't any other Wilders around here."

She stared.

"Do you want to go and see it?"

"Do I have time?"

"We have two hours before we have to leave for the domes, and the capsule is about a half-hour walk."

She was never going to get back to sleep, not with the puzzle of a mysterious object with her name on it whirling around her mind. "Let's go."

———

As they walked through the darkness, she got an inkling of what the thing might be. The description Steven had given reminded her of something she'd heard about very long ago. She'd never seen the item in question so she couldn't make a comparison. It sounded like the same thing, but everything else about her guess was impossible. Yet what other explanation could there be? Was Steven pulling a prank on her? That was even less likely.

Then she saw it. Even from afar and in the dark, the sight made her stomach flip.

"Do you recognize it now?" asked Steven in a hushed whisper. They crouched in tall weeds at the edge of the sand.

"I think I do, but I can't be right." The implication of what she was seeing had rocked her. And it did have her name on it and that meant only one thing.

"There don't seem to be any Scythians around," Steven said." You could take a closer look. I'll keep lookout."

"If that thing is what I think it is, I'll need to leave for a while, and I'll need your help to do it. Is that okay with you?"

"Huh?"

"Just trust me."

"Will you be back in time for Operation Rebirth?"

"I don't know."

"I guess you've got to do what you've got to do, but I'd appreciate it if you could explain. I'll have to tell the others something."

"Come with me to the water's edge."

It was a Fila capsule. There was no mistake. The transparent cover was open, revealing a single seat. There were no controls. The passenger didn't pilot it. She hadn't seen the ones Ethan and Cherry had traveled in during the early days of the colony, but she knew a little about them.

Her name was on the side like the name of a ship, the word written in a long, flowing script like Fila tentacles. She had no doubt what it all meant—her name and the appearance of the capsule on the estuary shore. It was an invitation.

"I have to get inside. When the lid closes, push me out into the water. That's all you need to do. You can go back to the hideout. I remember the way."

"P-push you out into the water? But there's no sail or engine or... What the hell is that thing?"

She was already climbing inside. "Just do as I say, please."

As soon as she lay down in the reclined seat, the cover automatically swung over and sealed. Steven gazed through the barrier, wide-eyed.

Push me, she mouthed. *Hurry.*

He disappeared from view. The capsule jerked as it broke free, and then the sand ground beneath it as it moved closer to the water. Its movement became liquid. The capsule lifted as a low wave caught it. Then she was floating free, bobbing on the surface. Wilder craned her neck but she couldn't see Steven. She hoped he'd left and wasn't hanging around out in the open, his curiosity making him forgetful of the threat of Scythians.

A sense of urgency hit. Perhaps there was time to call off Operation Rebirth. Perhaps there was another solution than all-out war, bloodshed, and massive loss of life.

Thirty-Nine

She was being carried out to sea, as far as she could tell. From her reclined, submerged position she could see hardly anything. The water above was dark save for glints of light that might be starlight penetrating the surface. She'd felt the capsule turn so her feet faced the ocean, but she hadn't noticed anything else except acceleration.

Of course she was being taken to the ocean. That was where Ethan and Cherry had gone, down to the metropolis on the ocean floor.

The Fila were back! It had to be good news for Concordians. They'd helped them so much in the past, introducing them to the Galactic Assembly and helping them fight the Scythians. The aquatic aliens must have returned to lend humanity a hand once more. She only hoped her meeting with them would be over in time for her to report to the Resistance before Operation Rebirth launched.

The capsule sank deeper. The glints disappeared and darkness entirely enclosed her. She began to grow cold and very aware of the fact she was in an extremely confined space, surrounded by water. How deep was she? How great was the pressure? Her breathing sped up and cold sweat bathed her. Years living aboard the *Sirocco* had helped her overcome her claustrophobia somewhat, but now it returned in a wave of panic. Her hands clenched as she resisted the urge to bang uselessly on the hull overhead and scream. How had Ethan and Cherry coped?

She had to find a distraction. She thought of Niall. Was he awake yet? Had Steven explained where she'd gone? What were Zapata and Maddox doing? Was Maddox still complaining about her ribs?

Wilder closed her eyes and imagined she was somewhere else. She was back in her treehouse outside Sidhe with her childhood friends. What an amazing time, so full of excitement and hope. How young she'd been. How innocent. The threat of the Scythians' return had hung over everyone's heads, but to her it had been a vague possibility. Her focus had been on the here and now. The future had been...

It was no good. Her treehouse melted into nothingness. Her eyes snapped open. She was in utter darkness and the chill of the ocean depths was invading her bones. She was trapped in a fragile bubble, a thin layer of material separating her from pulverizing pressure. It could crush her to death before she had time to breathe in a lungful of water and begin to drown.

Lights appeared. For a second she thought the capsule must have risen to the surface and it was starlight. Had the Fila decided to not meet her?

But the lights were colored and moving, undulating gently. And the colors were changing, coruscating, pulsing. A Fila was approaching. She was transfixed. Cherry had described the sight but words didn't encompass it.

"Wilder?"

"Yes!" She was no longer alone.

The Fila moved so close it was directly outside. It had been years since she'd seen one, and even now she couldn't see it properly, only the lights it emitted.

"I didn't know the Fila had returned. How long have you been here?" She'd imagined she was going to meet many of them. Why was there only one?

"It's so good to see you again."

A pulsing tentacle touched the hull directly over her head.

"It's good to...? Quinn! Is that you?!"

"I thought you had died, Wilder. Humans live such a short time."

Her throat swelled and she blinked back tears. Reaching up, she touched the hull opposite the tentacle. She and Quinn had never made physical contact in all the time they'd known each other. "It's good to see you too. I thought I would never see you again. What are you doing here? Are you living here alone?"

"There are many Fila on Concordia. You're traveling to our city now, but I wanted to meet you on the way. I have missed you greatly."

"How did you know I was back? I got the shock of my life when I saw my name on this thing."

"We monitor the human communications between Lyonesse and Suddene via the undersea cable. We have a policy of never interfering in land affairs, but when I heard your name had been mentioned in the messages I was concerned for your safety. I wanted to see you. I persuaded our authorities to organize this meeting."

"You have a policy of never interfering in land affairs? What do you mean?

Quinn," she repeated more urgently, "how long have the Fila been living on Concordia?"

"We returned not long after your ship departed. The biocide had worked itself through the oceans and faded out. The water was safe once more. But we made a decision to not become involved with humans again."

"I see," she said quietly. It was no surprise. Entangling themselves with humanity's problems had cost tens of thousands of Fila lives, wiped out by the biocide. "So you knew about the Scythian invasion? You were here then?"

"We were. The Scythians are aware of our presence but they tolerate us, providing we remain neutral. They have no use for the oceans."

In response to her silence he went on, "Planets that are habitable for my kind are rare in the galaxy, Wilder. Perhaps it seems disloyal, but..."

She swallowed. Her dreams of the Fila coming to the colony's rescue were crashing around her ears. "I understand."

"The communications implied your ship made it to Earth, but you've been gone a long time, longer than the voyage should have taken."

"We did make it there eventually." She explained about the jump drive failing. "Scythians are invading Earth too. They learned its location from the Guardian they salvaged from the wreck of the *Mistral*."

"I am sorry to hear that. Humans may have to accept enslavement for the time being if they are to survive."

"Do you know about Operation Rebirth?"

"We do. That was another reason I wanted to talk to you. I advise you not to take part. It is almost certain to fail and you might be killed."

"The same idea had occurred to me, but what choice do I have? The Resistance are determined to do something. Humans don't submit to slavery easily. At least, most of us don't. When it comes down to it, we would rather die."

"But all humans die. Your lives are brief. I don't understand why you don't value them more. Surely it's better to live as long as possible, even under another's control?"

"We don't see it like that. This one, short life we get, we want to make it the best we can. Otherwise, what's the point?"

Quinn's tentacles moved over the surface of the capsule as he considered her answer.

Each of them would probably never fully understand the other's viewpoint. Fila lived forever. Only accident or disease killed them, hence their unending quest to find new planets to inhabit. Maybe it made sense that a Fila would think a less-than-perfect life was better than dying. There was always the chance of a change of circumstances at some later point in time.

An idea struck, and hope surged in Wilder again. "Quinn, could the Fila contact the Galactic Assembly for us? We must still be members. They have a duty to come to our aid when we're attacked by hostile forces."

"The Galactic Assembly is already aware of the situation on Concordia."

"Huh? Then why haven't they done anything?"

"The Assembly re-classified the Scythians' actions. They applied to join and provided proof that they evolved on Concordia. What the Assembly previously judged to be an unprovoked assault has been downgraded to a territory dispute."

"What the...?" Air left Wilder's lungs. She couldn't have been more flabbergasted or more disappointed. Humanity's allies had deserted it. Humans were alone in the galaxy, doomed to choose between thralldom and death. "What about what's happening on Earth? That *is* an unprovoked assault."

"Not entirely unprovoked, considering that humans colonized Concordia without permission from the Scythians, but there may be a case to answer. I will ensure your point is made to the Assembly, but as I understand it, Earth is outside its jurisdiction."

"Nooo! No more, Quinn. I can't stand it."

"I am very sorry, Wilder. You know I want to help you. I am trying to help you now."

"What you've told me—is that what your authorities were going to tell me at the meeting?"

"I believe so. They were also going to ask that you do not reveal to the Scythians that we've been in contact."

"I won't tell them. Stars, that's the last thing on my mind. But if that's all they have to say, I'd prefer to skip it and go back to the Vimur. The Resistance attack will start soon. If I can get this new information to them it might change things. They could call off Operation Rebirth."

"I will have to—"

"I don't have time for bureaucracy. Please take me back."

The capsule's progress slowed, stopped, and then reversed.

Quinn said, "I may get into trouble for this, but it was worth it to see you again."

Wilder rubbed the heels of her hands into her eyes, and for some time she couldn't speak. The hopelessness of the situation had plagued her for months. This brief encounter with her old friend had alleviated it temporarily, only to dump her deeper than ever before. Finally, she managed to say softly, "I wish we could have met at a better time. Will I see you again?"

"I don't know how that will be possible. Human and Fila networks are no longer connected. We can't risk depositing more capsules on beaches just for you to pay me a visit. The Scythians will notice."

"So this is our last meeting?"

"I believe so."

Specks of light appeared in the dark water, separate from Quinn's luminescence.

"I'm glad I got this chance anyway," she whispered.

"Me too."

Water drained from the capsule's surface and it bumped as it hit sand.

"Take care, Wilder."

The lid opened.

"I'll miss you, Quinn."

But she didn't think he heard. His tentacles were already trailing out of sight.

She stood up, and the capsule rocked. It wasn't quite out of the water. She was forced to wade to shore.

What time was it? How long had her journey taken?

She looked up the estuary to where the Scythian domes stood, softly glowing silver. The night was still and peaceful.

An explosion split the air, startling her as the shockwave passed through her head. The explosion was quickly followed by another, and then a third.

Operation Rebirth had begun.

FORTY

Miki stiffened as she was carried aloft. Would it be the same as last time? Would the Scythian carry her to a dome and drop her in a cell of fellow prisoners?

Or had the aliens' method for dealing with humans changed? Would she be killed, ripped to shreds by their dreadful claws?

She'd heard the Scythians kept humans as slaves but she didn't know a lot more. Her only source of local information was the people of Chimera. What they'd said might not be accurate or up-to-date.

As the wind whipped around her, Miki peered at the field by the estuary, hoping to not see Wilder or Niall, hoping her actions had allowed them to escape. There was no sign of them, only ripples in the water. She breathed out heavily. If her friends had avoided capture, that was something. Her self-sacrifice would be worth it. But maybe she might be able to make more of a difference—if only she survived.

A dome loomed large beneath her, its spiral portal opening. The alien carrying her descended. She was in the airlock, the small Scythian aircraft lined up in rows. Quickly, her bearer swooped through a second opening. She was inside the 4main section of the dome. It was different from the one on Earth. The rooms had ceilings and doors.

Her Scythian dropped to the floor, opened a door with its foot, and pushed her in.

The other prisoners stared. She moved into a corner, regarding her new companions uneasily. They were dreadfully skinny, and their expressions weren't friendly or welcoming. They seemed suspicious, and no one spoke.

This place was different from the domes she'd been inside on Earth. There were beds—of a kind. Rows of stuffed cloth mattresses crossed the floor, walking space between them. There were no chairs or tables or other furniture, only the beds, but the prisoners were allowed possessions. A small pile of belongings sat on each mattress: clothes, combs, small oblong objects that might be bars of soap, dishes and spoons.

"Who are *you*?" A slight, bony woman with a high forehead and prominent cheekbones had spoken. She glared but Miki couldn't tell if she was fearful or angry.

"My name's Miki."

"And where are you from, *Miki*?" The woman stepped closer.

Miki suddenly realized all the fifteen or so people in the cell were women. They ranged from teenagers like her to gray-haired women even older than Wilder. There were no children.

"I'm from..." She hesitated. Most of the Chimerites hadn't believed she was from the *Sirocco*. If she told these women the truth, would they suspect she was lying? They already seemed to dislike her, even though she hadn't done anything to offend them.

"Did you forget?" The bony woman asked sarcastically.

"I'm from down south. Annwn."

This appeared to mollify her questioner. "Another runaway. The Scythians always get them in the end. You can have that bed." She jerked her chin at an empty mattress. "Just to be clear. We operate by strict rules here. Everything's divided equally. No one gets any more or any less than their fair share."

"I would never—"

"Yeah, everyone says that. Until the hunger starts to bite. We have ways of dealing with thieves and people who push their luck. You've been warned."

The prisoners' attention shifted from her. Conversations and other activities resumed.

Miki walked to the empty mattress. There were no sheets or other bedding. The cloth was dirty and greasy from the bed's previous occupants. She wrinkled her nose. The floor looked more appealing as a sleeping place.

A girl roughly Nina's age appeared at Miki's side and said quietly, "It doesn't look nice, does it? But you'd better use it or Margie won't like it. She'll say you think you're better than everyone else, and then no one will talk to you."

Miki weighed up the prospect of being ostracized against sleeping in someone else's dirt. It was a hard call to make. "What's your name?"

"Dana."

"Thanks for the tip, Dana."

"Can I sit down?"

"Sure." Miki perched on her new place of rest. Perhaps using it wouldn't be too bad as long as she kept her clothes on.

"My family are from Annwn, too," Dana said.

Uh oh.

"You might know them."

"Probably not. You know what it's like living under the Scythians. I hardly got to see anyone before I escaped."

"You escaped from a dome? That's awesome."

Miki wondered how else people got away from the aliens.

"How did you do it?"

"I...er..."

Margie had wandered closer and was making no secret of the fact she was eavesdropping.

Miki proceeded to relate the tale of the breakout she'd taken part in on Earth. The story fit the situation perfectly, providing things were similar on Concordia. It was clear they weren't exactly the same, but it was either use the story from Earth or make something up, which was even riskier.

Dana's eyes grew rounder as Miki talked. Her sense of her new acquaintance's resemblance to Nina grew stronger until Miki was forced to stop and swallow, hard.

Dana, most likely mistaking her emotion as relating to the escape, touched her arm. "You were very brave."

Miki concluded her narration, stating, "After we got out, we split up. I don't know what happened to the others, but I came north. I hoped I might find somewhere the Scythians didn't control, but they caught me by the estuary. And here I am."

Margie commented, "I never heard of any successful escapes around Annwn, but that isn't so surprising. We don't hear most of what goes on, and most of what we do hear is bullshit. But I believe you. Sorry for being harsh earlier. The Scythians put spies in the cells sometimes, to listen for dissenting remarks or escape plans. We can't be too careful."

"I understand."

A dull thump resounded from the door, and Dana ran to open it. A man stood outside holding a large metal container. Dana took the container, thanking him before he closed the door. It didn't seem to be kept locked. Margie supervised the portioning out of the food. Miki took her bowl and ate the scant contents—a porridge similar to the stuff she'd scraped in handfuls from the floor of her cell on Earth.

"How come there are only women here?" Miki asked Dana as they put their dirty bowls into the now-empty container.

Dana gave her a quizzical look. Apparently realizing the question was serious, she flushed. "Because...you know."

"I don't."

"Weren't the men and women segregated in the domes in Annwn?"

Miki became suddenly aware of Margie hovering close by once more. "Uhh, yes they were. I just never understood why."

"It's so they...so the Scythians can choose...who has a baby with who." Dana had turned deep red.

"Oh, yeah. That makes sense. I was stupid not to figure it out."

Dana looked at her as if she didn't quite believe her. "They haven't selected any pairs for a few years here. Maybe they're phasing out the breeding program."

"Why would they do that?"

Dana shrugged.

Naturally, the Scythians on Concordia had their systems all worked out. They kept the humans captive by a number of methods. Near-starvation was one. It was hard to stage a breakout when you were weak with hunger. Persuading the humans to police each other was another. The spies the aliens planted in the cells were probably rewarded with extra food or special privileges. And the sheer force of habit and lack of expectation for anything better from life seemed to be a powerful factor too. The women here in Miki's cell appeared to have accepted their fate. Dana had been excited by the story of an escape from Annwn, but her reaction had been as if she'd been watching an engaging vid drama, a fiction, not something that could ever happen to her.

A second thump came from the door. The man had returned to collect the food utensils. He handed Dana clean bowls and spoons in exchange for the dirty ones. No words were spoken. Perhaps it was forbidden.

The man pointed at Miki. "Come with me."

Her cell companions fell silent and watched as she walked to the doorway. "Where am I going?"

The man didn't answer, only grabbed her biceps to guide her. His other arm was wrapped around the empty container filled with dirty dishes and cutlery.

She felt like another consumable to be delivered. "Please, where are you taking me?"

"Shut up, or you'll get us both in trouble."

They stopped at a wall. The man positioned her so she stood exactly upon two spots marked on the floor. "Don't move. Not a centimeter. Understand?"

She nodded, and the man left.

Minutes passed, and still she waited. High above curved the upper shell of the dome. Scythians flew over wearing breathing apparatus. They were wearing breathing apparatus *inside*! This entire section had an oxygen-rich atmosphere.

Something grabbed Miki's waist from behind. She screamed with shock. Whatever it was, it was pulling her backward, into the wall.

It was pulling her *through* the wall.

She slid into the soft, porous material and out the other side, exactly as she had in the Scythian city. The thing gripping her was a set of alien's toes. As the creature's stench hit she turned and held her breath. The Scythian towered over her, peering down.

It released its grip. "Lie down. Do not resist or you will be restrained."

The voice she heard had been synthetic with a flatness to the tone. The creature's mouth had moved but the vocalization hadn't escaped the globe enclosing its head.

Miki recognized the circular platform she was supposed to lie on. It was the same as the ones they used on Earth. Steeling herself for what was to come, she did as she'd been instructed. A needle and syringe on a metal arm rose up from the side, pierced her arm and drew a sample of blood. She winced and blinked back tears. She'd thought she would be able to tolerate life in a Scythian dome again, but the rawness of her first experience was flooding back, full force.

What had she done?

The Scythian scientist—if that was what it was—had tippy toed in its harness over to a console and was ignoring her while consulting a screen. As quickly as it had arrived, the blood-drawing equipment disappeared.

Would she be allowed to return to the cell now, or were there more examinations to take place?

Beep. Beep. Beep.

Where was the noise coming from? It wasn't loud like an alarm but it was insistent. It also got the scientist's attention. It leaned closer to its console, and then its head swiveled to face her, the vertical-slitted eyes staring fixedly into hers.

"You are not from Concordia. You are from Earth."

FORTY-ONE

A new client arrived, waddling into the room.

Miki had soon been put to work. The day after her arrival she'd been introduced to her job: cleaning the skin of Scythians suffering from some kind of fungal infection. The humans called it Sticky Mold. What the aliens called it Miki had no idea. They didn't refer to it as she worked, though sometimes they spoke to her about other things. She had to wear a respirator as she had when she'd worked in the hatchery on Earth, and the device contained a comm or translator. She wasn't sure which it was. All she knew was that when the aliens spoke she could hear what they said, in English, in the same flat-toned computer-generated voice she'd heard in the examining room.

Her new friend, Dana, cleaned the aliens' skins too. She'd trained Miki, showing her which side of the crescent-shaped tool to use, how to draw it gently over the creatures' bodies and the wing webbing, and where to put the black, tacky scum the tool gathered. Next, Miki had to apply a soothing balm, rubbing it gently into the cleaned areas. Perhaps the ointment helped to protect against further infections. Again, she did not know.

The most important thing was that she was inside a dome again. If you wanted to learn about Scythians and their weaknesses, it was the best place to be. The only downside was that Wilder would be furious with her for the risk she was taking. But she had to do it for everyone's sake, and if she'd mentioned her plan Wilder would have stopped her.

Actually, there were two downsides. Dana reminded Miki strongly of Nina. Even their names were similar. Though Dana was a bit older than Nina she was just as sweet and gentle, and she'd taught Miki how to perform her duties inside the dome, the same as Nina had on Earth.

Dana and the other girl were already busy, whereas Miki's seat was empty. She drew back, bowing her head respectfully as the new client lowered itself to the chair and reclined, stretching out its wings.

She began work at the tip of its right wing. You had to start at the edges and work inward. Apparently, dragging the implement over large areas of mold was painful. This creature was quite badly affected. Its skin was almost entirely a dark, dusky gray, even its face. She would have to use a smaller instrument. She really disliked cleaning around their weird eyes and lipless mouths. Otherwise, her job wasn't too bad. The respirator cut out most of the smell, and it was better than dealing with vicious Scythian larvae.

As she bent down to drag her tool over the lip of the receptacle to clean it of mold, the alien said, "You are the Earthling?"

She hesitated before completing her task and returning to the wing. A small patch of bronze skin had been revealed in the gray. "No, sir. I'm Concordian."

She called them all Sir and none had corrected her. No one could tell whether Scythians were divided into two sexes like humans.

"You maintain your lie even now?"

When the scientist had challenged Miki about her origins, she'd pretended she had no idea what it was talking about. If she'd revealed she was from the *Sirocco* all hell would have broken loose. What might they do if they knew she was from the ship that had been to Earth—the ship had fired on the Scythian vessels? She would face interrogation, possibly torture. The aliens were desperate for the secret of jump drive.

"I'm not lying, sir. I'm from Annwn." It was the truth. She *was* Concordian and she *was* from Annwn.

"And yet no humans have been reported missing from that area," the Scythian challenged, "and your genetic code clearly demonstrates an association with the earliest phase of human colonization of this planet."

"I'm afraid I don't understand about genetics. All I can tell you is I was born in Annwn and my mother and father are dead, so I can't ask them about my heritage."

The statement she didn't understand about genetics wasn't true. Dad had taught her and Nina quite a lot, and when the Scythian scientist had told her she must be from Earth, she'd realized he must have analyzed her DNA. Had she been mistaken when she'd assumed the alien scientist on Earth deduced she was Concordian from the language she spoke? Perhaps it had a record of Concordian genetic patterns, and hers had matched.

Her client stretched its wing wider, increasing the tension in the webbing so she might clean it better. "It is beyond doubt that at least one of your parents belonged to the original settler stock. The only other possibility is that an Earther came here and mated with a Concordian. We know that to be impossible. No Earth ship arrived here at the time of your conception."

Though the creature had concluded she was lying, it didn't seem angry or even perturbed, though what those emotions might look or sound like Miki wasn't sure. She decided to take her chance. After a nervous swallow, she said, "Can I ask you something, sir?"

"Your request is granted. Perhaps I will not answer, but you can ask."

"Are you..." It had to be the best question. She might not be allowed a second one. "Why are you making records of our genetic codes?"

"To maintain healthy stock. Humans must be capable of performing all the tasks we require. Unfortunately, your colony is somewhat inbred. It lacks diversity, which is likely to result in the emergence of congenital diseases and the colony's eventual collapse. We have tried to mitigate against these effects by careful selection of mating partners. Nevertheless, our best geneticists predict we will only forestall the failure by a few generations." The creature turned its head to stare at her. "Does that answer your question?"

"Yes, sir. Thank you, sir. You seem to know a lot about humans."

"We have been studying your kind for many years. The research findings on a new, semi-intelligent species have been illuminating."

She started scraping the underside of its wing.

"Please apply the balm before you do that."

It had to be sore from the infection and wanted some relief. She put down her tool and dipped her fingertips into the ointment before gently massaging it into the wing's upper side. "May I ask another question?"

The creature's mouth had gone slack at her soothing touch. "You may."

"What is this disease that afflicts Scythians so badly? You are an advanced species, far superior to us." A little buttering-up wouldn't go amiss. "It seems strange that you don't have a cure."

"We're working on a preventative and a treatment. Concordia is the first planet where we've encountered it. The infection may be something humans introduced, or it may be due to the altered climate. We prefer drier conditions than exist on this continent, but we cannot live on..." The word came through the translator unchanged. "The climate there is perfect for us, but humans would find it unendurable. We must have slaves."

Miki recalled the arid atmosphere inside the Scythian city. The memory made her think of Wilder. How were she, Niall, Zapata, and Maddox getting on? Miki was glad that, as far as she could tell, Wilder and Niall had managed to escape. "Sir, I know it is very impolite of me, but may I ask your name?"

"You cannot pronounce my name, Earther."

"Is my service pleasing to you?"

The Scythian regarded her intently. "It is unlike a human to care about the quality of their performance."

"Your infection seems painful. I would like to suggest at your next treatment you ask specifically for me. I will do my best to ease your pain."

The creature held her gaze for long seconds. She stared back, frankly and confidently.

"I will bear your suggestion in mind."

"Thank you, sir. Shall I start on the underside of your wing now?"

It lifted the appendage to allow her access. Secretly, she smiled to herself. She'd begun to gain the creature's trust.

FORTY-TWO

His name was Klghurrshnn. That was the closest Miki could get to the correct pronunciation, which was way off. She couldn't reproduce that weird guttural sound Scythians made. Klghurrshnn seemed to like the fact she tried, however. When he came for his scraping and balm he always asked for her, and she was sure he timed it so he arrived she was on duty.

She thought of Klghurrshnn as a *he* but, even after all these weeks, she still didn't know anything about Scythian gender. It was just easier to think of him that way.

Over the weeks, she'd grown so used to seeing him she recognized him immediately. She'd begun to distinguish the other aliens too. When you saw them all the time, you began to spot differences between their faces and skin patterning. And they were different sizes, the same as humans. The girls who gave the treatments had made up joke names based on the aliens' bodies. One was Pot Belly, another was String, and they called one with particularly undefined facial features Gloop. Naturally, their giggles were saved for when no aliens were around. Scythians knew the signs of human insubordination and punished it severely.

One time, an alien with very short, bandy legs had waddled in, and a girl burst into semi-hysterical laughter she was unable to stifle. The creature had sliced her cheek open. She was forbidden from leaving or even to trying to stem the flow of blood until her workday was over. Miki and the other girls had cleaned the floor in somber silence.

The incident had left a strong impression on Miki. She was extra careful to always be polite and respectful, but especially with Klghurrshnn. Their relationship was fragile. Scythians had zero respect for humans and clearly believed them to be only one step higher on the evolutionary scale than dumb animals. A single wrong word, look, or movement could shatter the relationship she was painstakingly building. If it broke down, she would have to start all over again with another client.

She took every reasonable opportunity to probe Klghurrshnn for information, but she had to be subtle about it. He was smart. It wouldn't take much for him to realize what she was doing. Maybe he'd already guessed but was tolerating her for now. Maybe he enjoyed the special attention, and he was indulging her in kind, or he found it amusing that a human being might imagine they could manipulate a Scythian. Regardless, she was learning useful things, information her friends from the *Sirocco* and humans on Concordia could exploit.

One tidbit she'd learned was that some Scythians didn't mind the fungal infection too much because it provided some protection from the sun's rays on day patrols. Something in the fungus's hairlike fibers helped to prevent sunburn.

"Is the infection ever helpful to *you*, Klghurrshnn?" she had shyly asked.

"Not particularly."

"Is that because you...your job isn't to go on patrols?"

"I am a nursery supervisor. I avoid leaving the dome. Exposure to the external atmosphere makes my condition worse."

"I'm so sorry. I hope the scientists come up with a medication soon."

"Either that or I'll apply for a transfer off this dank, putrid planet."

It was laughable that a Scythian could refer to Concordia as putrid when they stank to high heaven.

Naturally, Miki did not laugh. Neither did she delve into the opening Klghurrshnn had created with his mention of alien movements offplanet. The information might be vital, but going after it immediately would be too suspicious. She forced herself to not respond and filed it away to bring up another day, as if it was something she vaguely remembered. "I used to work in a nursery."

"You did, Miki?"

Her heart skipped a beat. He'd used her name! He'd asked her it only once, weeks ago, and when she'd told him he'd mocked its simplicity. Not reacting had been hard. Dad had told her that Mom had chosen her and Nina's names. Her name was all she had left of her mother—about all she had left of anything. But she'd managed to keep anger out of her expression.

Klghurrshnn hadn't mentioned her name again after asking it, and she'd assumed he'd forgotten.

"I was in the..." she said. "I don't know what to call it. The starter room? I took the little w—" She gulped. Would he be offended if she called the first-stage Scythians worms? "The littlest ones out of the soil and put them in the nutrient solution. Then, when they grew bigger I would put them in the cages with the...the others." The savagery of the attacks the young aliens inflicted on each other was indelible in her mind.

"The early stages of our growth cycle are excellent at weeding out the slow and weak. Only the strongest and most intelligent survive. The human system is far inferior. You nurture every baby regardless of its deficiencies. It is no surprise your species has barely achieved space travel, or that we defeated you so easily."

"You're right, Klghurrshnn." She tightened her grip on the scraping tool as she drew it over the alien's skin, a line of gray-black sludge building up on the edge. "You're so right."

As the days passed, Miki gleaned more snippets of information, but she also became frustrated. Klghurrshnn was an ordinary worker. He didn't know much about the Scythians' long-term plans for the colony, their military capabilities, or anything vital to maintaining control over the slave population. Either that, or he was not so stupid as to give it away.

At first, she consoled herself that, even if she hadn't—and would probably never—discover a key that would ensure the success of a human uprising, she was learning quite a bit about the aliens' behavior and attitudes. They utterly despised humans, but they also didn't seem to like each other very much. No greetings ever passed between the clients. They ignored the other Scythians in the treatment room and outside of it, as far as she could see. Maybe it came from their strange, violent early stages of development. She had the impression that they barely kept their aggression under control, and that if they weren't vegetarian the species probably would have died out from cannibalism.

But what exactly she could do with what she'd learned, she didn't know. The prospect of escaping the dome seemed remote. When not working, she was with the other women in her group, eating, sleeping, or passing the scant free time in gossip or silly games.

Her situation on Earth had been far different. The Scythian invasion had only just begun and their security systems were slack. She'd also been working in an area with access to the outside, albeit through a metre of soil.

Here, the section for humans in this dome was central, surrounded by areas filled with CO_2 where the Scythians could move freely, and in the treatment room where she worked, the outer wall was solid. There was no way she could break through it.

Gradually, hope began to leave her. Her plan had failed. Maybe it had never been serious in the first place. Maybe she'd only wanted to punish herself for abandoning Nina. And she'd done a great job, consigning herself to a lifetime of servitude with barely enough food to stay alive. One day, she might even be bred, like an animal. She feared that she was turning into Dana, passively accepting her fate.

FORTY-THREE

Miki was in the process of finishing up at work, tired after a long shift, when Klghurrshnn walked in. She was about to leave, so Dana stepped forward to offer him a seat.

"It's fine," Miki said. "I have time for one more."

She hadn't seen him in a while. The fungal infection had regrown over his entire body. It would take at least an hour to clean it all off and rub ointment into his skin, but she decided to make the effort. She hadn't quite given up on the prospect of learning something from him that might one day put an end to Scythian control of Concordia.

He'd lost a lot of his reserve around her. She'd played her part as the subservient, admiring human well, and she was almost sure he believed it. Why should he be careful about what he said when the 'thing' he was talking to was in awe of him? Maybe today would be the day he finally let something significant slip.

"You must be uncomfortable, sir. Please sit down and allow me to help you."

He lowered himself into the seat and spread his wings.

"Have you just come from the nursery, sir?"

"Never mind what I've been doing. Be silent and do your job."

She was so taken aback she almost dropped her scraper, but she managed to compose herself.

"You're far too familiar with me, Earther," Klghurrshnn complained. "It's time to put a stop to it. Do you understand?"

"Yes, sir."

From his tone and the rigidity of his wings it was easy to tell he was angry. "It's time I left this miserable planet and its ungrateful humans. Do you know that if it weren't for us you would all be dead? Every single one of you would be dead by now. And how do you repay us? Laziness! Incompetency! Surliness! It's outrageous. We should wipe you out, give up the re-colonization, and leave. Concordia is a museum, a monument to our species' past, and that's how it should stay. Do you hear me?"

"Yes, sir," she timidly replied.

"After all we've done. All the trouble we've gone to in order to keep you miserable creatures alive..."

She could only guess at the source of his ire. Something to do with humans fighting back? She hoped so. She hoped that somewhere on Concordia, someone was taking a stand.

She started on the underside of Klghurrshnn's wing, taking care to keep her head low and avoid making eye contact. She was also especially gentle. He seemed to begin to calm down, his muscles relaxing under her hands.

"Perhaps it's nothing," he murmured. "Only a rumor. There are so many going arou—"

An explosion shattered the quiet.

The blast threw Miki into a wall and right through it into the passageway. She hit the farther wall and bounced off, landing heavily. Too shocked to take in what was happening, she stared stupidly at the scraper still in her hand.

She threw it down.

Concordians were attacking the dome. Split seconds after the first explosion she'd heard two more, quieter ones. All three domes were being attacked.

She leapt to her feet.

The treatment room wall was a jagged mess. Beyond it, she glimpsed the land outside the dome. There was the estuary in the distance. Starlight shone in, but she guessed it wasn't safe to remove her respirator. It would take time for the CO_2 to leak out.

Where was Dana? Where were the other girls?

Miki froze, uncertain about what she should do. The temptation to run outside was strong, but she should try to find her workmates or help to free the humans in the center of the dome. The Scythians would be trying to stop them from escaping.

A draft hit her from above, carrying with it the unmistakable odor her respirator could not entirely eliminate. She looked up. Klghurrshnn was hovering, glaring down. He'd survived the explosion. He must have either penetrated the wall too or flown over it.

She turned and sped away, but she hadn't gone more than a few paces before his toes descended on her shoulders and dug in like pincers. In another second she was aloft. Where was he taking her? Chaos reigned below. Aliens sprawled everywhere, some still, some moving, their wings broken, limbs missing, guts trailing.

There was the great hole in the side of the dome, debris piled around it. People outside were firing at still-living Scythians, but no one had entered yet.

Klghurrshnn flapped higher. The dome swarmed with flying aliens. Some flew haphazardly. One was on a collision course with them. Klghurrshnn narrowly avoided it, banking hard. Others were heading in the same direction as him.

There were the human quarters. A few brave people were venturing out. Scythians with breathing apparatus fired. The humans fell and were dragged inside by their cellmates. Doors slammed shut.

Where was Klghurrshnn taking her?

His flight was growing ragged. He dipped, as if he was struggling to remain airborne. The level of CO_2 had to be getting low. Klghurrshnn rallied, then dipped again. He was dropping steadily now, his wings outstretched so he glided rather than flew. His grip on her grew slack too. She gazed down in fear. If she fell from this height she might break her legs.

Flying aliens were converging on a large chamber, but most weren't making it. They plummeted, their wings and eyes closed, impacting heavily with the ground. One of them reached it, and then she understood why Klghurrshnn wanted to go there. The Scythian who had landed slit the ceiling open and slipped in. The ceiling was like the ones in the domes on Earth, covered in a translucent material to hold in the atmosphere. It would reseal automatically.

Klghurrshnn landed near the top of the wall. Apparently with his last gasp, he drew a claw through the ceiling. His hold on her was weak. She tore his toes from her shoulders and leaped for the edge. She could hurt herself jumping from this height but maybe not too much.

Toes fastened around her ankle and Klghurrshnn dragged her back. Together, they slid through the cut and toppled to the ground.

Only Klghurrshnn and the other Scythian had made it to safety—albeit a temporary one. The attack was continuing. An alien smacked into the ceiling and hung there, making the material sag. It had a hole in its head. Shots from Scythian guns rang out. The human attackers might have imagined they would kill a lot of the enemy by depriving them of CO_2, but the ones in the human zones had respirators. The battle promised to be bloody.

Klghurrshnn's hold on Miki had broken. He lay on his back, wings spread out, chest heaving. She crawled away to the nearest wall and pushed on it. It did not yield.

"No escape from this room, Earther." Klghurrshnn was regaining his strength.

She shrank into a corner.

"Your Resistance won't win. There is no doubt about the outcome of this attack. But in the meantime, if any humans happen to make it this far, you are my personal guarantee of safety."

He climbed to his feet and tottered closer. "We carry our own weapons, you see." His wings opened, displaying his claws. "Why is it humans are so helpless? You have nothing to defend yourself. Even your teeth are not sharp."

"I've been kind to you. I've tried my best to help you."

"Only because you wanted something from me. You wanted to trick me into telling you our secrets. I am not a stupid human."

She couldn't deny it. "You're right. I did want something from you. I wanted to help my people. The same as you want to help yours. You want to grow the best and strongest young Scythians. I know you think we're inferior, but we aren't that different."

"We are *very* different."

"If our circumstances were reversed, wouldn't Scythians do the same as us? Wouldn't they try to resist colonization and slavery?"

"And we would succeed!"

"My people will free some of their own today too. Maybe not all of them, and maybe some will die in the attempt. But they'll try. And they will carry on trying. On and on. You hurt us, and we fight back. What's the point? Why can't you leave us alone? I'm just a girl. My dad, my mom, and probably my sister are dead," she sobbed. "I don't have anyone. I just wanted to do something, just one good thing with my life. Why can't you treat me like a person?"

Klghurrshnn stared at her. She turned her head, avoiding his gaze. The next thing she knew, he'd grabbed her ankle and she was being dragged over the floor. He positioned her in front of him as he squatted behind her. One of his wings arched around, and the tip of a claw touched her throat.

He was just in time.

A figure appeared at the top of the wall. Its form was murky, indistinct through the translucent ceiling, but it was clearly human. How the person had managed to climb up there, Miki didn't know. She also didn't know why he or she wasn't escaping while they had the chance.

A knife bore down and sliced into the ceiling. Instantly, the cut began to reseal, but the figure quickly slashed a square and shoved a hand into it. The cut piece floated to the floor. Material began to ooze inward to close the gap, but the knife flashed again.

A face appeared in the hole.

Miki gasped.

"Miki? Is that you?"

"Wilder! I—"

Klghurrshnn's claw dug deep, making Miki wince with pain. She felt a trickle of hot blood.

"Tell him to stop doing that or I'll kill you."

It's not him, it's her. "She won't understand me. My respirator translates to Scythian."

"Then take it off."

"If I take it off I won't be able to breathe."

The claw dug deeper still. Miki inhaled and then pulled off the mask. "Wilder, it's me. He says if you don't let the ceiling self-repair he'll kill me." She slapped the mask over her face and breathed again.

Another person appeared next to Wilder.

Niall was here too.

"I can shoot him just as easily through the fabric," Wilder said. "I won't if he lets you go."

Miki related the message.

"I will slit your throat as I die."

She translated.

"Will he do it?" Wilder asked.

Miki took another breath and slid the respirator to one side. "I-I think so."

"She's just a kid, you bastard," Niall yelled.

Miki passed the words on, leaving out the bit about Klghurrshnn being a bastard. "Wilder and Niall are from the *Sirocco* like me. They're my friends. We went to Earth, but I'm not from there. My dad was. He was one of the first settlers. My mom was born here on Concordia. Please let me go. That way, neither of us gets hurt. They won't shoot you if you release me. I promise."

A pause followed as Wilder and Niall stared down through the closing hole.

The other Scythian, sitting in the opposite corner, only watched.

Klghurrshnn's claw didn't move from Miki's neck.

Then, suddenly, she felt movement behind her. Something hit her, propelling her forward. She landed on her knees. Klghurrshnn had kicked her.

He rose to his feet. "Climb onto my back, *Miki*. And take care not to fall, or I still might impale you."

He knelt, leaning forward.

She clambered onto him, gripping the powerful shoulders. Klghurrshnn straightened up, rising to his full height as she clung on. She had to climb onto his shoulders and balance precariously in order for Niall to reach in and grab her.

As soon as she was on the wall she tore off her respirator and tossed it down. All around, the battle was raging. Scythian and human bodies littered the ground. Pulses flashed, and the noise of Scythian rounds echoed from the dome overhead.

A grapple hung from the top of the wall.

"Another rope?" Miki asked.

Wilder replied, "I don't want to talk about it."

FORTY-FOUR

Wilder stared morosely out to sea.

They had failed.

The Scythians showed no sign of leaving, which meant was impossible to call Operation Rebirth a victory. Not only that, the Resistance had been decimated—more than decimated, according to the literal meaning of the word—in its failure to take control of Concordia. Casualty estimates were still coming in, but they already numbered in the thousands. Thousands of fighters were dead, permanently disabled, or seriously injured. The Resistance had also exhausted its equipment supplies. It was no longer possible to manufacture new pulse rifles or other weapons, so once they broke or fell into enemy hands they were gone forever, never to be replaced. If humans continued to fight they would eventually be reduced to using knives, pitchforks, and flails, like the farmers at the Vimur estuary.

Scythian casualties had been high too, no doubt. Many domes had been successfully blasted open. Plenty of aliens had suffocated. Others had been shot to death. But the Scythians could replenish their numbers from offplanet. The call would have gone out for more soldiers, more workers, more settlers. The human population could not replace itself so easily.

And reprisals had already begun. Concordians would pay dearly for their arrogance, for daring to challenge their masters.

More heartache. More bloodshed. More deaths.

At least Miki was back safe and sound.

Wilder had brought the girl to her little room in the cave complex. It wasn't really big enough for two. It wasn't, in fact, big enough for one. But it gave

Wilder comfort to have Miki close by. She would never let her out of her sight again, and she'd made her promise that if she had another bright idea about risking her life to learn the Scythians' secrets, she would discuss it first.

When the attack was over, Wilder had tried to stay upbeat for Miki's sake all the way back to the caves, but on arrival her mood had sunk low. It was hard not to despair when all you saw ahead of you was endless fighting, each side seeking revenge. It would never stop, not unless every last Concordian died or accepted unending servitude. And it would be the same on Earth.

Wilder glanced at Faina, her current companion. Miki was somewhere else in the complex. The android was activated and also taking in the ocean view. She was another depressing problem. Faina would never be able to move around independently. She also had no role to keep her occupied. She'd been designed and manufactured for a task that was long since over. An almost-human consciousness trapped inside a small receptacle, she couldn't improve her situation even a little bit. One day soon, Wilder anticipated, the android would ask to be deactivated and buried somewhere no one would ever find her.

Wilder said, "I don't think I ever told you—we met the original Strongquist on Earth."

"Another Strongquist? I didn't know there were two. Did he look the same as the one who came here on the *Mistral*?"

"He was the prototype the Makers built and identical to your Strongquist in almost every way, as far as I could tell. I didn't know the one from your ship very well."

"He was still functioning even now? His power lasted a very long time."

"The Makers deactivated him before they went into Deep Sleep. He reactivated when Niall and I entered their construction site. Do you remember it?"

"I do, perfectly. My memories do not fade as humans' do. But I was not aware of a prototype Strongquist. I would like to meet him if I could. Yet there is no possibility of returning to Earth, I believe?"

"We don't even know if the *Sirocco* still exists. If she does, I don't see how she could enter Concordian orbit without the Scythians blowing her to pieces. And the captain, Vessey, is unlikely to attempt it. She might go back to Earth, but that would be without us. I wish I could take you there. The Makers might be able to build you a new body."

"A new body would be very convenient."

"We're stuck here, unfortunately. I can't see an end to this conflict. It'll go on until I die."

"I've been considering the problem. It is a pity that humans have so little to offer the Scythians. All they can provide is their labor, and the aliens can take that by force. If you had something else, something the Scythians desired greatly from you, something they cannot take at will but must be freely given,

Concordians would have bargaining power. If that were the case, things might be very different."

Wilder froze.

Very slowly, she got to her feet. Then she had to hold onto the rock edge of the cave opening, her legs turning weak as a realization coursed through her.

Though she was only a little over thirty, she'd come close to death three times. The first time was when she was attacked aboard the *Sirocco* by four members of the Final Day Five. The second time had been when a Scythian had grabbed her and carried her aloft at Svalbard, the Makers' construction site. Her third brush with mortality had occurred in the Scythian city. Dying of thirst and exhaustion, alone in the dark deep within the ancient metropolis on Suddene had been a real possibility.

Never, in all those times, had her life passed before her eyes as legend said.

Yet now it did.

She saw herself on the *Nova*, hiding behind a pallet of cargo as her friend, Ben, snuck aboard the shuttle that would take him to a horrible demise in the First Night Attack. Next, she was building her treehouse outside Sidhe and a red-haired Woken man approached, carrying a bottle of sluglimpet repellent. Then she was leaning her forehead on the transparent barrier separating her from Quinn as the *Opportunity* carried her to the Galactic Assembly.

Scene after scene passed across her inner vision until in the end she was looking down at a teenage girl, her face covered by a Scythian respirator, sitting in front of a crouching alien who held a wing claw at her throat.

Right from Arrival Day Concordians had always been fighting, firstly for survival and then against the extra-terrestrial species whose planet they had unknowingly stolen. Decades full of destruction and murder had passed. So many loved ones had been lost, so many lives cut short.

Could it all finally, *finally*, be over?

She hardly dared to hope she was right.

She stooped and kissed Faina's burnt, mangled head. "I'll be back soon. You've just given me a brilliant idea."

She needed to send an urgent message via the undersea cable.

FORTY-FIVE

The air was thick with tension. And it was actual air. After days of negotiation leading up to the potentially watershed meeting, the Scythians had agreed to be the ones to wear breathing gear. It was a very positive sign.

The Fila, naturally, were forced to participate from the ocean, visible through a glass portal. Wilder had a feeling that this basement room used to be part of the Leader's Residence, where matters of state were discussed with the aquatic alien allies.

Three Scythians were here, perched on specially constructed chairs. Four humans were present: Wilder, two Resistance Council members, and Miki, who, for some reason, had insisted on coming along. It was becoming a habit.

Wilder wasn't sure how many Fila writhed on the far side of the transparent barrier. With all their tentacles, they were hard to count when they got together. She guessed Quinn was somewhere among them. The introductions were over, formalities out of the way. The Fila would bear witness to whatever agreements were reached and report to the Galactic Assembly.

Wilder cleared her throat. "I propose that we start with the big stuff and work our way down to the details." She actually planned on absenting herself for the smaller arguments. She'd always hated long, tedious meetings involving people arguing over minutiae. "Item one: we have something you want very much. Item two: we want to know what you're willing to give for it."

The central Scythian replied, "First, we must be absolutely clear about what this thing is that you are offering."

"All right. We call it a jump drive. It's a kind of starship engine. It enables travel across the galaxy in leaps rather than via regular propulsion through spacetime."

The drive.

The adaptation of Fila tech that allowed humans to bound across space, the drive that had failed and delayed the *Sirocco* a decade, the machine the Scythians greatly prized. It would allow them to explore the galaxy's farthest reaches and—who knew?—perhaps beyond. Only humans could give it to them. Would it be enough? How much would they be prepared to pay?

"As the Fila do?" the alien asked.

"The same way the Fila travel," Wilder replied, "but our drive works for atmosphere-breathing species like yours and ours. Miki and I have taken part in many jumps and we weren't harmed, the same as the rest of the *Sirocco*'s crew. I don't see any reason why it wouldn't work for Scythians too."

"You are the inventor?"

"The original design is the Fila's. I and others helped with the adaptation."

A pause followed. The aliens were probably talking among themselves.

Wilder coughed again. "If you're thinking you only need to capture and torture me to force me to tell you how we adapted it, that would be very stupid. Firstly, no agony you could inflict would make me betray my people. You've seen how recklessly and senselessly defiant we are. And, secondly, that wouldn't go down very well with the Galactic Assembly. I heard your application is in progress. I ask you again, what are you willing to give in exchange for the jump drive?"

Miki nudged her and whispered, "You're way too passive. Don't ask. *Demand.* Arrogance and pride are the only things they respect."

"Uh, okay." Wilder stood up. "We've waited long enough. You know why we're here. If you aren't willing to give us Concordia, we're done. Our discussion is over. There's nothing more to say."

"We were only considering our reply," said the Scythian.

"And what is your reply?" She remained standing.

"Concordia is our origin planet. It is our birthplace. We do not wish to leave."

"Then I guess it's no jump drive for you."

"Perhaps we can achieve a compromise."

"Wow," Miki breathed. "That must be a first."

Wilder sat down. "I'll listen, but—"

"No compromises!" a Resistance councilor spat. "You've killed thousands of our people, enslaved tens of thousands. You need to get off our planet yesterday."

"And many Scythians died in the recent uprising," the alien retorted. "We saved your colony from inevitable demise, and this is how you repay us."

The councilor leapt to her feet. "You enslaved us! What do you expect us to do? Roll over and accept our fate like obedient children? How were we to know all about Concordia's past when we came here? To us, it was an uninhabited planet, and all we wanted to do was to create a new home for humankind. How is any of this our fault?"

A Fila voice came from a speaker. "Scythians, humans, for this conflict to end, each of you must agree to unpalatable concessions. You must move on from everything that has happened between you. It may be impossible to forgive, but with the proper attitude it may be possible to move forward."

"And what if we aren't willing to move forward?" asked the Resistance woman.

"Then you are condemning your colony to repeat the same experiences it has suffered, without end and until its inescapable demise."

"Look, it's simple," Wilder said in an attempt to get the meeting back on track. "In return for the jump drive, the Scythians leave Concordia. You're going to have the entire galaxy at your disposal. So pack up and go wherever you want, giving us this one planet where you can't even breathe the atmosphere."

"Sounds like a wonderful idea," the Resistance woman commented.

Still, the aliens balked at the agreement. They sat still and silent, glaring at the humans.

The pause drew out, and Wilder began to despair. After abandoning their home planet for thousands of years, the Scythians now seemed to want it so badly they were prepared to forego tech that would revolutionize their future. The reason why was clear: they damn well didn't want another species to be in control of something that had once belonged to them. For all their long history and technological advancement, they were like toddlers, wanting something just because someone else had it.

"I know," Miki announced. "What if we divide Concordia between us? Scythians can live on Suddene. It's too hot and dry for humans, but the climate there is much better for you guys. Am I right?"

Silence from the aliens.

The Resistance councilor seemed to struggle with outrage, then she blurted, "Out of the question!"

"Why?" asked Miki. "What could we possibly do with Suddene? And we could trade with the Scythians. Sell them food and stuff. I'm sure they could think of something to give us in return. Surely that has to be better than a continuation of the war. Haven't enough people died?"

The two Resistance councilors began a quiet discussion.

Wilder gave Miki a hopeful smile, impressed by the girl's smart thinking. Knowing that the enemy aliens were living across the ocean would be uncomfortable. It would be far preferable for them to leave the planet. But, as the Fila had said, resolving the situation called for hard concessions.

Finally, a councilor said grudgingly, "I suppose it might work, providing we never have to set eyes another Scythian. All the domes on Lyonesse would have to be evacuated and destroyed, and its airspace has to be under human control. Perhaps the Fila could act as go-betweens."

"I think that's an excellent proposal," came the Fila voice.

Wilder said, "Given our history, Scythians living on Suddene is going to be hard for Concordians to stomach."

The Fila said, "Compromises often are."

"I can only speak for myself," said Wilder, "but I want peace. I want it almost more than anything."

"Me too," said Miki, her eyes shining with tears.

The Scythians conferred. The humans watched and waited. The Fila writhed.

Then the answer came. "We agree."

Wilder slumped. She felt like a taut string suddenly cut.

But, of course, it was not completely over. Not yet.

"There's still Earth," she said. "You're invading *our* home planet. Only it isn't empty like Concordia was when we arrived. Hundreds of millions of humans live there, and you're doing the same as you did here. Taking it over. Murdering people in cold blood. We want you to leave our world alone. Completely alone. No half-measures. You have no right to that place at all."

"But what will you give?"

"Give? We're not going to give you anything. I've already agreed to give you the jump drive. That's enough."

"That was for a half-share of Concordia."

"The land masses of Concordia," the Fila interjected.

Wilder was tempted to say the deal was off. She inwardly cursed for not including Earth in the original discussion. But too much was at stake. She'd missed her chance. "You can't just go around invading inhabited planets," she protested. "I-I bet the Galactic Assembly would have something to say about it."

"You are possibly correct in your assertion," said the Fila. "However, humanity's origin planet is far from the Assembly's area of jurisdiction, and if it decides to adjudicate it would require the submission of detailed evidence and testimonies. There would be hearings. The process could drag on for decades."

"Do you have other technology to offer?" asked the Scythians.

Wilder frowned. The idea of giving the aliens something in addition to the jump drive grated, but if the prospect of freeing Earth was on the table, she should take the opportunity. What else did humans have to offer? There was the Parvus's weapon, but she was damned if she was giving them *that*. Something else? Long ago, she'd won a lot of tech from the Assembly in return for...

"Do you have a-grav?"

"A-grav? What is a-grav? Our translators do not recognize this word."

"Artificial gravity."

A pause.

"You invented artificial gravity too?"

The aliens had a short discussion, followed by, "Would you consider a position working for us?"

"I would rather stick needles in my eyes."

Miki whispered, "That's a no, then?"

———

The meeting took hours and Wilder was unable to sneak off. Whenever she tried the Resistance councilors, the Scythians, or the Fila would drag her into the talks. But in the end she was glad she stayed, for there was an unexpected revelation, and somehow it meant more to her than securing the freedom of all the humans on Concordia and Earth.

The news came as they were wrapping things up. A timeline for the Scythians' withdrawal from both areas of conflict, reparations, and a plan for ongoing relations had been largely agreed upon. There were a few sticking points, but they could wait for later meetings. Wilder was itching to get out of the door. Sitting face-to-face with the creatures who had inflicted so much suffering on humankind nauseated her. The coming years of sharing Concordia were going to be very tough. Yet it was better than the alternative. They'd broken the cycle of reprisal.

Everyone was making a move to leave when the Fila stated, "There is one last item to discuss."

Wilder groaned. "Surely we've covered everything important?"

"The matter concerns the safe passage of human starships in the Concordian star system. You may wish to come to a formal agreement today, due to its urgency."

"Urgency?" Wilder asked. "But we don't have starsh—" She sucked in air in a whoop.

Miki leapt up. "The *Sirocco*!? She wasn't destroyed?"

"The Assembly reports your ship remains stationed in the nearest star system. She appears to have sustained considerable damage, and the crew has been effecting repairs. If her drive is intact, we believe it would be appropriate for—"

"Yes!" Wilder yelled. "Yes! Contact Vessey. Tell her the war's over and she can bring the ship here, and to bring the Ark too." She didn't bother asking the

Scythians' permission. If they didn't like it, screw them. Only a fool would jeopardize everything agreed upon today, and the aliens were not idiots.

Miki was weeping.

Wilder hugged her. "I'm sure Nina's fine. You'll see her soon…" She was weeping too. "She could be here in a few hours if someone flies the shuttle down. Dragan can do it."

But she didn't think Miki could hear her.

The news about the *Sirocco* meant even more than Nina and the rest of the crew's survival. It meant they still had all the material in the Ark. They could reseed Lyonesse and make it beautiful again. It also meant they could go to Earth. Wilder could see Cherry again.

The long years of struggle, the battles, the bloodshed, were over.

It felt too good to be true.

It was, of course. In reality, many problems lay ahead. Relations with the Scythians would be hard for a long time to come, perhaps forever. Replenishing Concordia's ecosystem would be difficult too. Such endeavors were complex and they'd lost Kes, their greatest asset in the field.

But they would try. They would try as they always had, right from the beginning when the *Nova Fortuna* had appeared in Concordia's night sky. Unknown, unforeseen difficulties would test them, and each time they would rise to the challenge.

EPILOGUE

It was a warm, sunny afternoon, perfect for a dip. Wilder walked down the beach to the ocean's edge, carrying her equipment. This area was clear of people. The holidaymakers and daytrippers were up the other end, where a pier stuck out into the sea and the water was shallow. Squeals of excited children and the loud conversations of their parents faintly reached her ears.

She needed to go into the deep water.

She pulled the equipment onto her back and slipped the respirator over her face, taking some experimental breaths before stepping into the waves. She wasn't too worried about the breathing part of the apparatus failing. That potential problem had a great solution. But the translation device was a new invention and untested.

The shock of cold water hit as she moved deeper. When the water reached her chest she dove under the surface and began to swim. Her body acclimating to the chill, she looked around expectantly. Visibility was good, but all she could see was stray seaweed and the odd crustacean side-stepping over the sandy seabed.

Then a tentacle prodded her foot.

"Quinn? You didn't keep me waiting." She swung around to face her friend.

His tentacles writhed and she felt the effect of their motion on her skin, but, of course, she couldn't understand what he was saying. He would also be generating electromagnetic pulses that she was unable to detect. He looked even bigger than usual in his natural element. If she didn't know what a Fila was she would have been terrified.

She hung still in the water, keeping the motions of her arms and legs to a minimum. What had her movements meant in Fila language? She smiled, imagining various ridiculous messages she'd inadvertently been sending.

Now was the real test. Fila could understand human speech, but humans could not interpret the complicated system of currents and electromagnetism that constituted Fila language. And humans could not 'speak' Fila. Until now. Maybe.

"Can you hear me, Wilder?"

She squealed. "It works! It works! I can hear you." The contraption on her back transmitted her words.

"That's no surprise to me. I was confident you could do it. Would you like to go for a swim?"

"I'd love to."

Her friend gently wrapped tentacles around her waist and arms, and carried her out to sea. Her translator only worked if the human and Fila had a full view of the other, so she could only talk to and hear Quinn if they stopped and faced each other. Their journey into the ocean had to be completed in silence.

It didn't matter. Despite her excitement about her new invention, Wilder found she didn't want to talk. She only wanted to be in this moment.

For now, the world was perfect. Word had arrived from the Assembly that the Scythians had departed Earth, and the Earthers were restarting their fledgling civilization. Meanwhile, rebuilding progressed apace on Lyonesse. Scythian domes no longer blighted the landscape and none of the aliens had been spotted in the sky for weeks. The scientists from the *Sirocco* had begun their reseeding program and, though it was early days, they'd already seen the first seeds sprouting through the soil. They had reported, however, that sluglimpets would play an important role in the ecosystem and had ruled out an eradication program.

Miki seemed to have entirely recovered from her time in the Scythian dome and the many ordeals of her childhood. Perhaps it was the resilience of youth. She spent every spare moment with Nina, and though Wilder missed her young friend, she didn't begrudge her the time one bit. The two girls were thick in their plans for Miki to run for Leader when she was old enough, and Nina was her biggest supporter. Kes would have been so proud of both of them.

The *Sirocco*'s repairs were nearly finished, and soon the ship would leave for Earth. Wilder's passage was already guaranteed. She'd asked that no one informed Cherry she was coming, so it would be a complete surprise. She would take Faina with her and give her to the Makers. The android had expressed unusual excitement at meeting the original Strongquist.

Quinn carried Wilder far from the shore, sweeping through the ocean as the sun blazed down, sending ripples of light from above. She felt completely safe. Her friend's care for her had been steady and unwavering ever since they'd met.

When he stopped, she turned to face him, floating in the deep blue water. "I'm so glad we can do this. It's better than talking through a glass pane, right?"

"I feel the same. Now you're in my environment and I can show you the ways of aquatic life. I hope we can do it often. And, when they're old enough, I will take your children into the ocean too."

"My children?" She lifted her eyebrows. "There's nothing like that on the horizon for me. I'm much too busy to have kids."

"How strange. Aren't you aware you are growing two babies?"

"I'm what?!" She touched her stomach. "No, I did *not* know that. Holy shit."

Pregnant?

With twins?

What would Niall say?

THE END

Thanks for joining me for the story of humanity's first deep space colony. I hope you've enjoyed reading it as much as I enjoyed writing it. For a different take on the future of humankind, check out: STAR LEGEND

Sign up to my reader group for a free ebook *Night of Flames,* the prequel to Space Colony One, and for more free books, discounts on new releases, Review Crew invitations and other interesting stuff:

https://jjgreenauthor.com/free-books/

Thanks to Patrons

With deepest thanks to patrons

Paul Hanrahan, John Treadwell, Joseph Lau, Peter Samuel Harness, Geeraline Marrs, Bobby Borland, John Stephenson, Chris, William Retsin, Dan Archibald, Grant Ballard-Tremeer, Dale Thompson, Jean Gill, Christopher E. Marshall, Cheryl Kuchler, Shan Shwe, Steve Glasper, Donald Swan, Wayne Lampel, Janette S. Mattey, Brian Kelly, Jim, Sarah Woods, Richard L. Adams, Frank Menendez, Patti DeLang, Elizabeth Hickey, Linda Liem, Russ Kirkpatrick, Kate Wilson, Duff Kindt, Catherine Corcoran, Shaun, John Gancz, Dave, Archie Strong, Struggle Session, Susan Cook, Annie Hsiao-Wen Wang, Julian White, Dane Elliot, Iffet a Burton, Gary Johnson, Tracey Paine, Randy Berlin, Ed Cleeves, Amaranth Dawe, Neil, Alex Green, Ann Bryant, Neil Holford, Michael Claremont

Copyright

www.ingramcontent.com/pod-product-compliance
Lightning Source LLC
Chambersburg PA
CBHW050559170726
48283CB00001B/22